Lesley Marie Mayo

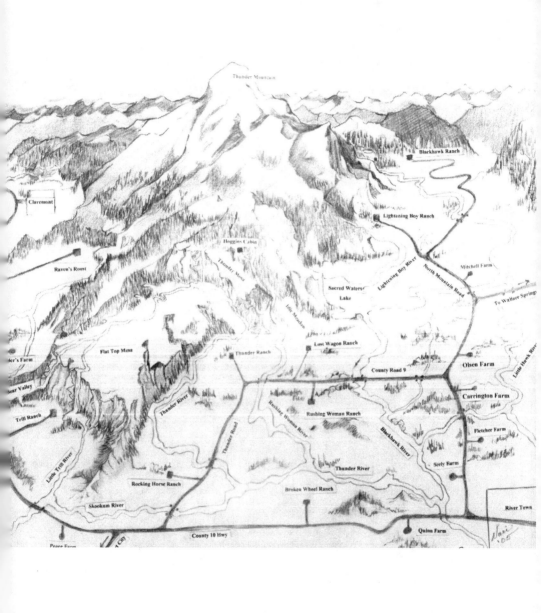

Order this book online at www.trafford.com
or email orders@trafford.com

Most Trafford titles are also available at major online book retailers.

© Copyright 2009 Ruby Nari Mayo.

All rights reserved. No part of this publication may be reproduced, stored in a retrieval system, or transmitted, in any form or by any means, electronic, mechanical, photocopying, recording, or otherwise, without the written prior permission of the author.

Printed in Victoria, BC, Canada.

ISBN: 978-1-4269-1670-0 (sc)
ISBN: 978-1-4269-1671-7 (hc)

Library of Congress Control Number: 2009935504

Our mission is to efficiently provide the world's finest, most comprehensive book publishing service, enabling every author to experience success. To find out how to publish your book, your way, and have it available worldwide, visit us online at www.trafford.com

Trafford rev.11/4/2009

 www.trafford.com

North America & international
toll-free: 1 888 232 4444 (USA & Canada)
phone: 250 383 6864 ♦ fax: 812 355 4082

Special Dedication

THIS BOOK IS DEDICATED to all the natural spirits that abide in the hills, in the mountains and in the waters everywhere on planet Earth and to our Native Americans.

TRUE HEART is also dedicated to my daughter, Edra (Eddi) Bonsall, who inspired me to fulfill my dream of becoming a published story teller. By her example I had the courage to overcome my hesitations and *go for it.*

My daughter Eddi has a true heart.

Acknowledgements

I WISH TO ACKNOWLEDGE the visions of the Sacred Valleys books that were gifted to me by those benign spirits, the Guardians.

My children, Eddi, Grant and Alan as well as my wonderful grandchildren have been very supportive of my desire to have a writing career.

To Lisa Lockwood who gave me the time and the space to finish writing True Heart. Thanks Lisa, my good angel.

Dorothy Seddon, my spiritual sister, has been my rock and constant friend through the years.

Maggie Enns, Dorothy's daughter, was the first to read the Sacred Valleys series and loved them. Thanks Maggie for your editing, advice and encouragement. Together these dear friends helped me to publish this first book for which they will always have my undying gratitude. Thanks for a new career ladies.

To Joan Marimi Lyman-Tollman, published author, my friend, helpful editor all rolled up into one super person; thank you for all your hard work.

No one writes a book totally alone without many helpers along the way. To all my friends thank you.

The Guardians

LONG, LONG AGO THE legend began when the Earth was young and before the coming of men, Advanced Spirits or Light Beings were asked by Mother Earth to come and serve as guardians for various areas of the planet. Many answered.

Four of these Advanced Beings were the Goddess of Sun and Beauty, God of Storm and Wind, God of Rain and Snow and God of Thunder and Lightening and agreed among themselves to combine their powers to protect the northwest lands called by Them the Sacred Valleys.

When Native Americans discovered these abundant hunting grounds the Guardians laid down three simple laws to them. First, no human blood was to be spilled on their sacred ground in violence by another human unless it was in self protection or in the protection of another person. Second, the land was to be cherished and not harmed. The third law was to honor and respect all animal life and only take as many animals as to sustain life. To fail these simple laws was to be driven out of the valleys.

Through the millennium many other Advanced Spirits had gradually left the Earth. Few remained among these were the Sacred Valleys Guardians because the people honored Them and Their laws and gave daily thanks for the bounty of the lands. And so the Guardians presence remained powerful and protective of all who dwelled beneath the awesome splendor of Thunder Mountain. Native Americans called them the Thunder Gods.

The Legend of the Thunder Gods continued.

Prologue

THE LUMINOUS FULL MOON of Aquarius hung from the midnight sky in awesome splendor. All was silent in the vastness of space. A figure materialized in a dark hooded cloak that concealing the features, so whether It was male or female or neither was unknown. It came to stand, tall and thin, before a dark vertical mirror suspended in space.

Fate! The figure was Fate, the one who decides the ultimate outcome and unpremeditated destiny of a person. A person would have to have great courage to look into the face of Fate and accept life or death. And, if it was for life, then to bravely accept the future for good or ill.

Fate drew a handful of shining stones from Its pocket and held them out over the dark glassed table. The moon revealed that some stones were black and some were white. Each stone had a symbol marked on it. Fate murmured an incantation then cast the stones upon the mirrored table.

"Ah, this one dies," Gathering up the stones It cast them again, "And this person also." Throwing the stones again and again for this particular family until It had completed the casting. Four to die and three to live and thus their destiny was ordained.

Gathering up the stones Fate put them back in the cloak's pocket turned and disappeared into the immense darkness.

Beneath a canopy of brilliant stars the Goddess of Sun and Beauty stood alone on the wind swept summit of Thunder Mountain in the far northwest. The Goddess turned in a circle looking down upon the surrounding valleys over which She and the others had guardianship. Her gaze dwelled for a time upon a ranch where an old embittered man lived. She communion with the Supreme One then sighed; She wasn't to interfere with the old man's fate for it was written in the stars. Well, She hadn't been forbidden from all action or from blessing him with a beam of hope that if he chose to face the truth of himself then he would find the peace he sought.

The Goddess's mind flew down the old man's bloodlines into the South and saw the death of two people and the tragic, desolated grief of three children. Compassion moved Her to extend her hand in their direction.

"It's time to come home, my children."

Then she sent an important line of investigation to a social worker who would know what to do at the right time. These children were needed in the Sacred Valleys to act as catalysts for the changes that must take the place of complacency.

"Yes," She murmured, *"Come to us little ones and be healed of your hearts' wounding."*

The Goddess lingered then with a wave of Her hand She disappeared into the wind that blew the snow into swirling mist off the Peak of Thunder Mountain. Only the whooshing sound of the wind broke the night's silence.

A new era was about to be set in motion; an ending and another beginning which was the unending cycle of life. These were the Sacred Valleys overseen by the eternal Guardians known as the Thunder Gods.

In Mike Kelly's opinion life generally sucked! Being blind-sided had felt like multiple hammer blows that had shocked his brother and sister and himself to their very souls. The foundation of their lives had been blasted to smithereens leaving them abandoned to the whims of Fate. How he knew Fate had dealt the cards couldn't be logically explained to anyone; he just knew that Impersonal Entity was responsible. Now, they were sitting in a courtroom numb with grief over the tragic loss of their parents.

Tragic? Now there was a mild word to describe what they were feeling thought Mike angrily as he sat on the hard bench holding his baby sister in his lap with his young brother Joe sitting tight against his side. Mike swallowed the lump of grief caught in his throat.

Mom and Dad were dead and that fact had placed them in the hands of the State of Texas. Now the state would decide what was going to be done with them.

Big damn deal, fumed Mike who rarely cussed, everyone was so concerned to obey the letter of the law that was being argued before the judge that no one was thinking about the emotional trauma that he and the kids were going through. They were all acting *very* unemotional as though we aren't *feeling* here. His deep brown eyes looked fiercely upon these do-gooders. D*amn* their impersonal hides!

The rational part of Mike's mind knew he was being unreasonable. Of course the lawyers and the judge had to be emotionally impersonal or they'd fail the law. These people *were* trying to do the best they could for them however somehow that didn't mean doodly-squat to Mike. He didn't want impersonal he wanted a hell of a lot of personal going on up there. He'd pray tonight and apologize to his folks for swearing, but he just was so *angry*.

The loud sound of the judge's gavel woke Mike to the present. Oh yeah, the judgment Fate had in store for them was about to be pronounced.

God help them.

In the trailer's small kitchen *was warm and scented with the delicious smells of dinner prepared for a hungry family. Laughter filled the small space. To Joe the trailer was full of light and energy tonight because everything sparkled. Mom and Dad especially seemed to sparkle with lots and lots of beautiful colors swirled around them like they were inside a moving rainbow. It was really beautiful and caused Joe smile. It must be because there is so much joy here he thought.*

Strangely, Carli sat unmoving in her highchair without talking, laughing or banging her spoon on the tray as she usually did. She was as still as a doll that had been propped up in its chair. Joe frowned; now that just wasn't right.

Joe was distracted from trying to puzzle out his sister's strange behavior by the conversation that going back and forth between his parents. He grinned as he watched them laughingly compete with each other in telling their children about a funny experience they'd had on their trip to the next county. What they were celebrating tonight was Dad's new job as a horse trainer and a better future for them all.

"Mike, in the near future you'll have a job training young horses. Something you can do after school and on weekends to earn a little money." Dad was saying. "And you'll be amazed where your music will take you in the future."

"That's good to know Dad, so when do we move over to that ranch?"

"Well, anytime is a good time to move on son. The change has already happened for your mother and me. In a larger sense we've already moved on. So, big changes are in the works for you kids too."

Joe looked at Mike and saw confusion and apprehension in his face. "Well, sure Dad," said Mike," "We're all together in this move so we're all changing at the same time too," Mike looked shaken, "Aren't we?"

Dad looked at Mother and hesitated just long enough for Joe to become fearful. What was wrong? Something surely wasn't right. They were all going to this other ranch together….weren't they?

Dad got up out of his chair leaned over and kissed Joe on his forehead. "I love you Joseph don't ever forget that. Make us proud of you and that golden voice of yours."

Joe opened his mouth, but couldn't get any words out. Then Dad moved around the table to Mike and kissed him on the forehead as well. "Take good care of the kids Mike, I'm counting on you." Then he kissed Carli and went to stand at the end of the table.

Mom kissed everyone too then she joined hands with Dad and smiled. "We love you all; remember you are part of us always, but we have to go now so be good children and make your lives a celebration. You'll be taken care of so don't worry about the future too much. Good times will come again when you get home."

While Joe and Mike and Carli sat frozen at the small round table their mother and father grew fainter and fainter until, at the very last moment, their parents raised their hands in a silent wave goodbye and disappeared.

Joe screamed and screamed, "Come back, come back, you can't leave us behind." He jumped up and tried to break through an invisible wall, beating his fists frantically against the resistance. Something gripped him like iron bands preventing him from fighting.

"**Joe, Joe wake up,** it's just a nightmare, wake up now. Come on boy, wake up now." Mike's firm voice finally got through to Joe. He awoke to find Mike holding him tightly against his chest. Joe was confused and looked around in bewilderment at the small dim room crowded with twin beds and saw Carli climbing out of her crib. Then he remembered the dream, the awful dream and burst into tears, sobbing like his heart was breaking which to him it was.

Carli crawled up onto the bed and sat beside Joe. "Joey, is you hurted? What's wrong with my boy?" Carli began to cry in sympathy as she patted Joe's wet face. Mike pulled her over into his lap and leaning back against the wall he managed to hold both of them close.

"Hush Carli, Joey just had a bad dream. He'll be okay now." said Mike quietly. It seemed to reassure the little girl as she sniffed and wiped her eyes on Mike's pajama top. He laughed and held out a Kleenex for her.

"Sorry guys, It was a really awful dream." Joe sniffed and wiped his eyes on his nightshirt sleeve. "I'm okay now. Thanks for waking me up." and took the Kleenex Mike handed him. After a good nose blow and more wiping up he took a deep breath and began to settle down.

"Yeah, it must have been one heck of a dream, boy. You were screaming and fighting me like I was a demon or something. Why, I'm sure to have black and blue marks all over me tomorrow." complained Mike, trying to light things up for Joe.

"I'm sorry Mike I didn't know I was hurting you. Geeze it was a wall I was pounding on not you." Joe gave a shuddering sigh.

"Hey, I'm just kidding you kid and there's no permanent damage. I'm pretty tough you know." chuckled Mike. "Can you tell me about the dream Joe? Can you remember it? At times it helps to talk about a bad experience. Mom used to say that sometimes angels visit us while we sleep and give us messages. If you tell me about the dream we can decide if you got a message. That would make the dream a good thing wouldn't it?"

"Yeah, it would." Sitting in the comfort of his brother's arm Joe told him about the dream. It wasn't hard because it was stamped clear as clear on his brain. "Honestly Mike, it was so real that it's hard to believe it was just a dream."

"I don't think it wasn't a dream kind of dream but a real vision Joe and those are rare and really important. Tell me again what Dad and Mom said. I think those are the messages they wanted us to hear. After all, in a way Mom and Dad are angels now aren't they?" said Mike quietly.

Joe teared up a little, but after a few deep breaths and more nose blowing he dutifully repeated the conversation. Mike hummed a bit and finally sighed, "It sounds to me like we'll be alright once we get home, but where is that? It certainly isn't here at the orphanage." Mike sighed again, "I just wished the folks had given us a better indication of where that future home was located it would give us a little more hope wouldn't it? Well, that's a mystery for right now. We just have to have faith in what the folks told us. It must have cost them something to come to you in that dream. Somehow, someway a miracle is waiting for us that we have to believe in."

They sat quietly together in the small dark bedroom until Mike got chilled. He roused up and realized Carli had gone to sleep in his arms. "Come on Carli Jean, let Mikey put you back to bed." whispered Mike as he picked up his baby sister and put her back in the crib and tucked the blankets around her shoulders.

Getting back under his own covers Mike looked over at Joe and said, "You snuggle down there and go to sleep. I don't think you'll dream anymore tonight."

Mike mind spun around and around trying to find more meaning to those last words of his parents. He knew they were trying to give them courage and hope for the future, but where was that future going to be? Where would they find a good home again and was this too part of their fate? Mike was filled with such anguish that he thought his heart would surely burst from grief.

"Mike, stop thinking so loud, I can't go to sleep with all that noise." murmured Joe as he turned over.

That shocked Mike and he laughed softly at that remark. Still Joe's words broke his mind out of its circuitous emotional downhill spiral. He snuggled himself back under his own covers and let go of worry for the time being. Mike soon fell deeply asleep.

~Devereaux~

THE OLD MAN WALKED wearily up the front porch steps and sat down in his favorite rocking chair on the wide front porch with his bag of mail that his foreman Hank had brought from town. It had been a long hard day and he was tired to the bone with ranch work that never seemed to get done.

"A man of seventy-eight has a right to get tired," he grumbled aloud, "After all I ain't no spring chicken anymore." He picked up the pitcher of cold water and poured himself a drink. Draining the glass he sighed in relief. Joseph Devereau swept off his hat and laid it beside his chair, gave his sweaty head a good scrubbing then slicked it back from his face and poured another glass of water.

He dumped the mail into his lap and dropped the sack on the floor beside his hat. Fortunately sorting the mail only had to be done three times a week for which he was grateful.

"Bills, bills and useless advertisements, I swear the United States Post Office could save a heap of money by not allowing all this junk mail to clutter up the system." Then he picked up a registered letter from Austin, Texas Social Services. He frowned. "Now what in the world is this all about?"

A strange chill ran up his spine followed by a deep fear of what that letter contained. He never claimed to have any of that psychic ability stuff, but his gut was suddenly in an uproar and it wasn't due to hunger.

He drew in a deep breath and let it go. "It's just one of those letters asking for money so just *open* the stupid thing." he said, trying to overcome his reluctance yet he still hesitated. His mind blanked as he stared at the envelope until suddenly he said aloud. "Why in tarnation would it be registered if it was just a solicitation from Texas? It doesn't make sense."

Impatient with his dithering he savagely ripped open the envelope and unfolded the paper and read. The blood drained out of his normally ruddy face and his head hit the back of the rocker with a whack. A groan of gut-wrenching anguish forced its way through his clenched teeth as he crushed the letter in his fist as if by doing so he could destroy the words that had hit him like lethal bullets.

"*My God, my girl is dead! My Jean is dead.*" He whispered and sat for the longest time clutching the letter to his chest trying to breathe passed his constricted throat.

May Tomlinson, housekeeper to Devereau and the wife of his foreman, heard that awful groan and rushed to the screen door where she stopped. No, she thought, he seemed to be alright now, however something in his ridged stillness told her not to disturb him. May waited for a few more minutes then walked slowly back to the kitchen with a frown on her pretty round face. Standing by the sink she looked out the window trying to decide what she should do because something definitely wasn't right with Mr. Devereaux. Finally she nodded her head decisively, took off her apron and left to find Hank who could always solve her problems.

Devereaux's tears flowed down his leathery cheeks catching in the many aged facial grooves to disappear under his shirt collar. He pulled out his handkerchief and swiped at his eyes and gave his nose a blow. When he could see again, he carefully smoothed out the crumpled paper and read the letter again.

"So," he murmured, "Kelly was her married name and they both were killed in a car accident in February and now their children, two boys and a little girl need a home." He whispered to himself, "I didn't know I had grandchildren? My God what have I done?"

Devereau put his head in his hands and sobbed. "*Why God? Why, her and not me? I deserve to die, not her.*" He howled his grief and anger at an unfeeling God. There was no answer.

Slowly he regained control of his emotions and wiped his face again with his red bandana. Devereaux looked down at the crumpled letter and laughing bitterly, "What kind of home could I give those children when I drove their mother away with my meanness? *Isn't this a dirty joke on me?* If those people knew the truth about me they'd think twice before sending those innocent kids here."

The day grayed out for him. The sun began to sink in the west with all its fiery glory brilliantly coloring the few fluffy clouds red and gold as it made the final descent behind the mountains. The old man was blind to its beauty; he was caught in remembering the past that had led his family to this tragic end. The horrible truth was he knew in his heart that he could have changed this outcome if he had only accepted her choice of a husband and invited them to share the ranch with him.

"*Damn* my hard heart! *Damn* my pride!" He beat his chest with one clutched fist as if that punishment would help ease the pain of guilt and loss.

He laughed harshly. Hind sight was always 20/20. Yes, he could have created a different outcome one where Jean would have lived on the ranch with her husband and had her children here. And he, their grandfather, would have had the joy of knowing and loving her babies. Grandsons that would have replace the emptiness caused by his son's death. Oh, and a sweet little baby girl to cuddle and cherish. *He* could have been filled with happiness. The house would have been filled with laughter and joy and noise instead of this empty silence. This house could have been a home again and life would have been......*so very, very good.*

Time simply slipped away before Devereaux gave another deep grief-stricken sigh and scrubbed his face and blew his nose again. He smoothed out the worst of the letter's wrinkles and read it through several times and each time hoped he had misread what it had said.

"*Stupid old man*," he said fiercely, as he folded the letter and inserted it forcibly into the torn envelope. "As if by *wishing* I could change what it says. As if by *wishing* I could change what I have done." He gave a harsh laugh. "All my grand plans are in ashes. Jean is dead and she will never, ever know what I have tried to do for her here. All the wishing in the world won't make this tragedy disappear."

The old man rocked with a mind gone silent. He rocked as dusk slid over the land. Suddenly a thought pierced the vacancy of his mind like an arrow hitting its target with a sharp impact. That thought had him sitting up abruptly. His heart picked up speed as excitement raced through his body. Maybe the Guardians of these Sacred Valleys were giving him a second chance to make up for the past. Maybe, just maybe, if he was kind to his daughter's children,

Jean would somehow know and forgive him and maybe then he could forgive himself. It would be an atonement of a kind, wouldn't it? He so *desperately* needed a way to atone for the harm he had done her.

He couldn't blame his meanness on his wife's death or the loss of his only son, for today, just like chickens, all his faults had come to roost right here on his head. "*God forgive me.*" and wept again for the loss of family and for his own loss of soul.

Hank Tomlinson stepped quietly up onto the front porch and got a shocking look at his boss and hesitated to intrude, but the man's anguish forced him to offer help.

"Mr. Devereaux, are you ill? Is there anything I can do for you?" he asked quietly.

Devereaux jerked then took his handkerchief, wiped his face and blew his nose.

"No, Hank, but thanks for asking, I just got some…bad news. I'll talk to you later." He pretended to be reading his other mail.

"If you need me before then Sir, I'll be around." and stepped back down the steps and walked around the house to the kitchen.

"There's nothing I can do for him, May, but something has hit him really hard 'cause I've never seen that man cry in all the years I've worked for him. I would have said he was too hard to do so." said Hank with concern written on his usually humorous face.

"The thing that might break him into tears is something tragic happening to his daughter. Do you think that might be it Hank?"

"Maybe, maybe so, we'll just have to wait and see if he confides in us." responded Hank and put his arm around her shoulders giving her a quick hug. "It's time to quit sweetheart so put his food in the warming oven and come on home. I'll see you there in twenty minutes." Then Hank went back out the door.

Devereaux sat and watched the darkness take over the day. It wasn't just the coolness that came after the sun took its warmth from the day and chilled the evening, but another kind of deep cold inside his chest that came like a fist clutching his lungs and heart while pain zipped down his arm causing sweat to break out on his forehead and nausea filled his stomach. He'd experienced these sensations several times in the past few months, but none as bad as this one. He snapped his hand as though to shake off the pain and finally it eased.

"Old age, that's all it is, just old age." He muttered fiercely trying to cover up the underlying fear that there was something bad happening. He gathering up the mail and got up and walked through to the kitchen to get his dinner only to peck at it with little appetite. Finally he gave up and retired to his office.

Hank stopped by as usual that evening to talk about what needed to be done the next day and to see if Devereau was alright. It didn't take long for Hank to see that Devereaux was distracted and left for his own cottage.

Now the old man sat quietly before the office fireplace soaking up the heat as the night was chilly with the cool wind blowing down off Thunder Mountain. The big house was still except for the occasional creak of boards or when the wind fluttered a loose shutter against the side of the house. In his sensitive state Devereaux could feel the house's patient sadness like a pressing weight as though it was alive and waiting for something good to happen; something that he was supposed to bring into it.

Out of his deep sadness came ghost-like thoughts began to stir the beginnings of anticipation. How would the arrival of the children change things? Well for one thing his quiet evenings would be rare as the kids would fill the house with their presence. As he gazed absently into the fire he imagined what it would be like to teach the boys about the ranch work and how to manage. A baby girl to hold on his lap of an evening and the stories he could tell them about their mother and the history of the ranch. Those thoughts made Devereaux smile for the first time that day. Yes, the children would make this old house sing again and he'd find and give love once more.

As he gazed into the fire another consideration came unbidden to him. What if this pain wasn't just old age, but something more serious? Maybe he was having small heart attacks? He disliked doctors fussing and pushing pills on a man, nevertheless Devereaux knew something wasn't right with him and it was time to quit putting off seeing the doctor because he had the kids to look after now. Much as he hated the thought of getting a physical he'd do it this week for now wasn't the time to flake out by being stupid.

But what if he did, flake out that is, before the children arrived? There was no one to explain to them the events of the past. A chill ran up his spine. Lord, he didn't even have a will to protect his grandchildren's future. Devereaux shook his head, appalled at having neglected such a basic necessity.

"I'd better take care of things right now; delay is no longer an option and I've got a premonition that time might be running out on me."

Talking to himself had become a habit of a man much alone. He got up and put more wood on the fire before going over to the old rolled top desk that had belonged to his great granddaddy and sat down. He opened the top drawer and pulled out some stationery. With pen in hand he wrote a letter to Social Services and enclosed a large check to cover the children's travel expenses then sealed the enclosed envelope and put it in the bag with the rest of the outgoing mail.

He leaned back in his chair and poured another brandy into his snifter. Now he would write his Will that would protect his grandchildren's legacy. It wouldn't take long for he was leaving everything to them. He also had a few other plans to work out with his lawyer that would further benefit his grandchildren. An hour later he was almost finished when he realized he would need witnesses for his signature. He reached over and picked up the phone.

"Tomlinson." said the man in a deep sleepy voice.

"Hank, I'm sorry to disturb you so late, but can you and May come up to the office for a minute? I need you to witness my Will."

"Is something wrong, boss?"

"No, no, nothing wrong, I'm just tying up loose ends and thought a man my age had better decide who he wanted to have his property when he died. Late night thinking perhaps, but I'm doing it now so would you both come up?"

"Be there in a few minutes." Hank hung up the phone and sat up on the edge of the bed as May turned on the light. "Devereaux is making out his Will and wants us to witness his signature. Wonder who he's chosen to inherit?" Hank got up and began to pull on his clothes.

"His upset *must* have been about Jean. I've heard that there was some trouble just before she left home over fifteen or so years ago.

Maybe she's why he's making his will. Could he be seriously ill? What do you think Hank?" said May as she dressed hurriedly.

"He's never spoken of her in all the time I've worked for him. As far as his being ill, well a man of his age that's possible I guess. Whatever this is about, May, it sure looks like there might be a change in the future for us so we'd best get set for it. I've got a feeling we're on uncertain ground from this point on."

"Oh, dear, I hope not." his wife murmured quietly.

Hank knocked on the ranch house front door then opened it for May to walk in before him. At the further end of the hall a light guided them to the open office door. At the office door they saw a brightly burning fire and the old man sitting at the desk busily writing under a tall lamp.

"Mr. Devereaux?" said Hank.

The old man looked up and motioned to them. "Come in, I'm sorry to have gotten you both out of bed, but I've just about finished the final draft." Hank and May sat down and waited until Devereaux finally laid down his pen and picked up the two sheets of paper and turned to them.

"This here is my last Will and Testament and in it I'm leaving this property to my daughter's children, Michael Devereaux Kelly, Joseph Devereaux Kelly and Carli Jean Kelly." He paused for a moment looking down at the document and murmured, "Jean named the boys after me and the girl after her mother. Well, I'm honored especially after all that has happened. Yes, I'm honored." Suddenly the man cleared his throat a few times, took another sip of brandy and continued. "I'm also giving you and May something for your services to the ranch and I haven't forgotten the men either. If you choose to leave in the future I'll have a fine personal recommendation ready for you. Judge Barker is to find trustworthy guardians for the children if that becomes necessary. Okay, I'm signing this thing and you two are witnesses. Please sign each page so there won't be any misunderstanding."

May and Hank stood up and walked over to the desk as Devereaux signed the paper and dated it then passed over the pen for May and Hank's signatures then Devereaux put the folded Will in a large envelope along with a letter to his lawyer asking for a meeting as soon as possible concerning estate management, sealed it and handed it to Hank.

"I want you to run this into town tomorrow morning and give it to Mr. Jensen to *immediately* file the will proper like with the court. I want *no* delay and tell him that this is to be his priority. Have him call me if there are any questions and to set up an appointment with me for later in the week."

"I'll take care of it first thing. Is there anything else, Sir?" asked Hank as he put the letter away in his pocket.

"Here, might as well take the mail bag. Goodnight and thanks again for coming up." Having dismissed them, Devereaux turned away and began writing. Hank gestured May to go ahead of him and closed the office door then guided his wife down the dark hallway.

The light burned on in the ranch house office until the early hours of the morning. Shafts of light poured out through the windows that cut into the dark night like stripes of white cloth laid down upon the ground. Page after page accumulated on the side of the desk until at last, with a sigh of relief Devereaux put down the pen and massaged his cramped right hand for awhile as he contemplated his work. He didn't reread the pages but simply put them in order and rolled the lot up and tied it with a red ribbon he took from his desk drawer where it had lain for years. Somehow it was appropriate to tie this bundle with one of Jean's hair ribbons. Holding the roll of paper in his hands he seemed mesmerized by the bright ribbon she used to tie her braids. Jean, his beautiful Jean would never return home again.

With a deep weary sigh Devereaux stood up, stretched his stiffened muscles then limped over to the side of the large stone fireplace and triggered the lever under the mantle that released a large rock that slid out revealing a deep drawer. Devereaux slipped the fat roll into the cavity with difficulty as the safe was practically full. Before he closed it he went back to the desk for the other red ribbon and placed it on the drawer's edge then closed it. All that was left to reveal the spot was a bit of red ribbon fluttering in the slight draft coming through the window.

"Now I can sleep, I've done all I can so if something happens to me before the kids get here I've made everything secure for them. They'll find the safe and the letter." The old man checked the fire and placed the fire screen securely in front of it and switched off the light.

As he slowly climbed the stairs to his bedroom he felt an easement come over him almost as though a *spirit* had laid its hand upon his heart giving him a sense of having received…compassion.

It had been years since he had eagerly looked forward to something good happening, but now he was excited and impatient for the arrival of his grandchildren and a renewed life for all of them. For the first time in many years he felt filled with a serene sense of peace.

Joseph Michael Devereaux slept deeply that night.

A week later May Tomlinson was busy in the ranch house kitchen just finishing the last pancake for Mr. Devereaux's breakfast for he was a stickler for everything being on time. Now there was a man who was so prompt you could set your watch by him.

"And if I'm the least bit late I hear about it too." She muttered aloud as she put his food in the warming oven and began doing up the dishes.

May was thinking about the morning work while she washed up the cooking dishes. It wasn't until she had finished that she suddenly realized Devereau hadn't called her to serve his coffee. She paused, but didn't hear any of his usual morning noises. The dining room was empty so May walked out into the hall to the bottom of the stairs and listened. The house was silent. A shiver run up her spine; it was too quiet and May knew something was very, very wrong.

She reluctantly climbed the stairs and walked along the upper hall to his room. She knocked and called through the door, "Mr. Devereaux, are you alright? Breakfast is ready, Sir." There was no answer. She knocked louder then hesitantly eased the door open and peeked in and saw the old man lying quietly in bed.

"Mr. Devereaux?" There was no response. He was too still; too quiet. "Oh, *Lord, have mercy.*" May whispered as she closed the door and ran for Hank.

Ten minutes later Hank walked over to the side of the bed and knew Devereaux was dead even before he touched the cool neck and felt for a pulse, of course there was none; death had paid a house call early that morning. Straightening up Hank pulled the sheet up over Devereaux's head then walked over to his wife who stood in the doorway with her hand over her mouth.

"He's gone May, probably not too long ago as his body is just now cooling." Hank said as he took his wife's arm and led her out into the hall and closed the door. "This is one heck of a way to start the day, babe. I'm real sorry you had to find him like that." Hank led his teary-eyed wife back down to the kitchen and sat her down at the table.

May sniffed. "I don't know why I'm crying for he wasn't a very pleasant man to work for, but I will say he was always polite to me. Oh, Hank, what are we going to do now?" she wailed.

"First of all you're going to calm down. We'll figure things out so stop worrying. You know I'll take care of everything just like you take care of me. You go on home now May, there isn't anything you can do here and I have to make some calls and see to things."

"I'm sorry Hank for carrying on like this and I know you'll take care of thing as you've always done before. Poor Mr. Devereaux, making his will just last week and now he's dead. Do you think he had a premonition, Hank?"

"That's a possibility I guess, but thank God he did make a will or we'd all be in a mess with the ranch left dangling. Even as it is there will be difficulties. Well, you go along May, and I'll come over as soon as I can." And sent May out the door.

Hank sat down at the kitchen table and heaved a heavy sigh before picking up the phone to report Devereaux's death to the police. After the call he just sat there with the phone in his hand, his mind whirled at the overwhelming responsibility for the ranch and everyone's uncertain future here. He just didn't know where to begin to tackle the added problems. Well, Hank desperately needed advice because he surely wasn't thinking very clear at the moment. He dialed his friend, Ben Strongbow, the rancher to the west of them.

"This is Hannah and a good morning to you." Her bright voice was like sunshine on a gloomy day.

"Hello Hannah this is Hank Tomlinson. Is your Dad still at the house? It's an emergency."

"Sure Hank, just a minute." Hank heard her put the phone down and call to her father. "Dan, Hank Tomlinson is on the phone and said it was an emergency."

"What's wrong Hank?" Ben said.

Just hearing that deep baritone calmed Hank somewhat. "Joseph Devereaux died this morning; May found him. I called the police."

"Good Lord, what a shock for poor May. How's she handling it?"

"Not too well Ben. She's a soft hearted woman you know and even though Devereaux wasn't any joy to take care of she said he always treated her politely which means he never yelled at her, which I wouldn't have put up with." Hank took a deep breath and blew it out. "Damn it, I'm babbling like a fool. I just don't know what to do now."

"You definitely have good reason to be upset. Now how can I help you?" Again Ben's calm voice helped steady Hank.

"Thanks Ben. We're going to have big problems here since the will the boss wrote last week hasn't finished probate and that means the assets of the ranch will be frozen. There is very little cash here in the office to run the place until the heirs are found. We might have to close down the ranch. Honestly Ben, I'm not sure what to do about all this."

"I'll come right over. We'll figure out a solution so just go on with the work at hand and I'll be there in ten minutes tops." and hung up the phone.

Hank held the receiver in his hand, and thought about how life could switch and change in a flash. The loud sound of beeping reminded him to hang up the phone. Yeah, life was about uncertainty and that surely was the truth.

No, Devereaux hadn't been easy to work for. As far as Hank was concerned, Devereaux had pretty much run this ranch almost into the ground with his penny pinching ways.

Hank sighed wearily and muttered, "I best go tell the men the bad news. God only knows what will happen next." Shaking his head, he heaved himself to his feet and left the house holding its dead.

~The Kellys~

Fate can be kind or cruel, even blind resulting in changes for good or evil.

THE EAGLE GLIDED ON the hot summer thermals rising off the land as she searched for prey. Sweeping back and forth across the immense valley the bird spotted the two small humans walking on the road below her. She had no interest in two leggers; she was after game to feed her young. Suddenly the eagle spotted several rabbits that had just left the cover of the roadside trees and were boldly running across the field toward the river.

Mike came to an abrupt halt as a Bald Eagle silently swooped across the road right in front of him. Mike watched with awe as the bird struck and all he heard was the squeal of the dying animal.

"Look at that eagle Joe! Boy is it big! I've never seen one this close." he exclaimed.

"Oh, wow, it's huge alright." They watched as the bird lumbered into the air with heavy down strokes of its huge wings with the rabbit dangling from its claws aiming for the awesome mountain ahead of them.

The boys began walking again.

The land baked under the hot July sun and was baking the boys to a nice crisp too. The long dusty road, undulating like a snake as it gradually ascended the rolling hills, lost itself only to reappear until it became like a thread in the distance. The heat seemed to be intensifying as the sun slid its way closer and closer to the western mountains. At least it seemed to get hotter to Mike. A fitful wind blew cool air down from the huge looming mountain with its snowy peak bringing them intermittent relief from the relentless heat. Melodic bird song mingled with the constant dissident rasping of crickets breaking the silence that gripped the magnificent land.

The boys topped a rise in the road then began descending into a shallow fold between the rolling hills. Mike, at fifteen, carried several heavy burdens; a backpack, a guitar case on one shoulder and a carry sack over the other that held his sleeping sister. Joe walked beside him. His young brother had turned seven in June and had only a small backpack, but seemed to be having difficulty keeping up with him.

Mike looked up the dusty road and wondered how long they could keep going. There was no doubt it had been sheer stupidity on his part to take his brother and sister on this long hot walk thinking that they could take care of themselves without help. After being under the control of the state orphanage, he had had his fill of strangers controlling their lives. He knew this was unreasonable, but it didn't lessen his resentment one little bit.

Mike was also angry with the caretaker, Brenda, who was supposed to have seen them safely to the ranch, but Mike didn't excuse himself for his decision to take this hot walk for it was evident that he'd gotten them all in deep trouble.

Brenda had left them high and dry at the River Town Motel and had not only stolen the rest of grandfather's travel money, but had cleaned out Mike's wallet to boot. After waiting for their grandfather to answer their message to come and pick them up he realized it wasn't going to happen. For whatever reason, grandfather hadn't gotten the message or else he would have come for them. Mike had been fed up with waiting and depending on others to help him, even the police. Now, wouldn't that have been a great way to meet your only relative; arriving in a police car. So Mike had asked the clerk how far it was to the Lost Wagon Wheel Ranch and she had said about an hour.

An hour she said! Mike kicked the gravel in disgust. How stupid can a guy be he fumed because after walking almost three hours even at Joe's speed he figured they had come six or seven miles, maybe. So he knew now that the clerk had thought they would be traveling by car. That meant there was still 40 to 50 miles to the ranch. No way would they make it before dark.

They had been trudging up the road with the snow capped mountains in the distance giving the illusion of white coolness and deep green shade with flowing cold rivers that drew a person's gaze upward seeking respite from the intense heat of the valley. That very sight seemed to increase their discomfort.

The hot sun *struck* with savage intensity on the boys' sweaty backs almost burning their left sides through their long sleeved shirts. The hard packed gravel road bounced the heat right back in their faces and added to their fatigue. The road was lined on both sides with tall scattered pine trees lightly coated with dust and cast their long shadows across the road in front of them creating patterns of light and dark to walk through. The boys lived from shade to shade.

The weight of Mike's heavy burdens was causing his shoulder muscles extreme pain that grew worse by the minute combined with the misery of hot swollen feet encased in cowboy boots. He'd been stupid not to have dug out their walking shoes; just another mistake to add to the others.

He didn't particularly want to think about their folks because that brought up too much bone deep grief. As tired as he was he'd probably break down and cry like a baby right here in the middle of the road which wouldn't help this situation one little bit. He was smart enough to realize he had an awful lot of rage at the world, at God and the drunk driver who had killed their parents. Maybe one day he'd find that, that…..stupid, selfish excuse of a man and beat the living daylights out of him. He gave a grunt and shifted his burdens once again. Not that violence would bring the folks back or that violence served any purpose other than a momentary satisfaction, but just the idea of a little revenge at this point felt good. At least he'd be in control of what happened and that thought was a channel for his anger for now. It purely ate at him that he was helpless to change anything.

For the last half hour Joe hadn't noticed the gradual slowing of Mike's steps. He didn't want to be thought a wimp, so he trudged on putting one foot in front of the other. He had been slow getting over the flu, but his pride just wouldn't allow any whining. He certainly wasn't feeling very well right now. He missed his mom and dad so badly that he often wondered if he would ever feel whole or safe or loved again like they had loved him. Joe pondered on his life and the more he thought about his parents the more depressed and tired he grew.

Joe remembered what it was like that *awful day* in court. He'd sat silently beside his brother and sister facing the judge. Joe was numb with fear as he listened to the man seated behind the high desk discussing their future. His heart was so *filled* with grief he couldn't bear to talk about it. He coughed a few times, a left over cold thing that hadn't gone away. Mike handed him a cough drop then put his arm around Joe's shoulders and snuggled him in tight to his side. Thank God for Mike, Joe thought, as he carefully pealed off the cellophane wrap as though how he managed the task was all important to controlling himself, and put the lemon drop in his mouth. Joe waited for the grownups to decide what they were going to do with them.

Life had taken such a sudden disastrous turn that it had left him bewildered and, and….*shriveled*. Yes, that's exactly how he felt, just plain *shriveled and almost invisible*. It was a very strange way to feel. The eternal question of why this *awfulness* had happened to them went unanswered. That question persisted in rolling around and around in his head like a whirling lasso.

The sudden bang of the judge's gavel startled Joe into jerking. Carli whimpered and hugged Mike tighter and hid her head under his jacket. Joe wished he could do the same thing, but he was too big to do something as timid as that. He looked bleakly up at the old man in black robes who was playing God with their lives. It hadn't taken all that long for the man on his high throne to decide their fate. They were going to The Austin Home for Children for the foreseeable future.

It was time for Mike to make a decision about going back. If they weren't going to be able to make the ranch, they'd best head back to the nearest farm right away. There was no sense in going any further.

He gave another hitch to the carry sack that held his sleeping sister and glanced down at Joe to see how he was holding up. Cripes, he hoped Joe could go back to that farm on his own two feet because if he pooped out Mike didn't know what he'd do.

After all, he was the oldest and he had the responsibility to see his brother and sister cared for and delivered safely to their grandfather.

Mike looked down at Joe and thought how like a handsome, masculine version of their mother he was. He had her mop of curly blond hair and deep green eyes while Mike resembled his father with his straight black hair and deep brown eyes; yet no one would ever mistake these two boys as being anything other than brothers. Now Carli was a mixture of both parents with black curly hair and green eyes. Yep, she was the beauty of the family and would surely break hearts when she was older.

Mike stopped abruptly. "I've made an awful big mistake, Joe. We should have gone to the police after all. My selfish excuse was I didn't want to have to explain to the police. Another excuse I gave myself was that I'd get grandfather into trouble. That was pretty stupid of me because I know the police would have helped us." Joe looked up at Mike and opened his mouth to speak when Mike continued. "It also dawned on me that the clerk thought we were going out to the ranch by car and not walking, which means the ranch is about 50 miles from town. Joe, I could just plain *kick* myself if I could reach my butt!" admitted Mike morosely as he hitched his sister up enough to change the slant of the carry sack strap on his aching shoulder.

"Hey Mike, remember I agreed with you so we're both to blame. We can't do much about that now 'cause we're here and there's no sense in going back to town. I guess we just have to keep walking. When you're out of options you just keep trucking, right?" the little boy sighed.

"Thanks for wanting to share the blame for this mess, but I'm the oldest and I should have known better. Unfortunately you're right, there's no going back to town. Dad always said when you make a choice you gotta' live with the results. Well, we're living it aren't we and are we having fun yet?" Mike said savagely.

"Well, no, we aren't, but misery loves company so we're not alone and that ain't all bad. You gotta go with a little humor in situations like this even though it hurts." said Joe with a weak grin. At least he got a bark of laughter out of his brother.

"I just can't *believe* grandfather hasn't come to meet us yet. Maybe he's gone out of town. If he has, won't that be just dandy. Yet surely you'd think someone at the ranch would check for messages? We're just going to have to change directions. We passed Carrington's Farm about a mile back so I think we'd better go back there because I can't risk us getting caught out here after dark."

"Sure Mike it's probably the smart thing to do too." Actually, Joe was relieved they'd stopped because if Mike hadn't Joe might have fallen flat on his face and that would have humiliated him to no end. He pointed over to the side of the road, "We can sit down over there under those trees for a few minutes and catch our breath before we head back."

"Good idea. I sure could use a sit-down I'm that tired. It's not that far back to that farm so we should be able to make it after we've rested a bit." said Mike, trying to appear unworried and positive, but he didn't think he was being very successful.

They crossed the ditch and Joe helped take Mike's guitar case and backpack off. With Joe's help he tramped around the big tree to see if any snakes had sought shelter from the sun in its shade. Finding the area clear of the creatures Mike gave a big sigh of relief as he took off his hat and dropped it on the ground before slipping the carry sack off over his head and gently laid their sleeping sister down on the grass. She never woke up, simply grunted and rolled over and continued to sleep. Joe dumped his backpack and sat down abruptly in the welcomed shade. Mike sat down beside him and groaned as the slight wind cooled him like a gentle hand. He rolled his shoulders several times, raising his arms over his head in a long stretch of arms and back muscles to relieve some of the aching. He wiped his sweaty brow on his shirtsleeve and handed Joe the canteen.

"Wow, sitting down is a relief, but man my feet are so hot I swear they're on fire. If I poured water on them they'd boil, but I'm too scared to take my boots off for fear I won't get them back on." Mike groaned again as he laid flat on the ground beside Carli letting all his muscles relax. It was bliss, pure heavenly bliss.

Joe pulled off his broad brimmed cowboy hat and tossing it on the ground and gave his sweaty head a good scratching that caused his curly hair to stand up which made him look like he'd stuck his finger in a light socket. Uncapping the canteen he took a few gulps of warm water, and while it wasn't real cold water, nevertheless it cleared the dryness from his mouth. Joe handed the canteen back to Mike.

"Yeah, my tootsies are fried for sure," It took Joe some effort to grin, but he managed it. "Now when we cross back over that river, just imagine how fine it will feel to put our hot feet in the cold water. Do you think the water would boil?"

Mike laughed and struggled to sit up to take his own drink of water and wrinkled his nose at the taste, drank a few more swallows before recapping it. "You know just how to torture a guy, don't you? Forget the feet, if we skinny dipped in that nice cool water it would definitely boil, but it would also clean our stinky, sweaty bodies."

Joe laughed and sniffed at his arm pit and groaned. "Yak, we sure don't smell so sweet right now. The idea of cold water hitting my hot body is really mean of you, Mike. Now, who's torturing who or is that whom? Mom would know, wouldn't she?" and the light of funning went out in his face like a blown out lamp. "Sorry Mike, sorry; it's just really hard for me to remember all the time that they're gone and we're alone."

Joe turned his head away and struggled hard not to cry, but grief simply welled up and choked him. Usually he had a better grip on his emotions and he wasn't a cry baby either. It was all because of trying to deal with grief, the children's home and being sick over these past months that had dragged him down plus being so tired right now. Well, it had weakened his grip on himself that's all. Joe was sure he'd be better once he got a good night's sleep. He sniffed, but couldn't stop the tears that seemed to have a mind of their own.

Mike put his arm around the small shoulders and pulled him into his side. "Yeah Joe, I know, and don't apologize for talking about Mom 'cause we need to remember all these little things. I think she'd be pleased to hear us. You know, I think she still can so we've got to keep talking about Dad and Mom just as though they were waiting for us down the road apiece." Mike stopped talking for his own throat had tightened up and he had to swallow several times in order to keep calm for his brother. It wouldn't do for both of them to break down at the same time.

Joe looked up at Mike through his tears and felt an odd kind of comfort when he noticed that Mike was fighting not to cry too, so he didn't feel so bad about crying.

"I'd give anything if I thought they were," sniffed Joe, wiping his face surreptitiously with his dirty sleeve, "Just *anything* at all." His shoulders shook with suppressed sobs and he laid his head on his arms that were braced against his draw-up knees.

"Me too Joe, me too buddy; hang in there and we'll make it together." sighed Mike and Joe sat leaning partially against him and somehow the comfort of that closeness helped. They had each other and Carli.

"We'll have a nice cool shower pretty soon and I bet that farmer will feed us too and drive us out to the ranch either tonight or tomorrow morning." said Mike, desperate to lift Joe's spirits.

"Yeah…okay….sure….that sounds great, Mikey."

Mike was surprised because Joe hadn't called him Mikey since their parents died. Mike figured Joe had decided he deserved a grown up name like their Dad's now. That slip of Joe's was just more proof of how beat the kid was.

The sun had disappeared behind the western mountains and a cool evening breeze felt good on their overheated bodies. Nature's own kind of peace calmed the boys a little. So here they were, sitting beside the empty road and taking those all-important deep breaths before turning back to Carrington's.

Mike worries increased as dusk would last only an hour or so before night came down on them like an avalanche. No rescue was expected as there hadn't been any traffic since they'd left town. At least the walk back to Carrington's farm would be cooler without the sun beating them half to death. Mike knew he had put them all in danger.

~*Rescue*~

CARLI TURNED OVER AND sat up. "Mikey, I is thirsty and hungry." Then the little girl looked around in a frightened and bewildered way. "Where is we?"

Her hair was squished flat on one side of her sweaty head making it look lopsided. Mike fluffed it up a bit before forcing a light laugh. "Why we're having an adventure Carli, now here's some water and I'll get you something to eat while we rest a bit more." While he was attending to her needs he thought he heard the faint sound of a motor and turned his head to look up and down the road. "Mike, I think a car is heading our way. Do you suppose we can hitch a ride?" asked Joe hopefully.

"Maybe, let's see who they are first." Then boys saw a big white truck come over the far hill from the direction of River Town. As it got closer the truck slowed down so it wouldn't spew dirt and dust all over them until it finally rolled to a stop.

A man put his window down. "Howdy kids! Can we help you?"

Mike stood up and after looking the big man over very carefully he took a long step cross the ditch onto the road and walked part way to the truck before he saw a woman sitting on the other side of the driver and breathed a little easier.

"Yes Sir, we've come from River Town where we were told that it was only an hour to the Devereaux Place, Lost Wagon Ranch, that is," said Mike. "How far is it from here now?"

"An hour walking as you are? For goodness sake, who told you that? Yes, it is about an hour's *drive* by car or truck, but not walking."

Mike nodded his head. "Yeah, I figured that out not too long ago. Well, that's that then. We were going to start back for the Carrington Farm."

Mike watched the couple speak softly for a minute then the woman got out and walked around the truck and over to where Mike was standing. She was a tall woman with a strong medium size frame, yet graceful in her jacketed calf length dress and boots. She had a lovely face and blond hair worn in a braid wrapped around her head like a crown just like his mother had worn hers. Mike thought she looked like one of those ancient queens he'd once seen in a picture book; regal was the word. Only her kind face was shadowed by a deep concern and for some unknown reason Mike tightened his stomach muscles as though preparing for a blow he knew was coming and was helpless to prevent.

"We're Ben and Mari Beth Strongbow and we have the ranch west of your grandfather's Lost Wagon Ranch." she said softly and hesitated for a minute. "What's your name, son?"

"I'm Michael Devereaux Kelly, ma'am; that's my brother Joseph Devereaux and our sister Carli Jean. We're on our way to live with our grandfather."

"Oh, my goodness, you're Jean's children! I knew your mother very well Michael, we were good friends. Now I recall Hank Tomlinson, Mr. Devereaux's foreman, mentioning something about a will and grandchildren."

The woman hesitated and glanced back over her shoulder at her husband before speaking again. "Michael, I'm so very sorry to have to tell you that your grandfather died suddenly of a heart attack ten days ago. There wasn't any way to notify Jean because we didn't have an address or phone number. No one knew you were coming."

It took a few minutes for her words to sink in. Dead? She said grandfather was *dead*? Devastation filled Mike's eyes and clutched his head. "*God, what am I to do now? What are we going to do now?*" he groaned in anguish.

Mari Beth put her arm around Mike's shoulders. "Michael, I know this is terrible news. I know and I am so very sorry." Mike breathed hard and tried to stop shaking while holding his head fearing it would fall off his shoulders if he let go.

"Now look here, Mike, Ben and I can't leave you children out here with night coming on." She squeezed his shoulders. "Sometimes you have to take help where you find it so it's best y'all come home with us. You'll get showered and have a nice hot dinner. After you've had a good night's sleep we'll help you sort things out in the morning. You're all tuckered out so let's get you into the truck. Go on now, get the children." Commanded the woman and gave him a little push to get him moving.

Mike walked back to the side of the road; after all what else could he do at this new turn of fate? When would the bad news end, he thought discouragingly as he stepped over the ditch, when would the bad times stop?

Mike bent over and picked up his sister. "I walk, Mikey, I walk." said Carli in a very clear voice.

"Sure, Carli, just as soon as I lift you over the big ditch." Mike fought to get a grip on his slippery emotions as he carried Carli over the ditch and sat her down on her feet. Squatting down on his heels he tried to say as calmly as possible, "See that nice lady standing over there? She's like a Mother and we're going to go home with her."

"Mother?" it was the only word Carli picked up on. "*My Momma?*" She tore her hand out of Mike's and ran toward Mari Beth with her arms up. "Momma, Momma, here I is, you baby! Momma, pick me up!" cried the little girl demandingly.

Mari Beth was startled then took a few steps toward the running child and scooped the little girl up and got her neck fiercely squeezed by the child's arms.

"You *bad* Momma, you *bad, bad* girl, you go away and I cried and cried." scolded Carli all the time holding on for dear life. "*Don't do that, I no like it; bad Momma.*" and began to cry wildly like her heart was breaking.

Mari Beth's heart was caught and she hugged the little girl tightly to her chest. "There, there my baby, I won't go away again, I promise with all my heart. I shall always be here for you now." said the woman recklessly while kissing the child's hot wet cheek. "Let's go home and I will give you a nice bath and a hot supper. Doesn't that sound good, sweet thing?"

Mari Beth carried the little girl over to stand beside the truck door and looked in at Ben with pleading eyes. Ben just shook his head laughing gently as he turned off the engine and got out of the truck.

"Got hooked again didn't you buttercup; got sucked in by a pretty face. Well, well, she's a beauty for sure." giving the crying little girl a pat on her bottom.

Ben looked over at the dumb struck young man whose mouth was still hanging open and had to grin. In his deep baritone voice Ben said, "It looks like your little sister has made up her mind young fella, so the best y'all can do is learn not to interfere with the ladies' choices." he clapped his hands sharply, "Alright, let's get rollin' 'cause supper's waiting. We'll take the baby up front with us and you two ride in the back with the dog 'cause we're loaded down with supplies in the small back seat. Now, don't you worry about Rosco, he won't bite you, in fact that dog is too darn friendly to even be a good watchdog."

Mike stood up and looked at the big dog hanging his head over the side of the truck with his tongue lolling out of his mouth and a furiously beating tail that wagged his whole black and brown body. Mike had to smile at the dog's eager body language. Glancing back at Joe's exhausted, anxious face standing on the other side of the ditch Mike knew that the offer of a ride and a place for the night was something to be profoundly grateful for. In fact, they were being rescued by two of God's angels.

The Strongbows appeared to be trustworthy, but whether they were or weren't he really didn't have a choice right now. He worried about Carli thinking Mrs. Strongbow was her mother, but there wasn't much he could do about that mistake either. Jumping back over the ditch Mike picked up his hat and slapped it on.

"Come on Joe, let's go. At least we won't have to walk another mile and we'll have that shower and dinner and a good place to sleep tonight. Let's be grateful." They gathered up their belongings and walked over to the side of the truck where the big man waited for them.

Ben Strongbow was as surprised as Mari Beth to see Devereaux's grandchildren stranded on the side of the road. It was only recently that Hank had mentioned to him that Devereaux had grandchildren. What in the heck were the kids doing way out here by themselves? There must be a story behind this. He helped Mike load their small packs into the back of the truck while admonishing Roscoe.

"Now behave yourself and don't slobber all over these boys." He turned and lifted Joe into the back while Mike climb in after him. He had to grin as the big dog got in a few licks when the boys sat down with their backs to the cab. He laughed as Roscoe tried to crunch himself small enough to squeeze his big body in between them and since he was so determined the boys laughed and moved apart just enough so the three of them could sit together.

Ben took a blanket from behind the front seat. "Here's a blanket if you get cold before we make it home." and handed it to Mike.

"Thanks Sir, we appreciate this."

"No bother son, no bother at all." Ben got back into the driver's seat and started the truck. He paused to look back through the window at the heads of the three passengers. Roscoe was about to apply his own form of comfort and sure enough, both boys had their arms around the delirious dog, petting him and talking to him like he was their best buddy.

Yeah, thought Ben, wordlessly communicated to Mari Beth with a grin and a head gesture toward the back, Roscoe was just what was needed and there wasn't anything better then a dog for comfort and instant selfless love.

She looked back then nodded as she smiled. "Maybe Roscoe has found something useful to do at last." Her observation spoken in such a droll voice made Ben laugh.

"Yeah, maybe he's found his purpose in life."

"Carli wants a doggie too, please?" the baby hiccupped on a sob and looked up through teary emerald eyes at Mari Beth. For months now Carli had been without her momma and poppa and it had left her bewildered and lost. She was so tired of traveling and being surrounded by strangers that she was in a state of constant confusion and fear.

"Yes my baby," said Mari Beth as she dried the child's cheeks, "When we get home you can have your very own doggie, but right now close your eyes and take a little nap." said the adoptive mother as she stroked the child's hair.

"Okay Momma, okay, I is a tired girl and, and my boys is tired too. I am really hungry Momma. Can I have a cookie? I love cookies." Carli took a waiver inward breath and closed her eyes though she clutched Mari Beth's jacket firmly in her little hands so her mother wouldn't disappear again.

Mari Beth patted the child's hands "Yes my girl, you shall have a big chocolate chip cookie. Hush now and sleep, you're home safe with me."

Ben looked over at Mari Beth holding the little girl snug in her arms and knew he would lose any argument with his wife's desire to keep the child. Well, well, it wasn't any problem for him because he liked kids, and truth to tell he missed having them around. So here were God's Gift of three forlorn children, maybe and *only* that if it worked out for the best. Hmm, I wonder who planned it this way, thought Ben suspiciously. He suspected that this happening had the fingerprints of those nosy Guardians all over it.

The truck sped quickly down the road in the gathering dusk and Ben switched on the headlights. Less than forty minutes later they were home as they drove under a wooden archway with a sign over the top that said, "Welcome to Thunder Ranch."

In the summer's twilight, that special, magical time just before full dark, the white truck purred along the graveled road revealed in the twin eyes of the headlights. His wife was holding the sleeping child and gazing out the window at the darkening land. Ben loved looking at her for she was the light of all that was good in his life, the all important substance of his foundation. They rarely had arguments, and for a long time married couple that was a rare thing in itself. Oh, they'd raised the roof a few times, but nothing that tore the fabric of their marriage apart. Mari Beth wasn't any patsy to placate a man and Ben had listened to her wisdom too many times not to know she *knew* things that often escaped him. He had a lot of respect for a woman's intuition because Mari Beth was more often right than wrong.

He turned his attention back to the road. The land had endured the changing of generations and the seasons. Oh, Mother Earth made changes, but usually it was a slow process, however once in awhile Mother Earth violently changed everything on the moment just to remind the humans that She was a force to contend with. Uncertainty was the key word for Mother Nature and a lesson never to take Her for granted and those who did were plain stupid. The Valleys had stayed relatively the same over the centuries because of the infinite care people gave the lands that lived here. The Guardians had a lot to do with that preservation too. Well, actually They demanded it.

Ben Strongbow believed in the philosophy that if you cherished the land and your family, everyone prospers. Daddy Strongbow had taught him that and as the story goes his Daddy taught him and on back to the first Strongbow to take up this land. It was written in an old, old journal about how the first Strongbow had made a covenant with the Guardians/Thunder Gods and the Chief Blackhawk of that long ago time. Who was he to doubt what was written in those old journals of past lives since he hadn't been there to personally verify it. He did believe in the honesty of his ancestors, however and their recording of their times.

His ancestors' journals had been kept mostly by the women of the family and were fascinating reading that told of the challenges, tragedies and triumphs of each generation. The first journal had been written in French on birch bark by one of the children who had learned to write from a Catholic Priest out of Canada. She had written the family history as told to her by her great-grandparents. Before, all stories had been orally past down through the family until the day this young person had written it down for posterity. Later on another ancestor by name of Little Bird had translated that history into English and onto parchment paper. She was smart enough to value and preserve the original birch bark document and had wrapped it in dry, un-tanned leather and stored it carefully in a wooden box sealed with wax to make it air tight. Ben had that treasure safely locked up in the bank along with the original land grant and the legal deed. One of these days he'd have a curator preserve the original bark writings in a more scientific way.

The story that intrigued Ben was about the first Strongbows and how they came into this valley with a child strapped to the woman's back and a pack of dogs dragging travois carrying all their worldly possessions. Both people had been of mixed blood and struck out into the wilderness with great courage to discover a place of their own and form their own tribe of Strongbow. In those times it was very dangerous to be alone in the wilderness because they would have been defenseless against attack by other Indians. That was why being cast out of a tribe was likely to be a death warrant.

The people here were another marvelous side to the magic of these Sacred Valleys; people took care of people just like now with these two lonesome boys and this sweet baby cuddled in Mari Beth's lap.

"**What are we going to do** about these three?" Ben asked Mari Beth.

"Do, what do you mean... do? Why we'll take them home and feed them a good hot meal and give them a soft bed to sleep in, of course. We'll tell them they can stay with us until their business has been settled." Mari Beth said in a positive manner that it had Ben smiling.

She was silent for a few minutes before saying sadly, "You know Ben, Jean must be dead or Carli wouldn't have scolded me for leaving her. It must have happened months ago for the baby to have forgotten exactly what her mother looked like. I remember Jean used to look something like me when I was younger and wore her hair as I do and she liked the same scent I have always worn so maybe to her I smell like Jean. I think babies remember their mother's smell more than what they looked like, but where is the father?" Mari Beth shook her head sadly. "Something tragic has happened or why were these children heading for Devereaux's? Well, you can tell they're worn to the bone so I say it's important right now to ease their worries because it's the only compassionate thing to do." stated Mari Beth emphatically.

"You're right my love and they seem to be good kids. I'll admit it will be kinda' nice having young people back at the ranch again. However, we don't know anything about them or their past so let's do what we can right now and wait before we take the next big step." Ben looked over at his beautiful wife and grinned then turned his attention back to the road and waited.

"I don't know if I can do that Ben; wait I mean. This baby-child thinks of me as her mother and if I abandon her to the system again she'll always feel rejected twice. In her mind Jean and I are one and the same. No, no, I really don't think I can wait."

Ben nodded. "Sure, I understand. Well, shoot and blast Mari Beth, that's the trouble with having children, they grow up on you and leave home. Now what do people like us do with all this kid-raising knowledge and vast wisdom gained from years of practice and no children to practice on anymore, I ask you?" grumbled the big man. "It's a waste of a valuable human resource. Yes, it's a rotten shame that's what it is."

Mari Beth laughed and punched Ben gently in the arm and he grunted appreciatively and cast a grin at her as she looked down at the sleeping child laying so confidently in her arms, yet her little hands had a firm grip on Mari Beth's jacket. Mari Beth smiled contentedly as she patted the baby's hands and knew that there was no way she would give this little girl up. The Gods had answered her prayers for more children.

"I should have given you a dozen children, Benji, and I'm sorry I couldn't, but that's an old sorrow. So maybe now we're supposed to watch out for these lost children with nowhere to go. We've raised three boys and three girls of our own, not to mention three great adopted children that desperately needed us at the time. Their all treasures Ben, they're all our treasures." She paused then chuckled, "Well, if we take these children in I will have given you an even dozen wouldn't I?"

Ben laughed at that. "Yeah, an even dozen kids sounds good. You know I like to think that we've made the world a better place because we raised our children with good principles and ethics to live by no matter where they chose to live."

Mari Beth was quiet for awhile then gave a heart felt sigh and casting a fleeting glance through the back truck window at the two boys with the blanket covering them and Roscoe and had to chuckle at the dog's acceptance though he didn't need the warmth.

"I miss the chaos and the fun of having a house full of kids and it sure kept us from being bored, didn't it? After the children left the peace and quiet was a welcomed thing for awhile. However, little birds must try their wings and fly away and what they make of themselves will be their doing. So far I'm happy that they're handling their lives just fine. Of course, one could wish that they weren't so scattered that we only see them on holidays and sometimes not even then as they lead such busy lives."

Mari Beth paused letting the thoughts come as they would. "Thank goodness Luther and Hannah chose to stay here in the Valley so I guess we should be grateful for that fact instead of complaining about the ones who aren't here." said Mari Beth in a quiet voice.

Ben knew his Mari Beth well enough to wait patiently while she worked out a situation. The quiet humming of the engine was the only sound for awhile as the ranch house came into view from the road's hilltop.

"These children now," said Mari Beth, breaking the silence. "Old Devereaux is gone and I while I don't like to speak ill of anyone I don't think he wouldn't have been good for these young ones at least not from our experience. The only thing good I can say about him is that he treated his land and his animals well. Of course, that's the only smart thing he ever did or The Thunder Gods would have kicked him out by now. Hmm, maybe the Gods had something better in mind for these young boys and this precious little girl besides a man like Devereaux."

Again silence settled in then she cleared her throat. "Now Ben, they don't have any place to go right now and I'll be darned if I will have anything to do with sending them to an orphanage. Who could do a better job of raising them considering all the practice we've had? It looks to me like these boys know something about ranching from the way they're dressed." She said defensively. "Besides, Carli called me Momma so I'm hooked and I just want you to know that I'll fight to keep them." When Mari Beth finished her jaw was set in a firm way and Ben struggled not to laugh at this very serious woman.

"True, true, it's not a good thing to let our useful child raisin' knowledge go to seed, so to speak. And isn't it handy that Devereaux's ranch is right next door to us, being that I think the kids will inherit the place? It's definitely logical for us to keep the children and then they'll be happy, you'll be happy and I'll be happy. You know I'll do anything to keep you happy sweetheart." said Ben in a mild unassuming voice as he glanced over at her with a somber face, but his eyes fairly sparkled with laughter in the soft light coming from the dashboard.

"Well darn you, Benjamin Strongbow; you're just leading me on. You'd already figured on taking these children in, haven't you? Come on, fess' up." She moved gently over to the center of the bench seat so as to not wake the baby and slipped her free arm around his neck and squeezed.

Laughing, Ben confessed. "Well, as I said, it's just logical. Of course a lot depends if they want to stay with us and if the authorities approve. I shouldn't think the authorities would be any trouble as we have proven to be good stable parents in the past. So yeah, I like the idea a lot. Let's just put this aside for later after we've become better acquainted and have talked it over with the boys. The bottom line is we'll help them do whatever is best for them now."

The road ran between pasture fences and Ben looked around at the darkened land that never ceased to delight him with its richness and it never ceased to fill Ben's heart with gratitude. The land was well watered by rivers and small streams flowing down from the mountains. They rode along in silence when Ben had a thought jump into his head of something that just hadn't clicked in before.

"I've just had a sudden thought. Looking back over the years there's been a real phenomenon happening right under our noses and we've been too busy to take notice. Do you realize how many homeless and abused children have managed to find their way here? Not just children, but adults too as though they were guided here by an unseen force. Not just the kids we've taken in, but look at people here and in the other Valleys that surround Thunder Mountain that have taken in children or adults. I don't think it's by accident, do you?"

Mari Beth opened her eyes wide as she listened to her husband. He amazed her with his astute ability to look at the big picture. "Goodness Ben, you're right! Now that I see the pattern, it is unusual for so many misplaced people to be attracted here to the Valleys. Well, well, well, I think the Thunder Gods are keeping Themselves busy, don't you?" she grinned.

"Something sure is acting like a magnet. Makes things kinda' interesting, doesn't it?" he smiled back at her, "We'll have to keep our eyes peeled for more of these *lost* children and adults and I'll bet we'll see more of them as time passes. However I've got a strange feeling that there is more behind this attracting of the homeless that either you or I can fathom at the moment. It's a mystery for sure, but if we keep the big picture in mind and sort of see what these people do or follow where these people go if they leave here, we just might understand a little of what the Guardians are doing. I think I'll do a little research and start keeping a journal and a follow up map on those who have left and those people who have stayed."

All Mari Beth said in reply was. "Hmmm, that should prove very enlightening." and looked down at the sleeping baby in her arms.

"Anyway, we're the best for these children right now and I'll tell anyone who thinks differently a thing or two."

Ben knew Mari Beth had made up her mind and when this woman said, *"Move,"* everyone who had any sense just naturally got out of her way. Mari Beth was kind and gentle of nature, but when she was on a mission it was best not to mess with her. Ben chuckled quietly and put his hand on her knee and squeezed it gently and left it there in a silent communication through touch.

~*Thunder Ranch*~

It was only a matter of minutes before they pulled into the well lit ranch yard and stopped at the back door. Turning off the engine and switching off the lights, Ben got out and came around to help Mari Beth out of the truck. Roscoe leaped out of the back and ran off to investigate his domain leaving the boys to stand up in the truck bed uncertain what to do next.

"Here, young fella', let me give you a hand down 'cause I bet it's been a hard day for you." Ben took hold of Joe's waist and plucked him out of the truck bed and whirled him up and around and around before setting him down on the ground surprising laughter out of the boy as he staggered dizzily. Mike quickly swung his legs over the side and slipped to the ground.

The brothers stood still for a few minutes gaping at the size of the beautiful ranch house. Off in the distance they could see the shadowy outlines of barns and other outbuildings with their outside lights.

"Wow, Mike, just look at all this!" whispered the little boy.

"Yeah, pretty neat, huh? Come on Joe, let's help Mr. Strongbow unload."

Ben looked surprised as the boys offered to help carry groceries into the kitchen.

"Sure you aren't too tired? Okay, here's a bag for you Joe and two for you Mike and I'll take three then we can make another trip or two for the rest of the stuff."

Mari Beth had already gone in with Carli by the time Mike and Joe walked into the warm kitchen that was filled with delicious smells. Their stomachs growled in unison as it had been a long time since breakfast and the small snacks eaten for lunch.

There was a woman standing beside Mari Beth, pretty and young and small in statue with a gently rounded figure and luxurious long black hair that reached past her hips and was held back by a red head band. Mike thought she had the largest, kindest brown eyes he'd ever seen and a full lipped mouth made for smiling. They set the bags down on the long counter and turned to face the women and took off their hats.

"This is our daughter, Hannah Truelove Strongbow. Hannah, this is Mike and Joe Kelly and they'll be staying with us until some of their problems get worked out."

"Oh good, more boys to feed and a baby in the house, you're truly welcome. Now Mother will have children to fuss over again which makes me very happy, being as how I'm the only chick still in the nest. I know we're going to be great friends." She smiled as she spoke in a soft velvety voice and sounded just like their mother's.

Hannah held out her hand to shake Mike's. "How do you do, Miss Hannah," said Mike politely. Hannah beamed at him and Mike had the strangest feeling as though he had just been hugged, and blushed.

Then Hannah held out her hand to Joe and as they clasped hands their eyes locked and something very profound seem to pass between them. Hannah whispered, "Son, you're home *safe* with us now."

Something shattered inside Joe and he completely lost it. He dropped his hat and took a long lunging step forward and grabbed Hannah violently around the waist and burst into anguished cries, digging his face into Hannah's chest. She calmly reached down and picked him up as though he weighed no more than a few pounds and walked away into the living room singing softly.

Mike blanched and rushed to follow, but Mari Beth stopped him with a firm hand on his arm. He looked up at her with the same anguish in his eyes that Joe was expressing out loud. Carli woke up abruptly and looked around wide-eyed at the strange place and the loud sobs she could hear from the other room. She clutched Mari Beth tightly around the neck, her mouth quivered and tears began to run down her face too.

"It's truly alright, Mike. I know this upsets you, but this is good for Joe and he must have needed to cry like this or it wouldn't have happened. Hannah's always had a way with the hurt ones. She's like a magic person that can draw the pain out of the heart. Let's leave them alone for a bit, she'll settle him down and he will be much better after awhile, you'll see." she said quietly.

Mike looked like he was about to cry too as he gazed after his brother, yet he sucked it in and ducked his head, settled his hat firmly back on his head and said. "Okay, you know best. Well, I'd better go help Mr. Strongbow with the rest of the stuff." and turned, swept up Joe's hat and placed it on a chair and escaped as fast as he could from the hot kitchen.

Mari Beth frowned as she rocked Carli and watching the tall boy slip out the back door. "Now there's another hurtin' boy if I ever saw one, Carli Jean," She said aloud to the child. "He's a real head-of-the-house kind of guy who had to be strong so he can take care of his brother and you. Something will have to give before he can heal his grief just like Joe is doing. Stuffing one's feelings is a very dangerous thing to do because eventually it invites explosions, usually at unexpected times."

At that point in her concern Carli began to talk a mile a minute. "Joey is crying. I no like Joey crying. What hurted my boy?" she sniffed.

"Now, now, baby girl, everything is alright and Joey will feel much better later on. How would you like a small glass of milk and a cookie before your bath?" she asked as she sat Carli on her feet.

"Promise, Momma, promise my boy is okay?" she frowned intently up into Mari Beth's face. The child was almost three and very precocious thought Mari Beth.

"Yes darling, I promise your boy will be alright and you'll see him in a little bit."

"Okay Momma, promise is promise. A cookie now, Momma, cookie please, okay?"

Mari Beth went out to the laundry room and brought in an old high chair that had a well used polish. She wiped it down then sat Carli in it and pushed the chair up to the table and got a washcloth to clean her face and hands.

"Cookie now, Momma!" demanded the child.

"Yes my love, cookie and milk coming right up."

Once all the bags and packages and the boys' packs were carried in, Mari Beth silently signaled Ben to follow her lead. He gave a slight nod and while he wasn't sure what she was about, he was willing to let Mari Beth deal with it and he'd catch on soon.

"Look, Mikey, cookie with choc'at. Bite?" and generously offered the last piece of cookie to her brother.

"Thanks, Carli, but you eat it. I don't want to spoil my supper."

"Okay." Then she looked back up at Mike with surprised eyes. "Supper? We gonna' eat more? I'm hungry, Momma, supper, please." and quickly shoved the last piece of cookie into her mouth.

Mari Beth laughed. "Supper after you had your bath sweetheart then you'll have lots of good things to eat."

Mike moved closer to Mari Beth and whispered. "Mom called her sugarplum."

Mari Beth smiled at him and gently smoothed his shirt sleeve. "Thank you Mike, indeed she is a sugarplum. Ben, why don't you show Mike your prize horses after you put the pickup away? Don't be too long as I want the boys to shower and put on fresh clothes before we have supper and we're running awfully late as it is. You've got about fifteen minutes no more."

"You interested in horses, boy?" asked Ben.

Mike lit up like a Christmas tree. "You bet Sir. Why, my Dad was a champion bronco rider and roper too and a mighty good horse trainer as well." Just as abruptly the light went out in his eyes and Mike dropped his eyes and stopped talking. Ben and Mari Beth exchanged speaking looks.

"How about a small glass of lemonade before you two take off for the barn? You've had quite a long walk before we picked you up and you must be fairly parched." Lifting her eyebrows at the boy got him to answer quickly.

"Yes Ma'am, I mean Mrs. Strongbow, I'd surely like that."

"Call me Mari Beth, Mike, just like everyone does around here."

"Well, shoot and blast woman, don't forget this old man could use some of that stuff too. I've had a long hard drive and I'm real tired with the fetchin' and carryin' you had me doing all day. Can't you see my tongue's hanging out?" said Ben in kind of a high whinny voice that had them laughing at his foolishness.

Mike thought how like his parents they were; down to earth loving people. Well, yeah, maybe so he thought cynically, but he'd wait and see. Still their fooling around brought another lump to his throat that he manfully swallowed along with his first gulp of lemonade.

That taste was so awesome that it shook him right out of his gloom. His eyebrows flew up and he exclaimed. "Wow, that's the best lemonade I've ever had. Golly, Joe should have some of this 'cause he's got a real thing for lemonade. Who made it?"

"It's Hannah's secret receipt and she won't let anyone in on it. We have to keep her chained to our kitchen so she won't escape." bragged her mother. "Why, my girl is the best cook in all the Sacred Valleys."

Mari Beth picked Carli up out of her chair and patted her back unconsciously and got some sticky kisses in return leaving chocolate smears on her face and on her jacket from the small hands. Mike cringed a little, but Mari Beth didn't seem to mind.

"Sacred Valleys? Where's that?" asked Mike quickly.

"Right here and all the other Valleys surrounding the huge old mountain you saw, but that's a story for later on. Now you two hurry up and finish that drink before you run out of time; get on with you." Mari Beth made shooing motions and the men hurried and finished their drinks in a rush.

"Thank you, Mrs., ah, Mari Beth, Ma'am, that was powerful good." Putting on his hat Mike followed Ben out the door.

Mari Beth sat Carli down and led her down the long hall and up the stairs to the big bathroom for a nice warm bath before supper. Carli didn't even cry for Mike or Joe, after all she had her mother again.

They drove the pickup into the garage and after closing the doors Ben and Mike walked toward the bigger barn and Ben was saying, "You see my ranch is both about cattle, horses and other products. The secret to my success is having a fine breed of Hereford cattle and I only feed them on good rich grass, natural grains and silage. None of this artificial stuff and growth hormones for my beef and they're certified organic. I would say that all the farms and ranches surrounding Thunder Mountain are organic and boy, let me tell you, it's made us all rich just by doing the right thing, isn't that amazing?" They walked a few more paces before Ben cleared his throat and continued.

"You see Mike I'm responsible for what I grow and how it affects people's health that buy my products. Besides that, the land must be protected from anything that would harm it or the animals. Well, I have lots of land and I don't overgraze." Ben chuckled. "Now I will admit my first love is fine horseflesh and for the most part they're Quarter Horses. Why, I got some of the likeliest colts and fillies you've ever set eyes on and once they're trained or partially trained I can sell them for a good price. I raise them gentle-like, discipline without harshness and that makes a mighty fine horse; responsive and quick without a mean bone in their bodies because they love what they do. I think the way I train my horses helps them grow in intelligence and in heart." Ben stopped and almost as though he was a bit embarrassed he added, "Of course, that's only my theory you understand."

"No, I think you're right, Mr. Strongbow; my Dad felt the same way and that's why ranchers wanted him to train their special horses." Mike grew quiet again after that short reply.

"Now that's mighty interesting and makes me feel....well, not quite so foolish, I guess. Say, while you're here, if you decide to stay awhile, maybe you can help me halter train a few of the young ones. I've got good men working for me, but these little ones take special patience and a loving touch that require time. This is a big ranch and we have our hands full most of the time, so I could really use a good man for the young ones. I'd like to see you work with them if you want to try. What do you say?" asked Ben.

"I can do that, Sir, why I used to help my Dad when he was training horses, at least some of the easier parts. I really love the little ones the best and he taught me the basics and I think I did fairly well with them 'cause my Dad was a patient teacher." again Mike stopped speaking and silence filled the next few steps.

"You kids lost your Father and your Mother, didn't you? That's why you were coming to live with Joseph Devereaux," asked Ben gently.

They reached the barn before Mike said bleakly. "We lost Mom and Dad in a car accident last February."

Ben put his arm around Mike's shoulders and hugged him gently to his side and said. "Now, that's a rough one son, a real down and dirty rough one. I lost my folks in an airplane accident twenty years ago and it still hurts." and said no more.

Mike found the big man's arm around his shoulders so comfortingly familiar that if he closed his eyes he would have sworn that it was his father walking beside him. Ben even smelled a bit like his dad too and that had Mike clenching his teeth and tightening his lips to keep from howling like Joe. He struggled to swallow the large lump in his throat. It was because he was so tired he reasoned, just plumb tuckered out and it's made him shaky is all.

Ben, with a side-wise glance at the grieving young man, opened the small barn door and gently pushed Mike ahead of him. Soft lights ran down the center alley between the horse stalls and inquisitive heads shot out to check who was coming and greeted the men with whinnies and snorts. Mike was immediately distracted from his sorrow by the familiar smells of horses, hay and yes, even manure.

Ben turned up the lights. "Here's a bucket of carrots; go make some friends." Grabbing the bucket, Mike went down one side of the alleyway stroking, snapping carrots and talking nonsense to the beauties who accepted love as their due. Ben watched and saw that Mike wasn't afraid of them and he didn't rush at them either. Horses frightened easily at sudden movements, probably left over survival instincts when living wild. It had something to do with the eyes in animals; predators had their eyes in the front of the head so they could stalk prey and the prey had theirs on the sides so they could watch for the predators while they grazed.

Ben noticed Mike talked softly and the horse responded calmly as he was feeding it a carrot while the others whinnied and stamped their feet at the slowness of the boy's progress. Ben thought this might be one of the ways Mike could heal his grief by giving him work that was familiar to him. These big animals had a way of grounding a person, and love was always given back for love received.

Exactly fifteen minutes later, Ben turned the lights down to dim and closed the barn door for the night. On their way back to the house, Mike was vocal about how wonderful the horses were and did he have a special stud and when could he see the colts and fillies. The boy's spat of questions delighted Ben's heart and he patiently answered each and every one.

They were almost to the kitchen door when Ben stopped and stood looking at the large farmhouse all lit up in welcome and said. "Mari Beth and I raised nine children in this house and it feels mighty empty now with only Hannah to keep us from rattling around like two stones in a barrel. Our son Luther lives on the southern section of the ranch. He calls it the Rocking Horse because he raises Tennessee Walkers. You'll meet him tonight because that's his pickup over there. Actually, he rarely misses supper at our house, not because he can't do without seeing us each day, you understand," Ben chuckled. "It's Hannah's cooking that brings him to our door most nights since he doesn't have a good cook. Actually Jude is a lousy cook and his men aren't happy and when working hands aren't happy with a cook, well, interesting things start happening. Jude used to be a regular hand and got shoved into filling in as cook when the last one quit. If the boys didn't personally like him so well they would have kicked him off the ranch a long time ago. Luther's going to have to change that real soon and employ a good cook or lose good men." Good Lord Almighty, he was rattling on and on.

Ben cleared his throat. "Mike, you're carrying a might big load for your age in caring for your brother and sister. From what I've seen, you're doing a fine job, but this is a hard, hard time for y'all so maybe you'll let us help you until things get straightened out. Ah, that is if you want us to? I know this is kind of sudden, but Mari Beth and I talked about this on the drive home and we agreed to wait to see how you kids settled in and if you liked us and vice versa. We like you kids just fine." Ben cleared his throat, not looking at Mike when he said, "Well, there's no rush about making up your mind, but Mari Beth and I more or less decided that we would be happy to have you kids stay here with us for a few weeks, if you'd like that or until we all agree on what's best. If it's permanent you're going to need guardians for awhile. In the meantime you'll be comfortable and best of all you'll be close to your ranch that's just over east of us." and gestured behind him. "It'd be a pleasure for us Mike. So what we'd like for you to do is think it over for the next few weeks and talk it over with Joe. Just take your time and get rested up."

Ben finally turned and looked down into Mike's stunned eyes and knew the kid was in shock because he just stood there with his mouth partly open. Shoot and blast, Benjamin Strongbow, you've startled the boy right out of his boots, thought Ben disgustedly. Now what do I do? Shoot and blast, he should have waited.

Mike used all his will power in an effort not to bawl like a baby calf in the face of such a generous kind offer. It was so totally unexpected that Mike had to wrap his arms tightly around his chest and turned partially away. Ben could see Mike's broad shoulders quiver and knew he was fighting for control. Ben shook his head and felt doubly bad about springing this idea on a kid who'd had just about all he could handle right at the moment.

They stood there like that for a bit with Ben patiently waiting for the boy to get a grip on his emotions. When it didn't seem like he was ever going to move again, Ben gently laid his hand on Mike's shoulder and gently pushed him toward the porch steps.

"Now I'll show you to your room so you and Joe can grab a quick shower and that should make you feel a whole lot better; wash off some sweat, dirt and fatigue all at the same time plus y'all will smell a lot nicer too." Ben chuckled forcibly trying to lighten the mood. "Don't forget dinner will be on in just a bit so you need to shower quickly. No one misses one of Hannah's dinners unless he's lost his wits."

Ben more or less pushed the boy into the kitchen that was bustling with last minute supper preparation. The man called Luther sat at the table talking with Joe as though they had known each other from pups. Joe, with red puffy eyes, seemed to be a non-stop motor mouth holding a glass half filled with lemonade. Carli was banging a spoon on the table and singing to her own rhythm all scrubbed and shinny looking and dressed in pajamas, robe and slippers dug out of one of those old storage boxes Mari Beth kept in the attic.

No strangers here, thought Ben, and looking over and winked at Mari Beth. "I hate to break up this riveting conversation between you three, but these guys have got to shower before supper 'cause it's getting real late. Luther, meet Mike Kelly." said Ben.

Luther stood up and Mike took off his hat and walked over to shake the man's hand. "Well, young man, if you're half as entertaining as your brother and sister, meeting you is a treat." The tall man smiled.

"I'm please to meet you, Sir. Mr. Strongbow's been showing me his beautiful horses." said Mike, striving to appear normal.

"*His beautiful horses*? Boy, if you want to see *HORSES*, you have to come down to my place. Why, I've got the best of the best of them, bar none. Tennessee Walkers, Mike, one of the easiest riding horse ever created." bragged the man with a wink and a grin for his father.

"There you go again, son, lost in your illusions." laughed Ben. "Come on boys, I'll show you to your room. Mari Beth, you might dig out some of those old clothes our boys outgrew and see if you can find something for them to wear tonight. Do you have other luggage Mike?"

"Yes, Sir, we left it at the bus depot thinking our grandfather would come in and get it." Suddenly Mike remembered. "I left two messages on the ranch's answering machine. I'd better call and tell them that we're here."

"I'll take care of that right now or we'll have Hank running up and down the road trying to find y'all. By the way your manager's name is Hank Tomlinson." And Ben picked up the kitchen phone and dialed Hank while Luther talked to Mike.

"Hello Hank, this is Ben Strongbow. Have you checked the answering machine up at the main house today?"

"Why, no Ben, I just got in from the north range about a half hour ago. I thought I'd eat dinner first before going up to the office. Why, do you need me for something?" Hank asked.

"No, but I've got some people here that belong to you. Seems Mr. Devereaux had grandchildren and they were coming out to live with him as their parents died last February. They called from town and left messages for their grandfather to come pick them up. They didn't know he'd passed away. You can imagine what an awful blow that was to them. Well, Mari Beth and I found them on the road about 7 miles out of River Town trying to walk to the ranch. I just wanted you to know they're here at our place. We'll be over in a couple of days once the kids are rested. Feel free to drop by if you want."

"His grandchildren are here? Well, darn it all, I should have been notified or something. Heck of a way for the kids to be welcomed. Devereaux said he had grandchildren, but he never mentioned where they were or that they'd be coming out soon. May and I just figured he was cutting Jean out of his will and putting his grandchildren in to inherit. Talk about a surprise! Please tell the children I'm really sorry not to have been there for them, but if they're with you then they're okay. Thanks, Ben, and give me a shout when you'd like to come over because I can't leave here right now seeing as how short handed we are. See you soon."

"Goodnight Hank." Ben hung up and turned to Mike.

"Mr. Tomlinson said to tell you that he was really sorry he wasn't available to pick you up today. He hadn't been up to the house to check any messages either. He's been up to his ears in work being as how they're really short handed over there. Well, boys let's get you settled. Tomorrow we'll go in and get your stuff, but for tonight you can do with some second hand clothes." Ben urged them out of the kitchen and through the hall to the curving staircase with its beautiful wide oak banister held up by mischievous animals carved into the thick supports.

Mike whispered to Joe. "Joe, look at those carvings, aren't they beautiful and funny?"

"Oh my, these are really, really wonderful. Hey Mike, look at this monkey, isn't he cute? And here's a parrot and a fat bear. Gee look at these others."

Ben grinned. "Yep, they're all treasures for sure. One of my great-uncles was a sculptor of some excellence and during the winter months he didn't have a lot to do so he practiced his art on the banister supports. There are other pieces of his work scattered about that are more serious than these. It was fortunate that he had an older brother who could run the ranch because his sculpting became a full time occupation. Remind me to show you his old studio that we've kept up because we're real proud of that old man; Able Truelove Strongbow was his name and his art was his passion and he was a natural like Rodin. One of my sons has a talent in that direction and has used Great-Uncle's studio. Now he's going to school to learn more about sculpturing. Hmm, he must have gotten the artistic gene from Able through our blood line. Now that's a thought."

"Wow, I bet he could have been rich and famous 'cause these are really pretty neat." Said Joe as he and Mike walked up the stairs all bent over as they tried to see each sculpture.

"What makes you think he wasn't rich and famous? Why boy, he had his sculptures in few city galleries around the country and people came from all around to get one of his pieces. Old Able lived to a ripe old age of 90." Ben laughed. "He set up a trust fund with his wealth for children of the family or any child of the Valleys that showed artistic talent of any kind so they could go to the right training school. That's what's paying for my son, Sweet's schooling."

"Gee, Mr. Strongbow isn't Sweet a funny name for a man?" asked Joe.

"You know cowboys, don't you? Well, they're the ones who nick-named him. His real name is Steve, but he has a real sweet disposition and the horses all adored him. Sweet doesn't seem to mind, 'course, he was nick-named when he was about four years old so he had time to get used to it. He said it was better than his best friend from over on the north side of the mountain who got the moniker of Stink." laughed Ben.

"Yeah, I can see that." laughed Joe. "Mike has a real fine talent for the guitar and I sing. Gee, maybe we're not such strangers here after all, being artistic and all."

Ben just had to lift the kid off his feet sling him over his shoulder and run up stairs whooping and that had Joe screaming with laughter. Mike had to laugh at their funning and something inside of him loosened and became less painful as he followed. The feeling was that, as Ben had easily lifted Joe onto his shoulders, he'd also taken some of Mike's burden off of his just as effortlessly. How very strange to feel so.....so much lighter. Maybe, just maybe they weren't going to be strangers for long after all.

At the top of the stairs Ben sat Joe on his feet and led the way down the hall. He opened the third door on the right into a large twin bedroom with an adjoining bath. Sand colored walls with brown multicolored braided rugs scattered over the floor and bedspreads in geometric designs of gold, orange and green; masculine yet warm in color and two easy chairs over by the windows.

"We figured you'd both be more comfortable in a strange place if you bunked together for awhile. We'll set Carli's crib in here for the time being too as she'll be happier that way as well. Now hurry up and shower, there's everything you'll need in there. I'll see you guys down stairs in ten, okay?"

"Thanks Mr. Strongbow, this is a really nice room. We appreciate everything you and ah…Mari Beth are doing for us. I mean, we're *really* grateful. Thank you." said Mike earnestly.

"Not at all, Mike, not at all. Y'all had better start calling me Ben or Luther and I will get confused when you holler for Mr. Strongbow. Hurry up now." He had just closed the door and almost bumped into

Mari Beth holding Carli by one hand and a stack of clothes over the other arm.

"I had to bring Carli along; I think she's worried her mother will leave her again if she doesn't watch me so it's going to take awhile for her to relax. I'm not sure of the fit of these clothes, but they should be able to find something in this stuff that will do until tomorrow. Be sure the boys bring their dirty clothes downstairs and I'll wash them tonight."

Ben knocked and opened the door and walked in. "Mari Beth has some clothes for you and I'll just put them here on the chair. I think there are a couple of night shirts in there as well. She wants you to bring your dirty things downstairs and she'll wash them up."

"Thanks for the clothes Ben; ours are really dirty and stinky. Well, we're pretty stinky too." Joe grinned as Mike helped him pull off his boots and held his nose.

Ben chuckled. "Hurry up and get yourselves sweet smelling because supper's waiting. Never mind putting on your boots again; socks are just fine."

"Well, once we have our boots off I doubt we'll be able to get them back on, our feet being swollen from the heat and all." said Mike.

Mari Beth, at Carli's insistence, stood beside Ben in the open door way so she could see her brothers. "Mikey, Joey, hurry, hurry. I hungry *now*! Suppertime, wash hands, Momma says. *Hurry*!"

"Okay, sis, we'll be there in a jiffy." replied Mike, laughing at his sister's demands.

Ben and Mari Beth walked quietly toward the stairs with Ben holding one of Carli's hands and Mari Beth held the other and he spoke in a low voice. "These kids lost both parents in an accident last February."

"Both parents killed at the same time? That's like how you losing your parents, Ben. Oh, that is so tragic. Poor Jean, I'd so hoped she'd come back someday and I'd see her again." She sighed and said a silent prayer for them. "I knew something awful had happened to bring these children way up here to that old man. The Guardians surely sent them to us, don't you think? We'd be much better for them than Mr. Devereaux would have been."

"You're right Mari Beth. I think Devereaux would have ruined them with his meanness let alone deal with a baby. I've asked Mike to consider staying with us and he was so stunned and shook up I thought he was going to break down and cry right there in the yard. It was stupid of me to have sprung it on him so sudden like."

"I thought he looked shocked when y'all came into the kitchen earlier. I'm sure he'll talk to Joe tonight so we'll wait awhile and let them settle in."

He and Mari Beth had stopped at the top of the stairs. Ben said, "I'll take Mike and Joe into town with me tomorrow and get their luggage. We'll call Social Services in Huntington tell them we have the children. I'm sure there won't be any problem making temporary arrangements for them to stay here."

Mari Beth bent down and picked Carli up as Ben said. "You should see him with the horses and they liked him too, he'll be a great help. Why he's a natural with them. I'm purely going to enjoy having them under foot. That Joe is something else, young and funny all at the same time. Understand, my love, Mike hasn't agreed to anything yet so we've got to give them time to make a decision. I think he knows that this would be a good thing for them, but they must have the chance to know us and for us to get to know them too." Just then Carli leaned over and made a grab for Ben.

"Me, Benny, carry me!" demanded the beautiful little sweet smelling tyrant.

Quickly he snagged her from Mari Beth laughing at this bundle of joy and tucked her tight to his chest with one arm and talk flowed between the two of them as they walked down the staircase.

Mari Beth smirked. "Way to go, Carli," she whispered. "Someone else just got taken in by a charmer with a pretty face. The bigger they are the harder they fall."

Sitting around the big kitchen table that night, Ben watched Mike look around with sad eyes and a slightly wistful smile that was filled, no doubt, with the memory of when his parents had been sitting at a kitchen table with them just like this.

Ben thought there was a spark of hope in Mike. Maybe it was just a glimmer, but there seemed to be a lessening of tension in the face and shoulders of the young man that spoke more eloquently than words. It was too soon for happiness on the short term, but if Ben had his way, happiness would be a sure thing in the future. Of course, it all depended on everything working out with the kids staying here permanently.

It was equally wonderful to see the glow on Joe's face as he sat as close to Hannah as his chair could fit. Now there was an instant bond if Ben had ever seen one, and Hannah seemed pleased that it was so too. For a woman who said she had no desire to marry, she adored children and Ben thought Joe was going to fill that place in her heart and maybe she would fill his need for a mother.

Ben became conscious that Luther was talking to him about the Huntington County Fair coming up the first week of October and questioning him as to what horses he would be selling. Was he going to sell any young bulls this year?

Ben looked over at Mike and winked. "Well, Lute, since I just might have hired me a likely young fellow who has had some training in handling young horses so I just might be selling a few colts and fillies. Mike's going to get them used to the halter and lead. He'll help me select which ones I will take to Huntington. I think he's got a very good eye. Bulls? Yes, I've got twenty-five young bulls that I need to sell and I expect top dollar for them for they're registered and they'll be fine breeding bulls for a rancher to use in upgrading his stock."

Mike's eyes lit up and smiled with enthusiasm and began to talk to Ben about his young horses and what had been done so far with them. For the first time Ben saw the strain leave the young man's face entirely. Maybe now Mike could begin to pass a little of the big load he had been carrying on to his own shoulders even if it was for this short time. However, Ben hoped everything would work out and the children would be staying. If they did, he'd praise God for giving him another family to raise, and he could use up some of his kid-raisin' knowledge.

~Blackhawk~

ISSAQUAH BLACKHAWK WAS THE Hereditary Guardian of the Sacred Valleys of Thunder Mountain and was accepted as such by everyone. His ranch house sat on a high bench beneath the mighty Thunder Mountain with the land sloping downhill in a series of large pastures. From his front porch Blackhawk, as most all people called him, could see all the way down his long, long valley with its rivers with glimpses of the road that led to his place appearing here and there as it wound itself around the rolling hills and trees. The land probably looked much the same as it had in the past centuries give or take a road or two and the fences.

He leaned one broad shoulder against the porch post with his hands tucked into his hind pockets. As he stood enjoying the view he thought about the burden of being the caretaker of these sacred lands and its people by decree of the Thunder Gods. It was a position that has been passed from father to son in his family, and sometimes to a daughter, since Lightening Boy came down from the Mountain with that duty hundreds of years ago. Someday, his son Tom would take over as that Caretaker/Guardian.

Blackhawk frowned and gave the post a sidewise kick in frustration and muttered to himself, "That boy needs to get a wiggle on and find himself a wife because this old man wants grandchildren by golly, and I want to be able to enjoy them while I'm still able." Then he sighed, "He's just being stubborn. He knows it's fretting me that he's not married by now. Kids! They just gotta' go their own way in their own time *I know*, but it doesn't help much. Tom's thirty years old and it's time he was getting hitched. Hmm, maybe when we go to the Huntington Fair he'll spot someone he'd like since he hasn't found any particular girl here in the Valleys." That was a hopeful thought, perhaps too hopeful, sighed Blackhawk. Well, no law against an old man dreaming.

Despite this nagging worry about off spring, there was a definite contentment in Blackhawk that was soul deep as he stood there in the twilight of the closing day. His blood had such deep roots in this land that if they were ever torn out, his world would cease to be as he'd cease to be. He drew his strength, power and purpose from these lands as his family had been on this very place for many, many generations, long before the white man discovered America. This was his turn to protect the land and watch the growth of families spread out to make sure they kept this sacred land a sheer paradise.

He was proud of these people, proud that they cherished the land as the Thunder Gods had decreed centuries ago. Of course, it helped occasionally to have the land itself re-enforce that. it would force owners to leave if they forgot to cherish the land.

Only four landowners and two men had been ejected in Blackhawk's time. The two men had been relatives of Joseph Devereaux. Then there was Hal Turner who had owned the farm that now belonged to Hank Seely. A farmer named Fletcher had died of heart failure, but his land had turned against him before that and his buildings had taken on an interesting fast deterioration. (Hmm, something had to be done about that land now that I think about it. I must stop by and check on things.) Another rancher named Binkster had owned Trill Ranch, a place over west of Luther Strongbow. He had been kicked out for abusing the land and the animals. Then down in the southern part of the valley another rancher named Sterns was forced out for the same reason. I must get down there too. Blackhawk had been busy traveling around the other Valleys but still that wasn't any excuse for neglecting his duties. Yes, he'd see to that as soon as possible. So much work to do and it seemed that the older he got the less he accomplished.

Blackhawk bought Trill Ranch four years ago by edict of the Thunder Gods. Man, the land had taken some major work to bring it back into health again. Part of the labor was fixing up the buildings and some of the fencing, but it was flourishing now. It was a mighty pretty place, just waiting for the new owner who would someday come to the Valleys. Blackhawk had been assured he'd know when the right man arrived. Well, that was sometime ago and he was still waiting and beginning to question if he'd heard right.

On the whole, the Valleys had prospered and hadn't had to reject anyone of late, still the people were very aware the land spirits' power, so they treated the Earth like a living thing, which it was. So many ills of the world could be solved if everyone treated Mother Earth with the same love, respect and care they gave themselves and their own families; well, most families that is.

The land was a sacred gift to humanity, vegetable, mineral and animal kingdoms. Humanity didn't have exclusive rights to Earth. People were blind not to treasure the planet that provided food and shelter let alone life itself. People just weren't aware that if they killed the planet they killed themselves along with it and it didn't matter how much money they had either. Unfortunately most people weren't very smart, but hopefully they were learning and getting more aware of the vulnerability of the Earth.

Blackhawk was coming into his sixtieth year, the prime of life for a man it is said. He was mostly of Indian blood with just a quarter Caucasian inherited from one of his white grandmothers. He was of average height and stalwart of build. He wore his long, thick black hair with its streaks of white clubbed at the back of his neck. If anyone had told him that his large, deep brown eyes were magnetically beautiful he'd have been embarrassed right down to his boots, even though they were, magnetic that is. People were *positive* that they could tell Blackhawk anything. So that became part of his job description, father confessor, for after all he was a Shaman. He wasn't a handsome man, being more rugged of feature with the strong bone structure that was actually more attractive than mere handsomeness. Dignity and power of his position radiated out of him like a beacon. Many people would call him striking in a masculine way, but that didn't tweak Blackhawk's vanity a bit. People will form their opinions by appearances which was a very primitive instinct for survival of the fittest. Beauty or handsomeness was attractive to the opposite sex and that was all. He only cared that he was still strong enough to handle the roughest jobs of running his ranch and capable of fulfilling the role of Guardian.

He turned away and walked across the porch to his old comfortable rocker and sat down and crossed his long legs. He took out his tobacco pouch and filled his pipe and tamped it down with a calloused finger while watching an eagle soar over his head going home for the night somewhere behind the ranch house. His eyes swept over the land as he struck a match and got his pipe going.

Just as he was beginning to puff contentedly on his first smoke of the day, Cat jumped up onto his lap, turned around a few times before settling down then turned his head and looked up at the man through amber gold eyes and meowed demandingly for his man to begin stroking him. The Cat's man laughed as he obediently began to scratch ears and smooth the big golden tiger and listened to its rumbling purr.

"Now why do I put up with you? You're supposed to be a barn cat not a lap cat, so what makes you so different from the others? You're arrogant, demanding and bossy you know; terrible faults in a cat and I've been meaning to speak to you about them. Think I belong to you? Hmmm, well, I guess I can stand that. I just saw a big eagle fly overhead, so you keep your eye peeled for it or you'll end up its dinner if you're not careful."

Smoking and talking to his companion were acts of a man who lived alone much of the time except for the resident cook. His beautiful wife, Rose, had passed away four years ago and he missed her presence as if he'd lost his right arm and deep in his heart he stilled grieved. Life went on as it should; perhaps not as happily as it had when Rose was alive, yet life was to be lived and lived as whole heartedly as a person could manage. A person's life didn't stop just because someone they loved passed to the other life. Blackhawk smiled sadly, that truth didn't bring him much comfort though it sounded real philosophical.

The sun was hovering over the rim of the western mountains transforming the bright southern land into patches of light and shadow that looked very much like a crazy quilt. As Blackhawk watched the sun sink behind the hills, it bathed the southern mountains and parts of the eastern hills with a bright rosy glow that was so beautiful. He sang the evening song that thanked the Father Sun for another good day.

This was a pretty time of evening; cooler now that the sun had gone from the sky taking its furnace heat from the day. After laboring in the open all day it felt good to sit and relax and enjoy the sunset and the coolness.

Blackhawk sniffed the air and hummed a bit; something was brewing weather-wise. Possibly they were about due to have a rip-snorter of a rainstorm or he missed his guess. After all they were into the last week of August now and at this altitude anything was possible.

Another day was passing and a very good day it had been too. He'd gotten the 20 horses selected for the sale coming up six weeks from now. It had been a hard task for he loved all the horses he'd raised from foals. He sighed; it was difficult to let go of someone or some animal you loved. All his horses had been gentled with love and was never struck or spurred. All his men here knew what would happen if he caught them abusing any of his children. For horses were very like children, and that called for lots of patience, love and discipline so they'd become fine animals trained to their fullest potential. Yes, his beauties were exceptional horses and most everyone wanted a Blackhawk Appaloosa. The sale should be a good one and ease the pressure of having too many horses on the ranch.

That thought reminded him to call his son and ask him about his selections. So the Chief of all the Valleys rocked and smoked and stroked his companion as he ran his thoughts over the day as the dusk of evening deepened.

The sharp ringing of the telephone interrupted his tranquility. "Blasted thing, can't it leave a man in peace? I wished I'd never put the blasted thing in!" he grumbled as he put Cat down and got up as the phone rang out another demand. "Alright, alright, I'm coming, blast it," and opened the screen door to pass into the house with Cat right on his heels.

"Hello, this is Blackhawk." he barked.

"Hello to you too Blackhawk, sorry if I interrupted you."

He laughed, a bit chagrined at his surliness. "Oh hello Ben, sorry about the growl, I was just relaxing on the porch and you know how I dislike this telephone contraption."

Ben laughed knowing Blackhawk's resistance to this necessary modern device called the telephone. "I told you about Mari Beth and me picking up three of Devereaux's grandchildren walking out to his place a month ago. Well, we've had them here with us since then and they seemed to have settled in quite nicely. The kids have had a rough time of it. I'd like you to meet the boys as Mari Beth and I want to take them in on a permanent basis and the kids seem to like the idea too." said Ben.

"Poor kids, poor kids, yes you told me they had arrived like so many have come our way, but man you're making it a regular habit of picking up strays. Aren't you and Mari Beth getting a little old for this?" chuckled Blackhawk.

"Frankly no, it's as though the Thunder Gods meant for us to find them just like we did the others we adopted. We've got this huge house you see, with just Hannah and us to bounce around in it. Well, it seems a waste of space when these kids could use a good home."

The earnest reply moved Blackhawk. "No, no, I can see you had to do just that. I'd do the same thing myself and have done, as you know."

"I'd like you to meet the boys, Blackhawk. Little Carli is not quite three years old and won't leave Mari Beth for hardly a minute. Did I tell you Carli thinks Mari Beth is her mother? She and Jean were somewhat alike. Mari Beth said she and Jean used the same scent so maybe that's part of it; anyways babies forget fast. Well, we'd like to come up tomorrow if you're not busy so you can judge the boys for yourself. And I have some other ideas I'd like to discuss with you."

"Sure, Ben, I'll be happy to see you tomorrow. Oh, if Hannah has any left over chocolate chip cookies, you know just sort of laying around that no one else wants, maybe she'd put a few in a bag for me. I sure miss my cookies and I can't make them worth a darn and my cook refused to humor me." Blackhawk grumbled.

"Well, fire the son of a gun. Imagine him refusing to make cookies for you, Chief Blackhawk of All the Valleys with the power of The Thunder Gods behind you." laughed Ben.

Blackhawk chuckled. "Yeah, I could fire him, but he's sort of grown deep roots into the place and he's too big to move and if I tried I'm afraid tearing him out of here would destroy the place so I can't shake him loose. My awesome reputation for fierce authority isn't helping me at all." Blackhawk was looking right at the cook standing in the kitchen doorway as he spoke and grinned and the big man snorted and returned to his kitchen.

"Shoot and blast man, you've got a great cook there not to mention a good friend too, so my advice is don't mess with perfection. I'll ask Hannah to bake a special batch just for you."

"Hah, so if he's so great why won't he make me cookies, I ask you? Thank Hannah for me and give her my heartfelt gratitude. Okay, see you in the morning only if the weather doesn't decide to turn on us. I must warn you there is a strong possibility that it will so watch out. We're due for a good hard rain now that we're moving into fall, I can feel it. Good night Ben." He let the receiver clang into its holder and walked out into the kitchen to talk to his friend, Mike Mitee otherwise know as Mike the Mighty.

The huge man turned from the stove and said. "Who's coming up?"

"Ben Strongbow with two young boys he wants me to meet. He and Mari Beth found Devereaux's grandchildren walking out to his place a month ago. I told you about that remember? Ben and Mari Beth still have them and from the sound of it they've keeping them. Handy you know, what with the Devereaux Ranch being just to the east of Ben's. Well, we'll know more tomorrow after we get a gander at these two youngens' and see what their made of."

"Those Strongbows are always taken in stray animals and people. It beats me how do they do it. All them kids they've raised and when they've finally gotten themselves a little peace and quiet they ups and gets more kids. How'd you figure people like that?" asked Mike gruffly. Secretly, Mike the Mighty admired both the Strongbows, but he had a reputation as a taciturn man to uphold. Besides that, he liked to think of himself as a hard one, an attitude that sort of went with his size.

Blackhawk laughed and poured a cup of coffee. He knew his friend would give the shirt off his back to any "stray" that came by all the while complaining about it so he could cover that soft heart of his. "Well, we'll get a good look at them tomorrow if the weather cooperates." said Blackhawk and sipped his coffee.

Cat circled around Mike's legs, stroking him and meowed loudly. "Oh, right, King Cat, I'll get your treat right away. My, how could I forget who's boss around here." and dug in the refrigerator for the can of salmon. No ordinary cat food for King Cat, snickered Blackhawk quietly as he sat at the table set for nine. His men always ate here with him in the kitchen.

He listened to the conversation between the cook and the Cat with amusement. For a man who declared his kitchen off limits to animals somehow this feline had gotten around that rule so now he had Blackhawk and the cook catering to his wants. Cats were notorious for being demanding, though some cats had more audacity than others, mused the boss as he watched Cat devour the treat. Maybe it was the extra food, but Cat was a huge animal and ruled the barn in no uncertain terms. Maybe he was part Lynx or something, he did have these little tuffs on the tops of his ears, but whatever his heritage, he was *big*.

Twilight closed down in earnest over the ranch, shadowed as it was by the huge mountain that looming over it. Lights were turned on in the main house and in the bunkhouse. Soon the sound of boots and men's voices grew louder as they came up to the back door of the kitchen and when the screen door opened, Cat, having finished off his dinner, scooted out before the men could enter.

Dinner passed with discussions of the day and the work to be done tomorrow if the weather held fair, which Blackhawk said was doubtful, but he'd know for sure at dawn. Before any of the men took off from the ranch they were to report to him for final orders in case the weather played its tricks and they got that storm.

As each man finished his meal, he gathered up his dishes, rinsed them before putting them in the dishwasher. No one wanted to get on the bad side of Big Mike as he had ways of ruining your day and making you wished you hadn't messed up. So the men strictly followed his kitchen rules. If you dirty a dish, you wash it and put away any food you got out if you came in late for dinner and wiped up after yourself too. Mike was a great and generous cook and hungry cowboys always valued that. Good cooks were beyond the price of rubies as far as they were concerned. When men worked physically hard, food became vitally important.

Dawn was faintly breaking the darkness in the east and a chilled wind laden with moisture came sweeping down off the Mountain bringing a foretelling of coming rain. Blackhawk walked out into the ranch yard and looked up at the Mountain top and sniffed a few times then contemplated the wide flat dark gray clouds developing in the northwest.

As Blackhawk gauged the severity of the storm that seemed to be building behind the north range of mountains he asked, "Is this going to be a really bad storm, O God of Rain and Snow?" and listened and when he heard the answer he said a quick, "Thank you."

He thought about what work could be done inside the barns today and decided he'd get the men to bring those 20 horses into the barn he plan on selling and work them over and secure everything else.

"Yep, she's going to be a devil of a storm. Best I get the word to Jake the weatherman or he's going to miss-call this as a gentle summer rain."

There was no sense in paying much attention to the weatherman in River City as he was mostly wrong. No real blame on Jake as he took the weather forecasting from the internet which didn't account for the diversity of weather around their mountains. At least Jake was smart enough to take Blackhawk's word and let people know what the Chief said.

"People of the Valley had best take cover today 'cause it's going to be a real gully washer," murmured Blackhawk. "I'd better call Ben and tell him to stay at home. Hades, now I won't get my cookies." He grumbled and went back into the house to make some phone calls.

Tom Blackhawk walked into the hall, picked up the phone. "Hello."

"Tom, there's a bad storm brewing over the Mountain so you'd better get set for it because it's going to be a bad one."

"Yeah Dad, I saw it coming when I stepped outside this morning and I've had the men busy buttoning things up. I've got the mares that are in foal in the barns and the other horses are shut up in the shelters so everything is good here. Need any help up there?"

"No, though Mike the Mighty might use some help making bread and stew in case the power shuts off." replied Blackhawk.

"Yeah right, and chance losing my good right arm? No thank you. By the way I'm sure you've called our good, but confused weatherman, Jake the Mistake, that we're in for a bad storm or we'd be hearing "It will be light rain and clearing by late afternoon" and everyone would be caught with their pants down. Why don't they just make you the weatherman? You want me to call anyone?"

"I'm calling Ben, Old Jim Waggener and I'll tell Bob Zeggler over to Claremont to spread the word too. And as for taking on the position of weatherman, not on your tin type, I'd rather give Jake a hard time as it's one of my hobbies." chuckled Blackhawk.

"Okay, I'll call Lightfoot and Ruble Peace though I'm pretty sure they can see for themselves what's heading our way. I'll call Seely's and have him pass the word to the others as well. The word will fly faster than the speed of light. Talk to you later. "

Tom got on the phone and it didn't take long to pass the warning to Seely's. He was a knowing man, Seely was, but he thanked Tom for the warning and he'd spread the word.

"Hey Dan, Tom here; just a heads-up in case you haven't seen the storm heading our way. I guess it will hit sometime this afternoon at the latest. Dad said it will be a bad one and best to secure things."

"Thanks Tom. Yeah, I thought it looked kinda' funny, but it's pretty early yet for a major storm isn't it? Do you think we'll have snow?"

"We're at four thousand feet and anything can happen even though we've just about to move into September, so being prepared is all we can do. If you have any cut hay still in the field you'd better get as much help as you can getting it all in. I'm set here so if you need help just say the word." said Tom.

"Hey, I could use some help if you have it to spare. I've got about two maybe three hours of bailing yet and I think I best haul it all in to the hay barn. No sense in soakin' good dry hay. It sure is right neighborly of you to offer, mister." Tom laughed at the old fashion usage.

"Sure enough, neighbor; I'll be right down with some of my men. I'll call Waggoner and see if he needs any help."

"That old coot? Man, he's a pain in the buttocks; grumpy old coot!" complained Dan.

"What's he done now?"

"He cut the fence on my side of the river so his mange cattle could get the better feed in my corn field. He says it was an accident, an act of nature." scoffed the other man.

"You gotta' give him points for being creative. Now, I wonder why he's trying to get your attention." Tom knew Jim Waggoner had prime white face cattle.

"Who knows, but if he doesn't quit it I'm going to get mad. Well, see you here in a jiffy; I gotta' mobilize the troops." and Dan hung up.

"Luther here, what can I do for you?"

"Hi, Lute, it's me, Tom. Did your Dad tell you about the big storm that's going to hit us by late afternoon?"

"Yeah, he said your Dad called him. I guess Ben was going to take the Kelly boys up to meet the Chief. This sure ain't the day for visitin'."

"Not hardly! I marvel at your folks, they never turn a kid away. Anyway back to business; have you got your hay all in? Do you need any help? I'm going to take four men to Lightfoot's and help him haul in his hay this morning as he's got several field to do." said Tom

"No, everything's under control, at least it will be shortly. I got my hay and corn in last week and the gardens are stripped. Maybe I'm getting intuitive or just suspicious of our extra fine weather and the trickiness of our resident Gods," chuckled Luther.

"Well, don't forget to pass on anything you get that's interesting in your crystal ball. See you Luther, gotta' go round up my guys and move it."

"Thanks for the call. Holler if you need any extra hands, I can spare a few and we'll buzz over. See you."

Instructing Henry to make sure there was plenty of firewood at each fireplace and to stock up on stews and such in case the power went out, Tom put on his heavy coat and started for the bunkhouse. The temperature was already dropping and the wind was beginning to breathe down his neck in a brisk way and appeared to be pushing the storm faster than it was thought to arrive. Tom saw one of the men heading his way toward the wood shed.

"It's time to really button up, boss. We'll have everything secured in another hour. I'm just making another couple of wood runs then me and the boys will hole up until the blow is over. If you need anything just give us a holler." called Mac.

"Well, Mac, I'm hollering. Get back to the bunkhouse and roust out four or five of the men. We're going down to Lightfoot's to help him get his hay in before this storm hits. Tell the others to finish up here and hurry up about it 'cause this storm is moving in faster then we expected."

"Okay, boss, I'm on my way. Now who do I partially dislike today." as he turned on his heels and ran for the bunkhouse leaving Tom grinning. Within minutes five men came out pulling on coats and hats and piled into the big farm truck. By the time they got to

Dan's and five hours of hard intense labor by nine fast working men got the job done. By the time Tom and the men returned home it was two o'clock in the afternoon. A thick grayness was settling over the day and a drizzle of rain had begun to hit the ground. "Man, oh man, we just made it under the wire. Just look at that sucker comin' on." Mac said as he looked out the truck window.

"Get under cover boys and thanks for the help, Lightfoot really needed a hand. See you guys in the morning if we're still afloat. Oh, you brave souls can take turns checking on the mares in the barn 'cause some of them are close to foaling." The men got out of the truck and made for the bunkhouse without wasting any time.

An aerie dark yellow gloom settled down over the ranch and the wind began to moan around the corners of the house sounding like lost souls wailing their lament. Tom stood on the covered kitchen porch with his back to the wall holding a hot cup of coffee in his hand, and watched in fascination as the storm came down off Thunder Mountain in a roaring rush of cold rain that swept across the ranch yard and filled the few pot-holes in short order.

"Oh, Gods, be not harsh to us humans. We honor You and the land. Be kind to us and our animal friends." murmured Tom.

The storm continued to roar and rain poured down as though someone had upended a bucket of water; a very large, oversized God-like bucket; Yep, God size for sure thought Tom as he glanced down his dirt road and hoped it didn't wash out completely and…. Tom straightened up and looked hard through the sheet of gray rain. There was someone struggling up the road and either that small person was very fat or carrying a heavy load. Just then Tom saw him stumble and fall to his knees.

Tom tossed his cup aside and was off the porch in a flash, running through the rain that soaked him right to the skin in a matter of seconds. The man was trying to struggle to his feet and only looked up when Tom grabbed his arm and heaved him to his feet.

"Oh, ggggracious, tttthank you. My car bbbbbroke down and I tttthought I could ggggget to Seely' farm if I hhhhhurried. I didn't know it wwwwwas such a lllllong way out hhhhhere." a female said breathlessly.

"Well, for heaven's sake woman, couldn't you see the storm coming before you started out? Besides, you passed Seely's thirty miles back toward River Town. Never mind that now, let's get into the house before we drown out here. You can explain the rest once we're dry." With that put his arm around her waist he practically dragged the heavy fat woman back to the ranch house. Coming in through the kitchen door, Tom turned and it took all his strength to close the door against the push of the wind.

"I ain't agoin' to mop that mess up, young man, so just you get busy. The idea dripping water all over my clean floor." said Henry indignantly.

Henry Tradeaux was of medium height, of slight build, bald as a qui-ball and wearing large size glasses that dwarfed his face, but that little man had authority in every inch of his skinny body. He was justifiably indignant as these people dripped cold muddy water all over his clean kitchen floor.

"Yeah, yeah, Henry, after I take care of this lady." Tom turned to the woman and said. "Wait here and I'll get you something dry to put on. There's a shower down the hall where you can get warm and change your clothes." With that Tom dashed through the living room and up stairs with his boots making squishy noises all the way to retrieve some of his long flannel underwear, a thick wool bathrobe and a pair of wool socks.

Hurrying back to the kitchen he stopped short when he saw a little girl of about four or five standing beside the woman. The lady had hung her dripping coat on a hook and was kneeling to take off the girl's wet outer clothes while Henry stood there with his mouth open.

All Tom could think was, 'she's not fat,' in fact, she was rather nice looking in a wet sort of way, just as pretty as a seal pup. The woman looked up and said with her teeth chattering. "Tttthis is mmmmy little nnnniece and wwwwe're expected at HHHank Seely's farm. If yyyyou have a ppppphone I nnnneed to call ssso tttthey won't think IIII'm lost in the ssssstorm and send out a sssssearch party."

"I'll call Seely while you two warm up in the shower and get dry. We can't have you catching cold or anything like that. Here take these things and go on into the bathroom while I go hunt up something more suitable for the young lady." The woman and the little girl disappeared down the hall and Tom heard the bathroom door shut.

Before Tom left the kitchen he turned to his cook. "Well Henry, don't just stand there, heat some milk and make tea for our visitors 'cause they'll need something to warm them up before they sicken."

"Sure, sure, Tom; I'm just kinda' stunned, you know. We ain't had us no females in the house before except once in awhile. Ah, hmm, let's see, I got my Apricot Brandy here. Do you think she'd like a sip of that? It's bound to warm the cockles of her heart and kill off any insipient bugs and then some. I'll fix hot chocolate for the little girl." Henry had a reputation as a tough guy, and he could be when it was called for, but he was a kind man underneath the facade. The cook whirled around and got busy.

Tom shook his head as he went back up the stairs. He knew that most of Henry's talk was cover up. He wasn't an easy man, but a man with a good heart and he made the best damn pies and cakes bar none plus being a number one all round cook. Of course his brandy was outstanding; a huge plus in any man's book. The real seal of approval were the men's opinion and they'd do anything for him. Tom sighed well I can't fire him which reminded him of his father's cook, Big Mike. That had him laughing at their similar situations.

All Tom could find suitable for the little girl was one of his softest flannel shirts, a thermal undershirt and another pair of soft wool boot socks guaranteed to fit her legs right up to her thighs. Before he left the room he picked up a wool/cashmere blanket his mother had given him.

Back downstairs, Tom knocked on the bathroom door and said. "Lady, I'm going to set these other things for your little girl right outside the door." Then Tom went back upstairs and grabbed a quick hot shower as he was chilled right down to the bone too. After changing into dry clothes he went back downstairs and threw more logs on living room fire. Just then another gust of wind rattled the windows so Tom walked quickly around the room pulling all the heavy drapes closed to keep the wind from sneaking in through the cracks and turned on the lights.

He made a quick call to Hank. "Hello Karen, this is Tom Blackhawk. Say I've got two of your relatives up here with me. They drove too far and with this sever storm they better spend the night. Hope this relieved your minds as to their whereabouts."

"Bless you Tom, we were becoming concerned that something had happened when they didn't show up over an hour ago. In fact, Hank was about to go out and start looking. Are they alright?"

"Sure, the car broke down and they got a little wet is all. They're showering now and getting into dry clothes. Anyway, we'll feed them and put them up for the night too. Of course I'll present you with a bill for lodging when I see you." and enjoyed Karen's laughter.

"Go on! Thanks Tom, you're a good man."

"I try and if I don't succeed Dad will skin me. Anyway, I'll drive them down tomorrow, but there is no time for man or beast to be out on a day like this. So we'll see you sometime tomorrow. Goodnight."

When the ladies came into the living room Tom sat them on the couch and wrapped the fire-warmed blanket around them. "Oh, my, this feels heavenly. Thank you, I'm sure this will take the last of the chills right out of our bodies." smiled the lady up at Tom. Before Tom could speak Henry did the honors of the house by bringing in a tray loaded with goodies. There was a mug of tea and two medium sized glasses of his special Apricot Brandy.

Tom raised his eyebrows at the sight of such generous proportions. And there was a Mickey Mouse Mug filled with hot chocolate that Tom remembered as being his favorite cup when he was a boy. Where on earth had Henry dug that up? The rest of the tray consisted of cookies, a couple of slices of apple pie and two custards.

"Oh, my, look at what Mr. Henry has fixed for us Luce, how delicious it all looks. Thank you Sir, this is very kind of you." smiled the woman at the blushing cook. Blushing? Tom had never seen such a sight in his life; Hard Hearted Henry? Blushing? Well, for mercy sake; and Tom just had to grin.

"Nothin' special ma'am, no, no, nothing's too good for our first lady guests is what I say. Ah, hmm, you want anything else Tom before I start supper?" asked Henry as he began to edge out of the room.

"No, Henry, this will be just fine, thank you." said Tom as he grinned at his cook. For that impudence Tom got a dirty look before Henry turned about face and stomped back to the kitchen.

"Now, help yourselves to anything on the tray. Luce, can I help you pick something out?" asked Tom as he handed her the Mickey Mouse Mug.

"Thank you. Oh, isn't this cute, Aunt Jeannie? Yes, please, may I have a cookie, Sir?"

"You can have anything on that tray. I think you'll hurt Henry's feelings if you didn't eat most all of it. Don't worry about spoiling your appetite as dinner won't be for another few hours. How about you, Aunt Jeannie, what can I help you to?" asked Tom smiling at the woman who was just as pretty dry even though her hair was still wet.

"I think that glass of brandy would be a nice beginning and the hot tea to follow. I will say I'm chilled right to the very core of me though that hot shower was a God send." reaching out a slender hand that trembled just slightly and took the glass from Tom.

Taking a healthy drink had Jean's eyes opened wide. She coughed and drew in a deep breath then coughed a few more times. "My, oh my, that's strong enough to light its own fire, but hmmm, very, very tasty. Here's to fire in the hole." she toasted Tom, laughingly and bravely took several small sips with a humming approval.

Tom laughed at her response which shocked him into a sudden silence. He hadn't laughed with a woman in a long time; not a woman who was a stranger that is. He didn't much trust women. Or maybe he didn't trust himself and his judgment of women unattached or otherwise?

Standing before the fireplace he drank from his own brandy snifter and gazed down into the fire. No doubt it was his past experience that had soured him on the feminine gender, though that was really foolish as his mother had been a wonderful trustworthy person and so were many of the women who lived in the valleys. Leaning his shoulder against the mantle Tom turned back to the two females and listened as they talked to each other while sipping his brandy and soaking up the fire's heat.

"No, Luce, you can't have a sip, this is definitely not for little girls. Why it would curl your toes and turn your nose bright red. Now, I'm all grown up and my toes are all conditioned to withstand this kind of fire. When you get older I'll give you a sip." smiled Jean.

"Will I be older tomorrow? Can I have a sip then?" said Luce in a serious tone of voice.

"I think tomorrow is a little too soon. It's going to take quite a long, long time for you to be old enough. Don't rush it, my love you'll be older soon enough."

"You're so funny, Aunt Jeannie. Okay, I'll wait, but remember you promised me a sip of Henry's fire when I'm older." Jean laughed and nodded her head.

Quiet filled the fire-lit room for a short time before Tom cleared his throat and said, "Just to clear things up my name is Tom Blackhawk and this is the Lightening Boy Ranch. You are exactly thirty five miles to the north of Seely's Farm. What are your names, if you don't mind telling me?"

"I'm so sorry Mr. Blackhawk. My name is Jean Hardwell and this is Lucy Ann Hardwell. Luce is five years old and is my brother's daughter and his wife was cousin to Karen Seely." Jean looked sad and with a quick glance at Lucy who didn't appear to be paying any attention to the adult conversation, she looked back up at Tom and shook her head then said cheerfully. "We've come to visit our cousin Karen and we might be staying for awhile." Tom caught enough of that understatement to realize Jean wasn't telling all.

He nodded and said. "I know the Seelys very well and they're grand people Luce, and you'll like Karen, she's a very nice person and her house looks just like elves or fairies might live there."

Lucy looked gravely up at Tom and said in a very adult way of an only child raised in grown up company. "Sir, please call me Lucy as no one calls me Luce except Aunt Jeannie because it's her own special name for me, you see. I'm glad my cousin is a nice person. It would be awfully hard to live with someone you didn't like, wouldn't it? My Daddy died a few months ago in a far away hospital. I really didn't remember him all that well because he was in the army and gone a lot. Momma died last month." Lucy turned to look up at Jean. "It was last month wasn't it, Aunt Jeannie?" At her nod Lucy went on. "I forget once in awhile. I'm awfully glad I forget once in awhile." and looking down at the Mickey Mouse Mug she clutched in her hands and then tears began to run down her cheeks.

Jean put down her glass and picked the little girl up and cuddled her on her lap and carefully took the mug from her hands. Tom went over and took it from her and caught sight of Henry disappearing into the kitchen.

Tom sat down in his chair by the fire and listened to the soft voice singing a lullaby into the child's ear while she cried. His heart was touched as it hadn't been in a long time. Lucy was obviously a very intelligent little girl and it was a hard thing to come to a strange place and have to live with strange people. Thank God she had her aunt.

Tom rocked and sipped his brandy and thought about his own romantic set back. It was nothing compared to this child's true suffering and loss. After all, he'd been a fully grown adult when he had been rejected. Yes, rejected in a very cruel way which he admitted now that it had been more of an ego wound than a true broken heart.

For the first time he acknowledged that losing that misplaced love was the best thing that could have happened. It certainly saved him from future misery of a broken marriage and possibly hurting his children. A broken romance definitely couldn't be compared to the loss of both parents. He must tell his father how much he loved and respected him. If his mother were here she would have given him a good talking to for thinking all women were like Becky.

Dinner had been over for some time and the girls were snuggly bedded down in one of his guestrooms. Hopefully a good night's sleep would mend a lot of grief that had gotten stirred up tonight. Tom sat beside the warm fire with Henry sitting opposite and each one was holding another snifter of Apricot Brandy while the wind whistled around the house and the rain pounded on the roof.

"You know, Henry, you could sell this brandy recipe and become a wealthy man. Companies would knock themselves out to acquire the patent. This is a pure-d gold mine." commented Tom after another appreciative sip of the hot flavor of apricots that slid easily down his throat and settled with a warm glow in his stomach.

"Who says I ain't a wealthy man already? You should see my portfolio." Henry laughed, "That sounds real important, don't it? Why son, I could buy my own ranch and stock it too without turning a hair if I was a mind too, but it's too much work for an old man like me." Tom raised his eyebrows and thought maybe old Henry had consumed a few more snifters of brandy than he had. He usually didn't prattle so openly. But was it prattle?

Henry talked on. "This here brandy recipe has been in my family since my great, great, great granddaddy came to these here shores and made his home in the new settlement of New France now New Orleans. He was a Frenchman you know and he made quite a fortune producing this drink in the past. Since then the recipe has been passed from father to son and on down the line. Eventually, being the last man in the family line, it came to me when I was a young man. The history and the original recipe are in an old journal I keep in a safe at the River Town Bank so some idiot can't steal it. It's been patented too and I renew that patent whenever necessary." Henry tapped his bald head and winked at Tom. "The recipe is right here in my head so it's extra safe. It's enough for me that I make up four or five barrels each year and store them in your basement as it has a good even temperature down there and I must say at last count, I've got close to thirty-five barrels aging and I only tap a couple at a time when it's ready to bottle."

Henry sipped and rocked, gazing into the fire before clearing his throat. "The stuff you're drinking now is close on to ten years old and I believe it's the best I've ever produced. I think the water here in the valley is superior to any water I've tried so far in other places. Strange as it may sound I'd say there seems to be a taste of…. *goodness* in the water that I hadn't experienced before. Maybe it's because the ground water hasn't been polluted. 'Course I go up to the falls back of here and bring down clean barrels of water when I'm making brandy. I really think the water makes the difference in the smoothness of the finished product. Maybe there's more love in the water here because the fire of the brandy is mellower, yet still has that explosion of flavor." Henry laughed gently, but didn't retract that interesting description. "While it's hot, it doesn't burn, but sort of slides down real easy like and warms the cockles of your innards. I think it also has some healing power in it. Of course that's just my feeling."

Henry took another good sip and looked into the fire a while before continuing. "Yes Sir, this is the best brandy I've produced bar none. No Tom, I ain't about to sell the recipe. I have a license to make and sell this brandy that's why I've got that special building outback to meet the standards the state requires. I'll sell a few bottles here and there and sometimes more depending on what I have available. I have several stores that want whatever I can give them and they pay top dollar too. I can get as much as $100 dollars a bottle at those fancy liquor stores. Surprises you, doesn't it?" Henry chuckled at the shock on Tom's face.

"When I die I'll leave you the recipe and the procedure. So you'll have to find the time to watch and work with me until you know how to make this beauty. I'm the last of my family since my only son died in the Viet Nam War." There was such a devastated look come over Henry's face that Tom hurt for him. What would it be like to lose your only child or any child for that matter?

Henry recovered himself quickly and swallowed the old pain. "Well, that was surely a sad, sad time for me, but life moved on. When I came here and found you and your family; let's see, hmmm, must be going on twenty years or so now. I remember you were just a young squirt of ten then. " Henry cleared his throat and took a hardy swallow of brandy and sniffed. "My gracious, it must be the brandy or the rainy night that got me to talking on about the past like this. Well, Tom, I've left you everything in my will. Yep, I'm a wealthy man to be sure 'cause I ain't got nothin' to spend my money on, except for barrels and the whatnot for the makins' of the brandy so my portfolio just keeps on growing. Mighty fine brandy, ain't it?" Henry's eyes twinkled at the shocked look on Tom's face and had the audacity to laugh.

"Henry, you've knocked the pins right out from under me, but you also have honored me beyond words. If I've haven't told you before how much I appreciate you and hope you never consider leaving, I should have done so a number of times. You're also an undiscovered genius, Henry Trudeaux, and never would I have suspected my great chef was a genius of finance as well. Of course, I knew you were a genius concerning this wonderful brandy and a fine man to boot, but the total sum of you boggles my mind."

Tom stood up and raised his glass and said sincerely. "Here's to you, Henry Trudeaux, a great self made man." Tom raised his snifter to the man opposite him and tipped the glass back and drained the remaining liquor.

Henry blushed. "Well, dadburnit, boy, you do know how to embarrass a man." He too stood and raised his glass to Tom, "Thank you, son. I'm proud of you too." and finished off the excellent Apricot Brandy by Trudeaux.

Through out the night the storm raged, but all was quiet and warm within the house of Tom Blackhawk.

~A Fly In the Ointment~

THE SEEDY LOOKING MAN sat shivering on a bench in New York City's Central Park. Dawn was just breaking over the city's skyline as he pulled a bunch of old newspapers out from under his jacket that he'd used in the attempt to keep the chill of the night away from his body. It hadn't worked too well, but it had been better than nothing. It was definitely time to move on to a warmer climate for the coming winter.

He was a medium sized man of around fifty years of age, but looked older. Once upon a time he had been fairly handsome, however the years of hard living and self indulgence had weakened his male good looks and coarsened his features. Still his blue eyes reflected a shrewd mind and along with that was an overly developed ego that felt superior to everyone else. He was a man with a naturally cruel nature that had grown in depravity over the years until now there was little he wouldn't do to accomplish his ends.

The man cursed and fought to control the *rage* that flowed through him as he thought about the man who had brought him to this low pitiful state. A con gone sour and it was Larken, his bloody partner's entire fault. He'd trusted Larken to do a thorough background check on Malovitch before the scam was set up. The scam had worked like a charm because of his own meticulous planning, but instead of the partners meeting afterward Larken had taken off to parts unknown with the money.

It wasn't just the loss of the money that burned the heart of the cold, blue eyed man, not that that didn't ring his bell, it was discovering that Malovitch had Mafia connection and now he was hunting him all over New York City. The only way Malovitch could have known that it was he who had masterminded the sting was if Larken had left evidence pointing the finger right at him. He knew if they found him they'd kill him and not quickly either. You don't con these guys and live to tell about it. He shivered, not just from the cold morning wind, but with gut wrenching fear.

He brooded over this betrayal, though he would have done the same thing to Larken only he would have waited to dump Larken when they had gotten out of town. Damnation, he couldn't even go back to his apartment and get his hideout money because they'd be waiting for him to show up there.

The man ground his teeth in frustration even as his stomach growled on empty and that just added insult to injury. He was used to fine clothes and fancy restaurants and having people see him as a successful businessman. First Class Elroy, that was him, never take second best was his motto. Now he'd have to walk, thumb or ride the freights to escape the city and even that would be difficult. That idea totally destroyed his dignity and his huge self-esteem. He'd do it, but someone was going to suffer for his indignation and it wouldn't matter who it was either.

He had to get out of town now because he had a feeling time had just about run out on him. Either he came up with a plan to get his twenty thousand dollars stashed in the refrigerator today or he'd have to forget it. Then all he had to do was decide in what direction to run. Well, that wasn't a hard one, head toward the warm south and the snow birds down there were made for easy plucking.

Elroy brooded and regretted that he didn't have any connections he could go to for help. Perhaps it had been short sighted of him to have cheated so many of his acquaintances, but even if he hadn't, his acquaintances wouldn't have lifted a finger once they knew who he'd conned. They'd figure out quickly enough that he was dead meat and they would be too if they helped him to achieve that end.

So here he sat on the cold park bench with an angry fire *burning* in his empty stomach while his body shook with cold at what fate had done to him. It would never occurred to Elroy to look closer at himself for the cause of his suffering because it was much easier to blame someone else for his failures. He failed to understand a basic law; *what goes around comes around eventually, or what you give is what you get.*

Suddenly his brain *fired* out a thought and it was so powerful that it brought him to his feet literally *shaking* with its revelation. There *was a way* to get into his apartment without triggering the watchers!

He slammed his hand against his head. "*Dummy, dummy*, all you have to do is just become the janitor in your building. Get him, get his keys and his clothes and *presto*, you're in!" He began to laugh hysterically and began to dance the boogie.

"Get the best of Elroy, would you?" He shook his fist at the sky. "Hah! Here's a fist in your face, *Fate, right in your puss!*" He shouted.

It was fortunate that the park was deserted at this dawn hour or someone might have reported a crazy man to the police. Elroy sat down breathing heavily and slowly calmed himself by taking many deep breaths so he could think clearly and figured out how to accomplish his goal without being caught. He was *very* good at planning; after all it was just like another scam where you did the research, got the details down, form them into a plan and then do it!

Tonight, Old Beason, the janitor in his building, would head for the local bar as usual. Elroy would steal a hat and coat somewhere and later that evening he would pick Beason up when he came out of the bar and they'd just be drunks going home and that's all the watchers would see. Once they were in Beason's basement apartment, it would be easy to tie the man up and gag him and take his work clothes. Then he'd let himself into his apartment, get the money and other portable valuables and get out. He'd leave the building, staggering like Old Beason going after another bottle and disappear out through the bar's back door. It was such a simple plan that Elroy feared that the last few days had softened his brain. He had only to wait until tonight.

Looking around for someone to panhandle, Elroy was disappointed to see that the park was still deserted; it was even too early for joggers. To help kill the time he picked up one of the months old papers he'd use to keep warm last night and began to read. He had read several pages when suddenly a short item caught his attention.

"Well, well, well, lookee here at this! Maybe my luck has just taken another leap upward." he grinned rather nastily. "Yes indeedy! Now that answers the question of direction, doesn't it?" and snickered at how fate had turned into Lady Luck just at the right time. "Oh, I'm *good*; I'm *very, very* good! I'm on a roll again."

Elroy jumped up scattering the newspapers as he did, and quickly walked away. He had to keep hidden just for today before he could begin the journey that would finally lead him to the pot of gold. Tonight he'd be on his way in Elroy Style.

He laughed in a most peculiar way and walked quickly out of the park and down to the corner of the quiet street. Then the street was deserted once more, waiting for all the people to begin their work day.

~Boys Meet the Chief~

"Come on boys let's go while the getting good 'cause you never can tell about our weather. She's as changeful as a woman with a closet full of dresses and she can't make up her mind which one to put on." The boys laughed and piled into Ben's truck, fastened their seat belts and were ready to roll.

It amazed both boys how easily they had settled into the Strongbow family in just a little over a month. It had begun to feel like home, but more importantly, they felt welcomed and wanted and that had been vital to their decision to stay.

They felt secure for the first time since their parents had died..

Having heard stories about Chief Blackhawk both boys were excited to meet him though they were a bit apprehensive as to what he'd be like. The stories about this Indian Chief sounded bigger than life. However, from the way Ben spoke of the man showed the boys how much Chief Blackhawk was liked by everyone so that was reassuring.

As they drove along Ben talked about the country. Mike and Joe both looked down the Lost Wagon ranch road as they passed and strained to see the Devereaux house, however they were disappointed that pine trees and small hills obscured it.

Ben observed their attempt and assured them. "We'll stop on our way back as I know you're both anxious to see the place. We should probably have gone over before now, but with one thing or another, well, it didn't happen. We also have to schedule a meeting with the lawyer now that probate is finished and everything legal seems to have been cleared for you all to inherit. Anyway, I called Hank to expect us this afternoon and we'll spend some time there. You've already met him and I know you both liked him. He's been an excellent foreman for your grandfather the past five years and I admire any man who could put up with such a difficult man as Devereaux was."

Ben glanced over at the boys and decided to tell them the truth. "Yes, kids, your Grandfather wasn't a congenial person, I'm sorry to say. He wasn't neighborly at all and resented having anyone dropping in on him and he never offered to help anyone either. Your Grandfather was a strange man and while I know he had family tragedies, nevertheless that isn't any excuse for turning mean. While the Valleys tolerate odd ducks and people's idiosyncrasies and we respect their choices as long as they obey the Guardian's laws, it's nice to have neighbors that one can rely on, you know? Devereaux never asked for help or offered any. Hank was always there on his days off if you needed him and there's the difference in men. Well, the poor man's dead now and it's to late to try for him to mend any fences. I'll get Mari Beth to tell you about what good friends she was with your Mother."

"I'd love to hear about Mom anytime. We never knew we had a grandfather until Social Services found Joseph Devereaux so you're the first one to tell us anything personal about him. The best part is Mari Beth and Mom had been good friends; that really makes things super, doesn't it Joe? When we go over to our ranch we'll see where she grew up. I think that's special."

"Oh, yeah, imagine Mom when she was little and living over there. I can't wait to see the place. Aren't we glad that we don't have to live with that mean old man?" Joe said, then hesitated, "Do you really, really think he'd have treated us badly? Somehow, I don't think so Mike, I got a feeling he might have liked us living there with him. I think we would have made him happy."

"Maybe so and then again, we'll never know will we? All we have to go on is what people say about grandfather and it doesn't sound like it would have been very good for us. I guess grandfather and I would have bumped heads a lot if he'd gotten mean with you or Carli. Gee, what if grandfather hadn't wanted to put up with having a baby around? Golly Joe, it sounds like we missed out on a lot of trouble after all." exclaimed Mike.

"Well, now, let me tell you a bit about the Blackhawk Ranch." Ben went on to spin some tales that kept the boys mind off imagining troubles that would never happen now.

The pickup turned onto North Mountain Road and sped along always climbing toward the mountains. It was a beautiful September day with enough warmth that they could roll down the windows and let the fresh mountain air flow into the cab.

It wasn't long before Ben made a right turn at the fork in the road. "The left road leads to Tom Blackhawk's ranch and this one leads to his father's place higher up the mountain. He and Tom raise the finest Appaloosas in the country, bar none. You know their usual colors are black, white, gray and brown with white or black spots on their rumps or, like the Leopard Appaloosa, spotted all over. They're mighty pretty and wonderful mountain horses too. At one time in the past the U.S. Army just about killed off the breed thinking it would subdue the Indian. Well, I'm sure the Chief would be delighted if you asked to see them."

The truck climbed up the hills drawing them closer and closer to the awesome mountain. Joe felt a shiver run down his spine and he got a strange feeling, a sense of an overwhelming…*presence*. He nudged Mike and whispered to him. Mike took a minute then looked at Joe and nodded. Yeah, the mountain felt alive.

"Ah Ben, is it our imagination or is the mountain alive?" said Mike in a hushed voice, hoping that Ben wouldn't think they were being silly.

Ben looked at Mike and after a moment he smiled and nodded. "Yep, boys, she's alive alright and that's where the Guardians live; up there somewhere at the top. It's interesting that you picked up on that. Most people aren't conscious of anything different about Thunder Mountain." Silence followed that leaving the boys very little to say.

At last they'd gained a large bench of land that butted up against the beginnings of a big cliff and that's when they saw a large, long, single storied log house with a wide covered front porch that ran around on one side facing the yard. The porch held rocking chairs, tables with lamps, baskets and other things hung on the walls with bright Indian blankets covering tables and chairs in a colorful eclectic way that was appealing in a homey country look.

They drew up in front of the house just as Chief Blackhawk walked out onto the porch letting the screen door slam shut behind him. The big man walked to the edge of the porch steps with his hands stuck in the front pockets of his jeans and waited. Ben turned off the engine and stepped down from the truck.

Blackhawk smiled and called "Howdy Ben, welcome and your boys too. Come on up and have a seat."

"Hello Blackhawk." The visitors walked up the porch steps and stopped. "Let me introduce you to Mike and Joe Kelly; gentlemen, this is Chief Blackhawk, Guardian of the Sacred Valleys."

"I'm glad to meet you both." and held out his hand. Taking off their hats the boys shook hands willingly if not a bit shyly, awed to be meeting a real Indian Chief.

"Now, now, youngens', I'm not going to bite or take any scalps this morning; I've been real civilized of late. I only scalp my men when they don't do a job right." Blackhawk stopped as though shot. "Dadblastit, now that I think of it, none of them have any hair left. Well, darn!" He frowned down at the boys with a twinkle in his eyes and they had to grin and dropped their nervousness.

"You just set easy now and give me the news from down yonder." Directed Blackhawk as he guided everyone to a seat around a table then went to the screen door and yelled.

"Mike, let's have some coffee out here and some lemonade for our young visitors and anything else you got to offer then come join us."

The man returned to his chair and apologized. "I can't offer you young men any cookies because my cook refuses to make them. Hey, speaking of cookies, did Hannah by any chance give you any for me?" asked the man with childlike eagerness.

"Oh!" said Joe, "I forgot. Yes Sir, Hannah sent a huge jar of chocolate chip cookies for you. I'll go get them." And ran down the steps and over to the passenger side of the truck and got out the commercial size jar that used to hold pickles. Walking very carefully with both arms wrapped around it so he wouldn't drop it, Joe watched his feet while the men held their breath. Joe cautiously walked up the porch steps and was almost to the porch floor when a huge man came out the front door, ducking his head to pass under the door lintel. Joe's eyes popped, his jaw dropped, his grip on the cookies jar loosened and the jar began to slip.

Blackhawk swooped to rescue the jar from disaster. "Whoa there little man let me help you with that. Ah, I've got it; why you almost gave me heart failure boy 'cause dropping my cookies would have made me cry." At Joe's look of embarrassment Blackhawk reassured

True Heart

him. "Now you're not to blame, Big Mike would startle anyone out of their minds if they didn't know he was a gentle as a kitten."

Blackhawk hear a snort behind him and the clatter of a tray hitting the table and the big man sat down. Joe wasn't paying any attention to Blackhawk's talk because he was mesmerized by the giant.

"Come on, Joe," and the chief took the gaping boy by the arm and led him back to his chair all the while Big Mike and Joe locked eyes.

"Gee, you must be the biggest man in the world, huh?" said Joe candidly. Even seated Big Mike towered over the boy who gazed way up in admiration at this huge man. "Do you think I could grow up to be as big as you if I set my mind to it?"

The amusement in the cook's eyes fairly sparkled. "Well, it's hard to say youngster," Came the deep rumbling voice." Maybe, but I doubt that. You see I come from a special kind of people; they're called giants. You know about giants, don't you?"

"Only in fairy tales Sir, and I didn't believe they were really, really real, if you know what I mean. Are there many of you?" By this time Joe had scooted his chair up close to Mike's and was watching him like a hawk. Big Mike laughed a deep belly laugh that surprised everyone there including Blackhawk. His cook rarely ever laughed like that. What a revelation into the man and just when you thought you knew him so well! The others watched in fascination as this little boy's admiration turn Big Mike the Mighty into Mike the Marshmallow.

"Ah, by the way Mike, this is Joe and Mike Kelly." said Blackhawk with a side glance at Ben and they both pressed their lips tightly together to prevent laughing at the scene. Joe stood up and shook the giant's hand and sat back down again. Mike moved around the table to do the same. Mike resumed his seat and couldn't help grinning as he watched his little brother charm the big man. Joe and Big Mike were holding an intense one on one conversation and the cook didn't appear bored at all.

Meanwhile, Blackhawk said to the others. "It looks like we've lost them, so I guess we'll have to entertain ourselves. I think you've got some questions for me, don't you Ben?"

Ben nodded his head. "You know that Mike, Joe, Mari Beth and I have discussed guardianship and the boys seemed to like the idea, so our lawyer, young Jim Jensen, is handling all the paper work and has made an appointment with Judge Barker for next Friday at 1:00

o'clock." Ben paused and sipped some coffee and eyed the tray of treats that Big Mike had put on the table.

"The day after the children arrived," Ben went on even as he continued to scrutinize the goodies. "I called Sheriff's Brandt and let him know we had them safe. Then I called the Social Services in Huntington about the children and spoke to Mrs. Dunsmoor, the social worker we'd worked with before. She didn't think there would be any problem with the guardianship as we've been through their system a few times and have proven to be good parents and providers. She's getting the paper work done and will fax it over to the courthouse in time for the court date. We want it finalized as soon as possible, don't we Mike?"

"Yes, Sir, we sure do. We couldn't have better guardians than you and Mari Beth. We're struck it lucky at last." replied a quiet Mike.

"These youngsters need stability and the boys need to get back in school. They've already missed a couple of weeks, but I've got all their school records. They're very smart, Blackhawk, so there won't be any problem with them catching up. I didn't want to put them in school right away because….well frankly, they needed some down time and Joe needed to recover his health." Ben stopped and took another sip of coffee and finally picked up one the pastries and took a big bite, hmm, hmm.

"I don't want to interrupt your concentration on the treats Ben, 'cause I know how important the final selection of the right pastry is, however get to the point because most of what you've said I've already heard from Tom and everyone else. You know there are no secrets in these Valleys."

Ben laughed and reached out to randomly take another pastry and pushed the plate toward Mike the Small who didn't hesitate at all figuring correctly that they'd all taste mighty fine.

"I was just giving you what they call an overview; a fancy word for getting all the facts straight in line. I wanted you to meet the boys here and after that I wanted to ask you to be co-custodian of Mike's Lost Wagon Ranch with me and Jim Jensen. I know you're a busy man so if you can't I'll understand. Anyway, I'm going to hire young Jim as we'll need someone to keep the records of profit and loss, control the bank accounts along with us and other such-like details. I'm thinking a mandatory of two signatures on all checks and any three of us can sign with another. It's cumbersome, but it's a safe guard for Mike. I want the cleanest record on file for custodial care that ever was." Ben finished his coffee and Blackhawk obligingly pour him another cup.

"So far it sounds alright to me so go on." replied Blackhawk and selected his own treat.

"Jim told me about Devereaux's will. The three children inherit equally, but Mike will no doubt be the primary head of the ranch. If after a period of time Mike has any objections to his manager we can hire someone else, but I think Hank Tomlinson is a good competent man and he has five years of experience working the ranch. I don't think we could find anyone better than he is. I'd like to keep him on as Ranch Manager with a sizable raise in pay because he'll be responsibility for the running of the ranch, which he's been doing that since Devereau died."

Ben sipped on his hot coffee. "Hank told me they've been short handed over there for some time because Devereaux wouldn't spend the money to hire more men so we'll have him hire extra hands. Mike and I plan on working closely with him, especially Mike, because he needs to learn the ropes. So what do you think?"

Blackhawk thought it over and the time commitment then he looked over at Mike who'd kept silent yet had listened to every word. This was a serious young man who would one day have his own ranch and the responsible for the care of the land. He liked the looks and the feel of this kid. "How do you feel about this Mike?"

"I know I'll need good custodians who will help me govern the ranch and give me time to learn how to manage it. I'd be honored if you'd accept, Sir." Mike said quietly.

"It would be a pleasure to help you Mike. I like your style and I think you'll make a fine rancher one day." Blackhawk turned his attention to Ben. "Sure Ben, you honor me and I'll be glad to meet you in town next Friday; probably everyone in the area will be there too so be prepared." Blackhawk paused and looked thoughtfully up at the mountain seen from the corner of the porch. After a few minutes he smiled and looked over at Mike and Ben.

"Now that I've seen these young men I think I'd like to be Godfather to them as well, that would give me a hand with the boys on other levels. Would you and Joe like to have a Native American

Chief as a Godfather?" asked Blackhawk looking directly into Mike's eyes and smiled when he saw them pop open and the kid's jaw dropped. Finally, thought Blackhawk, a child-like response from this serious faced young person.

"Are you serious Sir? If you are it would be past wonderful for Joe, Carli and me. That would really make everything really special. Hey, Joe, listen to this." grinned Mike.

"What?" asked Joe twisting around in his chair and looked at his brother.

"Chief Blackhawk wants to be our Godfather. What do you think about that?"

"Really? Why? I mean we aren't that special to have a real important Chief be our Godfather." said the bewildered boy as he looked at Blackhawk.

"Now young man, I don't offer to be just anyone's Godfather. I am the Big Chief of these Valleys so you bet you're special. Do you or don't you want me as your Godfather?" said Blackhawk with a serious face and sparkling black eyes.

"If it wouldn't be too much trouble, I can't think of anything I'd like more. Will that make us one of your tribe?" questioned Joe coming to stand beside Blackhawk and leaning on the chair's arm.

"I'll get out the adoption papers and make you and your brother and your sister Carli, honorary members of the Tribe of Blackhawk. Your tribal name will be given to you later, but Mike can have his anytime after he turns sixteen. We'll talk about that later Mike, as I'd like you to go on what we call "a vision quest." Perhaps next summer would be a good time."

"Whatever you say Chief is fine with me; you know best about these things and I'll look forward to next summer." smiled Mike and Blackhawk saw the light of deep pleasure in Mike's eyes and how much it meant to the young man to be included in belonging to something like a tribe.

"Geeze peeze, goodness me, I'll get my real Native American name too sometime." Joe was overjoyed and a grin spread across his face was worth a million bucks to those who watched him. "Mike, we get to have names just like Daddy had." whispered Joe to Mike.

"What's this about your father? Did he have a tribal name?" asked Blackhawk seriously.

"His full name was Michael Grayhawk Kelly, Sir. He was a half breed or so he thought, but Native American anyway." answered Mike.

"What tribe did he come from?" asked Blackhawk seriously.

"I don't know and neither did he. He was left at an orphanage with the name pinned to his blanket, Michael Grayhawk. The name Kelly was taken from an old priest that Dad really liked."

"Well, for sure you children need to belong to our tribe without a doubt so consider it done. I will officially bring you all under our Tribe's jurisdiction because that has to happen before any naming ceremony can happen." The talk went on for a bit until a silence came over the group at the table.

"Oh, Chief Blackhawk, can we see your horses? Ben said they were really special. Mike wants to see them too, don't you Mike? Mike is especially good with horses." said Joe as he leaned against his Godfather-to-be.

"Yeah, I love all breed of horses. I've only seen a few spotted ones in my life, but I'm not sure whether they were Appaloosas though." said Mike.

"Well, come along and take a good look; I've got some mighty pretty ones, boys." and the Chief and led the way off the porch.

"Aren't you coming Mr. Mike? It would be really neat if you did." Joe waited for the cook to answer.

"Well, I don't mind if I do Joe."

And got up to walk alongside this kid he'd fallen for. Me, the big man thought, tough Mean Mike, mush in the hands of a seven year old and burst out in a huge belly laugh. Although Joe didn't know what the man was laughing about, he took the big man's hand and joined right in just to keep him company.

The conversation flowed fast and furious on their way home from Blackhawk's. Now the boys were really in a quandary as to which breed of horse they like best. Arguing for this certain one and that certain one kept the boys busy with Ben chiming in with some facts here and there, but the bottom line was each breed of horse was unique and there really couldn't be any comparing one breed to another. It was just a matter of personal preference.

When they pulled into the Lost Wagon Ranch Road silence filled the cab as the boys watched the buildings appear and the house where their mother had been born and raised. They pulled up in front of the house and saw Mr. Tomlinson, a tall slender man dressed like a typical cowboy, standing on the steps of the front porch waiting for them.

As Mike got out of the truck he looked the ranch house over and quickly saw it needed painting yet it was in good repair. The fences were straight and in good repair also, at least the ones he had seen driving in. He couldn't see much of the out buildings to know what might need fixing. Mike had such a hunger to get started making this place their home.

Mr. Tomlinson stepped down the porch steps and Ben greeted him with a handshake. "Here are the new owners of the ranch come to see their domain at last."

Mike stepped up and shook hands saying, "It's good to see you again, Sir."

"I'm glad you've come to see your home Mr. Kelly, we've been waiting for you. Welcome." and then turned to Joe and shook his small hand and said the same thing.

"Why don't we go into the house and let you both look around. It's just as your grandfather left it. Your mother's room hasn't been touched since the day she left except for cleaning. My wife had cleaned the house regularly so it would be especially nice when you visited." Mr. Tomlinson led the way up the steps and held the door open for the new owners to enter. Ben winked at Hank and entered behind the boys.

While the boys took off to explore, Ben and Hank walked back to the kitchen for coffee. It didn't take long to locate their mother's room. When they opened the door they could smell her. Her perfume scented the room and it brought instant tears to their eyes remembering that unique smell that said "Mom."

All her things were on the dresser, just female stuff like jars of various creams, perfumes and brushes, combs and the like. A shirt and jeans were lying over a chair just like she had left them with her boots set beside it. The bed was a princess's bed, all white and pink with a canopy over the top.

"I can't stay here Mike, I gotta' go. Mom's here and I can't touch her. It hurts too much." he cried and ran out of the room.

Mike shivered and felt her presence too and lifted his hand up above his head as though to touch her spirit. "Mom, we love you and Dad so much. We miss you with all our hearts, but we're all right now." Mike swallowed hard. "Mari Beth and Ben are looking after us, so don't worry any more. Gosh, Mom, it's so *hard* to be without you both. I love you and Joe loves you too." and Mike turned and hurried after Joe and saw him sitting on at the top of the stairs. Mike sat down beside him and didn't say anything for while.

Finally Mike swallowed hard and blew his nose on his handkerchief. Joe sniffed and did the same. "Joe, you were right, she's here at least her spirit is. I guess she just wanted to know we were alright, don't you think? Actually, it's sort of comforting to know she's alive *somewhere*. But, yeah, I wished she was here and touchable too, but that's life I guess. Are you going to be alright?"

Joe sniffed and wiped his face on his shirt sleeve and gave his nose another hard blowing. "Yeah I guess so, not that we have much choice. It was kind of a shock feeling her there, I guess it spooked me, but it's kinda neat too, huh? Don't know if I could get used to that feeling, but I'm okay now…I guess."

"Okay, kid, come on, let's see the rest of this house. It sure is big." and giving Joe a hand up they walked back down the hall looking into the other rooms.

While the boys explored the house, Hank and Ben got themselves a cup of coffee and sat down at the table.

"Well, Hank, Mari Beth and I are going to be guardians of the Kelly children until Mike reaches eighteen and I've asked Blackhawk and Jim Jensen to be co-custodians of this ranch with me until Mike reached legal age."

"That's good to know. Those kids couldn't do any better than you and Mari Beth."

"Thanks Hank. Well, we've got young Jim Jensen to do the books, keep records and such. We want you to stay on as Ranch Manager with a significant raise in salary because you're going to be running the place. Don't forget Mike will be going to college, at least I hope so. That will leave you with at least six years of full management and maybe longer. For now and the next couple of years Mike will need to work with you as often as he can, so I hope you won't mind teaching him how to manage. We'll help you get this place up to snuff as I know you've been running shorthanded. You will have the authority to hire four or five new men or more if you need the extra hands to prepare this place for winter. What do you say, will you accept the position?"

Hank sat back in his kitchen chair and gave a deep heart felt sigh. "It sounds great Ben. I must admit your offer relieves me of a great anxiety. I figured the ranch would be sold and maybe the new owners might not want me to stay on. I'm glad the kids want to keep the place for it's a real honey. It's been difficult these last years working within the old man's restrictions. Believe me he didn't spend a dime he didn't have too. I was so frustrated at the amount of work just begging to be done that I was about ready to quit just before he died. I *know this place* and exactly what needs doing. Devereaux said he was leaving us something in his will and that was a surprise. He said he was remembering our two permanent men, Grumpy Tucker and Pike John in his will too."

Hank gave out another gusty sigh. "I gotta' say it's a relief to me that I'll be staying on. We love it here and think of the Valley as home. Now May can stop worrying what we'll do next. She can keep the cottage and I can put more money into retirement. Yes Ben, I'd be more than pleased to stay and thank you for the offer." and reached out his hand for Ben to give it a firm shake.

Ben grinned, "That's great Hank and it sure relieves my mind knowing you're here on the land. I'd sure hate to see you and May going out of the Valleys 'cause you're our friends and good friends are invaluable. After the boys get through looking around, let's do a quick tour and make some notes as to what needs doing before winter sets in."

"I've already got a list a mile long." smiled Hank as he got up to lead the way to the office. "Why I kept it up I'll never know unless it made me feel like I was doing *something* about the problems. Old Devereaux didn't want to spend the money on the kind of repairs this ranch has to have. Now that I know these needed repairs are going to get done I'll have the list updated with winter priorities at the top. When you all come over for that big meeting it will be ready and I hope it's soon because we pushing weather as it is. Snow could fly anytime now."

They entered the office and Hank pulled out the folder with his lists and they both sat down. "Ben, I've worked hard around this place with only two other men and Mr. Devereaux to help me so I won't kid you that there is a lot of repair work to be done that was impossible for us to accomplish. I think the ranch must have made money over the years I've been here, yet he rarely put anything back into the place that he didn't consider absolutely necessary. Don't mistake me he took care of the land all right and the animals too, if he hadn't you know what would have happened. Well who knows, maybe it happened anyway."

Hank pointed out several items and said. "I seriously need at least four new hands and a cook if I'm to pull this place together before winter. I'll need quite a load of building materials to do the repairs as well. We can go over all this later, but I've got to tell you it's a relief that this great ranch is going to get the care it deserves."

Hank gave Ben the list and they discussed it, made a few check marks here and there and agreed that after the guardianship and the custodial papers were signed, they'd immediately move to see the priorities got done.

"Why don't you put an ad in the paper for four ranch hands and a cook now?" said Ben as he looked at the huge amount of work that was going to have to be done as fast as possible. That meant hiring men immediately. "I'll give you permission to do that immediately."

"I'll gladly do that today. Lord knows there should be enough jobless men who are looking for a good place for the winter, not that I'll hire just any bum. No sir, I'll vet them really close because the ranch deserves the best and so do these kids."

Hank felt the weight of worries and frustrations slide off his shoulders and disappeared. He took a deep breath and the light of enthusiasm lit his eyes. *Now*, he was going to be able to run this ranch like it should be run and see it shine! They went on to discuss other items of immediate concern until Mike and Joe came into the office to join them.

As they left the house Hank pointed out some of the outbuildings and the barns that needed repair and they discussed other changes. Mike was delegated to take notes which made him feel included in the decision making. He even had a few intelligent recommendations to make that had Ben and Hank cheerfully agreeing. They got into Hank's Jeep and did a fast run around the property as it was getting on toward suppertime.

When they got back to the house, Mike shook Mr. Tomlinson's hand and said. "Thank you, Sir, I'll look forward to working with you as I have a lot to learn and Ben says you'll be a fine teacher. We'll be getting together for a meeting and give you what you need to do your job right. There is one thing I would like to see changed right away if you have no objection." Mike paused and looked at his foreman with intent dark eyes. "I want this ranch referred to as the Kelly Ranch from now on. I would like to have the sign out on the road that says "Devereaux" replaced. This is Kelly land from now on and people need to realize Joe and I are the new owners along with my sister Carli. Also, please tell your men I'll look forward to meeting them next time." Mike spoke with quiet authority and Hank nodded his agreement.

"Mr. Kelly, I can tell you're going to be a joy to work with. I'll have the sign taken down in a jiffy and a new one put up. Now it may not be professional looking, but it will say "Kelly" on it. We can get a sign done later that will be fancier. Yes, indeed, it's about time that we had a big, big change around here for which I am sincerely delighted." smiled Hank.

"Mr. Tomlinson, I'd also appreciate it if you'd call me Mike. I'm a little too young to have earned a Mister yet and I'm not the boss here either; you are." grinned Mike and Hank had to laugh.

"Mike you've got that straight for now and it's Hank to you too." shaking hands again. Then it was Joe's turn to say goodbye.

"Mike says I own part of the ranch, but he's really the one who will be the rancher and he's really the boss of us too. Carli and I are too young to know what to do, but Mike is really smart and I know he'll have fun learning all the ranching stuff. I know I am not going to be a rancher 'cause I think I will be something else, but I have to wait to grow up a little more before I know for certain. My home will be here and at Ben's and Mari Beth's too." Joe stopped talking; his jaw dropped as he turned to Mike and said in an awed voice. "Geeze peeze Mike, think of that, we're wealthy and we've got two homes." exclaimed Joe.

The laughter that greeted this bit of revelation put a nice period to the end of an eventful day. Waving goodbye as they drove away and Mike watched the old white house disappear in the side mirror.

" Ben, we got to get a wiggle on to see Hank gets what he needs before winter, don't we?" worried Mike.

"That we do son, that we do. Next Friday we'll keep that court date and get this guardianship approved. Yep, we got things to do and places to go 'cause time and weather waits for no man. We'll get a jump start on that by hiring men and ordering the supplies and lumber tomorrow ready for delivery on the afternoon we sign the papers." And the pickup whizzed along in the light of late afternoon.

"Isn't life funny Mike?" said Joe. "One day we're orphans, homeless, and the next we have wonderful guardians, a beautiful place to live and a ranch of our own. Myohmy, how sudden life is." Mused the little philosopher as he leaned his head against Ben's arm and closed his eyes. "Giants, imagine that; I know me a giant." And fell asleep.

Ben looked at Mike over Joe's head and with the meeting of their eyes both laughed as quietly as possible.

Yes, life was good. And now he knew what his folks had been trying to tell them when they visited Joe in his dream. This was the home they were speaking of. Angels really did give messages to people in dreams if we only knew how to listen thought Mike.

~Guardianship~

MIKE STEPPED OUT ONTO the front porch that special Friday morning just to be alone for awhile and to get a grip on his uncertain emotions 'cause they were bouncing all over the place; happy, sad, scared, blessed, and fearful. Geeze he felt ready to explode just so he could clear every feeling away. He felt panicky too most of all at how fast everything was moving. Was the Strongbow's guardianship the right way to go, the right thing to do for Joe and Carli and himself? This guardianship gave Ben and Mari Beth powerful control over their lives and that was a very scary thing. Trusting them was the bottom line. Mike felt responsible for making this lasting decision. After all, he was the oldest and Dad expected him to do right by the kids. The pressure was killing him.

Mike moved over to sit in one of the rocking chairs and leaning his arms on his long legs and looking out at the southern mountains. He sat there for quite some time trying to make sense of his life and his responsibilities without arriving at any conclusions. Life had just been happening too fast of late that he'd hardly had time to think about the results of his actions and how this decision of guardianship was so monumental that thinking about it's affect on them had him going around in circles.

His mind was far, far away when a cold nose was shoved up under his arm and a wet tongue slurp his cheek startled Mike into almost falling out of his chair. Roscoe gave a small woof and nudged him again.

"Lordy massy Roscoe, you *scared* the living daylights out of me. You idiot dog, you've got to learn not to sneak up on a guy this way. It's a good thing I'm young or you could have caused a serious heart attack here." All the time Mike was scratching and patting the dumb dog with Roscoe crowding in to lay his head in Mike's lap looked up at him with worshipful brown eyes and seemed content to stay there forever. And so they sat, boy and dog for awhile.

After a bit, Mike began to feel better about things as he stroked the dog's glossy head; he definitely didn't feel so alone anymore. Yeah, he felt calmer and deep inside he knew that Ben and Mari Beth would be the very best guardians for them until he could take over the ranch in a few years. He looked down at Roscoe and the contentment of the animal seemed to be giving Mike the same feeling.

Studying the animal, Mike got to thinking back to other times when he went around the ranch. Roscoe always seem to trail along behind as unobtrusive as a big dog could. He remembered asking Ben one time if Roscoe belonged to anyone and got, "No one in particular, he's just a young ranch dog and not good for much, but we like him."

Maybe Roscoe was looking for someone to belong to, thought Mike as he held the dog's face close to his. "Roscoe, do you want to be my dog, be my very own companion that goes everywhere with me? I'd like that if you would. What do you say? My dog Roscoe, My dog Roscoe." said Mike in a happy voice and shaking the dog's head enthusiastically had Roscoe going off into fits of barking. "Well, I guess that's a yes. I'll tell Ben you're mine now," but he spent another little bit talking to his new buddy.

Unknown to Mike, Ben had been standing in the front screen door out of Mike's sight and had been watching the boy through the screen with some concern. He had just about decided to go out and join him when he saw Roscoe sneak up on Mike and the rest, as they say, was history and Ben laughed quietly. Yeah, Roscoe had found something he could do; be a boy's dog. Ben turned back down the hallway to the kitchen to tell Mari Beth.

Ben was driving the big stretch truck so there would be room for all six people. They left the ranch as Roscoe howled mournfully beside Jacko who had put a leash on the dog to keep him from following.

Again, the truck was white just like the smaller pick-up and the boys, along with Hannah, were in the backseat all dressed in their best clothes, thanks to Mari Beth's trip to town to buy suitable ones for this grand occasion. Carli was up front between Ben and Mari Beth in her car seat.

Ill fate seemed to have finally passed away at least Mike hoped there wouldn't be any hitches in the guardianship hearing. At that thought his shoulders tensed up and he started worrying that with things going so awfully well lately surely something would pop up to ruin their wonderful new life. Mike talked in a whisper to himself saying, "That's negative thinking and Dad always said if you think negatively, negative will happen; it's the power of attraction. Like to like sort of thing."

"What are you muttering about, Mike? Are you worrying again? Mom wouldn't like that you know." said Joe laying his hand on Mike's knee. Mike had to laugh at Joe's ability to read people like a book, which broke him right out of his blue funk.

"No worries, mate, we've got this whole show on the right path. Whoo-Hoo! Tally-ho! Tally-ho!" shouted Mike startling Carli in her jump seat.

"Mikey, you stop. Yelling no good for babies." that set everyone off. Where in the world had she come up with that one, grinned Mike, maybe something Mom had said and she just remember it.

The drive to town reminded Mike and Joe of their long, long hot walk just seven weeks ago. He thought about how the best of luck had happened to them just because he had made the mistake of trying to walk out to grandfather's place. Maybe it hadn't been a mistake after all. And then again maybe fate or the Thunder Gods would have seen them cared for by the Strongbow's anyway. Well, my gratitude goes to whatever divine intervention happened to rescue us. Mike also believed that their Guardian Angels had a lot to do with the way things were working out. Gee, maybe these Guardians and Angels are the same thing? Whatever, at least they had protected them from harm.

Mike watched the passing scenery and said in the privacy of his mind. *"Mom and Dad, we're all right now. We're safe with good people and I'll take care of the kids. Bye, we love you."*

Mike keep his face turned toward the window and brushed the few tears that ran down his face and a small hand slipped into his and gripped it tightly. Mike looked down at his brother and saw that Joe had his head leaning against Hannah holding on to her hand too. Connections, it was all about love's connections and Mike breathed deeply and knew that today was the start of a whole new life for them.

River Town was a fairly good sized farming community; pretty as a picture and neat as a pin. Even before Ben pulled up in front of the courthouse he saw the empty parking space in a long line of parked vehicles with a sign that said, "Reserved for the Strongbows." Ben chuckled and wondering who the genius was that had thought of that. He parked the truck then just sat there for a few minutes looking at the crowd of people waiting for them on the steps of the courthouse.

Ben cleared his throat and said aloud. "Well, I guess we're the center of attention today, so come on kids, let's get this show on the road."

Once they were all on the sidewalk Blackhawk appeared out of the shadow of a tree and joined them. There was Luther, Dan Lightfoot and even the ornery Jim Waggoner and…and gee, an awful lot of strangers.

Tom Blackhawk walked up to stand beside his father. Joe whispered to Mike, "Gee, Mike they look just like twins except the Chief has white streaks in his long hair and Tom's hair is shorter."

The amount of turquoise Blackhawk was wearing would have bought another ranch, but to Joe, Blackhawk looked just like a Mighty Chief should look. Perfect! All the men were handsome in their suits and the women wore nice dresses with jackets or pant suits.

"We're here to welcome the newest members to the Sacred Valleys Ben, we all want to be your witnesses." called someone from the crowd.

"Mari Beth, you're the best." another voice piped up.

"Celebration time coming up." yelled another enthusiast.

Mari Beth, holding Carli by the hand smiled at all her neighbors and friends and said, "Thank you and you're welcome to join us inside. Ben and I are going to have a small celebration after the ceremony. Y'all are invited to Murphy's Place for refreshments and dancing at seven this evening." That invitation was greeted with cheers and applause. Carli looked like a princess in her new fancy pink dress and coat standing in her shinny Patten-Leather Mary Janes. She waved to everyone just like she was royalty and the crowd loved it.

Mari Beth, Carli and Hannah led the way up the steps at the slow pace of the child and the rest of the family followed them into the building. Mike and Joe gripped hands and got very nervous at the same time as Mike cast a quick anxious look around him at all the people following them.

Luther, just behind Mike, saw the sudden worry in the older boy's eyes and leaned forward and whispered." They're just nosy and don't want to miss anything. It's small town stuff so don't let it worry you. We're all here to support you guys and that's the bottom line. Come on Mike, we're all friends and we want to put the seal of approval on your adoption into the Valleys."

Mike smiled at the tall man whose kindness was deeply appreciated. So he straightened his back and looking down at Joe. They both grinned and dropped hands to walk forward and join the Strongbows at the front of the court room.

The actual procedure didn't take all that long. Ben and Mari Beth Strongbow, proven good citizens with a stable lifestyle as well as being excellent providers, were granted guardianship until each child reached twenty-one. Issaquah Blackhawk was granted alternate guardian in case the Strongbows were unable to finish the guardianship. Mike would gain control of the ranch and its assets at the age of eighteen with continued supervision until he turned twenty-one. Custodial care of the ranch would be divided among three men, Ben Strongbow, Issaquah Blackhawk and Jim Jensen, attorney. Judge Barker would do an overview once a year.

Everyone in the courthouse was surprised when another document was presented to the court that said Issaquah Blackhawk was applying to become the official Godfather to the Kelly children with all the rights of true parents and his obligation was to see to the spiritual training and the building of their character. Everyone burst out in loud applause causing Judge Barker to bang his gavel loudly and demand quiet in his court room and he got it too.

"Ruben," said Blackhawk to the Judge. "I know that there is a division between church and state, but since I represent my tribe and we are not a church, I thought it would be best to make this application for Godfather legal in the eyes of the law. I shall take great care to help form these children's moral foundation and help the Strongbows build their characters into fine citizens. Their characters are already just fine; their parents did a great job. I swear to be a very involved Godfather."

"Issaquah, you're to call me Judge Barker when you're in my court room and show some respect for my dignity here. Humph! Very well, so noted and recorded and it's now the law so behave Chief." said Ruben Barker looking over the tops of his half glasses and grinned at his friend.

"Yes Sir, your Honor, Sir." Blackhawk said with mock seriousness as he bowed several times and that little side show caused more laughter from their large audience.

"Court's adjourned. Now get out of here and go celebrate and I'll join you as soon as I attend to some other business. Congratulations to all of you." He banged his gavel, got up and left the room abruptly before anyone could stand to show that respect.

When all the legal papers were signed, wild applause, whistling and the stomping of feet broke out among the crowd. There was such an awesome feeling of gratitude at being so totally accepted and both boys just about lost it right there. Carli was enjoying the audience's attention and was clapping her hands and laughing too. To Mike and Joe it meant that they were no longer facing the world alone. They had a family and now more friends than they'd ever had before. God had blessed their lives with the abundance that really mattered; family and belonging.

After the crowd left for Murphy's, Ben turned to his closest friends and declared he was taking them all out to dinner before the dancing. With a whoop, Luther grabbed Joe and swung him high up onto his shoulders to the screaming delight of the boy and trotted out of the building with Joe bouncing on the big man's shoulders. Ben grabbed the baby and did the same to her screaming delight too. He might lose a little hair with her grip on it, but it was worth it.

Chief Blackhawk looked down at Mike and said. "Well, I'm too old and you're too big for me to swing you up in a similar style so why don't we present a little dignity to these here proceedings and walk out like gentlemen?"

Just as Mike was about to agree he was grabbed from behind and swung abruptly off his feet and planted on the huge shoulders of Mike the Mighty. "Now, why go for dignity when he can ride in style on the giant. Duck your head Mike as we pass through these doors or it will go missing."

And Big Mike strolled effortlessly down the aisle, stooped through the doors to assist Young Mike in preserve his head all the while the usual somber young Mike was laughing like a lunatic.

Chief Blackhawk gaped at the sight of his Mean Cook behaving in such an unexpected way then laughed and looked over at Mari Beth and Jim Waggoner.

"Well, I guess it's up to us to apply the dignity and follow the crazies." and presented his arm for Mari Beth. Jim, not to be left standing, offered her his arm as well and the three of them strolled out of the courtroom laughing.

Goodness, thought Mike sleepily, as he supported himself in the corner of the truck's back seat, this had certainly been a day and a night to remember. Even though the party at Murphy's had officially ended at five o'clock, the restaurant part of Murphy's had rapidly filled with the same crowd that swelled with the people who hadn't attended before and the party went on. Poor Murphy was beside himself to serve everyone as the room was so crowded there was hardly enough room to turn around.

Mike turned his head and saw that Joe was sound asleep with his head in Hannah's lap and Carli was asleep too. What a wonderful, wonderful time, the best that he could remember. It had been funny to see the very proper lawyer, Mr. Jensen, swinging Mari Beth enthusiastically in the Texas two-step. Mike had met so many other kids his age that he wouldn't be quite the stranger when he went to school.

The truck rumbled along and the quiet inside the cab gradually drained the last of the excitement out of Mike's tired body and he too slept.

~The Spider~

ELROY HAD ARRIVED AT last within touching distance of those obnoxiously rich children. He stood at the back of the courtroom and watched the whole guardianship proceedings and sneered behind his hand at the sickening show of goodwill by these country louts. Why, it made him positively ill.

Now that he was in town, he would have time to scope out the country and plan his first move; something subtle that would carry a warning that all was not as peachy keen in paradise as they thought. Of course, he would only stay in town overnight then move on to another town so no one would notice a stranger hanging around too long.

Elroy hadn't come up with a definitive plan yet, but he had several ideas and it was only a matter of which one he'd executed first. *Execute!* Now there was a word he could identify with. He wasn't leaving without his pot of gold and his pint of blood and these children were ripe for the plucking. He laughed at the thought of such a unique experience ahead of him. He'd never conned kids before. It would be a piece of cake!

He was still laughing when he left the courthouse on his way back to the motel. Oh, yes, they'd pay him sooner or later because Elroy would plan this business better than any scam he'd pulled off before.

He walked down the street in a leisurely way because there was no hurry, not until he had a sure plan of action. No, he chuckled, no hurry at all because half the enjoyment would be in seeing the fear in their faces and the uncertainty of where he, the mysterious marauder, would strike next.

He watched as the people flocked down the street to Murphy's to start the celebration before he continued on. He had some thinking and planning to do and that's what Elroy did best; a unique plot and an all over plan just for this delicious dish of settling old scores. Rubbing his hands together as he walk, the little man laughed.

He wanted….*revenge*. Yes! Sweet revenge would taste just fine for everything he'd been made to suffer.

Unknown to anyone in this small town, a poisonous spider had just invaded their kingdom.

~Spirits at Rest~

"**WAKE UP YOU LAZY boys**, dawn's busted and we've got to get over to your ranch by eight for that meeting. We've got chores to do here and more to do before the snow flies at your place, so ranchers *up and at 'em!*" Ben withdrew his head from the doorway and chuckled to hear the groans before he shut the door.

"Ranchers huh? Maybe I'll change my vocation and become a jet setter and get to go to all those fun places, soak up the sun, live the good life of leisure and sleep in on any morning I want." mumbled Mike as he rubbed his eyes and yawned.

"Yeah right, as if I believed *that* story! You'd be bored in no time. You're the Man now big brother and you're the official big property owner with lots of responsibility and all that tough stuff. It's bound to build a strong character, whatever that means. We're rich, but we've got to work hard, sweat and work some more. Come on, I bet we're having blueberry pancakes this morning too." said Joe as he jumped out of bed and began dragging on a clean set of work clothes.

Mike watched him for a minute through blurry eyes then asked. "How do you know we're having pancakes?"

"Cause Hannah promised me last night that we'd have pancakes this morning." And went into the bathroom and slammed the door. A moment later, Mike heard the toilet flush and water running in the sink and other assorted noises. He closed his eyes and dreamed of another hour's sleep when Joe came through the bedroom with his hair all slicked down and ran out into the hall and slammed that door too. Mike looked over and saw that Carli's crib was empty too.

"Geeze, what's turned that kid into a dynamo all of a sudden?" Mike yawned, stretched and reluctantly got out of bed to head for the bathroom. "I think it's about time I had my own room. I can't handle all this bounce and cheer first thing in the morning." grumbled Mike as he slammed the bathroom door.

Mike hurried his own washing and dressing. However, once awake his enthusiasm slowly beginning to catch up to Joe's. Just thinking about *their ranch* and all that waited for them for them to do. Yeah, their very own ranch, just like Mom and Dad had wanted! Somehow this morning's meeting made that dream officially solid. Such a huge thrill raced through Mike that he had to grin. Yeah, he laughed, I'm the Man.

At the top of the stairs he mounted the wide banister side-saddle and took a fast slide down to jump off onto the last stair tread before smacking his butt into the newel post carved as a big grinning gnome head which would have hurt immensely.

Strolling into the kitchen Mike saw Hannah at the stove with Joe pressed tight against her and talking fast and she was laughing and answering his questions all the while her hands kept busy fixing breakfast. Yep, there were pancakes for sure with sausage and bacon and eggs; his stomach growled in anticipation. Filling a glass with orange juice Mike sat down at the table opposite his guardian.

"Morning, Ben."

"Morning son, wasn't yesterday a grand day? Well, your fates are sealed now. You're our kids for the next few years and I'm real happy about that and I sure mean to see that you kids are happy too. Hannah, let's eat, my boys and I have to meet Blackhawk and Jensen over to the Kelly place by eight so let's get a wiggle on here."

Joe sat down beside Mike and exchanged smiling glances with him at being called Ben's boys, just like they really were his true sons, and even while they weren't it gave them a nice feeling to be considered so. "Nice, huh Mike, we really belong here now, don't we? Not like we're just visitors." Joe whispered as he waited for breakfast to be served and Mike nodded and grinned back at his brother.

"Yep, we've landed soft that's for sure. I guess fate has decided to be kind after all we've been through and that's a blessing." Mike whispered back.

Mari Beth came in carrying a wide-awake Carli. "Daddy, Daddy, you baby." She said and lunged out of Mari Beth's arms toward Ben.

"Whoa babe, easy there!" as he quickly grabbed Carli and hugged her to his chest, "We don't want you to fall and get squished on the floor, do we? How's my baby this morning?"

"Kisses, kisses, Daddy," Carli grabbed Ben's face and puckered up her little lips and smacked Ben on his lips.

"Wow, sugar lips, yummy, yummy." said Ben and hugged the little girl to him.

"Mikey, kisses too, kisses too, Joey." And Ben tipped Carli forward toward Mike who obliged her with a smacking noise that had her giggling. Joe was next and he kissed her cheeks.

"There sugarplum, you're kissed; now, let Daddy pull your highchair up to the table so you can have breakfast." said Joe.

"Daddy I hungry girl; I want pancake, pancake now!" Carli demanded.

"Okay, sweetheart here's your highchair, that's right, sit right down beside Mike and we'll have pancakes." Ben cast a worried eye over at Mike and Joe to see what their response was to their sister calling him daddy

"Kids," whispered Ben, "she doesn't know any better and babies forget awfully easy so please don't be upset; we'll explain it to her when she's older."

"It's okay Ben, really it is. We know she's forgotten Dad and in her mind if Mari Beth is her mother than that means you're her father so that's just logical, isn't it? We understand."

Mike looked at Joe to see if he agreed and Joe nodded his head solemnly. "It's not easy, but I agree with Mike. Honest Ben, it makes Carli happy and you *will* be her parents from now on in every way that's important and that's best for her, so like Mike said, it's okay with us."

"Thanks Joe, thanks Mike, I just want you guys to feel alright about this." Ben picked up his fork and proceeded to eat his share of the bountiful table.

Mike helped himself to the pancakes and everything else his plate would hold. He wouldn't let Carli's mistake ruin his appetite because he had a big day ahead of himself. As Mike ate he wondered if Carli *had* made a mistake. Maybe she had just moved on and maybe that's what mom and dad would have wanted all of us to do. Well, now that was something to think about later, but right now he had other things to occupy his attention so Mike resumed his breakfast with a hearty appetite.

They piled into their chores and were finished by 7:30, and just before they left the house Mike went back up to his room and came down carrying a heavy backpack and when he walked out onto the back porch Ben looked at the pack and raised his eyebrows in question. Joe had already climbed into the small pick-up as Mike explained.

"I have our parents' ashes in here and we want to scatter them on the land today. It will be our very first official act Joe and I do as owners of the ranch. We want Mom and Dad to be part of it all and a little closer to us too in a sense. We want our folks to have the ranch they'd planned and worked so hard for and it will mean *everything* to Joe and me to do this today." Ben was looking directly into Mike's eyes as he spoke and saw the tears gathered there, not quite spilling over, but very much there.

"Then that's what we'll do son, and I'm sure Chief Blackhawk will help you with a ceremony if you ask him." assured Ben and put his hand on Mike's shoulder.

"He's our Godfather so I know Mom and Dad would like that." They walked slowly down the kitchen porch steps when Mike said. "At the house, when we visited Mom's old room, we felt Mom's spirit was still with us. I guess blessing them when we scatter their ashes will help release them to go on. At least we think it will, we hope it will anyway."

"I'm sure you're right Mike, and you and Joe are fine sons to see that all is well with your parents' spirits. Blackhawk will tell you the same thing. Okay, let's get it done."

When they arrived at the Lost Wagon's ranch road, the first thing they spotted was a large, roughly painted board that said, "Welcome to Kelly's Lost Wagon Ranch."

"Wow Mike, look at that! I guess you could say we're the real official owners' now." said Joe in an awed voice.

"Yep, we're stamped legal and official owners of this here property with all the problems, responsibilities and money concerns and pride. Yep, yep Joe my boy, we're going to learn, work hard, sweat and have fun turning Mom's home into ours. That's a guarantee." laughed Mike and Ben grinned at their enthusiasm.

When they arrived at the house there was one car and a large black four-wheel drive stretch truck parked in front. Ben pulled up behind them and switched off the engine. "Okay boys let's go talk to Chief Blackhawk and isn't it grand that we have such a beautiful morning for the ceremony? It sort of puts a special blessing on everything, doesn't it?" said Ben and got out of the truck.

Hank opened the door and greeted them with. "Gentlemen, welcome home," and shook their hands.

"Thanks Hank, you couldn't have said finer words to Joe and me." said Mike gruffly.

"Yeah, Mr. Hank, it's like we've come home to Mom and Dad 'cause this place is hers if you know what I mean, and it's a real special kind of feeling." sniffed Joe. They went into the living room and said hello to Mr. Jensen and Blackhawk.

Ben spoke up. "The boys have something to do before the meeting that is very important." He turned to Mike and waited.

"We have our parents' ashes here in this pack and Joe and I want to scattered them on the property so Mom and Dad will be part of the ranch they always wanted. Chief Blackhawk, as you're our Godfather and spiritual leader of these Valleys we'd like you to perform a small ceremony for them. Would you do that for us and for them, Sir?"

Blackhawk got to his feet and put his coffee cup down and said with great solemnity, "You honor me by asking, young Kelly men; to be sure, let us go out and find the right place and we will hold this ceremony now. I'll join you outback in a few minutes." Blackhawk left through the front door. It was as simple as that. Hank led the way through the house and out the kitchen door to wait in the ranch yard for Blackhawk.

"Hank, you know this place better than anyone here therefore you could show us a private place where there are trees and maybe a slight slope that overlooks the ranch house that's quiet-like where not many people would go. We'd like you to pick that spot." said Mike.

"You honor me boys." Hank paused and looked north upon the land that gradually rose in a series of hills making up the frontal range of Thunder Mountain. He nodded his head. "I know a beautiful spot and I'll take you there." As they were climbing into the truck Blackhawk came around the corner carrying a small black bag and climbed in beside the boys. There was a back track of sorts that lead them up slopes and around stands of trees until finally Hank stopped and turned off the truck.

"That's Idle Meadow to our left and we'll walk up from here." It wasn't a strenuous climb and it only took ten minutes to mount the high knoll with its thick stands of aspen and pines trees. At the top end of the meadow was a small cup-shaped glen sprinkled with late fall flowers and tucked up against the trees. The best part was it was facing directly south and overlooked the ranch buildings that could be seen in the distance. There were several stones scattered about and one fairly large almost flat rock practically in the center. To the boys' minds it was as though that rock had waited all this time for this special ceremony.

"Yes, this is perfect. Look Joe, it overlooks the ranch just the way we wanted." said Mike as he looked down the long valley.

Joe nodded his head, "Yes, this is the perfect place, the most beautiful place ever. They'll like it here." he whispered and swallowed hard.

Mike placed the pack on the ground. Blackhawk said. "Wait here." He walked into the woods to gather twigs, small branches and a couple of handfuls of pine needles and came back to lay them on the flat stone in a nice little pile. Out of the small black bag the boys had seen the Chief take from his truck, came a headdress and a large eagle's wing and a bundle of tied sage. Chief Blackhawk put on his headdress and turned to face the others.

It was an odd thing, but somehow seeing Blackhawk in his headdress it really changed him in some mysterious way. "When I wear this headdress I become the Shaman, the holy man of my tribe. This ceremony calls for us to purify ourselves with sage smoke. When I light the fire and place the sage on it, each of you come forward to have the smoke waved over you. Then you will stand in a semi circle. I will tell you what to do next."

The Shaman walked over to the readied fire and lit it then faced Thunder Mountain. The wood that took hold and burned clean and bright and quickly ignited the sage allowing the aromatic smoke to lift on the air. With his eagle feather Blackhawk waved the smoke over himself uttering words that none of them could understand then he stepped to one side motioned for Joe and Mike to come forward. The boys dropped their hats on the ground and walked up to the fire.

Again, the shaman waved the eagle feather through the smoke and over the heads of the boys. He motioned them to step aside and allow the other men to come forward and repeated the process. Once they were standing around the fire facing the mountain again, Shaman Blackhawk began.

"Oh, Guardians of Thunder Mountain and protectors of these sacred lands we ask You to receive the ashes of these fine people, Jean Devereaux Kelly and Michael Grayhawk Kelly into Your keeping. Let them rest and mingle within the bosom of the lands of their ancestors. May their spirits dwell in peace within the Heart of Christ. Here is the final resting place of their physical remains and we declare this a holy place." Stepping back and to one side, Blackhawk nodded his head at the pack at Mike's feet.

Mike undid the flap and with Joe holding the backpack, he lifted out the wooden box. Opening it up, Mike pulled out the plastic sack of ashes and laid it on the ground. Tears began to run down Mike's cheeks as he took his pocketknife and slit the bag with Joe standing beside him crying so hard that sobs shook his small frame, but he helped Mike carry the bag as they slowly backed around the rock scattering the ashes. By this time both boys were crying hard, nevertheless, they finished. Mike placed the empty sack and the wooden box upon the fire to be consumed in its entirety. Stepping back Mike hugged Joe tightly and they grieved together. Ben walked up and took them both into the shelter of his big arms holding them closely.

Silently the men watched as the fire quickly burn the small box into ashes. Suddenly the last of the fire shot upward for just a second or two then it went out, completely out without even leaving one hot glowing ember.

The Shaman watched the last of the smoke rise straight up into the air before dispersing and smiled for in his heart he knew that the spirits of Jean and Michael Kelly were now free to go on. Their children were safely home.

Within seconds a vision flashed then was gone, but Blackhawk had seen a face of greed, veniality and a threat directed toward these young boys. Blackhawk bowed his head and clasped his hands tightly together and knew something evil had come their way and knew this man was even now present in the Sacred Valleys.

"Gods, be watchful over Your children for evil has come this way." murmured the Shaman. Blackhawk took off his headdress and carefully replaced it in small bag. He came over to the boys and Ben and stood silently there for awhile.

"It's time to leave children." Blackhawk said quietly. "This place will always be one of love and peace for you to visit in other times. This has been a wonderful blessing for your parents, especially because today you are officially on your own land from this day forward. Come, it's time to leave."

Blackhawk led the way down the hill and the men followed leaving Mike and Joe alone for a few minutes. They had calmed down enough to look around at the beauty of their parents' last resting place.

"Please take care of our parents Guardians, we love them and thank You for letting us put their ashes here; now they are home with us too." Joe whispered and sobbed a little, but bravely tried to control himself. They picked up their hats and walked down the slope after the other men.

Back at the ranch house, May Tomlinson had a light snack ready for everyone and it was welcomed. May was a round little woman with red cheeks and a generous smile and an understanding heart and wisely made no comment about the young owners red eyes and suppressed spirits.

"Well, young sirs, I'm really pleased to meet you at last and it looks to me like good times are here for sure. I personally want to thank you for making my husband your Ranch Manager and a very happy man which makes me happy too. We'll help you in every way we can, so be welcome to your home, boys. Now go into the dinning room and have your snack."

"Thank you Mrs. Tomlinson, but I think Joe and I are the lucky ones to have you both here. Thank you for fixing us the snack too. Joe and I want you to remember that this is your home as well as ours." Mike bowed his head to Hank's wife.

"Yes, we are ever so grateful that you're here to help make this our other home. Ah, Mrs. Hank, can you make cookies?" Red eyed or not Joe knew what was important at this moment.

May laughed and just had to smooth the hair away from Joe's forehead. "Why, darlin' I make the best peanut butter cookies in all the valleys as well fudge of all kinds and other yummy things; just you believe that I'll treat you like kings."

"Being a King is good, but I'd rather just be a boy who eats good things." Joe grinned.

That laughter lightened everyone's mood as they left the kitchen.

After eating an excellent slice of apple pie along with milk for the boys and coffee for the men, Jim Jensen stood up and pushed aside the dishes to make room for his briefcase.

"I'm going to tell you what is contained in the will. If later you want to read it word for word you will have your own copy." said Jim. "It's a simple will and as stated your grandfather left everything he possessed to his grandchildren; Michael Devereaux Kelly, Joseph Devereaux Kelly and Carli Jean Kelly. Whichever child took over running the ranch, he or she will hold the larger share which will become 40% and the other two children will receive 30%. Sale of the ranch must be agreed upon by all three children. No share of the ranch can be sold without the agreement of all the owners and must be offered to them first. I have been named executor of the will. To Hank and May Tomlinson he gives $15,000.00 for their steadfast service and loyalty. To Pike John and Grumpy Tucker, he leaves $5,000.00 each for the good work they have done for the ranch over the past few years. He asks me to provide guardians for his grandchildren if he should die before they obtained legal age."

Jim looked over his reading glasses and smiled at Ben. "I didn't have a chance to do that since certain folks got there first. Well, that's all folks; like I said, it was very simple and straight forward will. There are certain other legal protections that Mr. Devereaux wanted and they have been implemented."

May and Hank looked shocked. "Well, this is indeed a big surprise though Mr. Devereaux said he was leaving us something, but not how much. May and I are deeply grateful for the kind gift."

Hank looked at May and smiled as she fluttered her hands. "Ohmyohmy, I'm so flustered." Hank patted her hand and she looked at him with tears in her eyes. She sniffed and took out her handkerchief and gave her nose a delicate blowing. "I guess I'd better go fix some fresh coffee for you gentlemen. Thank you Mr. Jensen." and stood up, hesitated then turned around and was audibly sniffing as she left the room.

"I'll give the men the good news tonight at dinner and that will make their day." laughed Hank. "It sure made ours."

The rest of the meeting that took place was almost anti-climatic, still Mike had suggestions to make that were sensible. "One of the things I'd like to see done before winter sets in is to get the house painted. I know this isn't exactly a priority, however, to my way of thinking it will preserve the house from water damage. Also I'd like the roof checked if it hasn't been seen to in a few years."

"You're right Mike, those are excellent suggestions so we'll put the house on the list of priorities," said Ben. "While we're at it, we'll check out the other roofs at the same time unless Hank says that's already been done?"

Hank shook his head. "Not for several years and that has been a worry. Okay, on to the next item. We've been buying our hay from various ranches these past couple of winters. I had to put our mower away since it was being held together with chewing gum and bailing wire and too dangerous to put a man on it. Devereaux was holding off buying new as it was a big outlay of money. That means we haven't been cutting any grass and it's too late now for it to dry properly. Winter comes early at this elevation so we're back to buying hay again this year too." Ben and Blackhawk nodded agreement and Ben made another note to contract for hay.

Hank went on. "This is sort of beside our discussion here, but I've been doing a lot of thinking about this problem of aging machinery and I've come up with a possible solution that will save all of us money, at least I think it would. Dan Lightfoot has a brand spanking new mower and bailer and I thought next year we could rent from him; what do you think?' asked Hank.

"That's not a bad idea, not bad at all. Hmm, what if we expand on that a bit? What if all the ranchers and farmers here in this Valley combined their resources? You know we could set up a whole new business here and provide employment for our people too. To begin with we'd need funding, either investors or a bank loan. Initially we could buy used machinery, fix it up and as the business grew, buy new machines to replace the older ones and save those for parts. All in all, it makes better sense then for all of us to have the same machinery. Yeah, I for one like that idea. We can run the numbers and at least get an idea of what it would take for a start-up. If it's economical and feasible we'll present our idea at the next Farm Association meeting." With nods of agreement Ben made another note on his pad of paper.

Jim said. "This idea would make another business that anyone could buy shares in. The fees that would be charged would pay for the hire of a few mechanics, office help to keep track of scheduling, repair, operators and transporting, rental; all that stuff."

"Now, that's a logical follow through of a grand idea and definitely something for next Farm meeting and another way to provide jobs for our young people." answered Ben enthusiastically.

"Okay, back to this ranch. We need to build some new feeding stations pronto because if we get as much snow as we did last year, we'll be feeding longer. We lost some stock last year due to not having enough shelter for them. Next item: there is an immediate need to harvest twenty acres of corn. Who's got a silage machine? This ought to be done this week no later because I got a feeling this fine weather isn't going to hold for long. We survived that last big storm, but I wouldn't guarantee what that corn will look like if another one hits us before we can haul it in." worried Hank looking over his long list of things to do.

"I heard tell of a man over Claremont way that has a couple of silage machines and does rental service so I'll give him a call and see if he can't do you right away. I would say most all of us have our fields cleared already and could bring in a bunch of men to get your job done mighty fast. I'll phone right now and if we're lucky we could start in the morning bright and early. I can guarantee you that this fine weather won't hold past Saturday so that gives us five days to get the job done." Blackhawk looked around the table. "I can spare three men from my crew plus myself and I think Tom probably can too." Blackhawk stood up went to make that call.

"I can bring over four hands for three days then I'll have to cut that to two. I've got a couple of mares that are ready to foal, but Mike and Joe will be here to help and I'll ask Luther if he can spare a couple of men. No doubt Dan will want in on this as well. After that storm passes I've got to sign up a crew and drive cattle down off Flat Top Mesa which is going to take a few days work."

"You mean an honest to goodness round up and cattle drive, Ben? I mean, riding horses and with a chuck wagon and all? Do you think maybe Mike and I could help with that too?" said Joe all excitement at the idea of such an adventure.

Ben laughed. "Yeah, Joe, you both can come along and it's going to be a real roundup, probably by next week if our resident Chief Guardian gives us clear skies and fair weather we can get the job done fairly fast. We'll have to camp out for at least three or four nights and take four or five days to round up the cows and drive them down to the lower ranch. The Mesa is big with lots of small canyons and foothills that make great hiding places for cattle. After that we'll drive them down to the ranch. The chuck wagon is essential part of the plan and I sure hope you can ride Joe, if not we'll get you a Tennessee Walker."

"Oh, Wow." Joe was so excited he bounced in his seat. "I can ride anything with hair; that's what Dad use to say 'cause I'm like a burr in the saddle, just ask Mike. Besides sir, I'd rather ride a cutting horse for the cattle drive." said the confident boy.

"You can relax Ben, Joe can ride just about any horse. Dad taught us young on his cutting horse, Beau, and he was training me to do calf roping. Joe's a fine rider and besides that you could use his singing to calm the cattle at night so we might just as well use all his assets." Mike laughed and punched Joe in the shoulder.

"I don't know, Mike, cattle are mighty particular about singin'. Why I've known cowboys who would sing very well and the cattle would stampede so we've gotta' be careful." Ben said it all with a serious look on his face, but with a twinkle in his eyes.

Blackhawk walked into the dining room and sat down at the table. "What's this about singing?"

"Okay, Joe, show all these doubters how you can sing those cows to sleep easy like." smiled Mike and sat back to watch the fun.

Joe thought a moment, stood up and opened his mouth and began to sing, "The Streets of Laredo" in a soft, slow, plaintive voice that still carried power beyond his small form and it was almost like a lullaby so soothing and easy sounding that mesmerized and relaxed the men and at the same time Joe's voice absolutely astonished them.

Yep, Mike smirked, looking around the table at those gapping mouths. You go Joe, you go boy, and laughed quietly as he listened. Joe's voice seemed to smooth all the rough edges right off the men. He sure smoothed mine too, thought Mike.

Utter silence followed the ending of that song and Joe smiled at everyone then said. "And you should hear Mike compose music and write poetry and play the guitar 'cause he's *really, really* good! I'm going to go talk to Mrs. Hank because I don't know of anything I could say to help with your plans so I'll go along with whatever Mike says." and ran into the kitchen calling, "Mrs. Hank, do you have any cookies?"

Ben cleared his throat a time or two before opening his mouth. "He said he could sing and Mike could play the guitar, but *I'm flabbergasted!* Man oh man, we gotta' get him in the church choir soon as possible."

Hank said with admiration and a grin. "Now I remember when I first met Joe he told me he wasn't going to become a rancher because he had something else he thought he would be doing. I can guess what that something will be." Then Hank got serious. "Ben, you've got to get that boy some voice training 'cause if I'm right, and I think I am, that kid is going places. So what's this about your musical talent Mike?"

Mike grinned, "Sure I play the guitar and all the other stuff too. Joe sings and I play." Mike shrugged his shoulders and spread his hands. "We'll be glad to demonstrate anytime."

"Well, if I have a say about that, we're all going to have a musical evening real soon and it will be the first of many celebrations in this sad old house." said Hank emphatically.

"What a surprise; here we have two amazing young men and goodness knows what talent Miss Carli will develop." Blackhawk shook his head. "All I'll say that as a Godfather, I've surely hit the jackpot." and roared with laughter. It took some time to get the conversation back to business, but enough had been planned to occupy the labor force at Kelly Ranch for the next few weeks.

Blackhawk spoke up. "I've contracted Mr. Reilly for his silage machines and four trucks to haul it to the silo and he'll be here around 9 o'clock tomorrow. His charges are reasonable considering the last minute arrangements. While the contract isn't cheap it will still be cheaper than to buy silage and right now we can't afford to be picky or bargain too hard. The important thing is to get the job done quickly."

"As far as I'm concerned it's a bargain and the sooner we get started the surer we are to finish in good time." Ben said in a "let's get it done" tone of voice.

Jim Jensen, the quietest one of the group spoke up in a lawyer's command for attention. "Here's the synopsis of what we'll do this week, hopefully beginning tomorrow. We are hiring men, gathering and paying helpers to harvest the corn, assist in repairs, such as roofs, building storage sheds and feeding stations and etcetera. Since the materials have already been ordered, I'll get a quick delivery tomorrow along with fence posts and wire. Is there anything else?" said Jim looking down at his list.

"Here's a list of tools we must have." and handed it to Jim. "Also we have some 600 steers that have been culled from the main herd that needs to be sold. I need to hire four good-sized cattle trucks to haul them to the railroad to be taken to Huntington sale barns and that means reserving cattle cars. It will be worth it as cattle prices are high right now. This should pear down on the number of cattle we'll be feeding over winter."

"I'll do that when I get back to town." said Jim as he made another note.

"Well, this meeting is a wrap so let's get back home and get ready for tomorrow. I've got some work of my own to do as do all of you." said Ben, gathering up his own paper work.

"Now that this meeting is over I've just had another idea." Blackhawk said smiling. "Maybe next year we'll get the ranchers and farmers together and make one big cattle drive to Huntington market. It's only about three hundred miles across pretty open country. 'Course, we'd have to get permission from the landowners if we can't drive the back roads and if we do drive the roads, we'll have to have the state's permission. An old fashion cattle drive would make the news and bring the buyers flocking in so what do you think?"

"I think that idea could give us might big problems." said Ben with a serious look and shook his head and they all looked surprised at his obvious negative response. Then he grinned, "Big trouble with the sheer amount of cowboys and girls that will want to go along and all the evening parties and such like will make it one heck of trip. Oh, yes you're not going to keep the ladies out of that event. I just hope the cattle don't stampede with all the noise those folks are going to make. The competition among the young ones, not to mention us older fogies, as to who gets to go, will be fierce and could possibly start a minor civil war. Lordy, maybe even the Thunder Gods will want to go along. Gentlemen, it sounds like an awful lot of trouble and an awful lot of fun, but I'm all for it." Ben laughed along with the others.

"I vote we do it, ah, that is if I have a vote?" Mike looked around with such enthusiasm that Ben laughed.

"Yes you do, Mr. Kelly, because by this time next year you'll be an old hand."

"Gentlemen, unless there's something else I have to get back to town, set up accounts at the various supply stores. I'll get the lumber yard to deliver that supply order right away. Submit all invoices and bills to me and I'll have checks drawn on the Kelly account and two of you can sign them later this week. That reminds me Hank, I need a list of your employees, their social security numbers and wage scale, so I can get my accountant to do the taxes and all that and catch you all up on your wages. Ben told me that your wage as Ranch Manager is to be increased retroactive to Mr. Devereaux's death so I'll take that into account."

Hank looked surprised then very pleased. It seems they had lots to celebrate and that called for him to take May out on a first class date. She'll love that he thought. Better do that tonight because it looked like non stop work for the next several weeks.

"That reminds me Ben, you and Blackhawk and I need to file papers and sign documents at the bank for the joint ranch account. Let's take care of that within the next couple of days. Also I've put an ad in the paper for more men and gave it to the radio station. Hank, you should have a good response in a day or two."

Jim began to efficiently put things away in his brief case when he remembered something and laughed then looked slyly over at Mike as he closed his briefcase. "By the way Mr. Kelly, my father wanted you to know that you have exactly $1,870,483.65 in the bank, better than half of that has been invested in stocks and bonds and there are no taxes or debts against the estate as all had been paid before the death of your grandfather. He officially made you, your brother and sister co-owners of the ranch with him before he died hence you only had to pay death taxes on his share of the ranch." Jim frowned and looked down at his briefcase. "You know, I think he had a premonition that he was going to die. Well, it was a very smart move on his part to insure you had a good financial foundation. I strongly suggest that we get more of that money invested after we finish up the necessary repairs on the ranch." Jim smiled quietly at the astonishment on all their faces and then said. "So long boys, I'll see you in a few days."

Jim Jensen walked around the table and Mike stood up. Jim picked up Mike's limp hand and shook it firmly and laughed all the way out of the house slamming the front door behind him.

That woke everyone up. "Good Lord Almighty." Mike said in a shock, whispery tone of voice and collapsed into his chair. Just then Joe came strolling back into the room finishing off the last of his cookie.

"Mike, did you know Mrs. Hank makes the bestest peanut butter cookies just like she said? She promised me I could have all I wanted anytime I came over. Isn't that nice of her?"

"Boy, if she's going to bake you her special peanut butter cookies I'll have to beg some from you." Hank said in a complaining voice.

Joe laughed. "I promise to share mine with you, Mr. Hank. After all, it's all in the family, isn't it?"

Quiet struck the men at hearing those simple words from a young child. Yes, that was the secret of the Valleys. *It was all in the family.*

~*Luther*~

LUTHER STRONGBOW WAS A happy man and his life was just about perfect right this minute. Of course his parents thought it was past time for him to marry and beget grandchildren for them to play with. Mom and Dad had such big hearts for children or why else had they taken on three more? They were amazing people and he loved them dearly without question, but when would they stop taking in stray kids? Not to say that those Kelly kids weren't great and in fact he liked them very much, but it baffled him to understand his parents at their age would want to start all over again with young children? Well, it wasn't any of his business and if they were happy then he was happy.

Luther rode along enjoying being alone on a good horse on an absolutely gorgeous day not thinking about much of anything, just random thoughts that flowed through his mind like water.

That Carli was a beautiful charmer and dear Dad had better watch out for pretty girls attracted boys like bees to honey, Luther laughed. Of course, old Dad had had plenty of practice with his other daughter Rachel, but not Hannah who was too shy to put herself forward in order to catch a beau. Luther should tell Mike and Joe that when Carli grew up they'd have their hands full driving off the boys.

Luther was taking a slow ride around the ranch with the excuse that he was assessing the damage last week's storm might have caused. There was a downed tree over the west pasture fence. He'd get a couple of men to take care of that right away before any cattle got loose. The road would need grading in a place or two and the horse shelter in the east field could use some work before winter snows, but on the whole there had been little damage.

They had been working hard getting the Kelly Ranch set up for winter. Luther, being a big brother pro tem, had taken a few of his men over to help. This was his first day off in weeks so he was determined to enjoy it to the hilt.

All in all Luther felt good about things in general, hence his happy state of mind. To his way of thinking there wasn't anything finer than a nice horseback ride on a cool autumn day with the sun shining and all was right with his world. He felt the serenity of Mother Nature seeping into his bones. He took a deep breath of the pure air and smiled.

His cell phone rang.

"Well, shoot and blast, can't people leave a person *alone* once in awhile? Hello, what do you want?" he said impatiently.

"Now there's a greeting with a bite in it. What's set you off?" asked the deep voice.

"Well, dagnabit Dad, here I am having a nice ride on Midnight Racer for the first time in weeks and I was as happy as a pig in slop." Luther gave a short laugh at his own ill humor and eased back in the saddle and sat quietly for a few moments just drinking in the scenery while his father patiently waited. "Man, the beauty of nature just filling me right up and I was getting to feeling real good." Luther sighed, "I guess I was wanting more when the blasted phone rang. It's enough to put anyone in a bad mood, I should think. What can I do for you?"

"Gee, Lute I'm real sorry to have ruined your disposition."

"Don't worry about it, I'm mostly okay now so what's up?" Luther drew in the crisp air that was flavored with the smell of pine trees and country.

"Could you come up a little earlier tonight before super, there's a few things I'd like to talk to you about if you're not otherwise occupied."

"Sure, what's wrong? Anything you can tell me now?" Luther said as he began to frown in concern.

"No, it will hold until you get here."

"Okay, I'll be up around five, will that work for you?"

"That'll be just fine Lute. Enjoy the rest of your ride. Oh, by the way, another storm is expected sometime tomorrow."

"Well dang it all to blazes, another storm so soon? I haven't heard any news about another storm?" Luther signed deeply. "I guess we should be thankful we finished the work of harvesting at Kelly's and got the roofs fixed by yesterday. Okay, Pops, I see you around five." Then all Luther heard was a click at the end of the line.

Luther tucking his cell phone away. "Alright, my ride is ruined so I guess I'll go kick my men into locking things down again." And with that Luther swung his Racer's head around and kicked him into a run.

Man, oh, man did this quarter horse crossed back to a thoroughbred dearly love to run and he could jump too. Maybe he was just fast enough to win the three-quarter mile race at Huntington Fair this year. Luther tore over the pasture and Midnight Racer easily leaped the fence and the deep ditch beyond and landed on the road, turned and thundered toward the ranch going flat out with his rider screaming enthusiastically that would have put a wildcat to shame. The horse just laid his ears back and increased his speed.

Some of the men were repairing the big corral heard him coming and screaming like a whole attacking Indian tribe. They jerked around to watch in alarm at the stretched out horse and the big man who rode like a Cossack or a Red Indian and worried what disaster had happened to cause Luther to come on the way he was.

"What set him off? Good Lord, I hope it's nothing serious, but man, look at that horse run and him carrying that big man on his back. I'm for sure gonna' bet on Racer at Huntington that's if the boss enters him." commented Mac.

"Well if he ain't, we can talk him into it. We'll let Brown ride him 'cause with lighter weight on his back that horse will fly." said Sketter, referring to the slender, 5'7" eighteen year old Indian boy standing quietly at his side. This boy could ride anything with hooves and hair.

Luther came tearing into the ranch yard and pulled Racer into a sliding halt. Leaping out of the saddle he gave the horse a good few slaps on his damp neck. "You running fool I purely love you. Hey boys, should we enter him in the races at Huntington?"

"If you don't boss, you'll stand to loose a lot of money not to say we would too. So it ain't anything serious that set you off like that?" asked Jimson.

"Nope, I just felt like a run and this beauty sure gave it to me in spades didn't you old son." Luther patted the horse's damp shoulder as Little Brown came forward, took the reins from Luther and quietly talked to the excited horse as Racer snorted and dancing around as though he wanted to run some more and the horse had hardly worked up a good sweat though he was hot. Brown led him away to cool him down all the time crooning to him in a tone of voice that Racer loved.

"Thanks Brown, walk him until he's cool then give him a good rub down." shouted Luther and all he got was a disgusted backward look from the boy that had Luther laughing. "Okay, I'm put in my place." as he watched the young boy lead Racer off to the side yard. "You know guys, I've got to watch that boy or he'll be stealing my horse, or Racer will steal him. Hah, now that boy's a rider if I ever saw one and he'll take Racer right over the finish line with lengths to spare, mark my words." grinned the happy man.

"Boss, us boys will make a bundle on him so you'd better pay us just before the fair because we're going to put our whole wad on Racer." promised Brent. "Since he's an unknown we should clean up right nicely."

Luther looked at the older man who was roughly 45 and toughened from the constant hard ranch work, still this was a knowing man and as shrewd as they come. Luther watched the other fellows listen to him and how they nodded their heads in agreement. It was obvious that they showed respected for the man. Brent knew more about ranching than most people ever learned in a lifetime.

Luther turned to the waiting men. "Boys, Dad says we got another storm coming in tomorrow. We don't know how severe it will be so let's hope it isn't as bad as the last one. Personally I'm not ready for winter quite yet. You know the drill, button everything down and then some; prepare for the worse and we'll be safe either way. Most all the repairs have been done so get busy and finish up on what Brent thinks is priority. Bring the horses in first thing in the morning too. We've got a fair coming up the first of October so there will be some inside work to do on the horses we're taking for sale. Oh, I also want a 24-hour watch put on the foaling barn; some of our mares are very close. I'll go check and see if any of our neighbors needs a hand. Brent, you know what to do."

Luther walked toward the house only to turn around again. "Oh by the way, we have a tree down over the west pasture fence and as soon as this storm blows over I want it cleared." Luther took a few more steps when he stopped, turned around and called out, "By the way Brent, you're my new foreman as Dugan won't be coming back from his son-in-law's funeral on a permanent basis. His daughter and her kids need him on the farm over in Huntington. We'll sure miss him as he is a good man, but I suspect you'll do just fine so plan on moving into the foreman's house as soon as Dugan clears his stuff out. "

Luther walked toward the house and heard the sounds of yelling as the boys ganged up on Brent and when Luther looked over his shoulder he saw the new foreman being dumped into the big water trough. Luther covered his mouth to keep from shouting too. Man, oh man, that water must be near freezing to hear Brent shout, well, he scream really. Hysterical laughter of the men greeted the man's torment.

Luther turned away and was laughing as ran up the porch steps into the mud room, wiped his feet and went through the kitchen door and was hit with the smell of something delicious cooking.

"What was all that yelling about out there? You'd think a war was on or something the way you raced into the ranch yard. It scared me that something terrible had happened until I saw everyone laughing. By the way, you'd better enter that horse into the races at Huntington or you're going to have a very unhappy crew. Well, more unhappy then they already are that is." Hannah said to Luther as she stirred the large stew pot.

Luther had practically fallen over he'd stopped so fast. "What the heck are you doing in my kitchen, Hannah? I thought I was going to have supper at Dad's house?"

"You are! This is for that poor crew of yours out there who have suffered with Jude's excuse for cooking." she said as she added a generous cup of red wine to the beef stew. "You need a ranch cook *now* or your crew will rebel and go elsewhere. I'm warning you Luther, stop being so pig-headed and get an ad in the paper and hire someone. Now, I've got two big pans of biscuits in the warming oven and three apple pies in the pantry as well as a nice mixed salad in the refrigerator."

It wasn't until Luther had poured himself a cup of coffee and went to sit down at the kitchen table that he noticed Joe sitting quietly there with a glass of milk and some chocolate chip cookies.

"Hey Joe, how are you doing? I didn't see you there while Hannah was reading me the riot act. *Wait a minute*, where did you get those cookies?" Luther looked shocked and in an offended, childish voice said. "*Where* are you hiding the cookies Hannah? I *want* some cookies. Joe has some cookies why can't I *have* some cookies too?" Luther winked at Joe and got a grin in reply.

She laughed, "Grow up Lute, and look in the pantry, I brought a jar full." She said, tapping the spoon on the edge of the large pot before replacing the cover and turning the stove down to simmer. Luther made a beeline for the pantry and grabbed a handful of chocolate chip cookies and came back to sit down with Hannah and Joe.

Munching away, Luther said around a mouthful. "Yeah, if I can find a cook nearly as good as you, sister dear, I'll hire him or her on the instant. And just to keep you informed I've already put an ad in the paper so there." and ate another cookie.

"My goodness, a miracle indeed and it's past time too." Hannah said with a nod of her head and sipped her own coffee. Luther just grinned and stuffed another cookie into his mouth.

"Hannah said maybe you'd let me see a foal born. I almost did once, but it wasn't until the next day I got to see it, but it's not the same thing is it, Mr. Strongbow?" Eating the last of his cookies, Joey watched him over the rim of his glass of milk.

"No sir, it isn't. Call me Luther Joe since I'm more or less your oldest brother by adoption." Luther was a little bit startled by Joe's grin and enthusiastic nod.

"Yeah, Mike needs an older brother so he won't worry so much about me and Carli like he does now. I kinda' like the idea as it makes things extra special in a way too."

"Hmm, yes, ah, I'm really glad you think that way 'cause it makes me feel good to have little brothers to boss around. Back to the subject of babies; why Joe my man, it's a miracle to watch a foal being born then standing on his or her legs right afterward. Yep, it's a sight. I'll give Dad a call when we have a mare about to deliver so you can be here. Of course, it could be in the middle of the night you know."

"I wouldn't care what time it was, only Ben would have to wake up to drive me down. Gee, I don't know about night time. Maybe, if you think one of the mares is about to deliver, I could come stay here with you overnight just in case, maybe?" asked Joe.

Luther knew what a bold move it was for this boy who a short time ago wouldn't leave Hannah's side for long. "Sure you can, Joe. We're going to get a heck of a storm tomorrow so hopefully the mare won't give birth until after it's over, but sure, it's a done deal." and held out his hand for Joe to shake. The kid laughed and pumped Luther's hand enthusiastically up and down.

Hannah shook her head. "I can see you two are just alike, horses, horses, horses. Don't you think watching a birth might be a little traumatic for Joe? I mean what could he do to help you, Lute?"

"But Hannah, I can sing to horses and they like it really well. I used to help Dad that way with horses that wouldn't settle down. Honest, Dad told me I had magic." said Joe earnestly.

"Okay my man let's hear you sing just as a test." Hannah looked at Joe and waited.

Joe closed his eyes and thought for a moment then opened his mouth and crooned a lullaby soft and low. Luther and Hannah just about fell off their chairs as the glorious sound gently filled the room with the melodious tones of a boy tenor with an undertone of resonance. Shivers of joy ran up and down their spines as the boy sang. When Joe was finished he opened his eyes and looked at the stunned faces of his friends. He shrugged.

"See, magic and for some reason the horses love it and they practically go to sleep. I can sing much softer too if I have too." The little boy said without arrogance or pride. After all, his voice *just was* and that was that as far as Joe was concerned.

Luther cleared his throat and glanced at Hannah. "Yeah Joe, it's magic all right and I can see that you'd be a great help when the time comes for the mares to foal. Yes, indeedy you've got a magic voice for sure," and stopped not knowing what else to say.

"Well now, that was lovely, but we'd better get back home Joe. We'll have lots to do if this storm comes as predicted." Hannah stood up. "Luther tell the boys to come to the kitchen for supper in about 35 minutes as they know I've been cooking. I declare, I've been checked out though the window so many times that I've lost count. Come on let's go home Joe." She took her coat off the hook and slipped it on then handed Joe his coat and hat.

"Bye, Mr. Luther, remember our deal."

"How could I forget; see you guys at supper. Thanks Hannah for cooking for the men, they all love you, you know."

"Sure they do and their stomachs really adore me too." laughed Hannah as she walked out the door. Luther stood out on the porch and called out to the men. "Hannah has cooked you a fine dinner and she said to come up in 35 minutes." He waved to Hannah and Joe and heard various comments from the men.

"Thanks Hannah, you're a real life saver."

"Hannah, would you marry me please?"

"Ms. Hannah thank you for saving me from Jude's poison." called another audacious cowboy.

"I'll give you all my money for one good pot roast dinner." Bombarded with one offer after another kept Hannah laughing until she sent them a parting shot just before she closed the truck's window.

"There are pans of biscuits in the warming oven, apple pies in the pantry and salad in the refrigerator. Goodbye boys." At that the collective groans came from seven men's throats had Luther laughing as his sister drove out of the yard.

"Get busy you lay-abouts or I'll feed those apple pies to the pigs." shouted Luther. He laughed again to see such an explosion of fast action as those men deliberately crashed and bumped into each other as though to demonstrate how eager they were to get busy and their fooling around only increased Luther's laughter as he went back into the kitchen. Well, Hannah sure had given him a secret weapon to get his men to work hard and fast; apple pies. Now to find a good cook to make them was the next big problem.

Luther drove up to the old ranch house at 5 o'clock and parked his pickup close to the back door. He turned off the engine and sat there for a few minutes with worry sitting heavily on his mind that was growing in weight by the minute. What did Dad want to talk to him about? Luther was trying not to be scared that it might be something life threatening to his father or mother, maybe even one of his brothers or sisters.

"For petty sake Lute, get a grip." Throwing open the truck door he got out and slammed it shut just as his father stepped out the kitchen door. Since his Dad had his hat and jacket on and continued down the steps Luther walked over to meet him.

"What's up Dad?" Luther frowned with worry as he looked anxiously at his father.

"Well, nothing serious enough to put that worried look on your face Lute, everything's okay. Sorry if I gave you the wrong impression. Come, walk with me a bit."

Side by side the men strolled through the back yard, past the old basketball court and into the trees. Neither man spoke until they reached the private place his Dad always visited most every evening.

Luther grinned and remembered the day long ago when he and his brothers had followed him like Indians to see what he did, just like any normal kids would do. They saw him light a small fire then sit down on a big old stump. What in the heck was he doing, they whispered to each other? Big Ben caught them, and how he knew they were there they didn't know. Ben never turned around when he said, "Now you boys go on back to the house and I'll be there shortly, but since you're so curious, all I'm doing is thanking the Thunder Gods for our bounty." and they beat it back to the house 'cause they didn't want to communicate with any old gods. That was just too spooky and weird.

Luther laughed softly causing his father to glance over at him. "What's tickled your funny bone, Lute?"

"I was just remembering the first time the guys and I followed you out here to your private place and when you said you were talking to the Thunder Gods we spooked and ran for the house. How did you know we were there?" laughed Luther.

Ben chuckled, "Sweet never was very quiet in the woods and I hear you all coming along behind me. I can't blame you boys for being curious or spooked. I guess for kids it's hard to imagine a sensible man like me talking to something you can't see. It's a wonder you all didn't think I'd lost my mind. Yet people don't think it strange praying aloud to God in church or any other time and He's definitely unseen. Well, I guess it's just one's perspective as to what constitutes strange behavior."

Father and son walked into the little glen that held his Dad's old stump and the flat blackened rock that had held the ashes of many dead fires. Today, there were two stumps sitting beside that old rock. A funny feeling started to quiver in Luther's stomach and it wasn't because he was hungry either.

"Sit down son it won't take a minute to start a nice little fire here." Obediently Luther sat down on the newer stump and watched his father toss back a worn piece of tarp to gather up some dry kindling and small broken branches. He also saw the jug of water sitting beside Ben's stump.

The process of building and lighting the fire seemed almost ritualistic. Pine needles and dry moss were placed on the shallow rock then twigs and small pieces of branch were placed teepee-like over all.

"This is a fire I build each day or most everyday to honor the land and the Thunder Gods. I've told you kids some of this, but since you're the only son living on the land I need to instruct you in this ritual for the land your ranch is on. I'd like you to read the old stories your ancestors left for us especially the first journal. It tells of the long ago contract or agreement the first Strongbow made with Chief Blackhawk and the land grant that was given in the presence of a Spirit that Chief Blackhawk said was one of the Thunder Gods. One of the conditions to holding the land was to pledge to honor the animals that dwelled in the Valleys and the lands because they were sacred. There was to be no human blood spilled upon these sacred lands by another human. The Thunder Gods and the land spirits would judge that person and if that person was found guilty of aggravated assault with intent to do bodily harm, other than self protection for himself and or another person, he or she would be driven out and wouldn't be able to return without incurring severe penalties. This pledge was to be renewed daily if possible by building a devotional fire." Ben finished laying the fire bed before he continued.

"I believe everyone living in these Valleys gives thanks this same way, we just don't talk about it. Now they're all good Christians and have a strong belief in the Christ. I think you already know that the Guardians protect the lands and the people, They keep the peace, harmony and goodwill here and in turn we're better people because of Their presence. These Valleys wouldn't be the same without Them."

Ben turned to face Luther. "I'm teaching you this now Luther, because you need to start doing the same thing for your land. Up until now you've been holding land under me so I've been doing the pledge for all of it. Today I signed the land you call Rocking Horse over to you and it's yours in its entirety. I can't stress how very important it is for you to understand what we do here. Well, let's get started then we'll talk some more."

Luther's heart expanded at the very thought of owning his own land while watching his father light the small fire. As it began to blaze his father stood up straight and raised his hands to Thunder Mountain that could be seen clearly. "I bring You the fire of devotion for the gift of this bounteous and beautiful land, O' Mighty Thunder Gods. I keep the sacred pledge of my ancestors and will continue to cherish the lands and the animals. Thank You for Your gifts and for our good life that we have under Your care. I honor You, as did my first ancestor."

Lowering his hands, Ben took out of his coat pocket some grain and corn and some other seeds and scattered them on the fire where they burned quickly sending up a little smoke that seemed to move straight up in a circular spiral. Next he took some small pieces of various kinds of fruit that grew on his land; apple, cherry, and plum. These he put carefully on the fire one at a time.

When they had been consumed his father spoke once more. "Thus I make sacrifice of the goodness of this land to You. May You protect the people of this place, protect the animals that dwell on the land and replenish the waters the earth needs. Thank You and have a good night. I am Ben Strongbow." His father came and sat down on his worn stump and didn't say anything for awhile, just watched the fire burn joyfully until it grew smaller and smaller

"Well son, that's it. I'm sure you must think this is very primitive, yet I have seen people who have taken up land here and pooh-poohed this ritual. They didn't obey the laws of the Guardians or as the ancient natives called them, the Thunder Gods because they didn't believe in them. Those people lasted a year or so before the land closed up on them and their building began to fall apart and after that the people usually left in a hurry."

Ben was quiet for a time then looked over at his son and smiled. "Here's a story about someone you know. The man named Hal Turner, who owned the farm before Hank Seely, was more or less driven away. The land went barren and dry until they left. Blackhawk was just beginning to work with the land spirits to bring all back to normal when Hank Seely came to town looking for a farm. After he'd talked to the people in town about what was available they advised him to call Chief Blackhawk. Hank drove out to see him and what happened there I don't know, but when Hank came down off the mountain with Chief Blackhawk he had the papers for that farm in his hand.

There on that farmland Blackhawk built a fire more or less like this one, and Hank told me he put the offerings he had bought in town on the fire and pledged to the Thunder Gods that he'd honor the land and the animals and to the spirits of the land that he'd take good care of them. Then he and the Chief went around the land while Blackhawk blessed it with water and, well I guess you could say with Blackhawk's magic. He also blessed what was left of the buildings. Within a matter of a few weeks the water had come back and the grass grew green again." Ben smiled at his son's wide eyes.

"Of course, Hank had to replace most all the buildings, some he could save, but not many and I'm sure you've noticed that Seely's Farm is a picture book looking place now. Another example is the old Fletcher Farm which you've also seen. This happened just recently. Old man Fletcher wasn't exactly driven out, but he would have been if he hadn't sickened and died sudden-like. Now there was a very difficult man. In fact I got the Sheriff and we went out to confiscate his animals as they were being starved and generally neglected. The buildings on his place had begun their sped-up decay and the artesian wells stopped flowing too. The land suffered and refused to grow anything. It wasn't too long after that that Fletcher died in that awful house of his." Ben watched the fire burn down to flickering coals before he turned to look at Luther sitting beside him.

"So you see there is truth to this honoring of the land and its animals and it's not superstition. The land sustains us and nourishes us so why shouldn't we give it the tender loving care we give to our families? Why shouldn't we give thanks for the gift of the Earth as we thank the members of our family for their care and service? Why shouldn't we be reminded to stay in harmony and in balance with nature?"

They sat there for perhaps ten minutes before Luther spoke. "I always say a prayer to the Mountain Gods before a storm or just to say thanks for a good day. Never thought it was strange or primitive. I say the same thing to Jesus about blessing my men and my family." Luther laughed softly. "Maybe I'm unconsciously covering all the bases."

"That isn't a bad thing, for The Christ is the vital link to our spirit/soul. He is the Way and the Lord of Love. This that I do here is more like honoring the blessings of this land and giving thanks for the original grant. I do this ritual everyday if weather permits. I'm sure the Gods understand I can't build a fire in the pouring rain or in a blizzard. There have been times that I've done this ritual in the fireplace when the weather has been really bad." Ben chuckled, "Well, the Guardians are very tolerant about the substitute because it is the thought behind the action that counts. I've even thought about building a little roof over this fireplace, yet somehow it doesn't feel right out here"

"No, you're right, it wouldn't be right. So Pops, you're really going to deed the lower ranch over to me? Why now?"

"Because you're a man who has earned the right to his own place and I've always planned to do that when you first decided to stay in the valley. I got busy and kept putting it off. Well, I've done it now and here's the deed to the land and buildings of Rocking Horse Ranch with the land survey marking the boundaries and all just as we set them out originally." Luther watched his father pull out from an inner jacket pocket a rolled parchment tied with a blue ribbon and hold it out to him.

Pure joy filled flooded Luther and moved powerfully in his heart as his father laid the deed in his hands. Feelings so powerful that tears simply ran down his face and he couldn't say a word. Luther felt his father's arm around his shoulders and there they sat until the child-man could get his emotions under control again. He didn't feel so, well silly, when he heard his father sniff then cough a few times followed by a hard squeezing hug.

Luther sniffed and searched his back pocket for his handkerchief and blew his nose loudly and heard his father's watery chuckle as he did the same. Luther cleared his throat, coughed a few times. "Well, shoot and blast, Pops, you sure know how to show a guy a good time."

They both laughed together like idiots and that calmed the overwhelming sense of intense love to a manageable level. Love settled back into a warm glow in their hearts like the Rock of Gibraltar.

"Yeah, I always had a talent for coming up with something new. It was a challenge to keep ahead of you kids. Well, the fire's out, but I'll put a little water on it just in case of a spark or two." Luther sat there and watched his father finish up. Luther stood and looked up at Thunder Mountain, that magnificent overshadowing heap of rock and glacier and didn't have any trouble imagine Gods living on the top.

"Thanks Dad, you know how much this means to me. I guess it's like cutting the apron strings. I know *you* know this, but I just want to say it out loud. I love you with all my heart; never forget that."

"I've always known you did Lute, and your Mother and I couldn't be happier that you decided to stay in the Valley." Ben coughed and slapped Luther on his shoulder before turning away. "Emotions are kinda' hard for us men to handle, aren't they? Come on son, dinner is ready now and I've got a hunger on me that a horse couldn't match."

"Now that you mentioned it I could possibly choke down some of Hannah's cooking." Both men laughed as they walked back to the house with Luther's arm slung around his father's shoulders. They began discussing the preparations for the trip to Huntington in a few weeks.

"Breeding your quarter-horse mares with Suncatcher was sheer genius. In my opinion that Morgan/ Thoroughbred Stud is worth his weight in gold and even though your whole breeding program was a gamble the results are going to prove worth of the effort. I got to thank you again for giving me Midnight Racer. He's going to win lots of races. Racer is three and a half now and in full strength so I think he's well on his way to proving the worth of your program. He's not only fast and strong, but he's smart too with lots of fiery spirit and there's nothing mean about him. After the Huntington Races and we win big with him there, I'll take him around to other race tracks. I believe we'll win those and you'll get top dollar for any of his brothers and sisters you choose to sell, not to mention Racer's own progeny later on. I just purely love him and to say that about any horse other than my Walkers is high praise indeed."

They walked along for a few minutes until Luther chuckled and said. "I'm kinda worried though, I've noticed him casting eyes at Little Brown and sure as the day you were born, that boy's going to steal my horse away from me or vice versa." and Luther gave a big pathetic sigh that set his father laughing.

"Well, tell Brown to be patient and not take any offers from Racer 'cause I've got a couple of special mares waiting to foal and he can have one of the babies."

"You're kidding me! Wow, he'll go right through the roof." Luther chuckled as he imagined the stunned look on Brown's face when he told him. "Thanks Dad, anything that will keep Midnight Racer's affection mine is a good thing."

Little Brown had come to Luther when he was just turning sixteen, a lonesome boy with no one to care for him. Luther had taken him in, but insisted Brown finish high school which he did with honors. The kid deserved the very best and besides, this would give Brown something of his very own to treasure. Luther couldn't wait to see Little Brown's face when his father presented him with the next colt or filly. Revenge was sweet because that usual stoic kid was going to fall apart.

"I agree with you about the potential of this breeding program. It usually takes at least five years or longer to prove or disprove a new breeding. We need to keep records on each foal like you've done with Racer. Maybe you and I could do this special breeding together? If it pans out like we think it will, we've got hold of something mighty fine and it's sure to improve horse racing. I've been thinking we could possibly ring Mike in on it and put the new breeding program over at his place? He isn't doing any special horse breeding like we are. Oh, I'm not saying his ranch doesn't have good working horses 'cause they do, might fine ones too, but you know what I mean." said Ben.

"Sure Dad, I like your idea about bringing Mike in with us if he wants to and it would save us having to build another new barn and corrals here. Let's talk to Mike at supper."

"You've never said what you thought about your mother and me taking guardianship of the Kelly children." said Ben quietly. "Does it bother you?"

"It's really none of my business, is it? But to ease your mind, I think it's great and if it makes you and Mom happy that's all that matters. They're great kids and it's not a hardship for me to act like a big brother either. After all, I've had lots of practice." Luther grinned at his father. "Sure I'll help anyway I can and besides they deserve the best and that's you guys. I just want to say I'm really worried about Carli when she grows up 'cause she's going to lead us all a merry dance. That's what beauties do, you know; lead us poor men around by our noses so you watch out." Ben laughed and nodded his head in full agreement.

"Thank the Gods she'll have three big brothers to look out for her then which will keep me from getting more gray hair in my declining years."

Together they climbed the back steps and opened the kitchen door to the good smells of dinner filling the air and the talk of women and children.

~Joe~

LUTHER KEPT HIS PROMISE and called Joe the very next morning. Wouldn't you know it; one of the mares had chosen to drop her first foal just as a major autumn storm was due to strike.

"Hi Dad, I promised Joe that he could come down when one of our mares was about to foal. Mares' sure pick their times, don't they? Anyway, I thought I'd come and pick Joe up if he still wants to come."

"Just a minute Lute, I'll get him." and Luther could hear his father shouting. "Hey, Joe, Luther wants to talk to you." Then he heard the muted sound of thundering of feet on the stairs and a breathless. "Hi Mr. Luther, what's happening?"

"Hi yourself Joe, you wanted me to let you know when one of our mares was going to foal and I think it'll be today or tonight. She's in labor now so if you want to come down, I'll come pick you up. You probably better stay the night. Do you think you'd like to do that?" The man knew that if Joe did stay overnight that it'd be a major improvement in his sense of security.

The silence at the other end of the wire told its own story. "Sure Mr. Luther that would be super." Came the soft hesitant answer, "Ah, do you suppose Hannah could come too? I bet she'd like to be there to see the birth." Then more quiet.

Luther shook his head and guessed Joe wasn't quite ready to give Hannah a break and come by himself. "No problem Joe, run and ask her while I hold the phone."

There was a clatter as the phone hit the table and Luther snatched the receiver away from his ear with a wince, and heard Joe's muffled voice saying. "Hannah? Hannah, oh, there you are. Luther is asking me to come down to watch one of his mares foal. Ah, we wondered if you'd like to come down and spend the night with us." Clever guy smiled Luther, making like the invitation was meant for the both of them, not that he minded.

"Hello Luther what's going on?" Hannah's voice was all amusement. She'd seen plenty of mares giving birth, so she figured it was something else.

"Well, Joe wanted to come down and be here for the big event which will be this afternoon probably, however, I think he's a little worried about staying overnight alone. This place is still strange to him so he needs his "Mommy," and no snide remark intended. The kid is dealing with a big insecurity problem and he needs you here. I can drive you guys' back tomorrow sometime. Can't Mom handle things if you leave for one night?"

"Sure, you bet Luther, Joe and I wouldn't miss seeing this for anything. We'll pack and I'll drive down in the pick-up. Do you need anything else?"

"Well, you might snitch a few cookies on your way through the kitchen."

That was greeted with a laugh. "You mean the cookie jar is already empty? Well, I'll see what I can do and maybe I'll just bake a bunch while I'm hanging out with you guys. I'll even fix your dinner if you get at least seven chickens out of the freezer; that will be enough to feed everyone and they won't take long to bake. Stick them in the sink and cover them with cold water. If there is anything left over you can make sandwiches. See you in an hour unless the mare decides to foal early." He was chuckling as he went to hang up and caught the message light flashing on his phone.

First message: "This is Roy Smithers. Saw your ad for a cook/housekeeper. Well, I can cook, but I ain't doin' nothin' fancy and I don't clean nothin' either. I cooked recently for the Bar Z Ranch and a bigger bunch of dumb cowboys you never did see. Call me 734-0023."

"Oh yeah, that's great inducement to hire you, Mr. Smithers." Luther could tell by the guy's slurred voice that he'd been drinking. The men would instantly hate him and kick him out within a week if he was lucky to last that long.

Second message: "This is Amber Golight answering your ad for a cook and housekeeper. I am a very good cook and I have excellent references. Proof will have to be in the tasting, won't it, Sir? My number is 765-0589, same area code as yours, extension 104. Please give me a call if your offer is still open. I hope to hear from you soon. Have a good day."

True Heart

Third message:

"My name is Mrs. Rose Dooly and I'm only interested in being a cook. I'm getting too old for housecleaning so if you want a simple cook, I can do the job depending on how many people I have to cook for. If it's just for you there won't be any problem. I need to bring my husband with me; he's lazy, but he can still work if you need another hand around the place. I'm visiting my daughter in Port City so you'll have to call long distance. Call me at 934-6622."

Luther picked up the phone and dialed Ms. Golight's number. At least she sounded civil and coherent in that soft southern lady-like voice. Ms. Golight probably weighed 200 pounds and was older than the hills.

"This is Amber Golight." The woman's soft drawl actually caused goose bumps on Luther's arms. Hmm!

"This is Luther Strongbow of Rocking Horse Ranch returning your call about my ad for a cook/housekeeper." He said as calmly as possible.

"How do you do Sir, I am very interested in the job. I arrived in town yesterday and saw your ad. I have excellent references and job experience as well. Perhaps I could make an appointment to meet you at your convenience."

"You understand that you'll be cooking for eight men, Ms. Golight. Three meals a day and often called upon to pack lunches if the men and I are going to be away at lunch time. The house is fairly large with four bedrooms, three and a half baths, a den/office, large living room and kitchen with pantry and laundry room. I do have a cleaning lady come in twice a week to do general cleaning, but maintenance would be part of your job. There is a fairly large separate living space in the back attached to the house and if I hire you I think you'll like the privacy. It was actually meant as a mother-in-law house."

"That sounds wonderful. Let me assure you that I have cooked for hundreds of people as I have worked in several restaurants as one of their chefs so the numbers won't prove difficult. It's really quality along with quanity, isn't it? Don't worry, I can handle it easily."

"Do you drive, Ms. Golight?"

"I have my own Station Wagon, Sir."

"We've got a storm rolling in sometime in the late afternoon tomorrow. The storm should have already passed us, but I guess it got hung up on the Mountain. I've got some mares that are due to foal within the next twelve hours so I can't drive into town to meet with you. Besides, I think it would be best if you saw my place before you decide, don't you? Can you make it out here in the morning? Unless I'm helping a mare, I should be free to see you."

"Yes Sir, if you'll give me directions and depending on the distance I can be there by 10 o'clock if that suits you." the cool confident reply sounded in his ear.

"That sounds fine with me. Are you in River Town?"

"No Sir, I'm in Claremont. Is that a problem?"

"No problem, best to figure on a forty minute drive. Take the Claremont highway south to County Road 10 and turn left. Follow 10 along for about 10 miles until you see the road sign saying Thunder Road. Turn left and the first side road you come to will be my ranch road, the sign will say "Welcome to Rocking Horse Ranch.""

"Then I'll see you at 10 tomorrow morning. Thank you for giving me this appointment. Goodbye, Sir." And Luther heard the soft disconnect.

Well, mysterious lady, I wonder how that southern voice is packaged. Hmm, if she was half as attractive as her voice implied the boys would get something good to look at as well as good food. I hope! That reminded him of dinner and the frozen chickens. Luther got up and immediately took care of that priority and got out the chickens and sank them in water. Hannah was cooking tonight and the men would kiss her feet when they found out. He'd better call the bunk house and cancel Jude's plans for dinner if he had any that is.

He got busy in his office catching up on the paper work. "Why the government needs all these blasted forms filled out is beyond me." He heaved a heavy self-pitying sigh. "Well, I can bitch about it, but forms must be filled while I'm doing it, so get on with it Lute."

Three hours later he was relieved to hear Hannah's arrival as an excuse to leave the rest of the paperwork to finish later. Luther was seriously considered hiring a person to keep the books, after all he could afford it and it would be one less hassle. He got up and walked down the hall to the kitchen in time to see Joe carry in two small suitcases and Hannah following loaded down with supplies.

"Hail the Greeks bearing gifts. Hi guys, let me help you sister mine. Golly, have you stolen all this stuff from the folks? Shame on you and good for me; hmm, spices? What else."

"Lute, you really need to stock your pantry shelves with basic ingredients before the snow flies. Any cook who sees how limited everything here is will run out the door." said Hannah as she hung up her coat.

"Write down what you think I'll need to attract a good cook and I'll go shopping tomorrow if I have time, that is."

"Why don't you wait to see what your new cook wants before leaping in? Of course, some basic stuff wouldn't hurt, I guess. Okay, if you promise to fill the order right away." Hannah looked hard at her brother.

"Sure 'nough sweet thing, I promise." Luther swore and held up his hand then crossed his heart that had Joe snickering.

"Can we go to the barn now, Mr. Luther? I'm ever so anxious to visit the mare."

"Let me help you with the luggage first and show you where you and Hannah are going to sleep. I hope you don't mind sleeping in twin beds in the same room 'cause the other guest rooms aren't made up yet." with a wink at Hannah that Joe didn't see had Hannah quickly turning her back and begin unpacking the grocery bags.

"No, I don't mind at all if Hannah doesn't. Hannah, I really don't snore because Mike would have told me." Joe looked very earnestly at his adoptive mother.

"No problem Joe, sharing a room with you will be a treat." Joe grinned and turned to follow Luther and didn't see the laughing glance she directed at her brother. He winked again and had the audacity to snigger.

When they returned to the kitchen Hannah was already preparing the various fixings for the chickens when they'd thawed a little more and the sight of that made Luther hungry. Darn, he'd forgotten to eat lunch.

"Say Hannah dear, you wouldn't mind throwing a sandwich or two together for your hungry brother would you? Are you hungry enough to eat one Joe?"

"Well, maybe I could do peanut butter and jelly." volunteered Joe and Luther gave a small grimaced that had Hannah laughing.

"I'll throw some sandwiches together while you two run down to the barn and check on the mother." With a definite look that said 'get out of my kitchen.' Hannah continued working. "Give me fifteen minutes to organize myself then come up and eat. Once I get things started here I'll come down and watch."

"Right; come on Joe let's go." Luther grabbed his jacket and hat off the peg and was out the door before Hannah really got going. He'd learned never to mess with a busy cook not if you wanted a good dinner.

The big barn doors were shut so Luther entered by an ordinary size door cut in one of the sliding doors. Inside of the barn was warm, clean and well lighted because this was the nursery and delivery barn. Moving quietly down the aisle and stopping occasionally to check on a mare Luther finally stopped about midway at a stall and looked in at the groaning mare lying on her side.

Mac stood up and said quietly, "I was about to call you Luther, she's close, real close and I'm worried. She's not doing well at all. I sure wish Doc Grant would get here 'cause I think this is going to be one of those difficult deliveries. Ah, maybe the boy shouldn't be here if it is." and gave Luther a warning look. "Want me to give the doc another hurry-up call?

"Yes, speed him up if you can, I don't want to lose these two." Mac opened the stall door and hurried off to the barn office. Luther and Joe took off their coats and hats and slipped in as the mare struggled to get to her feet.

"So girl, easy there, that's my lovely it's going to be alright." The mare was sweating and looked frightened, but stopped trying to rise and Joe went to her head.

"Be careful Joe, she's excited and in pain and could hurt you unintentionally." cautioned Luther.

"I know Mr. Luther, I know." He knelt by her head and began to stroke her neck and head. A soft crooning issued from the boy's mouth; it was a sort of lullaby and there were no words that had to be spoken for the flow of sound was mesmeric and soothing. The Mare breathed deeply a time or two and then laid her head down on the boy's lap. Joe continued to sing and stroke in rhythmic movements.

The mare relaxed and it all happened within the first five minutes and the mare was completely calm.

Wow, thought Luther as he gazed in utter amazement at the miracle before him, what an asset this kid is! Talk about a magic voice! Luther just shook his head in wonder and closed his mouth. It was vital the mare relax so she wouldn't injure herself or her foal by the frantic muscle squeezing and it was obviously she wasn't going to give birth without help.

Within a few minutes Mac was back and reported. "I finally got the doc on his cell phone and he told me he'd left town twenty minutes ago and should be here within the next half hour or less. He said he was stomping on it and to tell you you'll pay his speeding ticket if he got one."

"No decent cop is going to stop a doctor on an emergency call. Good, I think we can keep Betsy here from doing herself an injury; Joe's got her calmed down." In fact, the mare looked like she was going to sleep. Mac raised his eyebrows at the sight and tuned into the soft mesmeric crooning of the boy hunched over the mare's head almost breathing the song into her ear.

"Mercy on us, do you think he'd pay barn calls whenever we have a difficult birth? He'd be worth his weight in gold." whispered Mac. Both men were quiet as they leaned on the stall door. "Just listen to that voice and look at that mare! I gotta' tell you boss I couldn't keep her quiet for the life of me, she was fighting me every which way and here I thought I was some punkins' with horses." Mac whispered then snorted softly like a horse at his own ego.

Less than twenty minutes later the sound of a racing truck penetrated the quiet of the barn followed by the skidding of the tires as they sought a grip in the gravel. A truck door slammed then there was the vet striding into the barn. Luther noticed he closed the door quietly behind him. However every horse had her head hanging over the stall doors.

Luther turned to greet him quietly. "Hi Grant, great timing and thank God you're here. I haven't checked her myself, but Mac has and he thinks we've got a breach birth."

Just then Hannah walked into the barn and joined them at the stall door. "What's the matter Lute, is she in trouble?" she asked quietly.

"Yes she is, but Joe's got her calmed down so we're hoping it's all going to work out, but I'm really worried."

Hannah listened for a few seconds then murmured, "Oh, my listen to Joe."

Dr. Grant Hennesey was of medium height and with his wide shoulders and strong physique he appeared almost square. He had brown hair, brown eyes with dark toned skin and the face of a cherub, all innocence looking, but he was one of the finest veterinarian surgeons in the west. His continence hid an acute intelligence and he was a champion chest player. Luther rather suspected he had a little crush on Hannah, but he wasn't sure. Poor doc didn't have much time for socializing.

"Hello Hannah, nice to see you again. We'll talk later, but right now this lady needs my attention." The vet took off his coat and hat and hung them on a hook then took off his shirt and tossed it over the stall door. Wearing only a short sleeved undershirt the vet entered the stall. He stopped and looked down at the quiet mare and listened to the awesome tones of the little boy who had put that horse to sleep and seemed almost to be in a trance himself.

"Well," he whispered, "it looks like you've found a new kind of anesthetic, Lute. Keeping her quiet is the best thing that could happen right now." The Doctor knelt down by the horse's rump and opened his bag. He took out a bottle of antiseptic and scrubbed his hands and arms down, wiped them dry then applied some oil.

Joe didn't stop his singing, though he roused enough to try seeing what the Doctor was doing which wasn't much from his end.

"Yep, she's breach; now to turn this little one around so he or she can make her entrance is going to be tricky. Betsy's awfully big Luther, she's either carrying one big baby or she's going to have twins. I wondered about that because sometimes I thought I could hear two heart beats from time to time. You keep on singing son and keep her really calm; that's the way," and went back to work. Grunting and with a lot of pushing and pulling that moved the mare around with his efforts yet didn't awaken her from her stupor.

"Okay, the baby's turned so you can stop singing boy, she needs to wake up and push."

Joe stopped singing and stroking and began to lightly slap the mare's neck. "Time to wake up Momma, it's time for your baby to come out. Come on now, wake up that's the girl, good girl" and slapping her a few more times on the neck. Betsy gave a snort and her eyes popped open and for the next ten minutes or so she labored hard.

"Here it comes! Oh, boy, look at this little girl, isn't she a hummer." The vet got busy and cleaned off her nose and the mare turned her head to lick her baby when she gave another grunt and a loud whinny and out popped number two. "Hey twins, by golly, one of each. No wonder she was having such a time." Grant laughed as Luther caught the second foal and busily cleaned its nostrils. Betsy got to her feet and helped finish cleaning them up.

Joe's eyes were wide with wonder. "I never saw twin horses before. Geeze Peeze, my first time watching a birth and *I get two*! *Wow,* wait until I tell Mike!" The men helped the little ones onto their wobbly legs and nurse their mother for the first time.

"They're so beautiful." said Hannah with a smile. "I'm glad I was here to see it all. Nice going Doctor. Well, I'm heading back to the house to finish fixing dinner. I'll pull out all the stops as I figured you gentlemen have earned a good one. Dinner at six so tell the men." and Hannah quietly left the barn.

An hour later the mare and babies had been cleaned up and moved into another stall deep in fresh sawdust. The babies were fast asleep while the mother ate her hot mash and settled down to sleep too.

"They'll require supplement feedings, but they're healthy and look to be fine little rocking horses." said Grant then sighed, "I gotta' get myself one of your beauties Lute, but it's hard trying to find time when I can get out here and make up my mind." Grant gave another tired sigh. "I'm thinking seriously about inviting another vet to come into partnership with me, maybe even two. There's only so much I can do and with all the animals in this Valley I'm running myself ragged. I'm getting overtired and the animals are going to suffer if I can't attend to them all. On top of all that I've heard that the vet, Dr. Jeffery, over in Claremont is close to retiring. It's simply too much work for one man to handle. Well, if I get any busier I'm going to run away from home just to get a rest."

"You *should* find another vet Grant, maybe two or three and expand your clinic and it's long past time. You shouldn't have any problem attracting the right kind of vets out here. Maybe you could advertise in several Veterinarian Magazines that there are openings here in the Valleys? People have a way of appearing when they're wanted you know."

"I'll offer my request to the Thunder Gods tonight and see what shows up."

"You just find the time to come out for a day old buddy and we'll do you a deal. I've got ten horses and one of them should suit you right down to the ground. In fact, you might want to look at them now because their going to be sold at Huntington."

"Yeah? Well, seeing as how I'm here now let's go see them." Grant perked up a bit and Luther led him out of the barn over to the other large barn. Joe trailed behind wanting to look at these other horses too. They watched the vet going from one horse to another and heard him groan repeatedly which made Luther and Joe grin and nudge each other at the vet's dilemma.

"They're all wonderful. How in Hades am I supposed to make up my mind? I can't afford to take them all like I want too. I like this handsome black gelding with the white feet and he's friendly too." Grant murmured nonsense and fed the horse another carrot.

"You've just picked the best of the bunch Grant. I've been seriously thinking about keeping him. So is he the one?" smiled Luther as he and Joe leaned on the stall door waiting for Grant to make up his mind. Luther had to laugh softy. This was the third time Grant had gone up and down the stalls inspecting each horse.

"This isn't easy, you know. It's a lot like getting married; you want to be sure it's the right partner, but…..yeah, he's the one. What's his name?"

"My sister named him Petunia." Luther said seriously and looked down at Joe and winked. Joe ducked his head and laughed quietly.

"*Petunia?* What kind of name is that for a handsome brute like this one?" Grant said indignantly and insulted for this beauty of a horse.

Luther laughed, "Actually, his name is Storm Cloud, Stormy for short. He was born in the midst on a real bad storm two years ago. It seemed appropriate at the time."

"That's more like it. Okay, Stormy is mine as of now, so let's make a deal." Grinned the vet as he left the stall. The men talked it over as they left the barn and struck a bargain. They arrived back in the maternity barn to check up on the new arrivals then just leaned on the stall door for awhile admiring the little babies.

"Thanks for the safe delivery Grant I sure wouldn't have wanted to lose those three. I'm glad I've got you on retainer because this is going to be a busy time. I guess all there's left to do is name them. What do you say Joe, since you were a large part of getting them born do you want to name the babies?"

"Me? Oh geeze, I don't know Luther." Joe frowned in concern at the responsibility. "Geeze, a name is *really, really* important because it's going to affect them the rest of their lives. Let me think for a minute." He looked over the stall door at the two little babies sleeping in the hay all worn out from getting born.

Both filly and colt were coal black except for some white markings. The female had a star on her forehead and the colt had a narrow white blaze all the way down his face and both babies had a white sock on the left front foot.

"I'd call the boy horse, Lightening Boy and the girl Star Chaser. What do you think of those names, Luther?" Joe asked worriedly. Sometime during the last two hours Joe had forgotten to "Mister" him.

"Why Joe my man, I think those names are perfect. Lightening Boy and Star Chaser it is. What do you say Grant?"

"I couldn't have done better myself. Those names sure beat your Petunia. Yep, those are two wonderful names for them to live up too."

"Tomorrow we will baptize them. For tonight, they just need sleep and their mother." However none of them made any move to leave, but just stood outside the stall door and looked down at the little beauties. Momma Betsy was getting in a few well earned winks herself when Mac walked up and joined them.

"Mac I know you've put some formula together so take a break. Tell Brent to set up a schedule for sharing the feeding times. Have Johnnie come in to spell you now because I don't want these little ones left alone for the next 48 hours. By the way Hannah's going to feed everyone the best roast chicken dinner known to man. Dinner's at six so pass the word."

"I purely *love* that woman, I sure wished she'd marry me and be my personal chef." grinned Mac who was already pushing fifty.

"You're *such* a romantic Mac and it just breaks my heart to tell you no way. She's declared herself marriage proof. We still have hopes for the future, but so far her eyes haven't lit on any particular guy." Luther pinched his lips together trying not to laugh as Mac gave a dramatic heart breaking sigh. They left Mac watching the new foals as they dimmed the lights and quietly left the barn.

Luther had his arm slung around Joe's shoulders as he talked to Grant. "You best stay for dinner as it's almost six now and no one wants to miss one of Hannah's dinners; roast chicken, mashed potatoes and gravy, hot biscuits and maybe a green bean casserole and all the other frills. The Lord only knows what fabulous dessert she has for us. Besides, if you drive back to town on an empty stomach you might get called out on another emergency and you'll faint by the wayside. You've got to keep up your strength 'cause you haven't got that other vet yet."

"Well, you've twisted my arm, Lute.... o*w, ow*, don't hurt me, I'll stay, I'll stay." Joe laughed because Luther hadn't even touched him. Dr. Hennesey was a funny man. "I guess I can be spared for an hour or two. Let me call my answering service and see if there's anything important." Grant grabbed his cell phone all the while walking up the slope to the lighted kitchen.

Joe was exhausted. He hadn't realized that helping the mare give birth would take so much out of him. My, but weren't they just the most beautiful babies you'd ever seen? Maybe if he were really good, Hannah would drive him down once in awhile so he could help feed the little ones. Joe yawned and put his arm around Luther's waist and hung on. Luther looked down at the tired boy who had worked so hard and only God knew where that wonderful mesmeric energy had come from to help that mare. Whatever healing power the kid channeled had tired him out. A good supper and early to bed was on the agenda. So he tucked his arm a little tighter around the tired boy and helped him along.

Grant Hennesey laughed as he disconnected his cell phone. "Hey Luther, guess what? A vet called my answering service and said our Dr. Valdez mentioned that I might be interested in taking on a partner. Seems Dr. Valdez met her when he had gone to that medical conference in Port City; she was a friend of one of his friends. Anyway she wants to know if she could come out for an interview. And there's another vet who wants to get out of the big city and work with farm animals for which he had trained. He might be okay, but a woman vet Lute? I don't know, still Dr. Valdez wouldn't have recommend her if she hadn't impressed him. I guess it's only fair to reserve judgment until after I interview with both of them. Gee, maybe the Thunder Gods are reading minds now and anticipating wishes too."

"Be careful what you wish for Grant, since you'll have to live with the results." his friend said slapped him heartily on the shoulder. "Maybe this female vet can take the load off your shoulders with the smaller animals while you other guys deal with the bigger ones. Of course, she would have to be a vet who understands farm animals too."

"Yeah, even if she can cut my load by a third it will give me some time to rest. By the way her name is Dr. Nancy Anne Ransom; doesn't that name have a nice ring to it?" Luther looked side-wise at his old friend and…hummed.

They scraped their boots clean on the cleat in the mud room then scrubbed the soles of their boots on a sisal rug. No tracking barn dirt into the kitchen when Hannah was cooking or she'd peel a stripe off their hides. That response seemed to be universal with cooks as far as Luther knew.

The kitchen counter held two large steaming peach cobblers and the smell of them caused their saliva glands to go into attack mode. Starved as he was, Joe thought the best thing of all was he got to tell Hannah how wonderful it had been to help with birthing the miracle babies. So before he washed up for supper, Joe gave Hannah a hug while telling her about naming the babies and glowed when she praised him. He thought it was just like coming home to a Mother who was patient and ready to hear all about his adventure even though Hannah had been there as a witness herself, he got to tell her *his* experience. He was awfully glad Hannah was here. Somehow she satisfied a deep need in him he didn't know how to describe. He guessed it didn't need words except to say…. it just felt good.

~Amber Golight~

HANNAH WAS COOKING BREAKFAST when Luther and Joe came into the kitchen from a visit to the new mother and the twins. "Hannah, I got to help feed the little ones; they're just the cutest things I've ever seen." said Joe enthusiastically as Hannah turned away from the stove and smiled at Joe.

"Luther sure has some pretty horses Joe; maybe he'll give you one someday."

"What with all the attention those twins are going to need I just might do that if Joe wants to help out down here." said a serious Luther with a decided twinkle in his eyes that had Hannah turning back to the stove with her shoulders shaking gently.

"You bet Luther, I sure would. Of course, Hannah would have to drive me down and then there's school after roundup is over and I'll be helping Mike over at our ranch too." Joe shook his head then looked Luther right in the eye and said, "Well, I'll just have to work it into my schedule." Just as gravely as if this was a major undertaking and that seriously stressed Luther's mouth to keep from laughing at this earnest little boy.

"Ahem," coughed Luther, "Ah, you let me know what days you can be here and I'll work around that. Say Hannah, we're starving here!" Luther met Hannah's eyes and both of them turn quickly away seeing as laughter wouldn't have been at all kind.

"You need a cook, Luther Strongbow." said Hannah severely as she served the breakfast.

"I just might have one sister dear. I made an appointment with a Ms. Golight yesterday and she'll be here by ten today. Hopefully she can cook as fine as she talks." As Luther filled his mouth with blueberry pancakes. Umm, umm, his sister sure could cook.

"It's about time. Wonder what she'll look like." said Hannah as she sat down.

"Who cares, if she can cook. What I *can* tell you is she has one of those velvety southern voices that could melt any man's hard heart into a puddle of goop."

"Oh, *really*! Better watch out, Lute, remember the old saying that the way to a man's heart is through his stomach." his sister said with a smirk.

"My dear sister, it's by far better to marry a great cook I always say or a man could die of acid-indigestion eating his own makings." laughed Luther.

"Yeah right, you've got a stomach like a cast iron stove. You're just lazy and have a huge appetite." Luther just smiled at her comment and kept on eating.

"Look Melanie Lee, we agreed we'd go someplace where we weren't known. We also agreed that we needed a big change. Well dear, this is about the biggest change I could come up with. You and Jack love to ride horses so what better place to live and have that pleasure than on a horse ranch? For goodness sake, we don't have to stay forever, you know." said Amber, exasperated at the resistance. Amber took a deeper breath and tried for patience as she busily picked up articles about the room and put them into a suitcase.

"I know what we said back then Aunt Amber, but we're out in the middle of *nowhere* and I don't think even God could find us here. Just give me an idea of how long we have to stay in this backwater place and I'll try to be patient." Melanie said, as she hurriedly packed her own bag while her young brother Jack sat in his chair listening quietly.

"All right, let's say six months or at least through the winter. Come spring we'll think the whole situation over again. Anyway, the nice thing about living in the country is you'll have lots of time for your painting and I'd think this beautiful country will inspire you to do that. We'll also have time to plan where you want to go to college. Jack and I will live somewhere not too far away so you can come home on holidays." Amber forcibly slammed shut a suitcase lid and turned impatiently to face her niece. "Honestly Melanie, it will give us a place to relax and heal and God knows we all could use a little of that."

Amber couldn't think of anything else to say that would make the situation any more palatable to Melanie. Frankly Amber just didn't have the stamina to persist in the argument. Either the girl would see the sense of what she was trying to do for them or she wouldn't. They would just have to trust her to do the right thing. Having finished packing and double-checking the rooms, Amber collapsed into the other chair and waited for a response.

"Alright Amber, I'm sorry I'm making things more difficult for you. It's just that I can't see any future for us way out here in this cow country." Melanie zipped her suitcase closed and dropped it on the floor beside the door. "You're a *five star rated chef* for goodness sake. It's bad enough that you had to give up a fabulous job to take care of us, but now you're planning on being buried up here in the sticks as a plain old ranch cook. That such a waste of your talent and it's down right humiliating for you. "

When Amber merely looked at her without comment Melanie threw up her hands in surrender and picked up her jacket. "Oh alright, we're here so I guess we'll just have to make the best of it. I'm going out for a walk. Do you want to come with me, Jack? We can see the town, which should take us about 10 minutes. Come with me and defend me against desperate cowboys. I'm soooo beautiful that I'll be in trouble in no time." Melanie smiled and held out her hand. Jack got up and put on his coat and followed his sister out the door without a word.

"Y'all come back in 20 minutes because we've got a ways to drive this morning." she said just as the door closed behind her niece and nephew. Amber laid her head back against the chair and took several deep breaths.

"Lordy, I'm tired." She groaned rubbing her face then pushed her fingers through her long hair. It wasn't just the physical fatigue that had drained Amber of energy, though that was certainly in the general mix. It was making all the decisions right or wrong. She'd had the full responsibility of settling all the family affairs, selling the house as well as packing and storing that proved painful. Their lives had been blind-sided by tragedy with the children as surviving victims. The trip up from Georgia had been long and hard. Each night when they stopped she'd question herself, "Have we gone far enough to escape the notoriety? Is this the place we can stop and begin to repair some of the damage to our hearts and spirits?"

It was weird that *something* always nudged her to continue on the next day angling in a northwesterly direction until she thought she'd never get to stop. She was worn out with the constant effort of keeping a positive attitude so these poor grieving children wouldn't fall into a blue funk. Starting life over again in totally different surroundings where no one knew them would hopefully be successful. She could only hope for the best.

"Lordy, I wish I had a crystal ball that showed me that I've done the right thing in dragging the children way up here. Dear Lord, help us find sanctuary where we can have peace. Help us to endure until we can heal our wounds." murmured Amber. After a time she gave a deep sigh and forced herself out of the chair to begin packing the Station Wagon.

It was going on 10 o'clock when Luther heard a car pulling into the ranch yard. When he opened the barn door and stepped outside he saw the driver's door and two back doors open and three people get out. Luther stopped in his tracks. Now who in the heck was this? Could it be that his possible cook had two children? Why hadn't she mentioned that little bit of news? *Well, we'll see about that!* He wasn't happy.

Luther walked purposely toward the car that stood by the front porch. Just then a chilled whippy wind picked up bringing a light scattering of rain that blew the lady's hat away. The woman's hair, free of its confine, flew out like a blond flag streaming in the wind. She reached up and to grab her hair as the same frisky wind opened her coat wide enough for Luther to catch a glimpse of a delightfully shaped.... lady.

Wow, thought Luther, his anger momentarily forgotten at the sight of this possible new cook of his and almost tripped over his own feet. My, ohmyohmy, *some southern lady*! The closer he got the better she looked and the stronger her brown eyes pulled him. As he walked toward her he bent and swept up her hat that was tumbling along the ground.

"Welcome to Rocking Horse, Ma'am, I'm Luther Strongbow." he was rather proud of being able speak coherently.

"I'm Miss Golight, Sir." Oh yeah, that smooth, velvety, southern voice was more potent face to face. *Lord, help me now!*

"Ah, come on in out of the wind. I guess the storm decided to arrive earlier than expected." he said politely and offered her hat back to her before leading the way up the porch steps. Now that he was somewhat over the shock of her appearance, he remembered he was angry. Man, oh, man, he didn't need a cook with complications.

Luther opened the front door and when she passed by him he caught a whiff of some light perfume that caused his nose to quiver like a rabbit's. Whoa boy, that's *not* a good sign, he thought and struggled to bring himself back into a business-like mode.

The two young people followed her. The boy might be seven or so and the girl was at least eighteen. Young pretty girls always caused problems around cowboys. Complications, that's what these women were; just plain complications. Luther slammed the door shut behind him.

"Let me take your coats." said Luther and hung them up on the coat rack standing beside the front door. "Please come into the living room. I have a nice hot fire going there and it will warm you up in no time. We're at about 4,000 feet so our fall and winter weather comes a little earlier than in the lower elevations. Sometimes the weather is variable, nice for a couple of days then *wham*, you get this kind of a blow off Thunder Mountain in a flash. Sit down, please."

Gods, he was babbling. Get a grip Lute, you idiot! And he went over to stand with his back to the fire while watching Ms. Golight sit down on the couch placing her briefcase on the floor beside her. The two children sat on either side of her forming a strong united front.

For the first time he got a close look at them and saw quiet faces, perhaps a little too quiet. The boy looked…..haunted and remote from what was going on; the kid just watched. What was wrong with him? His hair was a true red with dark blue eyes, fair skin and freckles. The boy should have looked happy or at least mischievous as red headed boys are supposed to look.

The girl was very close to being beautiful with strawberry blond colored hair and dark blue eyes, maybe even purple. And she would be more than pretty except for the strained, white face and dark circles under her eyes. She looked as though she had recently been ill. *Oh lordymassyme*, if she stayed she was going to break hearts for sure. Luther also picked up an air of desperation about them. Hmm, something definitely wasn't right which made him suspicious.

"Mr. Strongbow, let me introduce my niece and nephew, Melanie and Jack Golight. I am their guardian now so they have to stay with me. I am all that I told you I was; an excellent cook and competent housekeeper. Melanie and Jack will help me as well. I didn't tell you about them initially because I was afraid you'd refuse to interview me, not wanting a cook with responsibilities such as mine. You see Sir, we come as a unit and that's the way it must be. Here is my resume and my references." Amber pulled out a leather folder from her briefcase. "As you will see, they're excellent and you may phone these establishments for conformation." holding the folder out to Luther.

He stepped over and took it then returned to lean against the mantle. The fire felt good against his legs as he quickly scanned the information. She was a...*chef! An honest to God chef!* A five star restaurant called LaMonts in Atlanta employed here as an assistant to Chef Michael for the past four years. Before that she had two years training at Bleu Lorraine in Paris. Before that she had been cook and housekeeper for a Mr. Robert Clare Vega of New Orleans for two years. Hmm, a very classy resume if it was true he thought cynically.

When he looked up she was holding out a few more papers to him. Taking these he glanced over the letters of recommendation and the embossed letterheads verified the contents. Well, it was all pretty fancy for a ranch cook application which made him feel she was running from someone or something.

"Well, Ms. Golight, this resume is very impressive and way out of my class. All I wanted was a good everyday cook for me and my men. We really don't need or expect fancy cuisine here nor can I pay you the salary you deserve as a chef. Perhaps you'd better tell me the truth now as to why you want to hide yourself away from the world on a ranch?" asked Luther gently.

The reaction was instantaneous and totally unexpected. The girl, the very quiet young lady, burst into tears and sobbed. "I *told* you this wouldn't work Amber; I *told* you we couldn't get away. There is*n't* any place to start over. N*o peace, no nothing,* just more misery." Ms.

Golight took the sobbing girl into her arms and the boy just leaned in closer to Amber and watched Luther with wide scared eyes.

"*Hey* now, little lady," Luther quickly went over to the girl and putting the folder on the coffee table, knelt down to take the girl's hand and began patting it. "I didn't say I wasn't going to hire your mother I mean your aunt. I'm just asking questions just like a real employer would. Now…. now Missy, you just *stop* that caterwauling; everything's going to be alright." Luther said in a desperate attempt to calm the hysterical girl. "Now you *listen* to me young lady, you can't cry in here because that's a firm house rule and one I strictly enforce."

He continued to pat the girl's hand and desperately tried to think of something to distract her and had a brilliant idea. "Say, did you know I've got the prettiest horses you've ever seen right out there in the barn? Only yesterday one of my mares had twins, a colt and a filly. Now if you want to see them you got to quit crying or you'll scare the babies." Luther frantically looked at Ms. Golight for help and found her smiling at him. Oh wow, oh geeze, what had he just said?

Luther swallowed hard and stood up abruptly and walked back over to the fireplace putting a safe distance between him and the tears. He looked back over his shoulder and found that the girl had quieted down.

She sniffed and blew her nose delicately and wiped her cheeks then looked up at him and gave him a watery smile. "Twins? I'd love to see them Sir. I ride you know; I've ridden dressage since I was a child and helped train horses back home too. In case you're wondering, I'm eighteen and I can help Amber in the house as well as work for you with the horses if you want me too. Jack rides just as well as I do." Melanie had perked up a little while she talked about her experiences with horses. "I'm also an artist; I paint. Well, that's all about me except I'll probably go to college next year."

"Do you? Are you? I mean you ride? Then you should enjoy yourself here. I've got the finest Tennessee Walkers you ever laid eyes on. Hmm, yes indeed. Ah I could use the help exercising the horses and all."

He stopped. To say that he was down right flustered would be putting it mildly. "Hmm, well, ah, Ms. Golight, you obviously have a right to your secrecy as long as it doesn't involve criminal activities.

You look like a trustworthy person. Ah, let's give this a three month trial period and if you're happy with the salary I quoted and with us and we're happy with you all, I guess I've hired a real live certified chef."

When Luther heard himself hiring this woman right out loud in front of God and everyone, he blanched. His poor brain scrambled for something sane to say. All he could do was smile even while that smile was a trifle desperate it was the best he could do under the circumstances.

"Ah, ah, my biggest problems are my men. I'm afraid they're going to fall in love with you and your niece not to mention with your cooking too. Then if I have to fire you I'll have a mutiny on my hands and they'll quit and my ranch will fall apart and I'll be forced to go back and live with my Father and Mother. No, no, it would just be too humiliating." He caught himself up short and stopped talking. I am in trouble, thought Luther sweating and not just from the heat of the fire. Still the girl laughed quietly and even Jack cracked a small grin, but Ms. Golight just nodded her head smiling.

In her gentle, soft southern voice she said. "I'll see what I can do to prevent that mutiny Sir. Loyalty to the brand, I understand, is a western motto." Luther had to laugh at that and began to relax a little. Ms. Golight let Melanie go and stood up and walked over to Luther and held out her small yet strong hand and as he shook it gently she said. "You really won't regret your decision Sir, I'll see to that. Let me assure you that we are not running from the law or anything bad like that; we're just seeking a place like this where peace can heal our grieving hearts."

"Well, I never could stand to see a lady cry. It's all her fault that I couldn't maintain my gruff rancher's attitude." At least he got a nice laugh out of Ms. Golight and glancing over at the boy Luther saw another faint smile. A small victory to be sure, but it looked to be a beginning.

Now what had happened that a healing time was necessary for these troubled people? More importantly, why had the Thunder Gods brought them to his doorstep? He recognized wounded spirits when he saw them and the Gods were notorious for salvaging these kinds of people. Well, if the Thunder Gods wanted them here, what chance did he have of saying no?

Luther sighed as he led them down the hallway past the kitchen to a door that opened into the self-contained mother-in-law's cottage all the while Luther groused to himself. It was all Hannah's fault for pushing him into hire a cook, Well, shoot and blast, he had to blame someone and not his soft heart for hiring this troubled bunch. As sure as you were born trouble would follow if his gut feeling was right.

"Oh Mr. Strongbow, this is so lovely. I didn't expect anything so charming." Amber whipped around peeking into each room. "Look, there's a room for each of us. There now Jack, you've got your own room at last. My, this is perfect and once I get unpacked Melanie and I will see to lunch. By the way I've been teaching Melanie to cook and she's very capable so we'll give you and your men our very best even on such short notice, you'll see. So instead of one cook you've got one and a half at the same price as well as two housekeepers." She smiled at Luther and he turned to mush again.

"Always glad to get the best of a bargain, Ma'am." Luther jingled the change in his pocket. Before the silence could prove uncomfortable he said, "If I can have the keys to your car I'll drive it into the garage beside the cottage and get your luggage hauled in."

She handed him the car keys then turned to Melanie and with their arms around each other started cheerfully talking about room arrangements.

"**You're my man Jack**, so let's go get the luggage. It looks like you're going to be my newest cowboy." said Luther to the boy and the first look of interest on the kid's face said it all.

"Really? Do you think maybe I could learn to be a cowboy, Sir?" the boy whispered hopefully.

That's right Lute, open your dumb mouth and get hooked by a hurting kid. He gave another deep sigh as they left the cottage for the main house. Why me?

As they walked down the hallway Luther said, "Well Jack, we'll have plenty of time to train you up and all, won't we." They got their coats and walked out into the lashing wind side by side to where the car was parked.

"I really can ride Sir, so maybe I could help exercise your horses or clean tack or something else. I'll be willing to help out with whatever you need doing." Jack's offer was almost a plea to be acknowledged and thought useful. *Worthy* came the silent word into Luther's head.

"I'm sure we can find you lots to do around here Jack, because there's no end to the work around a ranch, you know." Luther hoped that would stem this kid's anguished plea because Luther didn't really have all that much experience in how to handle wounded children and this was an abused kid if he ever saw one. Where were his own mother and father when he needed them for advice? After all they were the experts.

Luther drove the Station Wagon around the side of the house and parked it in the garage. When Luther got out he caught the sight of Little Brown.

"Hey Brown, come give us a hand with the new cook's luggage." Brown changed directions and came trotting up the slope and stopped in front of the boy and looked down at Jack for a few moments.

"Meet the newest member of our elite group, Jack Golight. Jack, this is Jay Brown, better know as Little Brown and the best horseman on the ranch." Shyly Jack nodded his head to Brown. Luther continued, "Tell the boys we'll eat well at lunch and hopefully from now on. Tell Jude's he's fired as a cook and he can go back to fixing machinery which will make him and everyone else happier. Now let's get a move on here."

Brown smiled and said quietly. "I'll do that boss with pleasure. Always glad to be the bearer of good news, less chance of getting booted. I'd walk ten miles in a blizzard for a good meal and none of Jude's." Little Brown looked down at Jack and said with a smile, "Don't mistake me, Jude's a great guy, but a really terrible cook. Hi Jack." and held out his hand.

Luther watched in amazement as this young man who normally communicated by looks, grunts and gestures. Was this Brown, the taciturn young man of few words? Yet, was it really as strange as all that? Brown had a knack of knowing what needed healing and how to soothe a nervous horse. Perhaps it was all the same thing with humans.

"Hello, Mr. Brown," As they shook hands, "My aunt is a chef and she's a really, really great cook. Mr. Strongbow said I could be one of his cowboys, but I don't really know how to be a cowboy. Can you teach me? I ride very well and he said he had twin horses. Why does he call you the best horseman?"

Luther was utterly amazed at this explosion of questions. This kid hadn't spoken more than a few words before. Myohmy, Brown's magic was working right here and it was a shock in a way because Luther had never seen the "Brown's Touch" being used on humans before. If ever there was a bonding, Luther recognized one when it happened right before his eyes. Jack had Little Brown in his sights as his guide in all things important to life on a ranch. Poor Brown had just taken on a very delicate problem and knowing Brown, he probably knew that without words having to be spoken. Yep, magic was truly at work.

Luther turned away from the ongoing spat of conversation as the boys began to unload the car and looked up at the Mountain and murmured. "Well, well, well, what *are* You Gods up to now?"

~Strike One~

LIKE A GHOST A white Owl swooped out of the darkness and crossed the open pasture. Suddenly it dove to the ground and all that was heard was the squeak of a mouse's death. The Owl was startled by a sound from the road and quickly took off as noiselessly as it had struck, clutching the mouse in its claws.

The moonless night covered the subtle movements of a figure walking along the road as a cold wind blew mournfully through the trees. The man couldn't see the ranch buildings, but he didn't expect anyone to be around at this late hour. He could see the vague shapes of cattle as he climbed up the steep grassy bank toward the fence, slipping a few times in his slicked soled shoes until finally, panting with the exertion he made it to the top of the bank. Walking a few feet to the fence he pulled on thick gloves and began cutting the first of the barbed wire strands. Standing well away from the snap and recoil of the wire as it was freed he wrapped the wire around the post as best he could. It wouldn't be the neatest job in the world, but he was making a statement here. Once he cleared one section between posts he started on another until four sections of fence were down.

Cattle, curious creatures that they are, had begun moving in his direction ever since he'd started on the fence. Now he whistled low and made mooing sounds. It didn't take much more than half an hour to encourage the cows to go through the gaps and he saw more cattle trotting over to join their companions. It was a case of curious cows following the leaders. He figured he had about a hundred of the critters out of the pasture. Sure it was work, still he was laughing as he pushed the cattle further down the road. He quickly walked back to his car and used it to drive them even further along.

After five miles Elroy stopped and made a u-turn and headed back for Port City. He had to drive carefully because there were still cattle coming down the road. He would have rubbed his hands together if he hadn't had to hang on to the wheel. It had been a good night's work and the beginning of his harassment that would soon bring these kids to the payoff point. His gain and their loss he chuckled. He was on a roll.

The night again returned to silence with just the wind playing among the trees branches.

The phone woke the Ranch Manager out of a sound sleep. He peered blurrily at the clock that said 4:30 am. The phone rang again.

He sat up and lifted the receiver, "Tomlinson."

"Hey Hank, this is Dan Lightfoot. Are you missing any cows? I've got over a hundred head of cattle with your ear tags on 'em. They're on the County Road about eight miles east of my place. One of my men came home late last night and saw them. I've got my boys out there now keeping them from going any further east and nudging them back your way. Those cows aren't liking it much 'cause they appear to be in a real travelin' mood. So buddy, you must have a fence down somewhere. Best come and get them before they become a real nuisance." said Dan Lightfoot with a laugh.

"*Lordloveaduck*, how in Hades did *this* happen?" groaned Hank, "This is *not* the way I like to start the day. Well, tell your men I'll make it good with them. Thanks Dan, we'll be right down."

Hank hung up the phone and jumped out of bed and into his clothes. His only words to his wife's questions, as he pulled on his boots were. "I've got cattle loose on the road." and hurried out of the bedroom before May could say a word. He grabbed his heavy jacket and hat off the hook and was out the door heading for the bunkhouse.

Hank, Pike and Wolf Camden, the newly hired man, loaded the horse van and before they left Hank ordered Grumpy to begin checking the roadside fences as soon as it was light. When they turned onto the County Road going east, they saw the four sections of fence bare of wire.

Hank got on his cell phone and called May. "May go over and tell Grumpy the fence breaks are on the County Road just to the east of the ranch road and start him repairing it. Tell him to leave two sections open as we'll be driving the cattle back in that way. We probably won't be back until late this morning. Tell Grumpy I'll be back to help him as soon as I get this drive organized. I should be home within the next hour or two so would you make up some sandwiches and a couple of thermoses of coffee so I can take it back to the men?"

May laughed at her cranky man. "Honey, making a cattle drive will just relieve the monotony of your daily routine so make it as fun as you can." And she hung up.

"Fun? That woman of mine has a very odd sense of humor; besides how can a man have a sense of humor when he hasn't even had his morning coffee." he grumbled though he did crack a smile.

"Women! Who can understand them? But you're right, boss, this is a hard way to start the day without a couple of cups of coffee. It's down right cruel and unnatural. Just can't get my engine started without my coffee." said Wolf glumly.

Pike John said with indignation after having gotten a good look at the open sections of fence. "It ain't possible that four sections of fence go down all in a row like that. I fixed some small breaks in a couple of sections a week ago and checked the rest of this road fence and it was real tight and right. Honest, boss, that fence was solid. Somebody's messin' with us."

"I don't question your work or your word Pike. The fact that all four sections are bare of wire says vandalism to me. We'll check it out and maybe we'll have to put on a guard." said Hank and mumbled some not to be repeated words under his breath.

"With just Grumpy and me and Wolf here that's going to be difficult and cut into the day's work somethin' fierce." he said worriedly. "As it is we're still stretched pretty fine to get everything under wraps before snow flies."

"I'll be hiring more men in a day or two so we won't be short handed for long." replied Hank.

Even in the early gray morning light it wasn't hard to see the cattle as they were all over the place. They pulled over to the edge of the road and just sat in the truck for a few minutes watching the cows leisurely walking toward them stopping now and then to graze along the roadside until pushed on again. Thank goodness it was still too early for any major blockage just a few pickups that had volunteered to block the cattle from going further east while Dan's men were slowly hazing the cows back down the road.

"What's the matter, Hank, don't your cows like your grass?" laughed the smart-alex in one of the pickups.

"Hey, looks like they wanted to go on vacation. They must be bored with your entertainment and are out looking for fun." shouted some other smartass.

"Well, boys these here cows are exceptionally social and they like to take a walk-about off and on to visit the other cows in the neighborhood, you know? Real party animals just like y'all are." called Hank and that got a big laugh.

What else can a man to do? Grumbling wasn't going to make this mess any better. Honestly, the things people found funny, thought Hank. He got out to help unload the horses. Nothing like a cattle drive to whet a man's appetite for breakfast which they hadn't had before leaving.

"Start trailing them home boys. I'll send Grumpy down with coffee and something for you to eat 'cause it's going to take you awhile. I'm going to go back and help with that fence. Dagblastit all to hell and back! A whole morning wasted on this foolishness. Well, cowboys, head 'em up and move 'em out as they used to say." Nothing like leaving the boys laughing Hank said to himself.

"Hey, boss, no worries, it's just like the old cattle drive days. We're sure to make it home as we don't expect any Indian attacks or stampedes." called Pike as he and Wolf wove their way through the cows to get to the rear of the herd and joined Dan's men.

Just another smartass thought Hank sourly. Well, maybe May was right, it certainly broke up the boring routine of ranching.

Before he left he called Dan. "Say Dan can I borrow a few of your men to get these cows back home 'cause I only have two men I can leave here?"

"Sure, they'll enjoy the change. What happened to your fence? That's a sight of cattle to just accidentally go wandering." questioned Dan.

"Someone cut out four sections of fence bordering the road and must have driven the cattle out to get them started. We'll investigate and might have to set up a night patrol. Is this any way to begin the day, I ask you? I'll get back to you and thanks for the help." and hung up. He asked three of Dan's men if they'd stay with the herd. They thought it was a hoot and agreed.

Dubby Snow laughed and said, "Hank, all we were going to do was clean the barns this morning. I much prefer fresh air and an easy ride myself."

"Thanks Dub, the ranch will pay for you and the other men. Y'all plan on staying for dinner 'cause you're going to need nourishment by the time you make it to the ranch so we'll feed you like kings." Hank just got a grin and a wave before Dubby moved off.

It took all morning to drive the cows fifteen miles home 'cause they just wouldn't move any faster. By noon the cattle were back were they belonged and the fence was mended with new wire. That the wire had been cut and coiled around the posts was clear evidence of vandalism. Hank reported it to Sheriff Max Brandt and the good man had driven out to check on the damage.

While the Sheriff was talking to Hank, Wolf interrupted them. "Hey boss, I got something interesting to show you over here." Hank and the Sheriff walked over to where the cowboy stood and he showed them a shoe print that was hardening in a cow patty.

Sheriff said. "Looks like a town shoe to me; what do you say, Wolf?"

"Sure ain't no cowboy boot or any other kind of boot for that matter. This one has a slick sole. Now what would a townie be doing out here causing mischief?" mused the cowboy.

"Hmm, tell you what Wolf, you measure that shoe print for length and width, mark it down on paper then get a shovel and scoop that patty up real careful like and set it where it can safely dry. That there is evidence of trespassing, malicious mischief and destruction of property and must be preserved." said Brandt seriously then he frowned. "Yep, you just save that patty and when it's dried you give me a call and I'll come out and put it in an evidence bag."

The Sheriff paused and rubbed a hand over his chin looking down at the cow flop. "Hmm, guess it could be the first cow patty ever to be classified as evidence. It could be a real history making event, you know? A "Ripley's Believe it or Not," type of thing. I might get my picture in the paper holding that cow flop up and become famous and get on all those true life T.V. shows." Brandt said it all with a serious, sober face. "Possibly I'd make my fortune as well then I could retire and buy a condo in Cancun and live the high life."

The angry men who'd gathered around and were soberly listening to the Sheriff's speech began to see the humor of it all. By the time the Sheriff was finished speaking they were laughing their socks off.

Brandt's eyes just twinkled, but said seriously. "Now, now boys, all funning aside, this isn't to be tolerated so call me if anything else happens around here that's suspicious. I'll check around and see if we have any strangers visiting us. Now, y'all take care of that cow patty like I told you too 'cause it *is* evidence." Waving goodbye, Brand walked back to his car.

Hank entered the cook shack around one o'clock and washed his hands at the sink while May put a big dinner on the table for the men. The men soon came trooping in saying hello to Hank's wife and taking turns washing up before sitting down to eat like famished wolves. The quiet in the cook shack was broken only by the sounds of utensils making a noise on the plates.

When dinner was finished and the men were drinking a last cup of coffee Hank said "We'd still be driving cattle if y'all hadn't pitched in so thanks for your help. As I said before there will be extra pay for you guys as soon as I can get Jim Jensen to cut some checks."

"Well Sir, it ain't often that we get to eat such fine cooking as Mrs. Hank offers her men, so we're more than obliged. Not that our cook isn't good, but a pretty woman's touch just makes the food taste better somehow." said Dugan slyly and winked at the pink cheeked woman.

"Oh, you go on Dugan, if you think flattery will get you an extra piece of cake…you could be right." At that the other men began to voice such outrageous complements of Mrs. Tomlinson's person and cooking that she couldn't resist laughing at their foolishness and thus everyone got that second slice of cake. Men weren't stupid not to know that flattery would get most things for them.

Hank walked up to the house and into the office to make a phone call. "Mari Beth, this is Hank Tomlinson, I need to speak to Ben if he's there, please?"

"Sure Hank, he just now came in for dinner." After a few minutes as Hank listened to some background chatter Ben came on the phone.

"Hello Hank, what can I do for you?"

"We've had four sections of fence cut last night and more than a hundred head of cattle scattered down the road. Dan Lightfoot called me around 4:30 this morning and told me he had our cattle bottled up fifteen miles east of his property. I called in Brandt and he came out to investigate. Wolf found a perfect town shoe print in a cow paddy of all things. Brandt left instructions to dry it and he'll bag it as evidence. While we did get a laugh out of that possible history making event, this vandalism is worrisome. Some townie is causing mischief, Ben, and I don't know why. Not only that, why would a townie come all the way out to our place instead of hitting Sam or Seely or even Dan as they're closer to town? It just doesn't make sense."

"No it doesn't. Four sections of fence down, you say? No way is that a normal kind of break for sure." commented Ben.

"No it surely isn't, especially when the wire's been cut with a cutter and the wire wrapped around the posts. Well, we'll tighten up on security and I'm having a gate built on the ranch road and it will be locked. I'll post a guard on it to let in legitimate visitors as well as having one of the men ride the road fence during the night, but I don't think he'll pull that same trick twice or at least not in the same place. If we're the target of this sort of thing I might need more hands just to guard the place and still be able to get the necessary work done around here."

"You'll get whatever you need, Hank. Blackhawk and I will be over in the morning and we'll see what we can do to help you. Shoot and blast, just when things were going so well too, now this happens. Okay, Hank, anything else I can do for you right now?"

"No, I'm just reporting the event to you. I'll be interviewing several more hands this afternoon and if they're any good I'm hiring them. We'll see you all tomorrow then."

A half hour later Hank crossed the yard to the cowboy's kitchen. He walked in just as the boys had finished cleaning up the dishes. May cooked, but she didn't do dishes. Dan's men had already left so he grabbed a cup and poured himself coffee and sat down as he explained to his men what he was about to do. A guard shift was to be set up round the clock for today and they were to carry stun guns only.

"No townie is going to sneak in here to do any real damage boss without us being on his neck. After all the Kelly boys will be in and out of here all the time so we'd best take care of this person now." said Pike John. "Problem is we've got a few miles of fence along the road and I'm not sure whether we can cover it all adequately among us three. I suggest we electrify that fence line and run it on a couple of generators until we can connect it to our electricity."

Now Pike was a man of very few words. He wasn't a big man; more medium sized, but well put together. He was quiet and did more than his share of the work and was quick to loan a dollar or help out someone in need, still no one mistook him for a softy. Pike made a good loyal friend and a very bad enemy. The men didn't know where he'd come from originally; they only knew that he had been here a long time. This was his home and no one in their right mind wanted to mess with what Pike considered his.

"Thanks Pike, your idea about the electrifying the fence is one I'll run by the trustees and it just might save us a lot of extra work. Well, that's it for now; keep your eyes peeled and stay alert. Oh, by the way Pike, you're our new Foreman and I'm putting you in charge of these lazy boys and setting up the guard schedules." The cowboys laughed and applauded that and had some rare hilarious comments to make about their new foreman, but Hank could tell they liked the idea and once Pike got over the shock he would be a natural.

"There will be a raise in pay for you as Foreman Pike, because I'm going to have to rely heavily on you as my second in command. I'm interviewing three more men today and if they're any good y'all will get some added help. By the way Strongbow and Blackhawk will be here tomorrow to see what more we can do to protect this place. Well, that's it boys, so get on with your work." Hank got up and left the kitchen.

"Well, fellas', here's where we ride for the brand, as they used to say in all those old westerns. I guess what that really means is, you stand up and defend your place of work and your job so let's get this schedule down." ordered Pike.

"Yes Sir, boss, Sir." Pike looked up sharply at Wolf and when he saw the good nature grin he relaxed. Nothing much had changed really, just his official title. Pike knew Wolf was a rancher's boy and knew how to work hard. He and Grump were the old timers here. It certainly would be a big relief when they had more men. They'd be as tough as they needed to be.

That afternoon Hank interviewed four men; the first one to arrive was a young man named James Kilpatrick who brought his own horse with him. He was a likeable man and his references said he was a good if not an excellent working hand. Jimmy said he had worked for a rancher down in Nevada, but when the place was sold the old crew was fired. Stupid eastern dudes firing men who knew the lay of the land and what needed doing didn't show much in the way of brains. Jimmy had excellent references from the previous owner and Hank hired him on the spot.

The next candidate's name was Emmett Boggs who wanted the position of handyman or as cook. He said no one had complained to him so far about his cooking. Hank saw that his references were sound and he liked the jolly man's cheerfulness so if he could cook as well as he talked; well, that was to be seen.

"Why do you want to change jobs? It looks like you had a good thing going at the W Bar W?"

"Well Sir, my daughter's family moved to Claremont recently and I purely missed visiting them so when I read this here ad for ranch hands and a cook I came up to see if it would work out for me."

"Alright, you're hired on probation. If you can cook and the men like what you cook you'll have the job.

"Sure 'nough, Mr. Tomlinson. I couldn't expect you to buy a pig in a poke so the boys are goin' to love me, just you wait and see. I just wanted you to know I'm what you call versatile; I can do most any job on a ranch except maybe shoeing horses."

Emmett Boggs stood up, all 200 pounds of him, heavy for such a medium sized man, but Hank judged that very little of that weight was fat. The man was clean and neat in his attire and had clean nails, which was important in a cook.

"If I hire another cook you'll be hired as an all round hand. Is that acceptable to you?"

"Thank you Sir, that's certainly fair." They shook hands and Hank showed him out to the bunkhouse and the cook's quarters.

Later Hank stopped by their cottage to talk to May for a bit. "Man, this day is fried and I'm not going to accomplish any real work around here." he stopped and sighed,

"Well, that's not exactly true 'cause I guess hiring men is part of being a Ranch Manager's job. At least I've hired a cook for the crew on probation so you don't have to do that anymore. Actually honey, with the extra men to feed I don't want you working that hard. Now you'll just have me to cook for." and grinned wiggling his eyebrows at her which made her giggle.

"It certainly will be a relief not to have to cook so many big meals a day. Do you think the boys will like this new cook?"

"If they don't I'll hire someone else and put Mr. Boggs on a ranch hand's pay. Also May, if you still want to take care of the big house I plan on getting you some extra help as soon as I can get the overseers approval, but if you'd rather not do that anymore then they can hire a full time housekeeper for the boys."

"No, I like taking care of the house and it helps fill my day. Anyway, it's extra money for our retirement fund, not that you care what I do with my salary. Yes, I certainly would appreciate the extra help especially with the heavier cleaning jobs."

Hank heaved another self pitting sigh. "I guess I'll go do some paperwork and have it ready for the meeting tomorrow and I've got one last interview at 4:00 o'clock. Hopefully it will go as easy as the others did. I'll see you around five Sweetheart." and kissed his wife and headed for the ranch house office.

It didn't. The man was slovenly and smelled of liquor and his personality just wasn't what Hank wanted on the ranch. The man said he had been driving through and read the ad while at lunch. Hank thanked him for stopping, but told him that they had enough hands to do the work. Well, the man wasn't happy about that and got up without a thank you and slammed out the front door.

Hank was much happier with the next applicant who walked into the office. He gave his name as Hoss Charlie had a recommendation from Blackhawk who said Hoss was an all round hand and a good man with horses and cattle. Hank hired him after about six minutes of conversation.

It was going on 5:00 o'clock and Hank was about to call it a day and close the office when there was a knock at the front door.

When he opened it, he stopped and looked way up at the tall thin man standing on the porch with his hat in his hand. Hank couldn't remember having seen an uglier face. It looked like it had been put together with mismatched features left over that no one else wanted and stuck them in a long face. Yet despite those physical drawbacks to handsomeness, the man possessed the most beautiful, large, deep blue lapis lazuli eyes that were fringed with inch long eyelashes a woman would kill for plus they shone with a humorous light.

Hank had to smile, "Can I help you, Sir?"

"Well, Mr. Tomlinson, I surely hope so, maybe. Hank Zeggler sent me over on the off chance you might still be hiring?" The man's deep velvety base voice rolled over Hank like rich dark molasses. Hmm, an irrelevant thought appeared, I wonder if the man can sing.

"Sure 'nough stranger, come on in." Hank opened the screen door and the man ducked his head as he passed under the lintel. "Come on back to the office and we'll talk. Say, can you sing? You have the sort of voice that sounds like you could, coming as it does from such a long deep well." questioned Hank with a grin and the man laughed and it simply flowed out in a long wave that had Hank smiling without effort.

"Yes, Sir, I sang regularly in our church choir. Now they surely miss me as I could sing in place of the whole kit and caboodle of them if'n I was allowed to, that is. Yes sir, I do sing and the cows purely love me too." The man stooped again to clear the lintel of the office doorway.

"It's an asset if you do as when we ranchers and other farm people get together we have lots of music. Do you have any references? How long have you been a ranch hand and where did you last work? First, let's begin with your name." Hank busily got out a clean sheet of paper.

"My name is Conrad Divine Clive, but men mostly call me Divine, why I don't know, but it's my moniker now. I grew up on a ranch in Texas?" Hank could have surmised that from the way the man drawled and ended his statements with a question mark as all good Texans did.

"I've a degree in Animal Husbandry from University of Texas and I've recently work on the OK Ranch in Raton Pass in Colorado for the past seven years? I left there because the boss didn't want me courting his daughter? My heart being broken, I headed out west to find a new home. I did receive a good reference from Mr. Baker before I left and here it is along with my degree and all."

Handing over the documents as Hank struggled not to let his jaw drop. It didn't take long for Hank to read through the reference letter and look over Divine's degree. Well, this was a real asset for the ranch if indeed the man was all he said he was.

"You're hired Divine and glad to have you with us." Hank got up to shake the man's hand. Divine still sat in the chair and twisted his hat around a few times before looking up.

"Ah, thank you kindly Sir. There is somethin' else I think I should mention? Ah, I've got a little brother who just turned eighteen and I'm sort of his guardian until he's 21? Well, ah, I had to bring him with me. He's a real hard worker and magic with horses and all. He's a serious young man and his work is appreciated where we lived before? Ah, he plays the violin good enough to make the angels weep too." Divine smiled hopefully up at Hank.

Divine looked so like an ugly puppy begging for a kindly pat that Hank sat down and began to laugh. Divine grinned in response then ducked his head and twisted his hat around some more.

"Is he with you now?" chuckled Hank.

"Yes Sir, he's out in the truck waiting for me."

"Go get him 'cause I want to see this serious hard working young man before I commit myself." Hank commanded, but Divine was already out the door before Hank could finish. Hank laughed and wondered how the Thunder Gods figured in this comedy.

Divine and the serious youngster entered the office. Lordymassyme, thought Hank with his eyebrows breaching the heavens, I've got two giants on my hands now. Lordy, the grocery bill just went through the roof! Though tall and well built, the young man was a head shorter than his older brother and certainly a lot prettier too, however there was no mistaking the relationship.

"Mr. Tomlinson, this is my brother, Jacob Divine Clive? Say howdy to Mr. Tomlinson, Jake."

"How do you do Sir, it's a pleasure to meet you." and held out a strong hand and when Hank shook it he felt the calluses and the strength of the grip. Yep, he was a worker alright judging from his hard hand.

"Well, sit down and tell me about yourself, Jake." Hank couldn't wait for this revelation.

"I've worked on our ranch since I was a young pup until father died a few years ago. Connie, ah I mean, Divine became my guardian and I went to live with him? There wasn't much to the ranch so we sold it. I guess I'm a jack of all trades Sir, and I can lend a hand to almost anything having to do with ranch work, but I'm really good at horseshoeing? I apprenticed with a Ferrier for two, almost three years and I really liked it. Maybe I could help out with that sort of thing here along with any other work you might have that needs doing?" the young man cast an anxious look at his brother.

The long and the tall of it; Divine and Jake were hired on the spot. The only problem would be to find beds long enough to fit their frames, chuckled Hank. Well, shoot, we'll just have to build some he though cheerfully. He got up to show the men to their cabins and was delighted to find that they carried their own beds with them and guessed they'd learned the hard way about the discomfort of sleeping in ordinary beds. Best of all they had a horse trailer that held four big horses That too was a smart move on their part because finding horses big enough to carry these long legged galoots would have been a challenge.

Hank went home that evening in a much happier frame of mind considering the way the day had begun. He delighted May in describing their newest hands as they ate dinner. She got such a bang out of the Clive brothers and the others that she vowed to bake the new men a huge cake as a welcome to the ranch. Hank laughed and said they'd all enjoy that.

"The biggest problem I thought I'd have with the Clive brothers would be finding them horses tall enough to keep their feet from dragging on the ground, but they brought their own, thank God." They laughed at the picture that made.

Hank made the last phone call of the day. "Hey, Ben, just wait until you see my new crew. I've hired five men and one of them is a cook/handyman. Man alive, they're some of the funniest and best men I've had the privilege to have under me so y'all are in for a surprise." Hank waited for a few minutes then laughed. "No, no I won't say another word, I believe seeing a picture is better than a thousand words so I'll see you tomorrow." and hung up before Ben could ask anymore questions.

The sun had long gone behind the western mountains and night enfolding the land as Hank stood on his front porch and looked up at Thunder Mountain and said. "Guardians, I've got a hunch that we've got trouble heading our way and I don't know what it is, but I have a feeling it's going to get worse. Help us if You will, if You can. Harm to none is our motto for the Valleys, but what do we do if it turns out that we're dealing with a violent person? Help and protect us and our animals too. Thank you."

Hank walked back into the cottage and turned off the lights as he and May went early to bed for a well earned rest. Tomorrow would be a brand new day.

~Hank~

BLACKHAWK STEPPED OUT OF his truck and glanced around Ben's ranch yard watching all the activity for a moment then caught sight of Mike and a dog running toward him.

"Morning, Godfather, how are you today?" Mike smiled at the man with real warmth because there was something so solid, so enduringly strong about Blackhawk as though he was a giant Oak Tree with roots all the way to the center of the Earth. It was that essence of security that assured Mike that if he ever had a real problem this man and Ben too, would stand firmly with him. Mike thought yeah, I guess you'd call that real down to earth security and chuckled.

"I'm fine Mike, and you're looking good too. I see Roscoe had finally found himself a boy to take care of." Blackhawk said with a grin and greeted the big dog with some loving pats.

"Yeah, we've decided we're buddies and we're both happy about that; he's a really good dog, you know. Well, let's go inside." and led his Godfather up the front steps. "I hope this vandalism is one of those random kinda deals; some kid having a lark. I can't imagine why I'd be the only target. I guess we'll have to wait to see if this happens to one of the other ranchers." Mike opened the door and stood aside for the older man to enter first.

"I agree with you so let's wait until we're all together to discuss the situation." and proceeded down the hall to the kitchen.

"Good morning everyone, it's a lovely day and a special good morning to you Hannah, as if anyone could ignore the most famous cook in all the Valleys." Blackhawk said as he walked into busy kitchen.

"You're just saying that because you're out of cookies." Chuckled Hannah not in the least impressed with the compliment, but before Blackhawk could defend himself he got interrupted abruptly.

"God-Daddy, God-Daddy, hold me, Carli." she yelled. Blackhawk laughed at the little beauty holding up her arms demanding attention and scooped her up twirled her around a few times to her squeals of laughter.

"How can I resist such a demand from a beautiful girl? I tell you, Carli my love, no man is safe around you." and laughed.

"Kisses, God-Daddy, kisses," and puckered up so he smacked her once good and loud which set her giggling again.

"Girl, I'd walk a mile for one of those sweet kisses." and gave her a big hug. "There now, you sit down and finish your breakfast so you'll grow more beautiful." when Blackhawk look up he saw everyone watching him with grins on their faces.

"What are y'all grinning about? I'm sure you're all invincible to her charms, right? I'm just going with the flow here." He said with grave dignity and only the sparkle in his eyes betrayed him and that set everyone off.

"Joe, do you want to come to the meeting? You're an owner too." asked Ben.

"Yes Sir, I think I must even though Mike will be the real rancher I have to be responsible too don't I?" and Joe was very serious about that and no one laughed.

"Indeed you do Joe and your comments would be of great value I'm sure. Well so let's get on with it." Ben finished his coffee, got up, kissed Mari Beth and then Carli before she could demand one and said goodbye then got his hat and jacket and left the kitchen.

"Bye everyone, we'll see you all later." Blackhawk and the boys followed Ben.

Blackhawk stopped his truck abruptly when they arrived at the entrance to Kelly's Ranch road, shocked to see the beautifully newly designed ranch sign covered in red painted letters that said, **"It's only the beginning."**

Blackhawk muttered a word under his breath before he said, "How in the heck did I miss that on my way over to the ranch? I must be going blind in my old age."

"I guess I can say now that *we are* the target for the vandalism." Mike said in a quiet voice that covered his anger.

"This must have been done last night, but with the guard at the gate how did the man get away with it? Does Hank know about it?

Of course, the sign is about fifty yards away from the gate and that might account for no one knowing about it. Hmm, sneaky son-of-a-gun, isn't he?" murmured Blackhawk in a thoughtful way and drove on up to the locked gate where he was cheerfully greeted by a strange cowboy.

"Mornin' gentlemen, great morning isn't it? I guess we'd better enjoy it for it's looking nasty over the mountain. Oh, I'm Jimmy Kilpatrick, one of the Kelly's new hands. Nothing happened last night or so Grumpy said."

"Well, young man, something did happen here last night. Better look at the ranch sign out by the road." Jimmy's grim face said it all as he unlocked the gate and swung it open to let the black pickup drive through.

Parking at the front of the ranch house Blackhawk turned off the engine and turned to look at the sober faces of the young boys in the back seat and then at Ben sitting silently beside him. "Well, I guess we have trouble on our hands. Let's go see Hank."

Hank was upset when he heard the news. "I can't believe this took place right under Grumpy's nose. Give me a minute and I'll call him." Hank went to the phone and called the bunkhouse and his muffled voice could be heard by the others waiting in the living room.

When the manager came back in he only said, "He was asleep, but he'll be up in a minute." Then sat down and silence filled the room as each one thought about what could be done to stem the tide of vandalism and find the reason behind it. They heard the kitchen door opened and close then footsteps coming down the hallway and Grumpy appeared in the doorway with his hat clutched in his hands.

"Yes Sir, you wanted to see me?" Grumpy was still rumpled from sleep as he had only been in bed for a few hours.

"Come on in Grumpy and have a seat." The man sat down on the edge of the chair and wondered why he had been pulled out of bed. Something had to have happened and it made him nervous. "You're a good reliable man Grump and we all know that. Did you hear anything suspicious last night, any unusual sounds out close to the road?"

Grumpy looked startled then thought back and said. "Well, I thought I heard a car in the distance, but it was pretty far away, maybe half a mile or so. Like maybe it was coming from the east County Road just before it swings past Strongbow's and heads south on Thunder Road? Still there wasn't anything up close so I didn't pay much attention. You know how sound carries on a still night." Grumpy twisted his hat a few turns before he asked hesitantly, "Did something happen, Boss?"

"Yes, our new ranch sign was vandalized with words in red paint, 'it's only the beginning.'" said Hank.

"*Goldangit, boss*, I didn't hear a thing from the front of our road. Why, that sneaky *bastard*!" Using cuss words was extremely unlike the quiet and controlled Grumpy. They watched in amazement as he crushed his hat between his hands and turn all red in the face with shame. "*Goldangit* how am I to live down this….this *shame* in front of the men? Right under my nose this son of a no good horse thief, fence cuttin' bastard got away with messin' with us again." The man looked like he was going to break down and cry.

"Stop right there Grumpy, it wasn't your fault. Your job was to guard the gate and if you didn't hear anything it just confirms that he *is* a sneaky….so and so." said Hank forcefully and got up and walked over to the man and held out his hand for Grumpy to take and the shamed man stood and finally shook Hank's hand.

"I'm right sorry, Hank, right sorry I missed him. Judas Priest, I wished I'd caught him at it." Then he looked over at Mike and said, "I'm real sorry Mr. Kelly."

"It wasn't your fault Mr. Tucker."

"Well, that is as may be, Mr. Kelly, but I still feel mighty bad about it."

"I'll walk back with you to the bunkhouse and explain to the others what happened. I guess it would make you feel better if you were the one to take care of the sign and bring it up to the ranch so Sheriff Brandt can see it. Our next sign will be nailed high over the entrance and we'll see if that guy likes climbing up a pole to do his nastiness." grinned Hank. "We may be a step or two behind this guy right now, but eventually we'll catch him then watch what happens to this sneaky no good trouble maker."

Grumpy gave a short laugh which belied his nick name as he was a cheerful kind of man. Actually his real name was Grumstead Tucker, but he hated his first name, one of those family names that got passed down from long dead ancestors; hence the men had nicknamed him Grumpy which he didn't mind at all. Cowboy nicknames had a way that either matched the man's personality or as a complete opposite branding. Cowboy humor; you gotta' figure them for mavericks.

"Yeah, I could stand to see that and watch the so and so get splinters in his butt." Grumpy straighten out his hat and followed Hank out of the living room.

It was quiet until the sound of the kitchen door closing broke the stasis. "So much has happened this past week, what with getting this ranch ready for winter. This is just about the last thing we needed. I thought things were going just a little too smoothly. I purely hate to be a pessimist." commented Mike in a very doleful voice.

Ben looked over at the tired young man and felt the same way and sighed. "The timing of this certainly puts a clog in our wheel. Why we're the target is the question. Well, men, let's wait for Hank 'cause he needs to be in on this discussion. Does anyone want coffee? I bet May might have left something for us in the kitchen." They got up to investigate and kept the business buttoned.

They sat down at the kitchen table to wait and it wasn't long before Hank returned, got his coffee and sat down at the table.

Mike looked around at the quiet men, cleared his throat and said, "You know this is like what Dad would have called a "Round Table" where we'd discuss important matters. So, how did it go with the men, Hank?"

"Just as you would have expected Mike; they were mad as hornets, but not at Grumpy. I don't think Grump will get much sleep today, he's so upset. Other than that the men are all on alert and guards are posted which means there won't be much ranch work done today. Man, this is really screwing us up big time and we still have a lot to do before snow flies. I gotta figure that this man, who ever he is, knows what a monkey wrench he's thrown into the works. That's part of this harassment." Hank said in a definite way and drank some coffee.

"It appears we have a personal vendetta on our hands so I think we need to hire more men, don't you?" Mike looked to his manager.

"Yes Mike, that's for sure, but I've just hired five men yesterday and that makes us a total of eight workers including a cook, nine counting me. Maybe some of the other ranchers can loan us a man or two if they're all caught up on their work that is." said Hank in a depressed way.

"Whatever it takes to keep this guy out and everyone safe including our animals we'll do it. Maybe we'll get lucky and catch him in the act. I'm just fearful that his next act might be more destructive like fire or hurting the animals. Well, we're definite on the defensive side of things with no knowledge of where he'll strike next." commented Blackhawk.

Mike listened, however it was Joe who said. "I think the cattle should be moved to the back of the ranch and away from the road for awhile and maybe we'd better guard the back of the ranch a little bit more too."

"Thanks Joe, you're right and I also want to put on extra men to guard the ranch buildings, the house and the barns; I don't want any people or animals hurt if it can be helped." said Mike firmly. "We've got the money so hire extra men to do the job right."

Ben nodded. "I agree with Mike, one hundred percent. All right, we know that this vandal isn't a cowboy as the shoe print in that cow patty proved. Hmm, I think Hank's right too and we should ask the other ranchers if they can spare us an extra man or two from each place and we'll pay for their time while they're needed here that way they won't lose their permanent jobs. I don't want to hire men for just this emergency then fire them when it's over because that wouldn't be fair to men who need permanent jobs. I'll call around and see if we can shake loose a few good hands." said Ben, and then slapped his thigh angrily.

"Blast it all, I need extra men myself to get those cattle off the mesa this week. This good weather will be turning nasty soon and I won't risk losing cattle up there. Mike, remind me to contact Dusty Evan and see who he might have lined up to help us. We need to know how many men we're going to have to handle that big herd. Well, I guess this is one of those times when we're going to lean heavily on our kind neighbors. We're in a big bind. Hmm, let's back up here a minute, I'm galloping ahead too fast."

Ben rubbed his face and sat still thinking while the others waited. "What do y'all think about holding a large town meeting? It would be a way for us to tell everyone what's going on so they'll be on the look out for any stranger and at the same time we can ask for paid temporary guards. The more people that are involved the strongest we are. This sort of thing affects all the Valleys. We'll get the local paper to tell the story as well." concluded Ben.

"That's smart! Let's ask the ladies to call the ranchers and the farm people about the extra men. Hah, the gossip line will spread the word faster then the speed of light. Alright, this is Saturday and that storm is beginning to head in so how long will it last, Blackhawk?" asked Hank.

"It's going to blast through and be gone by midnight tonight so I'm suggesting that we make those calls today and ask everyone who can to come to River Town on Sunday and meet at the Preacher's church. Maybe Hank Zeggler can come so Claremont can get the word that we need men."

The men got quiet as each was thinking about what to do next when Joe spoke up. "Ben, I was just thinking about Luther's baby horses. This person is trying to hurt us isn't he?" Joe got nods so he went on. "Well, one of the ways he could do that would be to hurt our friends. Maybe we'd better get them to guard their places too." Joe offered hesitantly.

"Hey brother, good thinking." and slapped Joe lightly on the shoulder before turning to the others. "Joe's right, our friends might be in trouble even though these attacks have a personal feel to them and directed at us, but we don't want anyone hurt because of us."

"That's good solid thinking Joe. You bet this is personal and I can assure you that the Thunder Gods are aware of what's going on too." Ben said emphatically.

"Yes they are Ben, but they can't act unless the land or animals are harmed or human blood is spilled and that hasn't happened yet. They're letting us work out our own problems unless something happens to change that." said Blackhawk.

"Lord knows I don't want this vandalism to escalate so we'll do the best we can to handle the problem by ourselves." Ben said.

"Maybe Godfather could ask for a little protection for all of us from the Thunder Gods, sort of a prevention kind of prayer." suggested Joe in a quiet voice.

"Prayer or supplication never hurt and while the Gods won't actually take action They just might subtly direct our attention.

Hmm, yes that too is something we can all do. Thank you Joe for the reminder." nodded the Chief.

"Alright, let's make that list and get busy. Blackhawk, you'll want to get home before this storm worsens. By the way, it has been suggested that we electrify our boundary fences with generators and I think that's a good idea. At least it would help protect the property next to the road. However, we don't have time to do that right now. We'll deal with that after we do the cattle drive."

Driving back to Strongbow's they passed through the gate and saw Grumpy and a couple of other men putting up tall poles with an overhead support beam that would eventually bear the new ranch sign. Mike rolled down the window as Blackhawk stopped for a minute.

"Thanks guys, I sure would like to see that man mess with that sign, wouldn't you?" called Mike. "He's make a prime target for a shotgun loaded with rock salt."

"Hey boss, that's not a bad idea and it wouldn't draw blood… exactly, but it would be mighty painful in his nether parts, yes indeedy it would. I was thinking of doing what the old telegraph men used to do by pounding sharp nails into the sides of the poles and snapping off the heads to keep buffalo from pushing them over. It didn't work. The buffalo just thought the poles were good scratching places. However I had to give that idea up as it would have spilled blood. Darn, it was such a good idea to." Grumpy said mournfully. The other men were laughing as Blackhawk continued on down the road.

Trouble was on them again, thought Mike, just when everything seemed to be going so well. Who was this man and why had he chosen them to target? Something wicked was out there and he knew they hadn't seen the worse yet.

The storm was beginning to gather in strength and there was a noticeable drop in temperature as it began to sweep down though the Valleys warning them that winter was coming their way sooner than later. From the front porch Mike and Joe waved goodbye to Blackhawk then stood there in the cold wind watching their Godfather disappear down the road.

"Well, Joe I guess we've got another big challenge." worried Mike.

"Yep, we sure do, but we're stronger now and there are more of us than just you and me against the world which means, big brother, that nasty man is badly out numbered." Joe said emphatically with a sharp nod of his head.

Mike laughed. "Joe, can I say you make me proud right down to the ground without you punching me?"

Joe punched him in the arm. "Guess not." And they began to wrestle about knocking over chairs, hats flying and laughing like fools with Roscoe leaping and jumping on them in delight at the mayhem.

Ben watched them through the front window and felt relieved. Scared as they might be of this unknown vandal they were tougher now and more confident now than before. But more importantly their spirits were stronger. "You're alright kids, you're the best and I'm proud of you." said Ben, more or less to himself, not knowing that his wife stood behind him and had been watching the horseplay on her front porch.

She slipped her arms around his waist startling him for a moment then he relaxed. "And I'm really, really proud of you too, big man." They stood there for awhile before turning and walked arm in arm into the living room where a nice log fire was burning.

~Roundup~

IT WAS 5:00 O'CLOCK in the morning and as dark as the inside of a cat except for the flood lights that lit the ranch yard yet one sensed that dawn wasn't that far off. The stars had begun to lose their brilliance and a chill wind swept across the yard reminding them that summer was over and they'd be riding in the cold until the sun came up.

Mike stood on the back porch in his sheepskin coat and chaps with Roscoe sitting beside him. Joe was standing on his other side and Mike thought how like cowboys they looked now that they were similarly dressed. He knew he was going to be doing double duty for the next few days watching over his brother and pushing cows out of the bushes at the same time, but he didn't want Joe to miss this event for all the tea in China.

The all men were gathered in the ranch yard with their horses. Steam billowed out of the men's and horse's nostrils make it look like the ranch yard was full of small burst of many little smokes. Just then a large truck arrived pulling a big horse trailer and hitched to that was a chuck wagon and hitched to the back of that wagon was a big portable stove. The whole thing looked like a long gypsy caravan. When it stopped the men quickly unhitch the chuck wagon. The truck with the horse van drove forward ten feet or so before stopping. The men then opened up the trailer and unloaded four big handsome and sturdy Belgian Horses, blond as a Palomino, but four times as strong. Hitching them to the chuck wagon took only a few minutes as they were already wearing their harnesses.

The portable stove and grill on wheels was one of the inventions of the old line cook, Dusty Evans and good for events such as roundups, barbeques, hunting parties and fiestas. Dusty was the best in the business and competition was hot for his services. The older man had a reputation for running a first class operation and the cook was also boss of any camp. A superior camp cook meant good and plentiful food as well as a clean organized camp which made all the difference in lessening the discomforts of outdoor living.

There was another covered wagon of Ben's that was filled with bedrolls, tents, ground sheets, air cushions, blankets, extra saddles, harness, supplies , rifles and a good medical kit plus anything and everything else essential to camping out. Ben's work horses were already hitched up.

Mike had worked so hard on his ranch the previous week that Mike marveled that he wasn't asleep on his feet. Word had spread about the meeting at church and when one rancher or person was threatened everyone felt threatened and they came. Mike remembered clearly what Ben had said yesterday after church services.

Ben had stood up in front of the congregation and said, "Well neighbors, thank you for coming and I'm sure the Preacher appreciated the large turnout as well as the extra donations." The Preacher got up and bowed to the congregation they gave him enthusiastic applause. Ben waited until the clapping died down before continuing.

"I knew you would come for this is what we do for each other. You have no doubt heard what is happening at the Kelly place, Lost Wagon Ranch. A man has decided to victimize my young boys by acts of trespass, property damage and with threats that there is more is to come. Young Joe Kelly worried that this vandal would try hurting you all just to hurt them, so I'm warning you to be on the look out for a stranger who might want to do more than just malicious mischief next time.

Okay, here are the facts. Number one: We need extra hands to help the Kellys finish getting their ranch ready for winter so I'd appreciate it if some of you ranchers and farmers could lend us a few men next week. We did a lot last week and for those who helped us, we can't thank you enough. A couple more days of hard work should see them over the top of their priorities. We'll pay the salaries of any man who volunteers just as we have before.

Number two: We also need volunteers to help guard the Kellys property so their men can continue to do the ranch work. They just can't be in two places at once as I'm sure you understand. We need to protect the ranch. We'll pay good wages plus a bonus for any man who volunteers to help. I won't hire a man temporarily than fire him so I want men who have permanent jobs to go back to once this emergency is over.

Number three: Just as I have done in past years I need at least ten more men to help gather about six hundred head of cattle off the Flat Top Mesa and drive them down to my lower ranch. Under these unusual circumstances I don't dare stripe my ranch of men. I already have ten men I can count on, but I'll need another ten to do a fast and thorough job.

We leave for the mesa at 5:00 o'clock tomorrow morning from my ranch so anyone signing up now had better be there with bells on. The weather is turning fast and Flat Top Mesa is six thousand feet to eight thousand feet in elevation. We don't have time to dilly-dally around folks.

There it in a nutshell, we need your help and I'm willing to pay good wages for anyone who wants to help us. Okay, I've spoken my piece and we thank for coming. Now first off, we need at least six men for guard duty so see Hank Tomlinson over there at that table. The five men who will help finish work on Kelly's place please see Pike John, Kelly's foreman at that other table. For the cowboys who want a little bit more excitement, see me about the roundup right up here. Thank you all for coming."

The meeting broke up with men crowding up to the tables and it didn't take five minutes for the business to be accomplished. For the roundup, Hank was sending Jimmy Jumper, as the men had dubbed the young man, as a representative of Kelly ranch and personal bodyguard to the Kelly boys. Two of Ben's men would go along with Luther' two of his men plus Dan and two of his cowboys.

The funny part of this was how to deal with so many men wanting to go on roundup. It had Ben laughing helplessly at the crowd before his table. Some of these men had been in on his roundups before and a few new men had come down from the north valley specifically for this roundup. Ben finally signed on fifteen men, five more than he wanted or needed. Actually it was all fifteen men that had lined up waiting their turn. Ten men got signed right away and the last five men had actually gone down on their knees and gave such elaborate reasons why it was essential that Ben take them along, all the reasons being absolutely ridiculous of course, but they had Ben laughing like a maniac. Their strategy worked as he hired the jokers. Some of the

True Heart

extra men wanted to come along for free just for the fun of it, as it was a good excuse for joining in; crashing the party is all Ben would say as he laughed. However, Ben said if they worked he'd pay.

Mike was laughing behind his hand as he watched from the sidelines as money was quietly being passed off to one side. Mike nudged Joe's arm and head gestured to what the men were doing.

Joe giggled. "Dad used to say cowboys would bet on anything."

So here they were on a very cold dark morning waiting for Ben to give the signal to start. Within a few minutes he came out of the kitchen wearing the same kind of clothing as they did and stood with the boys. You can get mighty cold sitting a saddle all day if you weren't warmly dressed especially at the altitude on the mesa.

"Pull those gloves on, boys and keep your scarves wrapped around your ears under your hats, because cold ears hurt." Ben looked down at the dog. "Is he coming?"

"Yes Sir, because I don't think he'll stay behind, not unless I lock him up and that's no good 'cause he'll just follow me when they let him loose. He's done it before." replied Mike.

"He's your dog."

Mike grinned at that and stroked the dog's head; yep Roscoe was his dog and where he went Roscoe went most of the time and that's just the way it should be.

Ben stepped to the edge of the porch, cupped his hands around his mouth and yelled. "Let's head out." He and his boys along with the dog, walked down the steps to their waiting horses.

Ben had given Joe a brown cutting horse named Jigger, smaller than most of the cutting horses Ben owned, but he was fast, talented, mighty quick on his feet. One of the cowboys said Jigger could turn on a dime and give you back change. The horse was gentle and easy to handle plus being a good ride which was a little unusual as most quarter horses have a rough trot. Jigger also possessed a beautifully shaped head and wide between the eyes. Ben said that that denoted a larger brain and more intelligence.

Mike's horse was a big black except for four white socks and a white nose. His name was Sherlock because he was so clever. Ben claimed that the horse could think just like a man. One of the common traits in Ben's horses was their good dispositions. There wasn't a mean or dumb one in the bunch.

Ben, Mike and Joe took the lead up the north track toward the mountains and everyone else fell into line behind the chuck wagon and the supply wagon, at least those who weren't driving the extra horses.

They had thirty riders not counting the boys. There was no question that they had more men than they actually needed, but Ben had a lot of cows to roust out of the bush in the small feeder canyons and that took time and they didn't have much of that. The Mesa was a big, big place and they'd have a lot of ground to cover. The push was to get it all done quickly because the weather was definitely not going to get any better. These men worked hard at routine jobs and they wanted a little piece of what the old west had been like, being as they *were* cowboys after all.

Mike had learned about the fierce competition among most all the men each year to help Ben Strongbow move his cattle back and forth. Mike wondered if Ben knew that these men had already drawn lots to see who got to go on his cattle drives this fall. One lottery was held when Ben moved the cattle from the ranch's pastures up to the mesa and another lottery with different men to bring them back down again. Of course there was more challenge in the fall rounding up the cattle scattered all over the mesa not to mention into all those slot canyons too. Man, the competition was fierce and Mike was surprised to find out that it was Dusty Evans, a man all the men trusted to do the honest thing without argued about the results. Dusty's word was law and no one in their right minds wanted to mess with Dusty for some unknown reason.

Mike rode through the cold dark morning with his gloved hands stuffed in his pockets and pretty much allowed Sherlock to follow the other horses.

Ben had been concerned about his obvious fatigue and he had suggested Mike stay home for another day to rest then come out later. Mike vehemently said that he was okay and wanted to go so Ben reluctantly agreed. Right now maybe Ben had been right after all and that he should have stayed behind for another day. Well, he was here now and that was that.

Mike sat his saddle with his chin tucked into the turned up sheepskin collar. The rhythmic pace of his horse soon put him to sleep. Unknown to Mike Joe was watching his brother and worrying that Mike was much too tired to be starting out on days of even harder work. Mike was overdoing it was Joe's opinion. He was trying to work like an adult to prove to everyone he was responsible.

Joe had worked too, but all he had been allowed to do was to "gopher" and it had run him a little ragged. He was keeping up, but Ben saw him getting tired so he sent Joe to the house to see if he could help Henry or Mike the Mighty.

Yes, he was still a little tired from days of steady work, but not like Mike. Joe guessed he'd have to take better care of his brother and fetch and carry for him so he wouldn't collapse which would humiliate Mike to no end. Joe rode along beside his brother for awhile when a new thought came to him.

Golly, they had school next Monday. "Sure hope I don't fall asleep in class." mumbled Joe. He plodded along for awhile suddenly Joe let out such a hooting kind of laugher that it had Jigger dancing around a little bit. Mike sat up straight in the saddle, looked around then slumped back into a semi-doze.

Joe muffled his mouth with a gloved hand, his eyes fairly sparked with glee. Gee, the kids at school are really going to be impressed because we're the only boys that got to go on roundup. Ha, what a brilliant thought. Joe giggled. Man oh man, that's what I call making an entrance! He must remember to tell Mike about it.

It took the riders a little over three hours to make the trip up to the mesa. Once they got into the climb up through the gap there was only a very rough track to follow. The so-called road was so steep in places that riders had to rope onto the wagons to help   pull them up.

The sun had warmed the morning air just as they arrived at the selected campsite Dusty had chosen. The site sat back in the furthest northwestern corner snuggled into the north cliff and not to far away from the waterfalls.

"Why did Dusty set the camp so far back, Ben? Won't the noise of the falls disturb everyone's sleep?" questioned Joe.

"Well, it's necessary for the camp to be out of the way in case the cattle stampede. If that should happen chances are they'd likely head downhill toward the gap which would be okay. It would be much worse if they'd stampeded back south on the mesa and might run right off the cliffs if we can't turn them back. Cattle have a herd mentality, that's sort of a collective mind, so all that's needed to trigger a stampede is for a few cows to begin running and they're all up and running too and nothing had better get in their way. As far as the noise from the falls is concerned, it isn't that loud and it's actually quite relaxing."

The men dismounted and loosened the horses' saddle girths and threw off their coats. Dusty began setting up the camp and giving directions to the men helping to unload the wagons, chopping wood, digging a fire pit and starting a big fire. Dusty got busy preparing breakfast and soon hot coffee was ready and so were the men.

Mike and Joe walked out away from the hubbub, stomping their feet to get the feeling back in their stiff legs with Roscoe leading the way, sniffing at everything. Every once in a while he'd stop and look back to make sure Mike was following then would continue on.

"Roscoe, come here boy." Slapping his chaps with his hand and the dog immediately came back to sit beside him. "Good dog, you stick close now 'cause you can't tell what's out in those woods so you just stay with me, you hear?" and Roscoe gave his master his silly grin with his tongue hanging out that had Mike laughing and gently slapped the dog's shoulder.

"Looks like Roscoe is your dog for sure, which doesn't surprise me at all. He was always following you around hoping you'd notice him. I guess you finally did huh." said Joe smiling at the dog.

"Yeah I noticed him. Ben doesn't mind because Roscoe didn't belong to anyone so he's mine alright or maybe I'm his." laughed Mike.

From the small knoll, they look southeast through the steep gap leading down into Ben's upper ranch. Mesa was a Spanish word for table and a huge table it was too and the first the boys had seen up close. Ben said it contained over four thousand acres of good grass and water and was the summer pasture for his cows. It was a glorious pastureland bordered and protected on the north and west by steep mountains thickly covered with pine, maple and aspen trees.

"Golly Mike, isn't it beautiful up here? The air is so pure it makes you feel all tingly inside. It looks like it's been this way for a million years. Right now I feel just like an old fashioned cowboy. Why, we would have to watch out for Indian attacks just like in olden times." exclaimed the excited boy.

"Kid, you sure do have an active imagination kid, but I have to agree it's a super sight. Even though I'm pretty tired out I'm glad I came because this is adventure with a capitol A and not one to pass up."

"Oh yes, indeedy it is that for sure. You know, I was thinking on the way up here how the kids at school are going to be drooling in envy when we tell them about this 'cause we're the only kids among all these men." Joe laughed. "I'm taking lots of pictures and making notes too. It's all going to be frosting on the cake, Mike and we'll rub it in."

Mike slapped Joe on the back and joined the laughter. "Talk about an ice breaker, this should do it. Okay, bro, let's get back to camp 'cause I think breakfast is ready and I'm as hungry as a starving wolf. I can see some of the men already beginning to tighten their cinches so that means action, drama, adventure and cow chasing. Race you back to camp." With a whoop Mike took off with Joe thundering behind him and Roscoe again leading the way. Their legs were working just fine.

After a hurried breakfast Ben stood up and said. "Men, we'll start at the south end of the mesa and begin driving cows toward camp. Luther, you take a couple of men and select the best place to hold the herd. I suggest midway or somewhere close to that finger of land sticking out into the river. Dusty, we'll be back around noon for lunch and you better make it hot and a lot because we'll be starving men. Mount up boys and let's move cattle."

The horses moved out at a fast canter down the middle of the mesa with Ben riding beside Mike and Luther had Joe as a partner. The boys' excitement was a palatable thing and caused more than one man to feel responsible to look out for these two young boys, mostly young Joe, but that was okay with them as the kids gave the men permission to be excited too.

Once they arrived at the mesa's cliffs they had already seen plenty of cows. The men spread out and began hunting the bush. Mike and Joe along with Ben, Luther and Dan paused to look out and down upon the endless and glorious valley the lay before them like a map.

"Look Mike, we can see lots of ranches and some of the farms. Look we can see River Town way over there; see the smoke? Wow, what a view." Joe whipped up his camera that was hanging from a strap around his neck and began to snap pictures then turned and caught Mike and the men in swift shots as a record along with his journal so one day he could look back and live it all again.

"Alright, let's go help move these critters toward the holding area." Ben said as he turned his horse's head. "By the way boys, if you're chasin' a cow, watch out that you don't ride over the edge of the mesa. This is dangerous country and the ground is plenty rough around here so be careful."

It was hot, dusty and dirty work because those cows didn't want to leave. They had gotten as wild as deer. With a few other men, Mike and Joe pushed the cattle back up the mesa to the gathering place and it wasn't an easy job because the cows didn't take kindly to being driven. It was a revelation to see Roscoe turn into a cattle dog and his master had to laugh to see Roscoe driving a cow back into the herd.

"Good boy Roscoe, good dog, you keep them in line and I'll give you a treat tonight 'cause you're a working hand now."

At first Ben and Luther worked close with the boys to see how they handled themselves, but once they saw that they were excellent riders and knew what to do, they left them alone and went to driving cows out of the breaks.

It was a little past noon and quitting time couldn't come soon enough for Joe. Frankly four hours of driving cows and chasing them back into the small gathered herd had tired him out. He'd managed to use up several precious roles of film as the morning progressed. Now he began to worry he wouldn't have enough to last the three days as he'd only bought twenty rolls. Except for the men left to guarding the small herd the rest of them headed for camp. On the way in Joe though he better count the film he had left and divide the rolls into days so he'd have enough. Geeze peeze, he should have gotten double the amount of film for he was scared he'd miss a good shot.

When Joe climbed out of his saddle he could hardly stand as his legs were trembling with fatigue, but he unsaddled Jigger and gave him a good brisk rub down then turned him into the horse herd. Throwing his bridle over his shoulder Joe heft his heavy saddle and tried not to drag it as he staggered toward camp. He was one pooped out cowboy.

"Hey Mr. Kelly, let me give you a hand with that heavy saddle." said Jimmy. The young man possessed one of those old heads and Jimmy felt responsible for Joe. Joe thought maybe it was because he was technically Jimmy's boss, but Joe snorted at that idea.

"Well, I won't refuse a little help if I don't want to embarrass myself by falling over on my face. Thanks Jimmy." as the young man took Joe's saddle. They continued to walk toward camp when Joe said. "Say I think I caught a great picture of you chasing that ornery cow that had quit the herd. Man, she didn't want to go back without a struggle. When I get them all developed I'll give you a copy. I hope it turns out super." said Joe a little breathless as he dragged his toes in the grass a mite.

"Really?" Jimmy stopped short as though stunned. "Hey, maybe it will be seen by some big movie producer and they'll want my handsome face, great riding abilities plus my unmentionable and immense charm. Then I'll become rich and famous all because you, my buddy, took a picture of me. Wow, think of that?" said the serious faced cowboy. That sent Joe off into hysterical laughter causing him to fall down on his knees as Jimmy stood over him grinning.

Ben looked sharply over at the two when he saw Joe collapse then he saw Joe laughing fit to bust a gut and smiled. It wasn't fatigue so much as that joker Jimmy had put the kid on his knees with something he'd said. He had observed during the morning that Jimmy seemed always to be in Joe's vicinity much like a guardian angel and that relieved Ben's mind to know that someone else was looking after the eager young boy.

"Hey, Ben, I've just discovered something neat about Roscoe; he's a real cattle dog. Why you should have seen him turning cows back into the herd. Maybe he's not as useless as you thought he was." called Mike to Ben who was at the chuck wagon getting his lunch.

Ben turned around and grinned. "Well then, he's earning his food, isn't he?" Hungry men didn't talk while they consumed the generous portions of steak, mashed potatoes, beans, and corn with hot biscuits and Dusty had even made six huge berry cobblers.

Mike and Joe ate like their horses were doing, but Mike didn't forget to sneak bits of steak to the hard working dog and afterward he gave him all the bones he collected from the other men. That dog pigged out. When everyone was finished five men left to relieve the ones holding the herd so they could come and eat. The rest sat around talking while drinking another cup of coffee and resting. The guys had draw lots for the dishes after lunch. Joe pulled one of the short straws, and feeling more energized after that great meal he moved around collecting any forgotten cups and other dishes and took them over to the dishwasher.

"I forgot to warn you new fellows that we have an old mossy horn bull that lives up here. How he's escaped de-horning and roundup for the last ten years speaks of a very brainy bull. Usually he hides out in one of these small side canyons and doesn't come out to bother us. Last year was the first time we had trouble with the monster when he caught Ivan Jorgensen and horned him in the leg before his horse got him out of trouble; Do you remember that, Ivan?" that got a snort from the man. "So if you see him leave him strictly alone and get out of his way because he's as dangerous as a Grizzly Bear on the prod and three times as mean. Well, if you see him, give him all the room he wants. I let him live up here since he protects the cows from mountain lions and such, plus I don't want him down in the Valley mainly because he's just too darn dangerous. How he's managed to survive up here winter after winter without the wolves getting him or some other predator I'll never know. I want every man to carry a rifle and ride in pairs. If he charges anyone I want him killed and that's an order so pack your rifles before you go back out. Dusty has extra saddle scabbards and rifles in case anyone forgot theirs." Ben looked around at the gathering and grunted.

"Let's get going 'cause the light won't last much more than another four hours. Joe I want you to stay in camp this afternoon and help Dusty, he'll need firewood and other help. Get a rest and tomorrow you can chase cows again."

"Hey Joe, I heard tell you can sing real sweet so you can help ride night herd and sing our babies to sleep 'cause son, we sure want you to get all the pleasures of cowboy-ing." laughed Shorty Blaine, one of Dan's men.

"Yeah, I've heard rumors about these kids too. What are the chances of us having you both entertaining us tonight?" asked Miles Feather from Lightening Boy Ranch.

"Gee, fellas' I didn't bring my guitar. Sorry, but I'm sure Joe will be glad to sing for you." Mike apologized.

"The heck you didn't; guess what's in the other wagon." laughed Ben.

"Then Joe and I will put on a regular show and we expect great tips too." Mike grinned.

That got a rise out of the men. "Yeah, sure................." came an off color remark quietly spoken.

"What does that mean, Ben?" asked Joe in an aside.

"Never mind Joe, he was just trying to be funny and failed. Let's just say it wasn't nice." replied Ben fiercely frowning at the man and the man ducked his head and got busy finishing his coffee.

"Sorry Mr. Strongbow, it won't happen again." and the north valley man tossed the rest of his coffee on the fire and hurried away to saddle up.

Dan stood up and limped toward his horse and as he passed Luther, his friend stopped him and asked quietly, "How are you holding up Dan? Now don't go all macho on me, I really don't want you doing something stupid to that leg of yours."

"I'm doing okay Lute, honest. Sure it aches, but when doesn't it? I'll quit if it gets to bad and that's a promise. Heck, I'll come back to camp, sit on my butt and drink Dusty's cure all and that should fix things up real fine and I won't feel a bit of pain." and grinned at his friend, slapping Luther on the shoulder as he limped out to get another Tennessee Walker as he'd used White Boy that morning. That horse had held his own with the cutting horses even though he wasn't particularly trained as one. Luther had brought ten Walkers just for Dan's use because the man's leg just wouldn't stand up to the rough ride of some of the cutting horses. Luther just shook his head and followed along behind because there wasn't anything he could do about changing a stubborn man's mind.

Out on the mesa the afternoon was hazed with clouds of kicked up mesa dust. Back at camp Joe helped Dusty. The old man talked about the contrasts between when he was as young as Joe and worked the cattle ranches and going to the moon and the first space walks.

Joe wished he'd brought his recorder because this was history of ancient times, thought Joe in admiration. Of course he asked a thousand questions and Dusty patiently answered them all. Joe began taking a few pictures of Dusty at work. Dusty would smile when Joe tried unsuccessfully to sneak up on him for a few candid pictures. Finally he succeeded in taking one.

An hour later Dusty suggested that Joe go relax for awhile. Obediently Joe laid down on his bedroll, but didn't expect to fall asleep. He dropped off like a rock so fast he hadn't time to resist and didn't hear Dusty walk over or feel the blanket as it fell over his still body. Joe didn't wake up until he heard the men coming back to camp in the dusk of early evening which meant it was going on 5:30.

Groggily he got up and walked out to help Mike take care of his horse. Golly, Mike really looked exhausted with dark circles under his eyes too. After Mike dumped his saddle beside his bedroll Joe said, "Come on, Mike, let's get cleaned up for supper, it will make you feel a whole lot better too. You go on over to the falls and I'll grab our towels and soap."

"Okay Joe, that sounds good and the cold water ought to perk me up some." and slowly walked off toward the waterfall along with some of the other men who had the same idea. Joe decided he'd better speak to Ben and began looking for him.

Joe had to wait a few minutes until Ben finished talking to the men who would be going out on first evening guard before his foster father turned to him. "How you feeling Joe, get any rest or did Dusty work your tail off this afternoon?" Ben smiled down at the littlest cowboy.

"Oh no, Dusty was great and I'm glad I got to stay in camp because we had a good time talking and such and I took a nap too. Ah, I'm alright Ben, but I'm worried about Mike, because I think he's getting really, really tired. Isn't there something you can do about it without hurting his pride?"

"I've noticed that too, Joe, and I've kept my eye on him as well as having one other man ride with him to help him out, but that boy is a go-getter if I ever saw one and he doesn't slack for nothing. Yeah, I've got an idea of putting you, Jimmy Jumper, Sketter, Mike and two of the other valley men on holding the herd. Now it's not an easy job keeping those cows from breaking out, but it sure beats shaking the bushes for them like the rest of us will be doing. How does that sound?"

"Okay, we'll just have to see how Mike is at noon and if he's still too tired then it will be up to you to use the heavy hand and demand he stay in camp, I guess." said the worrier.

"Yeah I can do that. Now give over and go take care of that brother of yours." answered Ben and went on over to the campfire to rest his own bones for he sure was tired after a long day in the saddle. Shoot and blast, it wasn't any fun getting old.

"Here's your soap and towel, Mike," Joe said breathlessly. "I forgot where they were and I brought us some clean shirts and undershirts too. Maybe we can wash these dirty ones out. I guess they'll dry on the bushes. Oh geeze peeze, the water's cold. I bet it will wake us both up, huh." They stripped their shirts and undershirts and went to splashing, gasping at the shock then scrubbed until they both were clean and definitely stimulated and wide awake.

After they were dressing again, Joe laughed. "Hey, remember when we were so tired and hot on that long walk up North Mountain Road? Well, we finally got to put some of our body parts in a cold river." Somehow Joe's attention and sense of humor lightened Mike's fatigue and they was laughing and poking at each other on their way back to that warm campfire.

The sun had long disappeared behind the western range of mountains that cast deep shadows over their part of the mesa. With the sun gone it was definitely getting colder especially at this altitude. The boys flung their wet things over some bushes and hurried over to their bedrolls, grab their sheepskin jackets and headed for the big fire. Man-oh-man, did that feel good.

After supper the men sat around and Luther spoke out to the crowd. "We did great today and I think we rounded up at least 200 cows and more only because they were out there in large groups. It won't be as easy tomorrow, but we'll drag in at least that many because of an earlier start; say around first daylight which will be around 6:30 we'll be in the saddle and riding." *Groans* greeted that order, but with added laughter too.

"*Hey*, where's our entertainment? Now I was promised a good time if I would come out here and worked my butt off. *Come on* you kids, I need my music or I get real mean." growled Brent.

"Yeah, right, and didn't I see you carrying that little baby calf that was born too late this year? You could have shot it, you know." That wouldn't have happened, but it made a good way to rib Brent.

"Well you see, boys, I've known his mammy very well over the years and I just couldn't shoot someone's off-spring after such a long acquaintance now could I?" came the laconic response.

That set the guys up and the ribbing went on to include some of the other men. Meanwhile Mike got his guitar from Dusty and sat down on a log to tune it.

Mike began playing a Spanish melody full of passion and with complex picking and strumming that Mike had written and composed in Texas last year. The men quieted and Mike's music rolled out into the darkness with such beauty that those who listened didn't do it just out of politeness, but out of admiration. Wow, Ben grinned, that boy can play all right, and it was a treat because he hadn't heard Mike play before. Well, whowouldhavethunkit!

Mike rolled right over into another song he had written a few years ago. He and Joe sang it in perfect harmony. It was a beautiful moving song of horses and lonely men who had ridden the range long before anyone here had been born. Plaintive and simple, the music took the listening men back to those wild hard times and at the end Joe's tenor soared like the cry of a lonesome cowboy. Silence gripped the campfire and many a jaw had to be re-hinged before the burst of wild applause broke out. It was a good thing that the cattle weren't being held close or the noise would have caused that dreaded stampede. The boys grinned at each other then stood to take elaborate bows.

The next effort was all Joe's and Mike played "Ave Maria" all the way through as Joe stood up and looked up at the dark night sky studded with a billion stars. Then his beautiful tenor voice took up the Italian words. Joe sang from the very heart of his spirit infusing the music with such depth of feeling that it touched every man there. No words could describe this child's marvelous gift. It simply dug way down deep into the men's psyches and dragged out the yearning for spiritual union. For such a young boy to have such a voice range was phenomenal.

When the song was finished there was no applause, no loud whistling or appreciative response; just silence. Finally Joe smiled and said, "See? I told you guys I could quiet the cattle, just look what I did to you so now you believe me, don't you?" and laughed.

"Okay, Joe, you're with me tomorrow night and you can sing those beauties to sleep easy like." Jimmy grinned at his young boss who was not only phenomenally gifted, but someone he really liked.

Well, more music naturally followed that had an uplifting sort of fun to it and some songs the men could all sing to. Then as a finale Mike played and sang one of his favorites and it was well received. "Hey Mike, when are you going to record that song? I sure would admire having a copy." The evening only ended when Ben called a halt.

He stood up and waved his hand for silence. "We all thank you young fellows for the wonderful music, but it's time to call it enough. Four o'clock is coming mighty fast and we all need our beauty sleep, it's time to hit the hay. Good work today men. Thank you Dusty for the great food and now goodnight to you all."

~Strike Two~

"**Those stupid louts** think they can find me, well they don't know that I know my way around these hills just as good as anybody. Now I'm going to get mean and then we'll get down to serious negotiation. These people are so dumb they're easy marks, hardly any challenge at all for a brilliant man like me."

In a motel room out west of Claremont, Elroy dragged on his new walking boots, put on his down jacket and put everything he'd need into his backpack for an overnight stay. He got his twenty-two pistol out of the drawer with the silencer and checked to make sure it was fully loaded and put the gun and extra bullets into the pack. When he was ready he picked up the backpack and went out to his car.

Claremont was a small town so he'd dressed like a farmer and felt confident he wouldn't attract any attention or so he thought. He'd dyed his hair and had grown a mustache and beard to change his appearance just in case someone remembered him from the past.

Before Elroy left town he stopped at a small diner to have an early breakfast. He was so confident that he blended into the surroundings that he failed to notice the observant eyes of a waitress watching him with suspicion when he left. She turned to one of the men at the counter and whispered something to him. The man quickly got up and went to the door only to find the street empty. He remembered the warning that had gone out and thought if he saw the guy again he'd report it. Maybe the guy was just passin' through. He shrugged and went back to his coffee.

It was amazing how much you could pick up by keeping your mouth shut and your ears open. Just a few days ago he'd heard that the man who had owned the west valley ranch had died and the property was vacant and shortly after that he'd heard about the big man Strongbow's cattle gather upon Flat Top Mesa and the new plan had come into being and what a fabulous plan it was too.

Elroy got into his car and drove south until he saw the abandoned road leading into the ranch. He'd decided he could park his car at the deserted place and cut down on the time it would take for him to hike up to Flat Top from the west side.

He soon arrived at the old ranch and hid his car behind one of the barns. Strapping on his back pack he looked up at the steep climb ahead of him and didn't look forward to it, but if his plan was to succeed he'd just have to suck up his gut. Elroy began his hike into the foothills toward a valley that ran parallel to the mesa. He had to rest often due to his age and the fact that he was sadly out of shape. Lordy, he hated the country and he resented having to work so hard in order to get what he wanted. The little man had also heard all about the mean old bull having his own personal kingdom up on the mesa and how the hunters avoided the place. No one in their right mind wanted to mess with him.

Elroy laughed breathlessly, "*I'm* about to mess with him, and with all the activity on the mesa, no one will hear or see me. I just *love* surprises."

As he hiked along he figured he could get close to big mesa by tonight and tomorrow he'd drop down on the Flat Top side and begin seeking out the bull's hiding place. By late afternoon Elroy's plan was working just fine and he was tickled to find one of the small caves he'd discovered years ago when he was young.

He entered the small cave and took a careful look around to make sure it was empty of animal life before he took off his backpack with a sigh of relief and sat down to rest before fixing a fire. "This will do for tonight; shelter and a fire will suit me as I'm tired to the bone. Climbing these hills isn't what I call fun, but the fun will come tomorrow." He laughed. "Oh yes indeedy, tomorrow we'll see who survived after a nice stampede. Bet there's lots of damage." he said maliciously.

Just then the mountain rumbled and shook the cave causing Elroy to leap to his feet breathing hard. A few rocks and some dirty fell from the ceiling. When nothing further happened Elroy's breathing quieted and he sat down again.

"Just a little settling is all, just a little shaking; nothin' to worry about." he assured himself still it took him awhile to stop listening for that peculiar rumbling.

The next morning he got up groaning as his stiff sore muscles protested. It took him awhile to limber up. He ate a quick breakfast before gathering up his lighter backpack, leaving his sleeping bag and the rest of the food in the cave. There was always a chance that he could use this place in the future. Elroy began hiking up the mountain ridge bordering Flat Top on the west side. He started from the edge of the cliffs and moved slowly north in order to always be down wind of the bull. By late afternoon, having investigated several slot canyons, he was close to exhaustion with his leg muscles quivered like Jell-O. He was beginning to despair of ever finding the beast when suddenly Elroy came upon a very narrow slot canyon about midway of the mesa. He almost dismissed as it was filled with good size bushes and trees. At first glance it appeared to be uninhabitable when out of the corner of his eye he saw something massive move that made the bushes bend and shake. He stared for a few minutes before he saw the rear end of a big, very big brown Hereford bull that blended into the bushes with perfect camouflage.

Backing off the little man carefully made sure he was downwind before he cautiously worked his way down the steep side into the bull's domain as noiselessly as possible, sweating in fear the closer he came to the monster, Elroy stopped and took the time to settle his heavy breathing before continuing. This was not the time to rush and get careless. Carefully he inched forward and hid in a nest of rocks about twenty feet behind the bull.

Elroy pulled out his twenty-two and quietly screwed on the silencer and aimed at the bull's rump. *POP!* The bull bellowed and whirled around ready to attack whatever had bit him and Elroy had a full on view of a remarkable and deadly spread of horns that curled his guts in *fear*. The twenty-two wasn't powerful enough to kill such a heavy animal, but that was never the object of his intention anyway. He just wanted to sting the bull into running down the canyon and onto the mesa.

POP! Another stinging wound and the bull charged aimlessly around striking at the bushes with his long sweep of horns. *Pop! Pop! Pop!* The bull began to run down the canyon, blood running down his legs and side and Elroy jumped up and ran clumsily along the edge of the hill. Whenever the bull would stop he shot him again until finally, so enraged, the bull ran all the way down to the where the small canyon opened up onto the mesa.

Snorting, blowing and pawing the ground the bull waited for something to vent his pain, anger and frustration on. Elroy crept silently closer and caught a view of the open land ahead and the large herd of cattle being held there. Then he saw a small rider and his horse about to pass by the bull. The kid stopped and stared intently into the bushes that covered the canyon opening. As though realizing what he was looking at the boy was set to ride off when Elroy shot the old mossy horn again and the bull charged through the screen of tall bushes like a freight train. Elroy heard the boy scream then the pounding horse's hooves.

Elroy laughed and said. "*Bingo, I got the little one; my luck is running high.*"

He didn't stay to see the ending which he regretted, but laughed breathlessly at his success as he ran as fast as his weary legs would carry him back up the canyon. He heard rifle shots, but assumed the boy was dead or dying and the bull had been killed.

"Ha, too bad, so sad." he panted. Now maybe they'd listen a little more seriously to one Elroy when he made them his offer. He climbed swiftly out of the canyon and over the top of the ridge and was gone.

On that same day Mike and Joe, along with the other men, were riding guard around the growing herd as Ben had instructed. Men who were working the field would push cows into the holding herd from time to time, and it was a full time job to keep the cows loosely held. Dust rose in the air and the sound of cows bellowing and mooing added to the general noise. The tranquility of the mesa was definitely broken.

Once in awhile the cowboys would have to dash after cows determined to quit the herd and drive them back. A couple of hours later lunch came as a welcomed break. The men rode back to the chuck wagon stung out in two and threes. Joe was definitely ready to relax get off his horse and collapse. Just getting out of the saddle was a profound relief. Joe thought tiredly, well so much for the glamorous cowboy life of old. Pure bunkum! It was bloody hard work, but strangely enough he was having a wonderful time despite it all.

Ben saw Joe leaning against his horse and grew concerned. He walked over and laid his hand on the kid's shoulder. "How're you doing, Joe, need a break? Dusty might pose for some more pictures if you want to say in camp this afternoon." Ben looked hard at Joe's tired face, but the kid surprised him by standing up straight and laughing.

"Not for anything would I miss any little bit of this wild cowboy life. No siree Ben, I'm just fine. Well, I am a little tired for sure, but lunch will mostly take care of that I figure. I'll be riding Jigger again this afternoon and he does all the work anyway." assured the boy.

"Well okay boy, but if you decide to head into camp just holler." and Ben ruffled the boy's hair knocking his cowboy hat to the ground then went on to saddle his own horse. When it was time to get back to the job Joe gladly accepted help from Jimmy in saddling Jigger and trying to hide from him how tired he really was as he wearily climbed back into the saddle.

Lunch or rather the full meal Dusty served up did help Joe recover some energy so climbing back into Jigger's saddle wasn't so difficult as the getting off had been. By late afternoon Joe was making his umpteen circle around the herd for the umpteenth time with occasional bursts of riding to break up the boredom turning cows back into the herd. He was riding along the tree line when suddenly he pulled Jigger to a halt and peered closely at a dark form hiding behind a bunch of bushes. At first he thought it was a cow that had escaped then his eyes bulged and got a good look at what must be the huge Old Mossy Horn Bull.

Joe sat tight on a nervous Jigger, who already knew what was in the bushes, and was shocked to see the spread of horns that may not have been as wide as the old Texas longhorn, but were very impressive indeed. The boy and the bull must have starred at each other for a few seconds before it dawned on Joe to get the heck out of there and warn the others that they had a very dangerous visitor.

Joe tightened his legs around Jigger's belly and Jigger had started to move when Joe thought he heard a funny popping noise just before the bull came out of the bush and charged him like a freight train. Jigger leaped in a huge jump to one side as quick as a cat and it was a miracle that Joe wasn't thrown from the saddle right then. He would have been if he hadn't already closed his legs tight around the horse's barrel in preparation to ride away. Joe instinctively gripped the saddle horn with both hands which was the smartest thing he could have done.

"Look out! It's Old Mossy Horn. He's here. Look out! Look out!" Joe screamed repeatedly then concentrated on staying in the saddle. Jigger was small, but quick as a cat on his feet and was able to avoid the second charge with the same tactic, wheeling on his hind feet and taking off in another direction like a scared rabbit. Out of the corner of his eye Joe saw Jimmy racing to intercept the bull from the south side of the herd as Jigger dodged again and Joe hung on to the saddle horn for dear life and kept faith with the horse that knew a lot more about this game than he did.

Once more Jigger saved them from being gored by a fast move and raced away like a stone released from a slingshot, in other words *that horse got out of there.* There was the sound of a shot, then another. On a slight hill Jigger whirled around to face the bull that should have been coming at them and ready to dodge and dart again. When it was clear that the bull was not breathing down their necks poor Jigger just stood trembling, breathing hard and in a heavy sweat. Joe looked back through the dust to see the huge bull lying still on the ground with Jimmy riding up a few feet away from the monster with his rifle ready.

Joe didn't realize until then that the herd had scattered and was on the run. Shocked as he was, Joe felt the earth tremble with the pounding of many hooves of the fast disappearing herd. He heard men yelling and rifle shots as they rode to turn the cows away from the south leading to the cliffs and back toward the gap, but it wasn't a very safe thing to accomplish. They all could have fallen right over the steep cliffs. Joe frantically looked for Mike but didn't see him at all.

"*Oh God, please not Mike*! Please, you gotta' protect them all." And felt sick to his stomach thinking that he might have put the men and Mike in danger, maybe getting someone trampled. He started to shake just like Jigger.

He slumped over the saddle horn and laid his head on Jigger's wet neck. "*Jigger, you beauty, you!. You saved my life.* How am I ever going to repay you? God, *thank you* for this horse; Jigger I purely love you." Then Jimmy was dashing his horse up the knoll slidding out of the saddle and in one smooth stride and was there beside Jigger and dragging Joe off his horse by a fist full of jacket that knocked Joe's hat to the ground in the process. Jimmy hugged him fiercely until Joe thought he'd die from lack of breath. Joe was shaking right down to his toes and he embarrassed himself by bursting into tears.

"It's okay Joe, the bull's dead. *You're okay pal.*" said Jimmy. He hadn't been this been this scared since he'd met a grizzly bear face to face up in Montana. This had been a very close call. After all he was supposed to *protect* Joe. That was his job, not the bleeding cows! Jimmy knew his voice was shaking even as he tried to speaking lightly, "Hey Joe, I got Old Mossy Horn and just think what a great story you'll have to tell when you go to school on Monday?"

"I know, I know, I'm all right." Joe sobbed. "Jigger saw to that. Man oh man, Jimmy, he's a *Horse*; I mean he saved my life. Oh, Lord, *I was scared spitless*." as he clung fiercely to his friend then Joe turned grayish green. "I'm going to be sick."

Jimmy quickly dropped his rifle and bent Joe over and held his head as the kid knelt down and lost what was left of his lunch. Afterward, Jimmy half carried him over to lean against a rock.

"Spitless? Let me tell you, my young friend, you haven't *seen* spitless. You have no idea how *spitless* feels. I won't be spitting for several hours yet 'cause all my spit has plumb dried up. Lordy, Lordy, I never want to be that scared again." Jimmy ran his had over Joe's sweaty forehead and tried to say cheerfully. "Hey boy, *you can ride*! I saw how smart you were just hanging on to the saddle horn and staying right in the center of that pony while he danced, jumped and ran. I don't think I've seen a horse do acrobatics like that before. Yep he's some kind of horse. And I'd say you're a crackerjack cutting horse rider and no one could have done it better." said an admiring cowboy handing Joe his bandana and patting Joe on the shoulder. Jimmy got up and went over and got the canteen off his saddle and picked up his rifle on the way back. He handed the canteen to Joe so he could rinse his mouth. Having spat a few times Joe began to get some color back in his face.

"You think I did alright?" he asked in a shaky voice. "You know it was my Dad who taught me to ride cutting horses when I was really young." That comment made Jimmy smile as if Joe was a grown up boy now. "I just didn't dare fall off and Jiggers did all the work." Joe gave a big sigh, but continued to shake with nervous reaction. He looked up at Jimmy with a worshipful gaze and whispered. "Thanks for saving my life, Jimmy; if you hadn't killed that bull I'm not sure how Jigger and I would have come out of it."

Joe hurriedly wiped away tears that seemed to pour out of his eyes automatically. "Sorry to be such a crybaby. I'm kinda' leaky I guess, but I didn't pee my pants." grinned Joe weakly through the tears.

"You did just fine Joe, and you may be leaking a few tears, but I'm not sure my pants are completely dry." Jimmy grinned too and patted Joe on his shoulder again and got a small laugh out of the boy.

Joe heard the pounding of hooves and looked over Jimmy's shoulder. "Here comes Mike and just look at my brother ride. Isn't he a grand horseman? I'm so glad I didn't get anyone killed when that herd stampeded. I mean, no one else was hurt were they, Jimmy?" Joe got white in the face again.

"No, no one was seriously hurt, and that stampede wasn't your fault either. Blame it on Old Mossy Horn, Joe, or whatever started him on his rampage." Jimmy reassured him.

By this time Mike was racing up the small hill and in the next instant he was sliding out of the saddle on the run, breathing hard and kneeling beside Joe. Mike grabbed Joe into a hard hug. "*Oh God, oh God Joe, I almost lost you.* Mom and Dad would be *really angry* at me if I lost you. *Don't ever scare me like that again, you hear*?" and Mike continued to squeeze Joe hard. He felt Mike trembling as he breathed hard.

"I'm okay Mike, really I'm fine 'cause Jimmy saved us." When that didn't get Mike to let up Joe said in a squeaky voice. "Come on Mike let go 'cause I can't breath." all the while trying to comfort his brother by patting him on the back. Joe knew what a big a deal it was for Mike to protect him and Carli. "Geeze peeze Mike, give a guy a little *dignity* here." complained Joe in a shaky way.

Mike let go and gave Joe a shake. "*Don't do things like this, I can't stand the shock.* I've got some white hair for sure now; I'm too young for white hair." complained Mike trying to lighten up his deep fright though Joe could see the tears in Mike's eyes that he was struggling to hold in.

Joe managed a laugh. "Yeah, I can see the white in your hair right through the dust so you'll be an old man before I'm eighteen. Better get used to it 'cause if it's not me than Carli will do something else to give you white hair." Joe gave Mike another pat and wiping the last of his own tears away. Mike finally stood up and looked at the cowboy standing on the other side of Joe.

"Jimmy…Gods Jimmy how do I say *thanks* for saving Joe's life? I'm so *very grateful that you were there.*" Mike held out his hand and Jimmy took it with a laugh until Mike pulled him into a giant hug too. "God bless you Jimmy and your sharp shooter's eye. *There's nothing I can ever do that will repay you for this day.*" whispered Mike and finally let the red faced cowboy go and grip his hand again.

"Hey Mike, I was lucky to be on the spot is all, besides Joe rode like I've never seen before. That kid's more than just a voice; he's one heck of a horseman too. No worries boss, I ride for the brand as they say." joked Jimmy and Mike just nodded his head and squeezed Jimmy's hand hard then let go.

By this time other men, who had been out on the south end of the mesa and had ridden hard to help turn the herd, were now were riding toward where they had heard the shots and slowed down as they rode by the dead bull, Ben just glanced down as he galloped past and up the small hill where he saw three horses ground hitched and recognized Jigger by his smaller size. When Ben came up to the boys he stopped and stepped off his horse and walked up to the two boys that were now standing side by side and grabbed them in his strong arms and said breathlessly.

"What happened? *Are you're all right? Are you're all right? Tell me what happened?* Mari Beth will kill me if you two aren't all right. **Well blast it, say something**." he shouted and took each of them by a shoulder and shook them a little.

Joe sniffed and finally got calm enough to say. "Well Ben it was mighty close, but a miss is as good as a mile they say." And began to laugh hysterically at the choked exclamation Ben swallowed and then he grabbed Joe again and hugged him hard.

"Blast you boy, you're going to give me white hair before I'm due."

Jimmy Jumper laughed. "It looks like you'll have some company Mr. Strongbow 'cause Mike just said the same thing. Golly, it looks to me like Joe's going to be famous for giving men white hair too. I wonder what the hell he'll do next." and laughed at the expressions on their faces.

"I've certainly gotten more hugs today than I've gotten all year so maybe there's a plus to this, huh? Maybe I should do it again." Joe laughed again at the expressions on the men's faces.

"If you do that young man I'll rattle your hocks, but *good!*" Ben said sternly, not seeing that statement as funny at all.

"Truth to tell Ben, I won't because I really didn't find it fun at all. Please, don't be mad at me, Ben." It was Joe's turn to pat Ben's arm then he just tucked his head against Ben's waist and hugged him tightly with his small shoulders shaking.

"Okay boy, okay Joe, I'm not mad at you. Come on boy, you're all shook up and need some down time. Let's get you back to camp." Said Ben as he led Joe over to Jigger and effortlessly lifted him up into the saddle and Jimmy handed him his hat.

They rode down the hill together and stopped beside the dead bull. Joe slid out of the saddle and with Jimmy he wobbled over to stand beside the bull and took hold of his friend's hand.

Joe looked up at the tall young man and said. "Jimmy, I'll *never, ever* be able to thank you for saving my life, but thanks for being there for me. I hope we can be friends for life then I just might be able to do something great for you someday. I'll never forget you. Thanks Jimmy, you're the very bestest man ever." Before the red faced Jimmy could speak Joe said in an awed voice. "Geeze peeze Jimmy, *you're a hero!*"

Poor Jimmy got redder in the face and he'd tried to joke Joe's gratitude away because it embarrassed him right down to his boots. "I only did what any other man would have done under the same circumstances only I got to fire the shots. It's the luck of the draw kid and maybe the Thunder Gods give me a hand." Yeah, now *that* was a thought! "Well Joe my man, I can't have my boss killed while I'm on the job now, can I? It would look darn poor on my resume. Besides that, I like you and the Gods would never forgive me if I got you killed and ruined that fine voice of yours. So see, this so called heroic act was just saving my own bacon. You gotta' go with the bottom line, kid; that's save your own butt." instructed Jimmy in his serious voice that belied his laughing eyes.

"Jimmy, you're such a storyteller. I never knowed such an innocent face lying to a friend like you just did." Joe laughed a little, but his throat got kind of choked up. "Jimmy, I might be only seven, but I'm not stupid and I know a hero when I see one; just like in the storybooks so you're just going to have to bare the title 'cause you're my hero and don't you dare deny it." And with tears in his eyes, Joe squeezed Jimmy around the waist then turned and walked back to Mike who was waiting for him beside the horses. All of a sudden Joe felt like a big Mack Truck had rolled over him. How much flatter could a guy feel he wondered? "Mike," whispered Joe. "I can't get up into the saddle. Can you give me a boost?"

"Sure kid, no problem, if you're legs feel like mine, their pretty much like wet noodles." and Mike had to lift him up into his saddle.

Jimmy stood there looking after Joe absolutely stunned. Yeah, that kid may be young, but he was his friend. Life was purely amazing and he was now a real live hero, huh? Well, well, would wonders never cease!

Back at camp Mike got Joe seated on a blanket beside the fire and took off his boots and covered him with another blanket. Joe looked white and exhausted.

"Mike look after your brother while I ride out to check on the men." Worry sat heavily on Ben's shoulders. "I sure pray no one got hurt. That stampede blindsided us for sure. Now I've got a herd scattered from hell to breakfast and I just hope we can sweep them up before we run out of time." Ben stood there and looked around before he began to walk toward his horse. "I'll be back in awhile." He mounted and rode off at a fast clip.

Mike looked out over the mesa and watched Ben ride away. The dust that had been kicked up when the cattle stampeded had begun to clear off and Mike could see groups of men rounding up strays through the light haze. He too prayed that Ben wouldn't find any of the men badly hurt. Joe was probably shock. Maybe Dusty could fix him something and walked over to the chuck wagon to talk to him.

Ben finally came up on four of the men herding a dozen or so cows back toward the original holding area. Off in the distance he saw similar groups doing the same thing.

"Everyone here okay; no one hurt?" asked Ben abruptly.

"We're okay Ben," said Brent, Luther's foreman, "I saw only one man go down but I think he's okay as he was far enough out from the edge of the herd not to get trampled. I couldn't stop for these dumb cows were hot-footin' toward the eastern cliffs and we had to ride hard to turn 'em toward the gap."

The men looked fairly ragged thought Ben, but thank God they were all in one piece. He rode along side Brent for a bit before saying, "I surely hope no one got seriously hurt. I'm still checking that out.

This is the first time a herd has stampeded on me. Well, I guess cattle are unpredictable at best and stampedes can happen sudden like too. Thanks for your quick action men."

"Well, Ben," drawled Brent, "We all came up here for a taste of the old fashioned cowboy life. I must say you sure delivered that in spades. Can't tell you how much we appreciated your efforts to entertain us." At Brent's understatement the other men laughed and agreed.

Ben just shook his head and grinned. "I always suspected you were slightly tetched in the head Brent and now I know for sure. You boys get to work and stop lollygagging around." Ben rode off to the sound of laughter.

He spent the next hour checking on everyone and heaved a sign of relief to find that the most serious injury seemed to have been Sonny Little Man and that hopefully wasn't too bad.

After tending to their horses the dirty, tired men began coming into camp speaking quietly as though the effort of speech was too great an effort. Ben saw one of the men helping Sonny limp over to the chuck wagon and went to see how bad his injuries were."Not to bad Mr. Strongbow," said Sonny Little Man, "My horse stepped in a gopher hole and we both went down. Man, we were lucky not to have been trampled or badly hurt. Now *that* would have been the ultimate cowboy experience, wouldn't it?" Sonny tried to laugh, but gasped and grimaced in pain. "My horse has a sprained tendon, but he should be alright with time and as soon as Dusty cleans me up I'll go wrap his leg. Me, I'm just scraped up here and there, maybe a few sore ribs."

"Don't worry about your horse Sonny, I'll see to him. You take it easy 'cause I saw you limping." said Ben.

"Stop your chattering Sonny and take off your shirt and pants. That means strip off everything." At the man's shocked look Dusty snorted, "I good, but I can't tend your wounds through underwear. Now peel it off!" commanded Dusty.

"Right here if front of the Thunder Gods and the cowboys? Come on Dusty, think of my dignity." the injured man's face grew red and tried to laugh which ended in a groan.

"Yeah, Little Man, be brave and we won't laugh at your skinny body. Off with the duds and I'll help you with your boots!"

Ben turned away laughing quietly. You can believe that man striped without further argument. Dusty's Law: Do as you're told when I tell you or God help you.

From conversations with the other men earlier on had Ben fervently thanking the Thunder Gods for their protection for while there were bruises aplenty, sore muscles, and some scraps there hadn't been anyone seriously hurt.

Luther sat down beside his father and said wearily, "Well, Dad we've got cattle scattered all over the gap which isn't too bad as we can probably pick up most of them on our way down. Those we miss will follow along eventually. We've gotten over a hundred head gathered back in the same location. Those cows don't have any more run in them so they won't cause us trouble tonight, thank the Lord. Shoot, I think you could leave them out there alone without the men riding herd because their all laying down, but that's your decision, Dad. Other than some really close calls we came out of this unbelievably lucky."

"You got that right son, unbelievable indeed. I think we might have had a little protection from our resident Guardians. Well, go get cleaned up and I'm doubly thankful that you weren't hurt. Your mother would have laid me out if I got her first born injured." Luther laughed at that, slapped his father on the shoulder and went to clean up at the falls.

When the men came back to the fire they literally collapsed around it groaning and complaining and didn't pay much attention to the big kettle Dusty had heating on his grill; at least not until they saw him dip a cup into it, wipe it off and walk over to hand it to Joe.

"This is guaranteed to fix what ails you boy, so drink up."

Joe gratefully took a couple of gulps of the hot drink, took a breath, coughed and breathed deeply again "*Gosh All Mighty, Dusty, what in the heck is this?* I've never tasted hot chocolate like *this* before and my stomach feels all fiery." and coughed a few more times.

"Let's just say this is my favorite formula for shock, trauma, incidents, girls and sudden moves; it'll cure ailments of all sorts; snakebite, cow stomping, bad falls, a broken heart from an insincere woman, and most importantly, bull charges. So drink it down, my fine young warrior, and you'll sleep like a baby tonight." winked Dusty.

Now that got the attention of every man there and they sat up suddenly forgetting their aches and pains and watched young Joe with vast interest.

Joe drank up and the more he drank the better he liked it. Joe's face took on some needed color. "*Wow*, this is some hot chocolate! Hey Dusty, you gotta' give Mike some of this if it will cure worries and responsibilities above and beyond the call of duty for big brothers, sort of thingee." said Joe in a gay tipsy voice.

"If you will open your eyes young fella' you'll see that your big brother is well into his cup now and doesn't have a worry one." said Dusty and Mike laughed and asked for another fill up.

"Now, now, young man, this is the last cup you can have 'cause this here brew is potent fire and if I gave you any more you'd sleep like Rip Van Winkle for years." The men definitely perked up their ears and gave each other a *look* then looked speculative over at Dusty. Now there was some special treatment being handed out and before anyone could speak up Luther voiced all their complaints.

"We've all got aches and pains, fatigue, saddle sores and worries too, not to mention the shock and trauma of surviving a stampede that we've miraculously just lived through so shouldn't we have your cure all too Dusty, huh, huh?"

"Hey wait a minute, there's been a great strain on my nerves, body and trigger finger and I think my mind got strained too." whined Jimmy. "I'm sure Dusty's brew would cure me just fine and dandy. Besides, Joe said I was a *hero* and heroes deserve your famous brew, Mr. Evans, Sir." And that was greeted with a great deal of hissing and booing.

Dusty with great presence, served Jimmy a big cup of his "fixer-upper" and Jimmy saluted the gang with a mock bow and took a big swallow. The wide-eyed look on his face and the broad grin showed the men that it was a potent brew after all. "Yeah, eat your hearts out boys, this is for heroes and survivors only." and went over to sit beside Joe and that comment set fuel to the fire.

Dusty, that sober and serious man was laughing like a lunatic and said, "I've got a big pot here for you poor things and everyone will get a cup. Hey, now don't crowd so, stop pushing and everyone gets only one cup each." Needless to say, Dusty was a very popular guy.

Joe laughed and laughed and all his fears and inner shaking just seemed to melt away. He burst into a hilarious song that Mike had written sometime ago with Mike joining in. They had everyone in camp laughing and applauding. The boys just had to do a repeat performance with the men coming in on the tag lines. It was such a contrast from the near tragedy to have this evening end in song instead of sorrow.

Within the hour following supper Joe was fast asleep. Ben carefully picked him up from his place beside the fire. With Dusty's help he got Joe's jeans striped and leaving Joe's long underwear on, inserted him into his sleeping bag and warmly covered. This was one boy who wouldn't have nightmares tonight.

~Dusty~

LATER THAT EVENING, BEN walked away from the campfire to check on the boys and found them deeply asleep with their bedrolls pulled up over their ears so all that could be seen was the tops of their heads. Jimmy, who lay beside them, raised his head at once to see who it was and seeing Ben he turned over and went back to sleep. Joe's guardian was on guard, smiled Ben, and felt grateful beyond words for this young man's care.

Without Jimmy's crack shots today, this night would have been filled with deep sorrow and they'd have been taking a dead boy home in the morning. Ben *shuddered* at that thought. He'd have to see about an appropriate reward for being "Johnnie on the spot" and very tactfully too of course, or he'd risk offending the young man's pride. Maybe Jimmy would like one of Suncatcher's foals?

Ben was restless and when he had finished checking around the camp he walked back to the fire and sat down on a log. He rubbed his face hard before clutching his hands tightly together. Something was terribly wrong and the more he thought about it the more he suspected foul play. Ben didn't notice Dusty moving around until the man came over and sat down beside him and handed him a hot cup of coffee.

"This wasn't any accident Ben. Did you get a good look at that bull?" said Dusty in a low voice as men were asleep all around them. Ben shook his head.

"Well, Jimmy and I did right after dinner. I said I'd talk to you about it when we were alone."

"What about the bull?" Ben looked sharply at the old man.

"He'd been shot a number of times with a twenty-two and I bet the guy used a silencer otherwise we'd have heard those shots 'cause that canyon would have acted like a speaking tube and magnified the sound. Look, here are some of the slugs I dug out of the bull's rump. I left the others so if Sheriff Brandt needs proof he can come up and dig out some for himself and I think he should. We borrowed Joe's camera and took some close up shots. These are twenty-two's and that bull was shot enough times to drive him out onto the mesa. Normally that mossy horn avoids men like the plague unless someone disturbs him so someone had to have driven that bull out here to cause trouble and hurt. I think it's part of your ongoing harassment, only now it's getting violent."

"Lord All Mighty Dusty, this is an awful thing. I'll say my sincere prayers tonight especially for Joe's life. Yeah, you've figured it right and it's connected and it's not any of the Valleys' men for certain. I figure that this stranger has come here to get something from the Kellys boys and the way he's planned it is to cause a heap of hurt so he can get what he wants." murmured Ben as he took his first big sip of coffee, swallowed and gave a hearty cough and a whoosh of breath.

"Lordy, Lordy, what's in this, more of your ail-all?" questioned Ben looking aslant at the cook through the tears in his eyes as he coughed a few more times.

"Oh, a little this and a little of that and bound to cure boss's worries and helps the brain to function and stop going around in circles; a real cure all is this brew. I'm thinking of marketing it and making my fortune for my old age. 'Course, I'll have to hurry up as I'm getting on now right smart like." said Dusty and grinned. It was quiet for a time as the men sat together drinking their coffee companionably while turning their thoughts to the mystery of the attack.

"Anyway," continued Dusty quietly, "Tomorrow at daylight I'm going to take a horse and go have a look-see around in that slot canyon so you'll be on your own for breakfast. I'll have the biscuits done and I'm sure some of these fellows can cook eggs and fry bacon."

"Dusty, I don't mean to offend you or anything like that, but you're getting too old to be climbing around up in those rocks. Let me send one of the other guys."

Dusty fixed Ben with a gimlet eye and said softly. "Ben, nobody knows much about me and that's the way I've wanted it. Far as everyone knows, I'm just a cook. Fact is, when I was in the service I was a LRRP (lurp) in Viet Nam, that's short for Long Range Reconnaissance Patrol and when we came back into camp no one wanted to mess with us 'cause it wasn't safe. Let's just say we were specially trained to handle just about anything silently and alone. Well, I still have the training and I can track anything. Now it may have been awhile since those days, but you don't forget how it's done."

Dusty sipped his coffee and spent a few minutes looking back at the past. Then he cleared his throat and continued. "I'll be going out at first light. I'll see you around noon and tell you what I've found." With that Dusty got up and tossed the dregs of his coffee on the fire which caused it to flare up before it died down again. "Goodnight, Ben, don't worry about it now. There ain't anyone out there waiting to take a pot shot at us 'cause he's not into that direct a personal attack yet. No, this fellow wants to cause lots of trouble first. However put out a double the guard and have the men riding in pairs just in case I'm wrong and that guy is stupid enough to hang around. I wished I thought he'd be that stupid then I'd handle it." Dusty walked away into the dark.

Ben sat alone at the fire for awhile and thought about this unassuming man called Dusty until finally he shook his head at the mystery most people were and got up to awakened six men.

"Sorry fellas," Dusty thinks we'd better be safe than sorry in case this trouble maker is still hanging around, which he probably isn't. So here's the deal; guard duty for two hours and you're to ride in pairs then rotate. Wake up the next six and pass the word. This way everyone can get some rest. I'll take the last two hours so have whoever comes in wake me up." There was some groaning and grumbling, but nothing serious as the first group got up and went out to saddle their horses.

Ben waited until the men had left before seeking his own bedroll. He sat down and took off his boots, jacket and pants and climbed in the sleeping bag and sighed with bone deep fatigue. He didn't think he'd get much sleep, what with all the new worries. His body gradually warmed and relaxed though thoughts ran though his head like an express train. Then, as though someone had pulled a switch in his brain, he was fast asleep; no doubt due to Dusty's ail-all.

The next morning Ben rode in with the other guards and began breakfast. The men grumbled at having to cook their own breakfast as Ben handed out biscuits and helped dish up bacon and eggs along with hot coffee. Ben, tired to the bone, lost his hold on his temper, rounded on them and told them sharply, "Dusty is investigating the cause of the accident yesterday at considerable risk to himself. He'll be back by noon to fix lunch. I'm not in the mood to listen to your belly aching. This isn't a game we're playing." The silence after that was complete as the men ate their food they occasionally eyed Ben. Here was another man not to mess with.

Mike and Joe wanted to help with the rest of the gather and Ben decided they were safer being with him and Jimmy than alone in camp. The men saddled up in the cold dawn, mounted and scattered out to start the last of the roundup before beginning the drive to the ranch in the morning.

When the men trailed back into camp at noon Dusty was there and ready to serve a dinner with all the trimmings. The Old Cook must have put the huge roast in his oven before he left camp because he wasn't exactly hugged in appreciation, but the compliments flew fast and furious as they got their plates filled to overflowing.

That made the older man grin knowingly. "Absence does make the heart grow fonder especially when it involves your empty stomachs, don't it boys? See what I have to go through just to get a few words of praise?" Dusty laughed along with the men. After that the silence around the cook fire was almost deafening except for the clinking of forks and such like noise as the hungry men tucked the food away as though they hadn't eaten in days.

If anyone noticed Dusty's dirty pants with a torn shirtsleeve and tired eyes, no one was dumb enough to ask him. There was something about old Dusty that a man knew instinctively not to mess with him. They had heard stories about the cook and while they figured the truth might have been stretched a little here and there a might, they weren't stupid enough to ask for the facts. Dusty was easy going and friendly to a certain point, but there was something about Dusty that warned the men to walk respectfully.

After lunch, while the men lounged around resting their full stomachs and aching muscles, Dusty motioned to Ben and they walked away from the camp. "Well, it's like I suspected, our mystery man drove the bull out of his hideout with a series of shots. Now a silenced twenty-two doesn't make much noise and being back in the canyon we wouldn't have heard any of those shots because of the commotion out here. After the bull was at the entrance to the mesa the guy knew he'd keep going, maybe encouraged with another shot or two. Anyway, our shooter went back up the canyon and scrambled out over the top down into the next canyon west of us and wasn't being at all careful. I judged him to be about 5'7" weighing in around 160-70 and his left leg causes him to drag his toe a might. Now he might have hurt his leg climbing around the way he did so the limp might not last long enough to identify him by that. He's not a young man, probably in his late forties or early fifties and he's out of condition and mighty tired. He wears a climbing boot size 8 with rubber cleats and that's a mighty expensive boot. He's not a cowboy or a rancher. He was wearing brown denim pants and jacket to match. He put his right hand down in the dirt when he slipped and fell. He's got large hands for his size and his little finger is missing on his right hand. Anyway, he's heading for the west valley and Claremont most likely. I met up with Mr. Hoggins, our mountain man, who saw a man heading down in that direction at a fast clip yesterday. You might send one of the boys to look around Claremont and see if they've had seen any strangers of late that answers that description. He should be easy to spot. Curiously Ben, he knows his way around this country mighty well so I figure he's been here before."

Dusty drew out a piece of paper. "Here, I've drawn a picture of the man's hand and have noted other descriptions and where I found them. We'll sign this and dated it after we have someone witness our signatures. If it comes to court, we've got some evidence." Ben wrote that this had been given to him on Flat Top Mesa and the date.

Ben walked back to camp with Dusty. "Would you witness our signatures Jimmy? It's Dusty's description of the man he followed this morning."

Jimmy took the paper and read it then watched Ben and Dusty sign after which he took the pen Ben held out and signed it and wrote "witness" beneath his signature.

Ben said quietly to Jimmy, "Well, Dusty assures me that the shooter isn't from around here and it appears the man might be heading towards Claremont at least that's what Mr. Hoggins told Dusty when he saw him yesterday. Thanks Jimmy," taking back the paper and pen.

As Ben and Dusty walked away Ben said disgustedly, "My Lord Dusty, who in the world would come into this country and try to do harm to children?"

"As to that Ben, I don't rightly know what caused a man to do murder. I've known some evil men in the world who would do anything. I talked to Blackhawk a few weeks ago and he said he'd seen a vision of a man with an evil face. He thinks it's connected to Mike and Joe. His description was a medium sized man, with a short dark beard, mustache and light eyes, and not a young man for sure. Blackhawk said he looked real mean. Maybe we could get an artist to draw Blackhawk's vision and pass it around?"

"That's a good idea. When I get back to the ranch I'll look into Devereau's past and see if I can come up with any relatives or enemies who just might want a piece of the ranch. I'll ask Mike if there is anyone his parents had trouble with down in Texas. That's all I can think to do at the moment. Thanks Dusty, you're a good man to have around." shaking Dusty's hand and with a grin, "Remind me that I owe you a big bonus."

"Well I will, and I'll even tell you what I'd like. I'd like to ask Mike for a job as cook at his place. I know they have a cook already, but not in Mike's house and that's where I want to be so when the boys come over it might be handy for me to be around in case we have an uninvited visitor."

"Shoot and blast, I *never* thought of that. You've got the job and you can bet Mike will agree. The men will think they've died and gone to food heaven to have you there, Dusty." Ben grinned, "Hank told me that the cook he hired is on probation. He also said the man claimed to be a handy man so he wouldn't be out of a job."

"No false modesty Ben, I know I'm a good cook." Dusty chuckled as they walked back into camp, "Yeah, I can't wait to see the men's reaction. By the way, not to scare the boys or anything, but I never thought ignorance was bliss or safe, so everyone here needs to be told what we suspect. The more eyes out there to help us spot this guy the safer we'll be."

"I'll tell them right before we break camp in the morning."

And Ben did just that over the last cup of coffee. He told them what Dusty had found yesterday and gave them the man's description. Ben wasn't disappointed in their response for these were very angry men who vowed to keep their eyes and ears open. It wasn't just vandalism any more. Now it was attempted murder of a child or one of them because in a stampede men could have been killed real easy like.

Joe and Mike just looked at each other wide-eyed and wondered again who this man was. Ben asked Mike. "Do you think this man might have been an enemy of your parents down in Texas?

"I can't think of anyone our folks knew that would want to do something like this. Our father was generally well liked and to my knowledge he didn't have any enemies. Oh, a few disgruntled cowboys when Dad won the prize, but nothing more than that."

"Then that leaves only two other possibilities; a relative who wants a piece of your pie or just a blackmailer thinking you children would be an easy touch." concluded Ben. "Well, let's leave it alone for now and break camp."

Ben stood up and called, "Gather your stuff up and throw it in the wagon then saddle up. We'll do one last sweep from the southern cliffs to see if we can pick up any strays then let's head 'em for home."

Within the hour the men had the camp cleared and the wagons loaded. Then saddling up and began the sweep. It was going on eleven when Ben called the sweep finished. Lunch consisted of a quick sandwich and hot soup out of several big thermoses. Finally they started moving the cattle slowly toward the gap. As they moved along the men scattered out to gather up small bunches of cows and pushed them into the herd. This slowed them down, still they made good progress. When the grade got too steep for safety, the men roped the wagons to help put the brakes on the descent. It was a long slow day, but by early dusk on Friday afternoon the men had moved the big herd into the large northern pastures. They drove the one cow with her too young calf being carried over Brent's saddle, back to the ranch where they'd be safe in a corral.

Once more the ranch yard was full of men, horses, and noise as they began the job of loading horses and gear into the trailers. Before the men left they were served a fine dinner. More than one man commented how nice it was to sit down at a table with pretty ladies.

After the dinner was over Ben stood up and tapped his knife against his glass to get their attention. "I'm throwing the biggest barbecue and the biggest fiesta you've ever been too next Saturday; since Blackhawk said we'd have glorious weather then." That announcement got loud applause.

Once the whistling and clapping subsided Ben went on to say, " I said I'd pay you men a wage for a job speedily done, but I'm adding a nice fat bonus for the risk you took to turn those stampeding cattle. By your efforts you saved my herd from running off the cliffs. Thanks boys for the exceptional work. And thank the Thunder Gods for protecting us all from harm. Please keep your eyes and ears open and call me if you discover anything about our stranger. See you all next weekend. Thanks again men, and if you've nothing better do, we'll do it again next spring, minus the stampede of course." That got a laugh as the men stood and thanked Mari Beth and Hannah for a superior feast.

Laughter, good-byes, truck doors slamming and the throbbing sound of engines starting filled the yard as gradually the trucks with their trailers rolled away down the ranch road one by one until the Strongbow's yard returned to its normal state of emptiness.

Mari Beth had wisely hired a couple of women to clean up the dishes and straighten the dinning room. So the family went into the living room and sat down in front of a nice fire with coffee and hot chocolate so Mari Beth and Hannah could get an ongoing blow by blow description of the grand adventure from Luther, Ben and the boys. It was fascinating to hear the story of the roundup as each one experienced it

"Mom and I can ride just as good as any man so next year, I'm going along. "Declared Hannah and looked at her mother with a set chin.

"Don't look at me to disagree; I'm certainly not going to stay here either." stated Mari Beth. "I think I deserve an adventure once in awhile; besides, I must look after the boys. Just look at what happened without us, Hannah." exclaimed the boss's lady.

"Wait until you see my pictures, Mari Beth. You'll really like them I think, and I'm going to finish my journal and put some of the pictures in there too. It could even be a class project, couldn't it? Wow, that would really be different. Why, I've even got a picture of that Old Mossy Horn with Jimmy holding his rifle and me standing beside the bull. Geeze peeze, no one at school can beat this real life story for sure." Enthused Joe already planning out how the story would look.

"Yes my man, that's true, but what peaks my interest is what Dusty put in that hot chocolate of yours? Can you guess, Joe?" asked Hannah.

"Well, it tasted a little bit like…like, I don't know; lots of things I guess. I think I tasted apricots and maybe almonds and chocolate, maybe a little spice of some kind, the kind you put in cookies. Anyway, it was hot and made my tummy feel really warm. Dusty said it would cure anything and gave us a long, long list of ailments and troubles." Joe laughed. "He was awfully funny and whatever was in that chocolate made me laugh and boy did I sleep." as Joe slicking up the last of his ice cream.

Hannah raised her eyebrows and looked over at Mari Beth. "Apricots? Hmm, are we speaking of Henry's brandy? Well, I must buy another bottle from Henry next time I see him." said Hannah in a murmur. "Maybe I can experiment a little and come up with something close to what our Mr. Evans served."

That comment reminded Ben. "Oh, by the way Mike, I've hired a cook for your ranch, I hope you don't mind. Dusty thought you could use a good ranch cook and said he was tired of moving around. So what do you think?" asked Ben very serious like.

"Dusty? You're kidding, right? Wow, how did we get that lucky? Golly, the men are going to be fighting to come work for us, huh Ben?" Mike laughed and Joe nodded. "I'll have to talk to Hank about this of course. I know we just hire a cook, but I'd rather have Dusty than anyone else and I'm sure the men would too. With all the new men we're going to be feeding maybe it won't be so hard to keep the second cook to help Dusty; divide the labor, so to speak. We'll have to see." said the young rancher seriously.

"Yep, Old Dusty will make the Kelly Ranch famous 'cause he's a Great Man and famous in his own way." was Joe's astute comment that caused everyone's eyebrows to raise up and wonder what this child had meant by "a Great Man."

Mike and Joe went to bed early that Friday night almost beyond exhausted. A long hot shower felt great and did a lot to relax them from their strenuous four days; they were plumb worn out.

Ben, Mari Beth, Hannah and Luther sat around and talked seriously about expecting more trouble to come their way and what they could do to stop it. However, an hour later Luther left and the Strongbows buttoned up the house and retired to a well earned rest.

Ben groaned as he lowered his scrubbed body into the soft bed. "Mari Beth, I'm either getting too old for this kind of action or I need to get more riding in so I'll be in better condition for moving the cattle back up to the mesa come spring. Right now, I don't care whether shop keeps or not. This bed is as close to heaven on Earth as I'm going to get…for now." Mari Beth laughed, turned out the lights and was soon snuggled up to her sleeping husband.

The wind picked up and rain began hitting the windows like thrown pebbles as the predicted storm roared down from the mountain. The exhausted boys were warm and sound asleep under Eiderdown quilts and protected from the storm that brewed over the ranch and the mountains they had just left that morning.

The adventure was over, but it would live on in their dreams and in their memories for a life time. Each one had experienced something different over the past four days. There would be time tomorrow to compare notes whenever they woke up snd "when" was the optional word.

The storm strengthened and the night wind whipped around the walls of the sturdy house wailing like lost souls. Within the house all was serene, all was peaceful. They were safe.

~School Days~

THAT WEEKEND THE BOYS rested and got plenty of sleep so they were more than ready to leave for school on Monday morning. It was for Joe's sake that Ben was driving them to school. Mike could handle the strange environment easily, but Ben knew that Joe was apprehensive.

"Let's go kids, it's a good forty minutes to town and we need to be there by eight o'clock to get you registered." ordered Ben.

"One of us will pick you up at the end of the ranch road this afternoon." said Mari Beth as she handed them their lunch boxes.

Joe was ready to leave when he paused then turned around. "See you later Hannah…ah, you'll be here when I get home, won't you?" asked Joe trying to be casual about the question which didn't fool anyone.

"Sure Joe. I'll pick you up and we might sneak down to Luther's and visit the twins." She smiled as she gave him an encouraging pat on the shoulder.

"Oh hey, that'll be great," he grinned, "Okay, bye. See ya later, Carli." and Joe went out the door and Mike just shook his head, gave Carli a kiss on the head and followed Joe out the door.

"Where my boys going, Momma?" worried Carli as she stood up on her chair to watch the truck leave.

"They're off to school sugarplum, and one day when you're older you'll be going too. The boys will be back this afternoon."

"*You promise?*" Carli turned to frown at her Mother.

"Yes, Carli, I promise." laughed Mari Beth as she swung the child up and gave her a hug.

"Okay, promise is promise." and gave Mari Beth a smacking kiss.

Hannah laughed softly then said to her mother. "I'm not worried about Joe being so dependent on me right now. He's growing more confident all the time and soon I'll just be his auntie and he won't need me around all the time. That roundup was good for him, don't you think?"

Mari Beth nodded. "I can see the difference in him already and school is going to help a lot too. Next time Joe wants to visit the twins ask Luther to come pick him up. That way Joe won't depend on you always being with him down there."

"Good idea and visiting the twins will help break the clutching a lot faster."

"When Dr. Hennesy does his routine checkup on the foals next Thursday, let's invite the man to dinner." suggested Mari Beth innocently.

Hannah looked over her shoulder at her mother sitting at the table with Carli. And squinted her eyes and asked, "What's that all about? You aren't by any chance matchmaking are you Mother dear?"

"*Me*? Goodness no! I don't want you going off and getting married. What would we do without you?" and got very busy cleaning Carli's face and hands.

"Ah…right, sorry. I can't think what made me ask such an outlandish question like that. *Imagine* my mother trying to match me up with the ever so eligible Doctor Grant Hennesey. Why, it fair boggles the mind." clattered the dishes into the sink while her mother laughed softly and set Carli on the floor and taking her hand lead her out the kitchen to get dressed for the day.

Walking into a new school was always a tough experience though the Lord knew how many times Mike had done it before, but this would only be Joe's second experience and Mike could tell the kid was scared right down to his boots and hiding it pretty well.

Noisy children of all ages were streaming down the hallways with many a long look at the new kids. Joe and Mike had met some of them when they were celebrating their guardianship, but this was a lot of kids of all ages and it was rather intimidating.

Joe walked between Ben and Mike and wanted to clutch Mike's hand in the worst way, but he wouldn't allow himself to be seen as a scared baby. After all, hadn't he faced down a charging bull? He'd done *that* without having Mike hold his hand. Straightening up Joe walked bravely into the Principal's office.

The small talk between Ben and Mr. Cranston was friendly and the boys listened while Ben invited him and his wife to the dance and barbecue on Saturday and it was happily accepted. Regardless of the fact that the whole town has received an open invitation via the newspaper, this personal invitation made the principal feel special.

Once the paper work was done and class rooms assigned to the boys, Ben got up and turned to the young men and wink. "Remember, you're cowboys and have just come in off the range after a big round up, so *heads up* and I'll see you this afternoon." and started for the door.

Joe got a sudden empty feeling in his stomach as if someone had just pulled the rug out from under him. *Ben was leaving*! Joe swallowed hard and starred after the big man with huge eyes full of fear. Ben was *leaving* him here with strangers.

Then Ben stopped in the doorway and looked back. "Oh Joe, while I'm in town I'll get your pictures of the roundup developed and the ones you took of that huge mean old Mossy Horn bull you were bulldogging up there on the mesa where you narrowly escaped with your life. The kids here will really get a charge out of them."

Joe smiled weakly and it was interesting to Mike that Ben had waited to speak in an extra loud voice once he was practically into the busy hallway and the hush that immediately followed Ben's last words before the buzz of voices started up again.

Mike whispered to Joe. "I think that's our cue to act the big men." poking Joe in the shoulder and waggled his eyebrows at his brother and got a small giggle out of Joe.

It still wasn't fun having to walk into an already full class room and be the focus of every kid's eyes, but Mike waited by the door while the teacher greeted Joe. She appeared to be a kind woman so Mike relaxed a little more.

"Class, this is Joe Kelly; he and his brother Mike own the old Devereau Ranch. Joe, welcome to our school, we're really pleased to have you here. Now if you'll go sit down beside Tommy Lee over there (and Tommy Lee held his hand up), yes that's right, I'll look over your records then we'll start class."

Miss Ryerson nodded a smiling dismissal to Mike so he gave a thumb's up to Joe and left the class room feeling a little like he was deserting his brother. He knew how scared Joe was, but it couldn't be helped and maybe by noon Joe would have adjusted. Mike could only hope.

He walked into his Junior class to meet his home room teacher, Mr. Kilborn. "Hmm, excellent grades Mike, I must say I am surprised you've been able to keep such a high grade point considering the number of schools you've attended in the past. Well, now that you're going to be here all the way through high school, I expect you'll do even better. I see you enjoy music; guitar, is it? We have an excellent music department and if you want to, we'll get you into that today. It says here you compose and write your own music, well that's very interesting too. Hmm, I'd better give you Mr. Freedo's number," Mr. Kilborn wrote a number on a slip of paper and handed it to Mike. "He's a retired professional guitarist and plays the violin as well and perhaps he'll take you on as a student if you're interested."

"I'd like that very much Sir. I was hoping that I would find a music teacher to help me with composition and music theory." smiled Mike.

"Mr. Freedo composes music and that might make you more interesting to him as a student. What about sports, Mike, are you interested in playing basketball or football?"

"No Sir, I'm not interested in any team sports. You see, I have to spend time on the weekends with Mr. Tomlinson, my ranch manager, and learn how to run things so I won't have an awful lot of free time to spare. I ride of course, and at the Fair in October, I might enter the calf roping contest for my age group, but other than that, all the extra time I have will be for chores and my music."

"All right Mike, I understand. Since you've gotten a late start I'll mapped out past lessons for you to catch up on. If you need extra assistance with any of your subjects I'll be glad to help you. Also, when you are caught up there will be a test or two." Mr. Kilborn said rather austerely.

"I'd really appreciate you're doing this for me Sir, and thank you kindly for the offer of help and you can be sure I'll ask if I need any. I want to go on to college and get my degree in Business Management and Agriculture with a minor in music."

That response got a smile out of the serious teacher and Mike patted himself on the back 'cause ya gotta' start off on the right foot.

It wasn't exactly polishing the apple, but it was close. However he did have plans for college and those degrees.

The morning passed quickly and Mike was more than ready for lunch when noon came around. He had been getting acquainted with a lot of other ranch and farms boys as well as town kids and generally they were a friendly group; no sniping or giving the new guy a hard time and no challenges that a new kid usually had to meet out in the school yard. These kids seem genuinely interested in Mike's past and his experience with the rodeo circuit and the recent roundup. Before he knew it, he found himself to be somewhat of a celebrity and laughed about that, but he guessed there was a first time for everything.

On the bus ride home Mike was laughing when he told Joe about his day. "So, how did yours go?"

"Actually, it was great and that surprised the heck out of me. Golly Mike, I didn't know I was smart, but I am. The teacher was amazed that I could do what I did in the testing. Well after all, second grade isn't all that difficult, is it? I'm way ahead of the rest of the kids in most of the subjects. My math's okay, but it's not my best. Tommy Lee, the boy I sat next to in class, he's a whiz in math. Miss Ryerson is thinking of moving me up to third grade, but I don't know if I want to do that Mike, I'm pretty happy just where I am. I really don't want to change. See that kid two seats up, the one with the bright red hair? His name is Jack Golight and he lives at Luther's now 'cause his aunt is the cook. He's really, really quiet so I don't know him very well yet, but I will and when we go down to see the twins, I'll talk some more to him."

"Then he doesn't stand a chance of being a stranger for long with you on his tail. Poor kid, he's a gone goose and won't expect a thing until "The Joe Kelly Blitz" hits him." laughed Mike and Joe giggled at that too.

They rode along in silence for awhile then Joe said quietly. "We've been awfully lucky Mike, really, really lucky don't your think? Just look at what's happened since we arrived here. Doesn't it all feel like a miracle to you? We've got people who like us and will take care of us until we are old enough to do that for ourselves. I remember that dream about the folks telling us not to worry that we'd be fine when we got home. Do you think this is what they meant? I think it does.

Well, I'm glad we've got Mari Beth and Ben and Hannah because that means Carli and I won't be such burdens on you and I know we have. I never want to ever be a burden on you Mike."

Mike was shocked at Joe's words and felt a tweak of guilt. "Hey kid you and Carli could never be a burden to me especially not the way you mean and if I ever gave you that impression I'm real sorry. Yes, we're lucky to have the Strongbows and I do believe that this is the home the folks promised us. I will be honest and say it is a relief to me that Ben and Mari Beth and Hannah can share some of the care of you two, not all of it because I won't abdicate my role as older brother. I reserve the right to pound on you if you step out of line." and poked Joe in the shoulder.

Joe snickered and said, "Oh I'm scared, really terrified of that happening. *Right!* As if you've ever pounded on me like some brothers do."

Mike just shrugged. "Maybe I'm just saving it all up and when you least expect it; *wham*, gotcha." Now Joe did laugh then grew quiet again.

"It's amazing to me that we actually have a ranch of our very own, just like Mom and Dad wanted. Of course it's going to be mostly yours." Joe paused and thought over the many good things that had happened. "And I've got a new friend, Tommy Lee Quinn, he lives down on a farm close to River Town and he's a real nice guy. In fact all the kids liked me, and that was another surprise. 'Course, I promised I'd bring the pictures to class for show and tell and Miss Ryerson wants me to give a little talk next week on the roundup." Joe laughed and looked up at Mike with sparkling eyes. "Can't you just see me, the big experienced cowboy, talking it up big time?" He sighed and said in a pleased voice. "All in all, I'm happier than I have been in a long time especially with school as it is here. Are you?" Joe turned to look up at his big brother.

"Yes, I am." Mike looking out the bus window as the miles flew by with occasional stops to let kids off. "I've been so busy that I hadn't stopped to think about it much but, yes, I wouldn't want to be anywhere else now. This school is different from the others; no serious fighting and no teasing or bullying. Oh, there are a few kids who are kinda' snotty and standoffish, not liking a stranger coming to their school. On the whole…well, I can't just put my finger on it exactly, it's like everyone accepts you for who you are." More silence as they listened to the other kids talking.

"Say, let's do our homework now so after we get home and our chores are done we can watch a little T.V. We can do our reading assignments later too." suggested Mike. They got their books out and got busy.

The other kids noticed and asked, "Why are you guys doing homework now? Didn't you get enough work in school today?"

"Well," said Mike looking up from his book, "We figure that if we use this time for homework the more time we'll have to ourselves when we get home. Just makes sense to us since we're not doing anything right now as it is." Mike turned his attention back to the math problems. There was some whispering going on then some of them decided it was a good suggestion and got their books out too.

Hannah was there to meet them and after they climbed into the truck she asked, "Want to take a run down to Luther's now while you tell me how school went for you guys?"

"We sure do Hannah, I can't wait to see those twins Joe's been bragging on." laughed Mike. They took off after the bus and as they followed it along it got Joe to thinking about riding the bus with Jack on the days he wanted to help Luther.

"Hannah, I just had an idea. Why can't I ride the bus with Jack Golight on the days I can help Luther with the twins? He's the new kid living at Luther's and that way you wouldn't have to always drive me down there. 'Course, you'd have to come and pick me up. What do you think?" asked Joe

"Why that's a great idea Joe and maybe Luther could run you home once in awhile too. Yes, I think we can work that out with the school." Hannah was pleased as at another indication Joe was moving out of the clutching stage.

Both boys competed with each other telling Hannah all about their first day laughing and exchanging news passed the twenty minutes until Luther's place came into view and then they saw the roadblock. Hannah braked in front of the gate and before she could say a word, Johnnie Eddings came up to the truck

"Hi, Miss Hannah, we're on the watch for an un-welcomed visitor and it sure isn't you. Luther will be glad to see you all. Say, did you know we got ourselves a Chef? Yep, a real live, honest to goodness, certified chef. Man, we're all going to get fat 'cause she can really put out a meal and then some." Johnnie stopped talking; his mouth opened like a gasping fish. "Oh, ah, Miss Hannah, not that you need to fear any competition, 'cause you're the best in our book bar none. Ah, it's just that she's going to cook for us every single day you see? Not like we have to wait for you to treat us from time to time, you know."

Hannah laughed at the red-faced cowboy. "Not to worry Johnnie, I know what you mean and I bet Jude's a happier man too. See you later." For heaven's sake, what was a chef doing way out here in the country? And why hadn't her dear brother told them about her? She was going to burn his ears.

Trouble had come to the Valleys; guard gates and all. What did that *awful, awful* man want that he was terrorizing their boys and when was it going to end?

~Strike Three~

It was the dark of the moon again yet a barely discernible shadow slipped furtively along the west fence of Kelly's Ranch which was about a mile in from the road and not far from Rushing Woman River. The sound of the water covered any noise this ghost made. The dark shadow moved closer and closer until a man stood and paused to scan the fence line and surrounding area for guards and when he didn't see any he looked into the pasture that held the yearling stock.

"Now, they'll see that I can strike them anywhere and anytime I please." Elroy muttered quietly. "I'm getting bored with this waiting game."

He quickly ducked down and lay flat to the ground for he'd seen the rider coming out of a clump of trees and riding toward him and Elroy broke into a sweat and held his breath not daring to look directly at the man for fear his eyes would reflect light. The rider slowly came toward him then passed him by. Thankfully the wind was blowing toward Elroy so the horse didn't catch his scent. Sweating heavily, Elroy waited until the man disappeared from sight then waited another agonizing five minutes before crawling under the fence and moved a bit closer to his targets. There were four young bulls lying down together in the shelter of a small grove of trees fairly close to him. Snuggling heavy silenced rifle tight into his shoulder, Elroy sighted and took his first shot. The high caliber bullet took one young bull right through the head and it dropped without a sound. The other young bull raised his head and caught the second bullet.

Elroy crawled quickly back under the fence then in a crouching walk reached the cover of the pine trees before standing up to find his way back down to the road. He jogged and walked down the road for several hundred yards with many fearful looks over his shoulder until he finally reached his car. Breathing hard as he shut the car door, Elroy decided he was just about through playing Indian; it was just too exhausting.

Within an hour he was back in Claremont and tucked into his motel room on the outskirts of town. He laughed as he showered, at what easy marks those bulls had made. He could have killed a lot more, but decided two were enough of a demonstration. After all he wanted the boys' guardians to be afraid, but not so angry that they'd rather hang him than pay him.

Elroy laughed again, feeling more powerful then he had in many, many a long year. He'd just moved up a notch in his own estimation; he was now an arbitrator of life and death. Ah, revenge was getting sweeter and sweeter. He hummed a tune as he rid himself of the country dirt he had crawled through. Soon he'd be back in Armani suits, going first class and living the high life just as he deserved.

Tomorrow was time enough to make the next plan. He definitely was on a roll.

"Ben, this is Hank, this stranger has killed two of our prime young bulls in the back west pasture during the night. *Dagblast it all to hell and back,* how in the heck he snuck in on us I'll never know. No one heard any shots so he had to have used a silencer again. He's drawn innocent blood even if it's animal blood and this means he's pushed this harassment into a new level of violence starting with the roundup and I think it's more than likely he'll just continue to escalate. I believe he's gotten a taste for killing now."

"Shoot and blast that bloody-cold-greedy-no-good-evil-low-living-grub eating-son of a snake. He's dug himself a deep hole now" bellowed Ben almost beside himself at the waste and the fear that twisted his guts. He took a deep breath trying to control his hot temper. He spoke harshly, "All right, Hank, I'll be over as soon as I can shake loose from here. Check for tracks?"

"Yeah, he left a couple of boot prints and it will be interesting to see if they are a close match in size to the ones he left up on the mesa. *Dagnabit*, prime stock gone to waste and I can't even salvage the meat as the animals have been at them. All the cattle were spooked last night by the smell of blood and cause a minor stampede which was what caused Wolf to investigate. Let me tell you, that was one mad Indian."

"It's bad news alright and our boys will be upset, but you can bet we'll catch the weasel eventually. Anything else?" barked Ben.

"Nothing that can't wait for your arrival; I'm really sorry about this Ben."

"It's not your fault or the men it's that bloody man who won't stop at anything to get what he wants. I'll see you later."

"What's happened now, Ben?" asked Mari Beth wiping her hands on her apron as Ben slammed the phone down.

"*That bloody man has killed two young bulls over at Kelly's.*" Ben breathed heavily, "Two young bulls ready for sale at Huntington and would have brought top dollar too. It's a bloody waste! *And that man is causing me to lose aholdt of my temper.*" Ben growled and drew several more deep breaths hoping they'd calm him down; it wasn't working very well.

"It was bad when Joe almost got killed. I guess I shouldn't be surprised that he's killed again for he sure was aiming to do just that up on the mesa. Now he'd drawn blood and that shows us he's escalating his reign of terror. Mari Beth, I'm going into town and pick up the boys. I wouldn't put anything past this immoral man now; no nothing at all, not even the killing of a child."

Mari Beth put her arms around her angry man and felt him tremble as he fought to overcome his rage. She rarely ever saw Ben lose his temper and it scared her when it happened. "I think you're right Ben," she said softly. "Bring the boys home where we can protect them until that wicked man is caught. He has to be crazy for what he almost did to Joe therefore any children around Joe and Mike might be in danger too."

"Yeah, you're right, love." Ben held her tightly as he continued more deep breaths trying to get a grip. A man should have a temper, but have strict control over it at all times and never let temper control him. An uncontrolled temper could ruin your life. Slowly he grew calmer as he held his wife. Mari Beth had always been able to steady him. It mystified him as to how she did it, but it was if she drained the anger or the trouble right out of him. Ben hadn't really given it much thought; it was just something she could do that's all.

"Okay, I'm okay, I've got a hold of myself now. Thanks love. I'll report this to Brandt before I speak to the principle and the boys' teachers. I'll feel better about their safety if they're here." Ben heaved a deep sigh. "Thanks lovey, I'll leave for town after I see Hank." And giving his wife a big hug Ben walked out to the kitchen, put on his hat and coat and left the house without another word.

"Mom, what's going on? What's upset Dad so badly? I could hear him talking really loud on the phone." Hannah came into the kitchen with worried eyes and watched her mother sit carefully down at the table beside Carli who was big eyed.

"Momma, Daddy's really, really mad. It scares the baby." her lip quivered a bit.

"Oh, sugarplum, he's not mad at us; *No, no,* indeed he loves you like you were the best thing since chocolate, so no tears. And speaking of chocolate I've got ice cream with chocolate sauce for your morning treat." smiled Mari Beth.

"Sure, sure? Daddy's not mad at us? Promise?" Carli gave her Mother a frowning intent look. Carli's demand for promises was a sign she needed assurance.

"Yes Carli, I promise Daddy isn't mad at us, just at a very bad man."

Tears dried immediately on a sniff. "Okay, ice cream with choc'let now, Momma? Now please?" Her mother had promised everything was all right, so to Carli it was.

"I'll get it Mom and as soon as we have the little darling occupied you can fill me in on what's going on."

"That's me, little darling; I'm me, little darling, huh Momma?" Both women had to laugh and agreed with Carli. While she ate her treat Mari Beth quietly filled Hannah in on the latest happening.

Ben strolled briskly out to the barn and told the men what had happened over at Kellys. After giving them their duties for the day, he got one of the men to go down and set up a watch from a knoll in the south pasture overlooking the road armed with a rifle and a cell phone. Climbing into the truck Ben started for Kellys Ranch and arrived there within fifteen minutes because he wasn't picking any daisies along the way.

Hank and Ben rode out to the back pasture and looked down at what used to be young prime bulls. "Well Ben, here's what's left of the poor critters. They're really messed up now, but you can see they were shot right through the head at fairly close range. *Wouldn't*

I just LOVE to get my hands on this guy?" Hank fumed. "He's running circles around us and we're losing the battle."

The men looking down at the dead bulls and it wasn't a pretty sight for sure; one that he didn't want the boys to see. Yes, death and farm life went hand and hand, but not wanton killing just for the sake of killing. Ben shook his head; he just didn't understand how any man or woman could kill just for the sake of destroying a life. Ben guessed it might be a lack of any concept of right from wrong.

"I see you've moved all the cattle out of this pasture and further back of the ranch. That's a smart move as it's even further away from the road. Take pictures of this and any tracks you might find and get the men to wear gloves to dig out the bullets and put them in a plastic bag; there might be fingerprints on them. I don't know much about that sort of thing, but we'll take precautions." Ben shrugged his shoulders helplessly. "Also have them look around for the casings then bury these poor things right away. I'll be reporting this to Brandt when I go into town to pick up the boys. As of today I'm taking them out of school until we catch this fellow."

"Not a bad idea Ben. I've never seen an angrier crew. I'll take care of things here so you go on and try to keep our young boys from worrying too much."

"Yeah, easier said than done, Hank, I'm afraid I'll be worried about this mess until it's finally over and done with and mark my words, *it will be over soon* I guarantee that." he said grimly.

As the truck rumbled down the road toward River Town Ben got to thinking about what he was going to say to Mike and Joe. Whatever he said wasn't going to be a lie; the boys deserved the truth and maybe they'd be extra cautious. "Well, I guess I'd better give Lute a call and tell him the grim news. Just the way a fella wants to start his day." and picked up his cell phone and made the call.

"Hello Dad, what's up?"

"Lute, our man struck again and killed two prime young bulls in Kelly's west pasture last night."

"*Oh, for pity sake*, what kind of monster have we got on our tails? *Blast it all anyway*. Okay, what can I do?" asked Luther sounding as angry as Ben had been when he'd heard the news.

"Nothing, son, but I want you to watch your stock real close and move every animal back behind the ranch then ride guard on them.

At least the guy's going to have a long walk to do any more damage. Put night guards on from now."

"Sure Dad. Golly, the kids are going to take this mighty hard."

"I'm on my way into town to get them out of school. This man attempted to kill Joe and maybe more men in that stampede. Now he's killed two prime bulls. I wouldn't trust him not to try to harm the boys so I 'm keeping them home until we catch this sucker." Luther could hear the anger in his father's voice and under that was fear.

"Good thinking; okay, we're now on full alert. Call me if you need any help or anything, Dad. We're all yours and don't forget to watch your own back."

"Well, the Thunder Gods can't be too pleased about this latest event. Alright, I'll talk to you soon and spread the word for me son."

"Take care of yourself, Dad; don't let anything happen to you or the family." Luther hung up.

"Yeah, now wouldn't that be a fine kettle of fish." Ben muttered. "The children are to be protected at all cost. *Oh, Thunder Gods, take care of the innocent.*" Ben drove on down the road with an empty feeling in his belly.

~Dan Lightfoot~

FROM THE BIG BEND in the Rushing Woman River Dan Lightfoot cast his line out into the quiet pool of water as the main current swirled out and around the bulge of land. Fall weather was always unpredictable and chancy now that the winter rains had begun. However, today was one of those rare sunny, Indian summer days with a warm southern wind blowing gently across the land that fooled a man into thinking winter was a long way away. Any sane person would quit work and go fishing on such a day as this so that's what he'd done and had given the men the day off too which made him a very popular guy.

Dan reeled in and cast his line again and again in a steady whip like rhythm that never failed to soothe the wrinkles in his mind and caused him to forget any problems he might have. The wind moved its fingers through the grass and drifted the smells of late blooming flowers, hay and the scent of pine trees under his nose. Mother Nature was at her most outrageous as She blended trees with their leaves in a riot of vivid colors. The air breathed through the silence marked only by an occasional bird song and the sound of rushing water.

Dan Lightfoot was at peace with himself and the world.

He was a quiet man who had learned early to control his temper for he was an exceptionally strong man standing 6'4" in his stocking feet and weighing in at 210. He was thirty-years old with short blue-black hair that had already turned white over the temples giving him an older, more dignified appearance. The bright handsomeness of youth that he'd possessed before going to war was gone and now his face was marked with scars and deep lines carved there by pain. If you looked closely you could see past suffering in his eyes. It was a quiet, stern face for the most part, but when he smiled or laughed it changed into something very attractive indeed. His dark gray eyes had been inherited from one of his white grandmothers and his men swore that they could penetrate walls if he was angry or shine with humor whichever the case might be.

Dan had learned to take life pretty much as it was dished out and tried to make the best of it, however, he resented the leg that kept him from doing a lot of what he used to do with ease. Was he bitter? Was he disillusioned? Yes, for the most part he was and he had no one to blame for that except himself. He had chosen to go into the army with the bright idealism that he might be able to help bring peace to a war torn country, but instead he'd experienced only senseless death and destruction. He had lost too many friends in battle. Finally he came home wounded and in terrible pain as a constant reminder that he had lived while the others had died beside him. Why? What made him any different from the others that he was the one who had survived?

He fished on letting thoughts drift in and out of his head without clinging to any of them. The work was done and they were ready for winter. Of course, work on a ranch was never really finished, however he was at ease with the state of readiness they had achieved. The first early storm had come upon them so fast that it had caught him short without having finished his haying, but kind neighbors had pitched in to save his hay crop. He'd returned the favor by helping out at the Kelly's Ranch. Now the Kellys seem to have a mysterious and very nasty enemy trying to create even nastier harm. Attacking children had to be the lowest level any man or woman could stoop too; monsters for sure.

Dan's mind idled along as he worked the pool. He caught a few nice sized trout and put them in the bucket of cold water and continued to cast his line not really that interested in catching any more fish, it was simply that he loved the feel of the whole experience; sending his line zinging out across the slow moving current in a dance that was almost like meditation to him. The man, the fly rod, and the line were a slow moving symphony that made them one with the river.

The war had ended for him when his wounds had gotten him discharged only to arrive home to find his father had died some months before. No notification had come to prepare him for the shock. Probably the notice had been lost in the mail so the shock just doubled his pain. The real spooky part about his father's death was that he had died on the very day Dan had been severely wounded.

Sadness had piled on top of an already battered heart and body making his recovery very slow. And piled on the top of everything else was the guilt that he hadn't been here for his dad. Guilt was such a useless thing and only served to drag a person down for no purpose other than to destroy the will to live fully.

His ranch hands, God bless their hairy heads, had kept the place going and had worked for months without pay because the ranch was tied up until he could get home to sign the papers. Even after he had arrived, a wreck of a man, they had worked on carrying the full load of the ranch because it had taken the better part of a year to rebuild his strength. They had done more than their share to help him recover enough so he could take an active part in the work.

Dan called his men, his friends and named them: Mac McFarland, his foreman, Dubby Snow, Jasper Newley, Ozzie Cline, Dugan (Doubtful) Sloan, Mose Livingston and his son Little Mose, who was bigger than his father. Then of course there was Martha Longfellow his housekeeper/cook/surrogate mother and acting General of the Ranch. Dan had to grin because there was no question that Martha was CEO material.

When he had first come home, a shadow of the strong, confident and happy young man who had left, Martha comforted, nursed and worked with his disabilities and wouldn't let him lie down and quit. As he started to get better he'd have periods of depression and he wouldn't want to do anything, but sit in a quiet dark room that suited his mood. Then she'd nag him and force him to eat or move out of his chair and in those times all she lacked was an electric cattle prod though it hadn't been amusing at the time, he smiled. Now he figured if he had been stubborn about doing what she wanted, she would have used that little device very effectually on his rear end.

When he had regained what she thought was enough strength, she would irritate and nag him to get out and get to work. She said he was being lazy and selfish and letting self pity keep him from helping his poor overworked men. Dan would get so angry he'd storm out of the house to get away from her and walking as fast as his limp and his crutch would allow.

Dan chuckled at the memory; that wise old bird had known that to finish healing he needed to take an interest in something outside himself. Not once had it occurred to him that all he needed to do was fire her to shut her up and have his own way. Dan shook his head, how could he have fired the only Mother he had ever known? It just wasn't possible.

Dan liked remembering her cleverness as he worked the river. Yep, she was his CEO alright. He had given them all small shares in the ranch's profits to show his gratitude for their loyalty and each year the profits had grown. He encouraged his men to raise some of their own cattle along with his. So they were happy and Dan was slowly learning how to be happy again as well.

One of the joys he had lost was riding competitively in rodeos. He had been a champion bronc rider and calf roper; his father had been so proud of him. Dan had come home with a left leg that had been shattered below the knee and pinned together in so many places that he was lucky to be able to walk. His left arm and side had been easier to repair and he had worked hard with the physical therapist to rebuild the strength in his body, but his leg would never be strong enough to stand up to the strain of competing again. He would always limp and the pain would be a reminder when he'd done too much.

Dan knew he was lucky to even have a leg at all because the doctors had wanted to cut it off in the field hospital. They would have too, except for one surgeon, Doctor Henry Wright who had said that he could save it and he had worked like a demon for hours to see that Dan came home with two legs. Doc Henry knew how much Dan needed to be able to ride again. Well, he was grateful that he still could, not like he used to, but riding was part of his life and he never ceased to thank that man for giving him back one of his true joys even in a limited way.

"I just got to get Doc Henry out here. He'd love the fishing and hunting. Maybe I could get him and his family to move to River Town now that he's out of the service. We could sure use another doctor here and especially a man of his surgical talents. Yeah, and maybe we could enlarge the hospital too." Dan murmured aloud and he walked along the river. He'd write to Doc Henry today and give out the invitation. After all, the man deserved to see how Dan's leg was getting along if he needed an excuse that is.

Dan picked up his bucket of fish and walked along the riverbank, carefully placing his left foot so he wouldn't fall when he heard a horse snort and looked up to see Old Jim Waggoner sitting his horse on his side of the river watching him with his arm resting on the saddle horn.

"Howdy Dan, how's the fishin'?" came the gruff question.

"Pretty good and they're biting today. I've caught six nice sized trout for dinner. It might be they're stocking up on bugs for the winter." replied Dan in a reasonable tone of voice. His neighbor had a way of getting him riled without too much effort, but he had to admit the old man kept him interested and had never treated him like a cripple.

"Well, I caught me some whoppers down yonder just the other day at that next swing in the river; you might try it if you're a mind too."

"Thanks, Jim. How are you set for winter? Anything we can help you with seeing as how we're pretty much done over here?" Dan paused almost opposite from where the man sat his horse and flung out a test line to see if there were any biters here.

"Mostly all done as my place is a mite smaller than yours. Ah, I heard you might be going to the County Fair in Huntington this year?" Jim was looking off in another direction as though Dan's answer wasn't important.

"Yeah, I've given it some serious thought especially now that the ranch is good to go for awhile. I've got some excellent stock ready for market that I 'm having hauled into the sale barns on Monday. Cattle prices are up and I really don't want to hold too many cows over the winter. How about you, are you goin'?" Dan was amazed that he was actually holding a civilized conversation with the old coot.

"I figured on it. I've got three cattle trucks coming in on Monday to pick up my cows. You know Dan I've got me five really nice horses that I'm thinking of selling. I've been workin' on them for the past year or so and they are looking mighty fine. Ah, maybe if you're not too busy you could come over and give me your opinion on their worth. I hardly know what to ask for 'em."

Dan stopped fishing. Now why all of a sudden was this thorn-in-his-side being neighborly and asking for help to evaluate horses? This old man had probably forgotten more about horses then Dan would ever know. Hmm, now this was right curious.

"No problem Jim, I'm finished fishing for the day so I'll come over on White Boy here." The horse, White Boy had been following along as Dan had walked the river.

"Much obliged. Well, see you at the house then." Old Jim turned his horse and moved briskly off.

"Now if anyone had told me I could have civil words with that man, I'd have had to call him a liar. Something's happened to that old man and I guess I'm about to find out what that is. Do I really want to know?" Dan whistled for White Boy and began to unstring his fishing line and breaking down his pole into sections and once he had it back in its case Dan strapped it to the saddle with a tie. Mounted he hung the pail of fish up on a tree limb to collect on his way back.

Dan crossed at an easy river ford not to far away and moved at a good pace toward the Waggoner Ranch house. White Boy was one of Luther's prize Tennessee Walkers and a gift from one long time friend to another and a smoother ride wasn't possible to find. Dan with his bum leg, appreciated it every time he stepped into the saddle. White Boy could move fast so it didn't take long to arrive at the ranch house to find Jim standing on the porch watching him come.

"How's that Tennessee Walker for a ride, Dan? I've been thinking of buying one from Luther 'cause these old bones of mine don't much like the jolting trot of most of my horses, not even a little bit, yet I hate to give up riding all together." was the opening statement.

"Why don't you get up on White Boy and try him out? That will show you quicker than I could tell you about Walkers." and slid out of the saddle to land on his right foot and offered the reins.

Old Jim's face lit up as he stepped down off the porch and came over to the horse. Once Jim was mounted Dan said. "Wait a minute the stirrups are to long for you. Just give me a second and I'll shorten them a mite." Dan quickly adjusted the length. "Okay, you're all set to go." and watched Jim tear out of the yard at a fast gliding pace or with a Tennessee Quick Step is how Luther described a Walker's stride. Dan watched with amusement at the ride old Jim was getting.

When the old man came back into the yard ten minutes later his face was wreathed in a grin. He dismounted and helped Dan lengthen the stirrups again and loosen the cinch.

"I gotta' get me one of these here ponies. That's the smoothest ride I ever did have. Why my bones didn't complain once. I'm going to be down right discontented until I talk to Luther. Think he'll sell me one? He knows I treat my horses like children. Think maybe I could get me a nice one like White Boy here?" Child-like in his pleasure, Jim patting and stoking the horse's nose and showing Dan a whole new side to this thorny man.

"Why sure Jim, I know for a fact Lute is going to be taking fifteen or so Walkers to the County Fair next week. You might want to call him before you go up and he can give you the pick of that bunch." advised Dan. "I've seen the horses he's selling and they're real beauties, not a dud in the lot. The only reason he's selling them is because he's overrun with horses and he's got new fillies and colts on the ground too. I don't know how he can bring himself to sell one let alone that many of them."

"I sure will give him a call. You know, I could save him the cost of shipping another horse and that might lower the price just a tad and being a close neighbor and all he might make me a deal. Thanks Dan, for letting me ride White Boy; that was a treat. Now I'll show you those horses I'm taking and see what you think." leading the way to the barn.

It was obvious that the relationship between the two men had taken a 180 turn. Dan gave his advice, which he suspected wasn't really needed and waited for Jim to come out with what he really wanted.

"Come on up to the house and I'll give you a cup of coffee before you leave, I made it just before I took my ride." Once inside the small kitchen with its worn, but clean linoleum floor, Dan sat down at the vinyl covered table and sipped really, *really* strong coffee; Dan coughed and said. "I surely won't need a nap this afternoon, but it's really good coffee. Okay, Jim, what's up?"

"*What do you mean what's up?* Can't a man invite a neighbor in for coffee without being suspicioned?" Jim got a little red in the face.

"Sure he can, but I got a feeling maybe there's something else I could help you with and you're being shy as a girl about bringing it up, is all." said Dan peaceful like.

"Humph, I sure ain't no shy girl-child, but now that you mentioned it, there is one little thing." Jim fiddled with his cup a bit and tightened his lips as though gearing up to say something very difficult and Dan waited, more or less apprehensively.

"You see, I ain't so confident about making long drives anymore 'cause I get too blamed tired and I'm fearful of falling asleep at the wheel. If I kill myself, well that ain't no great matter, but if I'm hauling animals and maybe I hit somebody, well that worries me a whole bunch. I can't take a man from here to drive me because I need them to stay on the place to keep things moving. So I was wondering if I could go with you to the fair. I'm only going to take those five horses with me. Ah, do you think you would have room in your horse trailer for them? I'll help drive a bit and share the gas and I'll take care of my own expenses too." Dan could see the Jim was bending his pride to ask this of him. Well, between all the ranchers that were going and himself, he was sure he could squeeze in Jim's horses.

"Why sure, Jim that's no problem. You know Tom and the Chief are going to be taking some Appies, I mean Appaloosas and Lute and Ben are taking their horse selections too and I have a few nice mares and geldings I'm selling so between us all we'll have room for yours. That's what neighbors are for, you know. Sure I'll drive and you can co-pilot and I'll be glad of the company."

Jim flushed and mumbled a "Mighty kind of you, Dan, I'll help with the expenses and such like I said. Ah, when do you plan on heading out?" easing his way back into the comfort zone.

"This is Friday and Ben's big celebration is tomorrow, so let's talk to the men there about any spare horse space they might have. We may have to split your horses up among the trailers, but that's no problem. I guess we're all going as a caravan on Tuesday, safer that way too in case of breakdowns and such. I've already reserved a room at the motel close to the fairgrounds which you're welcomed to share with me if you'd like." Dan offered as he got up to leave.

"Thanks Dan, that's mighty kind of you and I'll sure take you up on that. I don't snore, least that's what my wife would have told you. There's nothin' worse than tryin' to sleep with someone beside you making sounds like sawin' a log. Well, I'm sure looking forward to the shindig of Ben's. Old Jasper isn't going, said he'll stay to watch the place, but the rest of the men wouldn't miss it. The Strongbow's sure know how to throw a party." as he walked Dan out to his horse and watched him mount.

"Thanks again for stopping by." said Jim and Dan touched his hat and turned White Boy for home and went like the wind just to show Jim what a rocking horse in action looked like from another point of view. He heard a departing yell. "*Wahoo, you go boy!*" Dan figured Jim meant his horse and not him, but who knew and laughed. He enjoyed the fast pace and the wind in his face. Life was sure full of surprises.

~Jacko~

Jack Olsen or Jacko as his pals back on Strongbow's ranch had dubbed him, leaned against the feed store building and looked up the street where their mystery man was just stepping into The Goodly Grub Restaurant. It was still early in Claremont, but the traffic was picking up; Friday's specials no doubt were bringing the buyers into town to stock up. He waved to a number of people as they passed by in their trucks.

Earlier that morning Jacko had searched several small motels in town without results until he was directed to the last motel out on the western edge of town called "The Sunset Inn." He was told it was being run by a widow woman.

"It's worth a try." murmured Jacko, "That fellow has to be stashing himself somewhere close by and he's not in Port City or River Town and he certainly doesn't sound like the sort to camp out."

Starting the pickup's engine Jacko drove out of town until he spotted the small, neatly kept little Swiss inn on the right side of the road with eight cabins scattered around a central garden. He must have passed it by a few times, but he couldn't remember having seen it before.

The tinkling of the little cowbell over the door warned the lady proprietor of a customer. As he entered the lobby Jacko could hear a baby crying in the background just as the owner came through the side door. Man oh man, this was some lady proprietor, he thought admiringly as he swept off his hat.

"May I help you, Sir?" And she had a very nice voice too, thought the cowboy; yep, mighty soft and genteel-like. For a few minutes the cowboy just stood and took her in. She wasn't too tall and not too round with shinning mink brown hair and amber eyes. Not beautiful, but mighty pretty all the same. Hmmm, then Jacko shook himself out of his muse.

"Oh, yes Ma'am, I'm looking for a fellow that might be stopping here. He's about 5'6" or a bit more, weighs about 160, has dark hair and a beard and I suspect he's a stranger to the Valleys too. Have you seen anyone like that recently?"

"Why do you ask?" she questioned with a suspicious look in her eyes.

"Well, Ma'am, we think he's the hombre who is doing a lot of malicious mischief up around our part of the valley, really bad stuff. We just want to locate him so the Sheriff can ask him a few questions."

"Yes, a man of that description is staying in cabin 4. His name on the register is E. J. Davies. I saw him drive toward town not too long ago. Is he dangerous? I have a baby here and I'm mostly alone during the afternoons and evenings." Now the lady looked worried and a tad bit scared, casting a glance back at the door where more crying… well actually screaming could be heard.

"Why don't you go pick up that little person and we'll continue to talk, I'll wait. Oh, I forgot to introduce myself; my name is Jack Olsen and I work for Ben Strongbow on Thunder Ranch over east of here." he smiled.

"I'm Mrs. Alexandra Armstrong, ah, I'll be right back." whirling around to pass back through the side door and within seconds the screaming stopped and Jacko grinned. Yep, that kid had it figured that if you screamed loud enough you'd get attention.

Mrs. Armstrong came back into the office and walked over to where Jacko waiting leaning his hip casually against the counter with his long legs crossed and his hat laid aside.

"Now, that's some boy you got there; good lungs too and he's almost as big as you are, Mrs. Armstrong."

She smiled, "He's growing like a weed and is big for a ten month old baby and he's walking which makes my life very interesting." and her mother's pride simply beaming. While they talked the baby eyeing Jacko with an intense gaze and for a few seconds man and baby held eye contact then suddenly the boy lurched forward toward Jacko with his arms outstretched and before the kid could hit the counter top, Jacko scooped him up.

"*Whoa* there fella," that's a great way to crack your bean. Howdy, partner?" Mrs. Armstrong just stood there with her pretty mouth in a nice O.

"What's his name?" just as though he handled babies everyday.

"James Gerald. For mercy sake, I've never seen him take to a stranger that way before. He has always been shy of strangers, especial men. For goodness sake, Mr. Olsen, give him back to me."

"No, no, he's alright for the moment and he seems to like my red scarf. Don't worry I put it on a clean this morning." Indeed the baby had a fist full of the faded cotton crammed into his mouth and was earnestly chewing away on the cloth.

"Oh my, I am sorry; he's teething and he'll bite anything; here give him to me." She came around the counter and tried to pry her son out of Jacko's arms and all she got was a grunt as the kid grabbed hold of Jacko's shirt and refused to let go. Jacko laughed, tickled pink as the boy snuggled down with his head tucked under Jacko's chin sucking like mad on the scarf.

"For goodness sake, Jimmy, you come here to momma right now." again she tried to pry her stubborn baby away from the stranger.

"Look Mrs. Armstrong, why don't I sit down in that rocker over there while we discuss Mr. E. J. Davies? It looks to me like this fellow is ready for a nap so maybe he'll go to sleep and you can put him to bed."

"Oh for goodness sake, he can be so stubborn. I guess I shouldn't be surprised. He's got a strong mind of his own, but you being a stranger and all; why he doesn't *like* strangers." she said again n a rather disgusted way. "This is embarrassing Mr. Olsen, what a way to introduce ourselves with my baby drooling all over you."

"Drool never hurt nothin' that won't wash off. Trust me, I've had worse." said the cowboy as he came around the counter to sit down in a rocking chair and began to rock; the kid never let out a peep. Jacko had to smile as he felt the baby's drool begin to soak into his shirt. Well, he'd had more disgusting things soil his shirt so baby drool wasn't a big thing.

They had an interesting talk while Jacko rocked the baby. He carefully unknotted his scarf so as not to wake the now sleeping child and let the kid have what scarf was left that wasn't stuck in his mouth. Mrs. Armstrong gently picked him up and carried him away and Jacko got up and went back behind the counter and took up his hat.

As soon as she was back he said. "I don't think you need to worry about Mr. Davies doing you any harm because he's not wanting any trouble here to attract attention to himself and right now he's concentrating on hurting some other folks; kids they are too. Well, it was nice meeting you and James. I'd best be getting back to town and keep an eye out for our man of interest."

Shaking her hand gently Jacko said, "I expect I'll be seeing you soon and fill you in on what's happening. By the way, does he owe you any money? If he does, I'll see that you get it pronto."

"No, he's all paid up through noon today. Thank you again for being so kind about the baby drool and all. I'll wash your scarf and send it back to you if you'll give me your address." smiled the pretty woman.

"No need to send it because I'll be by here next week sometime as I'm looking around for property to start my own farm or small ranch. Good bye Mrs. Armstrong it's been a real pleasure meeting you. Oh, in case you haven't heard, people here in the Valleys are always ready to help out if you have *any* problems you can't handle. Just you give a shout and you'll have more help than you probably would need and I guarantee that. You call Mr. Bob Zeggler who lives down south of Claremont a bit and he'll see you get that help quick like or you can call me at Strongbows and I'll come a-runnin'. We believe in being good neighbors." With a hat tip and a smile Jacko left.

As he drove out of the driveway Jacko waved to her as she stood in the door and said to himself, "Oh yes, I will definitely be back."

So here he was, leaning casual-like up against the feed store and waiting for Mr. E. Davies to finish eating his lunch when an old fellow came out of the feed store and stopped to chat. "Heared you fellows had yourselves that annual roundup out at Strongbow's. How'd go?"

"Hello Mr. Zeggler, how are you? Yep, we had us a time and we rounded up more than six hundred head off Flat Top. I declare we had us more cowboys than cows as it seemed like every man wanted in on the fun." Bob chuckled at that as Jacko continued, "'Course we kept it to men only, we'ens bein' the macho type and didn't allow the ladies to attend. How some ever, I got a feeling the females riders of our Valleys are about to rebel against that dictum. Strongbow is going to find himself with an ongoing party when those females make it known that they aren't to be left out of the bidding and that should make for a mighty interesting camp don't you think? It'll be a wonder if any work gets done." The men chuckled at that picture and Jacko went on. "We had Dusty Evans as cook and that could have been the attraction for many men as we didn't have any ladies present."

Mr. Zeggler laughed. "I agree Dusty might have been the main attraction, but I doubted it. It just gave the men a chance to cowboy like the olden days."

"Yeah, I'd say you're right there." They stood there in a companionable silence for a little while.

Jacko wasn't a handsome man according to the general standards, not with his reddish brown hair and a freckled angular shaped face with strong cheek bones, but his wide smile and straight white teeth were like a blast of sunlight that sparkled in his eyes and he could charm the birds out of the trees with his soft talk. His friends would say he had spaniel eyes, big and brown and trustworthy. Tall and strongly built yet slender, he was a horseman through and through. Jacko was a congenial man and liked most people, but when he didn't, that person knew about it in short order.

"I thought Old Dust had retired?" said Mr. Zeggler, breaking the silence.

"I think Ben bribed him or something because there he was with that big old portable stove and grill of his trailing behind the chuck wagon and *man* the cookin' was prime; why I haven't had better in a Five Star Restaurant in San Francisco."

"Don't say? Sorry to have missed that, but my 'rumitiz just won't let me fork a horse anymore and the wife would have had a fit kitty if I tried. Son, I love my wife, but sometimes it *do* get a might too interesting, if you know what I mean." the old man's eyes crinkled with humor.

"No I don't Mr. Zeggler, as the marriage bug never bit me. My advice to you is never let your wife hear you say that or you'll be sleeping outside with the dog." Jacko chuckled.

"That's so, that's so. Say, I heard tell that there was a lottery's been going on to see which men got to go on Ben's roundup, is that a fact?"

Jacko laughed. "Yeah, it's true only Ben Strongbow doesn't know a thing about it or at least he's never let on he knew about it if he did. I gotta' tell you Sir, the drawing is an exciting event. Dusty Evans runs it and no man wants to question Dusty as to the names he pulls out of the hat."

"No, I'd say that wouldn't be a wise thing to do." the older man chuckled. There they were, two men leaning up against the store front when Jacko saw Davies coming out of the diner and began walking the few blocks toward them.

"Well, tell me more about your round up."

"Well, we had us a little shindig up there when that old Mossy Horn Bull of Ben's decided to come out and join the party. He came barreling out of one of those small slot canyons and chased Ben's kid, young Joe Kelly, around some. Thanks be to God Joe was riding a real fast cutting horse and the kid knew how to stay in the saddle. Dead-Eye Jimmy Jumper Kilpatrick put that bull down with two shots and play-time was over for that he-bull. Yep, Jimmy shot him dead on Ben's orders if we ever saw him out among the cow-ladies 'cause that was one very dangerous mean bull and I've seen some doozies."

"You're jokin' me! You mean Jimmy killed that old varmint? Well, the country can rest easy now, especially the hunters. No man wanted to hunt up there 'cause you never knew where that big sucker would be hiding out. Is the boy alright?" inquired Mr. Zeggler, frowning in concern.

"Joe's okay and Jimmy's crack shots nailed that bull dead center in the heart from the back of a running horse. Sure as God made little apples, his trigger finger must have had some unusual help from You Know Who. It sure must have been a sight to behold, but I regret that I was way out at the south end of the Mesa so I had to hear about it from the others when I got back to camp. Of course the cows had to take exception to the noise and went to runnin', but we turned them away from taking a dive off the cliff edge back toward the gap and it actually made the drive easier 'cause we just picked them up on the way down to the ranch. Yes indeedy, it was excitin' for a time. Fortunately no one was hurt and that's another blessing of God, I can tell you. They're too many uncertainties when cattle decide to stampede. The men joked around saying Ben did it deliberately so they all could experience the old fashion cowboy way." commented Jacko while watching his man come toward the feed store.

"That Ben Strongbow, he's the man for sure. Say Jacko, you should tell that story to our news reporter and we could read something interesting instead of just that negative stuff about how our government is screwing the people. Heck, forget that, just tell me more and I'll spread the word; it'll give me a new profession as town crier." chuckled the old timer.

"Hush for a minute Mr. Zeggler, until this character passes." whispered Jacko and Mr. Zeggler mummed right up without asking why. They stood there quietly and looked away from E.J. Davies's approach and a few seconds later Elroy walked past them into the feed store as if they didn't exist; with no "howdy boys," or a friendly greeting like that. Jacko turned his head slightly and out of the corner of his eye he could see through the window as Elroy walking toward the back of the store.

"We suspect that he's the one who has been harassing the Kelly's ranch and shot those young bulls at Kelly's the other night too. Now, Bob this is real serious stuff and I might need your help. Let's just keep our voices down 'cause I don't want to scare this fellow off. After he leaves, I'm going to follow him and I want you to go in and find out what he's bought. Here's my cell number and you call me right away." Jacko reached into his shirt pocket and took out a small notebook and a stubby pencil and scribbled his number and ripped out the paper and gave it to his friend.

"Son from what you're saying, this is getting more dangerous than just mighty interesting; it sounds like a real, 'Who Done It.'"

Jacko laughed. "You just bet it is, Mr. Zeggler only in this case we're pretty certain *who done it*. You come up to Ben's place tomorrow 'cause he's having a dance and barbecue to celebrate the round up. I guess everyone in the combined Valleys who can, will be there." Jacko saw Elroy coming toward the front of the store and place a large bag on the counter.

"Let's just say we had a mysterious and invisible visitor out at camp one day and that old bull had been shot with a twenty-two to drive him out of his hiding place and he almost killed young Joe. Dusty Evans back tracked the man and gave us a very accurate description of him."

Jacko saw Elroy coming and nudged Mr. Zeggler's arm and they stopped talking until Elroy came out with the big bag over his shoulder and walked down the street toward the old livery stable that was now a parking garage. Jacko couldn't see what the label said.

"Now, I know more than most folks do about Dusty Evans and if he says that's your mysterious trouble maker you can take it to the bank which makes Mr. Davies a right interesting customer. Be sure you tell me the whole story son, until then I won't say anything, I'll just go in and find out what Mr. City Slicker bought."

"Thanks, Mr. Zeggler, that man's a bad dude, make no mistake. Give Ben a call if you see or hear anything else and call me when you find out what he bought and if by chance he gets away, warn people to watch their backs; this is a potential killer. By the way, I gave your name to a young woman by name of Mrs. Armstrong out at the Sunset Motel that if she needed any help she could call on you. Let me know." Touching his fingers to his hat brim, Jacko walked quickly away from the raised eyebrows of the crusty old timer.

"Sure will do Jacko; you mind yourself now." Mr. Zeggler called.

Just as Jacko reached the garage/livery stable's open double doors, a small rental car zipped out nearly catching his pant leg. "*Hey, watch it buddy*, this is a small town with lots of kids; *Slow down*." yelled Jacko busily memorizing the license plate number. He quickly wrote it in his small notebook and hurried to get into his pickup and follow after the speeding car. Jacko pulled out his cell phone and called Ben.

"This is Strongbow."

"Ben, this is Jacko, our man is leaving town and he's driving a blue four door sedan, recent Ford model and here's his license plate number." After Jacko gave Ben the information he continued. "Tell Luther heads up. I'm following him to see where he goes. Send up a red flare because I don't trust this snake not to do something really stupid. Well, he's doing the stupid now because he's working in daylight. He stopped at the feed store and left carrying a large bag. Mr. Zeggler had gone in to find out what he bought. Talk to you when I know something more." Hanging up he watched the car ahead disappear over the far hill. He wasn't particularly worried because there wasn't any turn off before County Road 10, except for other ranch roads and he didn't think this man was heading anywhere else except to Kellys.

The cell rang. "Hey, Jacko." said Mr. Zeggler.

"What did he buy, Dad?"

"You won't believe this, but he bought a bag of sheep dip and he told Fred he was doing a friend a favor by picking it up for him. Jacko this ain't good, that stuff is poison and will kill animals if they ingest it so you'd better stop him. I got a feeling he's out to poison some wells or the like."

"Gotcha, thanks Mr. Zeggler, I'll get back to you." as soon as he hung up he called Luther.

"*What do you want*? I'm busy here and up to my elbows in babies. State your business."

"Luther this is Jacko and I'm following our mysterious visitor, who is going by the name E. J. Davies, out of Claremont. He's carrying a mighty big bag of sheep dip he bought at Fred's Feed Store and heading your way. You'd better watch yourself; I surely don't want to see any of your horses going belly up. Here's his license plate number." Jacko rattled it off. "Your Dad will call Hank Tomlinson and have him put out look-outs because the feeling is that this is aimed at the Kelly boys again. Oh, you might give our local cop a call and tell him what's going on if Ben hasn't already seen to it."

Jacko listened in admiration to the descriptive words flowing out of Luther's mouth and not a cuss word in the bunch. It just proved to Jacko that that boy had him a good education.

"Yep I agree, but get busy we've almost reached the County road."

"Why is he acting as dumb as a post? He was being clever before this, why the sudden change? Well, whatever the reason it's our turn now. *Sun of a gun*, we're going to nail that sucker's hide to the barn door." and slammed down the phone.

"I don't know if I really like being out of school 'cause it was just getting interesting, you know? Ben must be really worried about us for him to pull us out like this. Even with time off we've still got studies. We'll get to go over to our ranch more often so it isn't all bad and I'll get to see Jimmy too." Joe said all enthusiasm.

"Yeah, I like it when we get to work around over there. Gee Joe, it's still hard for me to believe that we actually have our own ranch. Well, however thrilling as that fact is, Hank will have plenty of work for us to do so I think we'll have to give up the idea of lazing the days away."

Ben stepped out onto the porch and looked up at the sky. "Yep, it looks like it's going to be a great weekend for the shindig. The ladies are gearing up for it so we men had best get out of the way for awhile until it's our turn to work. Come on, boys let's roll." and trotted down the steps and raced the boys to the truck. At the end of the ranch road, Ben stopped to talk to Jeb Goggins who was standing guard with his rifle. Mike and Joe looked on with sober interest at this show of defense, scary too.

"I heard from Jacko and he said the guy was on his way with sheep dip so heads up." said Ben. "Luther called and said they're on the alert too. Jacko's on our man's tail and he won't lose him"

"Then we can't tell where he's heading for sure, boss, but it's more than likely here or over to Kelly's place."

"Where's Julep? I thought I sent the two of you down here?" said Ben, frowning.

"He's over in them trees Ben, just in case I need back up. *Hey Julep*, show yourself so the boss can see you." yelled Jeb.

"*Hey boss*, I've got a real good view of the road both ways from up here in the tree and nothin' coming so far," called Julep, a black slender young man that reminded Mike of a panther and he was just as quiet as one so you never knew when he was around until he was just there. Now he was totally invisible among the tree branches.

What fascinated the boys was watching Julep carve little figures of different sizes of just about anything. Miniatures, Julep called them, and they were so life like that he made a fair amount of money when he showed them at the fairs. Mike and Joe treasured the ones he had given them. Joe got a six inch craving of Jigger and there was no mistaking the wooden horse for any other one and Mike got a carving of a cowboy playing a guitar of about equal size. It eerily resembled Mike.

"I'm heading over to the boys' ranch and I'll be there for awhile so call me if you need recruits or something happens. I don't need to tell you boys that this guy is up to doing us a heap of hurt. He must have utter contempt for us as he's working in daylight now. Well, his ignorance is our advantage."

"Yeah, it sure does appear he's not too bright, but maybe it's more like arrogance. We're covered here Ben, and we've got some of the boys riding fence along the road. This guy hadn't better mess with us." Jeb said sternly and Ben believed him.

"Okay, see you later." Ben put the truck in gear and drove out onto the county road.

"Do you think this guy Jacko's following is the one causing all the trouble?" Mike questioned.

"Yes I do and so does Jacko. I think it's better than a good guess because he certainly answers to the description we have. As far as I know, most of the strangers we've had here have passed on through. Now this guy has been seen around in one town or another, always moving so we couldn't pin him down. It's becoming evident that this maliciousness is aimed at you and the ranch since all the damage has been done there and caused Joe and us grief on the roundup." Ben drove fast as he thought out the talk.

"It all started after you kids arrived which makes it more than likely that someone heard about your inheritance and decided on a little blackmail. He's doing the first really stupid thing by working in daylight. He must think we're all a bunch of dummies. Well, we'll find him and put a stop to this once and for all. Right now we've got everyone in the Valleys alerted to his description and car license. There are so many eyes watching him that he'd be shocked if he knew we've peg him."

Joe was silent while he listened to Ben talk. He was shocked that someone would deliberately set out to harm an animal or a person. The concept was so foreign to him and to the very air of peace here in the Valleys that it was hard to swallow. What was wrong with that man?

"The Gods won't like him being here. I bet he's going to hurt the water or the land and that means he's going to hurt more animals. No, the Thunder Gods won't let him and you can take *that* to the bank." both Ben and Mike looked down in amazement at this fountain of certainty sitting in the middle of the bench seat.

"I sure wouldn't bet against you Joe, that man is in bigger trouble then he knows." was the only comment Ben made for the rest of the drive.

Ben's cell phone rang. "Yeah?"

"This is Jacko. Our man saw the guys at the head of Luther's road and turned around and is now back on County 10 and driving towards River Town. He almost clipped me coming out of Thunder Road. I'm following, but I've got a hunch he's going to come around the other way so tell the boys. I'll give you a warning when he starts getting close."

"Good work, Jacko. Do you want Hank Seely or Sam Carrington to spell you at River Town and follow him north? We don't want to scare this boy off. He's going to be our meat."

"Good Idea. Yeah give Hank a shout and have him waiting at his farm road. I'll drive on into town and let him get ahead of me before I follow. If this guy changes his mind about taking North Mountain Road I'll give you a shout, but I can't figure where else he'd go other than that way."

"Consider it done." Ben disconnected then dialed Hank's cell phone.

"Seely's."

"Hank this is Ben. The man who's causing the Kelly boys trouble is coming your way. He's carrying a large bag of sheep dip and that means water poisoning to me or putting it on the land for the animals to eat. Jacko's following him from Claremont now. He turned up Thunder Road, but saw Luther's men at the ranch gate and turned around. He's heading for River Town and if our suspicions are right, he'll head up North Mountain Road. If so he'll be coming by your place in forty minutes or less. Can you pick him up from your road as he passes by?"

"Sure I can, it will be my total pleasure. Mess with us, will he."

"Okay, here's the description of his car and license number." Ben rattled that off. "We want you to follow him wherever he goes. Be careful because this is one mean dude and he carries a gun."

"Have you figured out why he's acting in daylight now? I'm betting that he's gotten impatient to finish. I think greed is pushing his buttons real hard and he's about finished playing around. Well, he's our meat now. Mess with our Thunder Gods and you're in a whole heap of hurt." growled Hank. "No worries mate, and I think I'll give a few of my neighbors a call too. Many eyes watching won't hurt."

Ben disconnected and looked over and said. "Well Hank more or less said the same thing you did Joe. That guy is in more trouble than he knows. Somehow I can't feel sorry for him. I don't have much compassion for anyone who deliberately and with evil intent, harms or kills the innocent human or animal just to destroy or out of greed."

Ben turned into Kelly's road and stopped to speak to the men there and give them an update. "Stay on your toes guys because our trouble maker is heading this way. I'm going to send a few more men out to keep the road fence under observation. We're doing it at our place too. We want the man to come on the property and then we'll catch him red-handed. Remember, the Thunder Gods don't want any human blood spilled in violence on Their lands, but if he gets nasty well, we'll have to take action."

"Shoot Ben, I'll just rope and hogtie him like a calf critter, might drag him a tad. Think the old Gods would mind that?" Jimmy didn't look like he was funning either.

"Jimmy you're a complete hand so just keep your rope handy then. I'll call you." and drove on up to the house.

"I'm calling Dan too; you never can tell what this dude will do. Like Joe said, he might do a hurt to one of our friends just to prove he can." Ben drove ahead as he dialed Dan's number.

"Hello Dan? Oh, Martha, this is Ben Strongbow, where's Dan? Okay, this is an emergency so find him and tell him our bad man is going to be passing his ranch within the next hour. We don't know what this guy will do, but we think he's coming to the Kelly's place to poison the water. Tell him to protect his boundary line. Yeah, he's a nasty piece of work. Bye Martha."

Hank walked out from the barn to meet their truck. "Howdy Ben, hello Bosses." and the boys laughed a little at that, but quickly sobered.

"Hi Hank," smiled Mike, "we already know who the boss is." That got a chuckle out of Hank and he slapped the boys on their shoulders as they got out of the truck.

Ben gave Hank an update on the progress of their man in question. "All I can say is he's going to *love* meeting Kelly's men if he's coming here, and I hope he does 'cause we'll be sure to give him a warm welcome. I've got men staked out in the short hills watching along the County Road that he won't see so he'll be in for a big surprise." Hank seemed unworried so that eased Mike and Joe's concern a little.

"Blast it, I forgot to call Brandt. Hold on just a minute." Ben picked up the phone and called the Sheriff. "Hello Max our trouble maker is on the way here……..Oh, Luther's already called you and you're on your way now? Well, wait up a bit until I hear from Hank Seely that he's picks up our man on the north road then jump on it…….. Right, we'll hold him when we catch him. Right, no blood on the ground guaranteed, but there may be a few bruises." Ben laughed. "I promise he'll be in deliverable condition. Yeah, right, see you soon."

Joe spoke up before the business talk could start. "I don't really know a lot about ranch business and book work so if it's alright with you, I think I'd like to go pick out my bedroom and then visit with Dusty, is that all right? Oh, is Mrs. Hank here?"

"I left her talking to Dusty in the kitchen just before you arrived." replied Hank.

"Sure take off Joe, I'll call you if you're needed." Mike watched Joe going off to hunt May's cookies or something of Dusty's which was his real objective and not picking out a bedroom. Thank goodness the kid had a metabolism that didn't run to fat, but the kid was growing and had finally put the lost weight back on so he was looking good.

"This is your future office Mike. I've been using it because all the ranch's records are here. Now pull up some chairs and I'll show you what's been done and the bills I've got here for Jensen to pay."

For awhile, they concentrated on the book work and the lists of jobs done and still to be completed. The house was contracted to be painted next Monday which pleased Mike then Ben and Hank got to talking about the next Cattlemen's Association's meeting.

After a few minutes of sitting and listening to the talk, there didn't appeared to be anything that required his input so Mike got up and wandered over to the fireplace to look at the long row of pictures on the mantle. There were quite a few pictures of people he didn't know, but must be related to him somehow. He came across a picture of a handsome man that was probably his grandfather. Joe looked a lot like him and would no doubt grow more in likeness as he got older, but no way would Joe ever look so stern. He saw pictures of his mother at different ages; in fact the mantle was mostly about her. For a father to display all these pictures of a child he supposedly had disowned was a very odd way to behave. You'd think there wouldn't be any pictures of Mom around. Yet he remembered her bedroom, how it had been kept just as if she'd left a short time ago.

Walking along the big fireplace he finally arrived at the far corner. He was about to turn away when a fluttering red ribbon caught his attention. He stooped and saw that the ribbon was caught between two large stones. Naturally, he gave it a tug with no results; it was caught fast.

"Ben, come here a second; I've found something curious." called Mike. Ben turned around and saw Mike standing at the far corner of the fireplace.

"What is it, Mike?"

"I don't know, but there's a piece of red ribbon stuck between two large stones."

The men got up and walked over to the fireplace and stooped to looked at what Mike had found. Each gave the ribbon a gentle tug with no response.

"My guess is there's a hidden safe here and your grandfather left you a clue. Lots of these really old fireplaces have safes because in the old days there weren't any banks handy to a ranch. I've got something similar over in my house." said Ben. "Hmm, let me poke around a bit because there should be a trigger or a lever maybe under the wood mantle." as he felt along under the mantel edge. Hank gave a grunt and did something and the large rock slid out.

"Yep, there's the lever right here just above the safe. What's in there, Mike?"

"Looks like a whole bunch of stuff. I'm going to start dragging things out if you'll put them on the desk." The first thing Mike got hold of was a thick roll of writing paper tied with the same red ribbon. Handing it to Ben, Mike delved deeper into the hole. Out came boxes, coin folders, jewelry boxes with worn velvet coverings and more papers in a small leather binder. When the safe was finally empty the men gathered around the desk and waited for Mike to open it all.

Mike hesitated then walked over to the hall door. "*Hey Joe, come here, we've found some things that you've gotta' see.*" The thumping of running steps came down the long hall and Joe popped into the office holding a half eaten cookie in his hand.

"What did you find? Is it a treasure? *What?*" he said excitedly as he shoved the rest of the cookie into his mouth munching fast and brushed his hands off on his jeans.

"We don't know yet, but I'm going to start opening stuff up." "Mike grinned at his brother's eagerness. Slowly Mike untied the red ribbon from the large roll of papers.

He read aloud: "**Dear Grandchildren: I have received word of your parents' death and cannot say how deeply I am grieved. I had hope that one day your mother would come home and she would have everything I have. It is never to be my dream.**"

Mike stopped and looked in shock at Ben and Hank. "It's been in the drawer ever since he heard. It's a long, long, letter." Mike stopped speaking and thought for a few minutes. "I think I'll read it later, if that's all right with you."

The men nodded and Mike carefully rolled the letter up and tied it again with the red ribbon. They must have been Mom's red ribbons. He sniffed and quickly blew his nose then picked up the first velvet box and opened it.

On the worn purple velvet cushion was a beautiful set of lovely pearl earrings with a matching necklace and bracelet. The clasps had small diamonds with central emeralds. The pearl bracelet was interspersed with small full cut emeralds and diamonds surrounding them. The set was just plain gorgeous.

"Wow, won't Carli look great in those when she's older?" said Mike and closed the cover. He opened other boxes of jewelry; there was a necklace with dime size gold nuggets and diamonds, a few rings that looked quite valuable with their green stones and others that appeared to be rubies and a man's large gold seal ring that Mike liked. There were several large gold bracelets and gold chains along with four sets of cuff links and shirt studs and several gold pocket watches with chains and fobs. Then Mike opened up the first of three coin folders and saw row after row of twenty dollar gold coins dating way back. There must have been at least 30 in each folder.

"Geeze peeze, I guess they must be worth a lot now, huh Ben?" whispered Joe.

"Yes indeed Joe, a lot of money. I don't think I've ever seen a collection like these, have you Hank? Well, if you decide to sell these, Mike, there's enough there to pay for everyone's education and then some."

"There's no rush about making a decision right now. Let's finish this." Mike picked up a leather bag that clinked and opened the draw strings and poured out more gold coins onto the table and quickly saw that the coins were randomly dated and some showed a little wear.

"Gee, wouldn't that make a great show and tell at school." They laughed at the boy who saw things as they were important to him.

"Yeah, it sure impresses me. Here Joe, take this one and do your thing, just remember to give it to Mr. Cranston so he can lock it up when you take it to school." Joe took a heavy coin and slipped it carefully into his shirt pocket and buttoned the flap down. He patted it for it was his very own personal treasure now.

"That's the lot and a treasure trove it surely is. My goodness, we just seem to get richer and richer all the time. Ben, don't you think we'd better put this stuff in a safety deposit box at the bank? I sure will be nervous knowing this was here in an empty house. Oh, it isn't that you couldn't protect it, Hank, but it's a worry you don't need."

"And right you are Mike 'cause I don't want to be responsible for all that." Hank assured him fervently. "In fact it makes me sweat to know that it was here all this time."

"I want you to have two gold twenty dollar coins Hank, because you're doing so much for me and Joe and before that for grandfather, so we'd really like you to have them." Mike carefully picking out two coins that had the least wear and handing them to Hank whose jaw just about came unhinged.

"You can't do that Mike! I mean those coins are very valuable and all. Why, you had better get those appraised before you hand them out like candy, not that I don't appreciate you wanting to give it to me." Hank was having a hard time of it and had his hands behind his back.

Mike sighed, looked down at Joe and raised his eyebrows. Finally Joe sighed too. "Mr. Hank if you don't take them now, you'll just find them in your Christmas stocking and Santa Claus will be really pissed if you try to give them back. Besides, it's a long cold ride to the North Pole for returns."

Hysterical laughter roared through the room as the men collapsed into their chairs. It brought May and Dusty out of the kitchen to investigate. When they looked in, Mike and the men were in hysterics with tears streaming down their faces. Joe looked up at her with a sober face. How he managed it Mike never knew, but they all heard Joe explaining to May.

"Mike tried to give your husband a present and he refused. So if he doesn't take it we're going to have Santa Claus put them in his Christmas Stocking." Joe held up the gold coins.

May gasped and Hank choked out. "And it's a long cold ride to return them to the North Pole." He went off in laughter again and May slapped a hand over her mouth as she too started to laugh. Dusty just chuckled at the scene in front of him. Joe just sat there with a grin on his face.

"Oh my, oh my goodness Joe, you *are* one in a million." Joe stood up, was still holding the coins, and walked over to May, took her hand and placed the coins in it. "Maybe you'd better hang on to them until Mr. Hank makes up his mind. Just don't go spending them all in one place 'cause I guess their worth a lot of money. Oh, well, it will help your retirement fund, won't it?" May grabbed Joe and gave him a hug that made him grunt yet he looked awfully pleased.

Mike got control of his laughter and chose two more of the best coins from the pile and handed them to Ben. "Now let's not go through another refusal Ben, or I'll sic Joe on you." And Ben held his hands up as though in fear and took the coins.

"Thank you boys, you're very kind and generous and I'll keep these in memory of this fine day." Ben put the coins in his shirt pocket and he too buttoned it down carefully.

"Take that as a lesson, Mr. Hank Tomlinson, be a gracious receiver as well as a giver. I for one thank these young men for their generosity. Now Dusty has lunch ready so come and eat." commanded May then with an audible sniffed, turned around and walked away and Dusty moved to follow her when Joe spoke up.

"Wait." said Joe and picked up another two coins and walked over to Dusty. "You're part of our family now Dusty, and Mike and I don't have too many in our family anymore so we want to thank you for finding out about that bad man and coming to live with us. These are for you."

Dusty looked down at the boy then over to the other men. "Don't look at us for help Dusty, or you'll just find them in *your* Christmas stocking." laughed Ben.

"Now boys, this is mighty fine of you, mighty fine. You don't owe me anything, but if you're adopting me into your family, well how can I say no?" and grinned at Mike and Joe, but there was a warmth in his eyes that said it all and accepted the gift.

"I knew you were a smart man, Dusty, and I know I can learn a lot from you too if you'd just talk a lot more." complained Joe, yet his grin spoiled the reprimand and that made Dusty laugh and shake his head at Joe.

"Mike, would it be alright with you if I gave Jimmy two of these coins, sort of a thank you for saving my life kind of a token, I mean?" asked Joe anxiously.

Mike picked up two more coins without asking Ben's permission and handed them to Joe and he carefully put them in his other shirt pocket and buttoned it down.

"We'll be ready for lunch Dusty just as soon as we get this stuff put away. Well, there has to be a bag around here somewhere that we can use. Mike, you want to keep your grandfather's letter, don't you?"

Once the treasure trove had been put into a shopping bag that Dusty found for them, they went into the dinning room and had a great lunch.

They had just finished when Ben's cell phone rang and silence fell around the table. "This is Ben."

"Ben, he's on his way to the Kelly Ranch or your place. He's almost to Black Hawk River where it crosses under the County 9 bridge." warned Hank Seely.

"Okay Hank, keep pace and call me; I'll get all the men out now."

Ben looked solemnly over at Hank and as he rose from his chair said, "He's on his way here I think so let's see what the man does, or tries to do. I think we need to round up the rest of the boys and cover every place he could squirrel in. He may not come by the road all the way."

Ben's cell rang again. "Ben, *he's stopped alongside the road*. I got my glasses on him and he's at that place just beyond the river where there's a large outcropping of rock and a bunch of aspen growing, you know the place? I'm sure it's on Kelly's ranch about two miles this side of their ranch road."

"Got it, thanks Sam." Ben stood up and spoke quickly. "Hank, get all the men mounted, he's here and parked on the county road beside that huge rock pile and aspen grove."

Hank leaped to his feet and ran through the kitchen to ring the giant ranch bell that signaled emergencies and fires and men boiled out of the cook shack and came running. "We've got that intruder on the property down near the road at the Old Rock Pile so get the horses saddled. *Move it*!" Then Hank dialed a number on his cell and said to the men on the road.

"Get over to the Pile of Rocks off the county road; our man is there. *Move it as fast as you can! We're on our way.*"

"I want you boys to stay here, understand?" Said Ben and ran with Hank to get a horse. There was fast and furious saddling made difficult by the excited horses, but the men mounted and were running all out with Hank and Ben in the lead. From the high porch Mike could just see the gate and Jimmy on his racing fool of a horse had jumped the fence bordering the ranch road and it looked like he was going to out distant the other riders by a mile. The men disappeared behind a hill leaving May and the two boys alone.

"I'm calling Luther." Mike went into the kitchen and picked up the phone.

"*What*? If this isn't an emergency, hang up the bloody phone. I'm having babies here!" said the sharp voice.

"Luther its Mike, I wanted to tell you that the guy's on my property down by that big pile of rocks beside the county road. Ben said it was about two miles east of my ranch road. Thought you'd want to know, anyway the men went blasting out of here and they should be there fairly soon."

"*Shoot and blast, I'm going to miss all the fun*. I'm on my way." the slam of the phone rang in Mike's ear.

Mike hurried out of the kitchen and stepped down off the porch into the yard, turned and said calmly and emphatically to May. "This is *my* ranch and nobody is going to cause harm here." and took off running for the barn. Within minutes they watched Mike tear out of the yard running his horse all out following the path the others had taken.

"Oh, my goodness, Ben isn't going to like this. No indeed he isn't, and that foolish boy has no sense at all and shouldn't be going after the men." exclaimed May ringing her hands.

"No, you're wrong Mrs. Hank, that brother of mine is as good as any man because my father trained him that way. Don't you worry Mrs. Hank, Mike can handle himself." Joe said it with such confidence that May almost believed him.

She hesitated then turned and went quickly into the kitchen leaving Joe standing on the porch looking down the valley where the men had gone. Sometimes it was very hard to be a young boy, he thought.

~Confrontation~

Mari Beth and Hannah were just finishing lunch and talking about the upcoming celebration when the phone rang.

"Strongbows." Hannah said in a cheerful voice.

"Hannah? This is May Tomlinson. I need to speak to Mari Beth. It's really important." May's voice sounded shaky.

"Sure May, just a moment." bringing the phone over to Mari Beth with raised eyebrows. "It's May Tomlinson."

"Hello, May, what can I do for you?"

"I really don't know, but I thought I had better call you and let you know what's happening here. Mari Beth, *THAT MAN* is here on the property! He's down at that big pile of rocks close to the county road. The men went out of here like they were shot, the whole kit and caboodle. Ben told Mike and Joe to stay with me, but Mike just left on a horse following after everyone. I *tried* to stop him, but he wouldn't listen to me, he said it was his property. Ben's going to be so *angry* with me, I just know it." Mari Beth could tell the poor woman was in tears.

"*No he won't,* May, he's knows boys so you *calm down* and take care of Joe. I'm on my way over there *right now.*" and hung up the phone.

"Hannah, listen for Carli," ordered Mari Beth as she threw on her coat and grabbed her car keys, "*That man* is on the Kelly ranch and all the men including Mike have gone running down to that big rock pile by the road." Hannah eyes opened wide for she had never seen her mother so angry. "*I'm going down there and give that creature a big piece of my mind and maybe I'll boil his gizzard while I do it!*" and slammed out the kitchen door.

Mari Beth drove faster than she usually did and skidded to a halt at the gate. "*Get that gate open now before I break it down!*" she ordered and the men scrambled to oblige her and barely got out of the way before she hurtled through. Mari Beth was determined she was going to be there to protect her new child from danger if there was any, regardless that all the other men would be doing the same thing. Right now she was one angry and frightened woman and that's a very dangerous combination as a wise person knows.

By the time the main body of riders got to the pile of rocks they saw that Jimmy had roped their man and his horse was dragging him at a stumbling walk away from the large feeding area and water tank. When the men got closer they heard the man screaming vindictive and very nasty words, threatening to report Jimmy to the police. Jimmy just kept the horse at a nice fast walk and grinned at the men as they rode up.

"Here he is boss, all pacified-like. 'Course the mouth on him isn't, but I figured you could cure that real quick like." And with a jerk on the rope the man fell to his knees. Keeping the rope taut Jimmy stopped his horse and being a good cutting horse it kept the rope tight and never let the man get up off the ground. It was funny to watch the man try to stand and the horse would back up sharply then *wham*, the guy was on the ground again.

"You'd better stay down mister or you're going to be mighty bruised on your neither parts." said Ben and dismounted as the other men circled around to enclose their prey and to get a better view of the action that was sure to follow. They didn't want to miss a thing. No one paid any attention to another horse that joined them a few minutes later.

"You've no right to do this to me. You're going to pay for harassing me this way. 'cause I wasn't doing nothin'; just looking around the place that's all and you can't prove anything else. There's no law against just looking around." yelled the man. Anyone with eyes could see how frightened he was as he twisted around to look at the silent men ring him.

"You're trespassing and there is a law against that. There is also a law about perpetrating malicious mischief on private property. *Now what is your name and what are you doing here?"* commanded Ben in a "don't mess with me," voice. He stood there looking as solid as an oak tree with his arms crossed over his big chest.

"I'm Elroy Stover Devereaux, son of Howard Devereaux who was a brother to Joseph Devereaux, that's who I am. Joseph was my uncle so therefore I have every right to be on my uncle's property. *I'm family!*" He screamed.

"Well, well, well… *Elroy*." said Ben in a gentle tone that had the men perking up their ears. The disgusted way Ben had said the man's name was as though it was a very bad taste in his mouth and he was trying to spit out. Whenever Ben got real quiet that was the time to pay close attention. "It has been a long time since I've seen you… *Elroy*; not long enough I might add. I didn't recognize you with your dyed hair. Of course, you are a few years older than me, fifty three or fifty five, aren't you? Don't you remember me *Elroy*? My name is Benjamin Truelove Strongbow, the Indian boy you used to play nasty tricks on when you visited your Uncle Devereaux. I also remember you taking my horse without my permission and almost crippling him. However, what got you kicked off Lost Wagon Ranch was being cruel to Devereau's horses and the other animals, not to mention being down right nasty mean to Jean. Now, since you're such a *stupid man* I'll tell you that the Thunder Gods don't *like you*. I don't think you remember too well what *They're* capable of doing … *Elroy*. I don't like you, *the men* don't like you and *you're* in big trouble."

"*That ain't so*! You're lying, I never did anything wrong and my uncle liked me; it was my father's fault we had to leave and….and I ain't afraid of any old gods who lost their power years and years ago; They're just made up *stories* to scare children, 'tis all."

Every man there felt a sudden shuddering cold winter wind begin to blow when there hadn't been any wind at all to speak of on this beautiful warm autumn day. It blew the dust in circles around Elroy like a miniature dust devil. He looked down, blanched, coughed and moved quickly on his knees and broke out of the dust circle. The wind remained chilled, especially where Elroy was, blowing his clothes and hair into fierce disarray causing him to shiver in its cold breath. The men also felt the drop in temperature, cold that made you feel as though winter's blast was right here. It didn't take a genius to know which Thunder God was causing it. They all knew they had Silent Witnesses.

"The whole Valley knew about you and your father…. *Elroy*, so don't try to convince these good men, who haven't had the displeasure of knowing you before, that you were a misunderstood boy. Now, *what are you doing here with that bag of sheep dip?*" Ben asked sternly.

"You know nothing about anything, and that bag *ain't* mine. Anyway, I don't have to answer to *you, you Indian,* this ain't your property." Just as he managed to stand up, Jimmy jumped his horse backwards spilling Elroy on his side again, very hard.

"Now boy, I'm a right peaceful man, but you keep a civil tongue in your head when you address *Mr. Strongbow* or I'll drag you all over this here field and it won't be a gentle trip." said Jimmy Jumper in a stern voice.

"*I am* the owner of this property so *you will speak to me,*" said Mike angrily as he pushed his horse through the men and dismounted and walked over to the man. "*Speak your piece and make it fast*; these men don't need to waste their time listening to a bunch of lies from *scum like you.*"

The men perked up when they heard their young boss's strong words. This would be their first real analysis of their new owner's character. Unknown to Mike it would prove something basic to these men. After all, they had their pride of place and they wouldn't work for a man they didn't respect.

"Let him go Jimmy, let this so called *man* stand up and explain what he's doing on my property." ordered Mike.

"Yes Sir." And walked the horse forward and gave the rope a flip that loosened the loop. Backing his horse up, Jimmy calmly coiled his rope loosely, but the men noticed he didn't hang it on his saddle horn.

"Shame on you boy for treating me this way; I just wanted to look around the place before calling at the house." Elroy got busy brushing off his clothes and didn't see the disgusted look on the men's faces.

Mike walked over and got right in Elroy's face and said in a low angry voice. "I told you *not* to waste your time lying to us, *Mr. Elroy Devereaux.* Now, what are you doing with that bag of sheep dip over there by the feed shed and water trough? I think Mr. Strongbow asked you the same question twice and if you don't answer it promptly, I'll have Jimmy show you the property in a way you won't enjoy." The men cheered that causing Elroy to look around in a panicky way. Jimmy began to play with his gathered rope while isolating the loop into his right hand in a hopeful way. Of course the grin on the young man's face wasn't something the Elroy thought as comforting.

"How *dare you* talk to me like that? How dare you threaten me? My uncle would have wanted me to have a share of this place as one of the only living close relatives he had." He said angrily then shifted to continue in a whining voice. "I know he wouldn't want me to be left out of the will. He was an old man and just forgot me is all because it's been awhile since we've seen each other. It's only fair that you share a little of the wealth with me and then I'll go away and I won't even contest the guardianship, being as I'm your only real living relative and should actually be your guardian."

Elroy looked furtively around and shivered before leaned a little closer to Mike and smiling slyly whispered. "If you'll give me $200,000.00 dollars I'll never darken your door again and I'll bring no harm to your sister and brother or anything else on the ranch."

The men heard what Elroy whispered because at that very moment of Elroy's speaking the wind picked up his words, amplified them and literally broadcast them around the circle of waiting riders. It was obvious that Elroy had wanted the threat to go just to Mike's ears, but the wind heard and grew colder as though it was blowing straight off the glacier. It was very *cold; very, very cold*. Frost began to form on Elroy's clothes.

Mike stiffened and drew back a step or two from this creature; scorn was evident in the lines of his youthful face as he looked down upon the lesser man. Young he may be, but Mike had firm integrity of character and he felt a blistering hot anger like he'd never experienced before. This was the man who had almost killed Joe.

The men looked at each other and nodded their heads in agreement; the Gods were definitely not happy with Elroy Devereaux. And just maybe the Guardians had been the cause of Elroy and his father being kicked off the ranch in the first place.

Elroy gave a convulsive shiver as his clothes crackled with frost. The continuous drop in the wind's chill factor began to crawl up his backbone, his breath puffed out in clouds, but he was intent upon pressuring the kid who he considered an easy mark and thinking he could use the threat to get what he wanted.

The Mike looked around at the men and said loudly. "Did you hear this man threaten my brother and sister and the ranch if I didn't pay him $200,000.00 dollars?"

"Yes Sir, Mr. Kelly, we heard him loud and clear with the help of the Thunder Gods. Remember them, Elroy?" growled Grumpy one of the older hands on Lost Wagon Ranch. "Well, some of us older hands talked about you and what we recall ain't a good report on your character."

"He still hasn't answered the question of what he's doing with that sheep dip, Mr. Kelly. It appears he isn't going to either. That would probably come under the heading of self incrimination. Now, I would suspect that being as how that bag is so close to the water tank over there, I just might suspect he planned on poisoning some cattle and horses just to encourage you to pay him off. That's what I suspect anyway." said Jimmy who was in the process of building a bigger loop on his rope. The men beside him moved aside as Jimmy began to idle swing it around and around.

"Now, now wait a minute, don't you dare try anything with me, cowboy. Why I was just going after some gypsum weed I saw over there and you can't prove I was going to do anything else."

Then Elroy moved closer to Mike while he kept his eyes on Jimmy and whispered. "Now, maybe I was asking too much boy, maybe just $100,000.00 would satisfy me and you can just call it insurance and write it off your taxes." smiled Elroy insincerely and if a man looked close enough he might notice the sweat beginning to run down the side of his face and freezing on his cheeks. In his state of anxiety Elroy didn't seem to notice.

"You really are stupid if you think we'll buy your lies. We don't run sheep and you don't kill Gypsum Weed with sheep dip either. You're a blackmailer and a low life that would poison innocent animals. I strongly suspect you've killed good stock besides being a trespasser. And worse of all, I suspect you sent that bull after my little brother and almost got him killed and that's an *assault* charge *Elroy Devereaux,* and for that last act alone I am tempted to let Jimmy show you around the land, but I don't want your blood polluting the ground and hurting my beautiful land spirits. You *will* go to jail and I *will* personally see that you do." Mike spoke in a harsh and angry voice.

The suddenness of Elroy's attack took everyone by surprise. He pulled a knife on Mike and before anyone could react Mike and Elroy were grappling. The action was so fast that Ben had only taken a few steps toward the struggling couple when Mike bulldogged Elroy just as he would a large calf, rolled him over his hip and the knife went flying. Mike threw the man belly down on the ground, knelt on his back, snatched his pegging string out of his rear pocket, wrenched Elroy's arms back behind his back, lashed them together then pulled up one of the man's thrashing legs and had him tied up just like a calf in less than 7 seconds. Stepping back Mike looked at Ben and said breathlessly. "And not a drop of human blood has been spilled on my land through violence."

Ben roared with laughter and stepped over to Mike whacking him on his back so hard that it practically knocked him over before Ben grabbed him in a bear hug. The men howled in laughter that had the horses snorting and dancing around at the sudden noise. Now they knew the steel in their young boss.

Jimmy yelled. "Time! And the winner is Mike Kelly. *Way to go, Mike!*"

It became noticeable that the cold wind had stopped and warmth now filled the inner circle. Just about then Sheriff Brandt stepped between two of the horses into the center, and as he walked past Elroy he looked calmly down on the trashing, cursing man.

"Hello Ben, I see you've got the situation all tied up." and that brought more gleeful laughter from the men. "By the way, who is this man and what's this fussin' all about?" said the big man with a smile as if he didn't know.

Sheriff Brandt listened to Ben with input from various others who would stand as witnesses; in fact the sheriff had far too many willing witnesses. Ben introduced the Sheriff to Mike and as they shook hands Mike looked into the most penetrating eyes he'd ever seen. He'd thought Ben had penetrating eyes, but this man's eyes could surely drill steel walls.

Sheriff Brandt turned back to Ben and commented. "I got your paper and description of the man who attempted murder on the Mesa and this man sure fits Dusty's I.D. Since it was Dusty, his findings will stand in any court. Of course, so will Mr. Hoggins sighting him in the immediate vicinity around the time of the attack. Let's see this bag of sheep dip." Sheriff walked away paying no attention to Elroy rolling around on the ground and yelling abuse and accusations and fearful denials.

Ben led Max down the pasture and stopped a few feet away from the bag and they both looked the situation over. The Sheriff saw that the bag had been partially ripped opened and was sitting right next to the water trough. He took a camera out of his pocket and took several pictures of the bag from different angles with the trough and the feeding station adjacent to it and the footprints in the damp ground leading up to the bag.

"One of you men put this bag in my cruiser's trunk and wear your gloves because I believe Mr. Elroy's fingerprints are all over the bag." called the Sheriff. "And maybe one of your men will drive Mr. Devereaux's car into town so we can examine it. That should prove enlightening. We'll also inspect his motel room too. Oh, don't step on these footprints either. I've got some plaster of Paris in my car that will do just fine."

They walked back over to Elroy and stood looking down at him for a few minutes as Elroy squirmed and whined that he'd been mistreated and attacked.

Brandt said, "I've heard about you, Elroy Devereaux, and it wasn't any good either. Obviously you ARE a very stupid man to dare to come back to the Valleys when the Gods are pissed off at you. Now, Mr. Elroy Devereaux, I'm arresting you on charges of trespassing, malicious mischief and blackmail, which I will testify to as I overheard everything and I also charge you with intent to poison and/or kill cattle and horses belonging to Mr. Michael Kelly. Now I'll read you your rights" And did so as he stooped over and slapped handcuffs on Elroy's wrists paying no attention to his yelling his innocence and claiming he'd been attacked by savage men while taking a walk.

The Sheriff loosened the pegging string and holding it up asked, "Who does this belong to?" as if he hadn't witnessed the neat tie up job of Mike's.

"It's mine Sir, he jumped me with a knife and I bulldogged him and tied him up." answered Mike stepping over to take the string back.

"Yeah, he did Sheriff, and in less than 7 seconds too." a cheerful voice volunteered.

"Very nicely done I see, and remarkably fast too, young man. Are you thinking of entering the roping at Huntington this year? Oh, by the way please put the knife into this bag for evidence." The Sheriff pulled out a bag and handed it to Mike. "Be careful to pick it up by the tip; fingerprints you know." The Sheriff hauled Elroy up on his feet and Elroy kicked the Sheriff in the leg, wrestled himself out of Brandt's grip and had taken all of two steps before the big man grabbed Elroy by his collar and the seat of the pants and lifted him up on his tip-toes.

"Now sir, I'm also charging you with assault on a minor with a deadly weapon with intent to injure him, striking an officer and resisting arrest. Judge Ruben Barker is surely going to have fun with you. By the way, do you remember the little boy you used to tease and torment when you visited here? Yep, that was Ruben Barker just to refresh your memory. He's our judge in River Town now and a very worthy man." and laughing sadistically at the whining voice of Elroy as the Sheriff walked him toward the fence with Elroy's toes barely touching the ground.

"Would a couple of you men help me get him through or over the fence because I can't give him any excuse for accusing me of police brutality." laughed the Sheriff.

Just at that moment, Ben saw Mari Beth in the loosened circle of horses as the men moved aside to let her through. "Oh, oh, I've got big trouble coming." He murmured to Mike as he watched his angry wife walk or more like stalk toward him. "Hi, honey, been standing there long? I didn't see you come up. No worries love, everything's under control now as you can see." Ben grinned and no one closer than Mike could see the anxious look in his foster father's eyes.

"*I've seen it all, thank you.* May called me and told me what was happening and she was worried sick about Mike being here. So I came over to see for myself how all you *great* men were protecting the children and the property while we *helpless women stayed at home* like *brainless little girls*. You didn't tell us the truth of what was happening as though we were *too fragile* to handle a crisis." Mari Beth said in an intense voice not taking her eyes off her husband all the time she was closing in on him. Mari Beth shook her head with a mixture of feelings written all over her face; grief, anger and disappointment.

The other men on hearing her first words had quickly taken their horses and walked out of earshot. They knew it wasn't smart to be in the same vicinity with a very angry woman. Innocent by standers could be injured.

Mari Beth whispered intently. "*I didn't think it of you Benjamin Truelove Strongbow. I thought you knew better than to under-rate me, humiliate me like this. And you, Michael Devereaux Kelly,* I'll have an explanation from you when you get home as to why you disobeyed orders and put yourself in danger. You could have been badly hurt if that man had struck you with his knife and we would have failed to keep you safe. *I'm disgusted with both of you.*" Mari Beth gave both of them a look of such repugnance that it turned them both into embarrassed little boys.

Without another word she turned around and headed for the fence. Divine took one quick look at Ben then he and Wolf hurried after Mari Beth to help her through the fence. It wouldn't do for Ben's wife to get hung up in the barbed wire and definitely not now 'cause as mad as she was she'd probably tear the fence down single handed.

"*Wow,* did you hear her? I haven't seen Mari Beth that angry in years. She's always so calm and collected. My, isn't she some humdinger? *My little woman* doesn't take a back seat to anyone." said Ben proudly yet sheepishly too, still stinging from her rebuke.

"Ah, Ben," said Mike quietly as he watched Mari Beth stomping away with anger flowing off her in waves with the two big men scuttling behind her, "I hope you're not going to treat this like she's having a temper tantrum because if you do, you're really going to be in hot water up to your lips." Mike paused for a minute before saying. "You know, once in a great while my Mom used to get really mad about something that Dad did or had said. My Dad, being a really smart man, walked very carefully around her for a time especially when he knew he was at fault. It was my observation that flowers are good and being really humble helped too. Also apologizing profusely is a must. If none of that softened Mom's anger, then Dad would almost grovel, but that was the last resort."

Ben rubbed his chin and glanced down at this young man and simply grunted as he turned his attention back in time to see Mari

Beth climbing through the fence with the help of his men and sighed deeply in relief when she was safely on the other side without tearing anything important.

Mike went on. "The thing is Ben, Mari Beth is right and we should have told her when Elroy was on his way here. I know I'm going to catch it because I disobeyed your order to stay at the house and I'll probably catch it from her too. That's okay; I'll apologize to her; not for coming down here, but for upsetting her. She's a fine lady and I'd never willingly hurt her for the world."

Ben turned to Mike and squinting his eyes at him. "Yes, now that you remind me young man, you had no business being here. He could have hurt you and if he had hurt you I would have drawn his blood without a second thought which would not have pleased the Thunder Gods at all. I came that close to violating Their law." Ben said sternly.

Mike faced Ben calmly. "I may be young Ben, but I'm not stupid or weak. Dad trained me in self defense because the rodeo circuit isn't for wimps. This is *my land* and it is *my duty to protect and defend it* as The Thunder Gods demand we all do. Blackhawk told me that so I did and I won't apologize for it. However, I respect your right to discipline me for my disobedience so whatever you decide to do, I'll accept it." Mike said in a sober voice. That statement pulled Ben up short.

"Well shoot and blast boy, you would have to go and say all that. I guess I can't fault you for acting the man and danged if you aren't right about being responsible to protect the land and all so there won't be any punishment. Still in the future, try giving whatever comes up next some real serious thought before you act. Like I said, I don't want any more white hair before it's due." Ben put his arm around Mike's shoulder and added smiling. "That was real fast work disarming and tying Elroy up; mighty quick and slick it was."

"My Dad taught me a few wrestling moves as well as boxing. Remember what I said about traveling the rodeo circuit wasn't for weenies; I had to know how to defend myself."

"You sure did that so fast that I didn't have a chance to move in. I think we better have you practice roping calves before we go to next year's fair. I sure think you could stand up and give the men some stiff competition. Your Dad was quite a teacher." Mounting up they all rode back with Hank, Jimmy and the other men.

"I am formally issuing a protest, boss." complained Jimmy, "All the fun was taken away from me 'cause I wanted to show cousin Elroy the land a little. It sure wasn't hospitable not to have done so seeing as how he wanted to take a sentimental walk around the property and all. I'm sure he would have gotten a howl out of it." The men laughed at their laconic joker. The mood was a lot lighter than when they had ridden down here.

"Jimmy, you've got a job for life." laughed Mike. "If there's a next time, you get to do just that and I'll watch."

"Remind me I owe you a little bonus for that roping, Jimmy. I know, I know, you enjoyed the whole thing, but you kept him from dumping that sheep dip into the water and really fouling up the spring that feeds it too before we could arrive and stop him. Man, with that horse of yours and your dead-eye with a rope, not to mention a gun, I'm betting on you to win at the fair. Yes, sir, we got a crew that's going to lick the rest of the contestants to smithereens." and the men all agreed to that.

Riding back Ben heaved a huge sigh. "Speaking of a licking, I guess Mike and I had better go home and get ours over with or Mari Beth won't be fit to live with." Ben gave another all-suffering sigh which caused the other men to quietly snicker at the big man. "I sure don't like eating humble pie, but when a guy has been married as long as I have and haven't had to eat humble pie often enough to remember what it tastes like, well, it's demoralizing for a man of my age." groaned Ben dramatically. The men were trying to be kind and not snicker too loudly in Ben's face, but it was a trial.

"Well Ben, you've just forgotten what it's like to be a kid. We're used to eating humble pie quite often and if Hannah makes it, well, it won't be too bad." and they all had a good laugh out of that one too.

All the chit-chat was just cover up for the relief they felt having gotten to Elroy before he could do any more harm. They all had felt that chilled wind though Elroy had gotten the brunt of it, at least none of them had frost on their clothes. Although it hadn't lasted long the look on Elroy's face showed a fear he couldn't hid from them and maybe now he believed a little more in the Thunder Gods, but of course he was basically a stupid man so maybe not. It seemed to the men that Elroy ignored the obvious if he didn't want to see or hear it.

Right now, riding back to the ranch, Mike thought the land felt different. A wave of good feeling washed over him as though the land spirits were thanking him for protecting them against harm. Mike listened and looked around as he rode and even held his hand out palm down as he'd see Blackhawk do in acknowledgement and maybe giving a blessing at the same time. He thought the land welcomed him in a noticeable way.

Whatever it was, this was his land now by having fought for it and it was savagely satisfying. Mike laughed, yep it was savagely satisfying.

~Mike~

THERE HADN'T BEEN TIME to read their grandfather's letter after they got home Thursday afternoon and the evening had been taken up with discussing Elroy and his arrest.

Mike gave a short laugh as he remembered Ben practically on his knees trying to make up to Mari Beth. He had even brought her some Indian Paint brush and some hardy daisies along with a bunch of ferns; it *was* a pretty bouquet. Mike was relieved to see that Mari Beth didn't carry a grudge for long. Once she had heard the sequences of events she kissed Ben and told him that in the future she was to be told everything. Ben, being a smart man, agreed fervently. She even kissed Mike and told him to use his better sense next time something important happened because she hadn't taken on another son just to have him injured in a stupid fight.

Mike had to give her a big hug which he had never done before and it surprised Mari Beth to no end, but she returned it in good measure. "I never want you mad at me Mari Beth, so I'll try to do better. I'm just grateful that you care so much about what happens to me. Just as though you really were my mother. I mean that sincerely."

"Oh, go on with both of you smooth talkers; honestly, I'm so sticky with all this honey flowing over me I'll probably have to go take another shower." laughingly, Mari Beth shooed them out of the kitchen and turned her back, but not before Mike caught a look at her tearful eyes.

Going back to school on Friday had been very exciting too, since every kid had heard about the arrest and wanted Mike's blow by blow description of the scene. However, popularity had its price and Mike began to slowly unravel. The capture of Elroy Devereaux had released him from worry that was true, but oddly enough that event had been like a catalyst that released his control on everything that had occurred up until now. It suddenly was all in his face; so much, *too* much had happened in a short length of time and Mike was feeling like he was about to burst wide open at any moment.

Mike was silent on the bus and that had Joe looking at him with concern but kept quiet. When they got home that afternoon they did their chores. Mike was almost complete silence. He felt Joe looking at him inquiringly a few times however he didn't ask any questions. Once they'd finished the chores Mike was barely able to keep the lid on his chaotic feelings. He knew the crisis point had been reached and he had to get away. In his room he put on his jacket, grabbed his guitar case and walked downstairs to the kitchen.

"I'll be back in a little while, Hannah. I'm going out for some air." Mike said abruptly.

"Sure Mike, supper will be in ready in an hour or so." and watched him leave with a worried frown on her pretty face. Quietly Joe watched Mike through the kitchen window as his brother crossed the yard heading for the far trees. Something definitely was bothering him.

Mike had found an empty cabin that had an air of long disuse sitting twenty feet back from the other men's cabins and close to another pretty white fenced cabin that looked a lot like a doll's house. He didn't understand why these cabins were separate from the others, but it suited his need for a place of retreat. He stepped up on the small porch and opened the door. Roscoe slipped in before Mike could close it behind him.

"Okay you can come in, but I don't want any conversation, you hear?" and stroked the dog's head before Roscoe went and flopped down in front of the cold fireplace. The cold musty air of the cabin wasn't pleasant so Mike set his guitar case down and left the door open when he went out to the wood shed with Roscoe walking tight to his side as though he knew Mike was upset. Mike didn't notice him as he gathered up an armload of wood and kindling and added three or four pine cones to his load.

Mike knelt down in front of the fireplace and carefully laid the fire then lit it. He watched as the fire got a good start then put on a few larger pieces of wood then stood and contemplating the growing flames for a bit. He turned and walked across the small room and closed the door. The room smelled better for the short airing and the small room began to warm quickly. Roscoe flopped down in front of the fire and laid his chin on his paws while keeping both eyes on the face of his master.

Mike didn't know what there was about rocking chairs in this country, only everyone seemed to have a lot of them. Mike had every intention of asking Ben how come everyone he knew had a few and that they all looked the same. He pulled the rocking chair up close to the fire and sat down.

Warmth permeated the room as he rocked and stared into the fire. He allowed his mind to drift while receiving comfort from his silent companion snoozing on the old rag rug. It eased him in a simple unconscious way. After a few minutes he took off his jacket and hung it over the back of the rocker then sat down and opened the guitar case. It took only a few minutes to tune the strings and when he was Satisfied, he closed his eyes.

Gradually he released the last of his emotional grip and allowed himself to touch the pit where his deepest feelings were stuffed; feelings of grief, anger, pain and indescribable sense of loss. Mike's fingers begin to stridently strum the strings discordantly, beating and pounding the guitar in raging sound. Roscoe tightened his ears flaps down.

Then the music came with unstructured violence, music he heard in his soul and heart. Always he had known that this was his gift! To be able to hear and bring into manifestation the music that came through his feeling nature. But this wasn't an intellectual endeavor; this wasn't a well thought out piece of composition; *this was the gut fire of released emotions. It hurt!* The passionate outpouring of all the penned up angers, fears, anxieties and sorrows he had *stuffed*. The guitar sounds were dissident and loud that pulled out everything in a deep cleansing.

Mike's face *twisted* into agonizing lines as tears poured down his face and sobs shook his body. He played as though his life depended on it, and maybe it did, for he felt it was *safe* to let go now. He could safely pour *everything* he was feeling into his music, and in the course of this purging it would set him free; to be safe around people.

There was nothing gentle about this torrent of noise, no one could call it music. This violence came out as a steady strumming and pounding out the deeper tones and higher notes that seemed to scream the frenzy of emotions. Yet strangely even as the buried fury was escaping and emptying the suppressed feelings, there was something *powerfully moving* with its expression of absolute freedom from form. It was a strangely..... *compelling battle* Mike was waging was full of undeniable authority and would have pulled anyone listening into full emotional response. It's a wonder that Roscoe didn't howl.

The guitar wept just like its master wept.

Unknown to Mike, the men in the main cabin heard him begin to play. Well, it wasn't playing exactly, for this sounded like a soul in agony burning up the air waves. Even with the distance muting the throbbing music, how could they not hear that volatile sound coming from the deserted cabin up the way? It was a miracle the guitar didn't go up in flames or break into pieces. Such were the men's quiet voiced comments.

They knew only that Mike was playing and from its ferocity the men also knew he was in deep pain. They looked at each other in concern as they listened to the anguish and the grief pouring out into the night. This was so unlike the Mike they knew, one who always appeared to be a quiet and controlled young man.

Without a word Jacko stood up and put on his jacket and hat. One by one the others did likewise and followed him out of their combined living room/ cook shack. Quietly they followed the growing sound of the music until they reached the porch outside Mike's cabin and silently sat down. They wouldn't disturb him, but somehow maybe their presence would comfort him on a subconscious level.

Roscoe lifted his head hearing the men's quiet arrival, but he didn't smell any strangers and as nothing further happened so he laid down again, but kept his eyes on his master and his ears tucked tight to his head.

The violent music ended abruptly. The sudden silence from within the cabin had the men looking at each other in speechless questioning. Was Mike finished? Then there came a melodious, spaced picking of strings in a tune that *grabbed* at a man's heart. If one could claim that an inanimate object could weep then the guitar did with its plucked notes that quivered with sadness. As the men listened, not a few brushed their cheeks as they remembered their own memories of loss and pain. Slowly the music began to strengthen with undertones of light and dark and soon it *soared into lightness*. When it was finished the men felt like all the suppressed grief had been released into the heavens; a purging of pain. If you had dared to ask them they probably would have sworn an oath that the music and everything it contained went straight up to the Gods on Thunder Mountain.

The cowboys gave a collective *sigh,* yet they didn't utter a word to each other. Maybe the reason was because the effect on them was all too personal. After that a number various melodies followed each different, each potent with possibilities until finally, silence fell within the cabin. They waited. Time passed until the men thought the playing was over. *Suddenly* there came a simple run of notes that built and built and flowed into a melody that was so poignant, so down right beautiful that it felt like a benediction after a dark storm.

Jacko looked up and saw Joe sitting on a tree stump not far from the porch with his hands clasped and with his head bowed, just sitting and listening. Upon hearing the last song repeated several times with minute changes here and there, Joe nodded and stood up. He looked over at the men, smiled then waved to them and walked back to the house. The men left just as quietly. Joe must have felt that it was all right to leave his brother now that he had gotten into the composing mode.

The men had learned something very valuable about this quiet young man; he was a deep one and didn't show much on the surface, but underneath was a whole different story and they knew Mike was a very special person.

Joe opened the kitchen door and saw everyone seated at the table.

"You're late young man. Where's Mike?" asked Ben. "All he told Hannah was he going out for awhile and that he was carrying his guitar case."

"He's in that old cabin down in the woods. He's playing Ben and we need to leave him alone. Don't worry, he'll be back in a little while," said Joe as he washed his hands at the sink. "That old cabin now, wouldn't it be nice if we could fix it up into a kind of music studio for Mike that is if you're not going to use it for anything else?" Wiping his hands on the towel and sat in his usual place beside Hannah. "You see, Mike has had an awful lot on his shoulders this past year and he hasn't had any time to himself. Mike has always needed a place where he could get away from everyone for awhile."

Joe looked over at Ben with such sad, wise eyes that the man immediately recognized just how very "old" Joe was. "You see Ben, Mike is a…..a…oh shoot, what's the word for being really above smart, real special kind of special person, Hannah?"

"Brilliant?" She suggested with a questioning look on her face.

"Yeah, that's it. Mike is brilliant and I guess you'd call him a very deep and private kind of person besides. I guess bright people need to be by themselves sometimes so they can think things out. Mike needs and uses his music in a very special way and I believe it's a way he empties himself out. That's part of his being brilliant and that's how he writes music, understand? Times of being alone are really important to him and really, really necessary too. Mom used to say music and aloneness gave Mike his balance. Yeah, I guess it's a kind of peace."

Hannah was filling his plate and nothing was said for a while. Joe began to eat hungrily. "Boy this is so good. I'm glad we have you Hannah dear, for sure I'm going to grow into a giant just like Big Mike." Laughter relaxed their concern and supper proceeded quietly.

"I don't see why we can't fix that cabin up for Mike as a surprise and make it into his special studio. We can put in a desk and a nice dresser for his papers and such." Mari Beth passed Hannah the potatoes.

"Sure we can," Ben added, "and I'll check around and see if I can get a recording deck for him. He should always have a tape running because one never knows when inspiration might strike. I'll make a few calls tomorrow." The table was quiet with only the clink of forks and such.

"Ben, you should have seen the men sitting real quiet like on Mike's porch." Joe paused while he took several more bites and thought about how he felt sitting there on the stump and listening to his brother's pain. Joe swallowed then said quietly. "At first, the music sounded really….*violent and sad. It made me cry.*" Joe put his fork down and swallowed hard and sniffed.

Hannah put her hand on his shoulder and he nodded, wiped his nose on his napkin and took a deep breath and ate a little more before he continued. "Mike was in such pain and I knew I couldn't go in there for he wouldn't have wanted that. I felt helpless to help him like he's helped me lots and lots of times. So all I could do was sit outside on a stump and just be there. I think the men were doing the same thing, just being there. *They knew*, Ben, they *knew* what he was going through; I know it sounds a little weird, but they *did* understand."

Joe looked down at his half finished plate, swallowed and looked up into Ben's eyes. "There's something else you gotta' understand about Mike. He's very, very… oh geeze, what's the word." and gave himself a little rap on the forehead. "Mom said Mike was a very controlled sort of person. He didn't used to be this way so much before Mom and Dad died. You gotta understand that Mike has been afraid to let go of his feelings because he had us to take care of and be strong for us. Well, his music helps him to let go in a safe way. Besides, Mike isn't really alone out there, he's got Roscoe in the cabin with him and a nice fire going and who can be alone when you've got a dog." grinned the young philosopher.

"Ain't that the truth, young wise one, ain't that the truth." Ben had to laugh at Joe. Lordy, Lordy, aren't we the lucky ones. We have much to thank the Guardians for bringing us these remarkable children. How many ways could a man feel blessed?

Dinner was over and the women were clearing off the dishes when Mike came in the back door with Roscoe right behind him and stopped, blinked a few times in the bright kitchen light. "Oh, mercy, I've missed supper! I'm sorry, I guess I just got caught up and didn't hear the dinner bell. It won't happen again I promise." said Mike apologetically.

"It isn't a crime, Mike. You were busy with your music and that's just as important as being on time for supper and you did tell Hannah that you were going out and Joe told us you were playing. Well dear heart, everyone needs time alone. Just let us know when you need to do that and we'll give you your space, okay? I also think it's time we gave you boys your own rooms and put Miss Carli in her room too. She's already taking her naps in the nursery Hannah and I fixed up and she seems to be happy there. Now Hannah's kept your supper hot so wash your hands and sit down." Mari Beth gave him a one armed squeeze around the shoulders and kept on cleaning the kitchen

Mike set his guitar case down by the door, took off his coat and hat and hung them up on the coat rack then walked down the hall to the bathroom to wash up. When he came back his dinner plate was on the table heaped with food. Mike sat down and he struggled to swallow the emotion at such understanding from people who knew very little about him; not the deep down important stuff.

He sniffed, blinked fast and began to eat hoping that swallowing some food might move the big lump out of his throat. He didn't look up until Hannah took away his empty plate and placed a piece of hot apple pie with ice cream in front of him and refilled his milk glass. Mike smiled up at her and said. "Thanks Hannah, you're a jewel."

She laughed and it was only then that Mike noticed Joe sitting quietly a couple of chairs away. Now Mike understood how everyone knew about some of his deeper needs; Joe had cleared the way. Mike's way of expressing gratitude was to reach over and lightly punch Joe on the shoulder and grin.

Mike carried his dishes to the sink and rinsed them off before putting them in the dishwasher. Turning around he saw Mari Beth puttering in the pantry.

"Mari Beth, did Ben tell you that grandfather Devereaux left us a letter?"

"*Drat that man*, how could he forget to tell me something that important? No he didn't Mike, 'course things have been a might busy around here. What did it say?"

"I don't know yet, but I thought I'd read it to everyone in the living room tonight if that's okay with you?"

"Sure son, you go get the letter and I'll corral everyone." She left to do that very thing and as she passed Ben leaning in the doorway she give him a little jab in the stomach with her elbow for his poor memory.

"Ow, ow, don't hurt me woman, I'm delicate you know. I am sorry I forgot honey, honestly." and followed her out of the kitchen as she cast a disgusting glance back over her shoulder at him.

Mike grabbed his guitar case and hurried upstairs to the bedroom. Getting the letter out of his pack he stood holding it in his hand for a few minutes and got the feeling of great sadness coming from that roll of papers.

When he came back into the living room his family, *yes his family*, were all seated with a cheerful fire snapping and popping in the big fireplace and Roscoe was again laying in front of it soaking up the heat.

Mike walked across the room to share the front of the fireplace with his dog and with a quick glance at Joe he untied the ribbon and stuffed it carefully in his pocket. Unrolling the papers, he cleared his throat before saying.

"We found this in a secret safe in the fireplace at the ranch the day we caught Elroy. Ben has all the other stuff in a briefcase that we'll take to the bank next week."

At that Mari Beth twisted around and looked hard at Ben. "*What other stuff, Benjamin Truelove Strongbow?*"

Ohmygosh, thought Mike, I've gotten Ben into trouble again and watched anxiously.

Ben said with a chagrined look on his face. "Ah, it's upstairs in our safe, sweet thing. I plumb forgot about it being there until Mike here unrolled that wad of paper. Gee, sweetie, *I really forgot.*" Ben's red face told it all.

Mari Beth laughed. "You're slipping big man; imagine not remembering something that important. Okay, all is forgiven if I get to see what's in the briefcase if that's alright with Mike and Joe."

"Oh sure Mari Beth, you can see anything we have." assured Mike.

"Yeah Mari Beth, I mean, you're like our mother now so there can't be any secrets. Mothers don't like it when kids keep secrets, do they?" said a very positive Joe.

Mari Beth laughed at that. "Most certainly not, as that would be a monumental mistake and even husbands should take that truth to heart." Ben nodded vigorously in agreement that set Mari Beth off into laughing again. Somehow the ordinary comments and laughter lightened Mike's hesitation so when he cleared his throat again, they quieted and Mike began to read.

Dearest Grandchildren:

I have received word of your parent's death and I cannot say how deeply I am grieved. I had hope that one day your mother would come home and she would have everything I have worked so hard for. My hope died.

This is a very hard letter for me to write, but write it I must. I am an old man now and I have the feeling that I may not have a long time to live, but I am hoping to live long enough to get to know you children.

I have not been a good man. Some will say I've been a mean man, a pinchpenny and they would be right. I could come up with lots of excuses for my behavior, but in the long run it's by the results that I must judge myself and be judged by my Maker.

Where to begin? When one comes to the point of purging one's soul of misdeeds and multiple mistakes it's hard to know where it all started to go wrong.

Well, I guess I was a pretty happy man when I married your grandmother. Yes, I was a contented man and I believe she loved me as much as I loved her. We were blessed with two children, a son, Jacob Joseph Devereaux and a daughter, Jean Ann Devereaux. When my son was eighteen he came home one day and told me he wanted to enlist in the Marines. I grew very angry and we had a terrible argument even after he said it was something that he had always wanted to do. I wouldn't listen to him. The ranch was supposed to be his life after I died. That day he left the ranch and never came back. I am sorry to this day that we parted in anger and never got to forgive each other. Eight months later we received news of his death in a far away war.

It changed my wife toward me and she blamed me for driving him away; she retreated. Jean was about twelve then and tried to take over running the house for her mother. Then one morning, my wife didn't awake up. She too had departed in anger.

I'm not proud of what I became then. I was harsh to my Jean and never allowing her to leave the ranch for any length of time as though by keeping her locked up she would stay with me. It was my treatment of her that finally drove her away. Who in their normal mind would want to continue to stay with a father like me, joyless and stubbornly set in my cruel attitude toward life and all people.

Jean was eighteen when she left and she was nineteen when she came back to the ranch with your father. I didn't know, at the time that she was pregnant with you, young Michael, all I could think of was her betrayal of all that I had worked so hard in order for the ranch to someday be hers. I drove her away again with my anger and rejection. I've regretted that act to this day. I hired detectives to try to locate her, but you see I had forgotten the married name she had given me and we couldn't locate her.

So the years passed and with each day I hoped to hear from her. I wanted her to come home with her husband. I saved money and worked hard on the ranch so she would have a fine legacy when she came back. The years passed and my bitterness grew. I became a recluse, a poor neighbor and an even poorer man.

When I received that letter from the Texas Social Services informing me of your mother and father's death, such horrible anguish filled my heart that I have no words to describe the pain and the sense of great loss to you children. Then I knew there would be no forgiveness for me from Jean, my beautiful daughter, in this life.

I learned then that I had three grandchildren, two boys and a girl. Perhaps when Jean gave each of you boys one of my names, Joseph and Michael, she may have forgiven me in her heart. I hope so and I pray that is true because I need desperately to believe she has forgiven me.

Do I want you? By the gods I do, more than you'll ever know. I think this might be the way to atone for my misdeeds and mistreatment of my Jean. I would love you and treat you kindly and you would bring the light of happiness back into this empty house and into my life as I would strive to give happiness to you children.

This evening I wrote a letter and enclosed a large check for your trip and sent it off to that social service address. It was then that I felt another chilling pain in my chest. It was a warning to me to speak now in case I don't live to see you. I pray I may live to see my Jean's children.

I made my will tonight leaving all to you, my grandchildren. I pray for forgiveness and hope the God of us all will have mercy on this old sinner and give me the chance to see you and love you. If *that doesn't happen, please accept that I love you children now and always shall.*

This letter is in case I don't get the opportunity to show you how good it will be for all of us. This letter doesn't do a very good job, but I know what I have been and I can only say I'm a changed man now that I know you will be on your way soon.

I welcome you. I need and want you here, but if I don't get to see you, please know that I welcome you and the house that has been so empty for so long will welcome you too.

God bless you, children, may you find joy in the legacy I leave. I hope to see Jean and your father Michael in heaven, if they'll let me in. Perhaps in another life I can make it up to my family the wrong I have done them. So be it.
With all my love,
Your grandfather,
Joseph Michael Devereaux

No one said a word for the longest time. Mike had had such a hard time reading the letter aloud because he kept choking up. Joe and Mike both had tears running down their cheeks feeling the anguish expressed in the letter. Mike walked over and sat down beside Joe and carefully rolled up the letter and tied it with their mother's red hair ribbon and handed it to Joe to hold. There was silence in the room for awhile until Mike spoke.

"Joe, do you remember the day when we were going with Ben to meet Blackhawk for the first time and we were talking about grandfather?" Joe nodded his head. "Do you remember saying that you thought maybe grandfather would have welcomed us and been happy that we were there, or words like that?"

"Yeah, I do. I sure wished we could have known him even if it had been just for a little bit. I think it would have made a difference in how he felt about life, don't you?" he said soberly.

"I should pay more attention to your feelings about things Joe, because you were right then and you're right now. Yeah, I wished we could have known him." and was silent.

"I have to ask forgiveness for saying all those bad things about that man even if at the time they were true, but who could have known that in Devereaux's heart there was a hurt spirit." Mari Beth sighed.

"Maybe we didn't believe enough in the redemption of a man's soul. We all would have helped him if we had only known."

"If he had let us Mari Beth we could have comforted him. Even though we regret our judgment of him he wouldn't let us get near him so he made the choice right then to isolate himself and be unhappy. We're only human and our experience with Joseph Devereau was not a pleasant one and he rejected all help. I guess the lesson here is not to judge anyone by appearances. I'm just glad these children know that they would have been welcomed and loved if Devereaux had lived; that's a big comfort." Ben spoke as he looked into the fire in a contemplative way.

"Maybe he knows that we would have loved to have had a real live grandfather too, someone who was a part of our Mother." said Joe, "Maybe we could visit his grave and have a talk with him. You know, tell him about how his daughter and son-in-law have come back home to the ranch now." Nothing was more was said as the family seemed lost in their own contemplations.

"Was Grandfather buried or cremated, Ben?" question Joe.

"His ashes have been placed in an urn at the ranch cemetery. It's the place where all the Devereaux's have been buried." answered Ben.

"Well, I think we need to dig them up and go put them in the same place with Mom's and Dad's, don't you Mike? I think he'd like that then he could be with her there and maybe it might ease his spirit 'cause I don't think grandfather's left yet." Joe looked at Mike and waited.

No one spoke. What could anyone say in the face of that? Old Devereaux's spirit was still hanging around? Why? Oh, they'd all heard about uneasy spirits and the Lord knew Devereaux had never been easy to be around. Maybe the old man was hanging around to be close to his grandchildren. Hmm, Ben frowned deep in thought.

"You're right Joe. Let's ask Blackhawk to perform another ceremony because I like the idea of happy spirits on our ranch. Ben, will we have to get permission from the state to move grandfather's ashes?" said Mike.

"I'll check, but I don't think that will be necessary as he's buried on private property in the family plot. We could leave his head stone where it is to mark his passing. Mike do you want to call your Godfather or should I?" Ben asked looking over at the two boys.

"We'll ask him tomorrow during the fiesta. We really have something extra special to celebrate now, don't we? It might be nice if we could do it on Sunday after church then we'll all go and Mari Beth and Hannah can see that beautiful spot we picked out."

Smiled Mike and stood up. "Would you like me to play my new song for you? It's a pretty one I think. Of course I still have to work on it a bit more as it's not polished yet."

"I think that's exactly what we need, a nice song before we go to bed." said Mari Beth.

"I'll get your guitar, Mike." Joe jumped up and raced up the stairs and within minutes raced back down and handed it over. Mike sat in the straight chair Ben brought out from the dinning room. After twiddling a bit with the tuning, he smiled and looked around at the expectant faces.

"This is for my new family, but the words aren't quite all there yet so I'll just play the melody. The song title will be, "Home Again."

And the music flowed out of the guitar in an uplifting cadence that truly lifted each heart. Joe sat with his head against Hannah's shoulder and smiled. Mike was okay now. Music had healed his spirit and Joe was content.

~Fiesta~

AFTER THE EXCITEMENT OF the past several weeks and ending with the arrest of Elroy Devereaux, the fiesta became a victory celebration. The women had been working hard for the past few days getting everything planned. As with all these valley get-togethers, everyone contributed food and help. A dozen women appeared early Saturday morning and the kitchen became a virtual beehive of organized chaos. The extra over-sized refrigerator in the large pantry was filled with dishes. Every available surface in the dinning room, including the table and sideboards, were covered with all kinds of casseroles and finger food that could be heated up last minute or left just as they were; after all this was supposed to be a feast!

The men volunteered their energy in preparing the outdoors. Yesterday morning the men had opened up the two big barbecue pits and had started roasting two whole steers and they would be done by the time people arrived around four o'clock. Another smaller pit was for chickens and pork roasts. Dusty's huge grill was pulled up close to the pits and he was making pies and rolls on the big chuck wagon table. Henry Trudeaux and Mike Mitee had their own stations set up beside Dusty's. Martha Longfellow was in the house with the ladies. The conversations were interesting if a person had time to stop and listen and it wasn't all about food either.

The men were setting up tables in the huge back yard using saw horses and placing 8x4 sheets of plywood on top. Stored chairs contributed from the many households were dragged over for just these occasions and set up. Varied colored oil clothes covered the table tops with dried flowers and Kerosene Lamps set out on each table acting as centerpieces. The men had also built a temporary dance floor from planks that would be used later on the ranch for other purposes.

These people had lots of experience in feeding large crowds and setting up parties. When they worked, they worked hard, and when they played, they played equally hard. Mike and Joe were astonished at what was involved in putting on such a large barbeque. Thank God for helping hands!

Ben laughed at Mike and Joe's comments. "People are coming from all the other Valleys today; Claremont, North Springfield, Port City which is south of us and over east is Wallace Springs. The ranches around here are hosting people from far away and campers galore setting out in a pasture or two. We've got room for at least fifty or so people right here. Yep, this here party is going to be the best and biggest blowout of the season's entertainments. Gotta' make hay while the sun shines or before winter closes the passes. We all have to get together and visit when we can because that keeps us all connected you know?" rubbing his hands together Ben took off to lend a hand with the big dance floor.

"Goodness Mike, there's so many people here already that I suspect the party has already begun. Geeze peeze, what's it going to be like tonight?" Joe said in amazement.

"I guess we'll have to wait and see, but I suspect we ain't seen nothin' yet." and stepped off the porch to join the mob of men. Joe looked around in wonder then followed on Mike's heels.

They volunteered their help here and there and generally made themselves useful for a couple of hours. Finally, the brothers withdrew to work on the music they'd perform that night. Later they took Carli around so she could see what everyone was doing and give Mari Beth a break while she worked in the kitchen.

About 3:00 everyone living close enough went home to get dressed and those who had come from far away and were staying with the Strongbows just changed their clothes in the bedrooms of the ranch or in the outlaying campers. The rest of the Strongbows gathered in the privacy of their den and relaxed before putting on their party dress. Carli had gone down for a much needed nap now that things were quieter.

"Wow, we've been to some picnics and family parties before, but nothing as big as this one that wasn't a county affair. I didn't realize how much work it took to put on a private party. It'll be a wonder if anyone will have the energy to eat and dance later." laughed Mike.

"Oh, we ranchers are a tough breed I can tell you; work hard and play harder that's our motto. This party will go on until the wee hours of the morning and then it's a late breakfast, more visiting before anyone heads for home. We don't do this very often, but when we do we make the most of it 'cause we get to see practically everyone in the Valleys and it's a lot of fun. It may take us days to recover, but it's always worth it."

Mari Beth smiled as she leaned her head against the couch's arm with her feet in Ben's lap and he obligingly rubbed her feet and that had Mari Beth groaning with pleasure.

"If I can get my feet rested I'll dance you down big man, just see if I don't. Right now this is about the best feeling in my world." Ben grinned and continued to massage his wife's tired feet.

"It's a good thing I got all my roundup pictures back. Mike and I have been choosing out the best ones and pinning them on a big board we're going to set up out on the back porch and Julep built me a tripod thingee to hold it. I sure hope the men like them." worried Joe.

"I plumb forgot about Joe's pictures. I've got to see them right now. Come on Mike, let's get that board and set it up on the porch and take a gander." Ben got up which meant the whole family had to have a preview too.

Mike and Ben carried the big board down the stairs and out onto the back porch and placed it on the tripod. Stepping back, they admired the shots of the roundup.

"Why Joe, these are great! Just wait until the men see them." said Mari Beth as she looked from one picture to another. "It's almost as good as being there."

"These are going to be the hit of the party. Wow, look at that shot of Mike on Sherlock with him rearing up and Mike just sitting there like it was no big deal and that cow running under him that way. Amazing shot Joe. Say isn't that Dusty?" murmured Hannah thoroughly engrossed.

"By golly Joe, a lot of these shots are excellent considering they weren't posed or set up. This action shot of Jimmy is beyond terrific and couldn't have been taken any better by a professional. Hmmm, maybe I'll send some these to the Rancher Magazine." Ben murmured as he examined the photos closely. They had all been enlarged to 5x7

True Heart

so they showed a lot of detail. "Look at this one of Dusty for instance. Did he poise for that Joe?"

"No, and that's the only one I managed to take without him knowing. That man always seemed to know when I was trying to sneak a shot. But there he was, just standing with one foot up on a rock beside the big campfire with the chuck wagon off to one side and starring off down the mesa. Yeah, it turned out really great, huh?"

"*Hey Dusty come up here, you've got to see this.*" yelled Ben. Dusty turned from his work and looked across at the house then dusting his hands, picked up a rag and was wiping them clean as he walked across the back yard and up on the porch.

"What air you hollerin' about Ben, I haven't gone deaf yet." said Dusty as he walked up the porch steps and stood before the board and hummed. "Well, well, it's a picture gallery. Now these pictures wouldn't be the work of our own personal photographer, would they?" He asked as he studied them closely. Joe was on tender hooks and was almost hopping back and forth in his anxiety.

"Dusty, look at this one, see it's one of you!" Joe pointed out the photo impatiently to the blind man.

"Huh, I didn't know you'd taken that. How did you manage to sneak up on me? I must have been distracted. Say, this picture has *good, good* composition young man. Ben, some of these would make a nice article in a magazine or newspaper now, wouldn't they? Why it would be hard for an editor to choose out the best ones. Myohmy boy, I knew you could sing, but you're right good with a camera too; I'd say you were a natural. Has Jimmy seen this one of him roping that cow? This one with his rifle and the dead bull could be titled. "Sure Shooter. It will sure set him up. Here's one of Mike playing the guitar and laughing. I sure like that one. Another one of Mike on that rearing horse, that's a fine, fine action shot." Giving Joe a pat on his shoulder, "You done good Joe, real good; congratulations boy." and he went back down the porch steps and over to his wagon.

"You can't beat that stamp of approval from the Great Man, as you call him Joe. Yep, these are definite good enough to send to a magazine. You could call it, "Roundup through the Eyes of a Child." Better finish that journal, Joe and we'll see." said Ben and Joe looked shocked and elated all at once as Ben went back into the house with Mari Beth.

"Oh geeze peeze Mike, my pictures might be in a magazine. Wow, just think of that! Well, I gotta' go finish putting copies into envelopes for everyone I took a picture of." and ran off to his room. Mike laughed and then looked again at the amazing collection of candid shots that spoke of all aspects of roundup action and felt very proud of the kid's ability. Here was a couple of him dogging a cow and another of him asleep in his bedroll as well as several others. Shaking his head, Mike went back upstairs to his room and closed the door.

His big bedroom gave him all the space he could ever want with a large double bed and placed in front of the window were two stuffed side chairs with a table between with a reading lamp. Of course the desk was against another wall along with his dresser and bookcase. It was definitely satisfying to have his own privacy and Joe had his too. Carli was happy with her brightly painted nursery with its animal figures close to Mari Beth and Ben's room. Yes, definitely a nice room of his own and somehow it made him feel more grown up and it gave him necessary breathing space for the preservation of his sanity. He liked his quiet and as much as he loved his brother, Joe was just too full of bounce in the mornings.

An hour later people began arriving by the droves and it wasn't long before the large ranch yard was filled with orderly rows of vehicles of all kinds and the overflow went into one of the smaller pastures behind the barn.

Well, the party was on and then some. Mike and Joe got to meet just about everyone and the only problem was trying to remember names. Mike got to meet a set of twins, identical and really great guys named Alan and George Graywolf from over in the North Valley. They were only a few years older than Mike, nineteen or twenty. The twins were as alike as two pees in a pod and it was near to impossible to tell them apart except when they revealed how different they were in their career choices. In personality they were very different; one was quiet, steady and grounded, Mike guess he'd have to say, and the other one was an imaginative and artistic person.

Mike particularly liked George or Geo, as he said his friends called him. Maybe because he was an artist and a writer while Mike wrote poetry and composed music. His brother Alan loved the land and it was obvious that he was bound to the earth.

Tommy Lee and Joe teamed up and were doing everything together along with some of the other school boys. Mike saw that as soon as Jack Golight arrived with his sister and aunt, Joe grabbed him and dragged him off too. Mike had to laugh because Jack didn't stand a chance of remaining a stranger with Joe around.

The picture board was a definite hit. Joe had been busy passing out copies to the men who had been on roundup and what shocked him was they were paying him for them. He told them they were gifts and he didn't want any money. That didn't change anyone's mind and money was just pushed into his hand. So Joe just shoved it into his pocket. When he tried to hand the money to Ben it got pushed back at Joe with a definite, "You earned it so you keep it." What could a boy do? So Joe stuffed the money into his pocket and figured he'd decide later what to do with it and went back to passing out copies.

Mike saw Jimmy and Joe talking up a storm in front of the picture board and walked over to hear what Jimmy was saying.

Jimmy slapped his thigh. "You're going to make me famous, Joe." And laughed like a hyena. "Hollywood, here I come; a rootin' tootin' cowboy and they said we were all dead." Jimmy grabbed Joe under the arms and swung him around a couple of times. Both of them were laughing at each other in complete accord.

Now Joe was busy taking pictures of the people at the party. This kid brother of his was going to get rich on his own hook before he turned eight and Mike shook his head. Joe just didn't know a stranger even if one came up and bit him. Mike shook his head again and wondered how two brothers could be exact opposites; one dark and one light in lots of ways, yet they got along so easy like. It truly amazed him.

Mike had found some of his school friends from River Town and got to show them around. Two of the guys were really neat, the doctor's son, Matt Valdez and the other was the local Ferrier's son, Ike Trumpet. The other guys sort of wandered off, but Mike and his two friends stuck together. They really liked horses and wanted to come out sometime and go riding if Mike thought Ben would okay that.

Later Mike excused himself from his friends saying he had to talk to his Godfather privately and after hunting through the crowd. Mike finally found Blackhawk sitting at a table with some of the local men. He waited quietly beside him until the men's conversation ended and Blackhawk looked up.

"Chief Blackhawk, can I talk to you privately for a moment?"

"Sure can son, let's walk down towards the field and visit all those curious beauties of Ben's lined up along the fence and watching us humans frolic."

It was so right that Mike had to laugh because a goodly number of heads were hanging over the fence. "Let's stop and pick up a bucket of carrots. After all one can't go visiting without taking a gift, can one?" Blackhawk laughed and agreed.

When they got to the fence they started snapping carrots and walking along feeding the horses as Mike told him about their grandfather's letter. "Joe and I want to take grandfather's ashes and scatter them up at the sacred site where Mom and Dad's are. We'd like you to perform a ceremony for him like you did for the folks. Joe feels that Grandfather's spirit hasn't left and it's still lingering around the ranch. I'd like to think a ceremony with all of us there might ease and free his spirit to go on."

Blackhawk leaned on the fence and watched the horses playing around in the green field while patting one that wouldn't go away and fed him another piece of carrot. The horse wasn't dumb and he figure if he hung around long enough he'd get fed. Only here came some other horses curious about what was going on.

"Mike, I'd be pleased to do a ceremony for Devereaux. When did you want to do it?"

"Tomorrow, if it's possible. School starts Monday and we're still pretty busy with work that needs to be done because the weather might turn on us anytime so I think the sooner the better." replied Mike soberly.

"Tomorrow it is! I'll come by in the morning and pick everyone up for church then we can go directly to your place afterward."

"Thanks Chief, that's great, and maybe you and Big Mike would like to stay for Sunday dinner afterward?"

"That sounds grand and Big Mike would love a break from cooking so I'll accept for both of us." Talking about this and that, they fed the last of the carrots to the horses before rejoining the party. Mike immediately went to find Mari Beth and Ben to tell them about the plans for Sunday.

Dancing had commenced at least for those who could still move after eating so much. There were a number of steel drums used as small fire pits for warmth as the evening cooled considerably. As it had gotten dark the strings of colored lights had been turned on all over the big back yard and the table lanterns had been lit. It looked festive and colorful with the addition of Tiki torches placed strategically around the dance floor.

It was going on ten o'clock when the band took a well-earned break. Ben got up on the dance floor and had the drummer do a loud roll that got everyone's attention.

"Folks, we are here in part to celebrate a successful roundup with no one getting hurt. My sincere thanks to a daring young man named James Kilpatrick who saved Joe Kelly's life from that old mossy horn bull. I owe a lot to the men who endangered their lives to turn a stampeding herd from going over the cliffs. A real live cowboy hair raising event I can tell you. If it hadn't been for their daring courage I might have lost hundreds of cows. Thank you men, I'd like y'all to stand up so folks can see what fearless cowboys look like." Ben applauded as the men sheepishly stood up and the crowd went wild. You never saw so many red faced men in all your born days. Ben was laughing and applauding just like everyone else.

Once the crowd quieted down he went on to say, "Also, as you all may know by now, we've caught the man who was causing so much grief to my Kelly sons." More applause stopped Ben for a minute and he stood there grinned. He knew how gossip could fly around the Valleys without the aid of a newspaper. "Added to all the above, this celebration is a thanksgiving to the land spirits that has nourished and given us everything we have enjoyed on this ranch. We celebrate life and the bountiful harvest and the coming of winter. We give thanks for our blessings and will do so again in church tomorrow and since Preacher Lyman and Father Donnigan and Rabbi Levi and Master Sing are here and we'd all better be in our holy places tomorrow; I'm sure they're counting noses." There was laughter greeting that statement.

"Now I have something very special to offer you this evening. For those of you who have not met our guardian children Mari Beth and I want to introduce Mr. Michael Devereaux Kelly, Mr. Joseph Devereaux Kelly, please come up here boys. The beautiful Miss Carli Jean Kelly you saw at supper is now sound asleep upstairs in the house. And now you're going to hear some amazing talents."

Applause broke out as the young boys mounted the dance platform with Mike carrying his guitar. Ben stepped down and rejoined Mari Beth on a bench.

People gathered around as the word spread out. Now the men who had been on roundup knew what to expect, but most of the other people who hadn't were whispering in varied ways the old complaint of, "Oh no, not amateur night?" or "Do we really have to sit through this?" However, like good guests the people sat down and resigned themselves to suffer through an amateur performance.

Mike dragged up a high stool and sat before the microphone with Joe standing by his side. Mike began to play and as the volume of music picked up in a rolling flow of the Spanish composition he'd written long ago the people quickly quieted down. It was full of fast plucked notes and strumming. When Mike was finished he quickly switched into another song that he and Joe harmonized. Joe had modified his voice to fit into perfect balance with Mike's and the results were fabulous. When they ended the applause was all that they could have wanted.

They bowed then Mike played the opening of another of his own country western songs that he sang alone and that too was well received. Now it was Joe's turn. Mike had written this one especially for Joe's voice.

Joe closed his eyes for a moment listening to Mike's opening phrases then look out at the many faces that surrounded the platform. He opened his mouth and the Spanish words poured out in such purity and volume all the while giving the words true emotional impact that people's eyes popped. The second time around Joe sang in English. There wasn't a person there who weren't caught up in the magic of a young boy's remarkable voice. There wasn't a sound when Joe was finished.

He smiled shyly and into the silence began his favorite, "Ave Maria." Sung in Italian and with great feeling and sung without

Mike's accompaniment. The song floated up into the air and seemed to draw the stars down closer to listen. The men who had heard it at roundup listened just as intently as they had before. With the divine music, Joe touched the hearts of everyone there. Again silence was his reward.

"Now can I sing in your church choir Preacher, please?" grinned Joe irrepressibly. Then the hooting and whistling and clapping broke out and loosened up the shocked crowd. Ben laughed and laughed as though he had pulled off one of the greatest stunts in the land.

Well, of course both boys had to do a number of other songs and the last one was that silly, funny tongue twister that the boys dueled back and forth with increasing speed that had the audience in hysterics. Mike stood up and he and Joe bowed and left the platform. You could say that they had been outrageously successful.

"Young men, if you don't join the church choir I will quit as preacher." Said the worth man. Portly he might be, but the energy of goodwill surrounded him like a cloak. "My name is Joshua Lyman or Preacher as they call me, I'll answer to either one so we will see you in church tomorrow, right?" and shaking their hands went over to talk to Mari Beth and Ben.

"Geeze peeze, Mike, it looks like we're going to get religion again." said Joe without enthusiasm.

"Looks like it Joe, but if it comes from that man it might not be too bad." replied his brother and with his arm slung over Joe's shoulder they walked off to get some of Amber Golight's special cake, if there was any left. Man, Luther sure had hit it lucky when he hired her, a real chef; can you imagine the luck of that?

It was very late or very early whichever way you wanted to look at it, when Mari Beth finally found Joe and Mike. "Goodness, boys it's after two in the morning and Joe looks half-asleep, I should have sent him to bed long before this. Most of the young people have gone home and the rest will be leaving shortly. Now y'all scoot and don't forget to brush your teeth. Thanks for the music boys, it was beautiful and made us all so proud of you and everyone loved it. Don't forget we have church tomorrow, so don't stay up all night talking." Mari Beth kissed their cheeks and rushed off.

Wearily Mike and Joe climbed the stairs with the sound of muted laughter and voices drifting up from the ranch yard mixed with the sound of starting engines. The boys walked over to Carli's crib and Mike pulled the covers up over her shoulders without waking her or the woman Mari Beth had hired to baby sit Carli. It wouldn't have been safe for the child to be left alone in the house.

"Night Mike, isn't it nice having our own rooms now?" said Joe standing in front of his bedroom door as he yawned fit to break his jaw.

"Yeah it is nice to have our own space. Night Joe, sleep well." Mike opened his bedroom door.

"Yep, we're both going to be rich and famous, I can tell. Gee, wasn't it fun?" and Joe closed his door as Mike laughed. Gradually the night fell silent.

~Mary~

In Maryland a woman's heart cries out for help and a silent voice answers.

VAGUE MEMORIES OF TALKING to a spirit about helping her find safety drifted through her sleeping mind. Pain awakened her and the voice with its reassurance faded and was forgotten.

She moaned.

Someone took hold of her hand. "Mary, you're alright; I'm Sally, your nurse."

"*What? What's the matter? Where am I?*" she murmured opening her eyes and tried to bring the person standing beside her into focus.

"You're in the hospital Mary and you've been hurt, but you're going to be all right. Your children are here and they're alright too, just waiting to see you. Take it easy, you're still a little groggy from the anesthetic."

"*What happened? Have I been in an accident?*" Mary said in a slurry voice.

"No, Mary, you were a victim of domestic violence. Your husband is in jail on an assault charge." said the nurse in a quiet voice.

"*Oh, God, I remember now!*" she cried, "*I was so afraid he'd kill me and the girls.*" Mary exclaimed then cried out in anguish as the pain grew unbearable

"Easy Mary; I'm going to give you a shot and it will make you feel better in just a few seconds." The nurse proceeded to insert the syringe needle into the I.V. line. She was right thought Mary as her pain floated away.

"Thank you, thank you so much. I want to see my girls. Are they all right? I want to see them please. They'll be so worried." murmured Mary in a disjointed way.

"I'll get them dear, but don't move around just lie still and I'll be right back." Mary drifted into a light sleep as she waited.

"Mom, are you awake?" Mary heard the whisper and opening her eyes and saw her daughters leaning over the side of the bed rail.

"Bliss? Yes, yes dear, I'm awake, mostly. Now girls I don't want you two to worry. The nurse said I was going to be just fine." Mary drifted for a few seconds then stirred back to the present and looked up at them. "Are you alright? Who's taking care of you?"

"We're fine Mom, don't worry, we're staying next door with Mr. & Mrs. Hubbard. The police have put Father in jail so we're safe. All you need to do is get better. We love you Mom, please get better quickly." Bliss leaned over and kissed her mother's cheek then Mary felt Stephanie kiss her too.

Tears began to roll down Mary's face. "I'm so *sorry* this happened and you had to see it." More tears leaked out of the corners of her eyes and soaked the bandage that was wrapped around her head. "My strong beautiful girls thank you for calling the police. I remember you shouting at your father that the police were coming and to run. I know you saved my life. I'll make it up to you, I promise. It's over now, it's all over." Mary drifted off into a deep sleep and didn't see her girls holding on to each other crying softly at the sight of their battered mother.

The nurse gently guided them out of the room, "Now girls, you listen to me. Your mother is going to be alright and will soon be going home so I don't want you to worry about her anymore. Come back tomorrow and you'll see a great improvement in her." The Hubbards were waiting to take them home and left the hospital with their arms around the girls.

The attack had come swiftly and unexpectedly; one she had feared one day might happen and he'd kill them all in one of his rages. Well, thought Mary as she lay in the hospital bed the next day, it had happened regardless of her carefully laid plans. She had come home from school yesterday afternoon loaded down with children's tests and other assignments to correct to find her husband waiting for her in the living room. Mary had stopped abruptly in the doorway. The hair rose up on the back of her neck in a primordial warning of *danger*. She saw the girls huddled together on the couch obviously scared stiff. Kevin was sitting in his usual chair; ice tinkled in the glass of whiskey as he drank. There was a half filled whiskey bottle sitting on the side table beside him.

"Girls, go get washed for supper. Have you done your homework yet? If not, you need to get busy." Mary said calmly and they quickly got up and left the room. Mary heard them close the bedroom door and heard the quiet click of the lock as she put her papers and briefcase down on the desk in the corner of the living room then turned to her husband.

"What's the matter Kevin? Didn't you get the job? I thought sure you would as it's right within your skills." Said Mary quietly, taking off her coat and laying it down on her desk chair before turning to look at the man she had grown to fear and, God forgive her, to hate.

"What do *you* care bitch, *you* with your fine education, *you* with your fine superiority! No, I didn't get the job because I didn't get the recommendation I should have had from Mr. Goody Two Shoes Collins, that's why." And Kevin took another long drink keeping his hard cold eyes on her.

"I'm sorry Kevin, I'm sure something better will show up. Now you must be hungry so I'd better start supper." and started for the kitchen.

"I didn't give you permission to leave the room, *Teacher!*" he shouted. "I'm not through talking to you, *woman!* What do you mean by serving me with divorce papers? We're *never* going to be divorced so make up your tiny little mind to that." Now Mary noticed how slurred his loud voice was and the fear grew as it rippled up her back as he followed her to the kitchen.

"Kevin, it's been over between us for a long time and I won't tolerate the abuse anymore. I refuse to raise the girls in a violent household. The marriage isn't doing either of us any good." Mary walked into the kitchen trying to control her breathing as she heard his hard footsteps close behind her.

What happened after that was an escalation of abusive words then the shoving and slapping started only this time she tried to fight back, but to no avail. He was so much bigger and stronger than she was.

Mary shuddered at the memory of the attack. The girls had heard her screams and Bliss had bravely left the bedroom, grabbed the cordless phone and ran back to her room and called 911. As Mary lay on the floor trying feebly to defend herself from the knife, she remembered hearing her daughter scream, "*The police are coming; the police are on their way. Get out now, RUN! RUN!*" And Kevin dropped the knife and ran out through the kitchen door.

Mary remembered struggling to remain consciousness fighting the pain because she needed to protect her children. How could she protect her children when she couldn't get up off the floor? Bliss was pressing a towel to her head and Stephanie was trying to do the same to her arms and chest. She heard them crying and pleading, but she didn't have the strength to respond, to do anything about reassuring them. She vaguely saw the paramedics and the police rush into the kitchen. *Now*, she remembered thinking, *now* it was safe for her to let go and leave her children; the police were here. That had been her last thought until she had awakened in the hospital.

This morning Mary had spoken to the police. They said that the girls had seen their father bolt out the back door. Within the hour Kevin was arrested while he was drinking in a bar and the bartender had called the police when he saw the man's bloody condition.

Today she was lying in white sheets in this all white room gazing out the window at the deep blue sky wondering why she had put up with the past years of abuse. Did she really think it would eventually go away or get better? Or had fear frozen her power to act? Over the past three years the abuse had grown from verbal attacks to physical beating. Each time he hit her he'd promised never do it again, but he always found some excuse to do so over and over. She reported him to the police and he'd been arrested. They went into counseling and for a few months he'd be good then the pattern of abuse would repeat itself.

One day she noticed bruises on Bliss's arms, deep bruises as though she had been roughly handled. Bliss admitted that her father did it. That's the day Mary woke up and knew that the mental, emotional abuse she was suffering had always included her children, but now that included physical abuse too. It was not to be tolerated. More important than her own welfare was the welfare of her children and she would no longer allow them to live a life of fear.

It had taken all her courage to make plans to escape and hide from this violent man. She knew what the probability of future attacks by an abusive husband was if she stayed in the same town. No, they had to disappear. She had contacted Mr. Coons, a lawyer, about her abusive marriage and how vitally important it was *not* to serve the divorce papers until that following weekend when she and the girls would be safely away.

The delivery of the divorce papers that afternoon had driven Kevin into this last attack. Mary had threatened him with divorce before but Kevin had always laughed and said she wouldn't dare, that he'd kill her first. Well, he'd almost succeeded and she knew she was awfully lucky to be alive and so were her girls. However, it didn't lessen her guilt that she had allowed the situation of violence to grow to this extent.

Mary cried with remorse for having put her children through scenes of violence because they'd carry those memories for the rest of their lives. She had come so close to causing her girls' real harm, maybe even their deaths and Mary was finding it hard to forgive herself for not having left before. It was the innocent that always suffered the most.

Someone knocked gently on her door and Mary carefully turned her head to see Mr. Coons and quickly wiped the tears from her cheeks as best she could. He came in with the most anguished look on his wrinkled face with tears actually pooling in his faded blue eyes behind his glasses when he saw the results of her wounds.

"I deserve to be horsewhipped Mrs. Dawson. Those divorce papers weren't to be delivered until you and the girls were gone. My secretary made a mistake by putting all the divorce papers and warrants together to give to the processor. Excuses are worthless and I take full responsibility for the harm that's been done to you through my carelessness. I am so very sorry. Please, I beg you to forgive me if you can." and as he spoke tears rolled down his cheeks.

"Poor Mr. Coons, I must look pretty bad to get you to cry over me." Mary smiled a little; a little was all she could manage as her lips were cut and her jaw was badly bruised and swollen, but thank God she still had her teeth, loose but still there. "I guess I should probably be glad they won't give me a mirror; vanity you know. I guess I'd be shocked right?" Mary looked down at her arms covered with bandages; knives were so nasty and painful. I'll have scars she thought in rather an abstract way.

"My dear brave lady, how can you joke at a time like this?" He blew his little nose, took off his glasses and swiped the handkerchief across his face. "You have every right to sue me for having helped precipitate this assault, you know. As a lawyer I recommend that you do just that." said the little man bravely.

"Mr. Coons, I am not going to sue you. Something like this may have happened anyway given his violent nature. The worse case scenario, as they would say in the movies, would have been his killing us all in one of his rages even if I had successfully divorced him. I don't think we would ever have been safe from him. When I came to you, you knew there was a likelihood of that. I did too. We're lucky in many ways that he can't touch us now and the divorce will go through and we will be free to leave. My girls are safe and I'm alive. I am so very grateful to God for that. So what do we do next?"

Mr. Coons pulled a chair up to the bed and sat down. "Nothing because any attack with a deadly weapon the state takes over and will prosecute him. With his past record of violence, it won't go easy on him. One of the nurses took pictures of you when they first brought you in for evidence. I've seen them and they made me terribly sick. Dear Mrs. Dawson, I'm so very sorry that this awful attack happened to you." He stopped and blew his nose again and wiped his cheeks, coughed and said firmly. "I will see that monster is put in prison for first degree assault. He's on record as having been arrested for domestic violence before this as well as other assault charges from before he married you. He won't bother you again, I promise."

Then he sort of lit up and grinned evilly. "My dear, Judge Lee had read his file and saw the pictures of your wounds. He was brought into her court and after the charge of assault with a deadly weapon and attempted murder was read she deemed him a danger to you, your children and society in general and denied him bail. Mr. Dawson went ballistic, struck the guards and pretty much wrecked the court room trying to get to the judge, calling her names and threatening to kill her too after he'd killed you and the children. He was finally subdued, cuffed and gagged and by the time the judge got through charging him with all the added violations, Mr. Dawson is going to be spending some prime time in prison. First degree assault with intent to kill you, striking officers of the court, threatening a federal judge; well my dear, they all carries very stiff penalties. The judge said she'd make an example of him. I think she will too."

Mr. Coons took Mary's hand gently in his and said, "You may have forgiven me my dear, but I can't forgive myself. I demand to do all the legal work for you absolutely free of charge. Please allow me to atone in this way because selfishly it will ease my conscience and my heart a little." Mr. Coons said in a pleading way. "And since you generously, and may I add, erroneously refused to sue my firm, I feel I must insist."

Mary smiled again and said. "I would never stand between a man and his conscience dear Mr. Coons, so I'll accept and now you may feel good again as I will very soon. I really would like you to call me Mary."

They looked at each other in complete accord. Then Mary said very seriously, "There's one thing I want above all; *I want my last name changed.* The girls have asked that their names be changed too, but I'm not sure if that can be done, but you'll know."

"You'll have no problem with your name change, but the girls? Well, Bliss is thirteen and should be considered mature enough to make that decision, however Stephanie is only ten. Hmm, I'll speak to Judge Lee about it. Because of the violence of the case, I think she will allow the girls that right. She understands the importance of you and the girls becoming invisible, so to speak. By the way, what is your maiden name, Mary?"

"It's Fletcher, but I think I will choose Van Cliveland, my great-grandmother's maiden name and a woman I most admired. I don't thing Kevin knows it because my grandmother died before I met him. I want to be rid of the name Dawson and I never want him to be able to find me in the future. *I want the record of the name change to be separate and sealed; that's vital to our future safety* if he ever gets out of prison." Mary was becoming agitated as she leaned up to look at Mr. Coons intently. "I want to take back my total freedom and independence from that man. I *need* to be free of the constant fear for my life and my girls' lives. *I never want to ever see him again*, do you understand?" Mary was crying as the emotions boiled over and painful sobs came from deep down. "We have to be free from this fear."

Mr. Coons reached over and rang for the nurse and then carefully slipped his small arm beneath her shoulders and leaned over to lay his head against hers and patted her. "There, there, my sweet little girl, there, there; I'll protect you and I will see that everything is done as you wish. Shush now, you're causing yourself more pain, my dear." He patted and stroked where he could without hurting her wounds.

The nurse came in and saw the condition of her patient and went immediately to get a shot to calm her down. Once that was done the nurse tried to get Mr. Coons to leave, but Mary was clinging hard to his hand. "*Don't go, please don't go yet.*" she sobbed.

Mr. Coons said in his forceful attorney's voice, which was really funny as it came out of such a small old man. "Mary is in need of a comforting presence and I will see that she becomes calm under these very trying circumstances. Rest assured she will be composed soon. I am staying with her as a representative father figure."

"Very well Sir, please call me if she's not better in a few minutes; she mustn't move around too much." And smiling at the fierce little man, the nurse left and closed the door.

Between sobs Mary laughed at her protector and that cracked her lips open. Mr. Coon grabbed a Kleenex and dabbed lightly to stop the blood. "Now, now, Mary, the nurse will kick me out if she sees the harm I've caused. Be calm, all is well; you and the girls are virtually free. Take a deep breath; oh dear, I see that that hurts too." The old man dabbed some more until the bleeding stopped, but he worried as to what he could do to distract the poor woman and had a sudden idea.

"Now if you're a very good girl I'll tell you a story. I have just run onto a very funny case involving two elderly people, neighbors of many years by the way, concerning three goats, a garden and a laundry line. You won't believe the dust up these people got themselves into." And Mr. Coons quietly and with a great deal of amusement told Mary the story that had her laughing softly. Between the shot and the story she listened to she finally fell asleep.

Mr. Coons slowly stopped speaking, patting her relaxed hand, tucked her arms carefully under the blanket and pulled it up over her shoulders. He walked over to the window blind, adjusted it so the room grew dim and with a last look at her, left the room.

Mary dreamed of a home far, far away and it was so beautiful that she felt peace fill her troubled heart.

Mary Dawson, now Van Cliveland, had been recuperating at home for the past month. Her wounds had closed and her head wound was healing as well and it was a relief to have the stitches out, but the scars were ugly so she was using a special vitamin E cream on them several times a day. Her long dark brunette hair had been shaved off on one side to attend the long knife slash through her scalp so it was logical to cut the rest very short. The scar started at her left eyebrow and ran above her ear and around to the back of her head. She had almost been scalped. The knife had missed her eye by a half inch and Mary shuddered. "Gods, I was almost blinded." The plastic surgeon had been very clever and the scaring on her forehead was going to be minimal he assured her, but right now it was just red and ugly.

"I guess it's better to lose my hair then my life; vanity, vanity all is vanity." She laughed at her reflection in the mirror. It was hard, but she did it. Her head was bristling with new growth; almost half an inch long now, but the new growth that was coming in along the scar was white. Well, it would be a reminder of her close shave. She had to laugh at that pun.

As Mary worked in the kitchen that afternoon and got to thinking about the funny dreams she had been having lately; dreams about talking to this shinning spirit. Yet in the mornings she couldn't quite recall what they'd talked about. Now, why was she dreaming of angels, because of course that's what they had to have been. Whatever the reason she always felt better, more positive when she woke up. Just then she heard the front door open.

"Mom, are you here?" The anxious call from Bliss came in the front hall.

"Hi, kids, I'm in the kitchen and getting some snacks fix for us." said Mary and went down the hallway to hug away the worried looks on her children's faces. "Now, it's cookies and hot chocolate time, I think. How did that test go, Stephanie?" asked Mary as she led them into the spotless and repainted kitchen. She felt Stephanie hesitate and Bliss flinched. They hated the kitchen.

Mary paused then said in a natural tone of voice. "Why don't you girls go wash up and put your books away and I'll fix hot chocolate and the tea and we'll have it in the living room?" Relieved, the girls backed out of the kitchen and went to their room talking softly.

Mary sighed and got busy. The truth was the kitchen bothered her a great deal too and it took an act of courage to work there. Sometimes she couldn't even do that without wanting to throw up, that's when she called for pizza. Something would have to be done about this situation and soon. There was no getting around the memories of that evening.

The phone rang and Mary walked over to the counter and picked it up. "Hello?"

"Mary my dear, I've got some sad news and some glad news, though actually I think it is all a God sent. Can I drop by in the next half-hour? I really need to talk to you about this wonderful event; at least I hope you're going to think it's wonderful. May I stop by?" said an excited Mr. Coons.

"Yes of course you may, you know you're always welcome. I was just fixing tea and hot chocolate and I'll save you either one." laughed Mary, and before she could ask what it was all about, Mr. Coons had hung up.

"Now I wonder what's got him so excited. At least it sounds like good news. Thank goodness." Ten minutes later she had a tray prepared with hot banana bread, fruit, cheese, tiny sandwiches and cups and saucers. The girls were always hungry when they first got home. They must be growing again she thought or the lack of stress had increased their appetites.

The girls came and stood in the kitchen doorway waiting until Mary had finished. "Bliss, please carry the tray in for me, I don't trust my strength yet. Stephanie, you carry the teapot. Use the potholders dear, because it's hot and I'll take the chocolate pot."

They sat everything on the coffee table and sat down while Mary poured them hot chocolate as she explained the phone call. "Mr. Coons is stopping by and he sounds excited about some good news he'd just gotten for us and I wonder what it could be."

"Well, it will certainly be a nice change, won't it Mom?" said Bliss and Mary looked over at her oldest daughter and frowned. Bliss was exhibiting a lot of anger and distrust of people and counseling was a slow process. Stephanie seemed to be handling past events a little better or maybe she was just clever at covering them up. Mary sighed and felt frustrated as to what would be best to do for them now.

Mary poured herself a cup of tea and replaced the tea caddy. Taking a piece of banana bread she sat back in her chair, sipping and nibbling and contemplated the nice fire burned in the fireplace. She looked over at her girls on the couch talking in soft undertones to each other.

"You know girls I've been seriously thinking about selling the house." Well, that certainly got their attention. Discussion of where they might like to live had just begun when the doorbell rang.

Before Mary could get up, Bliss jumped up, sat her cup down and went to the door. Before she opened it she asked. "Who is it?"

"It's Mr. Coons." She opened the door and let the old man in then closed, locked and chained the door after him; Bliss always double checked the doors to be sure they were locked. Yes, something had to be done soon, thought Mary as she got up to greet their visitor.

"Hello Mr. Coons," and kissed the man on the cheek, "Please sit down and let me pour you some tea. My neighbors have been most kind in giving us loads of goodies and hot dishes and Mrs. Hubbard is famous for her banana nut bread."

After Mary had served him, she sat down and looked over at his cheerful face and smiled. "It certainly must be great news to put such a happy expression on your face; what is it?"

"You see my dear it all began with Robert Morale who owns a good sized newspaper in the adjoining town of Stonyport. I play chess with him once a week and have done so for years. He's a very good player and he really keeps me on my toes. Ah, well, that's beside the point, isn't it?" Mary smiled at this dear little man who in a very short time had become her surrogate father.

"Hmm…yes…anyway, he had just received a legal item several days ago to run in his paper asking for any information leading to heirs of one Delaney Johnston Fletcher. Robert knew your father and that he had lived here in Midville. You see he had printed the news that concerned you as it made the national news; such a dreadful, dreadful thing. Well, he knew I was your lawyer and representing you in divorce proceedings so he thought maybe your family was connected to this Fletcher person."

"The probability of that is rather doubtful, don't you think? I mean, Fletcher is such a common name. There are probably tribes of Fletchers all over the country." Mary said in a surprised way.

"Let me go on, dear before I lose track of where I am, as I get older my memory gets spotty at times. Hmm, oh yes, to go on. I too wondered if perhaps you might be one of those heirs so I researched your family's genealogy and sure enough Delaney Johnston Fletcher was your great-uncle on your father's side and I didn't find any other Fletcher connected to him besides yourself, unless you know of any."

"No, no I don't. You see I was the last child born in my family line. My father was killed in Italy when I was eighteen years old and Mother died just before I married Kevin. Now I do vaguely remember Dad saying something about him being an only child too, so I don't have any close aunts, uncles or cousins that I know of." Mary thought for a few minutes then said, "I recall Dad talking about an Uncle D. who was the black sheep of the family; not a nice person he said. When I asked him if he knew where his uncle lived he said he'd gone west years and years ago. I guess the D. could stand for Delaney. Hmmm…Delaney was my father's middle name too come to think about it; one of those family things that get passed down." said Mary as she reflected on the past.

"Actually the man's legal name was Delaney Johnston Fletcher he just never used the first name once he got settled in the west. I do believe without question, that this is your great-uncle." Mr. Coons smiled like a cat licking up cream and sipped his tea and ate a small sandwich.

"My goodness, are you positive?" shocked and unable to take it all in, Mary just stared at her lawyer and he just nodded enthusiastically.

"I've already spoken to Mr. Jensen, the lawyer from Washington State who has been searching for relatives of Mr. Fletcher for the last two years. All I need to do is send copies of you and your father's birth certificate, a copy of your family's lineage plus a copy of your passport or picture I.D. as proof of your claim."

"Why is all that necessary?" Mary said in a surprised voice.

"Oh dear, I guess I forgot the important part, didn't I? Well, it's about your inheritance which is a good sized farm in The Sacred

Valleys region of western Washington. Now I understand the house isn't in really good condition, but the land is rich and has produced profitably in the past and it's situated quite close to River Town, a community of goodly size. When I spoke to Mr. Jensen I told him about you and mentioned that you were a teacher of seventh and eighth grades. He got excited and told me that the school district was looking for a teacher for the eighth grade and they needed one by the spring quarter. I assume it's very hard for them to find qualified teachers for such a remote area. The teacher they have is due to have her baby in the spring and she doesn't want to teach anymore as she has four children at home. My goodness, one can understand that, can't one? She must really have her hands full, don't you think? So they need a teacher by the third semester that begins in March I believe."

Mr. Coons put his teacup down and patted his lips with his napkin before going on. "They've asked me to make you an offer. They will fix up your house and finance your move west if you'll agree to come teach the eighth grade for no less than three years. I understand the salary is quite good as the Valleys are filled with prosperous farms and ranches." Sipping at his tea, Mr. Coons enjoyed the surprised and shocked look on their faces and had to laugh at the babble of voices.

Mary waved her hands for silence and. "Yes, yes girls, this could be our answer; sell the house and move far away to the west and leave all this unhappiness behind. What do you think?" Mary eagerly leaned forward and the girls began to whisper to each other in excited undertones. Mary left them alone and asked Mr. Coons for more particulars.

Finally she heaved a deep sigh and sank back into her chair. "This is indeed a miracle and I must say it looks almost too perfect to be true. However, I think this is the change we've desperately needed. It's a miracle coming to us in perfect timing." Mary paused then looked at Mr. Coons. "When is Kevin's trial date? That will affect how soon we can leave."

"Your husband actually did you a favor when he attacked the court guards and threatened to kill you, the girls and the judge because she's set the trial date two weeks from tomorrow. Your appearance will be done and over with, so by the time you sell your house and pack you should be free to go. Now, dear people, it's imperative that none of you tell your friends or neighbors where you are going and if you have to store anything please use my mother's maiden name so you can't be traced."

"We will be very careful. Girls, did you hear that? It's vital you don't tell any of your friends at school or other people where we will be going and especially don't tell anyone about our name change."

"On your last day at school I'll come and pick up your records and have them legally changed to your new name and cancel the old records. These records will also be sealed information." said Mr. Coons.

"Sure Mom, we'll be extra careful. We have cause to be don't we?" Bliss turned to Mr. Coons. "Will we have to testify against our father?"

"Only if you choose to do so as you're the only witnesses to the attack, but if you're afraid of facing your father, I believe the judge would question you in her office." Mr. Coons leaned forward to answer Bliss as he would have an adult.

"I am not afraid and if it will help put him in prison for a long time I'm more than willing." she said grimly.

"That is very brave of you young lady, I admire your courage. Yes, it would be very helpful. Because of his violent nature, he will be in restraints and chained to his chair so you won't have to be afraid of him leaping up and attacking any of you and if he gets verbally abusive he'll be gagged. We'll get together in a few days and I will prepare you for questioning, all right?"

Bliss nodded and said angrily. "I'd like to see him chained and gagged. Maybe that's not nice of me, but he's hurt Mom a number of times and this time he almost killed her. He deserves the worst that can happen."

Stephanie said quietly, "I will testify too if you need me 'cause I saw and heard it all too."

"Are you sure you want to do this, girls? You don't have to, you know." Mary said softly.

"Yes, we do and we'll do anything to see that the law takes care of that monster once and for all. It's time we stood up and told the truth." Mary flinched at that reprimand. "I hope he goes to prison and rots there for the rest of his life. From now on please do not refer to that man as my father." replied the angry girl and Stephanie gripped her sister's hand tightly and nodded in agreement.

"Me too Mommy, you can put me on the stand and I'll testify too." Stephanie nodded her head again to affirm her commitment.

"Oh girls, I'm so very sorry you have to go through all this, I'm so sorry." whispered Mary and struggled not to cry.

"Nothing that happened is your fault Mom, so stop apologizing; we're all in the same boat so let's just get it done and over with." Bliss said determinedly.

Mary saw in that instance that Bliss wasn't a child anymore; she had been forced to face the realities of an abusive life and no one could remain a child under those circumstances. Mary felt she had much to atone for.

At the thought of having to see Kevin again she shuddered even if he was restrained, but the jury needed to see the damage he had inflicted on her. Well, she was determined to see it through and if her girls were brave enough to face their father then she could do no less. Their bravery shamed her. The first step to independence was to confront the past and take their power back.

She straightened up and said in a determined voice. "All right then! One for all and all for one is our motto and we'll get this done and over with. Thank you girls, you're the greatest. Now, what do you think about going west?"

Bliss said firmly. "We would go anywhere as long as we don't have to stay in this town and in our school and in this house. Stephie and I say let's go because it's got to be better than here."

Mary nodded her head. "I agree. All right, I'll put the house up for sale this week. Yes, let's make a clean sweep and start our new lives in the west. Mr. Coons, please tell Mr. Jensen I accept the teaching position. I'll give you copies of my certification and whatever other necessary documents tomorrow. Oh, and please have my teaching certificate name changed too" Mary lifted her teacup in a toast to the future and everyone else did too.

Mary laughed. "Horace Greeley once said a long time ago when the west was young, "Go west young man go west". So I say to you girls, "Let's go west, young ladies, and start our new lives."

After Mary had shown Mr. Coons out she shut and locked the door as Bliss liked to do, then leaned against it and surveyed the hall.

In her mind and heart she had already left it. This house wasn't home anymore and truth to tell, it hadn't been for a long, long time.

People made a house a home or a hell, so like the pioneers of old she and her children would strike out into the unknown and hope for a better life. Mary was determined that they would succeed.

There was a lot to do to prepare for the move; a lot of sorting to be done. She'd have to pack Kevin's things and given them into the custody of the state, store the household goods and furniture they wanted to keep and hold a garage sale of everything else. If they sold the house right away, they could leave immediately and head out west. It felt liberating to get into positive action. She was taking her power back.

Mary walked back into the living room and her waiting children with a lighter heart.

~*Sunday*~

The boys trotted down the stairs for breakfast all dressed for church. Joe carried a small bag filled with their work clothes for when they went out to the ranch to dig up their Grandfather's ashes. Mike carried his guitar case.

"Hannah, you're coming with us when we scatter grandfather's ashes aren't you?" asked Joe anxiously.

"Sure honey, we're all going and being there will help us feel better about some of the hard things we've said about Mr. Devereaux. Best of all we'll make his spirit feel better too." Hannah placed the bowls of oatmeal on the table, along with bacon and eggs and toast. "Now, hurry up and eat or we'll be late for church."

They had just finished breakfast when the sound of a heavy truck came into the yard and within minutes there was a knock on the front door and Joe ran to answer it and was heard coming back down the hall to the kitchen talking to the Chief.

"We'll be with you in a jiffy Blackhawk just as soon as I take care of Miss Carli here." said Mari Beth.

"So, how is Miss Carli this morning?" said the Chief, smiling at the little beauty.

"I is a very, very good girl, God-Daddy." Blackhawk grinned down at the baby.

Mike and Joe burst into laughter. "Can we call you God-Daddy too?" asked Joe jokingly.

Mike watched a frown beginning to form on the Chief's face and hurriedly said. "You know Blackhawk; we don't have anyone to call daddy or even father anymore, so maybe you wouldn't mind if Joe and I call you……ah…just G.D. It would be our private name for you if you didn't mind, that is?" Mike said in a tentative way.

Blackhawk's face cleared and a grin formed on his mouth. "G.D. Hmm, okay, I'll accept that, but only Carli can call me God-Daddy."

Laughed Blackhawk and tickled the little girl under her chin and picked her up when Carli held her arms up.

Mari Beth said to Hannah in a low voice. "And another one bit the dust." which sent Hannah off into giggles.

As they were leaving the house Joe whispered to Mike. "Nice save, brother."

"Yeah, I was really inspired when I felt the sweat beginning to bead up on my forehead." Mike heard a snicker and looked down to see Joe's shaking shoulders as they climbed into Blackhawk's truck for the ride to town.

The church was situated right in the middle of the busiest section of Main Street as though it had been built first and the town had grown around it. It was a stately white building with broad steps leading up to the double doors that were wide open. The tower rose above the body of the church and the bells were melodiously ringing a welcoming peel. A huge garden surrounded all sides of the building with trees of all kinds and flowerbeds that had been readied for winter. The rectory bordered the garden on left side. Mike stood still for a moment and got the feeling that the whole church block gave off a vibration of unworldliness; a special place of peace and absolute harmony. He had never experienced a church in this way before.

This Central Church, as it was called, wasn't the only church in town of course; there was a Catholic Church over on First Street, a Synagogue on Maple Street and a Buddhist Temple on Downey Avenue and he had friends in all of them. It just showed Mike that all religions were accepted here without prejudice.

Church wasn't a new experience for the Kelly boys. With their parents they had attended many different churches and the boys felt that they were pretty much the same; in other words they had no connections or preferences with any of them. Well, they didn't like hell-fire and brimstone preaching, thank you very much. Being told that they all worthless trash and didn't deserve God's love didn't set well with what their parents said about them all being made in the mage of God and that He/She loved them. Dad had said that each person chose to be good or bad and had been given the right to decide and that was free will.

It was amazing to Mike how many people he knew now. Such a short time had passed since they had arrived and how *right* it felt now to be here. They were no longer strangers, but a very real part of the community. Mike was greeted by a number of people and got a wave and a grin from some of his school friends.

"Hey Mike, we heard the preacher had asked you and Joe to perform today. I gotta tell you I really like what you guys did at Strongbow's yesterday. See you after church?" asked Ike.

"Not today Ike, the family has a thing to do after church, but I'll see you at school tomorrow." with that Mike quickly ran up the steps to join his family. He laughed and thought he'd never got tired of saying "his family." It beat the heck out of "being alone to face the world" feeling.

Church began pretty much as usual, however, when the Preacher got up to talk to them it wasn't church as usual anymore. "Good morning everyone, you're welcome! Nice to see so many faces here today especially after such a wonderful celebration we all had out at Ben and Mari Beth's place yesterday. Those of you who couldn't make the barbecue really missed a treat."

Loud clapping followed his statement and Ben had to get up and bow then pulled Mari Beth up and she laughed even as she bowed. The Preacher grinned and waited until the church quieted again.

"Sunday should be a day of rest, but I know the Lord is forgiving as most of you are farm folks and have animals that have to be taken care of regardless of what day it is. I think it is more important to keep a sense of reverence every day rather than just reserving it for Sunday and then forget about it during the week.

"I welcome all newcomers or visitors to our Valleys, and I see a few of you here and there. Now you might not understand the significance of our protective spirits you may have heard about. The ancient tribes called them the Thunder Gods. These Spirits protect and sustain the energy of the land and its people even today. From my research into the Valleys history, these Guardian Spirits, or Gods as They have been called, have been here for a thousand years as far as we know." There was some murmuring and a whispering before Preacher went on.

"Let me make it clear that we do not worship Them. We do respect Them and keep Their simple rules and express our gratitude for the lands that provide us our abundance and prosperity. Rule One: no human blood is to be spilled in violence upon the valleys sacred land by another human. Two: respect and treat the animals well. Three: Do not harm the land in any way. These are simple rules that everyone can implement and practice no matter where they live.

I'm going to call upon our tutelary Guardian of the Valleys, Chief Issaquah Blackhawk, a direct descendent of a long, long line of chief guardians to tell you the beginning story of the Thunder Gods and their first interactions with humans. Chief Blackhawk, would you step up here please." The Preacher went and sat down with his family in the front row.

There were murmurs among the congregation at this unprecedented occurrence even as the dignified figure of Chief Blackhawk stood up and walked down the aisle with an air of great presence that could be felt by everyone. He was elegantly dressed in a black suit with his hawk pendent resting on his chest and large turquoise belt around his waist. He stepped up on the dais and stood behind the lectern and held his hands up to signal for quiet. The Chief's voice filled the silence in a deep authoritative tone.

"Blessings upon you," Blackhawk put his hands down on the lectern, "Let your hearts listen as I tell you the legend that has been passed down in my family from one Blackhawk chief to another and on back into the dimness of time."

Blackhawk paused as though listening to a silent inner voice then began to speak using his hands in the ritualistic storyteller's way. "And so it began long, long ago when oral stories were carefully learned to teach and instruct the people about the wisdom of its people and as with us stories about the Guardian Spirits that live upon Thunder Mountain. And so the tale begins before man first met the Thunder Gods, a name given to these Guardian Spirits at the very beginning of man's first contact."

The storyteller recounted the legend in an abbreviated form and completely mesmerized the audience. Blackhawk imbued the legend with emotion that colored the words with impact and drama with a true storyteller's magic. Of course, most people had heard the general basis for cherishing the land and the animals, but just not as it was being presented today. It wasn't the complete story, but enough to fill in some knowledge about the Guardian Spirits and to bring understanding to those who had never heard of the legend of the Sacred Valleys.

"Because we still honor Their ways and Their laws that were set down for anyone who lived within the Valleys of Thunder Mountain, the Guardians still reside with us. There aren't too many places in the world today that have the benefit of such wonderful Guardian Spirits protecting all who dwell beneath Their care. Because of Them we prosper, we have abundance and we live very well within the peace and serenity of our beautiful lands. We care for one another and thus everyone lives a better life." Chief Blackhawk raised his hands once more. "There is no quarrel between these Guardian Spirits and the Christ, Buddha, Shiva, Allah or any other worshipped prophet. This that we do isn't about religion. We have compassion for our fellow man; we serve where there is need; we give generously of our time, labor and profits to anyone who has that need. We respect each person's right to his own religious beliefs and we live in harmony with diverse ethnic groups. Everyone has the spark of God, The Creator within them. And thus we live in peace and in brotherhood and in balance with nature by cherish the land and the animals as gifts from the Earth Mother." Blackhawk raised his hands. "God bless you all through out your days and protect you on your journeys. I am Chief Blackhawk and I have finished." In silence he left the platform and returned to his seat.

The Preacher got up and resumed his place behind the lectern. "Thank you Chief Blackhawk. Now, I sincerely hope that any questions you might have had in your minds as to where this church stands regarding the Thunder Gods or Guardian Spirits, has been put to rest. To love one another as oneself, and strive to do good to all that come within our lands is our credo. We strive here in our valleys to live those basic teachings and no man can go wrong if he strives to live by those truths. Our very own Spiritual Guardians simply enforce them when we have had the occasional person or persons who abuse the land or the animals or a fellow human being. The Preacher bowed his head; "Loving God's Life should always be celebrated with a joyful noise. Let us repeat the 100 Psalm. There was a hush in the congregation and they followed the Preacher as they recited the Psalm with him. "Make a joyful noise to the Lord, all the

Earth. Worship the Lord with gladness; come into his presence with singing and unto his courts with praise…..."

When they had finished he raised his head and smiled upon the people. "I am going to ask young Joe if he would give us the pleasure of singing anything he wants to." and beckoned to Joe.

Joe walked up to stand beside the Preacher and whispered to him. Preacher laughed and gave Joe a pat on the shoulder and Joe stood alone on the platform waiting while the Preacher went over to speak to the organist then he went and sat once again with his family.

There was silence while the organist found the right music and Joe drew in a deep breath then he burst into song, "Joyful, Joyful" expressing the great joy that filled his heart and Joe sang it with such verve that he began to dance and the organist softly joined in on the speed and the heart-stirring rhythm then, without pause the organist started the music all over again and Joe gestured for everyone to join him and the church stood up and it rocked. When it was over there was shouting and applause until everyone gradually quieted down and were seated once more.

Mike came up and joined Joe and he played while he and Joe sang three old time hymns before sitting down to more thunderous applause. This was the most beautiful church service either boy had ever experienced. Why weren't more churches like this? Churches should express the love and the joy and spread that joy outward to other people. It was so simple that Joe couldn't understand why anyone would want to live any other way.

Driving home with Blackhawk Joe was very quiet. "What's going on Joe?" asked Mike in a low voice.

"I don't rightly know exactly…promise me you won't laugh?"

"No Joe, I won't laugh." promised his brother.

"Well when I sing I seem to be more *me* than just the ordinary little boy Joe. It's a strange yet right feeling inside of me when I sing. Anyway, something in me just breaks loose and I'm caught up in some sort of inner happiness that I have to express. I mean, I just *have* too, Mike 'cause something inside *drives me* to do that." Joe looked embarrassed as though he'd just taken off all his clothes in public and he blushed and whispered. "Gee, I'm not saying it very well, but I guess singing really rocks for me, you know?" looking anxiously at Mike.

Mike just had to hug his kid brother hard and scrub the top of Joe's head with his knuckles while laughing; not at Joe, but in amazement at this brother who didn't have a clue as to how his singing gave joy to people. "And you, being such a smart kid and all, have just come to that realization? Man, it sticks out all over you when you sing. People could tell you that that inner joy you feel just rocks them too."

Joe grinned. "Well, I guess that's better than having them throw tomatoes or sending them running for the door."

"Yeah way better Joe, way better. I know you take your voice casual-like as being just a part of you and that's a good thing. I sure wouldn't want you to get stuck-up or overly prideful about it 'cause stuff like that could become a problem in the future if you don't take care to keep your ego under your thumb. Your talent is like an untrained colt right now and it has to be disciplined like that colt so it can be all it's supposed to be. Your voice is your gift from God as sure as shootin' and God chose you to house it so that means you have a responsibility to train and use it well so everyone who hears you can take some of that joy into their lives and be better for having heard you sing." Mike said seriously then drew a long breath hoped to God he wasn't turning Joe off with his preaching and looked down at Joe with a little worried frown on his face.

"Yes, I know that all that Mike, and I'm really happy God gave me a voice because it makes me happy when I sing and I'd like to make people just as happy. I guess I always will, but just in case my voice gives out, can I come back home and be a rancher with you?" Joe laughed lightly even though that idea of losing his voice and never sing again was impossible to contemplate, yet he needed to know he'd be welcome back at the ranch; back home.

"Yeah you can come home any day and anytime you want because it's your home too and it always will be. And if the day ever comes that you lose your voice, which I strongly doubt, you can come home and I'll work your tail off. Even when you take vacations and come home, I'll still work your tail off just to keep you humble and grounded. It's my duty as your older brother." Kidding back and forth passed the time until they reached their ranch then they grew quiet remembering what they had to do that day.

When they arrived at Kelly's Ranch the boys went into the house to change their clothes before everyone drove out to the family cemetery. They found grandfather's headstone with the large marble urn sitting in front of it; no digging was required after all. Walking back to the ranch yard, Mike could only carry the heavy urn for a short ways and then had to pass it to Ben.

It took two trucks and a few other pickups to get everyone who wanted to go close to the sacred site. The men of the ranch were attending in force to support Mike and Joe and that touched the boys' hearts and made it seem more of a united effort to restore peace to their grandfather's spirit and to clear the ranch of any residual grief and remorse. Once they were up in Idle Meadow and gathered by the central rock, Chief Blackhawk, dressed once again in his headdress of Shaman, built a fire and placed sage upon it just as he had before. One by one each man, woman and child stepped up to have the sage smoke waved over them. Ben carried Carli and she coughed and waved her hand to disperse the smoke and that got a chuckle out of the others. Once this part of the ceremony had been completed, they formed into a large circle.

"Guardians of the Sacred Lands of Thunder Mountain, we ask you to help release the spirit of Joseph Michael Devereaux to go on to the other life. Help release him from his pain and suffering and the bonds that tie him to this land. We speak now to the spirit of Joseph Michael Devereaux: Your daughter and son-in-law's mortal ashes lay here on this dedicated sacred site on your land and we are about to place the ashes of your physical body here so that they may mingle with them. Together again, you will be able to leave this world behind at last and join your beloved wife, daughter, son, and son-in-law in the after life. We command this to be so in the name of the Christ."

Stepping back, he motioned Mike and Joe to step forward. With a sharp knife Mike broke the seal on the urn and once the top was off it took both boys to hold the urn tilted as they walk backward around the central fire shaking the ashes out as they went. Finally it was done and Mike sat the empty urn upside down against the rock and placed the cap on top of its base.

The fire burned brightly for a time as the wind blew gently across the small meadow. After awhile the small fire died out. Then all was calm. A deep voice sang softly into the silence, ***"Goin' home, goin' home, I'm just goin' home, it's not far, just close by through an open door, I'm just goin' home...."*** It was their new man Divine Clive with his gorgeous base voice rolling out of that deep chest and the wind seemed to pick it up until the little glen resonated with the feeling of total joyful release. When Divine had finished, quiet followed.

There was a sudden stirring in the energies around the small place with its central stone, and it wasn't just one person that felt it. There was sense of releasing, a sighing and a joyful freeing of a trapped spirit.

"This had been a very good thing you have done, my children. Your grandfather's spirit is released and at peace and a greater peace is now in the land. Yes, this has been a very good day. It is finished now so come, let us go." Chief Blackhawk led the way back down the mountain.

"Thank you Divine, you put a special blessing on our ceremony and Joe and I appreciate it very, very much." said Mike as he shook the tall man's hand and Joe did the same. Divine just smiled shyly, nodded his head before he followed the others.

For a few minutes Joe and Mike stood and looked down on the ground where the mortal remains of their only family lay mingled with the earth. They grieved and shed a few tears, not so much for their loved ones who were free from pain and sorrow, but for their own personal loss.

Mike sniffed and wiped his cheeks on the back of his sleeve saying softly, "Even though it hurts to have them up here instead of with us down there it feels.... different to me like maybe I'm more peaceful inside and out. I'm glad you thought to do this because they're together now, don't you think?"

Joe was silent for a few moments then nodded his head; nothing more was required. They turned away and walked down to join the living.

~*The Blunder*~

'**Stupid hicks**,' Elroy said silently and laughed viciously as he walked out of the jail and cast a furtive, fearful glance up and down the busy street. 'Yet it's good for me that they are, but now I've got to get out of town fast 'cause it's not going to take them long to discover their blunder. I've got to disappear.' He hurried down the street and turned left at the last corner.

He could hardly believe his luck when they'd turned him loose. Talk about being surprised, but he managed to act the part of the other stranger and he didn't even try to pick up his own valuables because they would have nailed him for sure if he had. The other guy's things were in his pocket which didn't amount too much, however, he'd taken it and even signed for them. Stupid hicks! Elroy nervously looked behind him and felt his luck had just about run its course.

Within minutes of fast walking he arrived at an old abandoned shed at the very edge of town and entered through the dilapidated doorway. Elroy had learned not to put all his money in one place, hence this hiding place. Going to the far corner he pulled up an old rotten floorboard and took out his sack of cash then he was out the door and walking away.

It would be a long walk to the next town unless he could catch a freight train somewhere south of here. He had to stay off the roads incase a search was organized so here he was walking cross country and freezing his hinny off. All the money he had spent on outdoor gear was wasted because it was all in his car and it had been impounded.

After hours of miserable cold and a rough hike Elroy found the railroad lines and eventually came upon a small maintenance shack where trains automatically switched tracks. The door was locked so Elroy broke a small pane in the door window then he was inside out of the wind. There was even a stove sitting in the middle of the floor and firewood stacked beside it too. Shivering so badly he had a hard time building a fire and once it got going he practically hugged the stove. He thought he'd never get warmed up, but finally the room heated and as exhausted as he was, the floor made a perfect bed. He curled up beside the stove and not even hunger could keep him awake.

It was just before dawn the next morning when he heard a train coming from the east. There was a train already waiting on the sidetrack heading east. Elroy couldn't go back east so he was seriously thinking about heading for warm California probably because he had had enough of cold weather. He knew that when a con turned sour it was time to get out of town. Yeah, maybe he'd head for California. Sure he'd love to stay and get *even*, but the odds weren't in his favor. He needed a place to think about what to do next. He needed a plan.

The westbound train slowed and as it crawled along Elroy heard the tracks being switched as he ran alongside the slow moving train. Climbing on between cars he snaked up a steel ladder and crawled along the stacks of lumber until he found a niche he could squeeze into between sections of lumber and within minutes the train picked up speed and began to clip along at a fast rate.

Elroy was freezing and pulled the thin coat collar high around his ears and stuffed his hands into the pockets and wished for his own fleece lined jacket instead of this worn wool coat of the transient. The coat didn't help keep him very warm, but it was a better than nothing. It wouldn't be long before he had himself a warm place to sleep and a decent meal.

At the first big town, a couple of hundred miles southwest of River Town, Elroy would find a small out of the way motel and buy a used pickup. He had enough money to rest up for a couple of weeks, besides he thought he was catching a cold which wasn't surprising since he had been chilled right down to the bone for hours.

At a cheap motel Elroy lay in bed shivering with a feverish cold, the result of being poorly dressed to withstand the hours of exposure to the bitter wind. Just remembering the long cold journey, the abuse of his person by those cowboys, being jailed which had never happened to him before, and going hungry for two days on top of all the rest simply fed his anger to a boiling point. So lying in bed, sick as a dog, he had nothing to do but fume and plot in the hours that passed until finally it built into a blinding unreasonable rage.

Nobody knocked him around and got away with it. *Nobody did dirt to Elroy.* If he couldn't get back at those people then he'd just find the next sucker to satisfy his need for revenge.

The very thought of how narrow an escape he'd had made him shiver and not from the fever either. No, he didn't think he'd be going back to River Town; it was too dangerous and Elroy had great deal of respect for his skin, but that didn't stop him from fantasizing how good it would feel to really hurt those boys.

He contemplated murder in his heart and if he couldn't kill the ones he'd like to then he didn't care who the victim would be.

~Mountain Man Hoggins~

ROCKLAND HOGGINS HAD LIVED up on Thunder Mountain for the past forty years and figured to die there. He didn't fear death for after all it was a natural event in the cycle of life. It was simply going back into the womb of the universe to be nurtured and born again in the proper time, hopefully a little smarter and a tad bit wiser than before.

People called him a hermit, a wise man, an odd one, and maybe just a bit on the crazy side. They all agreed more or less, that he definitely didn't think or believe the way the general public did which made him....different. Oh, yeah, they also said he was definitely anti-social. Chuckling, Rockland guessed he was all of those things, yet in a truer sense he was none of them. They were simply labels, but didn't touch the reality of his soul.

People did a lot of guessing and most of them weren't comfortable unless they could stick a person in a box and slap a label on it. He would say however that the people of the Valleys were a lot more tolerant of people who were different and let them be themselves as long as they followed the Guardian's rules.

The old man sat on his favorite bench beneath a large ancient oak tree at the edge of a small cliff. From this vantage point he could see in all directions except north because the big mountain was right in his back yard such as it was, and the long view of the west was cut short by Flat Top Mesa. The log cabin he had built when he was younger was sturdy and set back against the mountain like a baby snuggled up to its mother's breast. He had built up here before he knew about The Thunder Gods. He chuckled remembering the magnitude of the surprise when they had paid him a visit. Now that had been a red letter day to say the least. Rockland had almost fainted from shock.

Over the years he became at easy with the presence of these benign spirits and often fine conversations with Them. He chuckled to think how that knowledge would disturb people if they knew about it. The people of the Valleys paid homage to Them for the bounty of the land, but none of them had ever actually met Them up close and personal. Rockland enjoyed the rare occasions when one or another came calling.

He had found right here in nature's isolation a life of balance, study, meditation and physical survival. It had taken him his youth to figure out that everyone had a place in which to live, learn and have their being. This was his place and he had never regretted his choice. There weren't many things he needed from the world down there, nothing much that he couldn't make or grow except for a few essential staples and, of course books and clothes.

Fortunately he was rarely ill; in fact the last time he'd had a cold was years ago, so maybe his good health was the residual of living a quiet life, exercise, meditation and a good diet. The fenced in garden he had constructed down on Thunder Mesa provided him with fresh vegetables which he canned for the winter and occasionally fish from the rivers. He was primarily a vegetarian however he liked fish once in awhile. For his other needs he'd pan a little gold here and there then make a trip to town once a year to stock up on supplies. He'd buy grain and hay from the ranches for his mules and have it hauled up to his stable. He made rocking chairs that seemed to sell very well and it gave his hands something creative to do during long winters. He had been thinking lately about making small tables to go with them. A change would be nice.

The dogs and the two mules were his constant companions, his friends. The puppies, when there was a litter, were carefully given to good people as they were like his children and there was an obligation to see that they were protected and treated well. Since his adult dogs, Kit and Duke, were getting on in age, Rockland thought he'd keep a male and a female out of the next litter so he'd always have a reminder of his companions.

Rockland Hoggins allowed himself one bad habit and that was his pipe. The old man smile at the very human need to have at least one vice, not that he over indulged, but he thoroughly enjoyed one or two pipes a day. So he puffed away and contemplated life and his studies as he looked out over the beautiful land. He had to admit to another vice. Well, not really a vice so much as a mild sort of pleasure and that was Henry Trudeaux's Apricot Brandy. He allowed himself one bottle per winter; now that's not so bad, was it? He chuckled at this evidence of being human and fallible.

Writing certainly wasn't a vice; it was a very creative outlet and every man, woman and child should have a creative outlet and writing was his. Often his contemplations led to writing short essays on his insights and sometimes he'd get what he called, straight transmissions from a spirit of higher wisdom. That these journals might make a good bonfire didn't matter to him at all because he didn't write for other people to read what he wrote. His writings had gathered over the years and filled a number of his book shelves. He would carefully wrap each year's journal in brown paper write the date on them before putting them up on the shelf along with the others. In many ways, he was his own spiritual teacher and was guided by other Master's works along the self-realization path he trod. Maybe that was why the Thunder Gods tolerated his presence so close to Their abode. He was quiet.

His thoughts came to a sudden halt when he caught sight of a horseman entering the meadow below. Rockland watched the boy look around as though trying to figure out where he was. Being that the boy was surrounded by trees that enclosed this part of the meadow wasn't helping him with direction. It was obvious he was lost and it was already getting late in the day and too far from the Valley for safety.

Hoggins sighed and knocked the doodle out of his pipe into a clay jar sitting beside his bench, got up and walked to the edge of the small cliff cupping his hands around his mouth and shouted, "**Helloooooooo.**"

The boy looked all around then up the hill. Hoggins waved his arms to attract attention. The boy saw him and waved and started his horse in that direction. The old man shook his head at the foolishness of youth wandering out into the wilderness and getting lost at this time of day. Worse still was the changeable weather of late. It wasn't wise to go so far from shelter. Walking down the hidden switchback soon led him to the top slope of Thunder Mesa.

The young boy rode up to him and with a relieved smile on his face. "Oh Sir, I'm mighty glad to see you 'cause I've been really stupid and got myself lost. I rode out to visit my parent's sacred burial spot in Idle Meadow, just above Lost Wagon Ranch, and got to exploring a bit and now I don't know how to get back. Well, it was dumb and I've got to get home before they send men out to look for me and that will lead to a whole lot of trouble." It all poured out in more words than Rockland had heard in several months except for his short conversation with Dusty Evans a while back.

"Best get down and rest your horse a mite son and I can take you back in a bit. My name is Rockland Hoggins and I live up there." and waved in the general direction of the mountain.

"I'm really happy to meet you Mr. Hoggins." said Joe and shook the man's hand. "Wow, you live right up there with the Thunder Gods? My oh my, They must really like you. My name is Joe Kelly and I belong down there. Well, I really belong in two places, Lost Wagon Ranch that my brother and sister and I own. We stay mostly with Ben Strongbow as he and Mari Beth are our guardians. Neat huh?" grinned Joe.

The old man had to grin at the young person's innocent enthusiasm. "Yeah, pretty neat. Are you hungry or thirsty?"

"Yes, I am a little bit of both 'cause I've missed lunch, but I left a note saying where I was going and all. I guess I've got time if it won't take me long to get back." worried the boy.

"No, we'll have you back within the hour. Come on then, best lead your horse for the path is steep." Turning away the old man led the way back into the woods.

When they arrived at the cabin Joe's mouth dropped open. "Oh geeze peeze, Mr. Hoggins, this is a really, really beautiful house. How did it get here?" Just then two big dogs came barreling out of the woods baying like the Hounds of the Baskervilles.

Joe froze.

"*Quiet down!* Come here and meet our guest. Come on you dogs, and behave yourselves now. Just because we don't often have company is no excuse for being rude." The dogs stopped their noise and dropped from a run into a quiet walk as they came forward to be introduced. Before that could happen two puppies tore around the cabin and barreled right into Joe. They certainly were a lot friendlier than their parents and didn't have a shy bone in their bodies.

"Oh look, aren't you beautiful? Oh, just look at you two." Joe was on his knees as the puppies mobbed him and finally knocked him flat in their enthusiasm. There was laughter and more talk as Joe got licked and chewed on. Rockland and the puppy's parents stood side by side and watched the young ones wrestle around in the grass.

"Now, that's a friendly greeting if I ever saw one. Okay, pups, that's enough for now. Here, Joe let me help you up." Pulling the boy to his feet was harder than usual, but finally the old man pushed and shoved the pups enough to get the boy free. He brushed the dirt and debris off the kid's clothes as best he could while the pups didn't want to give up their new toy.

"Sit." Rockland spoke sharply and to Joe's surprise the puppies sat and panted. Mr. Hoggins he handed Joe his hat.

"Gee they're smart. You've got to tell me about this breed of dog 'cause I don't think I've ever seen any like these." Suddenly Joe looked at the two adult dogs that were sitting calmly beside Mr. Hoggins. "I'm sorry; I didn't get to meet you, did I? I'm Joe." And went up to the adult dogs and held out his hand politely to be sniffed.

"Their names are Kit and Duke and I've had them for six years now. As far as their breed goes I guess they're a mix of this and that and its all Big Dog, if you know what I mean." said Rockland and watched how easily the boy made friends with his dogs. None of them were strangers for long either and they finally made it to the porch so Joe could sit down in the rocker and finish carrying on his conversation with the four attentive dogs that sat around him in a tight circle.

The old man shook his head in wonder at the way this boy had charmed his usual fierce and stand-offish adult dogs, except for the puppies who were still knot-heads at this point in their growth. Bringing water, some bread and cheese and a wet rag out to the waiting child, Rockland told the dogs to go lie down so the boy could eat in peace. After wiping his hands and face clean, Joe got to work on the food.

"Thank you Sir, that was awfully good. I was really stupid coming away without food or a canteen and you can be sure I won't make that mistake again." He promised.

"You're the boy who tried to bull dog that old bull, aren't you?" questioned the man and beneath the trim white mustache and short beard there was a slight smile on his lips.

"I wouldn't say it exactly that way because it was Jigger who did the dodging and running that got me out of trouble. That's Jigger right out there," Joe pointed, "And he's one smart cutting horse. The cowboys said he could turn on a dime and hand you back change and he sure did that day. Anyway, we were just trying to stay out of the way of the bull's charges. I just sat in the saddle and hung on for dear life. It was really scary, but I didn't pee my pants." claimed the child proudly.

Hoggins laughed joyfully at this sudden child. "Yep, that's a real success given that most men would have."

"How did you know about Old Mossy Horn?"

"I'm not too far from Flat Top Mesa." And pointed south and west from the high porch, Joe saw big cliffs. "You can see the southern part of Flat Top from here. Now this house isn't on your land or Ben's. I'm just a bit north of the property line and I walk a lot.

The afternoon you had your run in with the bull, I was walking over west of here and close to the valley that's on the other side of Flat Top when I saw this stranger high tailin' it down the side canyon that leads off in the west valley direction. At first I thought he was in trouble because running downhill is a dumb thing to do and a good way to take a hard fall. At the rate he was going I figured he make Claremont before I could offer any help. So the next morning, me being a curious sort of fellow, I walked down there and that's where I met Dusty Evans."

Rockland amazed himself at the enjoyment he was getting out of this child's company. He rarely had company unless a hunter came by or someone got lost up here and he'd have to guide them back down.

"That man was Elroy Devereaux and he turned out to be…..the son of Grandfather Devereaux brother and that makes him some kind of relative to us I guess. Anyway he wanted us to pay him money to go away. He did some awful things besides just setting that bull after me. Well, he's in jail now and I can tell you that it's a mighty big relief that he won't be bothering us again. He isn't a good man." Joe's forehead wrinkled with concern. "Why do people want to hurt animals and other people?

"I think those kind of people have lost touch with their conscience, that's their Inner Guide or their Solar Angel who tells them when they do wrong. This man is one of those people and those of us who have a conscience, an angel, find it hard to imagine why someone would want to cause harm because it's foreign to our way of being. We just have to accept that there are those unconscious people in the world and watch out for them. The Thunder Gods won't let him do real harm if he ever comes back. It's a dangerous thing to offend Them, Joe, They're real and They aren't impotent."

"What does impotent mean?" Joe questioned.

"It means being powerless or lacking strength or being ineffectual and that means unable to take action. Well our Gods, our Guardians are not ineffectual and They have the power to make bad people leave. They generally use that power for good."

Rockland decided that this occasion called for another pipe and started in preparing it. There was a comfortable silence as the young and the old sat and looked out at the splendid view.

"Thank you Mr. Hoggins for finding me and feeding me and I'd really like it if we could be friends. I like your dogs really well too. Maybe I could have one of those pups maybe, someday." Joe said and Mr. Hoggins hummed. Then Joe thought about something that had bothered him for a long time. It seemed to him that this man might help him understand.

"Sometimes I don't feel like I fit in any place special, you know? Especially since I lost my parents and there wasn't any home any more. Maybe it's just a feeling of not being in the *right* place. Like I'm a square peg in a round hole, sort of thing. Gee, I can't really describe how I feel exactly. Before Mom and Dad died we traveled a lot during rodeo season. I felt full inside and safe and it didn't really matter where we were living, you understand? Then after they died I felt empty and…something *important* got shriveled, like it wasn't there anymore inside where it mattered." Joe heaved a deep sigh, sniffed and went on talking quietly. "Yeah, that's the feeling I had, *shriveled* and it's *not* a good feeling to have, but I don't know how to fill it up again and find my right place to be. I gotta say it worries me some."

Joe stopped talking and thought deeply about that shriveled feeling. After a minute or two he said. "You know, it's a curious thing that now I can actually feel some of that shriveled part being filled back up. Maybe it's because of Ben and Mari Beth and Hannah and having a real home again. Well, that's what's inside of me, but there's more."

One of the puppies had snuck over to sit quietly beside Joe, and without any conscious thought Joe's hand dropped down to stroke the young dog's head, the one with a white spot right between his eyes and as he felt….comforted.

Mr. Hoggins waited patiently puffing on his pipe and listened to a young boy struggling to understand himself and noticed when the young pup quietly snuck over to comfort the boy. Hmm, wasn't that an interesting connection.

"I've been aware for as long as I can remember that I've never felt at home anywhere we've been. I mean really being in *my place* sort of feeling. It's strange because my brother Mike fits right in here as the Lost Wagon rancher while I feel like I'm just a visitor there. After all, it's my home too only it isn't. Yeah, it does worry me some." Joe rocked back and forth while quietly taking in the view and stroking the pup's head.

"No, not strange at all, in fact it's very perceptive of you, Joe. Being perceptive means to be observant and noticing things. Not too many people are aware that there are certain places where they prosper and places where they don't. Don't worry about it, you'll find your place when you're older, mark my words. Just keep your eyes and heart open and it will find you when you least expect it. As far as this shriveled place inside you, well that's your center and you had your parents to fill that space for you, anchoring you as it were. When they died it got emptied so you didn't have an anchor. Now you're finding that you're the one who has to fill that inner space with your own spirit. That's when you'll feel full, safe and secure again. Of course right now the Strongbows are helping you do that. Don't rush that process, it will come to you as your grow older."

"Well, that's a relief! I've been worried about this stuff for a long time and I never really felt comfortable about spilling it all out. It's funny, but it felt okay to do that with you. Thank you Sir, I sort of knew you might have answers for me. I think maybe this place up here gives you wisdom or something like that. I guess I'll just have to be patient until I find my true place, huh?" Rockland smiled. The boy was a caution that was for sure, but the wisdom and intelligence just oozed out of that boy's mouth which was amazing in one so young.

"Would you like to see inside my house?" said Rockland searching for something that would entertain his young friend.

"Yes I would." and followed the old man into the simple log house. The living room was the largest and had an extra large fireplace with a thick rug covering the wood floor with several padded rocking chairs, side tables, lamps and against one wall was what passed for a kitchen, small and simple with a large wood burning Monarch Range, a small refrigerator, a small sink under a window and a long work bench with hanging cupboards with a small table and two chairs. Rockland led the way over to a wide doorway with no door that led into his bedroom. Joe peeked in and saw a noticeably high standing framed bed, shelves for clothes and a small round stove in one corner. The thing that really struck him was how neat and tidy the house was.

"Back here is the bathroom I added on years ago. I have a gas fired toilet and a nice shower and a large tank to hold water." chuckled the old man. "I had to concede to my old age because the outside privy was getting a bit too challenging in the wintertime."

"I bet it would!" Joe said in sympathy and laughed. "Just imagine dropping your pants when the weather would be down below zero and sitting on an ice cold toilet seat makes me shiver just at the thought of that. A man could get frost bitten really fast."

Rockland laughed and laughed. "Oh, it wasn't *that* bad since I had a heater out there that I keep lit when bad weather threatened, but the walk to get there could be mighty cold. I didn't mind roughing it when I was a young sprout, but times change, don't they? I have a large generator that provides me with electricity for the refrigerator, hot water heater and my lamps. I switch it off during the night. I live a simple life with just a few concessions to civilization. Now back here is my work room where I build things." Joe peeked inside the door and sure enough, he saw tools and wood and furniture in the process of being built. Hmm, they appeared to be rocking chairs.

Back in the living room Joe looked in awe at all the books on the shelves that covered two entire walls from floor to ceiling and marveled. "What are all these brown wrapped packages in this bookcase?"

"They're my journals that I've written over the years. Studies about what I've learned and realizations I've discovered." Rockland smiled down at the inquisitive boy. "A realization is what comes to you as a result of thinking about a subject and having a sudden clear understanding about it."

"Oh my, there must be a lot of wisdom in those packages. Would some of those writings help me?" Joe turned to look up at the man.

"Well, I don't know Joe you're pretty young for some of that stuff." Rockland frowned in thought.

"What about other people, adults I mean? Could they maybe learn some good things by reading your… realize…..real thoughts?"

"Hmm… maybe, I never thought about that one way or another because no one has ever asked that question before. This is just something I've done for years. I never thought much about publishing and I'm not sure if it's even publishable." Rockland continued to frown up at the dusty covers of the many journals tucked on the highest shelves of his book case as though he'd never seen them before.

"Mike said that everyone has a God given gift and so they were obliged to share it. Maybe this is your gift, Mr. Hoggins. When I get older maybe you'd let me read one or two of them so I could become wise like you."

Now that comment had Rockland laughing again. "When you're older Joe, when you're older." and slapped the boy gently on the back and led the way back out to the porch.

They rocked in silence for awhile and Rockland smoked until Joe spoke again. "They say my voice is God's gift. It would please me if you'd let me sing for you as a thank you and for rescuing me. Would you like that?" Joe looked over at the solid old man sitting beside him puffing on his fragrant pipe which was strange because most pipes smelled awful.

Rockland raised his eyebrows and looked back at this serious boy. "Why, sure son, it's been a long time since I've heard good singing. I play the harmonica, but I surely don't sing 'cause I'd set my dogs to howling if I did. Go ahead."

Joe stood up and walked over to the porch rail looking out at the wonders of the sunlit land. He closed his eyes and started to sing, "God Bless America." Rockland Hoggins almost dropped the pipe. His eyes widened and his heart opened equally wide as the lovely sound poured out of this child's throat and there wasn't anything forced about it. The words took on feeling and expressed such deep understanding which was amazing in itself coming from such a young boy. Rockland Hoggins felt a tingling along his spine and from the corner of his eye he saw a *Presence*.

When Joe had finished the unseen Presence disappeared. That's when Rockland noticed that his dogs hadn't uttered a sound, not even the puppies. Joe returned to his rocker and sat down. Silence held for the next few minutes and neither one seemed uncomfortable with the quiet broken only by the creak of the rockers and the sounds of birds and nature.

"Thank you Joe, that was mighty fine. You just hold on to that gift and you train your voice so that you can give many people joy in your talent for many years to come. When we're given gifts from God the one receiving that gift should honor it enough to use it for the benefit and wellbeing of humanity."

Rockland stopped abruptly on that last word; shocked as he heard what he had said....or had his spirit spoken through him? Hmmm, maybe it was time for him to think outside his own box and consider what he was doing with his own God given gift and the gift of this place and the years he had been given to develop it.

"I know your singing will be what you'll do in the world and your place will come to you as surely as night follows day. You're a good man Joe Kelly, your heart is pure and the Thunder Gods love you."

"They do? Oh my goodness, just think of that. Thank you for the advice Sir, I'll do just as you say and maybe you'll think about your gift for you are a very wise man, I know."

All Rockland could do was raise his white eyebrows and look over at the boy who was just gazing out at the beautiful view. The old man thought, out of the mouth of babes and a gentle reprimand that showed him how selfish he had been with his knowledge. I'm responsible for what I know, and if what I know can guide or suggest a better way for someone else to follow then I should think seriously about doing it. I'll admit I haven't been doing that. I know I shall be held accountable for not using my gift for the good of all.

More silence and more rocking before the child spoke again. "I've got another problem, just a small one. Ben said that the pictures I took and my experience at the roundup just might be good enough to be published in the Rancher's Magazine. He said to finish my journal and that's the problem. I'm only in the second grade and my journal is really simple notes about what happened day to day. I can remember clearly who said what and all the action. My problem is I can't write all the words I want to use. It won't be any good if I can't write it the way I know it. What do you think I should do, Mr. Hoggins?"

"Why don't you tell it to someone just as you experienced it? They can write the story down for you. It will still be your story only you will speak it and you'll acknowledge whoever writes it for you."

"Geeze peeze, now why in the world didn't I think of that? That's what I'll do and maybe Hannah can help me." Joe looked over at the man sitting calmly in the other chair and smiled in a brilliant, joyful way and said, "Thanks Mr. Hoggins."

"Well, youngen' I'll look forward to reading your story and seeing those pictures too, but right now we'd best be getting you back home so you won't get into trouble. Come on, let's be moving." Rockland tapped the doodle out of his pipe into another clay jar got up and calling the dogs as he stepped down off the porch. He led the way back to the path that would take them down off the cliff with Joe following with Jigger.

Mr. Hoggins led him down the small mesa to the path that snaked through the trees and would lead him back to the ranch. The path was more or less hidden and Joe saw where he had made the wrong turn. Well, he thought, maybe it wasn't a wrong turn after all. Mr. Hoggins and Joe shook hands and Joe gave a last pat to each of the dogs lingering a little longer over the puppies before he mounted Jigger.

The last thing the old man said was. "You know the way up here now, so come when you feel like a visit, but watch the weather and let your folks know where you're going. You'll be welcome here anytime."

"I will come again and thank you for the invitation. Maybe you could visit us at Ben's like when you go to town or something. You could call us from our ranch and we'd come over and give you a ride in to town and save you a long walk too. We'd sure enjoy having you stay for dinner 'cause Hannah cooks really fine. Goodbye, dogs, you take care of your master."

Mr. Hoggin's was laughing when Joe rode off at a brisk canter that would bring him to the ranch in half an hour or so if he kept the pace. It wasn't quite sunset so he felt he was going to be okay with the long absence. When he got to the top of the last hill, Joe stopped and turned to look back and sure enough, the old man was still standing on the far edge of the woods with his bright red shirt marking his presence there. Joe took off his hat and waved energetically and saw a response. Then slapping his hat back on his head Joe set his horse into a gallop heading for home.

"Golly Jigger, it's another miracle for sure and I've made a good, wise friend and I suspect he could be quite a teacher for me too. I'm not sure exactly what he'd teach, but living that close to the Thunder Gods has made him special. Wow, I made a real fine friend."

Joe arrived home in the nick of time and no comments were made for his long absence since he'd told them he'd be visiting his parents' sacred site that afternoon. Joe breathed a sigh of relief and hurried to do his share of the chores before supper.

Joe washed up and wandered into the kitchen where dinner was cooking. Hannah and Mari Beth were talking about this and that and Joe wasn't really interested so he sat and waited for the right opportunity to speak to Hannah alone.

Honestly, he thought in a disgruntled way, when you don't want a lot of people around they all come flocking in, as Mike and Ben stepping into the kitchen just as there was a lull in the women's conversation and Joe was forced to listen to more talk. Finally, Mike and Ben left to wash up and Mari Beth went to get Carli.

Joe quickly sidled up to Hannah and whispered, "Can I see you alone after supper? It's really important."

Hannah frowned down at her adoptive son and replied, "Why sure Joe, right after dishes are done I'll meet you in your room, okay?"

"That's great Hannah and, well no worries or anything serious like that, I just need to ask you something in private." Joe smiled.

"Now here's a mystery, and you've got my curiosity all stirred up and I'm like a cat until I know what the great secret is." Joe hugged her then went and sat down at the table.

Conversation was pretty general around the supper table. Mike was talking about the work he'd been doing under Hank's supervision. Yep, thought Joe as he watched his big brother enthuse over the new barn they were building; he's the rancher all right. Joe carried his plate and glass over to the dishwasher then went up to his room to wait impatiently for Hannah.

When the knock finally came he jumped up and ran over to the door and threw it open, dragged her quickly into his room then peeked out into the corridor to make sure no one else was around before closing his door.

"What's this big hush, hush meeting all about boy?" Hannah asked as she sat herself down in the overstuffed chair beside the window.

Joe dragged over a foot stool and sat down close to her as though he feared someone overhearing him. "You might think this is really silly Hannah, but I have been thinking about what Ben said that maybe I could submit those roundup pictures and my story to a magazine. I sure like the idea and I know some of those pictures would be really great for that. I'm only in the second grade and I don't write so well. That's my problem. My journal was just short notes to remind me of the action. Besides, I only print and it would take me forever to write everything down that I saw and experienced even if I knew how to spell all the words. I just can't write the way I talk." Joe looked properly worried then he suddenly lit up.

"Oh, by the way, while I was out visiting my parent's gravesite I met Mr. Hoggins. My, he's a really fine man and I believe he's now a friend of mine too." Joe wisely forgot to mention that he'd managed to get himself lost in order to meet the mountain man. "Anyways, I told him about the pictures and my journal and my problem. He suggested that I tell someone my story and have them write it for me. So can you do that please?"

Hannah felt as though she'd been steam rolled. "Gracious you've had quite a day haven't you sugarplum?" Joe grimaced at being called Carli's nick-name, but decided not to mention it as Hannah was frowning and thinking hard. He waited with baited breath for her answer. "To put it briefly, you want me to ghost-write your story of the roundup so you can submit it to a magazine, is that right?"

"If ghost-writing is the same as writing down what I say, I guess I do. Mr. Hoggins said I could put your name on it as having written it for me. So it would be both our names on the article."

"Hmm, when do you want to start doing this, Joe?" Hannah was growing amused at the earnestness of the request. Joe obviously felt very strongly about this project and it wouldn't be kind to embarrass him by laughing at the intensity of his need.

Joe gave a deep sigh of relief. "I don't know Hannah, I guess whenever you have the time since you're very busy around here and of course I have school and homework and helping Luther out with the twins and my chores to do." Joe heaved another heavy sigh. "It's going to be a problem, isn't it?" worried the boy and wringing his hands a little.

"Not really Joe, it's just a matter of juggling our busy schedules and making time maybe an hour a day sort of plan. Let's see what days we're the busiest and make time on other days, say right after supper. If you do your homework on the school bus that should help freeing up one or two evening hours a week at least, don't you think?"

"Yeah Hannah, that would work just fine. I really appreciate you helping me with this. I could ask Mike only he's so stretched with everything now that I really don't want to add another burden to the load he's carrying."

"Your right, Mike has enough to handle without this project, something that you and I are more than capable of managing. Today is Saturday so let's begin work Sunday afternoon or early evening. I've got a tape recorder that will help us because then I can type up your story during the day when I have free time. Evenings we can discuss and edit and change as we go along. So dear boy, is there anything else?"

"Would you help me select pictures that sort of point up my story? Maybe I need to tell the story from the pictures we select. See, this is why I really need you 'cause there is so much I don't know how to do." worried Joe.

"That's a smashing idea Joe. I think people would like you telling your story through pictures with your comments on what's happening. Hmmm…..besides submitting the article to a magazine, the story just might make a great children's book written by a child. Hmm, yes, there's lots of possibilities here young man. Well, we'll just have to begin and see what we end up with. We can always change what doesn't work can't we?" Hannah grasped Joe's tightly held hands and rubbed them until they relaxed and he could smile.

"I knew you'd know how to do it all. Gee Hannah, you're the bestest friend I've ever had and just like a real mother." Joe stopped and blushed as Hannah laughed lightly.

"You'd do the same for me if I had a problem, wouldn't you? What goes around comes around Joe. When you send good out, it always attracts good to return to you. Let's shake partner, we're in the writing business." and they stood up and shook hands heartily. Hannah just had to grab this child and give him a fierce hug making Joe grunt and laugh at the same time.

"We'll start tomorrow night." as she opened his door.

"I'll be ready, Hannah dear. Say do you think we'll become rich and famous?" Joe laughed.

"Maybe so, but I think we'd better get this epic written, printed, submitted, and accepted before we begin to count our money, don't you?"

Joe stood up straight and lifted his nose in the air and pronounced in a stilted voice, "My dear woman, miracles are happening all the time, so why not bout this? Have a little faith, Miss Strongbow." And she just had to laugh at this little old man.

Hannah and Joe were giggling as they walked down the stairs. "This partnership calls for hot chocolate with a special fix of mine, maybe it won't be as good as the one Dusty made, but I'll guarantee it'll taste mighty fine."

Oh boy, thought Joe, walking into the kitchen, we're really on a roll.

~The County Fair~

It had been extremely hard for Mike to choose the most likely colts and fillies to sell at the Huntington Fair and the task had taken him three days and even then he wasn't very happy with the results.

"Ben, I just can't pick any more than fifteen, honestly that's the best I can do. You should have warned me how hard this would be. I want so badly to keep them all especially those four over there. See how they sort of hang together all the time? Aren't they the best of the best?" Mike watched the young yearlings for a few minutes. "Ben, would you sell them to me?"

Ben laughed. "You do have a good eye for they are just slightly the better, and to tell the truth, I wasn't going to sell them either. Okay, I'll get Blackhawk and Jensen to spring for these four and you can keep them here and train them." He laughed at the joy in Mike's face. "That ought to keep you out of mischief if you *had* any spare time that is. Anyway, when they're older you can switch them over to your place."

"My very own little horses and while the rest are great too, I like those the most. Golly, I'll have to have Joe name them."

"You've picked us eight colts and seven fillies for sale and there's not a dud in the bunch either; they're great little horses if I do say so myself. Now I've got to choose six trained cutting horses and five half trained ones. I've decided to give Jigger to Joe because he loves him and I think they're a matched pair. After all, that little horse saved Joe's life and you can't sell a friend now can you? Do you want Sherlock? I'm keeping him if you don't want him because he's a fine, smart cutting horse. Now let's go and look at the cutting horses."

"Wait a minute! You want to give me Sherlock? I know he's one of the best and the men told me so too. Golly Ben, who wouldn't want a horse like him. Yes indeed I want him and thank you. I'll take good care of him."

"Your welcome Mike, I like the way you two look together too."

"You know in a way Sherlock reminds me of Dad's horse Beau. Not that they look much alike, but it's their personality, behavior and smarts." Mike brooded a bit before he said, "I surely hated to sell Beau because Dad had raised him from a colt and he was like family, but we needed the money. Then of course, we were going to the children's home and didn't have a place to keep him. He's a prince of a horse and won Dad lots of prize money. I purely loved that horse." Mike took off his hat and appeared to be wiping his brow with his shirtsleeve only the swipe was a little lower and Ben pretended not to notice.

"You know Mike, if you can tell me who you sold the horse to or the auction barn and the town where he was sold along with a description that would identify him, we just might do a search and buy him back. You can certainly afford to pay top dollar for him."

Mike was knocked speechless for a few minutes he stood there with his jaw dropped practically down on his chest then with a deep gasp he yelled. *"Well, for heaven's sake, why didn't I think of that?"* and gleefully pounded Ben on the shoulder in his enthusiasm while the man stood unmoved by the violence and just grinned down into the face of young joy. "Course we can. Oh, Ben, you just wait until you get a look at Beau, he's really something. He stands seventeen hands high and is a dapple grey Quarter horse with the sweetest disposition you've ever seen especially in a stallion. Wow, to have Beau back would just make my day." Mike simply glowed with happiness.

"When we get back to the house I'll call Luther; he's a whiz at this sort of research, besides he loves the computer."

"I still have the sale papers so that should make it a lot easier. I can't tell you how happy this would make me. Wait until I tell Joe." Mike walked with Ben over to the holding pen and the horses under consideration. Sitting up on the top bar he and Ben looked over the circling nervous horses as if they knew something was going on.

"How do you do this Ben, select and sell them; they're all so grand?" asked Mike quietly.

"It is hard to let them go and I dread doing this every year or so, but, this is a ranch and every rancher has to go through the same agony. Letting go is a fact of life; you can't hang on to everything you love. It's the same with horses. These animals need to find new homes and people who will love them. I make certain that the people who buy them will treat them right by demanding high prices; it's all I can do."

They finished the job of selection and the horses were led out of the corral to be groomed and curried. Ben had to smile at the boy's concern as he listened to Mike talking constantly to the horses reassuring them that Ben would see that they had good owners. You bet he'd would. He always carefully screened everyone who wanted one of his horses.

Now the animals were all bedded down in the barn, their last night at home and Mike couldn't help feeling sad for them. He knew how hard it was to leave your home and all that was familiar, and go out into the world not knowing how that world was going to treat you. Mike looked at the horses and prayed they'd have good lives. He guessed it was pretty much like having your own children grow up and leave home and all you could do was hope life treated them well. Before they left the barn Mike and Joe went around feeding the chosen ones little bits of apples and carrots and snuck a few lumps of sugar to each horse. It was all the comfort they could give them.

It had been decided that the ranchers and whoever else would be going to the fair, would meet at the River Town Park at six the next morning. That meant getting up at four and getting the horses loaded by five and heading for Town. Mike figured they'd make quite an impressive caravan going down the highway.

Ben said that it was about three hundred miles to Huntington and pulling horse trailers meant driving at a slower speed of which meant they'd arrive close to noon. The Valleys Cattleman's Association had reserved a whole motel close to the fairgrounds for them.

They got to bed early that night and when Ben woke them in the morning it was still dark. No problem with these boys, he chuckled, as he heard their feet hit the floor. For Mike and Joe it would be like old times when they had traveled with their parents to rodeos and county fairs.

Hannah had breakfast on the table and the suitcases ready to be put in the big truck. After eating Ben and the boys left to help load the horses. Mari Beth went upstairs to get Carli and came back to the kitchen carrying the sleeping child wrapped in blankets.

"Hannah, pack a good snack for Carli please because she won't wake up for another hour and she'll be hungry." Mari Beth said quietly.

"All ready done Mom and it's in that zippered lunch bag." Dishes were dumped in the dishwasher, lights were turned off and by five everyone was bundled into the trucks. It was cold this early in the morning and as dark as the inside of a hat when Ben slowly led the way down the ranch road with his large horse trailer and followed by two more with the men.

Jeb Goggins had chosen to stay home as he'd seen many, many a fair and that one was pretty much like another. He laughed and said he'd relish the peace and quiet after everyone was gone. Mike heard a mournful howl coming from Roscoe and felt bad that he couldn't take his dog with him, but that wasn't possible. He rolled down the back window and stuck his head way out and saw Jeb holding Roscoe on a leash waving goodbye.

"Close the window Mike before you freeze us out." said Mari Beth.

"Sorry!" and quickly complied.

Mike and Joe dozed on the way into town and only woke up as Ben pulled into the big park on the eastern edge of River Town where a number of other big horse vans had already assembled.

"Gee Mike everyone seems to be going to the fair. Why I bet we've practically cleaned out the Valleys." exclaimed Joe in wonder.

"It's a mass exodus for sure. Well, we're in for a long drive and it's just like old time, huh Joe?"

Carli woke up and looked around thoroughly bewildered. This wasn't her bed or her room. "It's okay sugarplum, we're going on an adventure with Mike and Joe and Daddy and Hannah." Mari Beth told her daughter.

"Gotta' pee Momma, gotta' pee now."

"Okay, let's go." laughed Mari Beth as she picked Carli up blankets and all and headed over to the park's ladies room. Once back in the truck Mari Beth dug out Carli's breakfast, but it was hard for the little girl to concentrate because so much was happening outside to distract her.

"What's that, Momma? Where's Daddy? Mikey, I not see Mikey!"

"See, Mikey's over there by Luther and there's Daddy talking to Mr. Lightfoot and those other men. Oh good here they come, I think we're going now and what fun we're going to have." Mari Beth said as she steadied the little girl.

"Mikey, Joey, we is going on 'venture, Momma says." an excited Carli jumped up and down on the bench seat while hanging on to the back then stopped and asked. "What's a 'venture?" as the boys climbed into the back seat.

"It means we're going to see new places and have lots and lots of fun." assured her brother as he sat down.

"Can I have my doggie now please?"

"Oh dear, I forgot I promised Carli a puppy of her own. Daddy will find you a nice doggie all your own, maybe for Christmas."

"Promise?" she demanded looking intently into Mari Beth's eyes.

"I promise, cross my heart." Mari Beth did just that and Carli laughed,

"Okay." she replied just as Ben climbed back into the driver's seat.

"Daddy, Momma says I can have my puppy Christmas time okay?"

"You bet, sweet girl, a nice puppy for you."

Now that the truck was in motion and things had settled down, Carli got on with her breakfast and after that Mari Beth got her dressed for the day.

With only two stops along the way at rest areas they arrived at Huntington Fair Grounds without incident. The caravans began to unload the animals and were taken to the appropriate barns. Once Ben's horses were settled and the trailers parked out of the way, they had lunch and took a quick tour of the fair grounds with Ben packing Carli on his shoulders.

Ben bought her a squishy toy puppy. "Just until Christmas and I will get you a real doggie, sweet pea." promised Ben.

"Okay, promise is promise, Daddy. Thank you for my puppy toy." and cuddled the fuzzy dog to her chest. By the time they arrived at the motel, checked in and hauled luggage up to the assigned rooms, Ben and the boys were ready to get on with another important errand.

"The boys and I are going to take these coin collections to an appraiser in town so we can insure them." said Ben.

"Don't forget everyone is going to meet at Clayton's for dinner around 5 o'clock, so don't be late getting back." Mari Beth said.

"This shouldn't take long sweetheart, so y'all have a rest and be ready for a nice evening. We'll be back to pick you girls up just before five." Promised Ben as he and the boys left the room.

It didn't take them long to find Wiggen's Appraisal and Gold Store. "Nice place." Ben commented as they got out of the truck and walked up to the steel grilled door. Ben rang the bell and within a minute the buzz of the door signaled the release and they entered through the double security doors.

"Gee Ben, it's just like the bank vault in River Town." said Mike and since he and Joe had never been in a store that sold gold before they were all eyes.

"Good morning Sirs, what can I do for y'all today?" said a cheerful little fat man. Ben put the briefcase on the counter and snapped open the locks.

"These coin portfolios came to these boys through an inheritance and we would like to have you evaluate them for insurance purposes." answered Ben as he opened the case to pull out the two large, heavy coin folders.

Mr. Wiggens opened one up in a casual way then gasped when he saw the years and the sequences of the mint condition twenty-dollar gold coins. Quickly he opened the other one. "Oh mercy me, I have never seen such a perfect mint conditioned coin collection in all my years and then only a few random coins and never so many in sequence. Oh mercy Sir, these are quite rare and very valuable." Then his customers lost him as he carefully looked coins over and took several of them out of their covers with tweezers to test the quality and the weight of the gold content. "Can you tell me a little about their history?"

"From the documents that I have here it appears the Devereaux family has been into coin collecting for over a hundred years so I guess that's why the coins are in mint condition. All of them had been sealed between glass and I suspect, when plastic came in, the coins were transferred to these new portfolios."

"How very ingenious your ancestors were." and the little man hummed and examined coins with great concentration. "Do you want to sell these coins, Sir?" asked Mr. Wiggens with a hopeful look in his eyes.

"I would first like to have an estimate of what they are worth for insurance purposes. Then we'll decide whether to sell or not." stated Ben.

"Roughly well over a million dollars or more at a guess, of course I'd have to examine each coin to be exact, but I think I am safe in saying that what you apparently have here is mint conditioned $20.00 gold coins of the 1800's in sequence. The fact that they are in a sequence without a break in dates increases their value. Oh my yes, these are real beauties. You should insure them for at least $2,000.000. Now, if you keep them in a bank vault that should reduced the insurance premium. If you choose to sell I can give you a very, very good price. To be sure it would take me a week or so to come up with the money as I would need to contact a few collectors I know." Mr. Wiggens hopeful expression said it all.

Ben turned to Mike and waited for him to speak. Mike was still trying to come to grips with the dollar amount involved. "Excuse me for a minute Ben." Mike took Joe's arm and pulled him across the room. "Well, Joe what will it be? Do you want to keep them or do we sell them now?" asked Mike.

"Geeze peeze Mike, that's an awful lot of money, isn't it? What would we do with it? Does the ranch need it now?"

"No, we've got enough ready funds to take care of the ranch and then some. We really don't need the money now and if we sold them we'd have to pay a big whopping tax." Mike said.

"Well if we don't need it why sell it?" said Joe and Mike laughed, slapped his brother lightly on the shoulder and walked back to Ben.

Mike looked down at what lay on the glass counter and slowly shook his head no. "We don't need the money now and they are sort of an insurance against hard times too, aren't they? No, we'll just put them in a safety deposit box and let them appreciate a little more." He had to grin at the disappointed look on Mr. Wiggens's chubby face.

"Oh dear, I was afraid of that, still you've made a wise decision young man."

"We do have some loose coins that aren't probably mint, but still very nice. Would you like to see them?" Mike said.

"Yes I would indeed." Mr. Wiggens waited eagerly for Ben to dig out the chamois skin bag and spread the thirteen assorted gold coins out on a felt pad. Mr. Wiggens with great care examined each one either nodding his head or shaking it.

"Some of these are very nice indeed, though they have been used. Five of them are worn around the edges, yet still fairly sharp. Well, there will be no problem selling these and as I said I have several collectors that would like to see them I'm sure. Would you care to leave them with me on consignment and I could notify you as to what they will sell for?"

Again Ben looked to Mike and Joe for their decisions. "You make out a receipt for each of these coins Mr. Wiggens and we'll leave them with you on consignment." said Mike.

"Very good gentlemen, it will only take me a few minutes to itemize and photograph these coins so you may have a record of what you left me. I'll be busy for a few minutes so look around. Christmas is coming you know." he smiled slyly and with a wink he got busy behind the counter. Ten minutes later Mr. Wiggens passed over the receipt and the photos of the gold coins to Ben along with his business card.

"If in the future you do decide to sell your coin collections, please remember me," he laughed and jokingly said, "If I'm still alive that is, I'll buy them immediately at their fair market value." With a sigh he closed the portfolios with little pat before Ben put them back into the briefcase snapping it closed.

"Thank you for your time Mr. Wiggens. What do we owe you for your evaluation?" asked Ben.

"No, no, nothing, it was a pleasure just to hold such rarities. It is I who should thank you, Sir. I think you can safely insure them for $2,000,000.00, allowing for the appreciation and all for they will continue to rise in value."

"Thank you Mr. Wiggens, you can be sure that when my sons decide to sell they'll come to you." and shook the man's hand.

"Good day and enjoy the fair. I will be in touch with you when I have a buyer for these other coins. "And personally saw them out the door.

"Next stop is the bank; I don't want to carry this stuff around like a lunch box any longer than I have to because it makes me sweat a bit too much." said Ben with an exaggerated gesture of wiping sweat off his brow.

"Me too so let's get going." said Mike.

By five o'clock they had returned to the motel to gather up the family and head for Clayton's.

It was noon when Dan Lightfoot pulled his trailer into the Fairground's parking lot close to the long line of barns. Tom Blackhawk's trailer was just to the other side of theirs and the big horse trailers were much alike except for the striping on the sides and the decal of a black hawk on Tom's.

Jim Waggoner slowly climbed down from the cab showing evidence of stiff joints and tight muscles from the long ride, but as soon as he and the other men began unloading the horses, he limbered up. Handling the nervous horses in a strange environment was a job and a half as they were being led to their assigned pens. The men talked and soothed the animals as they laid in water, feed and grain for them. The normal routine did a lot to gradually settle them down. All the rigs were parked out back of the barns along with the others.

"I'm for a hearty breakfast and that café across the street might still be serving it. Do you want to come with me?" asked Dan to the little man standing beside him.

"I could do with a bite as coffee just ain't cutting it; besides it's lunch time Dan." replied Jim.

"Food is food my good man, so let's not quibble about what we call it." Old Jim snickered and followed along to the restaurant that Dan happened to know was a good one and it was doing a booming business with all the new arrivals.

"Hey Dan, Jim, over here, we got a big table." yelled Tom.

"See? Luck is with us and no waitin' required." grinned Dan and strolled over to join the table. "Hello Zegglers; didn't see you joining up on the caravan. That must have gotten you up mighty early this morning to make the drive from Claremont." smiled Dan and shook hands with Bob. "Clara, you're as pretty as ever. Howdy, Blackhawk, Big Mike. Thanks Tom, for saving us a long wait." said Dan. Jim sat down and nodded his head at everyone and Dan had noticed that he tipped his hat to Clara before he put it under his seat.

"Say, Mike, who's cooking at the ranch?" asked Jim.

"Ain't nobody there to eat, except Holt and he's a fair hand at rustling his own grub and he'll take care of the animals. Besides, even if there wasn't I don't think anyone will disturb the Chief's ranch, do you?" Mike grinned.

"Not if they're smart they won't. Dangerous acts such as that could get a person in a whole heap of hurt what with the Thunder Gods watching over Blackhawk's place like broody hens, as I'm sure They're doing with Their Chief gone at the moment. Can't you just see any vandals wetting their pants when the Guardians showed up in the yard?" Jim smiled.

That comment from the Old Thorn in His Side had the table laughing and Blackhawk just grinned and winked at the old man. Jim perked up and looked like he was going to join the fun after all. Dan just shook his head, what was up with this usually cranky old man? Dan stopped and frowned in deep thought as he looked sidewise at Jim. Was he really an old crank?

"Looks like most everyone from the Valleys are here because I can hardly spot a stranger in the crowd. Looks like no one wanted to miss this fair for some reason." commented Tom.

Bob Zeggler spoke up. "Personally Carla and I wanted to get in a few more fairs 'cause one of these days I won't want to drive so far. Besides, it sort of puts a spark into our lives as it can get darn quiet out to our place."

"Anytime you and Carla don't want to drive just give one of us a shout and we'd be happy to have you come with us. Next time Bob, don't be so shy." Blackhawk said.

"We just may take you up on that, won't we Carla?" Bob gave a nudge to Carla.

"Of course dear, and it's mighty obliging of you, Blackhawk, but I question your motivation somewhat. It isn't because I make the best snicker-doodles or those vanilla cream filled chocolate layer cakes with whipped cream frosting, is it? Just need to know what the cost of the ride is gonna' be."

Carla spoke in a quiet laconic way as she cast a mild look at Blackhawk. What she said took a few seconds for everyone to catch it and the look on Blackhawk's face set everyone off. His love for sweet things was notorious. Blackhawk hung his head as though in shame, but the twinkle in his eyes belied that.

Poor Bob's jaw dropped in shock at his wife's response. *"Carla!"*

The Chief heaved a heavy sigh and shook his head. "Ah Carla, for me to be caught out in my wonderful ploy to get some of those snicker-doodles is beyond shame. I'm going to have to talk to the Thunder Gods about you as nothing I'm coming up with so far is doing the trick." Blackhawk gave another exaggerated sad sigh and placed his hand on his chest.

Everyone was cracking up by then while poor Bob Zeggler just gaped at his wife's rudeness. Carla just smiled and patted her husband's hand. "Now Chief, don't go into a decline or beat your breast that-a-way; you'll just make it sore. I never said I *wouldn't* give you all the snicker-doodles you could eat except Mike would skin me alive if I did. However you have a birthday coming up in January, don't you? Well dear man, I'll make you an extra special very large and very Decadent Chocolate Cake then."

Blackhawk leaped to his feet, knocking over his chair and dashed around the table to kneel beside Carla's chair and kissed her hand extravagantly many times and had Carla blushing even while laughing at his dramatics. To see this ordinarily dignified and reserved Indian Chief do such a silly impulsive act was both surprising and hilarious at the same time. It showed people a whole different side of the man they thought they knew.

After lunch folks went their different ways except Jim who was still tagging along after Dan a little bit like a lost puppy will do with a boy or man.

"We'd better get signed into our room and decide what we're going to do next. I've got a list of things I need to pick up while I'm here. River Town's supplies are good for the size of it, but I need to buy parts for some of my machinery." Dan looked doubtfully down at Jim. "Do you want to come along or have you something else you want to do?" Now why in the heck had he invited this tag-along to tag along?

"Not really, I could use some things myself. I'll just mosey along with you and see what I can find if you don't mind." Dan shrugged and so they moseyed.

It was suppertime and already the afternoon had turned dark by the time Dan and Jim had secured their boxes and bags in the horse van and decided they would walk down to Clayton's Ribs and Steak House. It was only about six blocks from the motel and the parking down yonder would be impossible this late.

Several blocks along, just as they were crossing a dark alley they heard a whine of a dog and a small whispered "Hush."

Jim and Dan stopped, looked at each other then carefully stepped into the alley a few steps. The light cast from a lamppost was enough to see trashcans all neatly stacked outside the stores back doors, but there was someone back there because the dog whined again.

"Hello there, we're friendly cowboys and we're about to go to supper. If you're hungry we'd be happy for you to join us and our families down at the restaurant. Come on out we're harmless, especially this old man with me. Why he is the gentlest man I've ever known." said Dan. Jim snorted, but remained quiet.

No answer. "Well now, you must be a real youngen' because a man wouldn't be afraid of an old man and a softy like Daniel here." Jim sighed loudly. "I sure wished we could do something for you, but I guess you've got the right to go hungry if you want."

Jim cleared his throat and said. "Come on Dan, we've bothered this person enough. Let's go get us some of those ribs and some apple pie with ice cream you were bragging about. Sure sounds like prime eatin'." Jim stomped his feet a little before turning away and Dan reluctantly followed. "Say Dan, did I ever tell you about that golden haired dog I used to have? He was the cutest thing you've ever did see and......."

"Mister...wait a minute....I'm coming." The men stopped and turned back to watch a young boy, maybe seven or so, step out of the dark shadows of discarded boxes and limped toward them into the light of the street lamp carrying a small puppy. The boy stopped and kept a safe distance while watched the two men with scared eyes.

Dan and Jim were shocked speechless for a minute. This kid's face was bruised and bloodied on one side and he bent over like his ribs were hurt too. The child's eyes were filled with fear, confusion, pain, and the gods only knew what else.

Dan stood still and let Jim, who deliberately stooped over like an old, old man, move slowly forward a bit while saying softly, "Hello boy, my name's Jim and I've got the bestest ranch in all the Valleys west of here. Why you should see my land, it's a humdinger. What's your name son, so as we can make friends while we have supper together?"

The boy didn't seem to be as afraid of Jim as he was of Dan. Well, Dan was a big man and that might have been a factor, but still for a child to fear him hurt him in the strangest way.

"I don't know my name," the boy whispered, "I hurt my head and when I woke up back there on the road this puppy was sleeping beside me. My head hurts and I'm really hungry Mister and so is Buddy. I call him Buddy because he's lost too so we're buddies." The boy stood there and the men could see that he was beginning to shake.

"Well then I think I'll call you Nino, that's Spanish for boy, just until you remember your own name that is. I'm sure that hit on your head made you forget for just a while. Let me help you for I can see that you're not really steady on your pins. I ain't too steady on mine either so maybe together we can stagger to that eatin' parlor. Why Nino, you remind me of a new born foal who's just found its legs." Jim gently took hold of the boy's arm and continued talking as he guided the child slowly down the street with Dan following.

"Dan, Mari Beth will know what to do so you go ahead to Clayton's and find her." Ordered Jim softly and Dan didn't argue just walked ahead as fast as his legs would take him.

"Why does that man limp?" asked the curious boy in a vague sort of way.

"Well, Nino, that boy was badly wounded in a war and when he got home all crippled up, he found his Daddy had died. Now Dan suffered something fierce, but he's better now and you don't need to let his big size scare you either because he's the bestest man you'd ever meet. He's got a ranch just to the north of me and I've known him since he was younger than you." Jim was talking softly when the kid suddenly sagged against Jim and almost went to his knees.

Jim took a strong grip on the boy's arm. "Here let me carry old Buddy there." and plucked the puppy out of Nino's arms. "Goodness he's a heavy pup and that means he's going to grow into a very big dog. Yes sir, you can tell because he's got these big feet. Now then, you hang on to old Jim and we'll be at the restaurant in a jiffy."

Jim quickly put his arm around the boy's back and under his arm and was practically carrying him by the time he got close to the restaurant. He was some relieved to see Dan and Mari Beth stepping out of the door just as they came within speaking distance.

"Is she an angel? She's all shinny like one. Do you think she is Jim? Am I seeing things or am I going to die?" whispered Nino anxiously.

"Well, she's not really an angel Nino, but a very wonderful person and you'll like her. No, you're not goin' to die and you have my word on it." he said reassuringly.

"Dear boy, whatever's happened to you? My name is Mari Beth and I am going to help you feel better. Now then darling, you've found good friends so that means you live under a lucky star. Come on in and we'll go to the restroom and I'll clean you up. Dan, you might find Doctor Jones. I saw him somewhere in the restaurant so get him to join us in the ladies. Now, now, no worries boy, the ladies won't mind if you sit in the powder room."

Without warning the boy collapsed, slowly slipping out of Jim's one handed grasp. Dan stepped forward and snatched the boy up before he could hit the cement and carried him unconscious through the door that Mari Beth held open. Dan walked straight back to the ladies room with Mari Beth right behind him. Jim left them to search out the Doctor while a waiter kept telling him he couldn't bring a dog into the place.

Dan heard Jim say. "You hush your mouth boy; I need a doctor so get out of my way." Jim stood still in the entrance and yelled. "Is there a doctor here?"

A man stood up in the back of the room and walked through the tables and over to Jim. "I'm Doctor Jones, what's the problem?" and looked down at the puppy. "I got to tell you Sir, I'm not a veterinarian."

"I don't need a dog doctor, I need a people doctor. We got a hurt kid in the ladies so follow me." Jim turned around and headed toward the restrooms.

When Jim opened the door to the ladies restroom, the doctor glanced sidewise at him before he passed through the doorway and saw a woman and man supporting an unconscious child seated on a red cushioned chair. Fortunately at the time, there weren't any other women present.

"What's happened to this child? Who did this?" demanded the doctor even as he gently raised the boy's head and began his examination.

"We don't know Doctor, Jim and I found him in an alley just a few blocks away. He looked like he's been beaten and tossed around some. He can't remember his name or what happened." Dan explained.

Just then the boy opened his deep green eyes and for a few minutes gazed at them without any real comprehension; then his eyes filled with confusion and not a little fear.

The doctor asked. "Did these men find you in an alley, son?"

"Oh, yes sir, they said they'd take me to supper 'cause I was awfully hungry. That's my puppy and he's hungry too." said the boy, trying not to wince when the doctor felt the large bruise on the side of his head and the cut that was still oozing blood.

"Well, it's hard to tell red blood from your red hair because they're so much alike," Doctor Jones said jokingly to the boy. "But I'm a real first class, A-number one doctor and I was taught to know the difference." Nino grinned at the funny man and split his lip open again. "Okay son, let's take your clothes off. Now don't be shy, we'll have the lady turn her back while I check the rest of you over." Nino eyed Mari Beth and she immediately turned her back.

"Okay, you'll have to help me because my arm doesn't work so very well." whispered the boy. Once stripped, the doctor examined the boy's bruised ribs and fortunately none were broken however, they might be cracked or separated. Running his hands down the boy's arms he discovered a sprained right wrist that could possibly be broken and had just reset itself naturally. Then he examined the boy's legs and found a big black bruise on his left hip and got a yelp out of Nino when the doctor touched the left knee.

"Your hip's taken a good knock and the knee is badly swollen. I know this is going to hurt so hold tight because I need to feel your hip and knee to see if they're broken okay? Ready?" Nino braced himself and nodded. Jim set the puppy down to put his hands on the boy's shoulders. Everyone sweated a little as the boy groaned in pain.

"Well, they don't appear to be broken which doesn't lessen the pain any, does it boy?" to the other adults he said, "From what I can tell, this child's bruises and injuries are all on the left side as though he might have been thrown out of a car or jumped out of a moving car; that's just a guess of course. He's got a mild concussion and probably one big headache too, a banged up hip, knee and shoulder, possibly a broken wrist and bruised ribs plus other contusions." Doctor Jones just shook his head. "Poor kid, well I'll get my bag and fix him up for tonight." and left the restroom.

The boy was crying and shivering even though it was nice and warm in the room. Mari Beth murmured "Equal parts shock, pain, hunger and fear I think. Dan, would you please go order some hot milk and put some sugar in it."

Dan left and Mari Beth took off her large thick wool sweater and wrapped the boy up and knelt down beside him and gently pulled him against her. "It's going to be alright in just a little bit honey and you'll feel so much better. Just hang in there." The boy Nino leaned his aching head against Mari Beth's bosom and felt comforted.

Within a few minutes the Doctor returned with his bag and the painful cleaning up and bandaging process began. "Sorry about this son, but there's dirt in some of these cuts on your face and hands that need cleaning; can't let any nasty infection get started can we? There, I'm almost done now then a few Band-Aids and a bandage around your head will take care of the worst. I'm going to wrap your wrist firmly in case you've broken it and I'll fix a sling for your arm and strap your ribs. I'll put an elastic wrap around your knee too to give it support. When I'm through I promise you'll feel much better." The doctor worked swiftly and when the bandaging had been completed, Mary Beth began helping the child back into his clothes. Surprisingly Nino didn't protest a woman's attention when he was still almost naked.

"This will keep you from moving your arm so you won't jar it by mistake." the doctor said as he adjusted the sling to cradle Nino's arm. Once that was done he pulled a small paper packet out of his bag and shook five small pills into it and handed it to Jim. "Give him one for pain every four hours if needed, preferably with milk. This should also help him get a good night's sleep. I would suggest soup and toast tonight that won't upset his stomach; concussions can cause nausea, you know. Take him home and when you give him a hot bath, don't let his taped wrist get wet and leave that bandage in place until we know for sure if it is broken or not. You can remove the knee bandage and the strapping. A good hot soak will help reduce his pain and relax him. Replace the bandage before you put him to bed, just make sure you don't wrap him too tight. You're horseman I believe so do like you would a horse. I want you to bring him into my office tomorrow morning for a more thorough examination and X-Rays. The boy will need several stitches in his head too. Right now these butterfly tapes will keep the cut together. Twenty-four hours of bed rest and good food should fix him up properly. His memory should return as these head blows usually only cause temporary amnesia. That means boy, given a little time you should remember everything so don't worry about it."

"What do I owe you, Doctor?" asked Dan getting out his wallet.

"Nothing, this was a case of my being in the right place at the right time. Consider it my good deed for the day. Here's my card, bring the boy in tomorrow and that *will* cost you." and laughed as he gave the boy a gentle stroke on the head and one on the puppy's as he left.

"Nice guy. Well youngen' I guess we'd better get you fed then tucked into a warm bed at our place for the night and you'll do just fine. Come on, this puppy has been mighty good and deserves a treat too."

Old Jim helped the boy up and handed Dan the puppy as he guided Nino out the door. Dan had to laugh quietly as the most important thing he'd done so far was to carry the kid in, find hot milk and hold the puppy. Oh well, he chuckled, we each serve the greater good no matter how small the task and followed Mari Beth out of the ladies room.

Finding a table took some doing, but folks generously moved over to make room at one of the long tables. Nino drank more hot milk and the puppy had some too along with a few small chopped up pieces of meat mixed with mashed potatoes which the dog slicked up mighty fast.

"We're going to have to get him some puppy chow tomorrow Nino, 'cause we can't feed him too much meat as he's a little young for that. We'll have to draw straws as to who gets up in the night to take him outside too." laughed Jim at Dan's grimace. "Come on Nino, finish up that soup and bread then we'll get you back to the motel." No need to encourage the kid for he was spooning it up as fast as he could.

Jim spoke quietly to Dan, "I guess we'd best talk to the authorities tomorrow, but I'm afraid the Social Services will pick him up. I don't want that. For whatever reason we were the ones to find him, Dan, I think we need to keep him with us for awhile until he settles down. Do you think they'll let us take care of him?" he asked anxiously.

Dan saw that Jim was really concerned over the child. "We'll get Mari Beth and Ben to vouch for us with Social Services and it's a done deal. I think I'd better keep him, Jim, as I've got Martha to take care of him during the day."

"I'm not going anywhere without Jim." said a small defiant voice that shocked the men. Obviously this boy had latched on to Jim Waggoner as his savior and it was also obvious he felt protected when Jim was around.

"Well, then I guess Jim's going to have to come live with us, won't he." Dan smiled as he looked sidewise at the astonished face of Mean Old Grump Waggoner, Dan laughed because Jim was speechless.

"Tarnation boy, I can't do that, I've got my own ranch to run." The boy teared up before ducking his head down and his small shoulders began to shake. "Tarnation, you just stop that cryin' now, just stop that caterwauling, you hear me? Mercy on me, alright, *alright*, I'll come stay with you and Dan." Nino sniffed. "Now, I said all right, didn't I? I'll have to go down every day to see to my own place you know." Jim fussed around with his fork before saying, "Ah.... maybe you could help me out down there once in awhile." Jim said desperately and sent Dan a harried look all the while patting Nino on the back. Dan didn't help one bit because he just laughed as quietly as he could at the spot old Jim had talked himself into.

Nino sniffed then looked up with happier eyes at the old man who suddenly was his world. "That's okay Sir, I can help you once I get over this headache. Can I have one of those pills the doctor gave you? My head hurts like the very dickens." Nino looked like he'd just realized he had a head and had turned an interesting shade of white.

"Sure," And Jim took the small packet of pills out of his shirt pocket and shook one out. "Here now, take this with the rest of your milk and as soon as we've finished our dinner, it's bed for you young man." The pill went down and within the next ten minutes that it took for Dan and Jim to finish eating, the boy and the puppy were both asleep. The kid's head was laid down beside his empty soup plate and the puppy was snoring under his chair. "Now what in tarnation are we to do? That pill really put the kid out." fretted Jim.

"I'll carry him. Now that he's asleep he won't be afraid of me, will he?" Dan didn't expect any answer.

Ben Strongbow walked up to their table as Dan was speaking. "No need to walk back Dan, I've got my truck outside and I'll give you a lift to the motel. I can come back for the family afterward so come on collect your baggage here and let's go."

Dan picked up the boy while Jim got the dog and they left the restaurant. "Ben, would you go with us to Social Services tomorrow? I think it would be better for the boy to stay with Jim, since he thinks the sun rises and sets with the old coot." Jim snorted at that. "You can put in a good word for us while a search is started for his parents. Personally, I'd like to meet the person who treated him like this, yes indeed I surely would." was all Dan would say.

"Whatever is in your mind to do, I'm sure it's too good for that person. You take him in to the doctor's first thing and get him fixed up then we'll go to Social Services afterwards. We'll help get you cleared to keep the boy until they find his parents or a relative." Ben and drove them to the motel.

It was hard getting the kid awake long enough to undress him and get him into the tub, scrubbed and dried off. Once bandaged and dressed in one of Dan's flannel shirts Nino was tucked into the trundle bed with the puppy snuggled in tight to his side and both weary children went into a deep sleep.

The two elected Godfathers stood for a minute looking down on the boy they had taken on. They both just shook their heads at the trick fate had played on them. Jim gave a big sigh. "I guess there's no help for it; we're stuck. Someone held up my hand and volunteered me and you to care for this lost child. I wonder how this is all going to turn out."

"I think it was better that we found him when we did, Jim for who knows what would have happened to the kid if we hadn't." Dan said.

"When you put it that way I guess you're right. It's just kinda hard for me to become a daddy at my age." complained Jim.

"The Thunder Gods must have taken a liking to you for them to hand you one of Their foundlings," chuckled Dan. "Maybe They thought your life had become a little too boring."

"Go ahead and laugh and we'll see how good you are at helpin' raise a young boy. You haven't had any practice at all and mine has been so long ago I've forgotten how. Well," Jim sighed, "I guess we got it to do."

It sounded long suffering when the speech was emphasized by a deep sigh of resignation, however Dan saw a sparkle of something like happiness in the old man's eyes at being needed. Hmm, mean old Waggener? Yeah right!

"I guess I'd better go out and buy the kid some clothes first thing in the morning. He surely can't wear those he walked in with because it would plumb put me to shame to appear before the social worker with a raggedy-tagged boy." Jim kicked aside the pile of dirty clothes contemptibly.

"I'll share the expense with you. I think we can count on having the child with us for awhile so we best buy him enough changes to last; good winter clothes you know, and a set of flannel pajamas."

The men sat on the edges of their beds and didn't speak for awhile; just sat there watching the kid sleep. Then Jim cleared his throat quietly. "Dan, I've been meaning to talk to you for some time and just never had the gumption to do so. Maybe it was just my stubborn pride." As Dan glanced over at Jim in a questioning way, the old man said defensively, "I've got pride you know only sometimes the darn thing gets in my way and trips me up. Well, I guess now is as good as another, so here it is. My property isn't as big as yours, I know, still it's rich bottom land and I put quite a few acres into hay, corn and some in garden products as well as cattle south of the county road. It's been a good paying ranch, and I've managed to put aside a bit of money here and there. What worries me is I'm getting on in years and too old and crippled up for the hard work it takes to keep the place going anymore. I don't want to hire more men either. Dan, I ain't got anyone to leave the place to when I die so here's the bottom line; would you consider taking the ranch into partnership? Not fifty-fifty, but maybe 40/60 in your favor? In my will, and in any contract we make up, I'll leave you my ranch when I die. If young Nino here doesn't come up with a relative to care for him, I might make him heir to my shares in our merger; it should be enough to take care of him in the future. Will that be okay with you?" Jim clutched his arthritic hands together.

For the first time Dan realized that this old man had real problems. How much had it taken for Jim to swallow his pride enough to make this offer? Quite a lot, Dan suspected, quite a lot indeed.

"Jim, you could knock me over with a feather springing this idea on me so sudden-like. I know you have good rich land and with all that water just adds to its value. Not only that, but it's priceless with the easy access to the main road and all. It sounds like a mighty fine business proposition. We'd have to decide how best to use that land since most of mine is grazing land with a number of acres of corn and hay down by the river. Your offer certainly opens up whole set of possibilities. I think it's definitely workable. Hmm… we'll have to hash all the details out later, but I'm thinking, if your willing that is, you could move into my house and make it the cooperate headquarters. We could turn your house over to a manager who would work for us once we decide what we want to do. It would be awfully inconvenient for us to have to ride back and forth every time we need to get together and talk especially in wintertime. As far as giving shares to Nino with the proviso that our merger would stay in effect; that's mighty generous of you and no problem at all for me. Also there a real nice little house attached to the main house that my Dad had added on for my grandmother if you don't want to live in the main house with me. So, what do you think?" Dan looked at the older man with keen eyes and saw how the man was trying to control his emotions.

"Glad you like the sound of it Dan." Jim heaved a soft sigh, "I gotta' tell you I've been a mite worried of late what to do. I know we've had our runarounds and that was mostly my fault, but I didn't mean to do no harm. It was silly of me to try to get your attention by making you mad. I never did have much social training." Jim cleared his throat a time or two and blew his nose. "About moving up to your place; well, I will admit I've grown mighty lonesome these past years since my wife died and I could possibly use more company for sure and it would definitely be more convenient," Jim chuckled, "And maybe then I might be fit to take out in society once I got some of the rough edges worn off." Dan had to chuckle over that one.

Jim stood up and walked over to the window and gazing out at the town's lights and the fairground's barn lights. He wiped his nose again and stuck his handkerchief into his back pocket then turned around to face Dan soberly.

"A man shouldn't have to die alone. I want my last years to be worth something fine. I want to be able to do as much as I can and know that it will be enough. I want a little ease of spirit too. So I'd admire to live at your place and I thank you kindly for the invite." Jim cleared his throat harshly then said. "All right, when we get home we'll get the details worked out. Thanks." And abruptly walked over and held his hand out. Dan stood up took it gently in both of his.

"A handshake and a man's word is all I need, however we'll do the paper work for the nosy state's benefit." laughed Dan and Jim lightened up. "Who would ever think that the Sour Recluse and the Old Thorn would get together in a friendly-like manner?"

Jim laughed delightedly and shook Dan's hand firmly. "Yeah, who would have thunk it? Well, nosy civil servants in the world need work too I suspect. Paper, paper, paper, what in the world do they do with all that paper? It used to be easier in the old days in some ways. I guess you can't stop progress. Well, well, I'll have to make my peace with these new times. Let's go to bed and sleep on it, not that it's going to get much better than this."

"Oh, I don't know Jim; we just might surprise ourselves and become successful entrepreneurs and be written about in all those fancy magazines. Like Joe says, we might become rich and famous." Laughter was a fine way to relieve a tense and a very delicate conversation.

The lights were out and Dan lay awake for some time wondering who was running his life. Now he had a kid and an old man to care for. Life was beginning to take on a whole new meaning.

~*Fair Days*~

THE DAYS THAT FOLLOWED were chuck full of excitement and activity of one kind or another and no one wanted to miss a thing.

Jimmy Kilpatrick had entered his horse Speedy in the quarter mile and the race was so fast that it was over before one could catch their breath. Jimmy flew across the finish line one length ahead of the second horse. Joe was so proud of his friend that he grew hoarse from shouting. He and Mike hurried down to the winner's circle where Jimmy was holding Speedy by the reins. Joe took several pictures of the horse and man. Mike shook Jimmy's hand and said. "They sure know who you are now Jimmy. Next stop Hollywood."

And Jimmy laughed. "Maybe with a few more horse races boss, but I'm happy at the ranch for now. Besides, it's you guys that are going to be rich and famous with your music, right? Maybe Joe will need me to hold his horse for him later on and I'll become famous by association."

"Nothing happens by accident Jimmy, so don't undersell your abilities to be right up there with the rich and famous if that's what you want. You're a grand man and good fortune will just follow you around. Believe it." said Mike very seriously too.

"Thanks Mike and maybe you're right, we'll just have to wait and see." Jimmy said with a pleased grin.

"Jimmy, I've been waiting for just the right time to give you a present; it's from Mike and me. I hope you'll take them and do whatever you want with them. It isn't payment for saving my life or anything like that. It's more like a little memento kind of thing and for winning the race too." Joe carefully unbuttoned his shirt pocket and took out the two gold coins that he had gotten from Ben that morning. Holding them out to Jimmy both boys had to smile as that cowboy's jaw dropped.

When Jimmy just stood there looking down at the coins and didn't make any move to take them, Mike reached over and lifted

Jimmy's hand so Joe could put the coins in them. Jimmy couldn't for the life of him find anything to say.

Joe began to laugh, "Hey Mike, we've accomplished a fine, fine thing; we've made Jimmy the Jumper speechless."

"You guys! You guys!" was all the stunned man could say. Jimmy sniffed, swallowed hard and finally grinned weakly. "You sure know how to knock a guy on his butt. That's quite a trick."

Jimmy kept looking down at the coins then very carefully, put them in his shirt pocket and buttoned the flap down with equal care. "Thanks bosses, I guess you could say this tops them all, even winning the horse race." With that he nodded not able to look at them in the eyes and led his horse away. Mike and Joe did a high-five and went looking for the rest of the family.

Next it was Luther's turn only he wasn't riding Midnight Racer. Little Brown and Racer ran the three-quarter mile like it was a cakewalk. Little Brown was so hunched over the horse's neck he was practically invisible. It was a joy to watch Luther in the winner's circle grinning up at the jockey like he was a king or something. Whatever Luther said to Little Brown had the kid beaming like the sun coming up in the morning.

Then there was the rodeo to take in and Jimmy came away with the calf roping money and Hoss Charlie, the small wiry cowboy, took first prize in the bronc busting. What a day the Lost Wagon Ranch was having. Jacko took the bull dogging with Whitey Cranefoot. James Bird from Blackhawk's Ranch took first in the Bull riding. Joe wanted to ride the calves, but Ben said better not this year, so they went on to attend the other events such as judging of stock and then the food and crafts.

The next day was spent at the sales barn where they watched Ben's bulls go for top dollar and Mike watched a few of their own go the same way. The horse sales were next and Mike and Joe were sitting with Ben in the first row seats that surrounded the enclosure. First out were the trained quarter horses. Then Ben's appeared one at a time with Jacko's fine demonstration of their abilities as the audience watched Ben's horse working a cow. Each quarter horse sold for a very high price as Ben's reputation for well behaved and trained horses was well known.

It was awfully hard to watch their young fillies and colts being sold. Four of the colts had been sold privately before the big sale and Ben had found good homes for them. These few hadn't been pre-sold so they were being led out, nervous and scared at all the noise and the strange enclosure. One by one they were sold to the highest bidder for good money.

Now Mike and Joe watched their last filly being led into the enclosure. She was a neat little sorrel and had two white socks and a blaze down her small nose. The handler yanked her lead rope when she balked and refused to move forward into the arena and that scared her so much that she reared and the handler began jerking her around trying to get her to behave and when she reared again and fell over backward. Before Mike could react, Ben had leaped over the wall into the enclosure ran over and grabbed the lead rope out of the handler's hands so fast that the guy must have had rope burns from the way he jerked his hands back.

"*Get your bloody hands off her.* You aren't a handler who understands nervous horses. *Get out of here.*" Crooning Ben leaned over to help the filly to her feet. The arena was hushed. He was brushing her off and checking her for injuries all the while the filly butted her head up against Ben's chest or back as he stooped over to check her legs and making distressing whinny sounds like, 'oh boy, my friend is back."

The audience began clapping and whistling their approval. The noise didn't help calm the filly and as Ben led her around to see if she was limping. The filly had her head practically tucked under his arm and walked so close to Ben she almost stepped on his feet.

"*This one's not for sale.*" Ben called to the auctioneer.

Mike stood up and yelled. "*You go Ben, she's ours now.*" And Ben just laughed and waved his hand and disappeared through the side door.

"Well ladies and gents, looks like this little filly has made her own choice instead of you. Looks like she's going back home." the laconic and humorous voice of the auctioneer got a huge laugh and a round of applause.

"*Yeah, way to go Ben*" Hooted Joe." They ran out of the building and around to the holding barn. There the little girl was being brushed and fed some corn as Ben talked softly to her.

"Is she alright Ben? She's not hurt is she?" Mike asked anxiously looking her over for himself.

"No, just scared is all and she's fine now." patting the filly while Joe fed her treats.

"So, Ben, what's her name?" asked Mike.

"I think Sudden Surprise fits her to a tee, don't you?" the man grinned at the joke of fate or the filly had pulled off.

"That's really good, Ben. How about if we shorten it to Suddi unofficially, that is?" commented Joe.

"Suddi she is." Ben took a little water from her water pail and dripped it over the filly's head. "I christen you Sudden Surprise and Suddi for short; may the spirits be pleased at your return." Suddi shook the water off then rubbed her face up and down the front of Ben's clean shirt.

"I think she'll make a good horse for Carli in a few years don't you?" said Ben and the boys added their welcome to the little horse that wouldn't leave home and if a horse could look smug, this one did it in spades.

In the hour before supper, Ben took the boys through the carnival and on some of the rides. They had done this every night so far as a private time with Ben. These times were special to the boys and somehow, mysteriously, Ben seemed to perceive this. It felt so normal to have a man so like their dad with them, sharing their fun and their joys. Ben appeared to be as much of a kid as they were.

That evening there would be the gathering together of all the people in from the Sacred Valleys to celebrate their combined victories. Life was good.

The Sacred Valleys' folks gathered together to celebrated that evening with a huge dinner and evening of entertainment. They had reserved a big restaurant and dance parlor for that purpose way in advance of the fair.

That night Joe got to meet Nino for the first time, even though he had seen the boy at Clayton's several nights before, he sure looked better now that he had new clothes and didn't look so sick. The boy still had a bandage around his head that Joe thought looked like a crown with the boy's red hair sticking out the top and his arm was still in a sling.

Joe walked over to where the quiet boy was sitting beside Jim Waggoner. "Hi, I'm Joe Kelly and we've got a ranch north of Dan Lightfoot's. I'm seven, how old are you?"

The boy jumped a little then looked up at Joe standing beside him smiling. "Well, I don't rightly know Joe 'cause I can't even remember my name."

"I'm sorry I should have remembered you had a bad accident. Anyway, you'll remember some time later then we can call each other by our real names huh?" smiled Joe. "'Course, Joe Kelly is my real name."

"Hi Joe, it's nice to meet someone my own age. This crowd really makes me nervous. Jim calls me Nino and he thinks I'm about seven or eight. I guess I'm going to live with Mr. Lightfoot and Jim's going to live with us too at Dan's house and that makes things nicer. I'm kinda scared of Mr. Lightfoot, he's so big and all." Joe had sat down beside the boy and listened. Jim was listening too and it was surprising to hear the usual silent Nino chattering away as though Joe was a long lost friend.

"Honestly Nino, Dan, I mean Mr. Lightfoot, is a really, really nice man. Mike and I like him a lot. We went on a cattle roundup with him and got to know him pretty well. You listen to me now; Dan wouldn't hurt a flea let alone a great kid like you. It just isn't in him, is it Mr. Waggoner?"

"Dan's alright and I've told Nino so, but we think Dan's size sort of triggers a forgotten memory or something like that." Old Jim then looked away as someone called his name.

"Well that sounds reasonable, doesn't it Nino. Anyway, Dan's a great guy so you just have to believe us." said Joe, nodding his head to reinforce his statement.

"Okay, if you say so, I'll try harder not to be so nervous around him. Jim has said maybe some big man like Mr. Lightfoot hurt me, so somewhere in my head I remember that part. Do you think so?" asked Nino anxiously.

"It wouldn't surprise me at all. The mind is a pretty complex thing or so I've heard. A bang on the head can really shake your brain up and it might take time for it to settle back into position." said Joe wisely.

Nino laughed. "Yeah it does that and gives you one heck of a headache too."

Ben had noticed Joe making Nino's acquaintance and nodded his head toward them to get Mari Beth attention. She looked and said. "Good, that poor boy needs a friend his own age. Joe will be good for him." and went back to talking to Mrs. Zeggler.

There was a loud banging that got everyone's attention. "Folks, we need some entertainment so I'm going to volunteer Mike and Joe Kelly first then we'll go on to pick on the rest of you talented people so be ready." Called out Mr. Zeggler, "They'll break the ice for you. Mike, you're first."

They used one of the big, long, heavy wooden tables as a platform and put two chairs on top. Mike laughed and got his guitar and climbed up on the narrow "stage." Joe dragged Nino over to the front and sat them both down beside Mari Beth and Hannah.

Mike started out playing a popular country western song that he sang and after the applause he played another old one that everyone knew and could sing together. The last song was one of Mike's compositions and all instrumental. Joe remembered parts of it from the night Mike had shut himself into the cabin. It was full of passion and pathos, so full of stored memories and feelings it touched many a cord in those who listened. The music didn't need words; the music said it all wordlessly.

There was a silence after the last note had been struck; Mike stood up and with a bow, began to step down from the table onto an equally sturdy bench and the sudden stomping and applause almost made him fall off. He grinned and waved and with one hand.

"Now wait a minute son, don't get so anxious to leave our fine stage here. You get back up there and let your brother do his stuff. Come on up Joe." The Master of Ceremonies, Mr. Zeggler, gestured to the young boy and Joe jumped up on the bench then onto the table like an agile monkey. Mike and Joe had been working on a new song. Well, it was an old song, but new for them. It was one of Joe's favorites called. "Send in the Clowns."

Somehow, Joe's voice lent the simple song something extra and sung in harmony with Mike it became a beautiful thing. There was sadness to it, yet an overall acceptance that life wasn't entirely all that one would wish it to be. The song evoked a response of, 'Yeah, I've been there and done that too', yet it also spoke of the courage to face disappointment and the courage to go on being one's self.

This time the applause was quieter and more prolonged and it in itself spoke volumes about the depth of feeling the song had drawn out of everyone.

The next one was hilarious. Somewhere Mike had found this old, old song with words so funny that he and Joe just had to add it to their growing repertoire. They took turns singing the lyrics back and forth like a duel. It was received with whistles and stomps and laughter as well as applause.

"Joe, sing Ave Maria." came a voice in the back. Joe looked around until he saw Jimmy wave and Joe grinned and nodded.

"Okay, Jimmy, just for you." And Mike played the piece through once before Joe began to sing in Italian. Again, the extraordinary voice coming from deep within a joyous heart sent chills down everyone's spine. When Joe was through he smiled at his friends and when he saw Nino with his mouth open he laughed.

Into the silence Joe said. "Ha, put you all to sleep, did I? Nice to know my voice acts on people just as it does on cows and horses; I guess you're too surprised to boo, moo or whinny." The boys jumped down off the table to the roar of laughter.

"Well, folks, I don't know who wants to follow that act, but come on, be brave and strut your stuff. Who's next?" Mr. Zeggler looked hopefully around the room. "Tarnation, I knew I had made a mistake by getting Mike and Joe to perform first after they were half way through, but come on, be fearless and stand up."

Dusty Evans stood up and said. "Never let it be said that I'm a coward and I'll play my harmonica if Mike, who is officially my boss and must support me, will join me up there. I figure if I can't beat 'em, I'll get 'em to join me."

Enthusiastic applause for that shrewd move, Dusty made his way to the front of the room, laughing as he shook Mike's hand and they both climbed back up on to the table. They whispered to each other, nodded their heads and started right in to rage. If "Dueling Banjos" can be played by a guitar and harmonica, these men did it. Dusty shocked and delighted the crowd with his ability. Who would have known that this old man had such talent? He and Mike jammed enthusiastically and had people at first clapping and stomping their feet that practically rocked the building. No one noticed other people sneaking in from the street to join the party. If they had they wouldn't have cared a bit.

Their next song was a foot stomping tune and that's when some of the men began pushing tables back against the wall, grabbing a partner and took to dancing the Texas Two Step. Another man climbed up on the temporary stage and began to fiddle along with the boys. Encouraged by that bold move a portly West Valley woman brought up her banjo and with a lot of assistance sat on the edge of the already crowded stage and added her talent to the rest. The entertainers were sweating by the time intermission was called.

While people helped themselves to refreshments and gossip, Mari Beth was talked with Jim Jensen. "Say, I've got some news for you Mari Beth. Come spring we're getting ourselves a new teacher from back east. Her name is Mary Louise Van Cliveland nee Fletcher." At the sight of Mari Beth's raised eyebrows Jim hurried on to say, "Now I know the name sounds stuck-up and all, but she sounded like a really nice quiet lady, a single mother with two young girls. I originally talked with a Mr. Coons, her lawyer, and he said she's just been through a very nasty time with an abusive husband that put her in the hospital with serious injuries; actually the husband almost killed her. Anyway, she's inherited the old Fletcher Farm from a great uncle on her father's side of the family. But Mari Beth what really worries me is that she and the girls are planning on living at the Fletcher place and it isn't fit for pigs." frowned Jim.

"Oh that poor woman, what she must have suffered." Then Jim's words seemed to sink in. "You said they were going to *live* on the old Fletcher Farm? Why, that's *crazy* Jim; it's falling down and living there is just plain *impossible*. That whole property is a disgrace to the Valley, a real eyesore. Well, *something* is going to have to be done about this. I'll speak to Blackhawk about this deplorable place, see if I don't." she said indignantly.

"Yes, I thought it impossible myself so maybe at the next town meeting we can suggest something to help her?" Jim waited expectantly, waiting for this good woman to explode and seriously restrained himself from breaking into premature laughter.

"*You leave this to me, Jim Jensen,* that *poor* woman *isn't* going to come out here and see that *awful* place; no she's *not!*" Leaving Jim without another word Mari Beth stalked off to find Blackhawk.

Jim grinned and rubbed his hands together and just thinking about the next town council meeting had him chuckling. They didn't know it yet, but he had just set a fox among the chickens. Oh, it was such fun to see Mari Beth on a mission. Jim bustled off to spread the word that the next town meeting wasn't to be missed. Fireworks were in the works.

One by one other people braved the platform and kept the mood going and the party went on. It was going on two o'clock when the manager finally cornered Ben. "Sir, I'm sorry, but I'll be breaking the law if I don't close now." Ben could see how tired he was, but the man was smiling nevertheless. "I want to say on behalf of the staff and myself how much we have enjoy this night; prime music and lots of fun. It's too bad I don't have a much larger place so a lot more people could have squeezed in. I guess you noticed that there are quite a few locals and other strangers that have managed to crash your private party."

"Why sure, more the merrier and glad they all had a good time. Hmm, well Mr. Prescott, maybe for next year's party you could rent us a bigger building or a larger hall and you can cater it. We'll really put on a show and advertise an open invitation, maybe charge a minimal entrance fee to cover food and the bar will be everyone's responsibility. We'll take care of the rent and your services."

"If you're serious about that Sir, here's my card and I'll see about renting the big Grange Hall down the way. It's not been used in awhile, but with a little fixing up it could be a grand place to hold big parties like yours. Hmm, it could just be the highlight of next year's Fair. I'll be in touch with you about that." smiled Mr. Prescott. He'd just made more money in this one night than in any three nights combined.

Ben climbed up on the table and whistled for silence. "The party's over friends and all you new friends. This establishment has to close and you're going to need your sleep so you can enjoy the rest of the fair days. Next year we Valley folks from over west of here plan on doing this same evening only in a bigger way and you town's people and other visitors are cordially invited. So goodnight, or really good morning to you all; see you when the sun comes up."

The following days had the same intensity of activities and everyone tried to do it all. Mike watched Joe as he and Nino enjoy themselves. Of course, poor Jim Waggoner got dragged here and there with them because Nino wasn't about to leave his guardian angel behind. That poor man was going to be worn to a frazzle before they got back home. Maybe they'd end up renting a wheelchair for Jim so he could keep the pace.

One afternoon Mike wandered down several lanes of avenues of booths to see what was being offered and eventually ended up at the other end of the fairway. He was about to turn back when he saw a booth displaying a number of musical instruments so he naturally stopped and got to talking with the booth salesman who also happened to be the craftsman. Hand made guitars with six and twelve strings plus banjos, mandolins, and violins.

"By the way, my name is Mike Kelly. I play guitar and yours are real beauties. Mine is an old Gibson and it's had years of hard wear. Frankly it's getting harder to keep it tuned and I haven't had time to have it repaired. Gee, these are really something." Mike looked like a kid in a candy store and the salesman had to grin.

"The name is Strat Jones and I appreciate an eye that sees beauty. These are my pieces of art and I take great pride in their creation." and shook Mike's hand.

The owner saw the hunger in the young man's eyes as he ran his hand gently over one particularly beautiful twelve-string guitar with its different wood inlays and mother-of-pearl shaped flowers on the neck. "Want to try it?" he asked Mike.

"Can I? Sure 'nough, Mr. Jones." Strat took a folding chair from the back of the tent and sat it out in front of his booth for Mike.

He watched the careful way the boy tuned the strings and then began to play the scales quietly at first, feeling out the difference and handling of the additional strings. He changed some of his cording, but once he got the hang of it all he began to experiment with the increased versatility the guitar gave him, not really playing any particular song, just trying new variations of his passionate song with more volume and added complexities.

True Heart

Thrills ran over Mike's body and he had such a look of quiet joy on his face that it struck Strat Jones with awe. He watched the young man lose himself in the music he was drawing out of the guitar, music that flowed fresh and new as the deep and mellow tones took the young man away from the world.

Within minutes people began to gather as the music swelled and drew people in like iron filings to a magnet. Mike didn't even notice there was a crowd standing around listening quietly. Strat got very busy selling his beauties all the while Mike just sat and played and if Strat was right, the young man was creating music unheard before.

Mike had to try all the guitars of course, but kept going back to the sweet twelve string guitar. What a deep mellow tone he thought, how much more versatile it was in its ability to express what he heard in his head and so he played on, lost to his surrounding again. Strat listened to the music while he briskly did business and his sales skyrocketed.

Finally Mike stopped and knew he couldn't play anymore. His creative juices had been drained for the time being and his fingers were sore, but oh, the music he could write now. He just sat there smiling with such a peaceful contented look that Strat felt his heart jerk. There was only one thing he could do.

"Young man you have a rare talent and you have made my venture here successful beyond what I expected, way beyond." Mike looked up at the man in a bemused way then seemed to come back to Earth. Strat Jones went on, "I wouldn't have sold half as much if you hadn't been playing. As it is, I only have four instruments left including the one you have. I will admit there isn't much of a selection left, but what instrument would you like? It's my gift to you."

Strat smiled as though he didn't know which one was Mike's first love. He had had a number of offers for that twelve-string Mike had been played, but Strat just said it was sold, but he'd be glad to take orders to make another one. And now he had orders for six 12 string guitars. In some cases that didn't work with a customer so he just turned the person's attention on to another instrument which he said was just as good. Strat lied cheerfully because that twelve-string was the best he'd ever made. It had magic.

"A gift for me, why for goodness sake? I had a wonderful time playing this beauty and I've got songs and music I can write now. On top of that you want to give me one of your creations? Mr. Jones, I know how much you could get for this particular guitar I'm holding and it's a lot of money be giving away even for any other of your instruments. Besides, I was going to ask you to hold it for me because I want to buy it. I have the money, but I have to get my guardian to pay you." Poor Mike was in shock and even as he spoke he was stroking the guitar like a pet.

"Well, you've helped me sell out my entire stock of thirty instruments not including these four I have left all within the last hour and a half. Secondly, I've got fifteen orders to fill. Mike, you play like a musical genius and when you become famous, you send people to old Strat to have a special instrument made for them. So you see Mike, I'm not being altogether altruistic because I know a good thing when I see and hear it. You're holding one of the finest instruments I've ever made; it has a magic that I've not been able to reproduce and it deserves to be owned by the very best musician. I've had that guitar for a number of years and couldn't bring myself to sell it because I knew it was special. I guess I always knew that someday someone would come along who deserved the very best I could make. That person is you and I can't put a price tag on that kind of magic! You and that guitar belong to one another. I'll even give you the case I made for it too." Mike was absolutely speechless.

Strat began sorting things packed under one of the tables and came up with a beautiful wooden case with gold latches that not only had a handle, but clips that held a wide leather strap which could be used on the guitar itself. Walking over to Mike he gently took the guitar away from the astounded young man and placed it in the case.

"Maybe next year you'll come by my booth and we'll do this all over again, huh?" Smiling Strat handed the case to Mike and held out his hand. Mike automatically took it and Strat applied a little pressure. "It's been a pleasure meeting you Mike. Here, take my card and you give me a call if you have any other needs. Besides, I'd like to keep in touch with you. Of course, if you really wanted to thank me you could send me a couple of your songs played on that guitar so I can play it for my customers." and handed his card to Mike.

"Thanks Mr. Jones thanks a lot. I'll remember you each time I play this beauty. I'll not only send you a tape, but I'll be sure to send

True Heart

some business your way too. I'll even get my brother to take a picture of me playing your guitar to put on the cover of the CD. Oh, I live in the Sacred Valleys over west of here close to River Town at Ben Strongbow's Thunder Ranch; he's my guardian."

"Always appreciate business, Mike. Goodbye and I'll see you next year."

In a daze Mike walked back down the fairway and didn't notice three young toughs following him until one grabbed him by the shoulder and shoved him hard up against a barn wall. Mike woke up fast.

"What 'cha got there, cowboy? Looks like a mighty expensive case to me. What'd ya' think, Moose?" said the taller boy to a big fat kid and reached out to grab the guitar case from Mike.

Moving fast Mike shoved the kid away and stuck the guitar case behind him and prepared to fight. "Not on your life buddy boy, it's mine and you can't have it. Get lost before I call the cops." threatened Mike.

The tall kid laughed. "Cops? There ain't no cops around that I can see, can you boys? Just make it easy on yourself, kid and give it over. Why, I bet I could get me a thousand dollars for that case and what's in it so I'm not going away without it."

The big young man started toward Mike and Mike got set for the fight of his life, but he was determined no one was going to steal this special instrument from him. His father had taught him a lot and following rodeos and Mike had learned early how to defend himself from bullies like these.

Just as the punk pulled back his fist a dog, a very large dog jumped in between them and snarled in a nasty, very serious way showing all his large teeth that scared them all into jumping back and even Mike stepped back against the barn wall. The bullies turned white with fear because this was a brute of an animal. Mike noticed that the dog wasn't snarling at him for which he was deeply grateful.

"*Watch it boys*, Ranger doesn't like violence and he usually solved his unhappiness by biting the one who's causing it. Now you guys get lost *real* quick or I'm going to knock your heads together and give you king size headaches. *Get out of here, now.*" They took one look at the tall broad shouldered man coming up on them and the so-called toughs couldn't run fast enough and quickly disappeared down the fairway.

Mike turned and watched the big man with a large backpack casually walk up and stand before him. Mike drew a deep breath and let it whoosh out. "Thanks Mister, I just got that case and guitar from the instrument maker down the way and I wasn't about to lose it without a fight. I might not have won the fight, but they were going to know they'd been in a battle. Thanks a lot for coming to the rescue. Say, that's some dog you've got." Mike said in a relieved tone of voice, still keyed up by the close encounter.

He looked down at the big dog sitting calmly at the side of the tall young man. You'd never have known that just a minute ago he'd looked like he was going to do some serious damage to someone's anatomy. The dog looked right back and opened his mouth. Mike would have sworn the dog laughing at him.

"Yep, Ranger is sure enough all dog, but here's the real fierce one." pulling the Chihuahua out of his pocket and held him in one large hand.

Mike laughed and Tiny's big ears perked up. "Can I pet him?" asked Mike.

"Sure, this little guy loves attention." and held the Chihuahua out for Mike to stroke.

"I don't think I've ever seen such a small dog; he sure is cute." Then Mike looked down at Ranger. "But you Sir, I owe you a big debt. Why, standing in front of me and being willing to bite those would-be bad guys deserves a treat." Ranger wagged his tail and Mike carefully held out his hand for the dog to smell. More tail wagging and Mike got the thrill of stroking the mighty dog's head.

"Wow, you're really special Ranger, it's a pleasure to meet you." It was only then that he noticed the missing hind leg.

"All that dog and only three legs; how did it happen?"

"I'm Pete Cameron, call me Pete. Well, I found him as a pup lying beside the road. Some one had hit him and broke his leg in too many places. I took him to the vet in the next town, but they couldn't save his leg so off it came. He gets along pretty well, don't you think?" smiled the big man.

"Hardly noticed it myself; it sure didn't slow down his action any that I could see. By the way, my name is Mike Kelly and I own a ranch west of here in the Sacred Valleys of Washington. It's called Lost Wagon Ranch not too far out from River Town. I'd be pleased if you'd stop by or come by Ben Strongbow's Thunder Ranch. You'd be welcomed at our places any time if you pass that way." Mike smiled as he held out his hand.

Pete shook Mike's hand and grinned. "You never can tell where the road will take me. Now let's get you and your guitar safely down this fairway and back to your people. Carnivals and fairs can get mighty rough on occasion as it attracts all sorts of people so it's safer to go in a group."

"Yeah, I know. My folks used to travel the rodeo circuit when they were alive. My father taught me how to protect myself, but I doubt I'd have come out the winner if those kids had ganged up on me."

They spoke some about Pete's journeys and how he had found Tiny until Mike caught sight of Ben and Mari Beth and waved.

"I want you to meet my guardians Pete." When they caught up to the Strongbows Mike said. "Ben, Mari Beth, I want you to meet Peter Cameron. Pete this is Ben and Mari Beth Strongbow, my guardians. Ben, this man just saved me a nasty fight and the lost of this new guitar."

Ben sized the young giant's hand and smiled. "Mr. Cameron, I'm indebted to you. I couldn't find young Mike anywhere. I never thought of going down to the other end of the fairway. Many thanks for being there for him."

"Glad to have been there, Sir. Well, it's been great meeting you all, but I've got to be moseying along. Bye Mike, I hope I'll be seeing you down the road sometime." Tipping his hat to Mari Beth, Pete moved quickly out into the moving crowd.

"Hey Pete, come back." called Mike, but his voice was lost amidst the general noise of the crowds and the man disappeared into the crowd.

"He's a sudden sort of young man, isn't he? Darn it all, I was going to invite him for supper too. Now how can we repay him for his kindness?" Mari Beth complained. "Mike, please don't go wandering off like that without telling us where you're going. You could have been seriously hurt. Oh my, where did you get that beautiful case?"

Mike told them about the instrument maker, Mr. Strat Jones, and how he had played for the man and had inadvertently helped him sell most all his instruments. "Mr. Jones said he'd even lined up enough future orders to keep him busy all winter too so he gave me the guitar."

"You certainly have had a busy afternoon haven't you? We'll have to hear something on this new fancy piece tonight, you know. Shoot and blast, we were going to buy you a new guitar for Christmas. Now we'll have to think of something else." Ben threw his arm around Mike' shoulders as they walked back to the motel.

Around noon the next day they pulled out for home with the little filly riding in solitary splendor in the big horse van. Both boys were exhausted, but so full of happenings that the conversations were quite lively for the first hour. The truck rumbled on and the singing of the tires against the pavement soon sent the boys into a deep sleep.

~Lightfoot and Waggoner~

They pulled into the ranch yard about seven that evening and Dan backed the empty horse trailer into its covered slot. Unhitching took little time, but once the truck was put away in the garage, Dan carried Nino into the house while Jim let the puppy do its thing in the yard which only took a fast minute as the pup hurried; maybe he was afraid he'd be left out again. Jim picked him up along with Nino's suitcase and following Dan into the house.

"Home sweet home, Nino." whispered Dan as he led the way up the stairs to a guestroom and laid the boy on the bed. Together the men undressed him without him even waking up and put him into new flannel pajamas. Dan rolled the boy carefully under the blankets so he wouldn't to jar his bad arm or his knee then tucked the puppy up against Nino's feet. The men laughed as the puppy had other ideas and crawled up against Nino's stomach and went to sleep. Neither one of the rescued pair woke up as Dan turned off the lights leaving the kid's door open with a night light burning in the bathroom

"I gotta say it's been one heck of a County Fair this year. We both sold our horses so we're both happier and richer. Frankly, I'm worn to a frazzle with Nino dragging me all over the fair grounds day after day. Well, it's just plumb worn me out." complained the old man.

"I'm frazzled too and I'm a bit younger man that you, old timer, so what's my excuse?" complained Dan and acknowledged that his leg hurt like a toothache.

"Becoming a father at your young age is bound to tire you out or maybe this old man is tougher than you young squirts. Besides, I've had practice so I'm way ahead of you." and laughed Jim, the transformed man.

Dan had to agree. "All the above I shouldn't wonder. Say, how does a sip of Henry's Apricot Brandy strike you before we go to bed?"

"I wouldn't say no to that; no sir-rebob, I wouldn't. It might help my 'rumitze some," grimaced Jim. "If you don't mind, I'll light a fire in the living room. There's something about a fire that not only warms the body, but relaxes the inner man or woman as the case may be. Now that may be primitive, but heck, it works."

"Sure go ahead. You know Jim, I have a liniment that might help you out. It's one that Blackhawk gave me for my leg some time ago and it has been a life saver a number of times. Delia White Bear a medicine woman made it. I'll dig it out for you. Of course, you aren't going to smell like a bouquet of roses, but it won't stink us out of the house either. Well, seeing as how you're sleeping alone I guess it won't matter. Put a clothes pin on your nose and you'll sleep just fine." Jim snickered at that and Dan went on to say. "It really isn't too bad a smell, but more like a pungent spicy odor, but strong. On second thought, it might attract the ladies now that I think about it." Dan grinned down at Jim.

Jim chuckled. "My boy, you must remember my dignity as an elderly gentleman. I'd surely admire to try that liniment and if I can get a little easement I'd be beholden to you. I tried hot mud baths and while they helped, the treatment doesn't last all that long and I can't see me going around like a permanent mud pie."

"Light the fire Jim while I bring in our suitcases and get us a brandy, though to speak of Henry's Excellent Apricot Brandy in the same breath as just an ordinary brandy is a sin, I'm sure."

Before long the men were sitting in the padded rocking chairs beside the brightly burning fire and sipping brandy in a contented way. A comfortable silence filled the room and Dan was amazed at how natural and companionable it felt with this Old Thorn sitting across from him. Funny, indeed, for it was almost like having his father back again.

"This boy is a hurtin' child, Dan. Who'd do such a thing like that to a kid? Such wickedness is beyond understanding. If I knew where to find that man I might be tempted to read him from the good book about treasuring children. I'd like to thump him for his wicked ways." grumbled Jim.

"Thumping would be good. Maybe a riding crop across his rear end might impress him a tad bit more. Well, Jesus said, "vengeance is mine, sayeth the Lord, I shall repay," said Dan, "And I've seen some might strange examples of that in my short years. I've seen men who were wicked, punished like I could never do and I didn't have to lift a hand against them. Maybe there is Karma, the balance of good for good and bad for bad sort of thing. Whoever did this to the kid is going to pay and I don't have to worry about how that's going to come about which is a big relief to me." Dan sipped some more brandy. Man alive it was good stuff; so good, it took only a bit to ease the stress out of the long drive.

"Of course, if the good Lord decided to use me as an instrument to punishing this varmint I wouldn't say no." Jim chuckled at that.

"You hold him and I'll administer a few good correctional whacks to his rear end my own self." said Dan.

Jim sighed. "You're right Dan, about leaving revenge to the Lord and all. 'Course being human, it wouldn't be as satisfying as taking that crop to his hind parts though it probably wouldn't do much good about straightening out his thinking, being that the head and the hind end are so far apart and all." Dan chuckled and agreed. "I like the idea of a Spirit or Something that has greater understanding of consequences taking over the vengeance or the balancing of the scales. It sort of eases a man's consciousness, don't it, knowing there is justice eventually?"

"Yep, on rare occasions my Daddy would have to resort to whoppin' my hinny for doing wrong, being as how that was the only way he could finally get my attention. He'd say it hurt him more than it did me, but I noticed it was my butt that hurt not his. Of course I know now that it did hurt him, for he loved me powerful much." Dan looked into the fire and grieved quietly. He sighed before saying, "Dad didn't like spanking, but sometimes it was the only way he could impress on me that I was doing wrong and the punishment just made that fact stick with me. I think that having my father forced to resort to a spanking hurt me more than my hind parts did. Sort of like when you see a mother bear applying her big paw to the cub's rear end when it didn't obey her immediately. Of course, she was only training them to be obedient in order to save their lives if she needed to send them up a tree for safety. I guess the whopping sort of acted as an exclamation point, if you know what I mean?"

"We weren't able to have any children, my wife and I, but we took in a couple of young boys long ago and loved them like we would have our very own flesh and blood. They finally left home to go their way as all children must do eventually. One was killed in the Viet Nam War and the other went into the Peace Corp. A couple of years ago, shortly after my wife died, I was notified that he had been killed by bandits in Africa. It just about broke my heart." Jim took a goodly sip of brandy before continuing. "They're deaths was years ago Dan, but it doesn't much change the deep grief at their loss. I was going to leave my ranch to those boys." Jim rocked and looked sadly into the fire.

Dan was shocked. Why had he forgotten about Jim and Sally's children? He remembered them of course though they had been much older. People forget and life moves on. Jim had given Dan a whole new insight into the soft inner man of his neighbor who would go out of his way to take on another lost child especially at his age.

"We'll give this kid a secure home and protection for now. When he regains his memory we'll know what to do next." Jim chuckled, "That little dickens cornered me into living with you as sure as I'm sitting here. Ha, well it's going to be a challenge for me to move after so many years in that old house of mine. Your idea about a manager living there makes good sense though. Well, well, all things change and I've been a lonely old man."

Jim contemplated his brandy glass then looked up at Dan and raised his glass. "Thanks for having me here, Dan." and drank a sip. Dan tipped his glass back toward Jim and sipped a bit more himself.

"Jim, did it ever occur to you that maybe it's you who is doing me a favor? I've been a mighty lonely man too, and I miss my father something fierce. It just might be that you're sort of easing that feeling of loss. Maybe we're both better off together then apart and alone like we were."

Jim looked up at Dan sharply then gave a sigh as though relieved that he had more to offer this young man than just land and a deal. Perhaps friendship wasn't all that hard to create. He liked that idea very much.

"Of course, the kid forced that issue, didn't he? He's a boy of definite mind and that speaks well for his future, I'd say. Still I think it just may work out for the best after all. Come on Jim, any more brandy and rocking before this hot fire is going to knock us both out before I can show you to your room. We'll end up sleeping the night right here. I think you'd better stay in the house until Nino gets used to us then if you want to move out into the cottage that will be up to you to decide. Either way suits me just fine. I expect I could use the company too, so don't be rushed making your decision." getting up Dan drained the last of his drink before reaching down a hand to help Jim from his chair.

"*Stop that*! I'm old, but I'm still able to get out of a chair by myself." He snapped then seemed to recollect himself and looked ashamed, "Sorry Dan, I guess I am just crotchety and tired. Pride you know goes before falling on your face, that's me. Thanks for the hand." and grasping Dan's hand firmly allowed the younger man to help him stand. Jim followed Dan upstairs to a nice large cheerful room with a double bed.

"Myohmy, now don't that feel just fine?" as Jim felt the mattress give easily beneath his hand, "So soft that my bones are going to love this bed. This here is mighty kind of you, mighty kind. Night Dan, see you in the morning. "

"If you keep on thanking me this way you're going to start worrying me and I'll have to fetch the doctor to see what ails you, Old Man. Be assured I can be a hard driving man and difficult to please too. I'm going to work your tail off so you can save your thanks for later if you still feel I still deserve them. You haven't seen the worse of me yet. Well, I'll go dig up that liniment for you and fetch the luggage up." Dan slapped Jim on the shoulder and closed the bedroom door quickly on what he suspected were tears in the old man's eyes.

How in the heck had he inherited an old man and a young wounded boy? Luck? "No," he muttered as he went down the stairs, "I gotta' figure it's those interfering Thunder Gods who have stuck Their fingers into my pie. Well, I'll know whether to thank Them or curse Them after a few weeks. My life won't be boring from now on, that's a guarantee."

Dan found the liniment and brought the luggage upstairs. Going to Jim's room he knocked softly he said, "Jim? I'll just set your suitcase and this bottle of liniment down by your door. Take a hot soaking bath and rub the liniment in real good. I hope it helps. Goodnight." and went across to his own room and shut the door.

Dan headed for the bed. He was tired out and five o'clock came earlier than it used to or was he just getting old and crotchety too? With a laugh, he turned off the lights.

~Mari Beth Strongbow~

MARI BETH HAD BEEN born in Claremont and though she had traveled all over the United States there was no place she loved as much as the Valleys. She had been raised on the western slope of Thunder Mountain and had met Ben Strongbow at a Country Fair as a young woman. She didn't know if it had been love at first sight, not that she doubted it could happen to people; she would rather say she recognized Ben in her heart and soul when he first came across the floor to ask her to dance. Mari Beth had wonderful memories and one of the best was Ben had felt the same way about her. She also recognized that what they had was a rare, rare gift therefore all the more reason to cherish and protect it. He was the center of her life.

She laughed while she rocked little Carli to sleep at how short their courtship had been, probably set some kind of record. Over the years she and Ben had raised nine children and now here she was with another little baby and two good boys to add to that number. She laughed softly again as she looked lovingly down at the sleeping child. This was one of those children of the heart rather than of the body and just as vital to her as her other children.

Mari Beth never worried about what she was supposed to do and there wasn't any angst about "finding herself" because she had always known who she was and what her purpose in life was from the very beginning. She loved her own born children without question, still the ones who had come to them, children who were lost, abused or alone in the world had simply found that special place in her heart. Rescuing these little spirits and helping them grown in love and security was part of her purpose.

Mari Beth knew she was the luckiest woman in the world because she was happy and fulfilled in her life and content to be herself and especially blessed with the man who loved and understood her. Yes, it was a rare, rare thing that two people should find and know such compatibility for what it was; *cherishing, honoring, and treasuring that said "love" in the fullest meaning of the word.*

Mari Beth slowly got up out of the old rocker beside the kitchen fireplace while Hannah hummed as she made a large torte as a surprise for the family's dinner. God love her thought Mari Beth, let her find her own fulfillment too. Hannah looked up as though she had heard her mother's silent blessing and smiled her radiant smile.

"Little one's asleep I see," she spoke softly. "You spoil her Mom. Of course it's hard not too, isn't it? I think she's grown a little in the past months and grown prettier too maybe because she's happy." Hannah turned her attention back to her culinary art.

"A little spoiling won't hurt this baby any and I'm sort of making up for what Jean wasn't able to do, but pretty soon she's going to be more independent. She's already better about letting me out of her sight for an hour or two which is a vast improvement. She's going to be all right soon." Mari Beth passed out of the kitchen and gently carried Carli upstairs for her nap.

When Mari Beth returned, Hannah poured them both a cup of coffee and sat them down on the table. Mari Beth took one of the chairs with a sigh of relief and gratefully sipped her hot drink.

"I will admit it's harder to keep up with a youngster now than it used to be. Well, I can't complain I'm not getting enough exercise." Chuckled the older woman and Hannah just laughed back at her.

"Mom, you could keep up with an army of these little ones and love every moment of it, however, as you're growing older and more decrepit I'll help you with Carli so she doesn't run you too hard." Hannah laughed as she watched the mock-insulted look on her mother's face.

"I'm not *that* old missy!" and laughed, "But my how busy we've all been. When I look back at how these past months have gone flying by I'm shocked. It seems like ever since the Kelly children arrived in the Valleys there's been one excitement after another. Before they arrived I guess we were all caught into a deep rut of doing routine jobs and living a routine life without much variation. Maybe the Thunder Gods wanted to shake things up a bit."

"It certainly hasn't been boring I'll say that much, but we're not the only ones who have gotten stirred up." Hannah leaned across the table and whispered, "Luther has that new cook. *Pardon me*; that new chef and her siblings living in the old mother-in-law's cottage behind the house. I really like her and she's the picture of a pretty southern belle if I ever saw one. Luther and the boys say she's some kind of *GODDESS IN THE KITCHEN*. Please note that that title is in all capitols." That had Mari Beth laughing.

"Well, it's true that she's a beauty and I regret that I didn't get to chat with Miss Golight at the fiesta. I certainly meant too, seeing as how she's part of Luther's household now, but it was such a zoo that I missed the opportunity. Drat that Luther for not bringing her to me and making the proper introductions." grumbled Mari Beth. "You'd think he didn't know any better."

"I think you'd like Amber Golight as she's a nice person and boy, can she cook! I'm a tad bit jealous. Hmm, you know Mom I think we need to pay an up-close and neighborly call on Miss Golight. Yes indeedy, that way you'll see what Luther is stacked up against." Hannah raised her eyebrows in a wiggle-waggle and Mari Beth, who had just taken a sip of hot coffee, choked then laughed and wiping her chin.

"*Yes indeed* my love, it's our duty to check her out so let's surprise Luther with an unannounced visit," smiled Mari Beth slyly. "We'll take her some of your ordinary, mundane chocolate chip cookies as a "welcome to the neighborhood gift" sort of thing."

Hannah eyes gleamed. "Hmm, good idea and isn't it fortunate that I baked today. Gee, maybe I'm getting psychic."

There was a quiet spell before Mari Beth came up with another surprising comment. "Did you hear we're getting a new teacher for the River Town School? No? Jim Jensen told me that a Mary Van Cliveland from back East has inherited the old Johnston Fletcher place." At Hannah's surprised look Mari Beth nodded in disgust. "Every time I drive to town I pass that disgraceful place with its falling down house and outbuildings. Blackhawk needs to do something about that. Anyway, Jim said Mrs. Van Cliveland had suffered serious injuries that put her in the hospital. She was attacked by her now divorced and imprisoned husband. She's going to be coming out here to start a new life with two young girls to care for and she's expecting to live in the old Fletcher house. Hannah my girl, *that is impossible*! Not that I think living there is even remotely possible. Don't you think we should do something about it? I mean the whole community owes it to her, given that it's hard to get good teachers way out here."

Hannah's eyes sparkled as she watched her mother begin to swing into action and nodding her agreement to everything she said. "It surely sounds to me like a community obligation to fix things up for her especially if they want to keep this new teacher happy and here. So what do you plan to do, O Queen of the Downtrodden?"

"Do? Why, the only thing a Christian Woman would do under the circumstances; light a bonfire under the feet of everyone in the Valleys. So I'm standing up at the next Town Meeting and getting a new house for Mrs. Van Cliveland." Mari Beth said in a no nonsense tone of voice.

"You propose it and I'll second it and the thing will be done in no time. However I think we should recruit some backup from our friends first before bearding the Counsel with our plan, don't you?" Hannah slyly winked at her beautiful blonde goddess of a mother.

Privately Hannah often wondered why she hadn't inherited her mother's blond looks instead of resembling her great-grandmother in her Indian appearance; not that it was bad or anything like that, it was just that she pined to be tall and stately and golden like her mother and Rachel. Well, it was a mystery of genetics for sure. She was the dark horse.

"Good idea! My you will make a marvelous Dr. Watson to my Sherlock Holmes, and between the two of us we can move mountains I'm sure, at least move the City Council. Besides which it's *just* the sort of thing the Thunder Gods would like us to do. Hmm, now maybe *They're* the ones that are calling this woman and her children here in the first place. You know how the abused and wound seem to appear in our Valleys." I must mention this to Ben, thought Mari Beth. "Well, gracious it would never do to go against what the Guardians wanted, would it? We just might mention that little item to get the board to act a little faster. Perhaps we should call on Chief Blackhawk to bring out the Big Guns, so to speak." That had Hannah giggling like a school girl. Hah, she thought, calling out the Big Guns indeed.

"Yes indeed, and wouldn't it be jolly to have the Thunder Gods make an appearance at the council meeting?"

"Ha! If I thought I could arrange THAT I would just to see the council's reaction."

Mari Beth tried to look serious, but only managed a few minutes of serous before they were laughing as they got up and put their cups in the dishwasher. When Carli woke up, they'd go pay a nice visit to Miss Golight. In the meanwhile, Hannah got busy preparing dinner to slow cook in the oven while they were gone.

It was just going on three o'clock when Hannah, Mari Beth and Carli drove into Luther's yard. Mari Beth walked up to the kitchen door and knocked, which she had never ever done before, but since this was more or less an informal-formal call upon a stranger she thought it polite to knock. The kitchen door was opened by a pretty young woman in a chef's apron.

"May I help you?' came the soft southern voice.

Oh deary me, thought Mari Beth, Luther is toast. She smiled, "Hello, I'm Luther's mother, Mari Beth Strongbow and you've already met Hannah and this is Carli Kelly my guardian child. I'm very sorry I didn't get to talk with you at the fiesta, but it was pure chaos that night. I do hope you'll forgive the neglect. If you're not too busy we came to welcome you to the Valleys."

"How very kind it is of y'all to visit me. Hello Miss Strongbow, it's nice to see you again, please come in and be welcomed." She led the way through the spotless kitchen that was filled with the delicious scent of cooking that had their mouths watering. What's that old saying about the way to a man's heart is through his stomach? Yep, Lute was toast, all right.

Once they were in the living room Miss Golight said, "I don't know where your son is at the moment Mrs. Strongbow, but he's always back at the ranch by four o'clock. Won't you sit down and I'll fix tea or do you prefer coffee?" asked Miss Golight.

"Whatever you have Miss Golight is just fine. Hannah has brought you some of Luther's favorite chocolate chip cookies. I do hope you don't mind." said Mari Beth.

"Cookies? Oh, dear, I'll have to hide them from my niece and nephew or they'll be gone before Mr. Strongbow gets to enjoy any." Miss Golight sighed as she took the cookie jar. "It's true that I'm a trained chef, but cookies have never been my thing. They're really not that difficult I know, but if you don't do them right they turn out like bricks, at least mine usually do. Thank you, I'll serve a few if it's alright with you." and hurried to the kitchen.

"My dear daughter," murmured Mari Beth, "Our Luther is a goner for sure or else he's totally deaf, dumb and blind, which I don't think he is. Imagine him hiring a sweet young thing like this lady chef plus taking on two young people as well. Hmm, it could lead to something very interesting, don't you think?" Mari Beth's eyes fairly sparkled in anticipation.

"Speaking of interesting events, if our resident Gods want Luther to marry then her arrival could have been a planned thing; a real God-like blindside, as it were. She's maybe 27-29 years old, beautiful and of marriageable age too. Now what is that wonderful smell we caught as we pasted through the kitchen?" said Hannah just as Miss Golight came in carrying a tray and sat it down on the coffee table and began serving them. She handing Mari Beth a small plastic cup half filled with milk for Carli and a big cookie.

"Cookies Momma, good choco'ate cookies." biting down on one.

"She called you mother? I thought you said you were her guardian, was I mistaken?" inquired Miss Golight, as she sat down on a chair she had drawn up to the coffee table.

"My baby here lost her real mother not too long ago and when she saw me she thought I was her mother and I didn't have the heart to say differently. Poor baby had been through a rough time losing both her parents and had only her brothers to take care of her. Now they did a fine job, but with babies mothers are very important, don't you think?" Mari Beth spoke very quickly and hoped Carli wasn't paying to much attention. She was wrong.

Carli turned and gave Mari Beth THE LOOK. "You is my Momma! Stop saying no! No is bad word, *don't do that*." and went back to eating her cookie.

The women looked at the little girl and Mari Beth hurried and said. "Yes indeed sugarplum, I am a Momma and all yours too." Trying not to laugh and get Carli all upset,

Miss Golight cleared her throat lightly. "How very fortunate you are to have such a beautiful child," smiling at Carli.

"I not beautiful child; I is sugarplum, Momma says." smiled Carli right back at Miss Golight and they had to laugh.

"Really?" Miss Golight said delightfully.

Carli turned around and frowned up at Mari Beth. "Momma says, Carli her sugarplum, huh Momma?"

"You bet you are a sugarplum and twice as sweet too." and gave Carli a big smacking kiss on her chocolate smeared lips making the little girl giggle then went back to more serious work on her chocolate chip cookie.

"Miss Golight, it is very nosy of me, but what do you have cooking in the kitchen?" asked Hannah.

"Oh, that's a baron of beef that I'll serve with a mixed green salad with raspberry vinaigrette along with a soufflé and other side dishes such as mashed potatoes plus green beans, a corn casserole and hot rolls. The dessert is a chocolate tort with raspberry fruit and Crème Brule'. The men seem to enjoy different kinds of foods I offer them. However, I do try to give them what they're more familiar with as well. Once in awhile I challenge them a little. They're so easy to please." Amber looked amused at the startled looks on her guests' faces and pursed her lips. "So far the only complaint has been that they're all going to die of overweight and swear that if I leave I'll have to take them all with me because they're addicted to my cooking."

She threw her head back and really laughed. "Luther threatens to tie them to stakes and starve them to death while torturing them by parading my food beneath their noses. Really, they are all so funny that it impossible to take any of these cowboys seriously. I have been very lucky so far because I've not been thrown into the water trough or fed to the pigs as they have done to other cooks or so they've said, so I guess I'm still safe."

"With that sampling of tonight's menu I'm sure you're in no danger; they'd probably throw Luther into the cold water trough if he fired you. Hmm, a chocolate tort you say? Isn't that interesting, because I've just made one at home. Maybe you and I can exchange some recipes for I'm considered a pretty good cook myself although I'm not a chef, but I can cook good food of the country." said Hannah modestly and leaning forward in her chair.

"Please call me Amber and don't think I haven't heard your praises sung by everyone here. I've plenty of questions and you're just the person I need. I don't know a lot about the cuisine of this country, but I would love to learn. Let's go to the kitchen because I have a recipe or two you might like to try."

True Heart

The two young women got up immediately and went into the kitchen forgetting all about Mari Beth and Carli. Suddenly Amber Golight rushed back into the living room full of apologies. "Oh, Mrs. Strongbow how very rude of me, perhaps you'd like to come into the kitchen where it would be more informal and friendly," said Amber tentatively.

"Just as soon as my baby here finishes her cookie we'll be out so don't fuss Amber, I know how it is when two people find a similar interest. Go on with you, I'll be there in a few moments." Amber smiled and hurried back to the kitchen where the women's voices joined in animated talk that had Mari Beth smiling. It looked like her daughter and Amber Golight were well on their way to forming a friendship and she was very happy about that as Hannah needed closer friends, especial girl friends. Mari Beth contentedly sipped her coffee while watching her child demolish the rest of her treat.

"All done Momma, I is all done." Mari Beth helped wipe Carli mouth and hands on a napkin before taking her by the hand and walked out to the kitchen to join the ladies elbow deep in recipes and arcane cooking talk. Mari Beth sat in a kitchen chair with Carli on her lap and listened for she wasn't a bad cook herself.

It wasn't long before they heard Luther's truck pull into the driveway then the sound of the truck door slamming and within a minute Luther came through the kitchen door. "Well, I was wondering why it had taken you two so long to pay us a call. Hello Mom, Hannah, Ms Golight." Luther kissed his mother's cheek with a knowing smile on his face.

"Lutey, me, me, say hi to Carli." Demanded the child as she slipped off her momma's lap and held up her arms. Luther scooped her up and whirled her around to her delight and gave her a smacking kiss.

"Hi, hi, Sweetheart, when are you going to grow up and marry me?"

"Is you my boy, Lutey?" As she held his cheeks tightly in her hands and looked intently into his eyes so close that Luther thought he'd go cross-eyed.

"You bet Sugarplum, I'm your boy." and gave her another big smack which seemed to satisfy her as to his devotion and laid her head down on his broad shoulder and sighed. Luther smiled and rocked her back and forth for a few minutes then turned to connect with the women's fascinated stares. "Well, I never could resist a pretty face." he grinned.

Mari Beth finally got around to talking about the Fletcher place and what she planned to do about it. "Sure, Mom, it's a great idea and I'll help you with your plan and I think I can." laughed Luther, using an old joke.

"You bet you will my son, or no more chocolate chip cookies 'cause I've got your number." Mari Beth said sternly, yet with that special look in her eyes.

"That's cruel and unnatural abuse! Okay, okay, I surrender. Gee, I didn't know I could be whipped into conforming to a dictator's wishes by threatening to withdraw my chocolate chip cookies. Say, not to change the subject, but what is that great smell that almost knocked me over when I came in?" Luther asked and adroitly changing the subject.

While everything *appeared* to be normal and the flow of days also appeared to settle into the same familiar rhythm, there were events both good and not so good that were developing and would relentlessly push everyone along with or without their agreement thus keeping people from becoming bored. These events would act as catalysts for growth and stimulate people's lives bringing about changes while entertaining the Gods.

The monthly River Town Council Meeting was an event no one missed unless they were sick or dying. There was the usual action and excitement that was generated by so many people when they got together to argue for or against an issue or just came to be entertained by all the arguments. Most everyone wanted their say as most everyone was pro-active in anything to do with their Valleys and the rest were just there for the gossip.

Mari Beth had already added Chief Blackhawk, Tom, Dan, and of course the Strongbow family and the farm holders close to the old Fletcher place to her list of supporters. Mari Beth was armed with duplicate enlarged pictures of the dilapidation of the Fletcher house and property that Sam Carrington had taken. Backed by her allies she sailed in with a no nonsense plan to place before the council members.

True Heart

There were greetings, conversations, visiting back and forth between people who had known each other all their lives for the most part, but that fact didn't diminish their love of personal one on one communications. And so the talk filled room making it resound like a lively beehive, just buzzing busily away until they heard Judge Barker's gavel hitting the table.

"It's eight o'clock so be seated and let's get the show on the road." a small man he might be, but he made up for it with the forceful strength of his character. A tough customer and putty in the hands of his wife to the mutual satisfaction of both of them.

People sat and gradually quieted down after another loud gravel whack echoed through the hall and the business of the Valleys began with the discussions of a new water main for the town. That went on for a time until the vote was taken to set aside specific funds was agreed upon. A youth center was being planned for the corner of Fifth and Main that meant taking down an old warehouse that was both a hazard and a danger before rebuilding could occur. It passed without opposition with the necessary funds for demolition and construction come early spring after the bids came in. The next order of business was complaints, counter charges, heated arguments until final solutions were reached. Now this was high entertainment indeed and the only things lacking were the popcorn and sodas.

When the call for new business came Mari Beth promptly stood up almost before the Judge finished speaking. When Mari Beth stood up in any Town Meeting, the people knew sparks were about to fly. Luther, who was sitting behind her, whispered. "Go get 'em General." Mari Beth turned around and gave him a frown and then a wink.

"The floor recognizes Mrs. Strongbow. All right Mari Beth, what bee do you have under your hat tonight?" asked Judge Barker with a decided gleam in his eye for the battle ahead and he was sure it would be a battle, but Mari Beth never bored him. If there was a particular wariness in the Judge's voice, it was because he knew Mari Beth for the steamroller she could be if she felt moved to take a stand.

"Judge Barker it has come to my attention that the school board has hired a new eighth grade teacher by the name of Mary Van Cliveland for this coming spring. Is this true?" Of course, Mari Beth knew it was because she'd already spoken to the school board, but this was the foundation for her case so she stated it.

"Yes that is a fact Mrs. Strongbow, what about it?" the Judge said briskly.

"Thank you for confirming that, Sir. I also understand the Mary Van Cliveland and her two daughters have inherited Fletcher's old farm. We are very fortunate to have attracted such a qualified teacher to our remote Valleys. Now that's all fine and dandy, but the condition of that neglected farmhouse, its buildings and the land is a disgrace to the community and an offense to the Thunder Gods. To ask a wounded, single mother with young children to occupy such a falling down house is a crime in my book. I have here recent pictures of that house and outbuildings and what they look like in case people here haven't had the opportunity to see it for themselves. I'd like to show them around. Luther, please pass these to the board and then pass a few around the room; thank you, son."

Mari Beth still stood not yielding the floor to anyone else, not that anyone would dream of contesting her while Luther did as he was told. She gave the people five minutes to look at the pictures that were being passed quickly along the rows accompanied by shocked murmurings and exclamations.

"As you all can see this is no place for a human being to live and certainly not the way we want our new teacher to live. I move that this house be torn down and a new one built and the farm cleaned up before Mrs. Van Cliveland arrives in the spring. If she sees where she is supposed to live, she'll turn around and be gone before you can wink your eye. I see this as a community project and I move we supply the materials and labor to bring that property into right condition as a gift to this poor woman and her children." and sat down.

Before Hannah could stand up, Chief Blackhawk stood to be recognized. "All right Issaquah, you're recognized." grumbled the Judge. He knew he'd lost before a vote could be taken.

"I second Mari Beth Strongbow's motion, Ruben. We as a community have always gone to the aid of anyone who was in trouble or needing help and to give whatever aid was required. The land and the Gods Themselves look with favor upon a compassionate community that takes care of its people and the land. I have visited this Fletcher land and I found it in deplorable shape and the land spirits are desperately unhappy and are becoming ill. Therefore as tutelary Chief of the Sacred Lands of Thunder Mountain, I say we have no choice except to support this motion and get the job done before Mrs. Van Cliveland arrives."

As Blackhawk sat down wild applause, whistles and stomping greeted his speech and the Judge was banging away with his gavel to no effect. He tossed it down and just glared at Blackhawk who grinned and winked at him. Finally Ruben Barker laughed and stood up and picked up his gavel and banged it a couple of more times. "All right, all right, settle down and let's finish this." He said at the top of his voice. Laughing the people complied and waited enthusiastically for the next go around.

"Now is there any objection to funding the new house and ground clearance of the old Fletcher place for the occupation of Mrs. Van Cliveland and her daughters?" Not a peep. With such whole hearted backing Mari Beth didn't think there would be a person who would dare object.

Judge Barker banged his gavel and said. "Motion passed. Please present your plan and expense list by the next meeting which will be November 10th."

Before he could declare the meeting adjourned Mari Beth stood up again. "I have another motion to put before the counsel."

"Well for goodness sake Mari Beth, haven't you started enough work yet?" Judge Barker said disgustedly.

"Now Ruben, you know the weather isn't going to stay nice this way forever. I move we start this project immediately. We need to pour the new foundations while the weather holds good and there can be no delay as we are already deep into late fall. The men of my committee have already drawn up a tentative list of supplies, lumber and other necessities. The money that will be needed to get this whole project finished has also been calculated. Mr. Jensen, Senior has volunteered to take contributions of financial support and keep the books for the project. I have here a sheet of paper asking for volunteer workers on weekends and days off and another sheet for what each person is willing to contribute. Storekeepers will be asked to help with plumbing, lumber and other necessary items for which they will be paid or they can contribute. We must move quickly to get the new foundation, the walls framed up and a roof on before snow flies." She sat down.

Luther stood and said, "I second the motion Judge, because I won't get any chocolate chip cookies if I don't." Roars of laughter greeted that statement and Mari Beth turned in her seat and cuffed Luther across his leg. He mimed being hurt and sat down and it took awhile for the crowd to settle down again.

"*Is this all, Mrs. Strongbow*? Is this the end of your requests? Is there any thing more you'd like this counsel to do for you?" Mari Beth shook her head even as she smiled at Ruben. "Are you sure? We're only here to serve your needs. No? If not, submit your estimates, plans and what have you. All in favor to begin the Fletcher project immediately say, yea." A resounding, 'yea" echoed against the walls along with laughter. "Opposed?" Silence. He sighed, "So noted and passed. This meeting is adjourned, now go home." and banged his gavel a final time.

But it was quite some time before the crowd dispersed. People wanted to talk over the new project, sign what they were willing to do, give, work or both. Mari Beth had to hang up two more pieces of paper to accommodate all the signatures.

"I'll get these typed up and send y'all a copy. We'll be scheduling the demolition and clearing of the property right away. Secondly, there will be the laying of the foundation. Thirdly, the building will begin." said Mari Beth as she gathered the signed sheets together.

People laughed and some smarty yelled, "You go General and we'll follow you anywhere."

"I know you Devil Mitchell, and you better believe you'll follow me 'cause if you don't I'll be right on your tail." laughed Mari Beth.

On the way home Mari Beth sighed and laid her head on Ben's shoulder. "Well, it went much faster than I thought it would and I will admit it surprised the heck out of me. I figured there would be more arguments. It's nice to have an important project like this backed by the whole community. Why it won't take any time at all with so many hands helping out."

"Sure sweetheart, but who's going to run the crew onsite day to day?" asked Ben in a mild tone of voice that had Mari Beth jerking erect.

"Well shoot and blast Ben Strongbow, how should I know? Oh dear, who can we get?" worried Mari Beth.

"We'll get Dan Lightfoot to oversee the demolition and the foundations. After all he had a degree in engineering before he went to war. He's the likeliest one to know how to go about it all." answered Ben quietly, with a slight smile on his face.

"I should have known you'd have the right answer. Sure enough, Dan is just the person we need to get us started so would you call and ask him tomorrow? Darn it all, I could have asked him tonight if I'd thought of it sooner."

"I already did when I saw that we'd need an onsite engineer and he agreed, in fact he seemed quite pleased to have been asked. I think maybe Sam Carrington might be the on-site manager. He's the closest to the property. Hope you don't mind that I did it without asking you first?"

"Not at all, not in the least bit especially when it answers a big problem for me that I didn't know I had. Thanks Benjamin my love, you never fail to fill all my needs." and laid her head back down on his shoulder.

He whispered softly, "That's what I'm here for babe, to take care of you and see that you're happy. I haven't told you lately how proud I am of you and how much I love you. I need to do that more often." Mari Beth reached up and pulled his head down so she could give him a big kiss.

Hannah sat in the back seat and watched her parents. How they loved each other. It was a joy to observe it and it was also a pain in her heart wishing she could have found a man who would be hers for the rest of her life too. Perhaps it was too much to ask to find such mutual love and respect as her parents had. She sighed sadly; maybe she should take a walk up the mountain and solicit the Thunder Gods help. She giggled at the thought of these mighty spirits playing match-maker to bring her a man to suit her qualifications. Well, she thought it wouldn't hurt to ask now would it?

Unknown to Hannah, one of the Thunder Gods had already figured out what she needed and the matchmaking was well underway. You could almost hear the sound of joyful laughter echoing throughout the Valleys. It seemed that the Gods loved a good cook as well as a good woman.

The truck hummed along the road with its headlights piercing the dark night.

~Seely Farm~

Tom was making a quick trip to town. Sure, he had shopping to do and business to attend to as well, but his main reason was to drop off the puppy that was now sleeping on his lap. Mollie's three month old puppies were ready for new homes. Now these Border Collies were sheep dogs par excellence and they'd herd anything from geese, sheep, cows, to kids. They were fabulous dogs; intelligent, loyal, gentle, loving and fiercely protective. Tom wanted Lucy to have this one, a white and gold pup with big brown eyes. He pulled into Seely's yard and sat for a minute admiring the neatness of the place. Everything in its place and a place for everything was Hank's motto.

Turning off the engine, Tom picked up the puppy and a small bag of puppy food then climbed out of the truck and shoved the door shut with a foot then walked up onto the porch, but before he could knock, the door flew open and there stood Lucy.

"I saw you with a puppy. Oh, oh, isn't it cute. Mr. Blackhawk, please may I hold it? I'll be very careful." asked Lucy of the hopeful eyes. Just then the puppy woke up and looked down at her and yipped.

"Sure you can Lucy, you see he doesn't have a home yet and I was going to take him into town to see if anyone wanted him when I thought I'd stop and say hello to everyone. Here you are." Tom handed her the dog and she carefully took him into her arms. Now if it wasn't love at first sight, Tom hoped never to see the real thing.

"Oh you darling, you're safe with me and I'll ask Mr. Blackhawk how much you cost so we can be together always. I'll save all my money so I can have you, yes indeed I will." crooned Lucy into the dog's fur as he wiggled and licked her face.

"Actually Lucy I'm giving the dog to you as a welcome gift."

Lucy's mouth dropped open and she could only stare at Tom. "Oh, my goodness, thank you Sir, this is the best present I've ever had and I'll take special care of her."

"I know you will Lucy only it's a boy dog. I'm sorry if that disappoints you."

"It doesn't matter to me at all because he's my dog, oh yes my very own doggie." and walked swiftly back down the long hallway leaving him standing at the open door grinning at the success of his present. "Aunt Jeannie, Aunt Jeannie, look what Mr. Blackhawk has brought me."

Voices were heard in the kitchen then Jean appeared laughing as she walked down the hallway toward him. "Please come in, I guess you know how very happy Luce is that she forgot to invite you in. Thank you, she's been wanting a puppy for the longest time."

"Every child should have a dog Miss Hardwell, there is simply no substitute for a dog who will love and comfort you and be a constant companion. I think that child needs a lot of that don't you?" Tom said seriously as he stepped in beside her and closed the door behind him and took off his hat.

"Yes she does. Karen has just taken several loaves of Poppy Seed Cake out of the oven and they're still hot. Come to the kitchen." Jean said as she looked up at him with a smile. A tantalizing scent was making his heart quiver; oh boy, it was her, Jean's scent standing right beside him. He followed her down the hall feeling totally knocked off his pins at the sudden awareness of …Jean. It was just too sudden, too fast; he had to get a grip. They entered the kitchen and the excited voice of one little girl. Tom sat the puppy food down in a corner.

"Hi Tom, so you're the master magician who brings gifts to little girls. I can't say as I'll mind having one of your collies around. We've been meaning to get another dog since old Butch, God love his spirit, died last month. Hank was going to give you a call when he heard you had some puppies at your place." Karen was talking all the time she was pouring a cup of coffee for Tom as Jean sliced the cake. Tom grinned as he listened to Karen who never missed a beat and could talk up a storm while her hands were busy with multiple tasks.

"For goodness sake Tom, hang up your coat and hat and sit down because you can't eat and drink with your coat on in my house." Tom quickly hung his things on the hook beside the back door and sat down.

"Heard tell Dan and the Old Thorn-In-His-Side are in cahoots these days? What happened? Well come on, give! How can I hold my head up with the ladies of the Valleys if I'm not in the *know*? So many folks went to Huntington this year. Darn it all this would be the one time we didn't go." Karen placed the coffee on the table in front of him and sat down. Jean was smiling as she served him a plate of cake smeared with melted butter.

"Now Karen, if you'd let me get a word in edgewise I'd be glad to fill you in on the latest. Aren't you two going to join me?"

Jean brought the coffeepot over to the table and two more cups. She glanced over to the corner of the kitchen where Lucy was playing with the dog.

"Lucy do you want a glass of milk and some cake?"

"Not right now Aunt Jeannie, I've got to think of a name for my boy." replied Lucy. Just then the puppy in his attempt to grab the small piece of rope that Lucy was holding lost his balance and rolled over twice before getting to his feet.

"Oh his name is Rollie, because he does that so well. Rollie is your name, my baby," laughed the girl as she hugged the squirming pup.

"Maybe you'd better take him outside for a bit Lucy it looks like he might need to after that long drive." Karen advised being wise to the way of puppies.

"Okay yes, I'll have to watch him closely for puppies have to pee a lot, don't they? Come on Rollie let's go out." Standing up Lucy picked her coat off the lower hook and put it on then picked the puppy up and went out the kitchen door.

Jean laughed and looked at Tom with sparkling eyes. "Now you've really done the magical thing, you've turned her attention away from her own loss and given her something else to be concerned about; excellent psychological therapy I might add, Sir. I congratulate you on your success." lifting her cup in salute and continued to look him in the eyes over the rim. Tom felt that strange feeling again and decided he'd better change the subject away from him to other things.

"Always glad to oblige Ma'am, now let me fill you in on the inside stuff. It all began when Dan Lightfoot gave Jim Waggoner a ride to the fair." So Dan talked between bites of cake and sips of coffee filling the women in on the happenings.

"Maybe Jim's not such a contrary man as we were thinking. Anyway, Dan told me that he and Jim are thinking of consolidating their ranches. 'Pears Jim doesn't have any relatives and is worried that he can't keep up with the work at his place. Ben and Mari Beth spoke for Dan with Social Services so they can keep the boy at his place until they find the kid's folks or a relative. It was a logical move because Dan has Martha, but the kid said he wouldn't go with Dan without Jim."

Here Tom shook his head at the courage of the little boy and laughed. "The end to that was Jim agreed to move to Dan's place. You'd have laughed to see the look on Jim's face when he realized a little boy had blindsided him." Tom took another big bite of delicious cake as the women laughed at that.

"Will wonders never cease and the feud between Dan and Jim is over. It's true that Jim is getting too old to do the work of a young man any more. Well good on them as the Aussies say, now that poor boy has two guardian angels, doesn't he? 'Course, I doubt that Jim would appreciate seeing himself as an angel." said Karen and Tom knowing Jim had to laugh at that idea.

Tom was almost ready to leave when Lucy came back in with the pup. "He's tired, Aunt Jeannie, I need to fix him a bed in my room so he can sleep." Lucy said in a determined way as though daring anyone to deny her the right to have the dog in the house.

Jean looked at Karen for permission. "Don't look at me, why should it be me to say no to the child? I'm not that stupid Jean." Karen turned to Lucy and said. "Honey I've got an old blanket that I should have tossed out long ago that's nice and soft. I bet we can make a super bed out of it." Karen left the kitchen followed by Lucy carrying her pup.

The little girl stopped in the doorway before leaving the kitchen, "Thank you Sir. This is the very best present I've ever had." then was gone.

"Well now I think I've been awarded the medal-of-honor, don't you, Miss Hardwell?" grinned Tom. "I do hope she'll let that puppy walk once in awhile just to give him some exercise or he'll forget how it's done."

Jean laughed, nodded and looked up at him with smiling eyes. "Tom, you'd better call me Jean. Rescues and puppies certainly earn the right to first names, don't you think?" Jean held out her hand to him and Tom grasped it gently in his and felt a charge of tingles shoot right up his arm. Jean jerked her hand away with a flush on her cheeks and apologized. "I must have built up a charge of electricity walking over Karen's hall rug." She tried to reason away that feeling of contact. Tom abruptly stood up and reached for his coat and hat.

"Maybe, but I don't think that's likely Jean. It will be interesting to see if that's true or not, won't it?" Tom smiled and Jean saw a peculiar light in his eyes. Tom looked intently at her for a few seconds then smiled and walked toward the front door with Jean trailing after him, speechless.

She stood on the porch and watched him drive away. Tom checked his rearview mirror just before the house dropped out of sight and she was still standing there on the porch watching his truck disappear. He smiled and began to hum along to the car's radio.

~Joe and Miracle~

BEN LOOKED ACROSS THE table and watched his boys eating fast as they could to make the school bus on time.

"Here's your breakfast Dad, better eat up before these little piglets get it all." Hannah put the plate in front of Ben and looked closely at him.

Something was on his mind as he said absently. "Thanks honey." Ben slowly began to eat. Hannah walked back to the stove and nudged her mother and with a gesture of her head indicated something wasn't quite right with father.

Mari Beth looked over at Ben for a minute or two then picking up her coffee and went over to the table to sit down beside him. "So Big Man, what's going on?"

Ben looked up. "What? Oh, just this and that I guess you'd say, well, a little more than that actually." Ben sighed and sat his coffee cup down and leaned back in his chair. "We've all been so danged busy what with the fiesta and the fair and all I need to bring everyone up to date on what's been happening. You knew Elroy got out of jail on a fluke after we took off for Huntington and has disappeared. I heard about it when we got back, but I'm not very comfortable with the general opinion that his disappearance is permanent and I've got this gut feeling I can't shake that he'll be back. Elroy is a vindictive man and I can't see him backing away from getting revenge so the men are back on guard at both ranches."

"Drat that man, now I wished I *had* kicked him when he was down." muttered Mari Beth and that got a small smile out of Ben.

"Sheriff Brandt finally told me this morning how Elroy got out. Seems the clerk got his record mixed with a transient in jail for panhandling and Elroy got released instead of the other man. Sheriff Brandt has searched the town and all the towns around and he can't find a trace of him anywhere. If Elroy is smart he'll keep on going, however, I don't think that man is smart enough and I fear once enough time has passed and his fear diminishes he'll be back. I guess it depends on how much he values his own hide. Just in case he's as stupid as I think he is, I want everyone to be on their toes and on guard." Joe and Mike looked at each other then down at their half-eaten breakfast and suddenly lost their appetites.

"That clerk was Corry, wasn't it? I really think it's time Max retires her honorably and hire someone who is just a bit younger and sharper. After all Corry is pushing 76 this year and hasn't been in the best of health lately. Eat your breakfast boys, you'll have to step on it to make the bus." reminded Mari Beth calmly.

"I'm not so hungry anymore Mari Beth and if it's alright with you, I'll go brush my teeth and be ready for Hannah to run us down the road." Joe pushed his chair away from the table and left the kitchen.

"Yeah, guess I'm ready for that tooth brushing myself." Mike got up and followed Joe.

"Why couldn't you have waited until after they'd finished eating to tell us the bad news?" asked Mari Beth in a disgusted way.

"Yeah, bad news does have a way of upsetting stomachs and my appetite is gone too. Sorry love, poor timing and maybe you can just blame it on worry." Ben shoved back from the table and put on his hat and coat as he left the kitchen.

"*Blast that Elroy*! May he have the itch something *fierce* in a place he can't reach to scratch it." Mari Beth gathered up the dishes and banged around in the kitchen venting her anger and worry at the same time.

Hannah drove the boys to the County Road and while they sat waiting for the bus Hannah said. "Luther called last night and wanted you to come down after school today Joe. Seems he's got a mare that may give him a lot of trouble and Lute thinks you can help ease her some."

"Sure I'd be glad to and maybe I can ride the bus back with Jack?"

"Sure you can. I'll have mom call the school and give her permission and I'll come pick you up if Luther can't get away. I'll be here to get you Mike because I know you have things to do this afternoon."

The boys jumped out of the truck as the bus came into view. As far as Mike and Joe were concerned the bus ride was time they could spend reading, doing homework or Mike entertaining the kids with his guitar. This morning it was a job not to worry about the disappearance of their archenemy.

School was an unending joy to the boys for the most part because this school was…friendly, inspiring the students to excel and of course the teachers made all the difference. Mike and Joe, both intelligent boys, zipped ahead and had no problem being on the honor roll. Mike had joined the school band, but that was the extent of his school activities. Once a week he and Joe had music lessons in town then Hannah or Mari Beth drove in to pick them up at five o'clock. By January Mike would be able to drive a pickup to school and save the others from having to fetch and carry them and Mike was really looking forward to that freedom.

On the bus that afternoon, Joe and Mike got their homework done except for the extra reading that they could do in the evening. The other kids who rode with them had caught on and liked having all the free time at home. That made points with the bus driver as it made a quieter ride for him.

Jacko was there to take Mike home. "Have a good time Joe and I hope the mare and foal do well." Picking up Joe's school pack Mike stepped down from the bus and climbed into the pickup with the cowboy.

When Jack and Joe got off the bus they were met by Little Brown. "Hey Brown has the mare delivered her baby yet? Am I in time?" asked Joe and Jack climbed into the ranch pickup.

"She's close, but you made it in time Joe. Can't do without your help buddy 'cause she's having a bit of a problem that's why I'm driving fast to get you there." Fast it was too. They pulled into the ranch yard and parked close to the barn and both boys piled out and dashed for the barn door.

Jack leaned on the half door of the stall and watched the action happening within the foaling stall and listened to Joe as he sang and stroked the mare's head in his lap. Dr. Hennesey was muttering and working on getting the foal straightened out so it could be born and he purely hated these breach births, they were so chancy.

This was one of the mares that Luther had had problems with once before and the mare hadn't given birth easily then either. This was the last one for her because she was too valuable a horse to risk again. It was going to be nip and tuck as to whether they could save either one. Luther didn't want to tell Joe this and he was sorry now he'd asked the kid to come down because it would go hard on him if they lost the baby let alone the mare. Dr. Grant had brought along one of the new vets he had hired, Dr. Nancy Anne Ransom, a seriously cute, petite woman who was watching the whole process.

"All right I've got a hold on the foal, now Luther grab hold of this rope and let's pull; she isn't going to be able to do this herself. This is one mighty big baby and Susie Q is just about out of strength. Keep her quiet Joe, this is important, I don't want her to fight me just now. Now pull Luther!"

Joe focused his attention on the exhausted mare and sang to her in an almost hypnotic way that had the mare half in a doze until the men began to pull the foal out of her. Then she tried to rear up her head as though to stand away from the pain.

Joe sang softly "No, no, sweet momma, stay still just another few minutes, stay still and just let go and you'll have the prettiest baby ever. Listen to old Joe, sweet momma, just relax and give us your baby." and so on, singing soft words had the mare flopped her head down again and appeared to be half unconscious that scared him white as he watched the men at work.

Finally Joe heard the vet exclaim. "I've gotcha' baby. Lordy, Lordy, get to work on him, he's not breathing." Grant said as he quickly cleared away the film on the colt's nose and began to breathe into its nostrils. Luther was pushing on its chest in coordination with the vet's breathing. No response as the minutes passed until finally both men sat back and Joe saw the look on their faces of sorrow.

"*No, he's not dead; he's not.* He just hasn't decided to wake up yet." And scrambled over to the quiet colt and grabbed its head and gave it a hard shake. "*Wake up now, do you hear me. I said WAKE UP.*" And put his mouth on the baby's nose and breathed hard into him. Again and again Joe worked with such total focus he wasn't even hearing Luther or Grant telling him to stop, nor felt them trying to separate him from the colt.

Joe vaguely heard the woman vet saying firmly, "Leave him alone, he knows something you two don't; give him a few minutes more." and Joe was conscious that the woman was down on her knees pumping on the colt's chest in coordination with Joe as he continued to breathe hard into the foal's nostrils. It seemed like Joe worked for a long time when in fact it was only three minutes when suddenly the colt heaved a big inward breath and opened his eyes and looked right into Joe's eyes and cough stuff out of his mouth.

"That's my boy, that's my beauty. Look at you, aren't you a wonder and your momma is going to be so happy to see you." Joe laughed as he stroked the little guy's head.

Dr. Ransom said, "See? I told you guys the kid knew something you didn't. Learn to pay attention gentleman, you almost lost a colt because you didn't believe in miracles." Grant looked at Luther with a long suffering "see what I have to put up with now?" kind of look, but he was relieved that the foal lived.

Luther just laughed and slapped his friend on the shoulder and said, "She's right and we were wrong, I can live with that." and Grant had to laugh too. The mare weakly raised her head, but was too tired to get up right away. While Joe and Dr. Ransom worked on the colt, Luther and Grant with Jack's help wiped the mare down with warm wet cloths then covering her with a blanket then gave her water followed by a hot mash. It wasn't long before the little colt was standing on wavering legs and Luther had gotten Susie Q on her feet at last.

As they watched the colt nurse, Joe suddenly broke down in tears and Luther held him tightly against his side as the boy sobbed then he reached out to gather Jack into his embrace too. Holding the two boys while they dealt with the drama of it all, Luther knew what it must feel like to have sons and daughters and he was surprised how the sudden hunger for children rose up and bit him hard.

"When you stopped working on him it just broke my heart because he was supposed to live; I *knew* he was supposed to live." It took awhile for Joe to settle down and by that time the colt had collapsed on the straw and was peacefully asleep undisturbed by the emotions that surrounded him.

"Look at him sleep as though he didn't have a care in the world. Isn't he a handsome one Jack? Now, what are you going to name him Joe?" As a distraction, it worked. Sniffing and wiping his face with his sleeve Joe took the handkerchief that Luther handed him, wiped his eyes and gave his nose a healthy blow. He figured he was going to have to start carrying his own handkerchief if these events kept happening. Then thoughtfully handed it to Jack who gave it a similar treatment then Jack courteously handed it back to Luther who took it cautiously and decided to place it on the stall door and collect it later.

For a few minutes Joe just stood there with his chin resting on the stall door and watched the colt sleep. "Well Luther, there is only one name for him and that's Miracle, what do you think?" and looked up at the man.

"I couldn't have chosen a better or a more fitting name for him. What do you say Jack?" turning to the silent boy who'd watched the life and death struggle and had wept too.

"Like you said Mr. Strongbow, it's a miracle he lived so Miracle is the perfect name. I like it which means he's going to grow up to be a fine horse. But another miracle is Joe 'cause he's a real healer, isn't he?" Luther raised his eyebrows at these many words from a usually quiet boy. He noticed that Jack wasn't moving away from under his arm either.

"Okay Miracle it is then. Alright boys let's let momma and baby sleep. We've got a good man in Sketter and he'll keep an eye on them. Dr. Grant and Dr. Ransom say the colt is in fine health despite the long time to get him awake. Actually it was five minutes and that is really pushing the clock of survival. Yes indeed, a miracle baby for sure. Okay guys and Lady let's go see what Miss Golight has for dinner."

Dr. Grant and Dr. Ransom led the way out of the barn talking in a rapid exchange while Luther watched and he thought he saw some interesting vibrations pass between the two vets. Now wouldn't that relationship be something interesting to keep his eye on. Luther and the two boys followed along through the chill of early evening.

Dinner was wonderful and the conversation involving the news about the country and what they had been doing since they last saw each other. "At last I've finally gotten myself some help. The other vet, Dr. Paul Gilbert, is just out of Veterinarian School and has graduated with honors. He's going to need some overseeing, but seems to love the versatility of the job. Dr. Nancy here is sure fire good with any animal and I'm still in awe of how easily she handles the big critters as well as the small ones. It must be her charming personality." Grant said laughing as he poked Nancy a little.

"Personality aside my dear Dr. Hennesey, it is sheer talent and empathy that gets the job done. I'm going to be you're greatest asset." laughed the small woman right back.

"Hmm, well that could be doc, that could be." they eyed each other until they became conscious that the table was silent and everyone was watching them.

"Say, are you two in love and going to get married soon?" asked Joe bluntly.

"What? Goodness Joe where did you get that idea." exclaimed Nancy, blushing like fire. Of course, it matched her deep auburn hair and made the others struggle not to laugh at this poor lady's embarrassment.

"Actually Joe, that has some merit as an observation. However, it is never wise to burst out with such candid words before the people in question have decided what's going on themselves." said Dr. Hennesey in a rather pompous tone of voice all the while trying desperately not to break apart at this boy's insightfulness.

Joe looked bemused for a bit then grinned. He'd caught enough of the meaning to understand he'd made a big boo-boo. "I'm sorry I'm just a kid and I don't know much about adults and the way they like to hide their feelings. I guess you'll figure things out without my help." and quickly went back to talking to Jack in hushed tones and was startled at the hilarious outburst that followed. He laughed along, but not sure what everyone was laughing about. Adults sure were funny and awfully complicated.

"Ah Luther, can I talk to you before I go? It's kinda' important you see." whispered Joe underneath the other on going conversations.

"Sure Joe." Glancing at his watch Luther saw it was going on eight o'clock and time Joe was going home. "Excuse us folks for a few minutes, Joe and I have some business to discuss." Just like that Luther eased them away from the table and walked down the hall to his office. "What's on your mind Joe." he said as he sat down in one of his rockers. Joe took the other one and clasped his hands.

"I guess I need to know if you've found our father's horse, Beau."

Luther slapped his forehead. "I knew there was something I was going to tell you before all this trouble with Susie Q came up."

Luther got up and went behind his desk to pick up the email he had received three days ago. He should have called his Dad about the success of his dickering, but he'd been up to his eyeballs in new foals, and just plain fourteen hour days. "Yep, here it is and good news and a done deal too. I bought Beau from his owner, a Mr. Kent Wood of Lubbock, Texas. The price was pretty steep, not too much for a trained, experienced cutting horse however, I'm just glad he didn't know how much we would have paid. Now that I think about it maybe he did. It took some talking to get Mr. Wood to release Beau because he really liked the horse. However, when he heard about you guys and how you had been forced to sell Beau well, he's a softy so he agreed. Does this answer your question?" Luther said with serious look that belied the twinkling eyes. Just to see the shinning face of this special child was worth all the hours of searching and dealing he had put in on this project and then some.

"Oh boy Luther does it ever. Geeze peeze, Mike is going to fly over the moon. When do you think Beau will get here?"

"According to Mr. Woods he planned to leave this week and possibly did on Monday or Tuesday latest. It is now Wednesday so he should be here in the next few days if all goes well with the trip. That trip was an added expense, but what the heck your ranch is going to reimburse me."

"Thanks Luther I knew you could do it. I'm ever so glad Beau is going to come home to us at last." If Joe leaked a few tears Luther ignored them, after all the kid looked like he had been put through an old fashioned wringer.

"Come on Joe you're all tired out. I'll call Hannah and tell her I'm bringing you home, but not before you eat the best dessert you ever put in your mouth." helping the boy out of the chair.

Back in the kitchen Joe went up to Miss Golight. "Hannah is a very good cook, but so are you, Miss Golight, just different and different is good, isn't it? Can Jack come up to my place sometime and play with me? I can show him my horse Jigger and we can ride horses and other stuff."

"Thank you for the compliment Joe. You'll have to ask Jack if he wants to go up to your place." Amber smiled as she served hot peach cobbler with ice cream to everyone. Luther was right this dessert was out of sight.

"Jack, do you want to come up this Saturday? I'm sure it will be okay with Ben. If the weather isn't nasty we can ride our horses over to our ranch and I can show you around. Ben put in a gate between our properties as sort of a short cut."

"I'd like to do that Joe and it sounds like fun." With that acceptance Jack took another step out of his withdrawal. Amber watched the small transformation and breathed a sigh of relief at this normal sign that Jack was healing at last.

"Maybe I can get Nino to come over from Mr. Lightfoot's place too. I'd like you to get to know him Jack, he's a nice kid, but awfully lost you know. We could help him feel more at home sort of and I figure a guy can't have too many friends, can he?" speaking with his mouth full of this delicious cobbler.

"No I guess not." Jack followed Joe's example and ate his dessert. Luther watched the boys' interaction than looked over at Amber sitting across from him and saw her smiling at the boys. Melanie observed Luther looking at her aunt with a "male sees female." It gave her a funny feeling of aloneness.

"Listen up ladies as I've got a proposition for you. I've got some horses I need to have exercised as their getting mighty frisky. Two of the mares are going to new owners at the end of next week and I want them suitably calmed down before then. I thought we'd ride up Thunder River and maybe have a picnic along the way if the weather is nice, that is." Luther looked over at the two women and waited.

"That's sounds wonderful, Mr. Strongbow. I've enjoyed riding ever since I've been here. Doesn't it sound like fun Amber?" Melanie looked anxious for Amber's acceptance.

"Couldn't think of anything I'd rather do. We'll make a picnic that will have Mr. Strongbow's eyes cross." laughed Amber.

"Hey don't leave us out of this treat, we can ride too. That is if I don't have any emergencies. Personally, I need to get back to riding again so I'm going to horn in on this proposition and ride my new horse. He's been missing me I'm sure. What about you Nancy, want to come along?" Grant asked. "Or don't you ride?"

Nancy took a sip of her coffee before slanting a look at her partner. "My, there's such a lot you don't know about me Doctor Hennesey, isn't there? I was All State Champion Barrel Racer a few years ago. I don't think I've forgotten how to ride."

"Now aren't you a surprise." And weren't the looks flashing between the two vets simply fascinating and had the other adults mesmerized for a few minutes.

Luther cleared his throat and said. "You'll both be welcomed and we'll have a fine time. I can always use extra hands exercising the horses." Luther grinned agreeably at his friend and his lady vet. Anyway you want to call it Grant was interested in his new partner and vice versa.

"So we have to earn our entrance fee to get into this trip, huh? The picnic basket should be a grand reward with Miss Golight's cooking." smiled Grant as Amber laughed.

"Whatever Mr. Strongbow wants, Mr. Strongbow gets as he's the boss, after all. It should be a great adventure." said Amber.

"I may be a veterinarian, but I also cook. I shall add my own little contribution to the picnic Ms. Golight, and we'll see if you like it. It's simply an appetizer served with a cold wine."

"Well Dr. Ransom, we must get out heads together over this presentation. I'm curious about what you are going to bring. Mind calling tomorrow to tell me? We'll have these men's tongues hanging out." smiled Amber.

"Not at all Ms Golight," smiled Nancy and the three women drifted across the kitchen and three heads converged.

"It looks like we are going to have one of those so called gourmet picnics Grant. I guess we can suffer though it, being that we're such big men and all." Luther sighed dramatically.

"Never underestimate the ladies is what I always say and don't undersell us either or our capacity to put away the goodies. It's a date Luther."

"Ladies and gentleman, if we're going to be friends I guess everyone had better go by their first names. No way am I going to continue this Miss Amber, Miss Melanie and Dr. Ransom stuff. We're friends now." Luther said emphatically.

"And you young lady," Luther pointed a finger at Melanie, "I'm paying you for helping exercise and groom my horses and you too Jack. Lordy children, I don't have enough time to give a good work out on some of my horses and I sure appreciate the help you've already given me. Melanie I know you have your art lessons in town and you are busy helping Amber, but I've noticed what you've done already so expect a nice check. You tell me the days or the hours you'd be available and we'll work around that. Jack it's about time I gave you your own horses to work with too and a personal mount as well. Can't have the Kelly boys lording it over you now, can I?" Luther took a long last drink of his coffee and stood up and was please that the Golight children's mouths were still open. "Come on Joe time to get rolling."

"I guess we'd better go too. There's no peace for the wicked or rest for the weary or so I hear. Thank you for dinner Amber and I for one look forward to the picnic on Saturday and we'll be there if the Lord's willing and the phone don't ring."

Grant picked up Amber's hand and kissed it gallantly to the astonishment of the two boys. What really set them off is when Doctor Grant did the same with Melanie. It was funny to the boys to see her blush. Dr. Nancy just laughed at his gallantry.

"You're most welcome Grant please come again." said Amber. Luther frowned as he watched the performance. Was Grant flirting with his chef? It looked like it and he didn't like it; no indeed, he didn't like it one bit. Ah, he must be mistaken because Nancy was right there and smiling up at the gallant vet. Luther saw him help her into her coat then take her hand. Well, old G.H. wouldn't trespass on another man's girl. Luther stopped short, shocked at his thoughts. His next immediate and uncontrolled thought was thank God Nancy was now in the picture. Good Lord, what was *happening* to him?

"Thank you Amber it was a wonderful dinner. I wished I could cook like that." Nancy shook Amber's hand.

"Don't forget to call, Nancy and we'll figure out a killer menu." laughed Amber.

"And we'll suffer like true men giving our all for the cause." Grant sighed and patted his heart.

Luther cleared his throat and said. "Come on Jack let's take Joe home before his face falls into that very empty dish. It was a great dinner as usual Amber. I declare I've put on twelve pounds since you started cooking and the boys are complaining they can't get into their jeans any more. I won't fire you because I really want to live to be an old man. Guess I'll just work them harder. Come on boys hustle it up."

As they were putting on their coats Luther remembered something. "Oh Amber, would you please call Hannah and tell her I'm bringing Joe home?" she nodded. "Thanks."

"Thank you Miss Golight for the great dinner, I can't wait to tell Hannah what we had for supper." Joe followed Luther and the others out the door.

In the truck the boys talked a bit about school and their own plans for a picnic.

"Hannah will fix us some fried chicken and such 'cause I'll ask her too. If Mike goes with us there will be four of us so we'll need lots of food. Hannah is a very great cook too." He said loyally and meant every word. By the time Luther dropped Joe off it was pushing nine o'clock.

"Night Luther I'm so happy the colt lived. Night Jack, see you in the morning." Joe went in through the kitchen door as Luther turned the truck around and disappeared down the road.

"How did it go Joe?" asked Hannah sitting at the table with a cup of coffee.

Joe gave a big yawn and slapped a hand over his mouth. "Sorry Hannah that just snuck up on me." Joe slumped down into a kitchen chair. "It was pretty hard and scary. Susie Q, that's the mare's name, was awfully tired and couldn't give birth. Dr. Grant and Luther had to pull the foal out. The foal wouldn't breathe no matter what they did. I just panicked 'cause that colt wasn't breathing. Did I tell you it was a boy horse? I knew that colt was supposed to live so I yelled at it, grabbed his nose and breathed really hard lots of times and he lived. I was so surprised that he actually lived. Honest Hannah, I was so happy because he is a miracle for sure." Joe yawned again.

"I'm so glad you saved him Joe and Luther must be mighty happy you did too. What did Luther name him?" Asked Hannah as she took him under the arm and encouraged him to get up and led him toward the stairs.

"I got to name him 'cause Luther said I saved him, so I called him Miracle and that's what he is, a really live miracle right there in the barn." Hannah stopped Joe at his bedroom door and gave him a hug.

"You did just fine Joe and I'm so proud of you. Now you get to bed as tomorrow's a school day and it coming on mighty fast. Goodnight son sleep well." she kissed him on his forehead and gave his hair a gentle stoke with her hand.

"Oh, I forgot to tell you. A kid got really sick in class today and threw up all over the place so we got to go to the library for an hour. I got this great book on "The Great Singers of the Twentieth Century; neat, huh? What do you know about this Julliard School?"

"I know it's a special school to train singers, musical students and all the truly gifted people. It's the best artistic school in the country or so they say. Maybe one day you'll go there Joe or to one of the other affiliated music schools that are equally good." smiled Hannah.

"Yeah maybe," Joe said pensively, "but not right now Hannah, not right now. I don't have to leave home yet do I?" Joe asked anxiously.

"Heavens no Joe, goodness what would we do without you? Besides I think you have to be older like fifteen or sixteen or so. I tell you what we'll do; we'll go to the town library one night and do a little research. There might be other schools of music closer to home. It will be our own little secret."

"Yeah that would be okay and then I'd really know what I would have to do to get into their school. I 'spect it will be a hard thing to do and maybe I won't be good enough. What do you think, Hannah, would I be good enough to be let in?"

"You'd be good enough for any musical school Joe. Why you've got the gift and you just keep on with your music lessons here and one day you will be more than ready and willing to take off and experience greater learning." reassured Hannah.

"Okay if you think so. I guess I don't have to worry about it just yet then. Anyway I'm pretty happy with Mrs. Rainbird. She's very good only it's a little boring right now with the breathing exercises and doing scales. She said it was all about foundation, whatever that is. Oh, she wants me to take piano lessons too and I forgot to ask Mike if he could get the ranch to buy a piano for me. Are they awfully expensive?"

"One thing at a time Joe, you're firing off questions faster than I can answer them. Breathing and scales is the foundation necessary for any great singer. It builds control and strengthens the diaphragm and trains the voice. Why I read that great singers do scales every day to limber their voices. So if you want to be a great singer, you have to be able to breathe right. As far as the piano is concerned I think we can find one without any problem. Now shut down that mind of yours and go to bed. Goodnight and sleep well."

    Joe went in and closed his door. He didn't mind Hannah hugging and kissing him if no one else was around to see. Joe yawned fit to break his jaw as he undressed and tossed his clothes on the chair. Pulling on his nightshirt, he crawled gratefully between the flannel sheets and pulling his comforter up tightly around his neck was soon fast asleep.

~Beau Comes Home~

MIKE AND JOE GOT off the bus Friday afternoon and climbed into the pickup waiting for them at the end of their road. "Hi Jacko, how come you're here to pick us up instead of Hannah?" asked Joe.

"She's mighty busy helping Mrs. Strongbow with her new project. Y'all know what that is so I stuck my hand up in the air and volunteered and here I am."

Jacko winked at them and whipped the pickup around and took off just like he was on a fast running horse. Yep, there was no wasting around when you were with this cowboy. "So how was school today, guys?"

"Not bad, just kinda' so-so, but it's Friday so we've got the whole weekend to do stuff. I expect Mike and I will be going over to help Hank with this and that on Sunday. I just fetch and carry mostly. If weather looks good tomorrow we're having our ride and picnic and that takes care of Saturday." Joe was rambling all the time thinking about his secret writing project with Hannah.

"Ah, has anything new happened since this morning Jacko?" The cowboy looked down at Joe and raised his eyebrows then glanced quickly over at Mike and saw him looking out the window and the horses racing the truck and smiling.

He winked at Joe and nodded. "Mostly just the routine stuff, you know." Joe just about came unglued though he manfully tucked his chin into his collar and turned his face away from his brother for a few minutes.

As they drove into the ranch yard they saw the strange trailer parked by the barn door. "Has someone delivered a mare for Suncatcher?" Mike asked.

"Gee I don't know Mike it passed me while I was driving down for you guys. Maybe you'd better go check it out." The boys were greeted by an enthusiastic Roscoe and Mike had to spend a few minutes renewing the friendship before setting his book pack on the porch beside Joe's. They entered the barn and walked back to where Ben was leaning against a stall door with a stranger.

As the boys walked up Ben turned around and smiled. "Hey Mike, look at this beauty that just got delivered." and stepped aside for Mike to move up closer.

Just then a nice shaped gray head appeared over the door with a loud welcoming whinny. The sight of the horse stopped Mike dead in his tracks. "*Beau? Beau*? Oh my gosh it's Dad's horse, Beau. Joe, its Beau." he cried in a broken voice and the men laughed softly and Ben hit Mike a little whack on the back.

Joe was just as happy to see this big horse again too. To Joe it was a special moment to be part of this wonderful surprise that had ever been sprung on his brother. Joe wept too just like Mike was doing as he watched his brother hug the horse's head. Beau whiffed Mike's shirt and made funny noises in his throat.

"Come on into the house Kent and have some coffee." Ben said to the older man. "You'll be staying the night or for as long as you like. That was a long drive so you'll need your rest before heading back, I suspect. Besides, I've got some beautiful quarter horses here and you just might find one or two you'll like." Ben threw his arm around Joe's shoulders and guided them all out the door leaving Mike to commune with his horse.

Joe looked back to see Mike open the stall door and close it behind him. Even while tears streamed down his own face it did his heart good to share in giving something really important to Mike who gave so much of himself to others. Joe sniffed and wiped his face on his sleeve and Ben's arm tightened. A white handkerchief appeared in front of his eyes all the while Ben kept on talking to the stranger.

"I must say Ben, I was reluctant to part with that horse, but seeing these young men's reaction, well I'm glad I did." said the quiet man. "Children should have something that connects them to their father."

"You did a fine, fine thing, Kent. Yes, that horse is important to the boys to say the least." replied Ben.

They entered the kitchen where Ben introduced the man to Mari Beth and Hannah. Under the cover of conversation Joe slipped away and ran up to his room and fell on his bed and cried. He had his memories of being carried in front of his father on long gallops and going like the wind with lots of laughter.

Joe heard the door open and close quietly then someone sat down beside him on the bed and a hand rubbed his back. Joe knew it was Hannah 'cause he could smell her special fragrance.

"You helped give a wonderful gift to Mike, Joe. I know it makes you feel both sad and happy at the same time because you have something that belonged to your father and Beau is that link to those good memories. Your dad would be so happy to see Beau back with you two."

"I know, Hannah, it's just.......I *miss him so much*......I can't tell you how much I miss my Dad and Mom.... Seeing Beau just opened it all up again." Joe sobbed like his heart was breaking. She gathered him into her arms, walked over to the padded rocking chair and sat down and held him while he cried. Maybe now the grief would become softer, Hannah thought as she rocked him until he became quiet.

Sniffing and using Ben's handkerchief gave his nose a good blow and sat up and Hannah let go. "Thanks Hannah, I'm mostly okay now." he took a couple of shuddering breaths and mopped up once more. "I think I'll go out and see if Mike's okay. He doesn't have anyone to comfort him right now."

"Sure he does Joe, he's got Beau and you'll see when Mike comes in the house with red eyes that he'll be really happy. So go wash your face in cold water and come on downstairs and I will fix some special hot chocolate for both of you."

"You'll make your special hot chocolate with secret fixings? Well, okay, I guess I could swallow some." slipping off her lap with a weak grin and went into the bathroom and washed his face.

Sniffing a little Joe took her hand. "You're a good woman Hannah Truelove and you're very special too." Hannah threw her head back and broke into huge gusts of laughter hugged him hard and staggered back to sit abruptly on the edge of the bed dragging Joe down with her and Joe had to laugh at her joy.

When she had caught her breath she had to borrow the Joe's handkerchief to wipe her cheeks free of tears. "Okay, I'm fine now." she gave a few more watery chuckles. "So let's let this good woman take you downstairs and see what we can treat ourselves to since you're a very good man as well, Joseph Devereaux Kelly."

Out in the barn Mike was grooming Beau which was totally unnecessary as the horse gleamed like a polished sheet of gray and black speckled tile. Grooming, talking, and stroking were all ways of communicating his love for this special horse.

"Sure sorry to have cried all over you Beau, but it was such a surprise. I told Luther to start looking for you, but I thought it would take months and months to find you." as he brushed the already smooth side. Beau whickered once in awhile as though joining in the conversation; a trick he'd always had with dad.

"Yeah, you're here just where you belong and you've make this all near perfect now. You're home with us and you'll never go to strangers again. Maybe next year we'll compete in the roping, how would you like that?"

Once Mike had settled down and finished fussing around the horse he closed the stall door and just watched the animal snoozing in comfort. It felt like a closure of sorts and having Beau back also felt like a continuance. A part of his father's love was here in this horse and in a strange way having Beau here comforted some grieving corner of his heart.

The sound of the dinner bell woke him as to how long he had been leaning on Beau's stall. It was time to go in and thank Mr. Kent for the safe delivery of his horse. Mike heaved a deep sigh of contentment. "Goodnight Beau, you rest well and we'll go for a nice ride tomorrow, just you and me and the country."

Mike watched the snoozing horse for another minute when a sudden memory popped in. "Well shoot, I forgot the picnic. Oh well, they'll all have a special treat seeing what a really good horse looks like. Oh not that Sherlock isn't a fine, fine horse, because he is, but you have a special place in my heart."

He entered the kitchen to the sound of conversations and laughter and good smells of dinner. Joe was entertaining the stranger who just laughed and listened like he had always known Joe. Well, not too many people didn't feel that way around his brother.

Joe looked up and red eyes met red eyes and they both grinned. Maybe a little more healing had taken place for both of them. Whatever they called it, it felt mighty good.

"Wash up everyone dinner is about to be put on the table."

The next morning the boys were saddling up for a day's ride. Fortunately it was going to be a fine Indian Summer Day, just brisk enough to make the ride invigorating.

"Beau, we're going for our ride and celebrate your arrival. Just like old times boy, just like old times." Mike finished harnessing the big horse and led him outside to join the others lined up along the corral fence.

"Ready to go guys?" asked Mike.

"We've got the picnic bags all strapped on. Geeze peeze, Beau looks good, doesn't he?" admired Joe and moved over to stroke the soft gray nose.

Beau snorted and rubbed his head up and down Joe's jacket in greeting. "Yeah, you remember me don't you big guy?" Gee, it's super to have him back, thought Joe and turned his back to his friends so they wouldn't see the tears.

Mike walked up behind Joe and gave him a pat on the shoulder. "Great isn't it?"

"Yeah it's really great. It kinda helps in a funny way to have him here, you know what I mean?"

"Sure I do and that's exactly how I feel too. It's just like having a bit of Dad back. I'm really sorry we couldn't find Mom's Molly, but it's been too long now and I don't have any way of tracing her. I just hope she's okay."

"We did what we could and I guess that's all we can be expect to do." sighed Joe giving Beau a last pat before turning back to Jigger.

"All right gang, let's mount up and get this show on the road." Mike said and swung up on Beau's back. The day sped by and Mike guessed that was the way it always was when you were having a good time. It wasn't until late afternoon and dusk was beginning to settle over the land that they made it back to the ranch.

Nino and Jack were going to be staying overnight so getting washed up created a lot of laughter and general noise.

They were all seated at the table which had been extended to accommodate the company when Mr. Wood asked Mike, "How did the ride go?"

Mike grinned, "It couldn't have been better Sir. It was pure-d joy to be riding Beau again. I can't thank you enough for giving him up because it's meant the world to Joe and me to have Dad's horse back home." Mike frantically tried to think of something else to say to the stranger. "Ah, Ben has some prime quarter horses you might like to look over and maybe take one back with you."

"Yes he does and yes I'm taking the one called Marky. Do you know the one I mean?" asked Mr. Wood as he took the bowl of mashed potatoes from Hannah.

"You're taking Marky?" Mike looked shocked. "Oh well, Marky is a favorite around here and he's one of the top quarter horses we've got. I'm just surprised Ben's willing to part with him. Well, that's a surprise for sure. Marky is one fine horse and you won't go wrong with him." Mike looked over at Ben as though to say, "How could you?"

"Marky is ready for the bigger world Mike. Mr. Wood is entering him in all kinds of competition down in Texas and will treat him well. I don't need another stallion here either since we have Beau. It makes for difficulties if I keep to many stallions and Beau will soon be going over to your place so that won't be a problem. Marky needs his own place and make his mark. He's too good a horse not to let him find his own success."

"Sure Ben, whatever you say, I just hadn't thought of Marky's future that way."

Mike looked across the table and said earnestly, "Mr. Wood maybe you'll write to us and let us know how Marky performs because we'd be really interested."

"Sure I will and I expect great things from that horse and you can be assured I treat my horses very well. I guess you know that from the condition of Beau. Marky will have a good home on my Circle KW."

The next morning the family said goodbye to Marky as he was loaded up and a final farewell to Mr. Wood. "You come back anytime and let us know when you get home all safe and sound." said Ben as he shook the man's hand. "Thanks for bringing Beau. You drive safe now."

"I will and it was great to have met y'all. You'll be hearing from me and I might even send a little business your way too. Bye now."

and got into the truck and slowly pulled out of the ranch yard. They stood there, the whole family and watched the truck disappear down the road.

Ben put his arms around the boys' shoulders and shared the heartache of watching a loved horse leave home. "Alright you guys let's get to work. We have chores to finish before church." Ben said gruffly.

Just before entering the barn, Mike cast a last glance down the road and sent a prayer after that big horse. "May life treat you well."

~A Man Comes Calling~

A LARGE RED DUALLY truck with a matching horse trailer turned into the Strongbow's ranch road and stopped at the closed gate.

"Howdy, can I help you, Sir?" said the man holding a shotgun.

The man in the truck raised his eyebrows at this show of protectiveness, but said mildly, "My name's Raven Chalk here to buy some horses from Mr. Strongbow. I'm expected."

"Yes Sir you sure are. Please go right on up and welcome." the man smiled, touched the brim of his hat and stepped back to open the gate. Raven nodded and drove on wondering what they needed a guard for? Raven looked over the land and the well kept wooden fences where a number of sleek horses trotted along the fence keeping pace with the truck.

He grinned. "Yeah, you're beauties all right. Well boys and girls if I'm lucky I'll be taking two or more of you home with me."

Raven Chalk stood 6'6" in his stocking feet and weighed in at 230 when he'd celebrated his 32nd birthday just a month ago. He was also single and planned to stay that way regardless of the pressure his Grandfather was putting on him to marry. He loved his Grandpa, but there was a limit to what a grandson was required to do to keep a grandparent happy. Until the day he found the woman he could happily live with, he'd stay single.

Raven was a big man and didn't have an ounce of fat on him due to an active physical life. He had startling deep blue eyes that contrasted sharply with hair as black as a Raven's wing for which he was named. It waved back from a widow's peak and swept over his ears n to his collar because he kept forgetting to get it cut on a regular basis. The only thing that kept him from being called handsome was his strong boned face that was full of character so he was merely good looking in a masculine way. His only vanity was a small neat mustache, other than that there was very little facial hair thanks to his Indian heritage.

Raven hid a sharp intelligent mind behind his quiet demeanor. He was also a man of few words, however when he did speak his words held meaning. Raven had learned early that his strength could easily hurt people so he held firm control over his temper. Fortunately he possessed a rare sense of humor that colored his whole personality.

He pulled the big truck into the ranch yard to the sound of a dog barking. Turning off his engine he watched the big black and brown dog racing toward him wagging his tail and barking furiously. Hmm, which end do I pay attention too, grinned Raven.

Just then the kitchen door slammed open and a small woman stepped out on the porch and yelled. "Roscoe shut up, now come up here and guard the kitchen." The dog stopped and raced back to the lady and plumped his butt down in front of her expecting a reward for his quick obedience and he got his pat and a laugh, "You nutty dog!"

Raven got out of the truck, shut the door and began walking toward her. The closer he got the funnier he felt and had a sudden vision flash before his eyes of an Indian woman waiting for him outside a teepee with her long black hair blowing in the wind and it stopped him in his tracks. *He knew her!* Shaking his head sharply Raven took a deep breath and admonished himself. This was not the time for visions especially about this woman who might very well turn out to be Ben Strongbow's wife. Now, that could complicate things a bit, he thought humorously.

The pretty woman with the long flowing black hair that was stirred by the slight wind twisted his guts like he'd never experienced before. What was it about long hair that could grab a guy by the throat and make him go all primitive? Raven laughed at himself, it must be caveman stuff.

"Hello and welcome. Sorry about the dog, but he thinks he's a watchdog and tries to impress us now and then. How may I help you?"

Yes indeed Raven thought ruefully, she would have to have a sexy voice and a nice full mouth made for smiling or kissing. *Whoa there boy*, best keep a lid on that thought. "I'm Raven Chalk and I'm looking for Ben Strongbow, is he around?"

"He's over in the maternity barn helping a mare in labor. You can go on down if you want, it's the one in back of the red barn." smiled Hannah.

"Much Obliged Mrs. Strongbow." Raven tipped his hat and as he started to turn away she spoke.

"I'm Ben's daughter, Hannah Truelove Strongbow." said the soft voice. Raven stopped and looked back at her to see her smiling. She was not too small and nicely rounded in all the right places and she was lovely in a quiet gentle way. Of course, all that long, long black hair didn't hurt either. I think I'm in big, huge trouble, he thought soberly, but managed to grin at her.

"Well, I'm very glad to hear that *Miss* Strongbow because I was thinking thoughts a man shouldn't have about another man's wife, so I'm doubly glad to meet you, Hannah Truelove Strongbow, daughter." Tipping his hat with a bow and a smile, Raven started walking toward the barn leaving Hannah more or less with her mouth open.

"My goodness gracious me, now what do you make of that man, Roscoe? Oh I wish mother was here, she'd know. Humph, he's probably just a practiced flirt." Yet she couldn't help standing there with her heart doing dye-dos as he walked away. "Come on in boy and I'll give you that bone I saved for you." She went inside with only one backward glance.

Raven stood for a few minutes in the doorway of the barn and looked around. What he saw was a spick and span place with large roomy stalls filled with fresh straw. He heard voices coming from the back area so he walked down the central aisle until he came to the stall where a new foal had just arrived in the world.

"Oh yes little boy, aren't you just perfect. Let's get you cleaned up a bit." murmured the big man who was on his knees beside the new baby. Momma horse was already licking her baby and almost knocking it down as it struggled to stand. Raven watched with a quiet joy in his heart as the colt finally found his feet and aimed for his mother's tit with a little help. Ben stood up and took up a wet towel to wipe down his arms and hands. "He'll do now, Brown, and there's your colt as promised, that is if you want this one."

"Yes, I most definitely want him Mr. Strongbow, he's a beauty. He'll be king of the race track, mark my words. I'll take mighty good care of him you can bet your last dollar on that. Thanks just don't cut it, but thanks anyway. I've never had a better present in my whole life." Brown looked to be a man in instant love.

"He's mighty cute with that pretty glossy dark gray color and the four white socks and forehead. What are you going to name him?" At the sound of a stranger's quiet voice had both men whipping their heads around to see a tall man leaning casually on the stall door. "Sorry, my name is Raven Chalk, I called you the other day about looking at some horses you have for sale. I missed the County Fair this year and I'm concerned you might have sold your best mounts, but you assured me you still had a few."

"Hello Mr. Chalk, I'm Ben Strongbow and this young man is Jay Little Brown, other wise known as Brown. In a minute we'll go look at what I've got available."

"Glad to meet you both. I've heard about Midnight Racer and the race at Huntington. Is this one of that new breeding of yours?"

"Yes he is. Brown rode the Racer and won by four lengths. We're sort of experimenting with quarter horse mares and my Morgan/Thoroughbred stallion, Suncatcher.

If the rest of these colts and fillies prove to be equally fast, smart and talented it should prove to be very interesting. This little fellow is one of the newest ones and Brown here is the happy owner and will help us with his training and proving up." Ben grinned over at the glowing face of Brown.

"It sure sounds interesting and I'm always looking to improve the horse breed. What are you going to name him Mr. Brown?" asked Raven.

"I should get Joe to help me with that one because he's really good at finding just the right names for these little ones, but I'll think about on it." Brown said, not looking away from the colt now sleeping beside his mother.

"Geeze peeze Brown, all you had to do was ask." said a quiet, breathless voice. "Darn if I didn't miss out on this. The bus was late getting started because Jack couldn't find his book bag. Golly isn't he the handsomest boy? Do you really want me to help you find a name for your colt?"

"Sure, Joe you're real good at nailing the perfect one." replied Brown.

"Thanks Brown, well dang if he isn't just down right beautiful, of course they all are, aren't they?" Joe seemed to go into a brown study for a few minutes and the men just had to smile at the serious boy.

Joe suddenly said, "Hah, I've got two names, Cloud Chaser is one and Thunder Horse is another. Doesn't he look like a dark thunder cloud, fast and powerful and full of go? If you don't like either of those I'm sure you'll pick a name that's just perfect." Joe peered over the top of the stall door.

Brown listened then contemplated the small horse and the potential he held within him. A Power name would help the colt live up to expectations. "His name is Thunder Horse and he'll be fast, steady, all heart and speed. He'll be the best of the breed, all that is good and a horse with kindness in his great heart; my horse."

"My, oh my, I can't wait to see him grow and live up to his name. Yeah, he's going to make tracks in the world for sure." said Joe enthusiastically.

"It's time to settle the new one in a clean stall. Julep will you and Joe help Brown while I take care of Mr. Chalk?" asked Ben as he stepped out of the stall.

"Sure thing boss, come on Brown let's get these two cleaned up and settled."

"Mr. Chalk, are you looking for young ones or trained horses?" Ben took the man's arm and led him out of the barn.

"Now that I've seen that little guy, I'd like to see Suncatcher before I make up my mind and please call me Raven."

"I'm always pleased to show Suncatcher off for he's a great horse and not a mean bone in his big body which is rare in stallions. I won't have a mean horse on the property. That's one of the great genes that he passes down to his offspring; gentleness with lots of fire and spirit. The mares are special too with more of the same great heart. Here's the big barn though he's probably out in his paddock. Let's go around the back and check."

Ben led the way until they came to a huge enclosure, more pasture than enclosure, and the men climbed through the fence. Ben gave a piercing whistle and a big light colored horse came running out of the trees at the other end. Swiftly the horse moved toward the men and straight up to Ben before putting on the brakes kicking dirt over Ben's boots as he slid to a halt, snorting the big horse put his nose in Ben's face and whiffed his hair and began searching his jacket for his treat.

While Raven admired the gorgeous horse Ben laughed and talked to the animal and pulled a few carrots out of his coat pocket. "There

True Heart

you go you greedy thing." As the horse crunched away Ben said. "He was a small two month old colt when I bought him over Tennessee way and it was the best purchase I ever made. You see, the owner was a mite upset when he discovered his Thoroughbred Mare had jumped the fence and had gotten mixed up with a Morgan/English Bred stallion and he didn't want the colt. He was so angry he told me he was going to shoot him. Can you *imagine* a man doing such a rotten thing? I wasn't about to let that happen so he sold him to me for a song when I offered for him. He even gave me papers on him and then had the audacity to say I saved him the cost of a bullet. I almost clobbered the stupid man. He was no judge of horses and he lost out on a great one. I had to put him with a mare who'd had just lost her foal so he didn't miss out on any feedings and fortunately the mare didn't object to the substitute. Suncatcher has won his fair share of races up and down the country; three quarter mile and the mile as well. He likes to come from behind and when he does that he simply blows right by the other horses like they were standing still. I've earned so much money that the cost of buying him has long been forgotten. So now he has a rep and his stud fees are high and he's responsible for the development of this new breeding too. Yep, the Gods were smiling on me that day."

"That speaks well for your sagacity Mr. Strongbow. He is truly a magnificent horse. Now that I've seen him could I see what his progeny looks like?"

"Sure you can however, you can bet I'm not letting any of them go just yet. Except for Brown who works for my son Luther, but he's in on our program and he'll ride them in the races too. After all, this breeding is still in the experimental stage. I have my son helping me as well as my adoptive son Mike, really my guardian child, but labels are just nit picking; he's my boy. You've met Joe and he's brother to Mike. They own the Lost Wagon Ranch next door. Luther and I are going to use Mike's place as the breeding farm because Mike isn't into specific horse breeding like Luther and I are. I raise Quarter Horses and my son raises Tennessee Walkers. So this new breeding program is a family business right now."

After looking at the few colts and fillies from the new breeding, Raven decided he really wanted to be a part of this if possible. "I'll be glad to bring over a few of my choice Canadian Quarter Horse Mares for you to look at that might work well with your breeding program. What do you say?" asked Raven. "I'll be glad to sign an agreement with you and hopefully you'll let me be part of this new program of yours."

"I'll have to discuss it with my sons before I make any decision. You'd better plan on staying a few days so we can all get to know each other and such like. It might be good to bring you in on the beginning program to see how this works with other breeds. If my sons agree we'll try three of your mares and you can board them here until they come into heat. Now, are you still interested in buying any horses?"

"I'll take two of your semi-trained quarter horses and four if their fully trained."

"I've got seven that are half trained and coming along fast, plus five fully trained ones that I think are exceptional. Come on over to the corral." It was a good two hours later that Raven made up his mind which horses he wanted. Finally they walked up to the house and entered the kitchen where Mari Beth and Hannah were fixing supper.

"Mari Beth, this is Raven Chalk from down California way. Raven, this is my wife Mari Beth and my daughter Hannah. You sort of met Joe in the barn, and this is Mike Kelly. As I've said, he and his brother own Lost Wagon Ranch next door to us.

Seeing as how we'll have business to discuss we'd be honored to have you stay with us for a few days and no one cooks like my girls." invited Ben.

"Now I'm not crazy enough to turn down a dinner with two charming ladies, not to mention the gentlemen too. I thank you kindly for the invitation. I've had a long drive today and it would be a blessing not to have to climb back into the truck and find lodging somewhere. If I could find a place to wash up, I'll sure be ready for that delicious supper." Raven was looking at Hannah while he spoke and only at the last did he bow to Mari Beth.

When the men had left the kitchen, Mari Beth looked over at Hannah and saw her daughter staring after Raven Chalk. Hmm, now I wonder what's going on in my dear daughter's head that caused that slight blush. Mari Beth was wise enough to keep her mouth shut, but oh my, the possibilities.

~Hello Mary~

"Hello?" Mari Beth heard the quiet voice cautiously answer on the other end.

"Hello, Ms. Van Cliveland? This is Mari Beth Strongbow of Thunder Mountain Valleys. I understand you're going to be our new teacher and that you've inherited the old Fletcher place? I just wanted to be the first to welcome you to our community."

"Hello Mrs. Strongbow, thank you for calling. I guess you must be close to River Town, am I right?" asked Mary in a more cheerful voice.

"We have a ranch about an hour from town. We're all so excited to hear that you're going to be living here. I think you'll like the Valleys, they're exceptionally beautiful, and the people here are very friendly too. I just wanted to call and say hello so that you'd know someone here before you came, besides Mr. Jensen of course."

"How very thoughtful of you, indeed it will make it less strange to be greeted by someone I've spoken to. The girls are excited about coming as well and they are nagging me to get them horses, but I said they'd have to wait until we see where we would be keeping them. I've seen the house Uncle Fletcher left us at least it is a picture I found among my father's things. I know I will have my work cut out to bring it into shape, however that too is a new beginning of a sort isn't it?"

"Now Mary, don't you worry about the house because the whole community is into refurbishing it for you to show their gratitude for getting a teacher as highly qualified as you are and we want you to be happy here with us."

"Oh my, that is kindness indeed and beyond what I expected. Why, that takes a great load off my shoulders to be sure. The girls and I really appreciate your goodness. Please thank everyone for me." Mary's voice wobbled and Mari Beth heard a few sniffles and she smiled. Ah sweetie if you only knew.

"Not at all Mary, not at all, and by the way everyone calls me Mari Beth. I hardly know how to answer to any other form of address and besides it makes our acquaintance much friendlier, doesn't it?"

Mary laughed. "Yes it does Mari Beth and isn't it interesting that we both have the same first names. How do you spell yours?"

"M A R I and B E T H the only difference is an "i" instead of a "y". My daughter Hannah and I were talking about painting the interior of your house and I know, being a woman, how important the right colors are. If you could give me an idea of the colors you like it would help a lot and not shock you too much when you see the finished job." Mari Beth said and chuckled a little. "Perhaps you could send me some paint chips for each of the rooms? Got a pencil handy so you can take some notes?"

"Oh yes just a minute while I get to my desk. To think of having a house that's freshly painted is going to be a treat. Okay I'm ready." Mari Beth looked over at her daughter who had the extra phone pressed to her ear ready to take notes too.

"On the main floor there is the living room, dinning room which has a fireplace as a divider, a kitchen, laundry room and a back bedroom with bath for a housekeeper/cook if you should have one. Opposite the living room and across the hall is the library/den with a half bath off the downstairs hallway. Upstairs is a guestroom, a bedroom for each girl, a bathroom for the girls to share. Then there's your room with your private bathroom and a study for you."

Here Mari Beth was really laying out the house in her head and she could almost see it. "Ah, the exterior can be natural wood, or painted in which case please state your preference. There is a wide porch all around with an attached garage."

"Oh that sounds so grand. I'm writing this all down. Would you repeat the rooms please?" Mari Beth did and then Mary asked. "Which direction is the front of the house facing? I presume the living room will be where the front door is and I need to know whether it is going to be hot in the afternoon or cool as it will make a difference in the color I choose."

"Why I never thought about that before. Let me see if I can remember the position of the house." And quickly covered the mouthpiece she whispered to Hannah. "Which way are we planning on placing the front of the house?"

Hannah had covered her mouthpiece when she saw her mother doing it. She whispered back. "West."

"The living room and library/den will be facing the west and the main road. There is an enclosed entrance like an old fashioned vestibule because of the cold winds in winter." Mari Beth looked at Hannah and shrugged. "However, please take into consideration you will have a large deep front porch that will shade the windows and keep out the direct strong light in the afternoons for the most part. You can add drop bamboo shades on the porch for that sunset time if needed. There are also some large shade trees in the front which will help break up the sun's intensity." Mari Beth wiped her brow in an exaggerated way that had Hannah silently snickering.

"Then the kitchen I presume will be on the eastside?" replied the happy voice.

"Yes it is, and there is a nice back porch there too, facing the back garden. It should be lovely in the morning light."

"I couldn't have wanted the kitchen anywhere else. Then the bedrooms will either be on the north or south side, won't they?"

"Oh yes upstairs, your bedroom will be on the south side the girls' will be on the north side of the central staircase. All the windows facing the west will have extended small roofs over them to shade them from the direct sun. Now you just think about nice size windows and four fireplaces, one in the living room shared with the dining room and one in your bedroom that will be shared by a common chimney. Another fireplace in the library/den will share the chimney with the upstairs studio. The rooms are of good sized, for instance your bedroom is approximately…" Mari Beth closed her eyes then said, "16x16, and the girls and the guest rooms are all 14x14." Opening her eyes she shrugged her shoulders at the silent laugh she was getting from her daughter.

"Mari Beth I'm so excited. Just wait until I tell the girls. We'll go downtown today after school and look at paint chips. Oh by the way, what is your number there if you don't mind giving it to me?" Mari Beth gave her their number and their address.

"So Mary what are your favorite colors?"

"I love yellow and autumn colors. Reds for winter times, you know the curtain and slipcover tricks so the rooms will look warm and welcoming in the colder months. I like some wallpaper in the bedrooms. I guess I'd better describe us. I'm blond with hazel eyes so that explains the choice of autumn colors. Bliss, my oldest is 13 and she has strawberry blond hair with almost violet eyes. Stephanie is 8 and has honey blond hair and hazel eyes more or less like mine. Their color choices are really eclectic. I'll get back to you right away by mail."

"Anything you can tell us about your likes and dislikes will help us make your home very welcoming. Are you bringing much furniture?"

"Just a few inherited family pieces. Would you like me to tell you about them?" She said in a hesitant question.

"I love to hear what you have that you treasure." and waggled her eyebrows at Hannah who was busy making notes. So Mary did while Hannah busily took down the description of the furniture.

"We're selling everything else." Mary finished in a decisive tone.

"Yes, sometimes when one is starting over they need to drop the old except for keepsakes and get new. There's something about changing the energy you know. By the way how is your couch covered?" and smiled at Hannah, "and what style of furniture do you like, Mary?"

So Hannah filled page after page of more details. "Goodness Mari Beth I'm beginning to get this nest building bug really bad. Perhaps when we get there you can help me decorate the house?" laughed Mary.

"No doubt you'll have all the ladies here in the Valley wanting to help which might be more of a detriment than a help." They laughed and chatted about valley events. "This gives me a general idea of where to start Mary, but do send me those colors and a selection of wall papers that you'd like and I'll try to match them here. In the meantime, God Bless and we're all looking forward to giving you a welcoming party when you arrive."

"I feel like I'm not coming to a strange place after all. Thank you Mari Beth, you have really lifted my heart and helped me immeasurably. I'll be talking to you. Bye."

"Bye Mary."

When Mari Beth hung up she grinned at her daughter. "We've gotten lots and lots of information of what she's bringing. Now we can get Sam working on the furniture pieces for the girls' bedrooms and the book cases. That man is a wonder with wood. We can wait to get her colors because that's way down on our priority list." Mari Beth looked up at the clock and said. "It's almost time to meet with Blackhawk and the others over at Fletcher's Farm. Also, since I've more or less laid out her house for her and the measurements I'd better pass those notes of yours on to Dan so he can incorporate the measurements into the building plans. I do hope this is not going to present a big problem."

"It should make his work easier than just building by guess and by gosh." Hannah stood up and went to hang up the extra phone.

The women put on their coats, dressed Carli warmly and took a drive all set for action.

"For pete sake, would you just look at this mess? It's worse than the pictures Sam took!" That shocked exclamation burst out of Mari Beth as she and Hannah drove cautiously down the farm road pitted with deep pot-holes that would have easily swallowed a smaller pickup. Finally they pulled into the weed filled farmyard and parked beside Dan and Blackhawk's trucks.

"Good morning gentlemen are you as shocked as we are at the condition of this farm?" asked Mari Beth when they joined the men.

"I knew it was this bad after seeing Sam's pictures, Mari Beth. I've had a chance this morning to look more closely before the Blackhawks arrived and this place is rotten to the core. What we have here my dear people, is a total demolition situation and we have to begin immediately to clear the whole property because there isn't anything that's salvageable. Come on and mind your step and I'll show you around." Dan led the way toward carefully toward the dilapidated house.

Blackhawk took Carli from Mari Beth and put her on his shoulders to her delight. There wasn't any use trying to get inside the house as the porch had collapsed leaving the doorway five feet up the building wall even if it was safe to do so. The barn was in the same state of fall-down and it was a mystery as to what was holding both structures up and most of the other outbuildings were already flat on the ground.

"What a sad, sad mess and how very dreary it must be for the land spirits. I'm so glad Mary Van Cliveland can't see this place or she'd high-tail it out of here pronto. Fletcher's been gone for four years so why is there so much decay now?" Mari Beth said shaking her head.

"You forget Mari Beth that Fletcher wasn't a kind man and he misused his land and you know how the Thunder Gods dislike that!" frowned Blackhawk. "I've been so busy that I've neglected my duty to this place."

"Even I can tell the land is desolated and the poor natural spirits are so very unhappy." Blackhawk looked with amazement at this woman who professed not to believe in the spirits period.

"Okay Mr. Engineer, How and when do we start?" Mari Beth smiled grimly.

"We start immediately with bulldozers, large dump trucks and ten men or more if we can get them to clear the property. We'll leave the trees and work around them. Gads, there's enough trash here to fill any dumpsite. Fortunately most of this can be burned right here. Let me make a few calls and get this started right away for I can't stand to see the land in this mess. Good property just let go to wrack and ruin." Angrily Dan dug out his cell phone and limped away.

Blackhawk put a comforting arm around Mari Beth's shoulders. "It's a beginning and in many ways it will be a clean beginning and clearing the property completely is the best thing to do, the only thing to do I think." Blackhawk looked grimly around as he spoke. "I have sadly neglected my duties as Guardian to have ignored the state of this place for as long as I have. It's a wonder the Thunder Gods didn't reprimand me. The energy here is appalling; in fact the land spirits are screaming at me to help them. Poor things are desperate so I'll see what I can do right now and once the land is cleared I'll bless it properly. Some of my men and I will be down tomorrow to help." Blackhawk handed Carli back to Mari Beth then walked away over the farm land making downward gestures and talking. Maybe he was telling them that clearing the rotten buildings was going to take place and to reassuring them that all would soon be well and help was on the way to bring the land back into harmony and wellness.

Mari Beth shook her head. Whatever her doubts about the existence of the Thunder Gods, she could not deny that there was something to the belief in them. "I'm going to call and get some volunteers lined up for tomorrow. They can give up a weekend once in a while for a good cause." She said to Tom and went back to the truck and tucked Carli inside. No way was she going to let her precious girl down on this filthy ground. She picked up her cell phone and called Sam Carrington.

"Hello Sam, this is Mari Beth. I'm over at the old Fletcher place with Tom, Dan and Blackhawk. Honestly Sam, this place is beyond awful! Dan says he's calling in the bulldozers to clean this place out completely. Can you come over and give us your advice and a hand? We want to start tomorrow if possible."

"I could have told you just how bad that place really was, but seeing and feeling that farm's condition speaks louder than pictures, doesn't it? It sounds like Dan is starting off on the right foot because sometimes a clean sweep is the only way. I'll be right over."

Mari Beth quickly put in calls to Ben, and Luther asking them to call as many men as they could so this clean up would go quickly.

She sat in the truck with her cell phone and looked around with sad eyes at the dismal farm where the sun's rays didn't seem able to penetrate the miasma of heavy dark energy that covered it like a blanket.

"It's a wonder the Gods didn't come marching down here and demand we all do something about cleaning it up before this." said Hannah to her mother.

"I know Hannah, but even as bad as this is, I can see in my mind's eye the potential and how it will look with a few months of hard work. Hopefully the weather will cooperate and we'll have the barn and house under roof before it gets serious about snowing. Everyone could continue to work indoors even in the worst weather."

"There's no time to waste bemoaning the state of things." And Hannah pulled the sheets of paper out of her large purse and they got busy again on their cell phones connecting people and resources.

Seven o'clock on Saturday morning and barely daylight, found two bulldozers working on clearing both the house and the outbuildings. A large scoop shovel was lifting debris into a series of dump trucks. Out in the back field men were throwing wood onto two huge fires.

Mari Beth was astounded at how many people were here. They were literally crawling all over the place. She saw women with rakes and shovels cleaning and dumping wheelbarrows full of trash into the big construction site dumpsters or throwing burnable items on the fires. She saw Sam talking to a few men and gesturing toward the barn and walked over to see what he was doing when he gave four loud blasts on his car horn.

He picked up a mega-phone. "Get clear of the barn, we're taking it down. Everyone move back now." Mari Beth watched several men run from behind the barn and waved at Sam an all clear.

"This is a second warning. Everyone clear the barn site; we're bulldozing it down now." Sam's magnified voice bellowed out and paused for a few minutes until another man waved that all was clear and to come on. Sam turned to the waiting man in the bulldozer. "Okay Lem go for it." Sam's amplified voice sounded over the idling of the engine. The big bulldozer roared and began its squeaking, rattling progress towards the barn and hit the corner of the building with a crash. The whole structure collapsed with groans and complaints like an old man seeking to lie down. Dust, dirt and debris flew everywhere. Once it settled the men began tossing wood into the trucks to be taken and burned. Others with chain saws were cutting up the longer pieces of lumber into manageable sizes.

At noon the work was broken up by the large lunch that several ranch cooks brought to the site. Dusty was there with his chuck wagon and big grill just like at roundup and doing steaks. That crew could eat and as it was all the pay the volunteers were going to get except a thank you, they made the most of it. By late Sunday afternoon the house site had been cleared, the old foundation broken up and the junk that couldn't be burned was hauled off. Three large fires in the back of the property were consuming the rest of the debris.

They shut everything down by four o'clock. One of the men volunteered to stay and watch the fires for a few hours until they burned down enough to be safe to leave. There wasn't much danger of the fires getting out of control as they had bulldozed a wide fire break around them all, but Sam wanted no accidents; sparks fly and could start fires in the trees.

Sam and Mari Beth were standing beside her truck and were the last ones left in the farmyard. "Progress Mari Beth, often begins with destruction. Tomorrow I have a steam shovel coming in to dig a larger cellar and a new septic field and we'll put in a new tank that will be environmentally safe. I'll have the bulldozer grade the farm road and drag the ranch yard. The backhoe will clean out the ditches. We'll lay a good bed of gravel over the road and the yard and steamroll it to pack it down firmly. Dan is going to oversee the foundations right away so there shouldn't be any problem with the cement curing properly before it gets to cold or rains." said Sam.

"It looks better all ready Sam. I guess I didn't expect it to be cleared so fast so I guess the old adage of many hands makes for fast work, and in this case fire purifies. I feel the difference in the land already, can't you?

"Yes I can and seeing as how I'm the closest to the project and to town, I think I'm the logical one to generally oversee things here and pass the bills on to the counsel. Hah, I'll bet I'll hear a few squawks, but the money is rolling in. Mike Kelly, with his guardian's approval, donated $5,000 dollars so right now we have about $30,000.00 in the kitty. The lumberyard and supply companies have been very generous too giving us really cut rate prices plus a lot of free stuff. Which reminds me I've got some house plans you'd better look at right away before Dan sets the basement and foundation walls. You'll know best which one will work." Sam went to his truck and dragged out a number of rolls. Sam was unrolling the first set of plans on the hood of his truck and anchoring it with rocks. "I've a flashlight, so we can see what's what." Sam said

Just then Dan Lightfoot's truck drove into the bare yard "Man this place looks one hundred percent better even if it is as bare as a baby's butt except for the trees. It feels mighty different or is that just my imagination?" said Jim Waggoner as he looked around.

"No you're right Jim and I felt it too, the land spirits are more cheerful." Then as though hearing what she had said, Mari Beth coughed and looked embarrassed and the men carefully smiled behind their hands.

"What's that you got Sam?" asked Jim walking closer to view the spread out house plans.

"I was just showing Mari Beth some house plans I happen to have by me. I picked up a couple more at the Fair pretty cheap. I can't seem to resist house plans though I don't have any intention of changing my house more than I already have. I think we can find something suitable for this site and save us the cost of an architect." Sam proceeded to show them the first set. By the time he rolled out the fourth set it was a sell.

"This is more like it. See those wide porches? See the layout of the floor plan? Very close to what I described to Mary over the phone. Hmm, I want a larger pantry and laundry room, but that shouldn't be too difficult. Hmm, a second story with four bedrooms upstairs and two full baths; excellent. That's a nice curved stairway; she'll like that. A full bath on the main floor off the kitchen a nice size room back beside the kitchen too. Nice size living room and look, a big fireplace shared with the dinning room, just like I said. Remind me that we'll need to get in a couple of cords of wood for her. And this other room off to the left of the main hall that she can use as an office/den sort of thing. This is sort of spooky because this plan is so close to what I imagined the house would look like. Hmm, do you think I had a little help?" They laughed and shrugged. "Well gentlemen, this is it except for a few modifications. So what's your opinion?" smiled Mari Beth.

"If you like it I'm sure Ms. Mary will too since you've talked to her you have a better idea than we would." Dan said wisely and knew better than to argue with a lady who has made up her mind.

"Dan, you've been trained as an engineer so you'll oversee the start of foundation work and you can have these plans to go by." Sam said, rolling up the set of plans and handing them to Dan.

"Boy, I call that passin' the buck, however you're right and the foundation has to be set right. Yes Mari Beth, I'll make sure there is an addition for the extension of the laundry room and pantry at the back of the kitchen." assured Dan.

"Yes, and I want an enclosed walkway or an attached garage with tool and wood shed on the side. So you'll have to include that in your plans, Dan."

"No problem, I'll have to watch the roof line and we've got to work fast because this good weather might not last and I would like to get everything under roof before the month is out. Now where do you want the barn situated?" They all turned around to look at the surrounding land. Even though it was dark there was a full moon and they could see well enough to make a choice.

"The original site is too close to the house and Ms. Mary wouldn't like that; smells you know. Let's move it over back by those trees aways and it doesn't have to be as large as the other barn was either. I understand they all ride so I figure a barn for three or four horses with a big loft for hay storage and a room for feed and tack. Oh, we'd better run a water line out there while we're at it. Later we can build another barn further back for cows if she wants. Is she going to farm the land Mari Beth?" asked Dan.

"I think we better wait until she settles in to ask her that, but would be a waste if she didn't at least grow enough for her own use or lease it out."

"Do you want to change the site of the house?" asked Dan.

"No, I told Mary the front of the house was facing west and the long driveway. That would make the garage easy to access as well as the barn. I want dormers over the upper windows and a wide front porch to shade the house from the western sun. You know how hot summer afternoons can get."

"That's it then, I'll have all the measurements down and the areas staked out by tomorrow or the next day at the latest." Dan paused then added. "This foundation job is for experts so I'm calling in Jake's Concrete and get him under contract. After the foundations are set, we can start building."

"It might also be a good idea to hire a good construction company to frame the house for us and lay on the roof and outer walls. We can do a lot of the inside stuff, but they will do a faster job of getting this baby under roof. We'll also need plumbers and electricians. We've all built enough pole barns that we can handle that project easily enough. Dan, you need to plan a cement floor for the barn too." said Sam and watched Dan make another notation on his list.

The following week saw great progress with the weather cooperating like a charmed maiden. Blackhawk came over before the foundations were to be poured and did the blessing ceremony. In the middle of the bare front yard, he built a fire and it was nice that so many who had worked on clearing the land were able to attend. Once the ceremony was over Blackhawk said, "I want a small circular flower garden built right here with a fountain in the center as it will be an affirmation to the land spirits that we will fulfill our promise to them."

Mari Beth said. "I'll see to it right now and that means we'll need a water line run out here Dan. I'm going into town and see what Mason's Supply has in stock; something very nice I think." she turned away before anyone could make further comment.

Within three weeks the first floor of the house covered the basement, the side walls were up and the second floor was laid and the roof was on except for shingling. A collective sigh of relief went up when it was all under cover. All the frantic work and long hours to get the house and the barn under roof before bad weather struck had been accomplished. That day was celebrated with another mini barbecue. The people firmly believed in "all work and no play makes for unhappy people."

They had been very lucky so far with the weather. They guess the Thunder Gods were being especially kind holding off severe winter storms until most of the buildings were under roof and the inside work had begun.

The whole Fletcher Farm resembled a hive of worker bees swarming all over the place. It's a wonder someone didn't get nailed into the walls with the carpenters working so closely together. There were plenty of men on the roof that it was also a wonder no one fell off for lack of room to stand. The amazing part of this endeavor was everyone was having such a great time being a part of creating something beautiful.

Meanwhile Mari Beth and Hannah had the women volunteers making curtains now that they had the window measurements. Mary's paint chips had arrived. Mary Beth, with tongue in cheek, had requested measurements of Mary's chairs and couch on the pretext that the room had to fit the furniture. Now slipcovers were in the works in a cheerful red for winter. Tablecloths, napkins and other assorted sewing projects made for busy fingers.

Sam was making furniture for the girl's bedrooms plus bookcases and providing a beautifully carved banister. Mr. Downey, a friend of Blackhawk's said he'd do a special newel post.

Mari Beth bought a butter-yellow paint for the kitchen with wallpaper of soft multicolored flowers around the kitchen table area and around the cornices of the ceiling that made a nice accent. The floor was laid in a deep brownish red brick tile. Colored flower handles and door pulls were a definite find that she gloated over. The kitchen, being on the southeast side, would be cool in the summer afternoons and warm in winter. Large windows over the sink and also around the kitchen seating area gave the needed light and openness. The living room would be a cool soft green color with white trim and cornices that would set off the colored fabrics of the living room furniture.

Whenever Mari Beth drove into the property she was astounded by the growing beauty of the place. She could almost swear she heard the land sigh and breathed excited expectation into the farm; her imagination of course, but she had to admit silently that the land did feel better and lighter.

Only another month before Mary Van Cliveland was due to arrive. "I hope we're ready for her. There is still so much to do and the yard looks pretty awful, so bare and all.

Hmm, maybe a picket fence around the front yard would add a nice touch and break up all that bareness and it would be a perfect frame for the central fountain. I was so lucky to find that sweet fairy holding a jar that eventually would pour water into the basin. Well, it's time to head for home and I'm tired as all get out." Mari Beth turned her truck around and left.

It was dark now and everyone had gone home. The Fletcher Farm was silent after all the activity. The full moon came out and shone down upon the quiet land and the new buildings. The Fountain Fairy posed in an attitude of…expectancy and the only movement was a cold wind moving through the trees. The moon watched as the land spirits materialized and danced around the fountain then ran out over the land, touching and sprinkling colored energies that sank into the ground leaving a soft glow that gradually disappeared. No one was there to see the elementals' joy as they blessed the land in a new profusion of renewed life that would come forth in the spring. The Thunder Gods were the only other witnesses.

~Kidnapped~

JOE WAS HAPPY TO have found a voice teacher. Of course, Mrs. Rainbird had insisted that he begin with breathing exercises which involved his diaphragm. He knew all that, nevertheless training had to begin with basics he supposed and if the big singers did it everyday who was he to say no to the daily practice himself. This has been his sixth lesson and it was mostly scale work though they had begun working on a song. It amazed Joe how much training and preparation went into perfectly singing a song. Needless to say he loved it, even the tedious repetitive parts. There was still the matter of piano lessons so he'd have to stop putting off asking for one; after all Christmas was coming wasn't it? Joe laughed, yeah, and Thanksgiving vacation was also coming next week.

It was 5:30 and dark now that winter was here and it had gotten colder after sundown which had been hardly noticeable for the sky had been covered in dark gray overcast. Snow was coming down steadily and as Joe walked through it he stuck his tongue out to catch the icy flakes. He turned around and walked backward looking at his footprints that marred the otherwise pristine white covering the sidewalk. Pretty neat, seeing where he had been and all.

Joe turned back around and looked ahead at the undisturbed snow and thought how like life it was. The future was a white blank without any marks on it and those marks would have to be made by him. Who knew what turnings he would make in the future? He'd only know after it happened and he could look back to see where he had been and what he had done.

He laughed at his funny thoughts. Joe pulled the ear flaps down over his cold ears. He could see his breath coming out of his mouth just for the fun of seeing it float away like smoke puffing it out like the old steam engines used to do. He walked on down the deserted, well-lit street toward the grocery store a few blocks ahead where he was to meet Hannah and Mike.

Thanksgiving was next week and school would be out for four days then he'd have time to visit Miracle every day. He and Hannah would be finishing up on his journal and they had finished selected the pictures to go with the story. Man that had been so hard because there were so many more pictures he'd want to use, but he had to stay within the space the magazine gave for each article which put a sever restriction on pictures and words. He prayed each night that all this work would be accepted by the magazine; "Roundup through the Eyes of a Child" by Joseph Kelly as Told to Hannah Truelove Strongbow with Photographs by Joseph Kelly. Joe giggled, man that was so cool just to see that written out on paper.

Everyone in the family had read it and made suggestions and corrections. Well, after all it was a family thing at least it was to Joe. Oh wow, to hopefully see it published would be just the greatest thing and the excitement of that thought had Joe running a few steps and skipping along through the snow making long dragging marks.

Mike was taking lessons with Mr. Freedo in music theory and composition and it was handy that they could have their lessons on the same night. Joe skipped along for a few steps just for the joy of it. Golly, they were both so lucky with the way their lives had changed from one of despair and grief to one of great contentment. No one could ever replace their parents in their hearts for that special place was reserved just for them, but that didn't stop the heart from loving others or putting others inside it. Joe figured love made the heart keep growing as one got older just like his gift had to grow; it was just the way things were. And he was ever so thankful for Hannah because she was almost like a mother. He purely loved Hannah and he loved Mari Beth and Ben and G. D., (Joe snickered at Mike's suggestion of calling Blackhawk G. D. and not God Daddy). Blackhawk told stories about the Thunder Gods and the times before. Joe wondered how much was really true. Well, he loved the stories anyway.

"I guess it doesn't really matter. After all the Gods have been here for thousands of years from what G.D. says, and he believes They are real and he's an honest man so I'll believe in Them too." He thought about that then said in a really loud voice. "*Hello Guardians, I'm Joe Kelly and I believe in You.*" Then laughed, a little embarrassed that he was shouting. Gee, people would think he was crazy or something.

Maybe someday he fantasized, he'd get to meet the Thunder Gods and sing for them and that would be a grand way to say thank you for bringing them to the Valleys. Joe giggled as he walked along; sure he'd tell everyone he'd sung for the Gods and they'd lock him up in a padded cell. Crazy Joe they'd call him.

Joe didn't notice the pickup following him until it pulled in ahead of him. Joe walked on by and didn't pay it any attention for pickups were common in a ranching community. He heard the guy get out and slam the truck door and he just kept on walking with his mind on so much more important things. Suddenly he was grabbed from behind and before he could shout something hard struck him an awful blow on the side of his head.

It was dark when he awoke. He could hear a rumbling noise against one ear felt himself being tossed about a little now and then. His head hurt something awful and he felt sick to his stomach too. He faded in and out of consciousness before he came awake enough to realize he was tied up tight in the small space behind the front bench seat. He looked up from where he laid on the floor boards and saw the back of a man's head and hat and fear ran through him like cold water.

"Mike," he screamed, "Mike, where are you? Help me!"

He heard a harsh laugh from the front seat, "You wished kid."

Then silence and the truck rumbled on and on. He was alone in the dark with a stranger. Why? Tears ran down his face.

"No one will know where to find me. I'm lost." he whispered. "Please help me Guardians, please help me." His silent plea went out into the night before he faded into unconsciousness again.

Hannah stood outside the grocery store with Mike and as they waited Mike suddenly jerked upright and looked frantically around and got an awful feeling, a gut wrenching feeling of loss. "Hannah, something really bad has happened......*to Joe*. I swear I heard him call my name just now. Hannah, *he's in trouble, I know it!*"

Mike's fear infected Hannah now because Joe was late meeting them and he was always on time.

"Maybe he got held over with his lesson so let's drive along the road to Mrs. Rainbird's and see if maybe he's fallen down and gotten hurt. Come on." They got into the truck.

Hannah drove slowly so that if Joe were walking they'd see him, but there was no sign of him and finally she stopped in front of the music teacher's house and they hurried up to her door.

"Hello Hannah, hello Mike, what's the matter, didn't Joe meet you as arranged? These boys, I tell you sometimes I don't think they know what time is." Mrs. Rainbow said smiling as they stepped into the house.

"You mean Joe isn't here? But where can he be? It's not like him at all to go off and not tell me where he's going." Hannah said firmly and now she wasn't just worried, but afraid.

"Mrs. Rainbird, Joe would have met us on time. He's a very responsible boy so I know something's happened to him." Mike spoke with such certainty that the older woman began to look panicky.

"He said he was meeting you at the grocery store and he left here a half hour ago." Wringing her hands helplessly, Mrs. Rainbow just stood in the hallway uncertain as to what to do next.

"May I use your phone please? I think I'll call Sheriff Brandt and see if he's seen Joe."

Hannah called Max Brandt and he promised to run through town and see if he could spot him. "Hannah, this could be Elroy has shown up again. I don't know that for sure so don't panic. Give me your cell number and I'll call you once I've gone through the town."

"Oh mercy Max, I think that might be what's happened. Elroy has taken Joe and it's all happened within the past half hour. Max please, get out a search party and scour the immediate neighborhood and I'll call Dad right away. Call us if you find him." Hannah hung up and looked into Mike's white face.

She dialed home. "Strongbows," Mari Beth's cheerful voice was in such contrast to Hannah's state of mind that she had to swallow hard before she spoke.

"Mom, Joe's missing and Sheriff Brandt said he thought it might be Elroy who has taken him. I'm scared Mom, Joe didn't show up at the grocery store and it's already been close to forty-five minutes. What should I do? Max is looking for him in town, but I've got an awful feeling that Elroy had gotten hold of him." Hannah was crying.

"Hold on Hannah, let me get your father." Hannah held on and waited with Mrs. Rainbow waiting anxiously in the background.

Mike put his arm around Hannah and gave her what comfort he could and himself too because he was scared right down to his toes. He knew how kidnappers treated their victims; usually the victim didn't come out alive. Would Elroy go that far?

"Hannah, come home, there isn't anything you can do there." Ben said after she repeated what had happened. "I'll call Max and have him get on to the State Police in case Elroy tries to take him out of the state. Come on home honey and we'll take it from here."

"Can't Mike and I help search the town for him? We can mobilize everyone here too if we have too. Please Dad, we've got to do something." cried Hannah frantically.

"Max will organize a search party so you and Mike come home now Hannah." commanded Ben.

"Okay we're on our way. I'm sorry I lost him, I should have driven over to Mrs. Rainbird's and picked him up, but I thought he be alright walking those few blocks to the store the way he usually does." she sniffed. "We can't lose him Dad."

"We won't and we'll organize a hunt here in the country and cover all the roads right away. Elroy wants to use Joe to get money from the ranch so we have to believe he won't hurt the boy yet. Now do as I say, come home."

"We're on the way." Hannah hung up the phone and turned to Mike. "There's nothing we can do here Mike, and Dad wants us to come home. Mrs. Rainbird, we'll let you know as soon as we get news." Hannah said on their way out the door.

"I'll pray for him really hard that he'll be okay. I'll call on our Guardian Spirits to protect him too. Please call me as soon as you hear anything." she stood in the doorway as they drove off.

Hannah sped along the road at a fast rate. Somehow she knew Joe and Elroy were no longer in town, but where would he take Joe? Obviously Elroy had had some time to make a plan. She opened her cell phone to call her father, but the line was busy. Frustrated she ended the call and drove as fast as it was safe to do on the snowy road.

~*Lost*~

THE MAN'S PANTING SOUNDED harsh and heavy in the silence. The boy's body slung over his shoulder seemed to have gained weight as the climb continued and just about did him in. After two hours of climbing, resting and climbing again in the dark, Elroy finally reached the cave he remembered playing in as a kid.

At this altitude it was hard enough to catch his breath let alone having to pack the kid's unconscious weight. He just wasn't in good enough shape to be doing this kind of strenuous work. He could have a heart attack for Pete's sake. The cave's entrance seemed to be a lot smaller now than it had when he was a boy. He was so exhausted his legs fairly shook under him as he staggered into the cave.

"Ha, let's see…..how smart they are now." he panted, "All I want…… is my money …….and then they can…..have the kid back." He muttered and carelessly tossed Joe down on the cave floor and up against one of the walls banging the boy's head against the unyielding rock. Elroy went out with his flashlight and gathered up dead branches and other stuff, and shook off the light snow cover. All he wanted right then was to get a fire going. He purely hated the dark and the cold.

Once he had the fire burning he looked over at the boy to see if he had regained consciousness. Nope, the kid was still out. Maybe he shouldn't have hit him so hard then the boy could have walked up here on his own two feet. Well, he didn't plan on doing this sort of thing again so he could forget about learning from experience.

After Elroy had rested awhile and had caught his second wind, he went back down to where he had hidden the truck and got his bed bedroll, backpack and a large canteen.

Joe woke up bewildered and disorientated and fearfully looked around. Shadows flicked and danced off the cave walls confusing him until his eyes fell on the man sitting beside the fire then he knew what had happened to him.

Joe licked his dry lips and croaked out. "I know who you are. Mike told me you were a very bad man. Mister, you have done a really stupid, dumb thing. Kids are supposed to do stupid dumb things 'cause they don't know any better, but I thought adults would have better sense. You haven't learned a thing have you?" said Joe.

"Shut up kid, you don't know anything about me. I've done some great things and made a lot of money too and all I want is my share of the ranch. I deserve that much from old Devereaux. I hated his guts, always so strict about everything and so protective of his precious Jean. She was nothing but a baby, just a stupid girl. Father said we'd have a chance at a good living if we behaved ourselves, but it was my *Father* who was always asking for money and there was *never* enough because he'd gamble it away, the stupid man; I hated him too." Elroy turned to Joe and screamed at him. "*This isn't my fault; it's on your brother's head that he's caused me to do all these things because he wouldn't give me what I deserve out of the ranch. I'm not to blame for all this happening.*" Elroy looked back into the fire and brooded over past slights and other injuries.

Elroy was suddenly hungry and dug bacon and bread out of the backpack. He put a small frying pan on the fire and placed strips of bacon in it.

"You're going to go hungry and I'm going to eat because there's just enough for me anyway. I will give you water though since I can't have you dying of thirst now can I?" Elroy laughed. "Thursday, that's the day after tomorrow, I'll have my money and maybe I'll tell them where to find you, then again *maybe not.*" Elroy really laughed at that. "That should even the score between your brother and me. Yeah, *sweet revenge* and he loses his baby brother because *money* meant more to him than you did. How do you like *them* facts?" Chuckling he fed some more wood to the fire.

Joe's stomach fought the nausea at the smell of frying bacon. Soon Elroy took it off the fire and soaked some bread in the drippings and stuffed the half-done bacon in between two slices of bread and ate the whole thing then he opened a can of peaches and ate that too. At last he took a long drink from the canteen. Just as he was about to recap the water bottle he looked over at Joe and got up to kneel beside the boy.

"Now you keep your words between you teeth boy and I'll give you a drink." Joe didn't say a word and Elroy grunted, grabbed Joe by the front of his jacket, jerked him into a sitting position and poured water into his mouth.

Joe gulped as fast as he could because he didn't know when Elroy would remember to give him more. Water escaped his mouth and ran down under his shirt collar, but he got most of it. "That's enough now go to sleep." and let go of Joe's jacket and let him slide back down on his side.

Capping the canteen, Elroy got up and went back to the fire and tossed some larger branches on it before he unrolled his sleeping bag and crawled into its warmth. Joe shivered with the growing cold as he was too far away from the fire to feel any heat at all. Gradually the fire died down and Joe felt half-sick and had a terrible headache pounding his poor brains to mush. The night passed with Joe slipping in and out of consciousness.

At home Ben was making calls and when he talked to Hank, the man hit the ceiling. "I'll get the men out and begin to search around these back roads. I'll call Bob Zeggler to alert the police in Claremont; maybe he went up there. Elroy knows this country pretty well. We'll find the boy, Ben, we'll find him." the man said desperately.

Ben and the men took off in their pickups and divided at the County Road, some headed east and some went west, however, there was no sign of a strange car or truck; in fact the roads were clear of any traffic. Whoever had passed on these roads the snow had filled in the tracks. An hour or so later the men returned home defeated and Ben came into the house with a grim set on his face.

"I've never felt so helpless in my life. Little Joe, that sweet kid to be put through this kind of terror horrifies me. I swear to God when I get my hands on Elroy......." Ben sat down abruptly and put his head in his hands. Mari Beth put her arm around his shoulders.

"Let's pray for him Ben." Ben grew still at her words then he raised his head and got up to call a very important man.

"Blackhawk, this is Ben. Elroy Devereaux has kidnapped our Joe and we have no idea where he is. Would you say prayers for him and if you get anything as to direction we are your men." said Ben grimly.

"He's kidnapped my godson? I shall go immediately to the Mountain." The sound of the disconnected line filled Ben's ear and he slowly hung up the phone. To his knowledge Blackhawk had never invoked the Gods in such a way before. The Chief was going to the Mountain which meant he was going up to the Medicine Wheel. Ben turned to Mari Beth and repeated what Blackhawk had said, and then he gave her a hug. "I'll be right back, Mari Beth." Picking up his coat and hat again Ben walked out the kitchen door with his flashlight. She knew where he was going and She knelt right there in the kitchen and clasping her hands, she prayed.

Ben lit the fire on his stone altar and once the flames were burning hotly, it melted the snow flakes as they fell into the fire. He turned off his flashlight and began his own supplication. "Guardian Spirits, great evil stalks Your lands. A wicked man has taken a child of great heart from us and is hiding him somewhere. I beg Your protection for this innocent boy and I place him in Your care if he is in Your lands. Joe Kelly is such a good boy. Thank You; I am Ben Strongbow." And Ben sat down and allowed tears to make their way down his cold cheeks as he waited until the small fire had burned itself out before returning to the house. He wondered how many other fires had been built this night praying the same prayer. Surely, the Guardians would hear.

The night grew long and then early morning came as they waited in the living room for some word to come, some clue as to a direction in which to search; to be doing something, *anything* except this deadly waiting. The sun came up and the light shone on haggard faces as Hannah and Mari Beth served breakfast.

"Joey? Where's my Joey, Daddy? Break'ist is ready. Call Joey, Daddy." Carli tugged on Ben's sleeve. He looked down at her and he could see the tears threatening to spill over. How she knew something wasn't right he could only guess that she had picked up on their despair.

"Joey is staying over night at a friend's house, sugarplum. He'll be home tonight." Ben's smiling reply seemed to relieve Carli.

"Okay Daddy, we be happy now. Joey always makes me happy." Then she started on her breakfast as though everything was all right with her world because her daddy had said so. Ben thought if it was only that simple. The family sat silently at the table and just looked down at the food sitting on their plates.

"Eat. You won't be ready to take action when it will be needed if you don't eat to keep up your strength and we're all overtired as it is. Now eat your food even if it chokes you." commanded Mari Beth in no uncertain terms and she dug into her own food and chewed and swallowed with determination. Slowly the others picked up their forks and followed suit.

By late afternoon, just as dusk began to fill the valleys, the Sheriff phoned and reported Joe had not been found in River Town, Claremont, Port City or the surrounding country. The State Police had set up roadblocks on the major roads. They were sending in a special search teams with dogs to be available if needed.

Max called. "Ben, the post mistress found a ransom note in with the outgoing mail demanding one million dollars cash by 1:00 Thursday. The money is to be placed in an unbreakable container and dropped by air. Last minute instructions would be given to the pilot as to where that drop would be. The pilot was to call this number for instructions at 1PM Thursday after he was airborne. If anyone else tries to use that number he will kill Joe. Only the pilot is allowed phone access. If Elroy doesn't get the money, you'll never find Joe. That's it Ben so from that we believe Joe hasn't been taken out of the state. We're still looking. Don't give up."

Ben hung up the phone and told the waiting family what Max had said. There was nothing to be done except try to work hard through the waiting.

It was going on five o'clock in the evening when the phone rang again. "Ben, Elroy is somewhere in the mountains north of you so I figure he must know of a cave where he can hide Joe and himself. The Gods have told Rockland Hoggins where to look and he's already started out. We'll meet you at the Kelly ranch within an hour. Get everyone to bring their horses." Blackhawk hung up.

Ben looked around at his waiting family with fierce eyes. "That was Blackhawk and he says Elroy is in the mountains north of us. He also said Mr. Hoggins had been contacted and was making a search himself. You remember Mr. Hoggins, don't you? He's lived up in those hills for years and Joe was talking about him a little while ago. The man's a hermit so how could Blackhawk contact him so fast when no one really knows where he lives? But, Joe knew, didn't he?" Ben rubbed his face hard then said,

"Does this all sound strange or am I losing it? Make the calls Mari Beth, and tell Luther we're meeting at Mike's place in an hour; I'm going to go get the men ready. Don't forget to tell them to bring their horses." Mike and Ben were out the back door before she could utter a word.

There was a flurry of activity as the men got themselves ready for a cold ride and saddled the horses. As soon as the horse trailers had been drawn out of the big garage the men loaded the horses. Mike went up to Joe's room and got a dirty shirt out of the hamper just in case Roscoe needed it to pick up Joe's scent. Coming back out into the yard he called Roscoe and finished saddling Beau. After putting on his heavy sheepskin coat he stuffed Joe's shirt into a large pocket and pulled on his gloves. His horse soon joined the others in the trailer.

Mike had been constantly praying that there wouldn't be any spilt blood on his land, Joe's blood, but the chances weren't good. He climbed into the back seat of Ben's truck and Roscoe jumped in after him. By 6:30 the trucks and horse trailers were pulling out of Strongbow's heading for his ranch. Mike felt sick to his stomach. He hadn't done a very good job of protecting his brother and he felt as though he'd failed his father in a big way.

Ben looked in his rear view mirror and saw the dim image of agony on Mike's face and knew what a beating the kid was giving himself. "Mike, for what it's worth, I'm just as much to fault as you or Hannah, or any of us for being so stupid to think you kids were safe; I'm to blame for that, not you. Now, stop it; it's not helping the situation and the next few hours will be tough enough without you going on a guilt trip and making yourself sick."

Mike met Ben's severe eyes in the mirror and nodded his head. "Okay Ben, your right and I'll share the guilt with you. Maybe it will make it easier for me to swallow my share." and got a grim smile in return.

Men, horses, horse trailers and trucks littered Kelly's flood lighted ranch yard and it looked to Mike as though an army had arrived. It was most all the men in the Valley. Why that should surprise him he didn't know, after all this time he should have known better. They got out of the truck and after Ben gave the order to unload the horses he and Mike walked over to join Hank who was standing silhouetted against the porch lights. It had begun to snow again.

Jimmy walked over and stopped Mike as Ben walked on. "Mike, we'll get Joe back. Don't ask me how I know that, but he's going to be found hurt, but okay. I know you're feeling guilty for not being there for him. Well, so do I and everyone here feels the same. We just want you to know you're not alone in this. We all have been violated. The Thunder Gods are angry 'cause every once in a while thunder rumbles and the earth shakes a little. It's been going on since last night. Haven't you felt it?"

"Now that you mention it Jimmy, I have. Is it Them then? I guess I wouldn't be in Elroy's shoes for anything if he's hurt Joe and his blood had been spilt," Mike swallowed hard then went on, "We'll find him and Joe's a tough little guy. You're such a good friend, Jimmy and if you believe we'll get him back then we will." Jimmy nodded and squeezed Mike's shoulder then went back to the group of men gathered around the corrals and Mike stepped up onto the porch.

"We're ready. Are we waiting for Blackhawk or do we start sweeping the foothills now?" asked Hank.

"As soon as Blackhawk gets here and gives us some specifics we'll head north. I know it's hard to wait when we're primed to go, but I'm not going chasing around in the dark and maybe not be in the right place at the right time. Maybe we won't need all these men, and then again, I'd rather have too many then not enough if they're needed. Besides I think it helps them to have a share in this hunt." answered Ben as he scanned the busy ranch yard.

Dusty stepped out on the porch letting the kitchen door slam shut behind him and yelled. "Y'all come get your coffee and some sandwiches; you're going to need fuel against the cold." and went back into the kitchen. For the next twenty minutes or so the men sat or stood around inside the house and ate, drank coffee and more coffee as Dusty made the rounds with his huge pot and talked in low voices.

There had been occasional thunder that would rumble in the high mountains, queer lights would flash every so often up on the mountain top and the ground would quiver a bit. The horses didn't like it at all and until it stopped they'd dance around some. The men would hush, listen and look up at the mountain they couldn't see for the falling snow except for the off and on brightness up there gleaming briefly through the snow storm. For sure the Thunder Gods weren't happy; no, not by a long shot.

They all heard the sound of a big engine coming fast. The men boiled out of the house like angry ants to see the headlights of a truck and horse trailer as they came up over the last little hill. Within a few minutes it swept into the yard slowly braking to a halt. Blackhawk got out and men hurried to unload horses. Big Mike got out the other side and walked up the porch steps and into the kitchen loaded down with bags.

Blackhawk stood on the front edge of the porch and was the immediate center of attention. You could have heard a pinecone hit the ground miles away it was so quiet.

The Chief said. "I'm not sure whether we will need all you men, however, I'm glad to see you because I'm going to cover all the bases. I want a long line of sweep riders to prevent even a mouse from getting down out of those hills. Men of Claremont have moved in to seal off the canyons on the west side incase Elroy tries to slip out that way. I've got Tom and his men as well as mine covering the eastside of the valley and any access to North Mountain Road. I've called North Springfield and they've got the roads covered over there. We'll move north from here and close this avenue of escape. As I said, this all may not be necessary for I don't think Elroy will escape the wrath of the Thunder Gods, but we all need to be doing everything we can as a back up strategy so I want all exit doors closed tight. Now, you all have heard of Old Mountain Man Hoggins, right?" Murmurs of assent and some that hadn't.

"He's a hermit that has lived up around Thunder Mesa and has been there for forty years. Well, you certainly know his rocking chairs." at that low laughter and nodding of heads greeted that piece of news. "I don't know how old he is, but he's a good man, a knowing man and one who is close to the Gods in strange ways. Well, Joe knows him and I guess you could say they're friends. Rockland Hoggins is looking for him and the way I heard it, he kinda' knows where Joe might be hidden. We move out now and I have cell phones here and men with one will be dispersed among the rest of you. I have a list of numbers for cell phones to give to each point man so he can pass the word. I'll call when I hear where Joe is. Don't ask me how I'll know, just that I will. All right, let's go get my Godchild back from that monster."

The moon was on the rise and the snow had stopped. The wind had also dropped as the men rode out of the ranch yard.

~Found~

IN THE MORNING OF the second day Elroy got up and rebuilt the fire. "Elroy, I've got to pee. Please help me or I'm going to wet my pants and stink up the cave." pleaded Joe.

That certainly got Elroy moving fast. He grabbed Joe up by the jacket and packed him outside the cave and untied his hands. It took a few painful minutes for Joe to get the feeling back into his swollen hands while Elroy had a firm grip on his coat. After he had attended to his need Elroy started to tie him up again.

"Please don't tie my hands so tight, I'm afraid I'll lose them."

Elroy snorted. "As if I really cared, but I won't just because I don't want to hear you whining." he tied him just tight enough that Joe couldn't break lose, but it was a relief to have better circulation.

Joe was real quiet during the day slipping in and out of consciousness which was a blessing in disguise. When he was unconscious he wasn't in pain, he wasn't cold and hungry or afraid. It was growing dark outside when Joe woke up and heard Elroy talking to himself. The man had kept the fire going all day so the cave wasn't so terribly cold. Even so Joe shivered, chilled to the very center of his body as he was to far away from the fire to really get any direct heat. "Can I have more water, please?"

Elroy picked up the canteen and shook it. "No you can't, there's just enough to see me through until tomorrow." and put the canteen down again and went back to watching the fire dance.

"Please help me, Joe prayed, *please find me so I can go home. I'll be ever so grateful. "*

Elroy stood up and took a few steps toward Joe. "You had better shut up kid or I'll give you another knock on the head and gag you as well. Maybe I'll just go off now and leave you here alone and no one will ever find you unless some hunter finds this cave by accident and your moldy bones." Elroy laughed even as he looked out at the dark night.

"The Thunder Gods won't let you to do that, Elroy. I know." Just then thunder rumbled long and low and lightening flashed repeatedly and the wind suddenly began to blow straight into the cave in a wintry blast that made Elroy jerk upright and look wildly around. Finally, he gave a shaky laugh before walking back to huddle close to the fire that was sputtering and flaring continuously in the cold wind.

"I think They've found you, Elroy." Joe spoke in a quiet dry voice and he began to pray. He was so awfully cold. He was constantly shivering now which made his head hurt even more, but he prayed harder. *'Please find me so I can go home. Please find me.'*

It suddenly grew very still in the cave except for the snapping and popping of the fire. A sense of breathless waiting for something to happen filled the atmosphere of the cave. Joe opened his eyes wide and saw a strange bright light appear in the cave's entrance that obscured the dark night. To his utter amazement he watched as four indistinct figures came into the cave flowing right through the rock wall to grow so tall that Their heads brushed the high ten foot rock ceiling. An intense Light filled the once dim cave in brilliance as these glowing Guardians became three tall men and one woman.

Joe's eyes flared wide at the visible appearance of these supernatural beings. His heart started beating like a trip hammer, literally knocking against his ribs. He quickly glanced over at Elroy who was crouched by the fire and saw the man's eyes bulge in fear and his mouth hung open in horror.

The Light Ones slowly drifting up to the fire and surround the huddled man. Joe couldn't see Elroy now because the great light formed a barrier and all he could hear was whimpering and pleading of a voice that was shaking in abject fear. Suddenly the ropes loosened and fell from Joe's wrists and ankles and he was free. He couldn't move because he was so weak and his stiff muscles were reluctant to obey, but valiantly he worked them to regain some strength.

Joe was in the back of the small cave and far from the fire, yet he could feel the powerful energy being emitted by these Gods and it made his hair stand up all over his body.

The Gods lived…..the Gods…lived! Boy did They ever live! Joe's thoughts stuttered repeatedly. *The Gods lived for real!*

Then Joe heard. *You were rejected from these sacred lands years ago yet you have foolishly returned. Now you have violated our most sacred law by shedding the blood of an innocent child. We waited to see if you would repent your wickedness. We gave you the opportunity to change your mind and take the child back. You have instead decided upon his death. Thus you have lost your chance of redemption here on Earth in this lifetime. You have crossed the line into true evil and now if you're allowed to go free you will become a murderer of the innocent to gain what you want in the world. Elroy Devereaux, you will not inflict more pain upon the living and we will save your soul from the stain of murder. Be gone, go to the Master to be sorted out. Be gone!*

A *scream* choked off abruptly by a flare of intense light and then silence descended. Joe closed his eyes and was glad that he couldn't see what had happened to Elroy. Then in the quiet that followed Joe opened his eyes and knew that he and these Beings were alone in the cave. Then the Gods turned and faced him. Joe trembled in Their presence, yet in his heart he knew he was safe.

He croaked. "Thank You, Mighty Ones, thank You with all my heart. I would sing for You if that would please You. It is the only gift of mine that I can give in gratitude for having save me only I haven't had any water in a long time."

The Guardians stilled then the canteen floated through the air and fell gently into Joe's lap. Opening it up was a hard task with his swollen hand, but he did it and drank deeply until finally he just held the glorious wet in his mouth before swallowing. Slowly his throat returned to normal after repeatedly drinking. His head pounded something fierce, but he had a performance to give and it was going to be the most important one of his life

Gathering up his courage and strength, Joe forced himself to stand and fought for steadiness as he slid up the cave wall wondering what he should sing. He looked over at the Gods waiting patiently and felt enclosed in the warmth of Their love and it took away all his fear.

Inspiration flooded through him on such a huge wave of joy he forgot his pain and weakness. Standing up straight he began to sing words to a song he had never heard before. Glorious sounds and words sung in praise of the Spirits who guarded these beautiful lands. Joy simply exploded in his heart and mind. It was minutes of sheer glory to sing for the Gods and that had to be the ultimate experience for any artist. Joe was in bliss, even as tears of Joy fell from his eyes, the music flowed out to fill the cave that was acting like a large amphitheater. He finished it was on a high note that dwindled as though it traveled away up into the heavens until silence once more filled the cave.

Joe slid down the wall and sat with a thump and leaned wearily back against the rock with his eyes closed and breathing heavily. He had given them all he had left of his strength. Joe felt heat and could see a bright light coming closer through his closed eyelids. When he opened his eyes it was to see a woman, the Goddess, standing in front of him. She smiled and said into his mind,

"Thank you small one. The song nourished our spirits with Beauty and brought us great joy. Your name is True Heart. Let it be known."

She took a gold medallion from around her neck and as She bent down and extended it, Joe watched it grow smaller and smaller until she placed the chain over his head. This wasn't a hallucination because he could feel the weight of the gold medallion fall upon his chest.

Joe looked up and smiled. "I'm going to think of You as my Mother now if that's all right with You, of course. I don't have an Earth mother anymore, so maybe a Sky-Mother would be great, huh?" The Goddess looked down at this human child and returned his smile. She placed Her hand upon Her heart and patted it then graciously bowed Her regal head.

From one second to another the Gods were there and then….. They weren't. The only light in the cave came from the campfire and as time slowly passed the fire curiously didn't need replenishing and Joe dwelled in the twilight of consciousness for some time. He wasn't worried about the cold or the pain or his hunger as they were distant things to him. Nothing seemed real to him and nothing outside mattered. He was in bliss.

He felt someone pick him up then lay him down and wrapped him in warmth and Joe opened his eyes briefly to see Mr. Hoggins. "Hello, how did you find me?" Joe whispered.

"The Guardians told me where you were. Now you rest easy boy, I'm taking you down the mountain to your family. Go to sleep Joe, all is well."

"They were here you know. The Goddess is my Sky-Mother now and I sang for Them too." Joe closed his eyes and fell into unconsciousness.

Mr. Hoggins smiled down at this remarkable child as he picked the limp boy up. "You have a Sky-Mother who cares a great deal about you. Now we'll see what other miracles come your way."

~*Going Home*~

BEN AND THE MEN were spread out along the northern line of foothills. After about an hour Blackhawk suddenly drew his horse to a halt and held up his hand and flashed his light to the left and to the right signaling everyone to stop. The light signal was passed on.

He appeared to be listening. "Joe and Elroy are in the old west cave. Come on, it's over this way." and trotted his horse ahead and the rest followed closely. Within the next half hour Blackhawk called out. "Leave your horses here men it's getting too steep for them." The men dismounted and loosened their cinches and followed Blackhawk up into the steep hills.

Rockland Hoggins had come quite a ways and had started down the last long incline when he heard the men coming up the hill, not noisily or anything like that, just the natural sound of lots of men moving through the woods as sound carries mighty easy on a still night. Rockland walked out of the trees carrying his heavy load.

In the beginning Joe hadn't weighed all that much, but as the climb down the mountain grew in length and time passed the boy's weight seemed to increase. Rockland stumbled a bit now and then as it was difficult walking in snow that covered pine needles making the footing very slippery. He kept on walking until he saw the line of men coming up to meet him.

"Rockland, is he alive?" yelled Blackhawk.

"Yes ……of course he's alive ……he's just ……sleeping." replied the breathless man and continued to carefully place his feet on the downward slope of snow. Sweat was rolling down his face and his legs were trembling from fatigue. "I'm getting too old…for this kind of….effort." He panted.

"God bless your hide my friend, I'm forever beholden to you." Blackhawk said with profound relief in his voice that it actually shook.

"Hello….Blackhawk…here's your boy…safe and sound….except for a bit of this and that ….but I figure…… time and rest will cure that." Rockland was saying as he gladly sat down on the closest boulder and rested his burden on his lap and sensibly waited there for the men to come up. "The Gods told me ……where to find him ……and sure enough he was there ……in that old cave up on the west face."

Mike sprinted forward and knelt beside the man and the boy and reached out and pulled the sleeping bag away from Joe's face and touched it. The moon was bright enough in the clearing for him to see that Joe was unconscious and one side of his head was bloody. Tears ran down Mike's face as Ben knelt down beside him and the other men gathered around.

"Now, youngen'…… there isn't much the matter….. with Joe here …except maybe a slight concussion….. loss of some blood, ….pain, hunger plus exposure…..It isn't serious…… at least it isn't for a western hombre."

Rockland Hoggins was gradually catching his breath. "You just watch him…he'll bounce right back as soon as he's warm and fed, just see if he doesn't…..The Gods love him, you know …….and he isn't near to cracking." laughed Rockland breathily as though he didn't have enough energy for a hearty laugh. The old man was more than willing to give up his burden as Ben stooped and picked up his guardian child.

"Come on let's get you two down to the ranch. Thank you is a weak word to express what we all feel Mr. Hoggins I owe you a life debt." Gently, Ben started down the hill while two men lifted Rockland to his feet.

"Now boys, you aren't going to… carry me, are you? Nonsense… I just needed a bit of rest to catch my breath. 'Course… I wouldn't mind…leaning on your arms a mite. That's a hard climb….down the mountain under these conditions…. for an old man like me."

"Well Mr. Hoggins, we all think you're a bit of a hero so anything you want you'll get, that's for sure." said Rio Three Toes.

So they clasped him around the waist and he laid his arms over their shoulders. "That's the ticket." Mr. Hoggins said as the men practically lifted him off the ground.

Back down the hill they all went with Ben having as many helping hands as could reach him to keep him from falling. Mike simply wasn't strong enough to carry his brother and struggle with the treacherous footing so when Ben tired he reluctantly passed Joe to Jimmy and after a bit Jimmy passed Joe to Jacko and Joe again was passed to Hank. Each man wanted the honor of packing Joe even if it was for just a few steps as they descended. If it hadn't been such a serious occasion the men would have joked about passing Joe around like a football. Well, maybe in the future they could retell this tale with a chuckle, but not now, their relief was too great at having found Joe alive. It took them forty minutes to reach the horses and by that time every man who had climbed the hill had had the chance to carry the boy except Mike, though he helped who ever was holding Joe at the time.

While the men were tightening cinches, Rockland Hoggins rested and talked to Blackhawk and Ben while Mike sat on a rock and held Joe cradled in his arms.

"Issaquah, I don't think you need to worry any more about that wicked man because he's been taken care of so call in all your men, they won't be needed anymore." Rockland said soberly.

"What do you mean he's been taken care of Rockland?" said Blackhawk quietly.

"The Gods took care of him. All that's left up in that cave is a pile of clothes and his boots. Elroy is gone from this world. Now I'm a mighty tired old man and I'm not used to hiking around in the dark on slippery ground and quite frankly Issaquah, I'm surprised I did as well as I have." he grinned.

"Okay Jimmy, take my cell phone and make some calls." After Ben was mounted Carl and Mike helped lift Joe up into his arms.

Jimmy put a call out on the phone. "Pass the word Joe has been found safe and Elroy had been dealt with. Call everyone back and they can go home now and tell them thanks for coming out, it was greatly appreciated. We're taking Joe to the Kelly Ranch. Everyone will get more news later." and hung up.

"Jimmy, call Mari Beth and give her the word that we're bringing Joe back to our ranch and to get the doctor out there pronto. Tell her Joe is basically okay except for some bangs and bruises so don't scare her." Jimmy did that once he was mounted.

Riding alongside Mike, Jimmy said. "See, I told you we'd find him all right and tight. That boy leads a charmed life."

"I'll never doubt your word again Jimmy, not after tonight." vowed Mike.

"Well Mike, don't get to feeling too bad about not being there to help Joe 'cause I wasn't either. Let me tell you this event has been mighty tough on my hero image." And Jimmy gave Mike's arm a good squeeze.

"Yeah, I can see where you'd be awfully worried about that." For the first time since Joe went missing Mike laughed at this crazy cowboy friend of theirs.

The riders rode into ranch yard where May, Big Mike and Dusty were waiting. May started to cry thinking the boy was dead when she saw Ben packing a wrapped up bundle until Hank called out that Joe was alive.

Once again Ben passed his burden down, this time to Jimmy before he dismounted. "Hank I need to borrow your truck to get this boy home immediately, my men will see to the horses."

"Sure, I'll get the keys." In a minute Hank came running out of the house with the truck keys.

Jimmy said, "I'd like to drive you and Mike home if you don't mind, Sir."

"Good idea young man, I'd appreciate that."

"I'll stay a bit and talk to the men and make more calls. Don't you worry about a thing Ben, just get our boy taken care of and I'll be over with Rockland after a bit." assured Blackhawk.

"Thanks Chief"

Mike climbed into the back of the truck with Ben in the front and Jimmy put Joe into Ben's arms, shut the door and climbed into the driver's side. You can believe that the ride home was done in record time. That Jimmy drove like he rode his horse; all out.

Mari Beth and Hannah were waiting in the kitchen when they heard the sound of a truck coming into the yard at a fast clip and skidding to a halt. Jumping to their feet they were out the door in time to see Ben carefully lifting a blanketed form out of the truck then Mike and Jimmy got out. Mari Beth almost fainted when she saw them, fearing real bad injuries they hadn't told her about. Hannah was crying quietly as Ben came up the porch steps.

"Now enough of that, Joe's going to be okay. He's no doubt got a concussion and he's been cold and hungry for the past 26 hours so let's get him into a warm tub of water and some hot soup for his belly. Come on ladies, this is your work." said Ben more cheerfully than he felt for he was worried about Joe's long unconscious state. "Did you call Dr. Valdez? Can he come?" asked Ben as he carried Joe up to his room.

"He's on his way and should be here any time now. Hannah, get a tub going while I strip Joe. Ben, go down and bring up some of that hot soup Hannah has ready, please. Oh, throw some blankets in the dryer to warm."

Mari Beth got busy unzipping the sleeping bag. She gasped at the sight of the blood on the side of Joe's head and shirt. She bit her lips and finished stripping off his shirt and saw the bruises and the raw wounds on his wrists showing her clearer than words what this child had suffered. As she rolled Joe over to strip away the rest of his clothes, he woke up.

"Mmmmom, is that you?" Joe said groggily through his chattering teeth, "I dddon't feel so ggggood Mom and I'm aaaawfully ccccccold."

Mari Beth paused and glanced over at Mike who was helping her and saw his white face. Then Mike said in an encouraging voice. "Joe we're going to make you feel better. Come on kid wake up and give us some help here."

"Mikey? Is ttttthat you? Wwwhere have you been? I cccccalled and ccccalled, but you were lllost. Are you ffffounded now Mikey? I'm ever ssssso glad." Joe mumbled. Mike looked stricken.

"Mike it's his concussion so don't worry, his confusion will pass. Come on Joe honey let's get you into a nice hot tub of water that will make you feel so much better." Mike and Mari Beth on either side practically carried the naked boy into the bathroom.

Just then Joe woke up. "Geeze ppppppeeze Mike, I'm nnnnnaked here and Hannah and Mari Beth cccan ssssee me all ooooover." complained the little boy as he staggered along. Mari Beth and Hannah laughed quietly relieved that Joe was back and once Mari Beth saw that Joe could stand on his own two feet, they both quickly disappeared from view leaving Mike to get Joe into the tub.

"Well kid, you're not much to look at right now and the women are gone. Let me help you into the tub." Mike lifted his brother into the water. "Come on swing that leg over, okay now the other one. I'll stay here so you don't fall asleep and drown." laughed Mike at his embarrassed brother all the while trying not to cry at the pathetic sight of Joe's injuries.

Joe hissed a little as the warm water hit his chilled body. He was so cold his teeth were chattering. Once he'd sunk under the water Joe gradually relaxed. "BBBBoy does this feel ggggood. I've bbbbbeen awfully ccccold for so long. Ddddumb Elroy wouldn't even lllllet me get cccclose to the fire." Joe shivered. "I'm ccccold all the way to my iiiiinnards." Gradually Mike added more hot water. As Joe got warmer he became aware of the pain in his head and wrists. He cried and tears streamed down his pale face. "Oh, man, I hurt real bad Mikey. I hurt all over."

"I know Joe; Hannah, can you bring Joe a glass of warm water please." Within a minute Hannah handed Mike a glass. "I want you to drink this water 'cause you need lots of liquids." Obediently, his little brother drank the warm water and only then did he realize how thirsty he was.

"Oh that's gggood. Can I have aaanother one? I haven't hhhad much to drink lately. How lllong was I gone? I've lllllost track of the tttime, I guess." he stopped talking while Mike helped him drink more water.

"You were gone over 24 hours. Thank God we found you. Actually it was Mr. Hoggins who found the cave and packed you down the mountain. Do you remember that?" Again Hannah added more hot water and Joe sighed as the heat increased and he relaxed more. Joe seemed to have forgotten worrying about the women seeing him naked.

"No not really. I think I rrrrremember him coming into the cave and then I ggguess I went to sleep. He's a nice man, isn't he Mikey?"

"He sure is and we owe him a real life debt, that's what Ben said. You and I will have to think of something nice to do for him when you're better."

All the time they were talking Mike was gently washing Joe's face and hair free of blood, but stayed away from the wound as best he could. Hannah ran more hot water into the tub and noticed Joe has stopped his constant shaking and only occasional shivers shook his small body. Mike carefully cleaned Joe's wrists and as the boy whimpered and cried out.

Mike bit his lip and said. "I know it hurts Joe, but we've got to get your wrists cleaned up. The doctor is coming out to fix you up so the more we do now the less he'll have to do."

Mike tried to distract him by saying. "So kid, you had yourself quite an adventure. It's amazing to me what you'll do to get attention so you can really brag about it when you go back to school. You'll be a real sensation, maybe even hand out autographs. By the way, where did you get the gold necklace? It's pretty snazzy." He could hear Hannah in the next room for which he was grateful in case Joe became unconsciousness again.

"The Gods are real, Mikey, *really, really real*! The Goddess gave me this gold medallion. She took it right off Her own neck too. She's so beautiful and really big, really tall, you know? She's going to be my mother now, my Sky-Mother. It's okay with Her 'cause She smiled at me and patted Her heart when I asked Her. Wasn't that nice? I sang for Them too. I wiss you could aaave been 'dare.'" Joe began to slur his words and his eyes grew unfocused. Joe sort of drifted a bit and Mike hurried with the washing in case he passed out. Joe roused. "You know how music sort of just comes to you when you play? Well, that's what happen' to me. I just knew the music and the words….. I can 'member some … if you'd like to hear. I can't sing right now……… but I haven't forgot…ten."

Joe drifted for a bit and Mike slipped his arm under Joe's shoulders and gripped his armpit to keep him from sliding down under the water.

Joe aroused and said. "Elroy's gone Mikey he's really gone, gone. They did somethin' in that awful bright light. I guess they just made 'im dis'pear. It was really scary…… Never make 'em mad, Mikey………don't never go 'dare." and drifted off.

"Hannah help me, Joe's going unconscious again." called Mike frantically as he gripped Joe to keep him afloat. Hannah rushed in and laid some large towels on the floor beside the tub and between the two of them they lifted him out and laid him down. Drying him didn't take long. They got him into warmed flannel pajamas then

Hannah went to the top of the stairs and called for her father to get Joe into bed.

Mari Beth brought up two heated blankets and came upstairs with Ben. She immediately spread one over the bottom sheet as Ben carried Joe in and put him into bed. She then spread another hot blanket over Joe and tucked the quilt over all. Hannah had thoughtfully spread a towel over the pillow so his wet and bloody head wouldn't soak it. Fortunately, five minutes later the doctor arrived and Blackhawk showed him upstairs.

"Okay people, bring me a basin of hot water and some towels and I'll see to our wounded warrior here. Hmm, he's unconscious." Dr. Valdez frowned. "How often has this been happening? Has he roused at all?" asked the doctor as he took Joe's pulse.

"Yes, he was kinda disorientated at first when he woke up before we got him in the tub. He talked quite lucidly for awhile then he sort of slid into this state again. What does it mean? Is it serious?" anxiously Mike questioned the doctor.

"After I examine him I'll know more. We'll hope he stays unconscious until I finish stitching him up. Now young man, you go downstairs and get some supper; your brother will be all right and the rest of you clear out too," commanded the doctor. "Accept you, Mari Beth, please stay and help me if you feel up to it."

"I've raised nine children Doctor and I've seen just about everything, so I won't faint on you." replied Mari Beth indignantly.

He laughed and looked at her over the top of his glasses. "It never entered my mind. Now, let's see to our boy here."

Downstairs Hannah served everyone stew and hot rolls she had readied for them earlier. Blackhawk, Tom, Luther, Ben, Hank, Mr. Hoggins, Jimmy and Mike ate like starving men.

Talk around the kitchen table was sporadic as they sat drinking coffee. Finally Mari Beth came into the kitchen with Doctor Valdez. The Doctor sat down at the kitchen table with a tired sigh and accepted the cup of coffee from Hannah.

"Now this is what I need," As he sipped the fresh coffee with pleasure.

"Would you like some stew doctor? It's hot and I have some nice rolls to go with it."

"Don't mind if I do though I don't normally eat this late in the evening. However I think I might need a little more energy for the long drive home. Thank you Hannah." She placed a bowl before him he dug right in. Everyone sat and waited as patiently as they could for the doctor to finish. With a fresh cup of coffee in his hand the doctor said. "Joe has a slightly more than a mild concussion from a blow to the right side of his head and I've put in four stitches to close the scalp wound. He's lost some blood; well head wounds bleed something fierce, don't they? It's not a serious blood lost, however, combined with dehydration and a mild case of hypothermia it does concern me. I would suggest hot bricks wrapped in towels and placed around his body to give him extra heat. Renew the hot blanket periodically. I've given him two bags of warm normal saline by I.V. and that's brought his blood pressure up nicely as well as hydrating him. His pulse is stronger. His wrists are abraded so I've bandaged those, but the other bruises aren't serious and there aren't any broken bones. I don't believe he should be rushed to the hospital. In my experience patients heal faster at home in most cases."

Doctor Valdez took another drink of coffee. "Normally, I'd take him into the hospital, but I'm sure he will get good care right here. I do want a 12 hour watch kept on him and because of the exposure he might develop a cold or even a chest cold in which case I want him in the emergency right away. I don't want him developing pneumonia. Now he's going to have quite a headache for a few days so I've left pain pills with Mari Beth. I want you to give him water and clear liquids as often as possible tonight. Keep him warm and in bed with regular food for the next three or four days. He can get up to go to the bathroom with help, but bed rest is imperative. If all goes well I want to see him in my office in four days. Call me tomorrow and give me an update. If by chance anything alarms you bring him into the hospital immediately, however I don't expect that will be necessary. Joe will come out of this a popular guy." smiled the Doctor said and watched people around the table relax. Mike got up quietly and slipped out of the kitchen.

"Now you all go home and go to bed. There isn't anything more you can do except wait for Joe to wake up and tell you his story which I hope someone passes along to me. I'm going to follow my own advice and go home. Goodnight and praise God Joe was found safe."

"Thank you for making a house call Dr. Valdez. I know physicians don't do that anymore." said Mari Beth as she helped him with his overcoat.

The Doctor turned to her and smiled. "I'm a country doctor besides you know I'd do most anything for you, Mari Beth. I wish y'all would call me Lyle, more friendly-like, isn't it? Goodnight people." Ben carried the doctor's bag and walked him out to his car.

When Ben came back into the house he said. "It's time everyone got some sleep and personally, I'm worn to a frazzle and the rest of you can't be any better off. Y'all can come back tomorrow and we'll talk to Joe. Hopefully he'll be making more sense by then."

Blackhawk got up and wearily stretched and he and the others said goodnight. "We'll be back in the morning, but not too early." With that the men left and by the time the sound of their engines had faded the Strongbows and Mr. Hoggins were climbing the stairs.

"Here's your room Mr. Hoggins with your own bathroom. I hope you have a good night's sleep because you deserve it. Thank you for bring our little boy home." said Mari Beth with a warm smile.

"He's my friend too, Mrs. Strongbow; besides the Thunder Gods want him alive and singing I would suppose." the tired old man said with a grin. Mari Beth stepped closer and hugged the man tightly and kissed his cheek. It embarrassed Mr. Hoggins to no end and he quickly ducked into his room and shut the door.

Ben chuckled. "I bet that's the first time in many years that a woman has hugged and kissed that man."

"Hannah, do you believe Joe when he said he'd sung for the Thunder Gods?" asked Mari Beth.

"How else could he have gotten that golden disk he's got around his neck? Yes, I believe him because Joe doesn't tell lies Mom."

"Enough! Let it rest until we talk to Joe. Hannah, you stay with Joe for a few hours then wake me and I'll watch him for awhile. Mari Beth, you've got Carli to care for early in the morning so you're exempt. Everyone is leaving their doors open tonight so if you need help just call, Hannah. I think that shot Lyle gave him will last at least four or five hours." said Ben as he gave a jaw-breaking yawn. "Lordy, I'm getting too old for all this excitement and hard riding.

Thank goodness Mr. Hoggins decided to spend the night; that must be another first for him to be in someone else's house."

Mari Beth and Ben stopped at Joe's opened door and looked in and saw Mike was sitting in a rocking chair beside the bed. Hannah walked on into the room and stopped beside Mike. "Mike, Joe's all right and snoring like a steam engine and I'm going to sit with him now. We'll all leave our doors open in case I need help. Go to bed and tomorrow he'll be must better. Dad will wake you around four and you can take your turn sitting with Joe, all right?" Mike got slowly out of his chair and pulled the covers up closer around Joe's neck and walked toward the door wiping his face with his sleeve.

"Sweetheart, you need sleep, why you're all tuckered out. Come dear boy and let me help you get into bed. I think a couple of aspirin might help." Mike, for all he was a young man now and almost sixteen, allowed Mari Beth to guide him to his room for it isn't only the victim of violence who suffers, but the ones who love them.

Fifteen minutes later Mari Beth entered their bedroom and got ready for bed then crawled in beside Ben with a deep groan of relief and he pulled her over to lay close against his side.

"My love, I don't want to go through these past twenty-four hours ever again. Poor Mike's feeling like he didn't protect his brother enough and we're all sharing his sense of guilt too, but who would have thought that Elroy would go so far as to kidnap one of them. If we had thought at all we'd have known that Joe, being the smaller, would be the natural target as Mike is too big not to have put up a good fight. Elroy killed those animals and sent a mean bull out to do harm. That should have warned us about the kind of man he was. Joe seems convinced that the Thunder Gods protected and saved him and I'm going to believe that too and I will give Them thanks for his safe return and our beloved Christ as well." murmured Mari Beth sleepily.

"And I say amen sweetheart, and again, amen." And the stillness of the night brought healing sleep.

There was a distant rumbling in the mountains and an occasional flash of lightening, then all became quiet and the night closed down on restless spirits. It began to snow again.

Joe woke late the next morning and the first thing he became aware of was his head hurt like the very dickens. He searched his mind, but couldn't remember how he had gotten hurt. When he put his hand on his head he felt the bandage. Wow, his head was bad enough to have a big bandage on it? "Geeze Peeze, what in the heck did I do?" Joe asked weakly.

"You got knocked on the head and dragged up a mountain among other things. The Doctor put four stitches in your scalp last night so you have less hair on that side too. It's a good thing you're such a hardheaded kid or you'd have been long gone." Mike's voice came quietly from the side of his bed.

"Mike? What happened? Gee, I can't remember." Joe fretted.

"Don't worry it will all come back to you real soon. Right now, I've got to help you to the bathroom as you've been asleep for over four hours and you must be ready to burst. Come on Champ let's stagger into the bathroom again." Mike pulled back the layers of blankets and slipped his arm under Joe's shoulders and lifted him into a sitting position.

"Geeze peeze!" Whined Joe as he grabbed his head to hold it on his shoulders. "My head's going to come off, Mike."

"Just sit still for a minute and the throbbing will calm down."

Patiently Mike waited until Joe opened his eyes carefully and gave a slight whispered, "Okay." Lifting him up Mike steadied him to the bathroom. "Geeze peeze, I don't have any legs."

Mike laughed at that. "Oh, you'll find them eventually."

Once back in bed, Mike propped Joe up with more pillows and covered him once again with blankets and put a heavy sweater around his shoulders. "You gotta' stay warm so you won't catch cold." All the while Mike was dragging the towel wrapped bricks out from under the covers. "I'll get the hot ones and bring them back."

"I don't mean to whine, but my head hurts something fierce, even my eyes hurt." Joe carefully breathed deeply and hoped the pain would soon go away. If it didn't, he was going to throw up. Joe's face had turned a whitish green. "I'm going to be sick." he moaned.

"Here Joe, take a long drink of water." Mike lifted his brother up so that he could drink a few sips of water. "Now drink a little of this milk shake with this pill the Doctor left you. The milk should settle your stomach."

Mike carefully laid Joe back down and covered him again. He got a cold wet washcloth and laid it over Joe's eyes and forehead. "Oh thanks, that feels great." he lay quietly until the worst of the throbbing abated and his stomach stopped churning.

"I've got to go down and tell Hannah you're awake so she can feed you a light breakfast, but I've set this bucket right here beside you in case you get sick."

"Could I have more water please? I'm awful thirsty."

"Sure Joe, but take it easy and don't jar your head. Here's the straw and all you have to do is suck." Joe drank water like he was a camel filling up for a long desert journey. "Hey, that's enough or you won't have any room for Hannah's breakfast which will really tick her off."

"Mike? If I can't remember, will you tell me what happened?" Joe asked in a fretful way.

"Sure, I'll fill you in on all the gory details. There's one thing I will tell you right now. You know your friend Mr. Hoggins? Well, he's here. Yes, right here in the house and he stayed overnight too. Now be good and he'll be up for a visit. I'll be right back." Mike left the door open as he left.

Joe could hear the sound of voices floating from the kitchen. It comforted him to know he wasn't alone anymore…Alone anymore? Where had that thought come from? The blank wall to his memory was still there. Gee this is weird, but at least he recognized people and his own name was Joseph Devereaux Kelly. Yeah, he had that much memory. Now he knew exactly how Nino must feel and it was really awful not to know what was what or who you were. He heard the sound of footsteps coming up the stairs which told Joe he was about to have company. An old man appeared in the doorway.

"Mr. Hoggins? Gee, it's great that you came down to see me." said Joe smiling in greeting.

"Well boy, what are friends for anyway? Glad to see you're doing better." The old man walked over to stand beside Joe and took his hand gently in his then cautiously sat down on the edge the bed. "I'm not going to stay long because you need your rest. I just came in to say good bye for now, but I'll be back down to see how you get on before long."

"Gee, do you have to go right away? I kinda need to talk to you about some things if I could only remember what they were." again a slight whine underlined Joe's voice.

"I'm not used to being around a lot of people Joe so I need to get back up on my mountain, you understand? We'll have plenty of time to talk when you're better. I'm just very happy you're safe. Why, what would we do if we lost that voice of yours, and of course you along with it." the man chuckled. "Don't you fret about not remembering exactly what happened, you will eventually. Getting a knock on the head can cause a fella' lots of interesting problems as you know."

"Yeah it does and it gives you a real peach of a headache too." Joe said with a weak grin.

"I'll be down to see you next week and that's a promise. We'll talk about all those things you can't remember right now, okay? Now my young friend, you take care and try to keep out of mischief." The old man grinned and patted Joe's hand gently.

"Please come back 'cause a good friend is hard to find. Thanks again Mr. Hoggins for coming even though I don't know why." Joe said sincerely.

"Friends *are* just that and age doesn't matter much between people who like each other and friends come when they're needed. You'd be surprised at how many friends you have in the Valleys. Now be good and I'll be seeing you soon I promise." Letting Joe's hand go Mr. Hoggins walked to the door and with a final wave he left the room. Joe heard him going down the stairs.

"Gee, he didn't stay very long, but I guess I'm lucky that he came at all 'cause that's a long trip just to see me for a few minutes." Joe pondered that and sighed. The next footsteps he heard he thought would be Hannah with his breakfast, but instead he got another surprise.

"My, just look at you, Mister Lazybones himself lying in bed at this hour of the mornin' just like a King with everyone to wait on him." laughed Jimmy quietly.

"Hi Jimmy, geeze peeze maybe you'll tell me what the heck is going on. Mr. Hoggins was just here and didn't stay very long and now you. What's happened? Am I awfully sick or something like that? It's worrying me a lot that I can't remember anything." Joe pulled off the washcloth and squinted against the light so he could see his friend.

True Heart

Jimmy also got a good look at Joe's scared and bruised white face. He also noticed how the intense light coming through the windows was bothering him. So he went around the room lowering the window shades until there was a nice soft grayness to the room.

With a sigh of relief Joe said, "Thanks Jimmy, that's much better. I've got an awful headache, you see." complained the little boy.

"Now look pard, I won't lie to you even if I could." Jimmy sat down on the edge of the bed. "You don't have anything wrong to worry about, honestly. Doctor said you had a hard blow to your noggin and it might take you a bit to recall things. Like Nino only you'll remember what's what faster I think. You remember your name so that's a good indication how fast you'll recover so stop all this fretting. Doc said to let things come to you as they will. I will only say that you had yourself quite an adventure and you'll be telling your grandchildren about it one day." Jimmy was smiling so relaxed that it relieved a bone deep fear inside Joe. He gave a heavy sigh of relief.

"Oh, is that all? Guess I'll just lie here like a King then and enjoy being waited on hand and foot. It's hard on a guy to be famous for daring-do, isn't it?" laughed Joe carefully and still winced at the pounding that started in his head. "Wished that pill would hurry up and take away this pain in my head."

"Here now, I'll get kicked out if you go into a decline or something. I'll wet down that cloth again 'cause that always helped my headaches." Jimmy went into the bathroom and Joe heard the water running and then a fresh cold cloth was laid gently on his hurting head.

"Oh yeah, that does feel good." and was quiet for a few minutes. "So Jimmy, what have you been doing?" For the next little bit Jimmy entertained him with the goings-on in the country and the progress on Ms. Mary's house until he heard footsteps on the stairs. "Well, Joe my visit is over for now. That's surely Miss Strongbow coming with your breakfast. Eat up and get back on your feet and we'll take us a nice horseback ride when you're feeling up to it okay? It's really beautiful out, what with the snow covering everything and the sun shining so bright that you have to wear sunglasses. See you soon, pard." And with a gentle pat on Joe's shoulder Jimmy left just as Hannah came in carrying a tray.

"Morning Joe honey, maybe you're ready to eat now." She sat the tray down on a side table. "Sir, I've got several things here for you to choose from. I'm not sure how your stomach is feeling so you get special treatment. I have custard, the kind you like, hot cereal, toast, eggs scrambled or poached and Juice or milk. What does your Highness desire?" said Hannah with a bow.

Joe laughed then put his hand on his head and Hannah waited patiently until he sighed and said. "I think my stomach says it would be happy with hot cereal, toast and milk this morning, and maybe the custard, my slave. Of course the rest of me would like pancakes, bacon and all that, but I'd better not."

"It's a good thing you have a sore head My Lord, or that slave remark might get you into serious trouble, but considering the state your in, I'll forgive you. Here now, don't strain to sit up and feed yourself Joe, I'll help you. The quieter you are the less your head will hurt." Hannah spread a towel under Joe's chin and proceeded to entertain and feed him at the same time. Hot oatmeal with cream and brown sugar was one of his favorites. Golly it tasted good and he ate most all of it too.

"I can't eat any more Hannah. I guess my stomach shrunk or something, but that was awfully good." Joe smiled sleepily and put his hand in hers.

"Happy stomachs are a piece of cake for me and I'm glad you liked it. Now I can tell you're just about to fall asleep again. I'm going to get a nice warm washcloth and wipe your face and hands then you'll take a little nap. I guarantee you'll feel much better afterward." Joe felt her removing some of the pillows and turn one over to the cool side. The next thing Joe felt was a warm washcloth moving over his face and murmured, "Just like Mom used to do." And that was all.

Mike came in the door just as Hannah stood up. He was loaded down with hot towel wrapped bricks and they managed to place them all round Joe without waking him up.

"He's sound asleep again and that's the best way to heal." said Hannah quietly as she entered the kitchen and sat the tray down on the butcher board with Mike right behind her.

"I guess we'll have to take turns visiting him then. Doctor said he'd sleep a lot at first, but if he isn't better tomorrow, into the Doc's office he goes." said Ben in a very no nonsense way.

"In the meantime I can call him and tell him that his patient is fine, no fever and only a bad headache so far. He's alert enough to joke with me this morning, but Mike said he hasn't remembered anything yet." Hannah began to clean up the dishes.

"I'll sit with him Ben and I bet within a few hours that kid will be hungry and thirsty so best fix him up some soup or whatever, Hannah." Mike stood up and went back upstairs.

Mari Beth was waiting for Carli to finish her breakfast and watched Mike leave the kitchen. With a worried frown on her normally pleasant face Mari Beth said. "I worry about the boy Ben, because he taking his failure to protect Joe too seriously. You might consider talking to him about it." Mari Beth looked at her husband and even though it was a suggestion sort of, Ben recognized a command when he heard one.

"Plan to Sweet Thing, I plan to. Right now I'm going to let him sit with Joe while I'm busy with some ranch business. I'll see you all at lunch." Ben took his hat and jacket off the hook, kissed his wife and daughter and was out the back door before either one could get a word out.

"Men! Honestly, Hannah, they just have to do things their way in their own time. It's mighty irritating, I must say." Mari Beth shook her head. "Well, it isn't my business to be telling him to do this and do that just because I think it should be done right now; or not too many times anyway. It's a failing I suppose, me being so downright bossy. I've got to watch that since that habit seems to be getting worse with old age.

"Momma all done. I want Joey Momma, I want Joey." Carli banged her spoon on her tray to get attention.

"Carli, Joey is sick and he's sound asleep right now so we have to be quiet. Come on Sugarplum, you need your nap too and when we get to Joey's room I'll let you look in on him, Okay? You have to be a very quiet little girl so Joey can sleep and get all better." After wiping her hands and face, Mari Beth lifted her out of her high chair.

"I want to see my Joey. He is hurted and I gotta' see Joey, please."

"Sure enough, let's go, but we have to be really quiet." holding the child's hand they walked slowly up the stairs. Mari Beth led Carli over to Joe's bed and watched the little girl examine Joe's face closely.

Then very gently, Carli patted Joe's blanket covered shoulder and looked up at her mother with tears in her eyes.

Mari Beth picked her up and whisked her out into the hall, whispered. "He's just got a bad headache sweetie, he'll be okay. After you've had your nap we'll go visit him again, all right? Now, there isn't any need to tear up love, your brother will be running after you in no time."

"Okay, Momma." And all was peaceful in the house for the next two hours.

"I see you're awake. How's the head?" Joe turned and saw Ben.

"It's a lot better now and hardly hurts at all. Well, not half as much anyway unless I move too fast. Gee Ben, can't I get up? I'm not really sick am I?" complained the boy as Ben came over and sat down beside him.

"No, you're not really sick, however the doctor wants you to stay in bed and be quiet for the next few days as you had quite a whack on the head. It's shaken your brains up a bit and it will take a few days for them to settle back into place, so don't be in a rush. You also got terribly cold while you were gone so we have to make sure you're kept warm. It's important Joe. If you're really good I'll ask the doctor if you can come downstairs for supper tonight if you lay on the couch so be really good, all right sport?" said Ben.

"Okay, I'll be really good. Ah Ben, I gotta' go to the bathroom now."

"Right, here you go be careful now, take it real easy like so your head doesn't fall off. I sure don't want to see it rolling across the floor 'cause that would really scare me something awful." Joe giggled. "I'll just guide you in and if you need more help, just holler, I'll be right outside the door."

But seeing how unsteady and weak Joe was Ben was afraid he fall down and hit his head again. Ben said. "On second thought I'd better hold you up and close my eyes so you won't shock me." Joe giggled at that and took care of business.

"Steady on boy, you look like you're a bit dizzy headed. Here, sit in this chair right by the window while I straighten your bed out." Wrapping Joe up in another quilt Ben sat Joe in the chair and quickly fixed the bed. Joe was glad the window shades were pulled or the light probably would have blown his head off.

Ben got Joe up and led him back to bed. "Boy, this feels good." as he settled in to the soft bed. "I thought I was ready to get up for awhile, but now I think this is better." Joe sighed as he laid back against his pillows his head thumping in tune with his heart.

"Yeah, when a guy's not feeling well a bed feels mighty fine. Let me get you another cold cloth." Ben fixed a cold cloth and placed that on his boy's head before he sat down beside the bed. "Let me tell you what's going on around here and fill you in on your kidnapping." Joe's eyes fairly bugged out and jerked him up abruptly. The cloth fell into his lap, groaned, grabbed his head and collapsed back against his pillows.

"*Blast my mouth*," Ben leaped up and placed the cloth back on Joe's head even as he saw tears streaming down Joe's face. Ben could have kicked himself for his thoughtless words that had jarred the kid so badly. Ben tucked the covers back up around Joe's shoulders. "I'm sorry Joe. Sorry boy, I shouldn't have said it that way. Now you just take it easy and breathe gently until your head settles. Lordy, Mari Beth will have my hide if I've given you a set back. I'll explain everything."

"*Kidnapped?* Gee, maybe they weren't bad dreams after all. I'm still real confused." He said through gritted teeth.

"Stay calm Joe and I'll tell you what happened. Elroy took you, banged you on the head and we found you. Let the rest of the details come easy-like. The important thing is for you're to rest and heal." Ben took Joe's hand and held it reassuringly.

"Okay, but it's hard losing a piece of yourself this way and I don't like it much at all." The boy complained and carefully opened his eyes a little. "I guess instead of complaining I should be really glad I'm home and safe and sound, huh?"

Ben grinned relieved that Joe was calming down. "Yeah, I know *we're* really happy to get you back. 'Course you *are* a lot of trouble, but heck, you certainly add spice to our lives." and squeezed Joe's hand. Joe could see the tears beading up in Ben's eyes before the man swallowed and cleared his throat. "You sure managed to scare us half to death so please try not to get yourself kidnapped again."

Joe squeezed Ben's hand hard. "It's okay Ben, big men can cry too. Anyway, it looks like I'm going to be around for awhile longer to plague you and give you some more white hair." That set Ben to laughing when a whisper came from the door.

"Joey, Joey, I come to see you headache. Momma said I could." whispered Carli. Ben and Joe looked over at the little face peeking through the door.

Ben frowned. "Come on in, Carli. I see you got yourself out of bed too. Now, honey I want you to always sit down on your bottom when you go down those stairs, step by step when there's no one around to hold your hand. Understand Daddy? You hang on the little animal spokes too. Daddy would cry big tears if you rolled all the way down to the bottom and hurt his baby." Carli giggled as she ran across the room and crawled up into Ben's lap.

"Hi, Joey! Gee you look funny. Is that a hat?"

"Hi yourself, Carli, it's not a hat, it's a bandage to make my headache feel better. I'm coming down for supper too, maybe." Joe smiled and looked hopefully at Ben.

"Supper? Is supper ready? I'm hung'y Daddy. Can I have a cookie? Please?" Big green eyes looked imploringly right into his eyes as she patted his cheek and Ben turned into instant mush.

Joe laughed softly. "Watch it Ben, little manipulator on the move there."

"Yeah, but she does it so well how can I resist. Okay pumpkin, we'll go get a small cookie and then I can come back and get Joe for supper." Picking the little girl up and giving her a toss or two caused Carli to scream delightfully causing Joe winced and put a hand on his head. Ben immediately shushed Carli. "No loud noises baby, it hurts Joe's head."

Carli slapped her hand over her mouth and then whispered. "I sorry Joey, really, really sorry, 'cause Momma said be quiet Carli, too." she pursed her lips like she was going to cry any moment.

"That's okay, it was Ben who started it all." grinned Joe through the flashing pain.

"Before I go I think I'll get you a couple of aspirin. I can't give you one of doc's pills or you'll fall down face first in your food." He let Carli bring Joe half a glass of water and Ben gave him a couple of pills while Carli very carefully handed Joe the glass.

"Thanks sis, you were a big help. You go get your cookie now and I'll be down soon."

"Daddy, can I prackis' going down steps on my bottom?"

"Okay, I'll see if you do it right, then I might give you permission to do it again another time." as they walked out the door together.

Joe had to smile as he listened to the commentary Carli was having with Ben as she thumped her way down the stairs.

Later Ben carried Joe downstairs and laid him carefully on the couch close to the fire and covering him up well with three blankets. If Joe was careful and didn't make any sudden moves, his head stayed on. Mari Beth gave him a pair of sunglasses that helped cut the glare from the lights and the fire.

"Boy, you look just like a Hollywood dude." laughed Mike as he caught sight of Joe laying in splendor on the couch.

"I'm just practicing the lounging act for when I grow up and become rich and famous." Joe snickered.

Dinner was served on the large coffee table so Joe could lay reclined and still be part of the family dinner. Afterward, they all sat around in the living room with Joe half-asleep on the couch. Mike was played soft music as the others had their coffee and spoke in low voices. Suddenly Joe gasped and turned white as a sheet and bolted upright.

Mari Beth jumped up and moved swiftly over to his side. "Honey, what's wrong?" Everyone had stopped what they were doing and gathered around.

"Everything! I've remembered everything! All of it!" Joe said in a dazed way with his eyes distended and his mouth slightly opened as the flood of memory flowed into his conscious mind. "Wow, oh wow." He groaned. "My head, geeze peeze it hurts something fierce." Joe sobbed and clutched his head between his hands, knocking his sunglasses off as tears ran down his face.

"Take it easy son, Hannah give him some hot tea." Ben said. While Hannah fixed sweet tea for Joe, Mike ran upstairs to get one of Joe's pills.

"I want Hannah, where's Hannah?" sobbed Joe with his eyes shut tight and Hannah came and sat beside Joe and slipped her arm behind his back and lifted him up against her chest and into her lap.

"There son, you're all right." taking the cup from Mari Beth, "Here Joe, take some of my good tea, that's my boy, sip slowly. Here's your pill and soon that nasty headache will go away." Joe took the pill in a shaky hand and sipped the tea that Hannah held for him. The family sat down and waited anxiously.

Joe gradually calmed down as the pill began to take away the pain and he completely relaxed against Hannah. "Thanks Mike, I'm sorry to be such a baby. I'll be better real soon." Joe closed his eyes and waited for the thumping in his head to reside. "Do you want to hear about it?" he asked without opening his eyes.

"If you want to tell us Joe, we're here to listen." said Ben. So he told it from beginning to the end. The end was pretty fantastic, but Joe described it in such detail that no one could doubt him. "She was so very beautiful, the woman spirit I mean. She glowed with…love I guess. Anyway, The Goddess, and that's the only word for Her, was the one who gave me this gold medallion. She took it from around her neck and then it sort of grew smaller as She bent down to put it around mine. I think She really liked me," his listeners chuckled at that. "They all disappeared at the same time. That's all. Oh, except I sang for them. Mike, listen to this."

Carefully, using soft tones in order not to jar his head, Joe began to sing and the words just flowed out and he sang for about a minute or so and then stopped. "That's all I can remember. I know there was more, but maybe you've caught enough of it to make a song out of it. Do you think you can, Mike? I can sing it for you again sometime if you need me too. I remembered most of it until I got so happy that things sort of faded out."

"Joe, that was beautiful. The Thunder Gods must have been really pleased with your "thank you". We'll maybe call it "Ode to the Thunder Gods" or maybe "Spirit Song." Hmm yeah, I've got enough to begin so don't worry about it now. We'll have time to work on it together when you're feeling better, okay?"

"Okay, I'm really glad I remembered most of it. Hannah, I'm awfully tired, can I go to bed now?" Joe was looking dazed so Ben came over and picked him up out of Hannah's lap.

"You bet my boy, you're for bed now." said Ben.

"Hannah, are you coming?" asked Joe plaintively as Ben was carrying him out of the living room.

"I'm right behind you, son." Hannah followed Joe and Ben up the stairs. Ben took him to the bathroom and left Hannah to tuck him in, and kiss him goodnight. Before Hannah left she said, "I'm leaving your door open and mine Joe, so if you need me just call, okay?"

"Okay, thanks Hannah. Oh, would you call Mikey for me. I want Mikey please." Joe begged for suddenly for no reason, he felt afraid to be alone.

"Mike, Mike! Can you come upstairs? Joe wants you." called Hannah from the top of the stairs.

Mike had been feeling left out which was silly he thought, but it hurt a little that Joe wanted Hannah and not him. When he heard Hannah calling his name he jumped up, grabbed his guitar and ran up the stairs. Ben and Hannah were waiting in Joe's room when Mike came in.

"I don't want to be alone right now Mikey, could you maybe play for me so I won't dream the bad dream?" asked Joe in a slurry voice.

"Sure Joe, no problem." Mike sat down in a chair beside the bed and began to softly play Joe's favorite "Ave Maria", Quiet, spiritual music that would ease his brother and give him peaceful sleep.

Mari Beth had been left alone in the living room sitting in her rocking chair. She listened to the faint music drifting down the stairwell and smiled as she picked up the sweater she was working on and began to knit.

Ben and Hannah left without Mike really being aware of their going. When he had played for ten minutes or so he looked over at Joe and saw that he was fast asleep, yet Mike continued to play quietly. Mike wasn't sure whether the music was to soothe Joe or himself. It didn't really matter for the music was relaxing and filled with peace at the same time, so he played on.

Ben and Hannah came back into the living room and said Joe was good for the night and as they sat down together, they listened to the soft soothing sounds of Mike's guitar coming from Joe's room.

"That was quite an adventure for a seven year old, not one you'd wish on any child. Joe saw the Thunder Gods and sang for them. No one will believe that, of course, or not many accept us anyway, but certainly Blackhawk will. It has been written that there is more to be believed that ever was seen, or something of that sort. Perhaps it would be best if no one else knew about this part of the kidnapping. What do you think Ben?" said Mari Beth quietly.

"I think you're right. Let's keep it in the family. I believe the less said the better. Maybe we can tell Blackhawk, but no one else. Now, let's call it a night as we've all been under a terrible strain. I think I'll go have a talk with Mike now." Ben got up and went upstairs while Hannah and Mari Beth put the house to bed.

Ben stuck his head in Joe's door and saw that the boy was sound asleep. "Mike, let Joe sleep now. I'd like to talk to you for a bit, if I might." Ben said quietly.

"Sure, Ben, what's the problem?"

"Let's go to your room so we won't disturb Joe."

Mike opened his bedroom door and Ben walked over and sat down in one of the overstuffed chairs and Mike took the other one and waited. "Well, it's been a scary time, hasn't it? I can't remember the last time I was that personally afraid. I can't remember when the Valleys had such a near tragedy and I sincerely hope it's a long time before another. You know it's funny Mike; life I mean. There's a lot a man can do to prevent accidents from happening, but there are those times when there's nothing one can do to prevent or stop what comes down. It's a scientific fact that says a person cannot be in two places at once. So no matter how badly you feel about not being with Joe at the time of his kidnapping, you couldn't be in two places at once. Accidents happen to good people all the time. Why, is a good question and there aren't any real good answers to that. I do know it's wrong for you to take the blame for Joe's kidnapping because you aren't superman nor do you possess a crystal ball to foretell the future." Ben looked at Mike straightly. "It isn't good for Joe to have you hovering over him as though you thought he wasn't smart enough to row his own boat. You, being the oldest, have done a grand job taking care of your brother and sister and I'm sure you'll continue to do so. I'm really proud of you Mike, never doubt that. However, you've got to ease up on yourself and understand you cannot always stand between your siblings and trouble; that isn't the way life works. No one and I mean no man, woman or child blames you for Joe's kidnapping; it just not possible." Ben reached over and took one of Mike's hands in his.

"Awful things sometimes happen to our loved ones and that hurts us something fierce. Now, I want you to let it all go. In many ways you've got to train yourself into letting go being overprotective

True Heart

just like you'd train a horse out of a bad habit. Can you do that for yourself and for Joe?" Ben sat waiting for Mike to answer.

Mike sighed. "It may take awhile, but I'll try. I guess it all started when Dad died because there was only me and I knew he would want me to take care of the kids. It's gotten to be a habit just like you said. I can see if I carried it too far it could hurt the kids instead of helping them. Maybe that's the lesson Grandfather didn't learn with Mom; you know being overly protective and not letting her off the leash so she had to run away. I don't expect it will be easy. I'll think a lot about what you've said Ben, and thanks for the good talk." Mike smiled at the big man who cared so much about him.

"That's it boy, just thinking about it and knowing what needs to be changed means it's already changing. Go to bed and sleep, son. Rest assured you're growing into a fine man, one your father would have been very proud of. Sleep well Mike." And when they both stood up Ben gave Mike a quick hug and left the tall boy alone.

Mike closed his eyes and prayed. "Dad, I guess I got a little tight on the reins, huh? Boy, this being a father is a tough job so I think I'll wait a few years before I try the real thing. But I want you to know Joe and Carli and I have found another father in Ben. I know you would have liked him a lot I know because you're so much alike. You were the greatest and he's the second greatest father. I miss you Dad, I miss you so very much. Say hi to Mom for me. Love you guys. Night." quickly scrubbed the tears off his face, Mike got ready for bed.

Turning off the light he laid his head down on the soft pillow and pulled the covers up over his shoulders. In the silence of his room he became aware of feeling strangely light as though Ben had taken the last of the burden from his shoulders and a lot of the responsibility for Joe and Carli onto his own broad shoulders.

"God bless this house and everyone in it. Thank you for the safe return of my brother Joe. Thank you Thunder Gods for Your continual protection." Mike fell into a dreamless sleep.

Soft thunder rumbled in the mountains and the wind blew gently around the boy's window. The sound of faint laughter floated through the night air then the night was silent. The snow made no sound as it fell.

~The Legend of Lightening Boy~

THE LAND SLEPT BENEATH the late November snow making a sharp contrast to the deep green of the pine trees showing shyly through the white covering on their branches. The sun gleamed off the white fields like millions of brilliant diamonds that had been cast over them and were painfully bright to the eyes.

A long caravan of vehicles moved slowly up the North Mountain Road toward the far hills. Today was a special day of giving thanks to the Thunder Gods for the bounty of their lands. Thanksgiving Day was on the calendars all over the country, but for the Valleys it was traditional to give thanks in community, at least for all those who could make it at Blackhawk's ranch. It was an event not to be missed if at all possible. Travel from the north side of the mountain wasn't always possible if the passes were closed so in that case the Valley there held a similar celebration at North Springfield.

Noon found Blackhawk's yard and the adjacent field filled with parked cars, trucks and pickups. A huge barn like building had been built long ago and situated just to the west of the main house. There were two massive fireplaces on either end of the huge room and two more on either side of the building to warm the interior. The ceiling was deliberately low in order to conserve heat. The people gathered, gossiped and moved about the huge room in their sweaters and boots, having hung their coats on a multitude of wall hooks. Warm spiced apple cider helped comfort their stomachs and warm their hands. The space was large enough to hold 500 people and it often had. When it came time for the feast, long tables would be set up and benches provided for seating.

Outside were several fire pits barbecuing beef, chickens and two lambs. Several barbecues were cooking turkeys. Everyone attending had brought three or four dishes for the feast that would follow and a feast it would surely be.

Actually it was one of those mild sunny days that often happened in winter. It was cold enough to hold the snow in place, but with no wind to speak of. This was probably due to the Gods moderating the weather and no doubt They enjoyed a party now and then or so people liked to think. If any strangers were noted in the gathering, they were cheerfully made welcomed and served as though indeed, a Light Spirit was visiting. Who really knew? Better to err on the side of possibility then to flub up and insult a God or an angel.

Chairs were brought out of storage and placed in semi-circled rows around one end of the room. Many of the men stood against the walls while the ladies and children sat. When all were seated that could be seated, Blackhawk stood up and the crowd quickly grew quiet.

He presented a striking picture in his black pants, boots and black leather shirt with his huge turquoise belt buckle and wrist bands with a large gold hawk medallion around his neck that simply made him an altogether majestic figure. His long thick black hair with its white streaks were allowed to hang loose about his shoulders with only one braid from the top hair dropped down on one side with several hawk feathers tied to it.

"Thank you for coming friends. Once again we celebrate another year of goodness and prosperity. We are gathered here to express gratitude for all that these lands have given us. We express gratitude to our Valleys Guardian Spirits who protect us and our children." People knew most of the story behind Joe Kelly's kidnapping and murmured an agreement.

"Now today I will tell you the legend of Lightening Boy and the first medicine wheel. Some of you have heard this story before, many of you haven't. I haven't told this story in years, but something urges me to tell it again today. It is such a beautiful day for us to go up to the original medicine wheel where centuries ago Lightening Boy danced for the Thunder Gods for the first time. It isn't far and the way has been made easier and cleared of snow. That is where we will hold the Thanksgiving Ceremony."

Blackhawk stood still and raised his hands once then they fell to his side.

"Hear now this true story of Little Bear who became our first Chief Guardian. He was a young Indian boy who had gone on his vision quest. He was gone a long time and his people began to fear he had been killed. Little Bear entered his village a week later weak from fasting. His tribe's home was to the east and south of us out in the plains. Little Bear went directly to the shaman's tent and asked permission to enter. When permission was given Little Bear entered and closed the flap behind him. People quietly gathered around outside and waited for a long time before the Shaman came out and spoke.

"Little Bear has until next summer to complete the preparation his vision requires of him. Only then will he receive his new name. Nothing more will be said."

And the people said, "Haw!" and went about their business. Spiritual matters were respected and no one would question Little Bear.

Little Bear had been told what he must do before the next journey into the sacred lands of the Thunder Gods. Now here are the seven things Little Bear was to prepare as gifts for the gods that ruled the Sacred Valleys. There was to be an arrow like none other and never used and a white buffalo robe of young calf. A perfectly adorned buffalo horn, a deer skull decorated with sacred symbols, a hand drum unlike any drum seen, an unusual necklace never worn and lastly, a large shield that depicted all Four Gods. Little Bear was to wear new garments of white leather for the ceremony.

Little Bear prepared a small lodge for himself a short distance from the others. For a week he meditated upon these gifts and as a gift revealed its shape and composition to him he began the work. All through the summer, late fall, winter and spring, Little Bear labored to complete those items he had seen in his vision. His fingers grew sore and his back hurt for the hours of labor. When his eyes blurred with fatigue he rested.

He had so much to do that he didn't have time to join any of the games or hunt that winter with his friends. He barely had time to accomplish all the gifts before the summer journey to the Valleys of the Thunder Gods. He labored hard and long.

He asked his young sisters to make white deerskin garments for him. They quickly began the process of bleaching the deerskins. A few months later they were done and his sisters put them in a new deerskin pouch. His ceremonial dress was complete.

In the common storage tent he found a perfect silvery gray buffalo horn. He spent hours polished it until it gleamed. Little Bear was pleased with its beautiful silvery shine.

You must remember that in that long ago time people had to make the tools first to suit the job. From a captive southern Indian, Little Bear had learned how to work silver and he decided to use it in his decoration. In order to melt the small chunks of silver he first had to find a small rock and chip out a round basin. When he was finished he set it in the fire and put in the pieces of silver. After it was melted he covered his hands with wet skins and pulled the rock out of the fire and poured the silver into a hollowed out wooden bucket of cold water. Once cool enough to handle he took the flat silver and shaped it to fit around the horn rim and its tip. He carved scallops into the silver edges and smoothed out any roughness. The final touch was decorating the horn with strings of polished shells, beads of colored rock and feathers. He carefully stored it away. Tired beyond fatigue, he slept.

He made ten arrow shafts before he was satisfied that the one he held was about as perfect as he could make it. The fletching was done with a multitude of colored feathers Little Bear had collected over the years. All the work on the arrow was very carefully done until it too, was finished and he bound the head to the shaft with narrow strips of white leather and laid it away.

Next, Little bear prepared the robe from a white buffalo yearling he had killed some years ago as a young boy. Carefully he brushed the fur then he got some ochre colored rock and red Pipestone and ground them into powder and added a little oil to make a liquid paste. Little Bear turned the buffalo robe skin side up and painted his right hand in the red/orange mix then put his hand down hard in the center of the robe. It too was finished.

The deer's skull still had its antlers and this took two moons to clean and polish before he painted the antlers red from the juice of dried berries to symbolize Storm and Wind. The skull he painted in white clay and he cut flowers of mother-of-pearl from shells he had traded for and glued them to the long frontal bone. On the sides of the skull he drew, in deepest blue from the flax flower, the symbol of rain, snow and deep green of the grasses. He drew the thunder and lightening. The gold of the mustard flower created the sun at the tip of the nose. The horn points he capped with more silver.

Now little bear was almost finished so he took a break from his labors. His mother treated his hands for injuries and fed him nourishing meals.

Next he made the drum that was shaped from the barrel of a young tree. Long was the labor of cutting, chopping and carving the sides of the one piece cylinder. It was ready for the tight white deer skin, the wood decorated with the symbols of the gods. Blue, red, yellow and green feathers hung from the strips of leather binding the leather to the hollow drum. He carved a beater out of the same wood, padding it with a piece of white leather from the buffalo's leg and bound with white leather scraps.

It was coming on melting time when Little Bear began work on the shield. He chose a long willow branch and patiently heated it above the fire until it was limber enough to bend in a circle and bound. The inner layer was of tough bearskin that he hardened in water and the heat of the fire several times. The final two coverings were two skins of the deer that he hardened in the same way. On the shield Little Bear painted a dark blue outer circle then a white circle then a red circle than white again and finally a bright yellow center. And through it all he drew a diagonal black lightening bolt.

The approaching spring was pushing Little Bear harder. The small necklace had twelve medium colored stones, polished and patiently drilled. Fortunately he already had the beginnings of a necklace he had been working on for the past few years.

Again he visited the supply tent and found four bear claws that he polished with oil until they were smooth and shinny. Little Bear capped the claws with beaten silver with a hole punched through the silver top. Small beads of silver interspersed the colored stones and the final touch was a large, brilliant blue feather from a country far away to the south and now hung from a large silver bead right in the center of the necklace.

He was finished. For the remainder of the spring, he rested from his long hard labor, healing his hands and body. He could only hope that the Gods would find the gifts acceptable.

The people of Little Bear's tribe knew that this was going to be a special summer. Before they began their journey, they purified themselves. No one touched Little Bear's large bundle of wrapped gifts leaving him to put them on the travois.

Once the tribe arrived at their usual campsite in the valley of their choice, which is right here where we now sit, Little Bear and the Shaman went apart to build a sweat lodge. Three days they were gone from the camp and no hunting was allowed to take place during those first days. When the Shaman and Little Bear returned to camp, they were dressed in their finest clothes and the people stood and watched in silence as they entered Little Bear's lodge. Then the Shaman's voice rose in a cadence and the sound of his rattle could be easily heard. When Little Bear emerged from his lodge into the quiet of the waiting village the people began to chant and drum as he walked slowly by them carrying his burdens on his back and vanished into the forest

The people sang as he went out of their sight. They knew it was possible that Little Bear would not be returning. To face the Gods was dangerous. The village went quietly about their business as they waited through the days for Little Bear's return, if he returned at all.

Little Bear climbed, weaving his way up the mountain, until he reached a spot where he chose to camp beside a small stream. Setting down his burdens he climbed another slope until he came to a small plateau where he could plainly see the summit of gleaming white glaciered mountain hovering right over him. Here he paced out an area 12x12 feet and cleared the area of debris. Then he carried rocks of good size to make a medicine wheel. In the center of the wheel he built a round pillar of rocks 3x3 feet and 3 feet high. Little Bear went back to his camp and got mud from the banks of the flowing river and carried it back in a leather skin which he plastered over the top of the pillar.

On the next day he returned to the medicine wheel and found the mud on the top of his altar had dried firm. Then he collected pinecones, pine needles and small dried branches from as many different trees that grew on that part of the mountain. He arranged the materials carefully on the altar. He drove a prepared stake of shaved wood into the ground on the north side of the altar and secured an equal length of wood across it with a leather tie. As his last act, Little Bear took a pine bough and swept the inner circle clean of his footprints and anything else not wanted and stepped out of the medicine wheel.

That evening, he bathed himself in the cold stream and walking naked back to the fire and purified himself with burning sage smoke. When the moon rose up round and full Little Bear, wearing his old moccasins, picked up two bundles and walked naked up the mountain. Leaving one bundle on the ground outside the wheel, he opened the first one and dressed himself in his white tunic and pants. Then he prepared his hair with its eagle feather and beading. He took white clay from a small pot and drew a line down the center of his face and another white line across his eyes. Little Bear opened up the large bundle and picked up the white buffalo robe that held all the other gifts.

Putting them under one arm he took his own drum, beater and flints and slipped out of his old moccasins and stepped into the sacred circle.

Quickly he arranged his gifts upon the cross of wood. Stepping back, he marveled at the beauty that had come from his hands and heart and he prayed that the Gods would find them acceptable.

Little Bear struck the sparks that set the wood on the altar blazing. Casting sage upon the fire he turned and cast his flints out of the circle. He turned and faced the Mountain. Standing still for a few moments he knew that when he had finished he might not be in this world anymore. So be it, he was resigned. Little Bear began to drum and sing to the drum beat, dancing around the inside of the medicine wheel until he and the dance became one.

Time flew by until he at last came to a stop at the entrance of the medicine wheel. His white robes were now drenched with sweat and his hair looked like he had just come from the water. His head hung low as he breathed in heaving gasps. When he could speak he said aloud. "Oh, Thunder Gods….. I have made gifts for You to the best of my ability…… I have danced for You ….to express my people's gratitude…..for the bounty You share with us in these sacred lands. Oh, Thunder Gods, do with me as You will……. I am Little Bear and I have finished." He bowed his head in submission.

In the silence of night time passed. When Little Bear had regained his strength, he looked up and saw the Thunder Gods standing on the other side of the fire which had continued to burn brightly. He froze for a brief moment then fell to his knees and bowed his head for to see the Gods surely meant his death.

"Arise, man of spirit. We accept your beautiful gifts and the gratitude of your tribe. This is the first of many ceremonies to come. It is our command that each tribe do this in remembrance of this first day. We find you worthy of being named First Guardian of these valleys to oversee the men who will come within our boundaries. The Guardian will decree a special day at the end of each year. Such power as needed to regulate men's activities we bequeath to you on this day of naming and the power shall be passed on through the eldest child of your family, be they male or female. You shall be called Lightening Boy. This name shall live and die with you and no other Guardian shall carry this name. We decree that the name of the future Guardians be called Blackhawk."

One of the Gods drifted over to stand before Little Bear as he knelt there in the medicine wheel. Little Bear was compelled to look up into the face of the Thunder God. *"I am the God of Thunder and Lightening and I am your friend as are the others. The Goddess of Sun and Beauty, The God of Rain and Snow and the God of Wind and Storm. Be blessed young warrior."*

The God of Thunder and Lightening smiled down into the young man's wide eyes then He laid His hand upon Little Bear's head. Little Bear fell to the ground unconscious. When he recovered he knew himself changed. The boy Little Bear lived no more and the man Lightening Boy was born. He got shakily to his feet and immediately noticed he was wearing black leathers where the white ones had once draped his body. A golden medallion hung from his neck in the shape of a large striking Hawk.

Lightening Boy looked around at the empty medicine wheel. The gifts and the Gods had disappeared and the fire had gone out leaving all in darkness except for the light of the full moon. How long he stood there in the silence of the mountain he would never be able to recall except that the moon was on the wane when he at last descended the mountain back to his campsite.

A boy had gone out of his village and with the dawn of the fifth day a man returned. The man walked into the village in his black leathers with a golden medallion hung from his neck in the shape of a large striking Hawk. A large brilliant blue feather dangled from his long white streaked hair replacing the Hawk feather he used to wear. His face shone with a light the people had never seen before. It frightened them and they silently greeted the transformed man. The young man came to a halt before the Shaman's teepee.

"Shaman come out; I have returned." and waited. The door flap was whipped back and the Shaman stepped out in full ceremonial garments.

"I was told you would come today. What do you wish of me young warrior."

"I wish to tell you my true name as given to me by the Thunder Gods. I wish to tell our people of the great ceremony and my meeting with Them and what was said to me. I have a story to tell if any wish to hear. My name is Lightening Boy."

Women came and spread buffalo robes for the Shaman and Lightening Boy and the other elders. Once they were seated, the people quietly gathered around and the new man told of his journey to the Mountain."

Blackhawk paused then said, "The legend of Lightening Boy has been told. I have finished."

Chief Blackhawk stood still for a few minutes in front of the fireplace as though he had come back from a long journey. That's when the crowd finally connected the golden emblem of a striking Hawk in the story to the one upon Blackhawk's Black leather shirt.

Blackhawk continued. "And so even after many, many generations have passed since that day we of the Blackhawk Tribe still honor the ceremony each year at this time. I welcome anyone who wishes to walk with me to the sacred medicine wheel that Lightening Boy built." And raising his hands once more he walked out of the building.

People gradually stood up and gathered their coats and followed Blackhawk. Those who could went up the mountain, those who couldn't would remain and follow the others in spirit. For they had heard a true story and one they wouldn't forget again.

The path up to the medicine wheel had been made easier by the addition of railings and stone steps that each generation had help build in the hardest inclines. It made it easier for people to attend this ceremony without struggling up difficult slopes or plowing through snow drifts.

The medicine wheel was old. Only constant care over the many years had kept it in shape. The original rocks forming the circle were worn and in several places they had been replaced. The energy was still there; oh yes, it most definitely was there and even the least sensitive of people could feel the aliveness of this sacred spot. The central altar had survived its long usage with only some of the smaller stones and the renewal of the mud top needed replacing from time to time.

The people moved around the outside of the circle until there were three to four rows deep. The front row obligingly squatted down. Only Blackhawk would enter the center. He stood at the southern entrance where he took off his boots and socks before stepping into the circle where the snow had been brushed away. Chief Blackhawk,

Hereditary Guardian of the Valleys walked to the altar.

He struck two flints together creating several sparks that flew into the dried moss and twigs. As the fire blazed upward he placed sage upon it. Clouds of sage smoke bellowed up as Blackhawk took his large eagle wing and waved the smoke in all four directions and then over himself. Picking up a small drum and beater Blackhawk began to move in slow dance steps around the central fire singing and beating the drum for perhaps ten minutes before stopping.

"Oh Thunder Gods, I am the Blackhawk Guardian of my generation and I have come before You to give thanks for a good and prosperous year. We are gathered here, people of Your Valleys, to offer heart felt gratitude for the bounty of these lands. May You always remain here and continue Your protection for all who dwell under Your Mountain."

From a bag hanging on his belt, Blackhawk took grains and fed them to the fire. He took pieces of dried fruit, dried meat, grass, hay and all manner of tokens of bounty placing them one by one upon the fire. From a small canteen he sprinkled drops of water. "These are small samples of the bounty of our harvest. Come join us in our feasting and our dancing. You are welcome, You are welcome, You are welcome. This is a celebration in Your honor. I am Blackhawk, the Guardian of the people and the lands of the Sacred Valleys by Your decree."

He bowed to the Mountain, then stepped back, turned and walked out of the circle. There was a rumbling in the mountain and a slight shaking of the ground accompanied by flashing lightening then all was quiet. It startled the people and they looked fearfully up at the Mountain. Though they had experienced similar responses when this ceremony was performed it was always…startling.

"Be calm; be at peace; it is only our Guardians thanking us for our offerings. Go now, go down to the feasting."

Mike and Joe stood beside Blackhawk as they watched the people go back down the path to the ranch. There was a tall young man, Indian by his looks, who hesitated then slowly, reluctantly followed the others. Just before he stepped down the first of the steps that would obscure his sight of the medicine wheel, he looked back in wonder before slowly continued down the slope until at last he disappeared from sight.

"I know that man G.D. That was Pete Cameron. I met him at the County Fair. I didn't know he was here in the Valleys, but it's great he is here at last and I can't wait to talk to him."

"Yes, isn't it interesting how he didn't want to leave here? Hmm, well more of that later. He has the Trill Ranch now so you'll see him again. Let's go down and get on with the party." said Blackhawk as he pulled on his socks and boots.

Mike was standing in line for the roast beef when he looked up straight into the eyes of the stranger. The stranger grinned and reached out to shake Mike's hand.

"Mike, remember me? Well, I took your advice and came to the Sacred Valleys. Ever since I arrived here miracles have happened, a miracle called Trill Ranch, can you beat that?" laughed Pete as the two young men shook hands. It was noticeable, that tall as Pete Cameron was, Mike was only two or three inches shorter. It more or less shocked Mike as he hadn't really realized he had grown so tall.

"Hello to you, Pete Cameron, it's good to see you here. I thought I recognized you up at the medicine wheel. I heard we had a new rancher in the valley, but I just didn't connect it to you. I'm happy you've found a place. I can't tell you how happy I am for you. Say you're almost a neighbor of mine. I sure would like to help you if you need any help getting settled in, that is?" Mike spoke enthusiastically.

Again Pete laughed and said, "Boy, I've had more help than I know what to do with. Do you know an old man by the name of George Chambers Roosevelt Downy?"

True Heart

"No, I don't think so, but maybe Blackhawk does; he knows just about everyone."

"Sure he does, he's the one who sent that old man to me. He's around here somewhere." Pete grinned. "I must say he's down right entertaining and that son of a gun can cook too and I really needed fattening up. So my miracles are numerous. Well, life certainly hasn't been dull since I got here. Blackhawk has seen to that." They talked about Joe and how he was doing after the kidnapping than they drifted apart with promises to meet later on.

Joe sang for the first time since his kidnapping and that was just two weeks ago. He assured Ben that he was "good to go" and wanted to do his part in the celebration. Just as he prepared to sing he swore he saw some strange glimmerings in the back of the room. He caught a flash of light like sun off a white rock or off a gold medallion or, or, something bright coming from an otherwise dark corner and where there weren't any people standing. Oh my, he thought, They're here.

Joe switched and began to sing that same song he had sung in the cave. He sang to Them. Joe was filled with such overwhelming joy at the very idea that They were listening that he gave it his all. Mike fortunately caught on and accompanied his brother rather mystified as to why Joe switched songs without warning him.

Joe's performance was greeted with people standing and prolonged applause. There was no whistling or stomping or shouting, only the continuous clapping that had him taking numerous bows until finally he sang another couple of songs before he left the fireplace hearth. A little while later Mike found him sitting back in a corner with his head resting on the chair back and his eyes closed and got concerned.

"Hey Joe, are you alright?"

"I'm alright Mike, I'm just a little tuckered out is all and just a little headache. Amazing how much energy it takes to sing. I never noticed that before."

"Why did you change our program and switch to that song we haven't had time to work on?"

"Oh, I don't know. I guess I just felt like it. Sorry not to have warned you." and looked warily at Mike.

"You're entitled to switch directions only give me a heads up next time so I can get my jaw off the ground and follow along." Mike grinned then frowned looking at his brother's white face. "I should have stopped you taking those added requests. It was just too much too soon for you. I thought you were okay with it and you seemed to be having so much fun. Sorry about that."

"I was having fun, you know that. Well, I guess that biff on the bean sort of slowed me down some. I sure hope I get over this soon, I hate feeling like a wimp." Joe groused.

Mike laughed, "Yeah, you're such a wimpy guy standing up to kidnappers and having the guts and strength to sing for the Thunder Gods when you were suffering and all. Sure, They just love wimps." Joe giggled.

"Well, maybe I'm not a wimp exactly." Joe paused and looked at his brother in a serious way. "Say Mike, I'll tell something if you won't tell anyone."

"I promise I won't tell a soul. Now what's the secret?" asked Mike with a slight smile on his face even as he leaned forward.

Joe leaned forward too and looked around to make sure no one was paying any attention to them then whispered, "They were here; right over there in the back of the room. I saw Them."

Mike frowned, "Saw who, Joe?"

"Them! You know, The Thunder Gods! I'm positive because I saw this brilliant flash of light like it was coming off a medallion or something gold and it was in that empty dark corner of the room with no people there either. There was this white misty kind of look to that whole back area too." Joe pointed over to the corner where he had seen the apparition and nodded emphatically.

"No kidding? Gee, I wished I had seen that too. Are you sure? Yeah, you'd know, wouldn't you? You've been up close and personal with those Guardians. Wow, Joe what a way to begin your new singing career. How are you going to top this huh?" and punched his little brother which got retaliated and the horsing around helped pull Joe out of his exhaustion.

"Come on big guy, let's get you something to eat and that will perk you up." Mike hauled Joe to his feet and led him over to the groaning tables filled with food. Yeah, food did help a guy regain his enthusiasm while filling his stomach.

~Holiday Parties~

WINTER WITH ALL ITS sports, parties and visitations were upon them. Especially Christmas was going to be celebrated with joy this year by the Kelly children. School was out and the Mike was enjoying overnight stays with his friends, but Joe wasn't up to this much activity. Besides which he felt the need to stay safely at home, at least for the time being.

It had taken Joe weeks to regain his strength. He was in and out of school periodically as he had caught a bad cold right after Thanksgiving, but with all the TLC he recovered fairly fast, then he caught a 24 hour bug that kept him home again. Slowly however, he was making progress back to being his sturdy self. Yet there was an air of fragility about him that hadn't been there before his kidnapping. It worried his family and they sought ways to keep him warm, occupied without smothering him with attention.

It was fun to help cut down a Christmas tree and get it set up in the living room. They had a decorating party that very evening and adorned the tree with lights, ornaments, popcorn strings and tinsel. Even Carli got to put tinsel in clumps on the lower branches. Hannah kept driving the boys out of her kitchen as she said they were robbing her of the delicious treats she was fixing for later.

There was no question that they felt the joy of Christmas, however along with that were the memories of the last Christmas with their parents. They tried to put those aside, but they were like shadows following them, haunting them with sadness.

Mike and Joe were offered a chance to invite all the neighbor children to a party that following weekend. The big problem was the list kept getting longer. All their special friends were invited, but of course there were the River Town kids as well as young friends from Claremont and all the other kids that rode the school bus with them from the smaller farms. It just wouldn't be fair not to invite them all.

"Ben?" Ben looked up from his ranch books to see Mike and Joe standing on the other side of his desk with Mike holding a sheet of paper. He leaned back in his chair and waited. "We have a big problem. We have a list of all the kids we want or need to invite which is really long. However we can't just invite the kids because their parents will have to drive them way out here and then go back to town and then return to pick them up later in the evening. It just isn't going to work. So Joe and I would like to have your permission to throw a party for the kids *and* their parents. I know it's a lot of trouble, but Joe and I will work really hard and I think our ranch should pay for everything too since it's our party. In fact, I will insist that it does. I want to invite the Tomlinsons and all the guys at our ranch too and, and our people here too. I mean, gee Ben, I don't know how we're going to work this out."

They stood before Ben's office desk and he just looked at them. As the minutes went by Mike and Joe started to fidget. Joe looked up at Mike who finally broke out with. "Maybe it's too much right now. Joe and I can figure something else out, maybe. Like we could give a party in town, or something like that, maybe." Mike felt a let down coming as he slid the paper back and forth through his hands. It was really a lot to ask the Strongbows to give such a large party after that big fiesta two months ago.

"Call everyone and tell them it's an open invitation to a buffet supper, dancing and general party. That way you won't miss anyone. Is that all you need?" Ben spoke soberly, but they saw that twinkle in his eyes.

"Geeze peeze Ben, you scared us half to death. *Don't do that!* You know my delicate health can't handle shocks like this." Exclaimed Joe and wiped invisible sweat off his brow then ran around the desk to give Ben a big strangling hug.

Mike shook his head and heaved a deep sigh. "Thanks Ben, it means a lot to Joe and me."

Ben just laughed. "Go see Hannah and Mari Beth. Make whatever plans you want and I'll go along with it. Now get on with you, I've got work to do here," waving them out of the office.

"A Bang Up Party, that's what it will be called. After all, the Kelly's have to hold their heads up in society or our names will be shamed, won't it Mom?" said Hannah with her lips tightly pressed together,

her nose in the air and her arms folded tightly over her chest. Joe looked at her with his mouth open.

"I certainly agree, my dear Hannah, we'd never live it down. It is going to be an *awful bother, you know*. What we have to go through to please these children." Mari Beth heaved a theatrical sigh, patted her heart then turned and gave Mike and Joe a sorrowful look. Then she broke out in laughter at the expressions on their faces.

"*Gotcha!*"

She immediately turned to Hannah. "Now for the menu, let's have lots of finger foods as well as three nice big, really huge Prime Rib Roasts with all the trimmings and lots of fried chicken or maybe several baked hams. Hmm, what do you think Hannah, fried chicken or baked ham or both? I can help you boys make calls if you'd like." said Mari Beth.

"You two are as bad as Ben. One more good joke and Joe and I will run for the hills." breathed Mike with a relieved smile.

The day before the party they moved all the living room furniture into the den, rolled up the big rug so there'd be room for dancing. The dinning room table was extended and pushed against one wall so the food could be set out for the buffet. Of course, the women of the Valleys insisted on helping out with added casseroles and side dishes as usual. There was just no stopping them.

"Lordy," exclaimed Mike, when he saw the amount of food being set out. "It's going to be another feast! Joe, we're going to grow into giants just like you wanted to."

"We Strongbows and Kellys never do things halfway." returned Mari Beth, again with her nose in the air she returned to the kitchen with a swish and a sway of her hips that had them laughing at her absurdity. Gods, he loved this family thought Mike.

Well, the party really rocked. Ben fixed up one of the big hay wagons with runners to be used for hayrides. The first to go for a ride were all the kids. The sleigh took off with bells ringing and loud laughter. When the kids got back, the adults insisted on their ride too. Mike watched closely to see who was sitting with whom. Whom? Wasn't that one of the questions Joe had asked him so many months ago? Funny how the mind remembers little things like that.

Hmm, Tom had Jean Hardwell then he saw Luther lift Amber Golight up into the hay, climb in after her and covered them both with a blanket. Melanie had been reluctant to go, but Jimmy grabbed her by the waist and hoisted her up into the hay bed and jumped in after her.

"Now sit down Miss Golight, and I'll let you share this blanket with me. I'll protect you from bears, wildcats and wild cowboys."

She laughed as he covered her legs and pertly replied in her southern drawl. "Yes indeed Mr. Kilpatrick, but who is to protect me from you?"

"Me?" he said in a shocked insulted way. "Why, I'm the most discreet and honorable escort of ladies in the Valleys and extremely shy. Have no fear, Jimmy is here." Melanie burst out in laughter.

Dan lifted a hefty Martha up onto the hay wagon despite her protest and climbed in after her. "Now hush Martha, or everyone will know we're courting." Dan's loud voice boomed around the yard. She laughed hilariously and everyone joined in.

Other couples climbing in were Ben and Mari Beth, Bob and Carla Zeggler, Hank and May, and Suzie Quinn with Sam Carrington. Mike suspected that Suzie and Sam were just good friends. Then the Seelys joined the jam. Well gee, there couldn't be much more room in the hay wagon without getting rid of the hay that is and as it was they were all squeezed together. No one seemed to mind though.

"That's it, or our horses will flounder in the next hundred feet. Anyone else wanting a ride will have to wait their turn. Hang on, here we go. Hup, you beauties, Getup." Shouted Jacko and the large wagon rigged out with lights and bells took off with a lunge that had the ladies screaming and laughter floated back from the wagon as it disappeared into the darkness

Inside the house Henry Trudeaux, Blackhawk, Big Mike, Pete Cameron and a couple of strangers were comfortably sipping brandy in the living room before the fire.

When Mike entered the room Pete turned around and Mike went forward to meet him. "I'm awfully glad you could come Pete, we never did find time after we met at Blackhawk's to get together, did we?" smiled Mike and shook hands with the taller man.

Mike liked Pete instinctively and they weren't that far apart in age. Pete was nineteen and Mike would be sixteen next month. Pete always acted so much older than his years; well so did he. Guess it was all about having tragedies and responsibilities heaped on young shoulders. Anyway, Mike thought he and Pete had a lot in common.

"No we didn't I'm sorry to say, but I've been mighty busy on the ranch too. I got a new hired hand now besides the cook. Let me introduce you. Mike I'd like you to meet Mr. George Downey and Tony Cassel. Gentlemen this is one of our hosts, Mike Kelly of Lost Wagon Ranch."

Mike shook hands with the gentlemen. Actually, Mike towered over the small Mr. Downey, but he didn't make the mistake of judging the smaller man as being weak or ineffectual, oh my no, not by any stretch of the imagination. If Mike was any judge this Mr. Downey was a unique, forceful character.

"You're very welcome and it's a pleasure to meet you, sirs." smiled Mike shaking their hands.

"Likewise young man, I've been hearing a lot about you and your brother lately. Hope all is well with the boy now?" said Mr. Downey.

"Yes Sir, thank you for asking. Joe is coming along just fine. He'll be singing for you later too." Then Mike turned his attention back to Pete.

"Well Mike, needless to say things have been moving a might fast over at my place which doesn't give us much time for socializing. I hope you can come over soon and see what we've done. It's a beautiful place." said Pete and Mike could see the joy shining in Pete's eyes.

"I've been hearing rumors, but it isn't like seeing it for myself. Can you tell me some of it now?" asked Mike.

"Better you see for yourself, Mike. Say, do I get to hear that new guitar of yours, the one you almost lost to those bullies?"

"You bet and there's also some very good musicians here too so we'll do our best to make this party rock. I gotta' go check in on the kids upstairs, but I'll catch you later."

"Sure 'nough Mike, have yourself a good time like I am." Mike left and Pete returned to the men's conversation. Mike ran up to join the younger set playing video games.

These were times to remember. The party didn't end until the wee hours of the morning. Pete Cameron got to hear Mike's twelve-string sing and applauded like mad. Joe sang and that was received enthusiastically. With so many good musicians present the success of the party was a given. No wonder no one wanted to go home.

Later Pete complimented Mike on his playing. "I'm glad Ranger and I helped save your new guitar that day or I'd have missed out on something fine tonight."

As the evening wore on there were so many people needing attention that Mike didn't get back to talk to Pete again. Finally, when there seemed to be a break in Mike's hosting duties he asked Blackhawk, "Have you seen Pete Cameron G.D.? I sure wanted to talk to him again."

"He and his men had to leave, but he said he'd give you a call since he couldn't find you to say goodbye and to thank you for the party. He said he'd make up for that slight by having you and Joe over for a day."

"That's great and we'll look forward to that."

Of course, there followed a string of invitations to other ranches and farms and a huge community dance as December days moved toward Christmas.

Winter was the ideal time to entertain because it wasn't as busy as in the other seasons, but of course a rancher was always had work to do.

Christmas Eve was celebrated quietly with just the family. Mari Beth and Ben were disappointed that none of their other children had been able to make it home, though there were promises of a visit around New Year's. Well, that was to be seen.

Bedtime finally rolled around and as the house grew quiet Mike sat in his room unable to sleep. Memories swamped him along with grief for his parents' absence. Roscoe whined and laid his head in Mike's lap and looked up at him with brown understanding eyes.

"You're such a good dog Roscoe, I'm so glad I have you. You're really the best present I've ever had. Well, there was the new guitar and of course Beau, but you weren't really a present because it was more like we found each other, huh?" stroking his dog's head when he heard a soft knock on the door. Mike looking up as the door open and Joe's head appeared.

"Come on in Joe, I'm not sleepy and I can see you aren't either." said Mike quietly.

Joe came in and closed the door quietly. He walked over and sat in the chair opposite Mike. He at least had on his pajamas and robe though he had forgotten to put on his slippers.

"I couldn't sleep." sniffed Joe. "I guess I got to remembering last Christmas and Mom and Dad." The woeful look on Joe's face echoed what Mike was feeling in his heart.

"Yeah me too, and I think we'll miss them all our lives. Christmas will be one of those times when the grief will just about choke us. They say time heals all grief, what do you think?"

"I don't know, maybe it will 'cause we'll be older and maybe that will help. I just wished Mom and Dad had lived to share the ranch with us. It just isn't fair that they had to die so soon. Couldn't God have waited for awhile?" Joe hid his face in his hands and began to sob.

"Come here Joe." Joe got up and Mike pulled him down to sit in his lap. As he held his young brother, Mike realized Joe had grown some in the last months just like he had; at least he was longer and felt heavier too. Mike held Joe tightly and at last he allowed himself to let go enough to cry with him for a bit. Digging out his big handkerchief he had Joe blow his nose and wipe his face then Mike did the same thing.

"Well, that's one well used handkerchief and I think we won't use it again if you don't mind." Mike shifted over so Joe could squeeze down in the chair beside him. It was a tight fit, not that it mattered.

"Well, one more nose blowing and I'm tossing this thing on the floor." And that got a weak laugh out of Joe as Mike did just that.

"Why did it have to happen that way, Mike? I just can't find any reason that they had to die right then. Do you know?"

Geeze, this was a test if there ever was one, thought Mike. I'm supposed to answer such a huge question before I turn sixteen next month? He heaved a deep sigh and said, "I'm not sure if there is a reason. Maybe it's more like each person has a certain amount of time in which to do their work or fulfill their purpose before they die. When that has been accomplished they're ready to move on. Maybe that's what Mom and Dad have done, moved on. Now, a lot of people don't believe in reincarnation. You know, after death the spirit moves out of the body and goes into another life somewhere. After awhile they can be reborn again in another life here. I've been reading about it and I do believe it. Jesus said we have life eternal. Gee Joe, can you imagine dying, going to heaven to sit on a cloud and twiddle your thumbs for an eternity?" Mike exaggerated his appalled look.

Joe laughed. "It sure sounds awful boring to me and not fun at all."

"Yeah, it does to me too. If we only have this one life to live and don't get anymore chances to put to use what we learned this time around, I can't see the point in all the hard work acquiring wisdom, goodness and becoming a better person just to die and, poof, gone for good? No, I think God is smarter than to waste perfectly good souls that are learning and growing by limiting them to one lifetime. How can these souls that have grown so wise be wasted sitting on a cloud when they could come back to Earth and help us out here? Anyway, I prefer to believe that Mom and Dad will come back to Earth in another life." Mike was quiet for a minute then laughed. "Hey, maybe they'll come back as our children. Wouldn't that be a gas?" and Joe laughed again.

"I like that idea Mike, don't you? I'm going to believe like you do. Hey, I believe in the Thunder Gods or Guardian Spirits, why not believe in life after death? It's not too big a stretch is it?" said a more cheerful boy.

"Okay little brother, let's shake on that. You get one parent and I'll get the other. That way we'll give our parents the very best we have for them just like they gave us their very best." and solemnly they shook hands.

"Thanks Mike, I feel a lot better so I guess I can sleep now. I hope you do too. Thanks for being a super brother." Joe got up and ran for the door remembering to close it quietly.

The big brother had to smile. "Thanks Joe, I do feel better now too." Mike gave a sigh and got up to undress and when he climbed into bed he felt his heart fill with peace in place of grief.

"Goodnight Mom and Dad, we'll love you always." Mike closed his eyes and slept dreamlessly.

It was early Christmas morning when Joe and Mike crept downstairs to slip their presents under an already crowded tree. They heard Hannah in the kitchen rattling pans preparing breakfast. It was going on 6:30 and that was late as most mornings they were usually up by 5:00 at the latest. Joe ran out into the kitchen still dressed in his pajamas and robe and gave Hannah a hug. "Merry Christmas Hannah dear, wait until you see what I got you for Christmas." laughed Joe.

"Merry Christmas to you too Joe, but you didn't have to spend your money on me, but I bet I can guess what you got me." She grinned down on him.

"No you can't. Guess anyway."

"Well, it's a new toaster; this one is all worn out. No? Well hmm, new slippers. No? A book, oh I know, you got me a box of candy. I'm wrong? Gee you're a tough one. I guess I'll have to wait and be surprised, handsome. I can hear Carli from here thumping her bottom down the stairs at a fast rate and yelling her head off. You'd better go see she doesn't tumble head over heels." Joe ran off to find Mike already waiting for his excited sister.

"Daddy, Momma, Santa Claus has come. Hurry, hurry, I want my stockin'! Momma, Daddy, hurry, hurry." Carli yelled in a piercing voice.

"Lordy what a big voice for such a small person, it's loud enough to wake all the farmers around here. Hey, not so fast or you'll slip." Mike reached up and grabbed her, swinging her around in circles as she screamed with laughter.

"Shoot and Blast, can't a man sleep in once in awhile? I declare Mari Beth, there is neither rest for the weary nor peace for the wicked this morning." grumped Ben tying his bathrobe belt around his waist. "Humph, Merry Christmas everyone and look at that sister of yours. Stop her Mike before she's torn all the packages open." Ben instructed with a hearty voice and with Mari Beth, wrapped in her bathrobe with hair all which way, came into the living room to accept hot coffee served by their darling daughter; well anyone who could hand her coffee was her darling.

"I'll remember you in my will my girl, you just saved my life. With coffee maybe I'll survive the chaos." Ben and Mari Beth sat down to watch the fun.

Soon enough paper was flying as Carli went from one package to another as Mike handed them to her. She suddenly jumped up and yelled. "Gotta' pee Momma! Quick, gotta' pee."

"I knew it! Come on sugarplum, let's hurry." Mari Beth hurriedly set her coffee on the table and rushed the little girl to the bathroom off the kitchen. Luther came in the front door loaded down with gifts just about then and saw the flurry of torn paper spread over the floor.

"It sure looks like a good time is being had by someone. Merry Christmas, here are my packages to add to the heap already there." And placed them down where there was room. "I gotta' have a cup of coffee or I won't wake up until Christmas is over." As he headed for the kitchen Carli barreled out of the bathroom and almost ran into Luther.

"Whoops there darlin'," he quickly swung her up before she could smack into him. "Where's the fire?"

"Santa Claus Lutey, lots of presents. Let me down. I gots me presents, lots and lots." And giving him a big kiss she squirmed until laughing, he set her on her feet.

"Look out, here comes demolition baby."

And he went on his way to the kitchen only to meet Hannah bringing more coffee to the living room. Luther followed his sister trying to snag a cup before she could set the tray down. They had to laugh at the mess of paper and presents Carli was sitting in. Joe and Mike were gathering up torn paper and putting it in a sack or else Carli would have soon been buried. Luther found a place to sit and sip his coffee while watching the chaos and remembered back when he was a kid and Christmas was the best of times.

Joe hadn't noticed the large lump over in the corner until Ben got up and walked over to pull the dark blanket off the grand piano. "Merry Christmas Joe, this is yours from all of us." Ben laughed at the sight of Joe's dropped jaw.

"Oh wow, a piano! Wow, my own piano! Geeze Peeze, this is the very bestest present I ever had." and burst into tears. In some ways, Joe was still a little frail from his kidnapping and while the doctor assured them that the trauma would eventually disappear, it was hard to see the little guy upset even joyfully.

Ben picked him up in his burly arms and laughed and laughed. "I can see you're really happy Joe; nothing else gets you to cry. Hey, Mari Beth, hey guys, he likes it."

Ben gave Joe a Kleenex and after blowing hard he hugged Ben around the neck and once he got set on his feet, Joe hugged everyone else too.

"Thanks, oh, thanks, it's great and now I can learn to play like Mike does." running over to the piano to stoke its sides.

"Okay, its Mike's turn." Ben plucked a large white envelope from a tree bough and handed it to Mike. "I couldn't get your presents into the house so here is the next best thing." Mike opened the envelope and saw a picture of a year old colt and filly. The official paper gave their names and their breeding and the date of transfer of ownership. Mike's mouth fell open.

"They are the results of that new breeding program Luther and I are working with. Your babies were born from two of my best Quarter Horse mares; Easy Girl and Dawn and sired by Suncatcher. We'd like you to join us in developing our new stud farm over at your place and we'll see what kind of great horses we can breed."

Mike just held the picture and looked at the great little horses; he sniffed and swallowed hard. Joe came and looked over his shoulder. "Oh Mike, aren't you going to have fun with those two."

Mike looked up at his new family and just couldn't get the words out. He just shook his head and got up and left the room and they heard the kitchen door slam shut.

Ben looked worriedly at Mari Beth. "Shoot and blast Mari Beth, I thought he'd be happy. What should I do?"

"Don't worry Benjamin our Mike just couldn't get the words out is all. Let him go see his presents and he'll be back full of appreciation; he's just overwhelmed right now. That was a really big present." Joe snickered. "Couldn't get them in the house, right? Well, I wished you had done that just to have seen the look on Mike's face." He did manage to get a laugh of relief out of everyone.

More presents were opened and had exclaimed over and appreciated. Five minutes later Mike came back into the living room smiling and went over to Luther and shook his hand and shook Ben's hand too. "Thanks, they are real beauties and I'm very proud you want me to help you with the new breeding. Gee, it's going to make Kelly Ranch famous. Have you thought up a name for our amazing new breed?"

Ben and Luther looked blankly at each other then burst out laughing. When Ben could get a grip on his mirth he said. "No, neither one of us has thought of naming our new breeding. Maybe you and Joe can think of one?"

The men watched Mike and Joe talking softly with their heads together. There was a nod or a shake of the head until they grinned at each other and smacked hands in a high-five before Mike said. "Well, we think a good name would be Sun Racers. Take the first part of the sire's name and the last part of Luther's horse, he being the first of the breeding, and you get Sun Racers." Both boys waited and watched anxiously as Luther and Ben put their heads together and whispered.

"What's taking them so long?" questioned Joe of Mike as they waited for what seemed an age. Ben turned a sober face toward the boys and paused. Mike and Joe waited apprehensively.

"We think that's just about says it all. We'll officially register that logo and start putting it on our business letters and such. It's down right perfect." Ben and Luther laughed at the boys' expressions as they collapsed back against their chairs.

"Oh my goodness, you are just the greatest jokers we've ever known." exclaimed Joe and they laughed.

"More to celebrate; golly, this is turning out to be a great Christmas isn't it?" said Joe. Once the excitement lessened they got back into delivering presents.

Ben opened his from the boys. There on the velvet bed of the case was an old gold pocket watch with a gold chain that had a golden horse as a fob at the end. It was engraved on the back. "To Benjamin Truelove Strongbow from his children, Mike, Joe and Carli Kelly, Beyond Love and Gratitude." Ben clutched the watch and coughed, sniffed, stood up and walked out of the room.

Joe grinned. "Yep he sure liked it a lot, didn't he Mari Beth? Gee, I've never seen so many people crying as I have this morning, including me. Yep, and he doesn't even know the watch chimes the hour and plays "Camp Down Races." Mike said it was a really, really old song." Just then, from down the hall, a tinkling song could be heard.

"Guess he knows that now, Joe." laughed Mike. Ben came back into the room and grabbed each boy and just about crunched their bones.

"You knew I hated wearing a wrist watch. Well now, I won't have any excuses for being late, will I?" Ben chuckled as he sat down beside Mari Beth to show her his new watch and listen to Camp Down Races play on his watch.

"Now Ben, don't wear the thing out before it can be useful." cautioned Mari Beth.

"Luther here's one for you." It took Mike and Joe both to lift and carry the large package over to Luther and put it in his lap.

Luther grunted. "Man, that's heavy. What is it, a new car?" He ripped open the awkwardly wrapped package as enthusiastically as Carli had hers and saw a huge old golden weather vane with a trotting horse on the top that sat on a rocker bar. The crossbars had the four directions, north, south, east and west.

"Oh, man, you got this at the fair, didn't you? Shoot and blast, I was going to buy this for myself then I plumb forgot about it. Thanks Joe, Mike; you guys really know how to please a fellow," said Luther as he stroked the thing. "I'm going to put this right up on top of the barn."

"These kids have sprung some surprises on us, Lute." Ben said. "But, we ain't finished yet."

Luther put the weather vane down then walked over to pluck a similar white card off the tree and handed it to Joe. He tore it open and a Merry Christmas card fell out and it said. "To Joe, my new master; thanks for saving my life, Love Miracle."

"Geeze peeze Luther, you're giving me Miracle? Oh my goodness, Miracle! Mike, Luther just gave me the colt, Miracle. Ohmygoodness, where will I put him?" Joe was all confused. "Gee Luther I didn't do anything to deserve him, did I?"

"Miracle is alive because of you and I think you two are meant for each other so he's yours. Hey, I want some more presents." And laughing, Mari Beth began to toss presents at him so did Hannah and the boys. More paper flew and gasps along with laughter greeted the opening of gifts.

Mari Beth looked up after setting aside one of her presents to see Mike and Joe stand in front of her.

"Mari Beth, Joe and I want you to have this." She opened the wrapping and saw a worn purple velvet box and inside was a beautiful old gold locket with diamonds and a two caret emerald in the center. Inside was a place for pictures. "It was our mother's and her mother's and I guess on back a ways; we're not sure how far, but Joe and I want you to enjoy this as you're our mother now."

Now it was Mari Beth's turn to tear up. "Oh dear, I'm too old to cry, just think of my wrinkles." She sniffed and brushed her cheeks. "I'll wear this from now on boys, and when you see it, know that I love you just as your mom loved you, Okay? Here Mike, come and fasten it for me." Mike did as she held up her thick braid and then she grabbed him and just about broke his ribs. Then she turned and gave Joe the same treatment.

To Hannah, Joe gave their mother's baroque pearl ring; a lovely one inch long pearl encircled with small sapphires and diamonds all in an antique setting. "This is from Mike and me too. Mom said this ring belonged to her mother's mother, so it's really old. It was the second thing she took with her when she left home and Mike kept it for us. If you'd rather have something newer, I'll have to ask Mike for the money so we can buy it for you. But, I thought you'll like thisssssssss….." Hannah grabbed Joe and squeezed the rest of his words right out of him. Man, his ribs were going to be sore for a week.

"Oh Joe, you all should be saving these things for your future wives, not giving them to us. Really, think about it sweetie." sniffed Hannah.

"We have and we decided this was the way we wanted it. So, let's see how it looks on your finger, Hannah." Hannah slipped the ring on and it fit like it had been made for her. "Oh Joe, it is the most gorgeous thing I've ever owned. Mike, thank you so much. Mom, just look at this beautiful ring Joe and Mike gave me." While the women admired each other's jewelry they heard Ben saying.

"Okay, here's another present for Mike. It's been sent by Federal Express and it only got here the other day. Open it up Mike and let's see who your secret admirer is." Ben handed Mike the long bulky heavy cardboard box.

It took a knife to slit the box open and inside was a case holding a beautiful banjo with mother-of-pearl inlays over the whole front of the box and neck. A card in the box said. "Merry Christmas Mike, from your friend Strat."

"He's sent me a banjo. This is the one I tried out and really liked; I thought he had sold it. Why would he do something like this? How beautiful it is. Look he's put my name on it too." Of course he had to tune the strings right away after putting on the finger picks and immediately began to pick out a tune that led to a fast tune. "Oh man, I need to really drum up some trade for this artist. Isn't this just too grand?" grinned Mike as he caressed the banjo.

"Mighty generous that's for sure. Well, we'll put an ad in the paper for him advertising his hand crafted one-of-a-kind instruments that ought to get him a few customers. We'll send a copy of it to Huntington too. We'll put your name in as a satisfied customer, Mike."

"Let's go have some breakfast. After all this gift giving I'm exhausted and hungry. Oh dear, Miss Carli has fallen asleep. Doesn't she look cute lying practically under the Christmas Tree? Hannah, where's the camera? We've forgotten to take any pictures." Hannah took a picture of Carli then turned to the boys and did some quick shots. Mari Beth ushered them all into the kitchen.

Carli still hadn't gotten her puppy, well; more of a six month old dog Ben had waiting in the mud room. "Dang it I didn't forgot to bring him in. When she wakes up she'll just have another surprise." amended Ben with a quick glance back into the living room.

Later, Mike took Joe out to the barn to show him his new horses. They played with them for awhile discussing how their training should be started with halters and such. Brushing the colt and filly was a case of stroke and chase that had both boys in hysterical laughter and the little ones loved it too.

The men from Rocking Horse, Lost Wagon, Thunder, and Rushing Woman Ranch were all invited up for Christmas dinner that evening. Fortunately the Strongbow's dinning room was huge so the table could be extended its full length of 24 feet. Another table of almost equal size was squeezed in that would seat the rest of the 46 people. Ben and the boys had brought in the extra dinning room chairs and folding chairs for the occasion. Mike had invited Pete Cameron, but he said thank you only he and his crew were to go to Blackhawk's for Christmas.

The tables were beautifully decorated with Poinsettias and red and white candles for centerpieces. On all the place settings, and that included the family too, were found little gifts from the family for all five ranches. If the gifts were to big to put on the table, the man or woman got a white Christmas Card with the description of the present waiting for them in the barn or on the back porch. When Little Brown opened his card, it had a picture of the small colt he had been given and the certificate declaring the lineage and the new owner of Strongbow's newest breed with the colt's name duly inscribed. Little Brown just stared at the picture and grinned to beat the band.

Brown had been an orphan when he walked up to Luther's ranch at age fourteen with nothing much in the way of possessions except for the clothes on his back and a small satchel. Luther took him on and insisted that Brown go back to school and graduate if he wanted a job with him. Now, Brown was the proud owner of his very own horse. Life was good and Brown's chin quivered at that thought. Luther's men saved the day with outrageous bets for the racing future of Brown's colt.

"So what's his name, Brown?" asked Wolf.

"His name is Thunder Horse." The young man said as he held the picture of his beautiful colt in his hand. "I wanted to name him Miracle, but since Joe already had already named a horse by that name, he gave me the name of Thunder Horse and I liked that really well." That brought a resounding applause from everyone.

There was a lot of laughter as the gifts were opened. Each gift was something that man or woman had been wanting, but since it was more or less a luxury item, they'd put it aside for later purchase.

Jimmy got real quiet when he saw the new spurs with the California bell that tinkled with each step a cowboy took.

"Jimmy, Ben said I could give this to you now and I hope the rest of you fellows will wait a bit for yours. Open it up so the guys can see the work of a cowboy in action." And Joe walked around the table to hand Jimmy a flat, square wrapped package 24x24.

Jimmy stood up and tore the wrap away and gasped. Jimmy finally turned it around so everyone could see the picture Joe had taken at the roundup of Jimmy riding all out, chasing a cow with his rope swinging. The picture breathed action and one could almost expect the figures to burst right out of the frame.

"Wow!" was the general comment. The picture got passed around for everyone to get a real close look until finally Jimmy put the picture carefully up against the wall out of harms way.

Then he turned to Joe and shook hands. "I was kidding when I said that stuff about you making me rich and famous in the future because I really feel that you've achieved that goal. I feel rich and famous right now. Thanks Joe."

Joe blushed and grinned at his best friend. "Well, it would be very impolite of me to say I told you so. It was one of those shots in a lifetime, Jimmy and the one of Mike is just as good I think."

"Hey, when do I get to see mine?" said Dusty.

"The framer got all jammed up with orders and forgot about mine until it was too late to get them all done by Christmas. Gee, if I thought they'd be so darn popular I would have started the project months ago. I'm real sorry guys." said Joe looking down in the mouth.

"Hey Joe, half the pleasure is in anticipation so no worries mate." Said one of the men, "We know we'll be getting ours soon then we can hang them up in the bunk houses."

"Now Joe here's your present." said Ben and pulled a small slim package out from under his chair. The men passed it down the table until it finally arrived at Joe's place. He eagerly tore off the wrappings and opened the envelope and froze.

Everyone was watching him and finally Jimmy said "Well, Joe what is it?"

Joe looked up and said, "It's my story; it's the magazine Hannah submitted my story too with pictures of the roundup. And just look at the cover." and gazed down at the Magazine he held in his hands.

"Come on fella', share it around for crying-out-loud!" Johnnie yelled. Joe picked up a magazine and turned it around for everyone to see. On the cover was the picture of Jimmy with the caption "Roundup, Through the Eyes of a Child."

Ben came up with a large box of magazines and began to pass them around the table. Joe sat still just holding the magazine like it was a lost treasure. Then he looked over at Hannah with such glowing eye and said. "We got published Hannah, we got published."

"Yes we did and I've got the check to prove it. I've had a hard time not telling you sooner. It's a terrific story. Congratulations." She grinned and toasted him with her wine.

"But I couldn't have done it without you." In awe and wonder Joe quickly turned the pages to where the story began. There it was in big letters, "Pictures and story by Joe Devereaux Kelly as told to and written by Hannah Truelove Strongbow". "Oh wow, it's so beautiful."

By this time the talk was loud and comments flew. "Look, there's Dusty" or" Mac I didn't know you could fall off a horse like that, so graceful like." Actually Mac was doing a flying dismount to tie up a calf. "Here's one of Mike. Say he can ride; just look at horse rearing up and him just a sittin' there like it wasn't nothin' a'tall. It's as good as the one of Jimmy. Powerful, I say."

The men were enthralled at the many pictures of them and by reading what Joe and Hannah had written. The magazine actually had made an exception because of the unique story and had given them more space.

"Jimmy? I think you're now famous. I don't know about rich, but you finally made the headlines." Laughter and joshing followed Ben's comment, but Jimmy sat silently and just held the magazine gently in his hands as he stared down at the cover. When he looked up his sober eyes met Joe's and he just shook his head, speechless.

"So Jimmy, when do you leave for Hollywood?' grinned Joe so happy he could hardly contain himself.

"Pard, I ain't never going to beat this moment; this is beyond great. You've made me famous and I'll treasure this all my life. No matter where I go from here I'll always be your friend and ready to come at a moments notice if you need me. That's a vow, Joseph Devereaux Kelly." Jimmy said solemnly and none of the men laughed or made any ribald comments.

Needless to say the dinner was an outrageous success. "I say Joe, there's a nice art gallery in River Town, it's small, but it's got real quality. I bet you could do a neat show there when all the pictures you like are framed. People would come from all over to see them." Hank Tomlinson said. "You could write little captions underneath each one to describe the action and the man's name."

"I know I'd sure love to see them all. I'd never ever seen any pictures of a real roundup before I say Joe's and many of the pictures are really fine, fine work. Congratulations Joe on the quality." said Amber Golight.

Joe blushed again. "Ms. Golight, it's really just a hobby I love, you know. Not like I was a real photographer or anything like that."

"Don't underrate yourself boy, the pictures I've seen are excellent." said Dusty. If Dusty said so, it must be so and no one argued with that statement.

Mike looked around at the people gathered at the tables and wondered again at the miracles in their lives. These people were friends, real honest to goodness friends. Lordy, Lordy, they were lucky boys. His heart was so full that it felt near to bursting. It kinda' scared him right down to his toes just how lucky they were and joy shouldn't scare you like it did Mike. Then the 'scare' soon went away and left only sheer contentment behind. He'd said many times when something is too good to be true then it usually was. Well, he began to believe that this was a unique place and the good *was more than* believable.

The dinner celebration was over and Mike entertained with his new banjo then gave it to Dusty and switched to the guitar and of course, once Dusty proved he wasn't any slouch on the banjo, the boys laughingly demanded "Dueling Banjos" so what could Mike and Dusty do, but hit it hard. After that they all sang Christmas carols.

Mike turned off all the electric lights and with only the soft illumination cast by scattered candles and the tree lights setting the stage for Joe as he sang "Silent Night, Holy Night," without any accompaniment. There was silence when Joe had finished. It was a hard spell to break out of and it left all those there with a heart full of completeness one would have to say. That put the cap on Christmas.

It was a clear and very, very cold night as their guests departed. The family stood on the porch in their coats and waved everyone off. When the tooting of horns finally faded away, Ben stepped inside and switched off the inside and outdoor lights then rejoined the family on the porch.

"Look up my own, look up at the glorious stars of God's universe and may the Christ return to Earth some day!" Wordlessly they absorbed the magnificence of the star studded night sky for awhile. Then one by one they went into the house and closed the door except Joe and Mike.

They stayed a few minutes longer with Mike's arm around Joe's shoulders and he said. "Aren't we the fortunate ones? Somehow Joe, a simple thank you just doesn't seem to cover what I'm feeling. We'll keep trying to find other words, but it just doesn't do the complete job."

"Yeah, I know what you mean. I guess Jesus and our Guardians can hear our hearts though, don't you."

Mike nodded. "With all the fabulous and thoughtful gifts we've gotten today the greatest of all was coming here and finding this family. God is awfully good. I think Mom and Dad know we're alright now. That thought makes this all just perfect." After a bit, Mike led his brother back into the warm and welcoming house.

~The Goddess Appears~

Joe was sound asleep and dreaming of riding Miracle.

"*Joe.*"

He sat straight up in bed and his eyes snapped opened and there at the end of his bed was…. *SHE! THE GODDESS! MY SKY-MOTHER! Right here in my bedroom, for goodness sake!*

"***Joe, Mr. Hoggins is hurt. Go to him.***" She patted Her heart and disappeared.

"*Oh my goodness; oh my goodness, I'm awake, I know I'm awake, oh my goodness.*" Joe leaped out of bed and without turning on a light ran to his door, flung it open with a crash and ran down the corridor to Ben and Mari Beth's bedroom. Without even so much as a knock, he thrust the door open and ran to Ben's side of the bed, stumbled over Ben's boots and landed with a jar on top of his adoptive father.

"Oomph! What?" Ben was instantly awake and sat up swiftly to see Joe sliding off his chest. "What's the matter Joe, did you have a nightmare? What's wrong?"

"What's the matter? Oh Joe dear, are you ill?" Mari Beth raised her head off the pillow on the instant. Ben grabbed Joe and lifted him up to sit on the side of the bed feeling his forehead for fever.

"No, no Ben, *She* was here. I mean, *She* was really here, right there in my bedroom, right there at the end of my bed. I wasn't dreaming." Babbled Joe all excited.

"Who is she, Joe? Come on boy, make some sense here." Ben frowned. Mari Beth looked concerned and wondered if the concussion Joe had experienced was having some late side effects and reached over to turn on the bedside lamp.

"*SHE*, Ben, the Goddess, *the Thunder Goddess*, right there at the foot of my bed and She spoke to me too."

"Joe, are you sure you weren't dreaming? Sometimes dreams can seem real you know." trying to comfort the boy out of his excited state.

Joe frowned at Ben and said fiercely, "I wasn't dreaming and *She, my Sky-Mother was really in my room.* She said "Mr. Hoggins is hurt. Go to him." Then She patted Her heart. Oh, did I tell you about that part when I asked Her to be my sky-mother up in the cave? Well, She patted Her heart then too, so I know something awful has happened to Mr. Hoggins and we've got to go up there and rescue him *now*!"

Ben looked at this little boy, this boy who had been specially marked by the Thunder Gods and strange as it sounded he decided that the kid was telling the truth. Ben also had the distinct feeling that if he didn't do something immediately Joe would get on his horse and go himself.

"The Goddess was here in *my* house and I didn't even get a chance to welcome Her? Well, I feel cheated, yes I do. Y'all had better get dressed and go see if Mr. Hoggins needs help." Mari Beth threw back the covers and grabbed her dressing gown and turned to the men who were just starring at her abruptness. "Get a wiggle on you two, Mr. Hoggins must be in a bad way for the Goddess to wake Joe. I'll get dressed and fix some breakfast after all it's almost 4:30." and disappeared into the bathroom.

"My woman says to get dressed and get on with the rescue mission so I guess we'd better get busy." Joe scrambled off the bed and ran from the room. Ben groaned as he got up rubbing his head hard he looked over at the clock; yep, it was 4:30. "It figures, well I'm definitely awake now." He went to the closet and dug out his warmest clothes. "Mari Beth, has it dawned on you that our Thunder Gods are becoming more up close and personal lately? I wonder why now?" said Ben as he dragged on his long underwear.

"Hmm, there's always been Blackhawk of course and maybe Mr. Hoggins, what with living up there close to Them for so many years that doesn't seem so strange to believe, but now there's Joe. Hmmm, it is interesting, isn't it?"

Meanwhile Joe burst into Mike's room and shook him hard. "Mike, Mike wake up."

"What's the matter? Joe? What's going on?" Coming out of a deep sleep so fast could rattle a guy's brains and then some.

"Listen, the Goddess appeared at the foot of my bed and said Mr. Hoggins was bad hurt and we've got to go rescue him. Ben and Mari

Beth are already up. Honestly, it took them long enough to believe me." Joe said in a disgusted way.

"Who appeared? Joe, are you all right?" Mike sat up and was about to lay his hand on Joe's forehead only Joe ducked impatiently away.

"I don't have time for this nonsense. Either you believe me or you don't, Ben and I are going up the mountain and if you want to come along you'd better get up and dressed warmly because we'll be leaving shortly." and Joe dashed back out the door and slammed it hard enough to wake the dead.

Mike sat there for a few minutes and let everything soak in. The Goddess had paid a house call on Joe? Mercy, with all the strange things that had been happening to the kid, it wasn't hard to believe. He sighed and got out of bed as it looked like the day was beginning a little early and on a Saturday morning too.

Ten minutes later Ben, Joe and Mike arrived in the kitchen and saw Mari Beth and Hannah busy fixing a hot breakfast. "I'll have four of the men come up for breakfast so fix plenty." The men of the family pulled on their coats, hats and gloves to go roust out the men and saddle the horses.

After breakfast Ben told Mari Beth, "Honey, I'll call you from Mr. Hoggins's place when we find out what's wrong then you call for an ambulance because I really believe Joe that Mr. Hoggins is hurt and will need to go to the hospital, but we'll make sure of that first before calling for an ambulance to come all the way out here. By the time we have him back the ambulance can run him right into town without delay."

Joe glowed to hear them express such absolute faith in him. It gave him a funny feeling of, well, being trusted like this and it did something funny to his stomach and maybe his heart too. Before full daylight the big six-wheel dually truck, with men jammed inside were pulling the large horse trailer out onto the main road.

"Joe knows the back way from the Kelly Ranch to Mr. Hoggin's cabin. Being able to drive the back road leading up to the sacred site will make getting Mr. Hoggins out a little easier and fortunately the snow isn't too deep yet." said Ben as he drove. "Mike, give Hank a call and tell him we'll be driving through without stopping and the reason. Can't have him stewing about what's going on." Mike took the cell phone and made the call.

Hank was standing on the high porch and waved as they passed through the ranch yard and then, after they opened the gate, they were on the old back road and it was four wheeling for sure. Finally they'd reached the end where Ben turned the truck around so it was heading back down the road. They got the horses out of the van and mounted up. With Joe leading the way up the long slope and past their parents resting place where Joe had to stop for a minute to orient himself as it was still quite dark then moved off to the left where he found the dim trail through the trees. Praying he'd remember all the twists and turns easily, Joe moved on. He gave a deep sigh of relief when he finally came out on Thunder Mesa where Mr. Hoggins had his garden further north.

"His cabin is up there on a big bench." he pointed, "We can ride up the mesa until we reach the end then we have to walk because the path is very steep. Best leave the horses though 'cause the path's probably deep in snow."

Joe led the way up the mesa with the horses bucking drifts occasionally and finally arrived where the path was visible. The men dismounted, covered the horses with blankets before following Joe up the snow filled trail. It was hard going and Joe just wasn't up to opening the trail filled with snow so Rio took the lead and broke trail. Ben had a hand under Joe's arm to help him, followed by the others. With a short time they arrived at the cabin to be greeted by the baying of several dogs in the house.

"Yep, that's our welcoming committee," laughed Joe breathlessly. "Better let me go ahead 'cause they know me." Knocking at the door Joe had to yell over the fierce barking. "Mr. Hoggins, Mr. Hoggins, it's me, Joe Kelly, we've come to help you."

"Quiet you dogs and lie down. Come on in Joe and welcome." Joe could hardly hear the weak voice of the older man. Joe opened the door to see Mr. Hoggins laying in front of the fireplace with his dogs guarding him; all four of them, the adults and the two half grown puppies.

"Oh goodness, Mr. Hoggins, whatever happened to you?" Joe came over to the dogs. "Hi doggies, remember me? I'm Joe and I sure remember you." There was a reassuring thumping of tails. "Yeah, that's the way. Now you be good so we can help your master." Ben had already moved around the dogs shedding his coat and hat on the way and tossing them over a rocking chair. "What happened, Mr. Hoggins? Darn, it looks like you've broken your leg. You did a fair job of splinting I see. Well, we've come to get you down the mountain and to the hospital where they can do a better job."

"I'm sure glad to see you, Ben. I've been laying here since late yesterday afternoon. I went out to get wood and slipped on the icy back step and came down wrong. Stupid, that's what it was." grumbled the old man and they could see he was in a lot of pain and struggling to cover it up.

"I never heard of an accident that was smart." Ben smiled and that comment had Mr. Hoggins giving a short barking laugh before hissing as he moved his leg.

"Okay Mr. Hoggins, I'm going to give you three of Joe's headache pills left over from when he had his concussion. I figure your weight is at least three times if not four of his so three pills should do the trick. I guarantee you'll be pain free within just a few minutes. It won't hurt you so much when we take you down the mountain and I guarantee that isn't going to be a lot of fun."

"I just bet so I won't say no to a little painkiller. Thanks Joe." as Joe handed him a glass of water and Ben gave the man the pills. The other men were gathering up clothes and stuffing them into a pillow case while others went about putting the cabin to bed, so to speak, because as far as Ben was concerned Mr. Hoggins wouldn't be coming back here after he got out of the hospital and certainly not until he could do for himself so that was that.

Mr. Hoggins began growing groggy, but was instructing the others as to what he'd need in the short term; long term was what Ben whispered to the men. They waited until the old man was gently snoring before they began to bundle him up in blankets.

"Say boss, I found this small box sleigh in the shed out back along with his mules, but I want you to come take a look at the contraption and see if you think we can take Mr. Hoggins down in it." Jeb stood just inside the kitchen doorway.

"Might just be the answer if it will work. It will be less painful for the old man so let's go see." And putting on his coat and hat he followed Jeb out the door.

When Ben came back in he said. "Yeah, the sleigh will work only he'll have to sit up, but his leg will be protected. We can tie him so he doesn't slip on the downgrade. Rio, go get those mules and put the pack saddle on one of them. We'll hitch the other one up to the sleigh 'cause it looks to me like Mr. Hoggins has used them this way before so they shouldn't give you any trouble. Okay, let's get the man's things loaded and that sleigh padded up and head down the mountain. We can always come back for anything he wants later and finish closing up the cabin 'cause he'll be staying at the ranch this winter if I have to sit on him." Ben pulled his cell phone out and gave Mari Beth a call.

Finally, the cabin was shut up tight and the old man had been gently lifted and carried out of the cabin and sat in the blanketed, pillowed sleigh. He was secured tight with ropes found in the barn and they had also tied another couple of ropes to the back of the sleigh to help ease it down the steep path. Rio led the mules down first followed by the sleigh and the dogs. In Joe's back pack were Mr. Hoggins's pipe, tobacco, several of his books and several journals that looked like the man might have been using.

The trip down the steep slope was easier as the trail had already been broken, still it was a challenge. When they got to the bottom Rio hitched one of the mules up to the sleigh and with the reins in his hands he mounted his own horse thus the caravan got under way. The rescue was almost completed.

From the ranch's front porch Joe heaved a relieved sigh as the ambulance pulled out of the driveway. The dogs howled mournfully and he got busy reassuring them all was well.

"Alright, we need lots of hands to get grandmother's cottage fixed up for Mr. Hoggins. I figure we've only got three days at the max to do it in. Let's start by putting his things around and shutting the dogs in the cabin. Maybe that will settle them down. Joe, lead them over there while I get Mari Beth and Hannah."

"Come on doggies; let Joe take you to your new home. You're going to like it ever so much. You'll have company when you want it too, and lots of treats because you're such good dogs." The conversation went on and surprisingly enough the dogs followed Joe obediently.

The cottage was set a ways back into a grove of pine trees and it was as pretty as a post card with a tall fence all around because old Grandmother Strongbow had loved her gardens and so had the deer.

True Heart

Of course, it might be a bit *too cute* for a rugged mountain man, but it was private with all the facilities indoors so Mr. Hoggins wouldn't feel too hemmed in. Mike had his cabin not to far away.

It was fun making it more like the old man's home. The ladies cleaned and made up the soft bed up with flannel sheets and comforters. They stocked the pantry and within two days it was a nice comfortable living space. Ben had sent the men and Joe back up the mountain to pack a few books and anything that looked like a personal mementos. They cleaned out the refrigerator and cast out left over food. Back at the ranch the women filled book shelves, scattered other objects around the cottage making it very more familiar. Even the dogs relaxed more with the familiar smell of Mr. Hoggin's present.

On the third day, Ben and Joe went in to pick up the invalid at the hospital. When they got to his room the man was practically crawling up the walls. He frowned at them fiercely and barked. "I want out of here now."

"That's what we've come to do Sir, we're taking you home. Now you can be happy again." smiled Joe and watched the grumpy man lighten up.

"It's about time Joe. Just because a man throws a little fever doesn't mean he has to stay in bed. I declare, I've spent more time in bed these past three days then all my life long. It's disgusting for a grown man to lie about like this. Let's go." and pushed himself out of the chair and stood unsteadily on one leg.

Of course, the other leg was encased in plaster and being a wise man, Dr. Valdez had put on a walking cast. He fiercely told the old man he was to elevate that leg most all the time and use a crutch when walking if he wanted to walk in the future without a painfully limp.

"I can't wait to get away from people poking at me with needles of this and that medicine. I tell you Ben, I've had all the coddling I can handle." just as the nurse came in with a wheel chair.

Before the old man could burst into indignant speech Ben said, "Ah a ride, now this should make it easy for us to get this good man into our truck. Climb aboard Mr. Hoggins, and we'll be off."

Mr. Hoggins glared at Ben's smiling face and Joe's struggling not to laugh when the older man finally gave a deep self-pitying sigh, "What's a man to do." and ungraciously sat down in the wheel chair.

Once in the truck and whizzing down the road, Mr. Hoggins lightened up considerably. "I apologize for my attitude and I'm really grateful for the rescue. I guess I'm not showing much of that now, am I? A man my age can forms too many bad habits. You have to watch out for those because you can really get stuck in some deep ruts that way. Guess I found a few of mine, huh Joe?"

"None of us are perfect yet Sir, or so my dad used to say."

"Hah, you're dad was right too; being perfect is near impossible; besides who could stand to be around a perfect person." laughed Mr. Hoggins. After a while he continued. "Say, not to get off the subject of my imperfections, but how did you know I needed help?"

Joe looked up at him and said, "She came and woke me up. She said "Go to Mr. Hoggins. He's hurt." The Goddess, you know the one who is my Sky-Mother now."

Mr. Hoggins eyebrows couldn't have climbed any higher. He looked bemused as he starred at Joe intently. "Hmm, I guess there's nothing like having a Goddess looking after me is there? I'm one fortunate man so I must say a great big thank you next time I happen to see Her." It was all he had to say except he took Joe's hand in his and squeezed it.

Joe heaved a sigh of relief; his friend believed him just like that with no questions asked. Joe wasn't stupid and he knew how flaky it sounded to say, "Hey, I just had a visitation from a Goddess." Booby hatch for sure.

They pulled into the ranch yard and instead of stopping at the kitchen door Ben just kept on driving until he pulled up in front of grandmother Strongbow's cottage.

"What's this? Whose house is this Ben? You know I don't really feel much like visiting anyone right now."

"Let's just say this is your winter home until you're all healed up and back on your pins again. No arguments Mr. Hoggins, no one is taking you up the mountain until winter is over and you're healthy once more. You can be as private here as you wish. Just hang out the "Do Not Disturb" sign on the gate and you'll be left alone. Come on in your dogs are waiting for you." Ben jumped down and slammed his door and went around and helped the speechless old man out of the truck.

The barking of the dogs could have been heard in River Town as they ripped around the corner of the cottage to jump up on the fence just belling like fire sirens.

Mr. Hoggins laughed and shouted, "Hush up you beasts I'm home now and no jumping up." Together they helped the old man onto his crutches and opened the gate. Ben and Joe defended the old man from the attention of his animals as he hobbled toward the porch talking a blue streak to his dogs. Once in the house Mr. Hoggins sat down in a soft overstuffed chair before the fire. Joe shoved a foot stool close and lifted the man's leg up to rest on it. Then the dogs crowded around to be patted and reassured of their master's well being. That took some time so Ben and Joe sat down to wait for the greeting frenzy to quiet down. The panting happy dogs finally agreed to settle down by the fire, their eyes never leaving their master's face.

Mr. Hoggins looked around the room spotting many of his possessions on the shelves and other possession here and there. He didn't say anything; just looked.

"I brought your pipe and tobacco down too. See, it's right here on the mantel. Would you like a pipe now, Sir?" asked Joe.

"Now that would be just fine, Joe. I've missed my pipe; another bad habit I suppose, but nevertheless a man deserves at least one vice."

Joe brought the pipe and tobacco to his friend after which he went into the kitchen to fetch a box of matches. He watched Mr. Hoggins pack his pipe and light up, drawing until the pipe was going well. "Ah, just what was needed to make me feel at home; thanks Joe."

"We'll be going Mr. Hoggins, I hope you'll find everything you need here, if not give us a call at the house and we'll fetch it over. The number is right there beside the phone." Mr. Hoggins looked aslant at the modern convenience and sighed then nodded.

"Thank you Ben, I appreciate what you all have done for me. It will just take a little getting used to, is all. I'm not so dumb that I don't know I couldn't have managed by myself up there at the cabin with a broken leg. Oh well, I guess I'll have to concede that I'm not as young as I used to be. When I was lying on the floor up there I was wishing mighty hard that I had a two way radio to call for help. Maybe that's when the Goddess paid a call on Joe. Guess I'll buy one of those cell phone things before I go back. Never can tell when I might need a hand. Thanks for everything; it's down right gratifying to know I've got friends in all the best places." He smiled and was more relaxed now and obviously tired out from the trip.

Ben laid a bottle of pills on the table beside him and Joe brought in a large glass of water. Ben shook the man's hand, "Mike will bring your dinner over and Joe has already fed your dogs so you rest, read a good book and I'll come by after dinner to see if you need anything and let the dogs out. Be welcome here Mr. Hoggins and I think this is sort of like pay back-time, isn't it? What goes around comes around. You saved Joe and now we've saved you. Ain't that just a wonderful thing?" grinned Ben.

They left the cottage with Mr. Hoggins laughing up a storm and that had Joe grinning up at Ben. "That was very clever of you Ben. That really turned the tables on him, didn't it? I guess he'll be okay after awhile. We'll not bother him too much at first, but I really think he's been kinda' lonesome of late and hadn't realized it. We'll just have to see how it goes huh? I want him to be happy with us."

"Change is always hard on older people Joe. We tend to get set in our ways and that's something like what Mr. Hoggins said about getting into a deep rut. It's not a good habit because then you can't be spontaneous or open to expanding your mind and allow better ways to happen. There is one constant in this world and that is the Energy of Change. You can't stop it. However you can resist it, but that only causes a blockage, like trees jamming a river and eventually the dam will have to break. Yep, this will prove very good for the man and I wouldn't be surprised if he doesn't make this his winter home from now on. Well Joe, I'm hungry so maybe a slice of that cake I saw Hannah working on before we left for town would go down real well just about now. You ask her 'cause you're her favorite, but just make sure I get a big piece." making Joe laugh. Joe was glad his friend was just a few hundred feet away and he'd see to it that the man didn't get too lonesome, after all, what were friends for?

In his mind Joe said, "Thank you Sky-Mother for telling me about Mr. Hoggins."

~The Frosting on the Cake~

BY THE FIRST WEEK of January Mary Van Cliveland's new house was complete. The barn stood just where the builders had envisioned it nestled in a family of pine trees with a newly fenced back pasture. Natural cedar siding eliminated the need for exterior paint on both the house and the barn. They had painted the house trim white with doors and shutters cherry red and with white porch railings. It was a warm and inviting looking house in the country style that they all thought Mary would love.

The first thing Mari Beth did upon entering the house was to turn up the heat from the low setting so by the time the other women arrived the house was cozy warm. Now the women could work and finish the interior in comfort. Another week saw the walls painted and the bedrooms papered. The bathroom fixtures were in and all the curtain fixtures in place. By that weekend, the work force arrived to help carry in the furniture that Sam had built and lay the area rugs over the pretty pine wood floors.

The women got busy making sure the slipcovers fit on the bedroom chairs and hanging the pretty curtains throughout the house. Most of the people in the valley had touched this place in one way or another. This last act was just the frosting on the cake.

The ladies made the beds with new sheets and comforters. The bathrooms had new towels hung up with green plants placed around the wide edge of the tubs, candles, flowers in colored vases and a large shell filled with nice smelling soaps placed along the countertop. Very feminine the men thought and pretty as all get out.

Mrs. Tubs from the large grocery store in town stocked the pantry with a variety of spices and other basic foods plus an array of canned goods. The freezer was stocked and refrigerator would be filled just before occupancy.

The men hauled in two cords of chopped wood and stacked it in the woodshed. No porch was complete until there were six red painted rocking chairs on it with the accompanying tables dressed with large clay flower pots filled with plastic flowers for color until the real flowers grew in the spring. After the welcome party the porch furniture would be stored away protecting it from the weather.

Nothing could be done about planting grass and flowers until spring. For now snow covered everything in snow hiding the raw earth and creating its own kind of beauty in the stark whiteness surrounding the house and outbuildings.

Finally the place was as ready as they could make it. Everyone was about to quit for the day when the moving van with Mary's stuff arrived and the workers groaned seeing their escape impossible now. Immediately the call went out for strong backs and soon men arrived to help with the unloading which didn't take all that long. They decided to leave boxes and furniture in the appropriate rooms and finish the sorting and arranging for the next morning. Fortunately it was the weekend and with many hands helping, short work was made of unpacking the kitchen things and other odds and ends and arranging the furniture.

Standing in the hallway late Sunday afternoon the tired people walked through the finished rooms more than pleased with the results. Mari Beth decided that personal boxes would just be stacked inside the bedrooms and Mary could take care of those once she moved in. At last the volunteers waved a weary goodbye and left for home.

The house was beautiful. That next week Mari Beth held one morning open house for everyone who had contributed money, supplies, time and energy could walk through and see the finished product. Pride burst a lot of buttons that day as it should have. What a labor of love it had been and of course, there was Joe taking the finishing pictures as the unofficial photographer.

Two days before Mary and the children were due to arrive Mari Beth and Hannah had the refrigerator stocked then did one more walk through the house that love had built to see if all was as they remembered it. They placed the final touch upon the coffee table which was an album of before and after pictures of the construction.

"Isn't it amazing how one can have a beautiful vision and have that vision turn out even better than the dream? Just look how warm and inviting the living room turned out. Well, really the whole house is better than my dream. My, it's pretty."

Mari Beth admiringly patted a cushion into better shape and placed it with the others on the couch. "I'm so glad I had Joe take pictures of all the work phases so Mary can see the beginning and the final product. It makes a nice picture book for her coffee table, don't you think? I know she's going to be overwhelmed. Lord knows we are and we've been in on this from the beginning as well as everyone else, but we've had the chance to grow along with the transformation. Golly, I hope Ms. Mary doesn't faint on us."

"Mom, if she doesn't love this house she's one crazy woman. Sure, she's going to rearrange things to suit herself and the girls, but that's different from walking into a cold house with everything in boxes, isn't it? Especially if she tried to walk into that old falling down house of Fletcher's if she could have gotten through the front door, that is. Lordy, that would have been an awfully shock for her. This shock will be much more beneficial don't you think?" They both laughed at that.

Hannah put her arm around her mother's waist as they walked from room to room, so very proud of everything everyone had contributed to this project. In the hallway was a framed 30x30 plaque hanging close to the entrance.

The House that Love Built.
Welcome here where Harmony Abides

Around the wide border that surrounded the central writing were all the signatures of everyone who had helped with little messages scribbled here and there. Around the edges of that were fantastic little figures of fairies and elves that were hammering, sawing, carrying lumber, and lady elves painting and sewing. There were unicorns, sprites in the flowers gardens and all were beautifully detailed and meticulously executed water color drawings. It was a pretty thing and the idea for the plaque had come from Melanie Golight and showed extraordinary talent.

Walking up the curved stairs, Mari Beth ran her hand along the banister that Sam had created in lovely curved smooth pine to match the flooring and the newel post was of a carved head and upper body of a whimsical grinning Elf holding a pot of gold.

"Isn't this a piece of exquisite art Hannah? Mr. Downey did this. Hmm, you know it looks a little bit like an exaggeration of him, all puckish humor, wise and sneaky too or is it my imagination? You'd swear that little impish elf was going to speak right out."

"Now that you mentioned it Mom, it does resemble that sly old man somewhat. Hah, used himself for inspiration I bet; what a talented jokester." laughed Hannah. "I wonder if he's waiting around to see if people are sharp enough to pick up on that likeness."

"Well, knowing Mr. Downey for the sly boots he is, I shouldn't wonder. Let's go look in the girls' bedrooms again." They opened doors to peek in as they went down the hall. They loved the results of all their hard labor and couldn't see one more thing that they needed to do. "I hope they like these rooms. I tried to follow what Mary told me about their likes and dislikes."

"Momma, if I were a girl again I'd love the double bed with all the frills. Hopefully they will too and I'll guarantee they'll love these rooms. From what I understand they've been hurt, unhappy and probably worried about moving to a strange town. They must think they're coming to a savage country full of smelly ranches and primitive people. Well, you know what most Easterners generally think who have never been west in their lives. Of course, it isn't as bad as it used to be what with everyone moving around so freely these days. Still is like civilization stops at the Mississippi River and jumps right over to California." Mari Beth laughed at that.

Hannah went on. "I was looking at the expense sheets the other day and considering all the work we've done, the overall cost wasn't outrageous with everyone donating money, supplies not to mention the backbreaking labor. Labor, besides the contractors, would have added twice the expense if we'd had to pay everyone. Come spring we will help her plant her lawn, flower beds and garden if she wants us too. I think we need to back off a little now and not overwhelm her with too much more help, you know what I mean?" said Hannah as they walked down the stairs. "We don't want her to feel like she's a charity case or O.D. her with smother-love. Well, the house pretty much does that all on its own, doesn't it?"

"I think this place expresses physically what Jesus said, "Do unto others as you would have them do unto you." Just imagine if we were Mary and under great stress, injured and responsible for two young children coming to a strange land and expecting nothing but hard work to make a home. Then we found *this house* waiting for us. Yes, Hannah, I think we'd be in overwhelmed too. I just hope we haven't overdone it and cause her to break down."

"It certainly *is over the top*, but it definitely makes a statement of what the people of the Valleys are all about, doesn't it? Like they say, a picture speaks louder than a thousand words. Well, this house rather shouts instead of merely speaking." Hannah got a chuckle from her Mother.

"Then we've been successful."

They left the heat at sixty-five and went out the front door shutting it and locking it after them. Mari Beth looked at the key ring with the shinny new house keys that had a medallion of a large sunflower smiley face.

"Let's go home, I'm tired." said Mari Beth in a rather dead tone of voice as she dropped the keys into her purse. Hannah looked with concerned at her Mother as they walked toward the pickup. Her mother hardly ever complained of being tired, yet now that she was taking a good look at her he could see the fatigue in her face.

"Are you all right Mom; not getting sick are you?" worried her daughter.

"No, it's just that I've been so busy so long that now the pressure is off I suddenly feel it all. Just old age I guess." laughing depreciably at herself. "I'll take me a little nap when we get home if you'll watch Carli for me. Now don't go telling your father for if you do he'll drag me into the doctor's and there isn't a thing wrong with me that a little rest won't cure. Come on sweet, let's go home and relax and maybe a little of Henry's nice Apricot Brandy will rest my bones a little faster, huh? We have cause to celebrate my girl"

As Hannah started the pickup they sat for a few minutes while it warmed up and looked at the house and grounds. "And by the way thanks for all your help, you've been a great assistant director. All I can say is this place must take the record as the biggest housewarming present ever." Mari Beth said and laughed.

"All it needs is a big red ribbon wrapped around it and it would be garishly over done." laughed Hannah. "You can't beat this country for generous gifts of the heart, can you?" and the drive home was fairly quiet with only occasional comments.

"Oh that reminds me, Blackhawk is coming down tomorrow around 1:00 o'clock to do the final blessing on the land, the house and barn. We mustn't forget to call and tell everyone; it's important that they be there if they can."

"I'll get on the phone and spread the word while you take a beauty nap." Mari Beth sighed anticipating doing just that when she got home. She couldn't remember when she felt this worn out to the point of tears. For five straight months it had been one thing after another to keep her jumping. Yes, she was bone tired.

Once they were home Hannah poured her mother a little snifter of brandy and shooed Mari Beth upstairs. Once in her bedroom Mari Beth closed the door and leaned briefly against it until she got up the energy to walk across the room and set her glass down beside the bed. She took off her clothes laying them across the chair and took her hair down. Unbraided it she massaged her scalp which relieved some of the tension in her head and gave her hair a dozen strokes of the brush before loosely braiding it. She went to the closet for her gown and warmest bathrobe as she felt strangely chilled, no doubt it was from fatigue more than anything else, she thought. Sitting on the edge of the king size bed she slowly drank her brandy and finally set the empty snifter down on the night stand she pulled back the covers, crawled into bed and gratefully laid her head down on the pillow and pulled the thick eiderdown comforter up around her neck. In a matter of minutes she was sound asleep.

When Ben peeked in two hours later she was still deeply asleep and he carefully closed the door and went back downstairs. He sat down at the table beside Carli and frowned with worry. "What's the matter with your Mother, Hannah? She never naps, except when she was sick. Is she sick? Do you think I need to call the doctor?" questioned Ben anxiously.

"I don't think there's anything wrong with Mom that a little rest won't cure. You have to admit that these last five months have been extremely busy as well as traumatic with very little let up. She's just not used to the fast pace any more; after all, she's no spring chicken,

True Heart

Dad. I think we need to consider getting someone in to take care of Carli for six hours a day and maybe put an ad in the paper this week. Also, this is a big house and you can afford to hire a full time housekeeper because Mom needs a little more care and less hard work and I can't do it all either."

"You're right and I've neglected seeing her better cared for. Well, that's going to change now. I'll see to it right away."

Hannah was busy fixing supper. "Here, have some of Henry's fix-er-upper brandy; a little bit won't hurt you either and Mom had hers earlier. Now sit down and tell me about your day."

Ben had to grin at his daughter's taking charge just as Mari Beth would have. So he began to tell her about the new foals and the plans they were developing for Mike's new barn.

Mari Beth didn't come down that evening and when Ben checked on her again the only change was Mari Beth had rolled over on her other side. Everyone was very quiet so as not to disturb her and they were all concerned. The boys took over caring for Carli.

"Where's my Momma? I want my Momma now, Mikey." whined Carli with a pout.

"Momma isn't feeling well Carli, so we have to let her sleep. Be a good girl and before I put you to bed I'll let you peek in on her okay? Now, how about if I read you a story?" said Mike.

"Momma's napping? Okay, story time, Mikey. I see Momma then, okay?"

When the boys got up the next morning they trooped down to the kitchen to see Carli sitting in Mari Beth's lap talking up a storm with the woman's face alight with amusement when she looked up and saw their serious faces. "What's the matter now? You look like you've just heard the worst news ever. Come in and sit down, Hannah has breakfast all ready and your sister has already eaten, haven't you Pet? In fact, Ben and I had company in our beds somewhere toward morning. Goodness, we almost squished her between us."

Carli laughed. "I got squished, didn't I Momma. I yelled too."

"Are you alright now Mari Beth? I mean, if there is anything we can do around here for you, you just have to tell us. We can take care of our own rooms and the bathrooms. We're really sorry we've let you get so tired. I'll take care of Carli more so you don't have to all the time." Mike said anxiously and Joe nodded his head.

"Yeah Mari Beth, you're maybe getting so you need more rest like Carli and take naps like her and I'll take care of her better too." added Joe and came over to feel Mari Beth's forehead. "Are you feelin' all right now, dear?" just like Ben would have said and that set Mari Beth off into slight hysterics.

"Boys, boys, I'm not dead yet and I can have a sleep-in once in awhile without being at death's door. Now I'm as fit as a fiddle so sit down, quit your fussing and eat your breakfast. We've got a ceremony to go to today remember? Blackhawk is going to bless Ms. Mary's property at one o'clock."

And so it was that there were a lot of people there to attend the Blessing Ceremony for the land and the buildings. It was also an act of completion for all their efforts. People brought small bouquets of fresh flowers and placed them in the rooms. Sheaths of Wheat and corncobs were hung on the barn doors. Luther had stabled three horses that were on loan until Ms. Mary could choose their own. The barn was fully provisioned with hay, grain and oats. Three saddles and bridles in the tack room waiting for eager riders.

The Van Cliveland Farm was ready with its white picket fence around the house and large white fences paralleling the farm road. It was finished and it was a thing of beauty. Tomorrow the Van Clivelands would arrive.

Mary Van Cliveland and her girls drove into River Town around three Saturday afternoon. It had been a long trip on snowy and often icy roads. Frankly Mary was exhausted. They were to meet Mr. Jensen at his office and he'd give her the keys to the house. That house was a big worry to Mary because she had seen the picture of her great-uncle's house and it had looked pretty run down. She had found it in a box of her father's things. Maybe it had been renovated in recent years? If not, how could she afford to refurbish it? She had the money from the house sale, but that was going to be put aside for the girls' college. Mari Beth had said they'd paint and fix the house up so it must be livable and maybe it wouldn't be too bad. She'd decide when she saw it and if it wasn't possible to live in they'd rent a place in town. It was just one more decision she'd have to make.

True Heart

So many decisions right or wrong and still more work would have to be done today before she could rest. Mary sighed glancing over her shoulders at the girls sitting quietly on the back seat and looking out at the town. 'God, help and strengthen us to make this new beginning one of blessed peace and healing,' prayed Mary. 'We need it so very much.'

Her wounds had healed with only the ugly scars to remind her of what had happened and the doctor had reassured her they would gradually fade. Her hair had grown out almost three inches and resembled a boy's short haircut, yet the light golden hair curled softly over the scar on the side of her face. That scar would fade into a white line eventually and until then makeup hid most of the visible damage. The wounds in her heart were something else and fear of violence had to be gotten past. Her counselor had said only time could finish the healing. Well, they'd see if that was so too.

"It looks like a nice neat town, doesn't it girls? Oh, there's Mr. Jensen's law office on the right so let's go see what this farm we've inherited looks like."

She pulled into a parking space in front of the office building before continuing her cheerful talk. "If it's too bad we'll sell the farm and rent while we look for a house to buy here in town. Come on, babes, this is a new start and a new life for us far away from the past. Cheer up, please." begged Mary in an exhausted voice.

"Sure Mom; you know it's a relief to be here and not back there so let's go see this lawyer fellow and get the bad news over with." Bliss and Stephanie unbuckled their seat belts and got out.

Mary sighed deeply as she stepped out and shut her door. 'It's going to take time' she said to herself; 'I must have patience.' Together they walked into the office out of the cold wind and saw a pleasant woman sitting at the front desk.

"We're here to see Mr. Jensen so would you please tell him that Ms. Van Cliveland and her children have arrived." she said to the receptionist.

"Oh Ms. Mary how nice to meet you at last, I'm Lesley Schultz. I'll tell Jim you're here. Please have a seat." She got out of her chair and whisked through another door closing it behind her.

Ms. Mary? Wasn't that an odd way to address a stranger? "Sit down girls, though after all that driving my sit-down is a little tired of sitting down." Mary smiled and remained standing and so did the girls.

Within a few minutes Jim Jensen came out of his office all smiles holding out his hand to Mary and shaking hers enthusiastically. "Hello, hello to you all, how nice to speak with you in person, Ms. Van Cliveland. If you'll just step into my office we'll take care of the last details." He ushered them into his office.

"Mr. Jensen, I need to see the property and decide if it will be livable. If not, then I want to rent a house here in town for the duration." Mary sat down in a soft overstuffed chair, the girls sat on the couch placed against a wall. They talked as Mary passed over her identification papers and signed the documents that made the farm officially hers free and clear. Mary put the deed and her papers into her large purse.

Jim stood up with a smile. "Now I will lead you out to the farm which is just about twenty minutes from town. In good weather the timing should be a little shorter than that and should make your daily drive to school and back easy. Just follow me ladies."

Walking through the front office he told his secretary/receptionist that he wouldn't be back and to close the office at five, Mary didn't see him wink at the girl and she just smiled and nodded saying. "I hope you like the farm, Ms. Van Cliveland." as they left.

"We've been having mild weather for February. We usually have some pretty good snowstorms between now and spring, so don't be surprised to wake up to snow flying around some morning. We'll go on through town then turn right on North Mountain Road Ms. Mary. Oh dear, forgive me Ms. Van Cliveland, but Ms. Mary is what everyone has been calling you, I do hope you don't mind. Well just follow me." Jim opened his car door and jumped in while Mary and the girls hurried to their van to follow him out of town.

It was truly a beautiful day with the sun shining off the snow even though there was a cold wind blowing. The mountains rose majestically to the north calling to one's heart in the strangest way, she thought. "Wow girls, aren't the mountains awesome? Maybe we'll explore them when summer comes." They followed Mr. Jensen's jeep up the snow covered road admiring the neat farm on their left as they passed.

"That looks like a fairy book farm, doesn't it girls? Seely's Farm, hmm, I wonder if we'll be friends."

"I noticed a funny thing, Mom; ten miles or so east of River Town the roads became graveled. The streets in town were paved, but once we left town this road is graveled again too. You'd think a main road like this would be all paved too." observed Bliss.

"Now that you've mentioned it, it does seem strange. We'll have to ask Mr. Jensen." Just ahead of them Mr. Jensen's jeep signaled a right hand turn and Mary followed.

"Aren't the white fences pretty? That gives me the idea of doing the same thing at our place one-day if it's suitable. I wonder why Mr. Jensen is stopping at another farm before we go to ours. Golly, I hope it's not one of those impromptu welcome parties. I have to say I'm just not up to it as tired as we are." worried Mary. The farm road curved around a large stand of maple trees until a house came into view. One vehicle was parked in the driveway

"Oh my, isn't this a beautiful house, girls? Maybe one day ours will look something like that. I can't say I like the idea of calling on a new neighbor with us being so worn out and all. There's Mr. Jensen motioning to us. Darn! All right put on your happy faces and let's go meet our neighbors and I'll make it very plain that we are not staying." Mary shut off the engine and got out.

"I just wanted to stop here for a few minutes," Jim grabbed Mary's arm firmly to escort her through the front yard gate and up the porch steps and opened the door for her without knocking which Mary thought was very odd behavior.

"Welcome home, Ms. Mary and ladies; welcome to the Van Cliveland's Farm." Jim said pushed Mary into the front hall. A very tall lady with a cornet of blond braids walked toward them from the living room.

"Hello Mary, I'm Mari Beth. I wanted to be one of the first to welcome you to our community. This house is a gift to you from all the people in the southern Valley. Welcome home ladies, we're awfully glad to see you at last." Mari Beth smiled at three shocked faces as she went forward to pick up and shake Mary's limp hand.

"Lots of people will be here in a couple of hours to celebrate your arrival, but we thought it would be easier on you if Jim and I were the first to greet you. It will give you time to get over the surprise." Mari

Beth spoke gently to the pale faced woman. Oh deary me, worried Mari Beth, I hope she's not going to faint on me.

Mary looked around the cheerful living room with a fire burning in the fireplace then she saw her furniture placed about with the red slipcovers. Mary burst out in loud sobs and slapped her hands over her mouth and almost collapsed right there in the hallway. Mari Beth pulled the smaller woman into her strong arms holding her tightly. The girls were crying too hugging as close to their mother as they could get. It was quite a huddle of weeping women.

Jim quickly stepped out on the front porch and closed the door firmly behind him because he couldn't even handle one crying woman let alone four. He figured he'd wait in his car until they settled down. It was cowardly of him, he knew, but Mari Beth was better geared to handle situations like this then he was or so he rationalized.

"There, there, my girls, that's enough or you'll all have red swollen eyes to greet your friendly neighbors later. Come on now, let's go into the kitchen and have a nice cup of tea and hot chocolate that's ready for you. Once you're calm I'll show you the rest of the house." Mari Beth practically had to drag the crying ladies that were hanging onto her like limpets into the sun yellow kitchen where Mary again broke out in loud sobs at the sight of it.

Mari Beth sat the girls down beside her mother. "Goodness, I never thought the sight of this beautiful kitchen you described to me would put you into tears again Mary. This is the kitchen just the way you said you'd like it, isn't it?"

"Yes, oh yes, but it was a dream," she sobbed. "And I tttthought it would ttttake me years to accomplish it. We've dreaded cccoming out here because that pppicture of the house was so awful. Please forgive our loss of control," Mary struggled to regain some sense of balance. "We're all so tired…..you know and …shocked. Well, I'm overwhelmed that's all, just overwhelmed…… It's so beautiful." breaking down Mary cried some more.

"Here now drink your tea; you girls drink your hot chocolate, take some deep breaths and settle yourselves because there is more." laughed Mari Beth encouragingly.

"More?" Sobbing harder, "Goodness……I can't stop ccccrying….. do you have anything stronger than tea? I'm not a ddddrinker, in fact I ddddislike it immensely, but this calls for drastic aaaaction,"

Hiccupped Mary, as she mopped her eyes again and put her arms around her crying children and sat all three huddled up.

"Now ladies we've got to stop this or we'll surely look a sight" Mari Beth wiped a few sympathy tears from her own cheeks.

"Oh my, look at our beautiful kkkkitchen so golden with bbbbrick red tile floor and flowered paper. Isn't it beyond our ddddreams?" Mary sobbed harder and that triggered more crying from the girls.

Mari Beth hurriedly poured Henry's Cure All Brandy into a snifter and handed it to Mary and she downed the whole thing without stopping. When she took her first breath she gasped, coughed, choked and coughed again, beating her chest with one hand and fresh tears streamed down her flushed cheeks.

Mari Beth laughed while the girls looked in astonishment at their mother's reaction. Well, at least it stopped them crying for the moment anyway.

"Gracious me." said Mary hoarsely. "I swear that was the ...... whew,....most interesting liquid fire I've ever swallowed. Whew, what in the world was that?"

"That's from our local genius who makes the finest Apricot Brandy and sells it at the finest prices too. We call it Henry's Cure All; guaranteed to stop hysterics, cures fatigue, shock and overwhelm." Mari Beth laughed gently at the flush on Mary's cheeks, but it had succeeded in stopping her crying jag. That in turn, helped the girls settle down too. This time the tear wiping, nose blowing had the desired affect of stopping the hysteria.

Once the hot drinks had been consumed with some fill-in small talk, Mari Beth stood up and said," Okay up and at em', we've got the rest of the house to see. Come on now, before the gang descends upon us. There's a welcoming party planned for you at five o'clock."

The Van Clivelands looked at everything in the kitchen, the back bedroom with its bath, inspected the stocked pantry, the laundry room. They even went out the back door onto the side porch to view the adjoining full woodshed and the adjacent garage. Mary just shook her head in wonder at the completeness of everything.

"There is something very special I want to show you before we go upstairs." Mari Beth said as she led them back down the hall to read the plaque hanging on the wall.

"Wait until you see the pictures of before and after you'll be amazed, that's the book on your coffee table. Why we had so many people helping with this project it's a wonder that we managed to squeeze all their names in on that plaque." Mary just put her hand over her mouth and read as her shoulders shook.

The House that Love Built.
Welcome Here Where Harmony Abides

"Now, this isn't supposed to be a sad thing and you've cried enough for years of future tears I'm sure. I'm more than happy though that you love everything. Of course, you'll want to rearrange things to suit yourselves and we didn't touch your personal boxes or trunks. They're all in your rooms." Mari Beth guided the shocked woman into the den. "This room off the living room we thought you'd like to have as a den/library thing. As you can see, your books are all on the book shelves, cozy chairs by the fireplace for reading and your desk over there in the corner. You can change this if you want too. Now, come on up stairs."

"Oh, mom, look at this cute elf; isn't it darling? Who did that?" asked Stephanie as she stroked the grinning elf's head on the newel post.

"The furniture and the banister were crafted by your neighbor, Sam Carrington who lives practically across the road from you." answered Mari Beth, "The elf was carved by Mr. Downey, a very gifted sculptor. It is unique, isn't it?"

"His name is Mickalo McGee because he's definitely Irish just like we are." said Stephanie in a pleased voice as she stroked the elf's head and she would have sworn the elf winked at her. None of the ladies questioned the child through Mari Beth took a close look at the little girl. Hmm, very perceptive she thought.

The view of their bedrooms had the tears gently flowing again, happily now than the first shocky ones. The girls actually squealed as each one said, "Wow, look at this" and "Oh, how super, "over the set ups.

Mary smiled at this first show of enthusiasm from her sad girls. Mary's room was beyond her power of speech. She just walked around, patting this and that, but the luxurious bathroom had her crying again and murmuring, "Oh it's just too lovely. Just look at that old fashion long tub with claw feet. Where on earth did you find such a treasure? The glassed in shower is perfect too. Oh my, isn't this beautiful beyond belief."

Mary Beth laughed and said, "We're glad you like it. We women had such fun with it and now our husbands are going to have some remodeling to do in our own homes." and got a nice laugh out of Mary. By the time five o'clock rolled around Mary and the girls had washed their faces and fixed themselves up. Mary had taken one look at her bare, tired face and scrambled for her purse to repaired her makeup and brush her hair to cover the scar.

With clean happy faces they were ready to meet the inflow of people. It was amazing to Mary how the fatigue she had been feeling had simply vanished. She guessed happiness could do that kind of instant healing.

For the next three hours, Mary talked to the women about the little things they'd created for her. She got to look through the picture book and was deeply shocked at the original ugly house and found it hard to imagine anything that bad had been in the same place as this lovely new house.

She talked to the men about the construction and what they each had done. Finally she cornered Ben about the cost of building so she could pay them for their hard work.

"Pay us? There aren't any bills that need paying Ms. Mary. Here in the Sacred Valleys we are responsible to keep the lands well and this place had not been kept that way. Why, it was an offense to our Thunder Gods, our Guardian Spirits up there on the mountain and it was definitely an offense to our tidy souls. No, no there was nothing else to do, but to clean it up because our dignity demanded that we do so. Besides, it makes a very nice housewarming present, doesn't it?" Ben grinned gleefully at the opening and closing of their new teacher's mouth that closely resembled a fish. He just loved shocking people in a nice way.

Before Mary could collect her wits Ben went on to say, "We couldn't get a big enough red ribbon to go around the house so it's come to you unwrapped, but we didn't think you'd mind. No, Ms. Mary, there are no bills so cease asking for one. Why, it would insult us to the very depths of our cowboy boots if you refused our present;

it just wouldn't be kind of you." Then Ben took Mary's hand when he saw the tears pooling up in her eyes and smiling kindly down at her and said very gently, "We want you to feel welcomed here. We hope you and the girls will be happy living in the Valley. Besides, it's hard getting good teachers to come to such a remote place so we know how to cherish them when they do."

Ben turned around and pointed, "Let me tell you about Mrs. Carmichael standing over there to the left of the fireplace, the woman wearing the purple hat? She was a professor in an eastern college and finally had it with the college political in- fighting and city life in general. We hired her sight unseen and built her a nice house in town which she preferred. She's teaching 12th grade plus college preparatory classes and adult classes. So you see, it's just what we do and one day, if the opportunity arises, you'll be volunteering your time and energy to someone who needs you to help them. What goes around comes around, my dear."

Squeezing her hand, Ben excused himself and walked quickly away while Mary still hadn't been able to get a word in edgewise.

All he heard before he entered the kitchen was, "For heaven's sake."

Grinning, Ben winked at Mike as he passed saying quietly. "Quick, go play something," and walked out the kitchen door to stand on the enclosed porch to gossip with some other men.

The sound of Mike's guitar beating out a strong compelling rhythm had Ben smiling. The harmonizing of two young voices hushed the loud buzz of the many conversations in the room. There, that baritone/bass voice joining the others had to be Divine's adding a deeper beauty to Mike and Joe's voices. Ben leaning against the porch rail with the other men and listened. It was turning out to be a grand house warming.

The women cleared and cleaned up after the party, talking to Mary while many hands got the job done within a short time. Mary got to meet all the other teachers too so when she began her job she wouldn't be a stranger there either.

Joe saw Mike talking to Bliss about her music and they seemed to be hitting it off really well. Well, that grand piano must belong to her. Maybe Mike was gonna' get him a girlfriend though she was pretty young, but you never know thought Joe.

"You'll have no trouble making friends here, Bliss," Mike was saying to the shy girl. "I worried about that when Joe and I first came here last summer, but it was easy. I've been to many different schools when I was younger and this one is unique. The kids are great and I suspect you and your sister will be really popular. You two are going to love it here. Hey, have you seen the horses out in your barn that Luther Strongbow loaned you?"

"We have horses in our barn? What kind of horses are they? Can we go out now and see them? Stephanie, come with us, Mike says we have horses out in our barn." grabbing their coats off the hall coat tree they were out the back door in a flash.

Entering the new barn, the girls saw three horses stick their heads out over their stall doors and greet them with snorts and whinnies. The barn smelled of new lumber and hay and now, horse.

Mike turned on the lights, as it had already dark. "Here, I've got a bucket of carrots for you to feed your new residents. Let's go visit them." Mike had to laugh because the next half-hour was an "OO and AW" time.

"These are Tennessee Walkers, the sweetest ride you've ever had. This little mare is called Sweet Baby. Do you like her Stephanie? I think she's just the right size for you. She's a small horse, but she's gentle."

"Oh Mike, she's a beauty; what's not to like." Stephanie grinned as she stroked the velvety nose.

Mike and Bliss walked down to the next stall where she fed a gelding his carrot while Mike introduced them to each other. "This guy is a grand horse and Luther calls him "Pacer." His gait is so smooth you'll never even know you're riding faster than the wind. Your mom's horse is another mare and she's a big one and her name is "Little Blackie". Do you think she'll like her? Of course these horses are just on loan and you can have your pick of all the different breeds from the ranches around the valleys. Can you take care of a horse? I mean do you know how to take care of a horse?'

"Yes indeed we do, all of us. I can see it's going to be a pleasure living here. Thank you Mike for showing us these beauties and I must go tell Mother so we can thank Mr. Strongbow for the loan. I'm afraid we'll fall in love with them though." said Bliss, giving Pacer a final pat, a kiss on the nose with another carrot just for good measure. Moving over to Little Blackie, who wasn't so little, being she was sixteen hands high; Bliss gave her a carrot and a few pats so she wouldn't feel left out.

"I wonder if Mr. Strongbow would consider selling them to us. Is it alright if I ask?" Bliss looked questioningly at Mike.

"It certainly won't hurt to ask. You might wait awhile and try them before making up your mind. Come on let's get back to the house." Turning off the lights, Mike closed the barn door and held on to the girls' arms to help them back along the snowy path so they wouldn't slip in their slick soled street shoes.

They got back to find that most of the crowd had left. The women who had stayed to help neaten things up had just finished and were putting on their coats saying goodbye as well. Mike waited with Joe while Hannah, Mari Beth and Ben said their good-byes while Bliss and her sister had Luther cornered. He was laughing, nodding and talking before he finally moved away towards the door and with a wave to the boys he went out into the dark evening.

On the drive home the family exchanged news and conversations they had had. Mari Beth told them how Mary and the girls had cried for the first hour over the beauties of the house. It was a satisfying end to their project and a wonderful beginning for their new neighbors.

The Thunder Gods must be pleased as they were at this successful conclusion. The healing of the land and harmony restored to the spirits that dwelled there and a place for wounded hearts to begin a healing new life.

Mary closed the door behind the Strongbows and walked back into the living room to bonelessly fall on the couch. Her girls had curled up in the overstuffed chairs on either side of the burning log fire just watching the flames, completely relaxed. In the quiet of the room surrounded by the warmth of such loving generosity, Mary felt she had at last come home.

After so much fear, pain, suffering and struggle, peace flowed in and around her. All worries, anxieties and problems had dissolved into thin air. Mary gazed into the fire feeling as limp as a wet noodle and decided not to move for the next few hours.

God was good and so were these amazing Valley people, but she didn't understand them. No, she didn't understand such openhanded generosity for the sheer sake of giving. She knew many good people, but this, this was beyond her comprehension. This beautiful gift was beyond her intellectual capacity to grasp such goodness to a stranger. What had she done to deserve this stupendous outpouring of compassion? She was too tired, too content to work up the energy to cry about the wonder of it all.

In times of disaster people rushed to help the victims, to help each other; that was a given. Maybe she qualified as a victim though she hated that term for it implied helplessness and she certainly didn't feel helpless now; besides she disliked labels of all kinds. Still all this for just one woman and her children boggled her mind. And they refused to take anything from her though she had tried to pay them for it; more than willing to pay for this beautiful house.

God grant she could return the blessings someday to someone else in need. The plaque said, "The House that Love Built. Welcome Here Where Harmony Abides." No truer words had ever been written. She and her daughters were living in a house that love had built.

~Mike and Joe~

"Come on Joe let's go out to my studio." Putting on their coats Mike told Hannah they'd be gone for a while and she nodded her head and returned to preparing dinner.

Stepping out of the warm kitchen into the cold of late afternoon was a bit of a shock. They could see their breath bloom white against the dark of the late afternoon. Joe tucked his chin into his coat collar.

"Boy, this is some different from winter in southern Texas." Joe's voice came out muffled by his coat collar.

"Yeah it is that, but you know I kinda' like it. Just look at that sky."

The sky was magnificent with the fire of zillions of twinkling stars. There was no moon tonight so Mike snapped on his flashlight though he probably could have found the way in his sleep. The snow made the path easily discernable making the flashlight redundant so he snapped it off. Roscoe certainly knew the way and all they had to do was follow the dog.

They passed by Mr. Hoggins cottage with the lights gleaming in the darkness. Once inside Mike's cabin they hurriedly built a fire. It roared to life and within minutes heat filled the small space sufficiently that the boys could take off their coats, hang them up and pulled rockers up close to the fireplace.

"I guess I forgot to set the new thermostat to keep this place warmer. It isn't good for my instruments to get cold like that." Mike got up and did the job right, setting the temperature at 65 degrees then came back and sat down.

Mike looked around the room still marveling at the transformation of his own private space. Mari Beth and Hannah had scrubbed it to a fair thee well and Ben had bought him the recording table for his birthday. It sat in one corner and there was a writing desk with a good lamp, a soft easy chair, a bookcase and his three stands holding his guitars and the banjo and two rocking chairs on each side of the fireplace. Curtains covered the windows in a warm shade of red and there were scatter rugs on the floor. The one in front of the fireplace Roscoe claimed as his own. Mike had his very own space to retreat to when he needed quiet and to create his music. Here was another surprise from his loving family. Blessings kept pouring in.

Joe sat watching his brother looking around the room. Surely thought Joe, Mike should be used to it by now. Granted it was only a month past Christmas, but Mike looked just about as surprised as when he had seen it for the first time.

"What's going on Mike? It's not often you ask me into your private hideaway. I mean, not that that's bad or anything like that. Do I have to start worrying about something I've done right this minute?"

Mike seemed to come back to himself, shook his head and smiled over at his little brother. "No Joe, nothing to worry about. I guess I just wanted to be alone with you for awhile. Seems we've come an awful long way in a very short time, doesn't it? Tomorrow I will be sixteen years old and this seemed like a good time to clear the board sort of thing is all."

"Yep, we've traveled many roads together, but this past year was the toughest of them and the best of them all. Talk about the highs and the lows of it, goodness, it fair boggles the mind. It will be a year, come next month that Mom and Dad passed away. Are we going up to their place when that day comes?"

"It's on the calendar and we will if it's not in the middle of a blizzard or a bad storm. We'll say a little prayer that the weather will be just fine."

"Maybe it would be alright if I talked to my Sky-Mother about it, do you think She'd mind?"

"She loves you Joe, so I don't think She would mind at all. Of course, She might not be able to guarantee good weather for that day, but I guess it won't hurt to ask." Mike smiled at the earnest boy.

"Yeah, like Mom would say when you ask for something and she's say, "maybe." said Joe and Mike laughed at that comment. Mike proceeded to rock for awhile as his thoughts drifted here and there. Joe waited patiently and rocked too.

"This *has* been quite a year, hasn't it? From absolute despair to great joy and who would have believed it possible. I sure didn't.

You're right Joe, talk about extremes. When we walked down that long, long road to grandfather's place, who would have predicted that we'd end up in such a wonderful home with people who really love us? Not to mention meeting such great hearted people as there are in these Valleys. Sometimes I think I'm not living in the so called "real world" anymore because who would believe such a place as this even existed? Man, it's like Utopia or like the author Hilton who wrote "Lost Horizons." This place is right out of a fairy tale, "And they lived happily ever after." It's a big miracle Joe, a really *big, huge, awesome miracle*. So huge I'm still in wonderment and bewilderment. How did we deserve all this goodness?"

"I think God had a lot to do with this miracle and I think those wonderful Guardian Spirits had a lot to do with our miracle too. Sometimes Mike, there's just no figuring out the why of things so we just have to be grateful when good things happen and bare with the times that aren't."

Mike laughed and said. "Yea, old wise one, yea!"

Joe giggled. "Now, you're poking fun at me."

"Not really little brother because I agree with you that sometimes the really big things are the hardest to talk about without bursting into tears and for two guys like us that would really be embarrassing," chucked Mike, "unless we both did it together."

"Well, I've shed a lot of tears in the past and so have you. Hannah says it clears a lot of grief out of the heart so it's okay for guys to cry once in awhile without us becoming total wimps. It just shows that guys have feelings and all. It becomes awfully painful if you stuff feelings inside for too long. Mr. Hoggins said that feelings fester and become like stinky garbage if they're not dumped out periodically. I guess that means fairly often huh? Ben said stuffed feelings can come out all at once like a log jam bursting in a river and the water gushes through. It's sure to be hard on a body."

Mike laughed and nodded agreement. "Yeah, heaven keep me from stinking like old garbage 'cause that sure wouldn't attract the girls would it?" and they both laughed about that one.

After a bit Joe spoke up again. "I'll tell you something else if you promise not to laugh." and looked over at his brother who was just rocking easy like in his chair.

"I promise I won't laugh. What is it?"

"I say prayers every night to the Guardian Spirits, especially to my Sky-Mother 'cause She's really special to me. I don't think Jesus would mind as They are really good Spirits and They've lived here for a long, long time. They're sort of more real to me 'cause I've seen Them so that makes Them really real to me, understand? They saved my life and sent Mr. Hoggins to rescue me too and then the Goddess sent us to rescue him." Joe paused and a shocked look came over his face. "Geeze peeze, I just remembered to tell you what They, I mean She called me. She said my name was "True Heart" and I was supposed to tell people that, but I forgot until just now. Well, geeze peeze, just think of that! I've got my own Indian name!"

"True Heart? Yes, that describes your spirit Joe, right down to the ground and I'm glad you told me. Be sure you tell Ben and Blackhawk, they'll be so pleased. Well, I guess you won't need a vision quest like I will. I'm actually looking forward to doing mine this coming summer. Perhaps in a way you've already had your vision quest kind of prematurely. Think about it Joe, a lot of testing went into your experience of being kidnapped. We'll just arrive at our true names a little differently then most people. I'll tell you something strange too Joe. I pray to Them ever since that night we found you unharmed, but it will be our secret and we don't need to go blabbing it around. Besides, Blackhawk says I need to start give thanks for our ranch. I'm not sure how I can get over there every night to build a fire and all. Maybe Ben would let me do it from here. Hmm, now that's a thought so I guess I'd better ask and get that taken care of right away."

The boys rocked. "You know Mike there's something else that's kind of strange too. You and I get along just grand even though you're older than me by…" Joe stopped and counted on his fingers, "by eight years. You've never treated me like a nuisance or a baby nor do you beat on me like some older brothers do. Maybe we have another miracle to be thankful for that we just took for granted; you know, like us being such good friends and all."

Mike looked over at Joe and slowly nodded his head. "Yeah, we are that for sure."

Joe pursed his lips then sat a little straighter in his chair and looked at Mike right in his eyes. "Anyway, I've always liked having you as an older and wiser brother; it comforts my heart." said in a serious, old man's voice.

Mike gaped at him and then Joe burst out into laughter and Mike reached, punched him lightly on the shoulder and laughter filled the cabin.

"Comforts your heart, you little idiot; I'll comfort you, bro." Laughed Mike and punched Joe lightly again.

They rocked some more with sheer peace and quiet surrounding them. "Another thing Joe, I've been watching the people in the Valley and the way they act with each other. Have you noticed anything special going on between certain men and certain women lately?" asked Mike.

"No, can't say as I have, but then I'm just a little guy and not as wise nor aware as you are, Michael Devereaux Kelly." came the smart reply from Joe.

"If you find cracker crumbs in you bed tonight, don't be surprised. I'd get ants only they're all asleep. No silly boy, I mean like Luther and Amber. Then there's Tom and Jean Hardwell. And I think our Jimmy might have his eye on Melanie. Well, that might present a problem for I noticed Pete Cameron does too. When people get together a natural pairing off begins to happen. It will be interesting to watch what happens."

More rocking and more contemplation of the fire before Mike said. "Peter Cameron is another real mystery. I wished I knew how he came to have Trill Ranch for instance. Blackhawk knows and isn't saying anything. Blackhawk just told me there would be time for Pete and my friendship later, but how long is later? Oh, that reminds me, we've got an open invitation to visit Pete and I think we'll do that real soon, don't you? It will satisfy our curiosity and you know it isn't good for the digestion to stay curious too long, or so I'm told." he added with a grin.

"Well, well, well, all this happening right under my nose and I didn't twig to it at all. I guess that means you're growing up fast, mister. You'll have to keep me in the loop sort of thingee, 'cause now I am really curious and I don't want to ruin my appetite cause I want to grow up to be a giant like Big Mike." said Joe thoughtfully not paying any attention to Mike's snickering. "Tell me more about the mysterious Peter."

"You know how I met him at the fair in Huntington then the next time I saw him was at Blackhawk's on Thanksgiving, then here at our party. I haven't seen nor heard from him since. Oh, I hear gossip about some of the what's going on over there at Trill Ranch, but not coming from the horse's mouth, so to speak. There is definitely something that Blackhawk knows about Pete that none of the rest of us has knowledge of. That's why I say Pete's a mystery man."

"Hmm, for sure there's a lot going on in these Valleys, isn't there? You know, I used to think it would be kinda' boring living in one place all the time. It's really different from the constant traveling we always did with the folks where you'd expect new and interesting things to happen on a regular basis. I've come to the conclusion that this ain't no boring place, but a place of happenings and possibilities. It's like reading a mystery novel. You just can't wait to turn the page to see what happens next. 'Course, I wouldn't want to be kidnapped again, but even that wasn't all bad considering the way things turned out and all; I mean with me being able to sing to the Thunder Gods. Hey, I bet no one has ever done that before. I'll admit it scared me enough to almost pee my pants until I got into it. I don't think any other performance I may do in the future will ever beat that one." Joe said with all seriousness that had Mike's mouth twitching.

He got such a bang out of Joe's sudden and unexpected pronouncements and they always, or most always hit the nail on the head.

"No, even the bad times somehow turned into some kind of good." Mike said, "You know Ms. Van Cliveland was badly hurt by her husband, don't you? You can see the scars on her face and once when she pushed her sweater sleeves up I saw awful long cuts in her arms. Imagine a man doing that to anyone? Makes me shudder! Well, the Valleys will heal her. She's another wounded person to find shelter under the Guardians care. She'll be safe here just like Nino will be safe and like we are and the Golights too. I suspect something awful happened to them too Joe. Why would a first class chef bring her niece and nephew all the way up here from Georgia just be a ranch cook? Now there's another mystery." said Mike.

"Hmm, I thought maybe Jack had been through something pretty bad because he didn't talk much and watches people real careful like. I think maybe he's been badly abused. He's better now, but still there's this watchfulness about him. Goodness, I didn't notice Ms. Van Cliveland's scars, but the girls are nice only they're really quiet especially for girls. Now I know why." Both boys rocked awhile until Mike turned to Joe and asked.

"Have you been over to see Mr. Hoggins lately? I'm awful glad he's settled in at the cottage while his leg heals. I've talked to him a few times, visited you know, and we sometimes play music together."

"I was over there this morning and brought in some wood for him. I sure love those pups of his. Funny, I don't even know their names. Mr. Hoggins said one of the pups is going over to Luther's for Jack 'cause Jack really likes the one pup. Gee, I hope it isn't that all black one with the white spot on his forehead, smack right between his eyes. I'd really like to have Target. Oh wow, that's his name and maybe Tag for short. Hmm, of course I'd have to ask Mr. Hoggins though I don't think that will be any problem 'cause he saved the fair-haired boy here" laughed Joe

Mike stood and with a commanding poise issued his statement. "Yes indeed, saving the fair-haired boy was a big thing. Okay, we'll ask Mr. Hoggins, we'll gather forces, we'll mobilize the troops and go forth and conquer and the pup will be yours. It'll be a done deal."

Joe laughed and jumped up. "Aye, Aye, Captain, I'm your man!" and they both laughed at their play-acting.

"Let's just say, we'll talk to Mr. Hoggins and Ben and see what they say, but I really don't see any problem. Every boy needs a dog. Last thing if they don't agree, we'll take it to the Thunder Gods. Hmmm, *you'll* take it to the Thunder Gods since you seem to have the inside track with Them, my boy."

"Agreed!" nodded Joe and they shook hands.

"Oh did I tell you that Mr. Hoggins is writing a book? Yep, he said that it was selfish of him to tuck away all his knowledge without sharing any of it with others. So that's what he's doing this winter, isn't that neat?" Joe really felt good about that. Of course, he wouldn't be able to read it or even understand a lot of it until he was older, but Mr. Hoggins said he'd give Joe a copy to keep until he was.

"Yep Joe, we live in exciting times and I can't wait to see Pete again and solve that mystery once and for all, that is if I'm suppose to know. Well pal of mine; let's go to dinner; Hannah's going to be ringing the bell for us any time now."

Placing the screen tightly over the dying fire, the boys put on their coats and hats, turned off the lights and closed the door behind Roscoe.

One long journey had ended and a New Year opened up all kinds of new beginnings and possibilities that Joe had mentioned. Wonder what miracles were waiting to be sprung next, thought Mike, as they trudged through the snow on the way back to the house. Whatever they were, they would be here to help and be of use to the general good just like everyone else in the Valleys were. Mike felt the sense of belonging, of being in his "right place" and again thanked the Thunder Gods for directing their feet to this Valley. God preserve us all, he thought.

"Want to hear something amazing Mike? I'm not afraid anymore. I feel so safe here, even after that awful Elroy. I'll never feel afraid to go anywhere alone again. Well, not outside the Valleys just yet because I need to stay here and ripen a little more."

Mike gave a shout of laughter and grabbed Joe and began to wrestle with him, but before they could tumble into the snow bank the dinner bell rang. He and Joe raced to the kitchen door and quickly knocked the snow off their boots and followed by Roscoe went inside shutting it behind them, closing out the cold night air.

~The Thunder Gods~

ON THE TOP OF Thunder Mountain's snowy crest, the Guardians stood like gleaming pillars of Light looking down upon Their huge Valleys with satisfaction and felt the peace and goodness that filled Their lands. To the east, south, west and north all was serene.

Their work wasn't finished and hopefully it never would be. Now at last a special man was here, a man who had been seeking to come home for a long time. Thunder God had succeeded in drawn him back to the Valley after many, many long lifetimes living in other lands. Other souls that were troubled and seeking peace were destined to be nurtured into wholeness just as had others before them.

The people of the Valleys still treasured their Guardian Spirits. It was an acknowledgement of the good guardianship by these benign Masters of Light and Love.

Gradually the large forms of the Thunder Gods dissolved like mist into the whipping wind that blew a stream of snow off the crest of the Mountain.

And all that was left to oversee the Sacred Lands were the millions upon millions of brilliant stars in the dark sky.

Peace

Epilogue

To many people, the existence of these valleys
Would not be believed.
To some, this place would remain
A wished-for-paradise
Unobtainable in this lifetime.
To those who were being drawn here
It became a hope, a striving and a deep
Inner hunger for peace
And a new way to live.
To the souls living in these valleys,
It was simply
HOME.

And the magic continues

Turn the page for a preview of

"Blue Feather"

Ruby Nari Mayo's second captivating novel in
The Sacred Valleys Series

A young Peter Cameron is struggling to learn to be strong and achieve a way to protect himself against the abuse he suffered as a child. To become a whole man requires him to let go of his anger and revenge. At the age of seventeen he leaves the orphan's home in search of his true place. His adventures begin as he makes his way toward his destiny; his home in the Sacred Valleys.

~The Beginning Journey~

A COOL WIND BLEW in through the pickup's open window bringing with it a heady sense of freedom that thrilled Pete right down to his boots. He was singing, which he rarely did except in the shower even though he had a nice baritone voice.

It was a perfectly beautiful spring day, sunny and filled with bright promise as he drove out of Pennsylvania and down a long winding road toward Kentucky; driving in his very own pickup that he'd earned by a winter's hard work. Pete laughed as he thought about celebrating his upcoming eighteenth birthday. Legal age and no one could haul him back to Virginia. He was free.

Granted his pride and joy was an old, *very* old pickup with red rust rimmed around the dull green fenders that rattled like a box full of nuts and bolts, but it was all *his*. He laughed at himself for that prideful thought 'cause, while this old pickup wasn't exactly a thing of beauty, however it did have the distinction of being his first car and what seventeen year old man wouldn't get a kick out of that. No, this old heap wasn't pretty yet it gave him the gift of freedom and that *was* beautiful.

At the Pennsylvania farm where he had worked last winter he'd found the old thing abandoned behind one of the barns practically covered in vines. While he didn't know anything about mechanics, it didn't look too bad on the outside and just might have unknown possibilities inside.

That evening he'd asked Mr. Weiner, the owner about it. "What, that old thing? If you want it it's yours. It's worthless to me and I warn you boy, it isn't any good and not worth fixing to my way of thinking, but maybe you can sell it for junk."

Well, it was doubtful that the pickup would ever run again, but Gus, one of the old men he worked with, consulted with Pete over its innards. Gus poked and pulled at this and that and did a lot of humming, muttering, tisking and shaking his gray head while Pete stood by thinking how like a doctor examining a patient he didn't expect to live. Pete waited patiently for Gus's diagnosis; life or the junkyard.

Finally Gus turned and looking up at the tall boy and grinned, "Well Pete, it will be a challenge, but with a little of this and a lot of that, not to mention money and hard work plus the Car Angel of Loss Causes taking a liking to you, I think you could get more mileage out of the engine; not overly long mind you, for her engine is fair worn out and won't last much longer, but maybe long enough to get you down the road in the spring and maybe even to where you're aiming for." Gus shrugged his shoulders. "Well, boy, I'll help you fix her if you want to."

So they hauled it into a shed and began doing a little of this and a lot of that, scavenging for parts in old vehicles, not to mention new tires, brakes and what all, over the winter. Pete had a quick course in mechanics and at the end of all their efforts the old pickup went just fine. Well, fine might be a relative word, but the pickup passed inspection and was duly licensed that spring.

Shortly after that Pete woke early one spring morning and felt that tugging in his heart and knew beyond question that the urge to head west was on him again.

So here he was cruising down the road that still had a scattering of snow in the shade of the roadside trees heading south to Kentucky with a letter of introduction to a friend of Mr. Weiner's who owned a horse farm. Pete needed another job as he had very little cash left after fixing the pickup.

Going south seemed to be an indirect way to go west, but since Pete didn't know exactly what spirit intended as his final destination he'd continue to follow that silent voice inside his heart. It got him out of the Home in Virginia and that landed him in Pennsylvania so why stop now and question Its wisdom?

Pete drove along with his mind wandering from one thing to another as an unattended mind did to entertain itself. Powerful memories of before……before he had been shut up in the Home; memories of pain and suffering and profound loss and grief were indelibly printed in his mind.

He remembered.

True Heart

It was the night of his ninth birthday when all hell broke loose. The screams woke him out of a sound sleep in the camper.

"Mom?"

When she screamed again Pete jumped out of the top bunk and ran to the door and tried to open it. It was locked. He looked out and saw her lying beside the road and Dick was walking back toward the camper. As the man approached the door he looked up at Pete and smiled before going on by. The truck opened and slammed shut then the engine started.

"*No, no, you can't leave her there. You can't. She's hurt!*" Pete frantically pounded on the door and finally managed to break the small window, but it was too small for him to crawl though.

"*Momma!*" he screamed, "*Momma!*"

He could only stand there helplessly gripping the broken window frame without noticing the glass was cutting his hands and watch his mother's body recede into darkness as the truck accelerated. She was dead! He knew she was dead and Dick had killed her.

It was dark when he woke up to find himself on his back with his head pounding so hard he couldn't seem to think. Gradually, he became aware of being cold and jammed up again a….bridge railing. He couldn't remember how he had gotten there.

Struggling to sit up brought instant nausea and vomiting. The dry heaves sent his head into a thundering roar. He didn't feel the pain of hitting the cement as he had already passed out.

Time slipped by as the cold wind blew uncaringly over the small heap of clothes, ruffling them like leaves on a tree.

He drifted awake again, this time it didn't take him as long to get his mind to working. Breathing deeply caused instant grabbing pain in his side. The boy groaned and slowly, cautiously inched his way up to finally leaned against the bridge railing. He could hear the rush of the water beneath him and found it strangely soothing. When he had his headache under manageable control, he opened his swollen eyes and looked up and down the deserted road. It was obviously very late at night or very early in the morning. He couldn't see very far as it was so dark, but the land around felt…..empty, like he was in the country.

He sat unmoving for awhile held in a space where nothing happened. Nothing moved outside on the road and nothing moved inside of him either. Interesting sensation, this nothing-place, thought the boy sluggishly, a place of no memories or much feeling; it was a pretty cool place. A flash in his mind dragging him out of his comfort zone and

he shuddered as that thought awakened his pounding headache with a vengeance.

"Gods, I remember now. Please, I don't want to remember now." Tears of pain, anger, fear and loss rolled down his dirty bruised cheeks as he sobbed.

"Mom!" he cried in anguish. *"Momma?"* There was no answer. He hadn't expected one because she was dead. After all he was sure she was dead when he had seen her lying so still beside the road. The beast had killed her and had driven away with him still inside the trailer.

How long ago was that? How many days of beatings, more beatings and starvation? How had he escaped? Where was he? A grip of sudden fear made him feel for the small box he had tied to his waist…ah, it was still there and unbroken. He took a deep relieved breath and groaned as pain swept him almost into unconsciousness again. It was so much worse now that his body was coming out of shock. Breathing in shallow breaths so his ribs didn't grab him again, he let himself drift for a time. Gradually more memory returned and he knew how he had gotten away.

He had been on the floor of the large camper and conscious of the truck's rumble in his ear and felt the sway of travel. He guessed he'd drifted off only to be jarred awake by his mother's voice.

"Peter, get up and get out now; Dick forgot to lock the camper door. Get up and jump now." commanded the voice.

"Mom?" Pete looked around in a bewildered way, but didn't see her, *"Mom, where are you?"*

"Never mind that, just do as I say right now. It's your chance to escape. Do it!"

"Okay, geez don't yell so loud, it makes my head hurt. I'm going, I'm going."

And indeed he did, crawling across to the door and reaching up twisted the knob and the door flew open and banged against the side of the camper. That scared Pete enough that he didn't even hesitate, but leaped as far out from the vehicle as he could and landed hard on the road and rolled a number of times and fell over the verge and into the ditch. When he woke up he was alone. Struggling to his feet took him awhile, but he finally made it up the slight bank and began to stagger away from the direction that the beast had taken.

How long he walked he was never able to recall later only that it seemed to be a very long time before he fell down the first time.

Now he knew it was urgent that he get to his feet so he pulled himself up by the iron railings and began staggering along holding onto the side of the bridge for support. It was harder to stay upright once he had left the bridge behind, but he kept on until he fell the second time. He lay panting on the cement trying to get up enough energy to continue on and that's when he heard a truck coming. Motivated by sheer terror he rolled over and over down an embankment into another ditch filled with bushes. Crawling among them Pete hid before unconsciousness took him under once more.

When he awoke he was looking straight up at the coming of dawn. He felt no desire to move because when he did he hurt something awfully so he stayed where he was and listened uncaringly to the occasional car passing by.

"Peter, get up from there. You must get up onto the road. Your angels can't find you down there hiding among the bushes. Move it Peter, or you'll miss your angels."

"Geez Mom, I feel sick when I move and I'm comfortable here." whined Pete.

"Peter Little Bear Cameron, I told you to move. Do it now." the invisible voice commanded.

"Okay, okay, I'm moving here. Geez, you don't have to get mad." Painfully Pete rolled over and crawled up the slope to the edge of the road and promptly passed out from the effort. The ground beneath his ear vibrated with the sound of a car engine close beside him scared him awake. He jerked and tried to get up and only managed to scramble away on hands and knees a few feet before he fell hard. The beast had found him again.

He heard footsteps and began to scream, *"Don't touch me, don't hurt me anymore, please, don't! Don't!"* he sobbed hysterically.

"Easy boy, easy there, we're not going to hurt you, we're policemen and we're going to help you so just calm down now. Gods Zack, this kid's in a bad way. What kind of person would do this?" said an angry voice even as gentle hands stroked the boy's hair away from his bruised face.

"Not any human in my book abuses children." another gruff voice reply.

"Okay son, okay now, I'm going to pick you up and take you to the hospital where they'll make you all better and the pain will go away. Who did this to you, boy? I personally want to meet the person who did this to you." said the cop grimly.

"The beast, the beast, don't let the beast get me, please. He killed my mother. I know he killed my mother. *Don't….*" the boy pleaded.

"No, we won't let the beast get you. I'll just shoot him if I see him, okay?"

"Okay, yeah, thanks. Are you angels? My Mom said angels were coming for me and I had to get up out of the bushes so you could find me. Are you them?" asked the boy, trying to see through his swollen eyes. "Am I going to die and go to heaven now?"

He could see the fuzzy outline of a tall man bending over him and heard quiet laughter. "Angels you say? Well boy, we've been called a lot of things, but not angels, have we Zack?"

"Not that I can recall; lots of other names which I won't mention, but I don't think I'm any kind of angel either or else my wings have been hidden for a long time." replied Zack with a grin.

"However, in this case boy, I guess God appointed us to be your angels and that does make for a nice change. No, you're not going to die, but you are going to the hospital to get well."

"What's your name, son?" asked the other policeman as his partner gently lifted Pete up in his arms.

The boy had to think a bit about that question before he burst out with, "My name is Peter Little Bear Cameron…….because that's what my Mother calls me. I've got to go home now, way out there…. ..I know my home is way out there somewhere." he was babbling now, lost for a few minutes in the vision of his inner eye. "I can see it, I can see it right there under the huge snow topped mountain." The policemen looked concerned as the boy seemed to be slipping into delirium.

Then the kid looked up at the man who carried him and said lucidly, "Thank you for finding me, Angel. I'm ever so grateful." Peter Little Bear Cameron felt safe now to let go and passed out.

His spirit once again walked the high mountain trails and communed with Light Beings who seemed to be calling him.

"Come home. It's time to come home now, Peter Little Bear."

"I'm coming, please wait for me," the boy murmured, "I'm coming home."

Pete had been at the Clement Home for Children in Norfolk, Virginia for the past month recovering from his injuries. This would be the day Pete would meet the man who would turn his life around.

Returning from the first day at school Pete was being bullied as he walked along the street toward the Home and finally got his nose bloodied and knocked down to land at the feet of a small Oriental man standing on the steps. An amazing thing happened right before his eyes. Pete saw this small man take down the big bully with a swift move and that was the end of the conflict. The boys ran.

The man introduced himself as Chin Lee, Karate Master and invited Pete through the door behind him that said, **"The Red Dragon Dojo."**

After they had talked awhile Pete, so full of fear, anger, and rebellion, begged Master Chin to show him a way to become a stronger and better man so that no one would ever abuse him again or anyone else that Pete could protect. The Master gave him that way plus a philosophy to live by.

For the next eight years Pete worked hard at Karate and earned his Master's Black Belt. Along with working at the dojo for Master Chin he managed graduate early at the age of seventeen.

The calling to *"come home"* was getting stronger and his dreams were repetitive of talking to Light Beings on a huge mountain covered in snow. The pressure to leave was becoming unbearable. Finally the day came when Pete couldn't stand the walls of the Home any longer.

Saying goodbye to his one friend and mentor, Master Chin, Pete left promising to write his Sensei from time to time. Now his adventure had begun and freedom beacon him to take the road west.

When Pete Little Bear Cameron left the state of Virginia he was seventeen years old and stood 6'3" and weighed close to 185 pounds. He appeared to be a mixture of Cherokee Indian and possibly Scottish blood, considering his last name. His shoulder length hair was coal black and his eyes were a dark gray with broad cheekbones and olive skin. His was a face that would increase in good looks as he filled out and matured.

The most important thing about his physical appearance was he looked and acted older than his age and that meant he wouldn't be bothered by bullies. Being a Black Belt he knew how to protect himself. There had been a few conflicts, however they were brief. After all one can't be on the road without bumping into men who wanted to test themselves against a stranger.

Fortunately there had been lots of changes since he had left the Home; mainly getting older, taller and stronger due to his vigorous life. He had found a winter job on a farm in Pennsylvania and worked hard at any job he could find.

He had years to think about what direction he would while he lived at the Home. He loved Louis L'Amour's books and somehow that connected to a place inside of him that said west was his direction and he never questioned the rightness of that instinct. The west wouldn't be the same as the times the author had written about, but it still had enough open space that Pete wouldn't feel shut in and he desperately needed that freedom. He knew in his heart that somewhere out there he would find a home and begin to build a life for himself. He was looking for that big snow topped mountain that said the Rockies or another big mountain range.

**For Peter Little Bear's
adventures had just begun.
As a man they would lead him
far, far away from his eastern birthplace.**

LaVergne, TN USA
10 January 2010
169475LV00002B/4/P